ENTERING EPHESUS

ENTERING EPHESUS

Daphne Athas

NEW YORK / THE VIKING PRESS

First published in 1971 by The Viking Press, Inc.
625 Madison Avenue, New York, N.Y. 10022

Published simultaneously in Canada by
The Macmillan Company of Canada Limited

SBN 670-29716-x

Library of Congress catalog card number: 75-150120

Printed in U.S.A. by Vail-Ballou Press, Inc.

PART I

CHAPTER 1

Packed in among the blankets, linens, and Loco Poco's dolls, the three girls and their mother sat upright like bankers. Their faces were shaded and dark in contrast to the scorching glare of the sun, but their eyes betrayed a certain eerie wildness. Cars passing in the opposite direction jerked away from the Pontiac, giving it a wide berth. The grilled hood was lined with suitcases. Three mattresses, two bedsprings, and a carton box were roped onto the roof. The valves in the engine were worn, and in the airless heat the pistons pounded monotonously.

"I see no sign saying Ephesus," said Irene, the oldest, a beauty of fourteen known as the family fool.

"We're only at Richmond," answered Urie derisively.

"How far away is home now?" asked the youngest, Loco Poco, in a lonesome voice. She was ten years old and clutched a doll on her knees. Dark curls matted her temples.

No one answered.

"Will the moving van get there before us?" asked Irene.

Again no one answered.

They had left their old home two days ago, at six-fifteen, August 18, 1939. Irene had taken a picture of that moment. Urie, Loco, and Mrs. Bishop lined up before the Pontiac, the great white house behind, the ocean its infinite backdrop. Urie, thirteen years old, had stood like a general with one foot on the running board, her grandeur mitigated by the *Grapes of Wrath* car. This moment was entitled "The End of Their Oceanic Life." They had gotten in, slammed the four doors, and left.

The Indian's nose pointed south. For two days they had been traveling, passing through New York, New Jersey, Delaware, Maryland, Virginia. Urie told everyone that the wheels clicked the following words: "Wrong South Wrong South Wrong South Wrong South."

Mrs. Bishop allowed these remarks to pass without comment, but she had to restrain herself. She needed all her energy to nurse this Pontiac to P.Q. at Ephesus.

The girls commented lugubriously on everything.

"Look at that woman sweeping the yard with a broom!"

"Whoever heard of such a thing! Sweeping a yard!"

"She's white trash."

"Mamma, is she white trash?"

"Why does she do it?"

"Because it's a dirt yard. They don't have any grass. See!"

"Who ever heard of dirt yards?"

"What good is sweeping dirt?"

Or:

"Look. Negroes with umbrellas. And it's not even raining!"

Or:

"Look. Red dirt."

"Who ever heard of red dirt?"

"Dirt is supposed to be brown."

"Red dirt stinks."

"What does red dirt make you think of?"

"Old rusted stoves."

"Red dirt comes from real iron rusting in the ground," Urie informed them.

"It makes me think of the earth having an operation," said Loco.

"Yeah. Trenchmouth!" spat Urie.

Or:

"Look at that high grass."

"It looks like upside-down brooms. See how dull and boring it is."

"Will you people keep still!" exploded Mrs. Bishop finally. "We're coming to a town!"

It was Richmond.

At the moment of Mrs. Bishop's words the radiator began to steam. Billows of smoke poured out.

The Pontiac picked up speed on the descent. It wobbled down onto the long James River bridge. Smoke heaved up over the roof of the automobile and down each side of the red-stained railings of the bridge.

"Get the milk bottles out," barked Mrs. Bishop.

"But there must be a gas station!"

The automobile plummeted into a long street of houses.

"Try to make it through town," said Irene. "People are staring."

"Since when does Mamma take your orders?" asked Urie.

"Yes. What does our family care what people think?" parroted Loco.

Blankets, dolls, magazines twitched spasmodically as Urie and Loco fought to unearth the milk bottles.

"They're empty, Mamma," said Loco.

"After I told you to fill them on Grandfather Mountain?" said Mrs. Bishop in a shocked voice. Rusty water began to spit on the windshield. The smell of hot metal threatened.

A red-necked man on the sidewalk dropped a chocolate ice-cream cone in surprise. They passed through Tin Town. Two Negroes backed into their shack-yard.

They turned into a street of brick houses with black wooden porches. People turned their heads. Expressions varied from pleased suspense to the hope that this incipient Mount Vesuvius would erupt farther down the street.

Cords stood out in Urie's neck until she looked like a quivering airplane of the Lindbergh era. Loco clenched her fists together and sucked the mouth of the milk bottle. Only Irene was impassive. She hid her fear under the creamy imperturbability of a sacred cow.

Suddenly Loco Poco screamed, "There's a Sears Roebuck!" The sound, given Biblical authority by its descent into and emanation as echo out of the empty milk bottle, caused Mrs. Bishop to slam on the brakes.

The Pontiac jerked sidewise like a crab. Mrs. Bishop piloted it bumping and stuttering past the row of brick houses to the brand-new yellow Sears Roebuck sitting in a bulldozed red gravel pit.

She swung fully around, holding the wheel and holding the motor in a pronounced idle, facing the back-seat three as if from a pulpit. Clouds, sun, and sky were blotted out by the billows of wet steam.

"Why did you tell me to stop here?" she demanded.

Loco Poco rolled her eyes up into her head.

"She didn't tell you to stop," said Urie, but seeing the expression in her mother's face, improvised rapidly: "There's water in Sears Roebuck."

"Oh," said Mrs. Bishop. She turned off the key.

Outside, people seemed to be running, and a crowd gathered.

A man's face appeared in the steam and said, "The engine ain't got no air to breathe with all them suitcases lined up against it."

"You, Loco and Urie, hurry into Sears Roebuck and fill those bottles,"

[5

whispered Mrs. Bishop, her hand on the door handle. "You, Irene, get out and help me unload this stuff."

Assuming a brave, gallant, elegant, "so glad you are helping me, how wonderful you are" expression, she opened the door.

Urie and Loco sneaked out of the car and threaded their way through the curious faces, clutching their empty bottles. Just as they stretched out their hands to push, the Sears Roebuck doors swept open to usher them into an automatic embrace. They were welcomed from limbo into a new, hushed, shiny, impersonal world. Lawnmowers, light bulbs, refrigerators glowed in indirect lighting. People were moving up and down the appliance counter, slow and reverent as in church.

"It's air-conditioned," whispered Urie.

They walked down a green carpet. A thousand automobile tires hung above them, some black, some pure velvety, others wrapped modestly in fluted brown paper. Everything smelled unreal. They did not question the unreality. They accepted it naturally, as if they had not lost their home forever, as if they were not eight hundred miles away from their Oceanic Life, on their way to their father P.Q., to a home and life they could not imagine.

Suddenly Loco Poco stood in front of a gigantic suspended trailer-truck tire.

"Look! It's the kitty of the Little Cat's Paw!" she breathed. She drew her finger over the tire tread. Outlined against her fingernail, a small rubber cat was cut to the pattern of the tread. It lay sleeping in a bed, its nose and one paw exposed. "If I ever have a chance to buy a tire, I'm going to buy the Cat's Paw Tire. Isn't it cute!"

"We're supposed to be in here getting water!"

"This little kitty is home in bed. If you put ink on it, it would make a hundred little cats all the way down the highway!"

Searching the labyrinth of the store, Urie suddenly spotted something at the end of Straw Seat Covers. "Look, there are two fountains!"

Forgetting the sleeping cat, Loco darted forward. "One has colored water, Urie!" Pink, she bet.

She had the milk bottle ready, aiming it under the spout. But before she had time to push the handle, a horned finger touched her shoulder. It belonged to a bony middle-aged woman. "You're not supposed to use that fountain," she informed Loco in a low voice.

There was such strangeness in her disapproval that Loco was frightened. She backed away.

Outside, having delivered plain old white water without having spilled a drop, having for fifteen minutes maintained careful, minuscule footsteps like a serving girl's on a Greek vase, Loco paid no heed to the honks and brays of her sisters. She was only faintly pleased at Mrs. Bishop's diatribe: "All right. If you older ones don't know how to behave in a public place, you can just get right in the car and stay there until we get to Ephesus."

In this case the Truth Urie had told was a Lie. Maybe only Negroes were supposed to use the fountain, but Loco had been prevented from ever finding out what color the water was. Was it pink? Was it blue? Was it iridescent? Secretly she still thought it was pink. Forever she would be dedicated, like Ponce de Leon, to looking for the pink water in the magic fountain she saw so clearly in her mind's Garden of Eden.

It was more than an hour—restarting the motor, pouring endless milk bottles of water in—before they could repack the suitcases and wobble onward again, halting and starting out of Richmond, out of sight of the crowd of waving helpers.

Hours passed. Everything descended into monotone. The family's personalities became dissolved until they became a Pontiacal zoom upon the universe.

Toward evening they saw a sign pointing to Ephesus.

They stirred. Their faces were dusty, and they became slightly scared. It was like awakening. At once they thought of the ocean. They could not believe it was lost. And they thought of P.Q. They had not seen him for more than a year. Mrs. Bishop had the address of the house he had taken for them on a piece of paper.

It was dusk when they entered the town. Mrs. Bishop squinted over the steering wheel and went slowly. The stores were flat. The gravel sidewalks were gullied by erosion. Trees clutched their hands over the automobile. The lights of the town came on. They passed a gas station in front of which there was a large magnolia tree which stuck out its blossoms through vulgar, shiny patent-leather leaves, like tongues. They turned right, passing the post office and the Ephesus Inn. Then, following the directions carefully, they entered an area of houses. Lights from the windows twinkled obscenely through large padded leaves. Bushes were overgrown in the yards. The fruitfulness of the Judas, quince, dogwood, honeysuckle was a disguise, and the fragrance that permeated everything was overpowering.

Suddenly a bell from a bell tower rang: "O Love That Will Not Let Me

Go." The F-sharp was flat. Urie made a face at Loco. Behind this ritual their hearts were sinking.

The houses became closer and closer together. Mrs. Bishop veered toward the curb. "Nineteen Ransome Street," she said.

It was a squatting bungalow set in a gully. Bushes hid everything except the light inside and two fat orange columns which held up the porch.

Mrs. Bishop looked at her paper again to make sure.

"It can't be!" said Irene in a shocked voice. "This is a residential district!"

Their old house had been splendid, private and white, with fourteen rooms and forty-nine windows, fronting on the harbor, its back toward the ocean. P.Q. named it Thalassia. It stood on Eastern Point, an area of estates. The green blinds opened from white clapboard above the breakwater and Rafe's Chasm. Sea gulls cried in the morning, pure and merciless. Through the spring leaves of their cherry tree on a clear evening they could see Minot's Light and the Portland steamer heading on its weekly way to Maine.

At first they were summer people. The moon rose over the Atlantic, a shattering glister on choppy waves. Mrs. Bishop played Brahms and Chopin and the music drifted up to the girls' bedrooms at night. The wind sang through long grasses. The leaves of silver poplars sighed in the sun. The milkweeds wept tears of milk when their stems were broken. Sudden lightning storms erupted and broke bolts over the ocean.

After the Depression they became winter people too. One winter a storm came. The wind ripped the eaves. Warning bells lashed by fifteen-foot waves called from the ocean. The Leggetts' bathhouse, green and lonely above the empty swimming pool, was torn off its rock and tossed away to sea. The girls laughed.

Blizzards piled up ten-foot snowdrifts on the hills. Brace's Rock became encrusted with salt-water ice. The harbor froze, and ice cutters had to come in so that the gill-netters could make their way out to the Grand Banks. They put on their skates in the house and walked out to the pond which separated their house from the ocean. Holding burlap bags between them, they sailed at fifty miles an hour. They played hide-and-seek in the winter-deserted estates, hiding behind snow-covered naked Roman statues of gods and goddesses imported from Italy. They walked the winter beach. They followed the leader.

Urie was the leader. She made them go over cliffs and through woods.

Ghosts of snow pretending to be trees watched them. They learned purity in the winter. They had to be strong to enter into eternal, merciless freedom. They tramped all the millionaires' estates, fake Tudor castles, Norman turrets, Italian rococo mansions, glass piazzas gleaming in the snow, and one carved French palace, its windowpanes etched white upon the vicious ocean.

They broke and entered with the confidence of kings. Forgotten locks and rusty hinges were a challenge. They gazed with rapturous awe at the acres of deserted rooms, furniture shrouded by sheets as if in spectral imitation of the snow. White congealed in hypostasis the powerful absent owners. Who had stood where? What had they said, these dead rulers of the universe? Everything was haunted. Once Loco discovered some left- over cheese-cracker crumbs in a great dark kitchen at Maynards'. They ate them, all three, thrilling to this actual evidence of the absent owners. They were like mice taking Communion and becoming lords. Their kingdom was endless and undisputed. Trespass made them gods.

Illuminated by a consciousness of what this experience meant, Urie became a preacher as well as a leader. She waited until they were at the farthest extremity from home, in the bleakest room of the Ramparts, or at the last stone of the Point, looking at the figure of Mother Ann, a granite, bosomy stone facing the sea. Then she turned to them, her breath supernatural with enthusiastic steam, her eyes very blue.

"You see, there is no boundary to us. We are completely limitless. We are just like the ocean and the sky. We own everything in the world!"

"I want to go home, Urie," said Loco in a scared voice.

"Where do you think you are?"

"At the lighthouse."

"No, you are not at the lighthouse."

It was because Loco was the smallest against the endless waste of snow that she was scared. Once she had got stuck for four hours in a snowbank at the Ramparts. Irene and Urie had not been able to pull her out. They had had to leave her and go for help. March lay upon February's back and the sea stretched away to infinity. The wind was tugging at the sky. All Loco could see was endless miles of granite, mansion and maze overwhelming her.

"Where am I, then?" she asked.

"You *are* at home!" crescendoed Urie, stretching out her arms to embrace all power.

"No. I'm at the lighthouse!" said Loco, beginning to cry. "I want to go home, Urie!"

"Go home, then!"—petulantly turning away, knowing none of them would go alone.

"Make her go home, Irene!" Loco held her mittens pleadingly before her chin, her tears beginning to freeze on her cheeks.

"Oh, lily-livered cowards," scorned Urie. She led the tramp back, etching her mittens into the sky into huge gestures of espousal. "Home. Home. Everything is home!"

All through the years of losing the house Mrs. Bishop called the family "aristocrats of the soul." They did not take this as compensation for losing paradise, for they were not aware of losing it. The banks closed. The Bishops lost their money. Four of the millionaires whose mansions the girls explored jumped off skyscrapers in New York and Chicago. But the girls did not notice that Mrs. Bishop no longer brought them toys. They were surprised when she talked about it. They went to school. They did not associate with other children. They were too far from the school. They were the only ones who rode to it in an automobile. The townschildren spoke with bad grammar. The Bishops spoke with good grammar and made top grades. The bank did not believe the Bishops would never pay off the mortgage. So they were allowed to stay in hope. For five years they stayed, owning their house, the millionaires' estates, the Point, the ocean, and the sky. And then the bank made the first steps toward foreclosure.

They got out of the car. They fanned through the shrubbery, creeping toward the bungalow with the repulsion and curiosity of wary soldiers ordered to capture a hill. Through the screen door they saw P.Q.

He was sitting in an empty living room in the glare of a naked 150-watt light bulb. The only stick of furniture was the camp chair upon which he sat. His left leg was perched on his right knee. He was reading Plutarch. He looked like a marooned tyrant ruling fathoms of polished floor. The only articles in his emptiness were a string rug, upon which his foot was carefully placed, and books, neatly lined along the wall from one end of the floor to the other.

He sensed the forces outside and stepped out the screen door to look, the book in his right hand, his forefinger marking his place. His cheeks had acquired squint lines from sun. His face had grown sharper and hollower. His nose had grown longer and more sarcastic. His bald head was more imposing than ever, giving a new, total authority to the uniqueness that made him unable to get along in the world.

He saw them. "Ah! So you got here at last!"

Such gladness spilled through these words, punctuating his old dashing knife-smile in the darkness and his foreign accent, so strange, yet so familiar, that suddenly they felt as if it were yesterday.

Loco Poco, squealing with delight, ran up the wooden steps and half tripped. He caught her in his arms.

The others came more slowly and shyly.

All this time they had not even missed him because his dominance, in abeyance, was always felt. But now his presence was overpowering.

"This is a crazy place, P.Q."

"You bet your life it is."

They walked around the empty room to inspect. To talk about anything was irrelevant.

"We saw white trash sweeping dirt yards."

"We saw Negroes with umbrellas and it was ninety-eight degrees and the sun was out."

The repetition of what had been flotsam to their mother was suddenly recognizable as the coin of Bishopry. Bishopry against the world, Bishopry dancing in enlightened ecstasy upon the wet spots of ignorance, stupidity, craziness, and dumbness. Bishopry, wise as owls witnessing the wonders and absurdities of the world.

"The moving van didn't come," said Irene.

"There's nothing here but floors."

"What a funny house, P.Q. It's so small I feel like I'm a doll in it."

They came into possession of hysterical euphoria, laughing insanely. They walked like goslings about P.Q. They went from one room into another. Their footsteps echoed on the plaster walls. Echoes pursued them from room to room. They repeated rooms as if to make the place bigger. Unreality became total reality. Their Bishopry thwacked over the echoes of themselves, over the emptiness, over the meaninglessness of their footsteps, into the very workings of their leg muscles.

"No furniture! Insane!"

"Where are we going to sleep?"

"Where do you sleep, P.Q.?"

He opened a last door. He was poker-faced.

In the empty room on the empty floor lay a mattress. It was dressed in sheets. A pillow was its head. It wore a blue blanket. An alarm clock sat next to it, pointing to nine-five.

"You sleep on the floor?"

"Of course."

"We can sleep on the floor too, can't we, P.Q.?" asked Loco Poco.

"You bet your life. That's the way I slept in ninteen-oh-eight on my first day at the University of Illinois."

"Come on," said P.Q. from the hallway, after they had unloaded everything. "Let's go for a walk. We'll get some ice cream. I want to show you the university."

"At this time of night? It's eleven o'clock," said Mrs. Bishop.

"Mamma!" breathed Loco.

"You only live once," said P.Q.

P. Q. Bishop, born in Khartoum and originally named Pavlos Episcopoulos, had dropped the name of Paul because of Saint Paul, whom he hated. He was Greek but had never been in Greece. Sometimes he claimed to be a Jew, but no one in the family knew whether to believe it because he told lies and truths with the same straight face. He laughed at Christianity but literally translated his name into English as Bishop. He had come to America at the age of sixteen, though he told some people it was at twelve.

He was a combination of opportunist and utopian. When he was young he worked as bellhop, shoeshine boy, and grocery clerk to put himself through college. The mythology of America opened his eyes. If a man was smart in this country, he could make money.

But education was the guide light. Ignorance kept people down. As a student P.Q. tried to organize the Greeks of New England, to make them learn English and read American history to get them out of the mills of Lawrence and Lowell, out of the ghettos and raise them up. He did not believe in work. Horatio Alger was folderol, the Puritan ethic nonsense. Understanding operated through enlightened self-interest (business) with technology and relieved man for higher spheres of service. This was the lesson of America.

Before the First World War he tried to enlist in the Canadian Air Force but was rejected for being underweight. He entered law school. There he met Clara Parsons, the daughter of Hector J. Parsons, sugar broker and owner of real estate. The Parsons family went back to the *Mayflower*. P.Q., always separated from the rest of the Greeks by his slow-burning egotism and the arrogance of messianic idealism, began to straddle the bridge between immigrancy and the cream of Yankee society. Hector J. Parsons took a fancy to him. The irascible old man liked to pit P.Q. against his relatives who had never made a bean themselves. He liked to watch him drop neatly turned bombs in society and reveled in his wicked, young delight at flustering men and women. P.Q.'s flair turned strong-willed, generous Clara Parsons' head, and winning over her divinity-student suitors, egged on by her doting old father, he married her. He never finished law school, for he was drafted and spent the war teaching English to immigrants. Hector J. Parsons died, and P.Q. went into the banking business with Clara's money. His new affluence proved his ideas. Outward circumstances mattered little to him, and he fitted himself to the life of golf clubs, roadster, club memberships, and the summer house on Eastern Point as easily as he had once lived in boarding houses.

The first child, a boy, died. When Irene was born, P.Q. was disappointed. A second girl changed his disappointment into transcendence. He began to conceive of women as potential Athenas, superior to men. He began to teach his daughters manners, ideas, and philosophies as if they were not children but the leaders of future generations. At three years old, Urie was taught to repeat after him man's progress from the animal: "Man has progressed from being an animal. First he was a savage. Then he was a barbarian. And at last he became a social man."

By the time Loco was born, P.Q. had sated his desires for inculcation, so she became his favorite and looked to him just like a little Clara.

When the Depression came, he could not believe it. Clara came to the fore. She buoyed him up. He raised himself out of a paralysis of inaction, cutting down on their way of life, moving into the Eastern Point house. He started a business making radio casings. The NRA closed it up. None of his former associates had anything to do with him. He began a new business in wool. It failed. Years passed. He started two new ventures. The more he failed, the more he became convinced of his belief in free enterprise as panacea. He preached. He became more stubborn and more enthusiastic. But bitterness began to turn the edges of his enthusiasms brown. He grew hard in his preachings.

Every Friday each girl deposited twenty-five cents in her bank account. During all their school years the three had amassed three hundred dollars. When it was evident that the family could barely make a living, and that ultimately they would lose their house, P.Q. decided to leave New England. There was no opportunity. The textile industry, shoe industry, and banking had gone down the drain.

The children drew out their saved money. In a ritual of family solidarity, it was given to P.Q. He said good-by and made his way south. A year passed, during which Mrs. Bishop supported the family by the cliché stratagem of baking and selling apple turnovers. P.Q. existed by raising tomatoes.

"What are we doing here? Separated?" Clara Bishop wrote him in June.

"You have been gone a year, and all the girls are calling themselves Little Orphan Annies. If we are going to starve, we might as well do it together."

Nevertheless, it was not until a man in a gray business suit visited them at ten o'clock that summer morning, that they left the Eastern Point house. The children huddled at the end of the long living room, trying to understand what the businessman was telling their mother in low, soft tones. There was an air of unreality in a businessman from the outside world establishing the reality that they had no home, finally. The unreality was a delusion, and they had to go.

P.Q. led them like a Pied Piper. His bald head gleamed in the street lamps. He extolled the sights of Ephesus, which were invisible because of black night. The fact that the girls could not see the buildings he pointed out made them magnificent in imagination.

"Turn left. Cross that gutter. Watch out the root. Turn right."

In a Greek café their eyes were blinded by the dim lights. A wet rag wiped off the marble tabletop. P.Q. ordered: huge mounds of raspberry ice cream in silver dishes.

But sleep was catching up with them. On the way home a slight melancholy crept through the seams of their euphoria. The items of fact which had made them so happy to be together, and which had proved their Bishopry, now began to be seen in another light. Through the muting waves of their laughter, their silly hoots, the glamour of P.Q., the freedom of this existence where beds were no longer a necessity and the future was no longer known, there came a gnawing doubt. No money. No future. The lamplight glistened in the soft darkness. P.Q. and Mrs. Bishop fell behind. As the three girls walked ahead, they overheard words and phrases which floated over the sound of their footsteps.

"Wonder if we did the right thing. . . . Tomatoes . . . Fifty dollars a month . . . But can we keep it? . . . At least . . . How long? . . . Here they'll be able to have a college education anyway. . . ."

Urie thought of Mr. Micawber. She was glad there was no such thing as debtors' prison in this day and age. She knew her mother was asking practical questions. P.Q. was trying not to hear. He was trying to walk faster to catch up with them so that he would not have to think about facing facts. A vision of the beauty and frailty of Bishopry assailed her. She thought of the raspberry ice cream they had just eaten. Now the raspberry ice cream was gone. P.Q.'s money was gone.

"Stop here," commanded P.Q. "I want to show you something."

They turned. Outlined by the street lamp, a massive imitation of the Parthenon, stood a fat Baptist church with Doric columns. He pointed. "Look at that Baptist church."

They stared at it.

"Go up the steps."

They followed his order. But they climbed slowly, for they did not know what came next. At the top they stood. They were directly under the huge columns.

"Now, knock the column."

"Which one?"

"Any one of them."

They approached the columns gingerly. They put out their hands.

Loco knocked first. The monolithic column clinked like a penny. At this ludicrous sound she bent forward, with a wicked smile. "It's not stone at all! It's not even cement."

"It's made of tin cans," said P.Q.

He turned and walked away.

Enchanted, the three girls began knocking and rapping as if the columns were kettle drums. Their laughter punctuated the metallic clangs which gave out various notes, like wanton ghosts. They rapped until their knuckles were sore. Incognito they had arrived, only to discover the tin behind the stone. P.Q. always knew the secret!

They ran down the steps. They flung themselves gaily into the darkness, trying to catch up with P.Q. and Mrs. Bishop.

Suddenly they heard their mother say quite clearly, "You mean you spent your last penny on that raspberry ice cream? We don't even have enough to get a loaf of bread in the morning?"

Bread. Jean Valjean stumbling through the night.

Something was necessary, Urie thought. It could not be that Mamma and P.Q. were weak or middle-aged. They were not growing old. They were not invalidated by lack of money. They were not afraid. They were not at sea in the world. They were true pillars of Bishopry. They could not have lived so long without understanding the workings of the world. It was the bad luck that their mother called it. Something was necessary that moment. Something small but pivotal, like that last inch in the air of the pole-vaulter, the minute upfling of ankle or knee that broke free, so that the crossbar could not fall.

"P.Q.," she called. Her mother and P.Q. stopped and turned around, and she thrust out her chin. "We're going to crack this town wide open!" she breathed, pushing the gallantry, like the last inch, through a constriction of tears.

She was rewarded with the crashing sound of Bishop laughter from her two sisters, her mother, and P.Q., furious, victorious, hosannas.

CHAPTER 2

The Bishops did not remain in the house in the residential district. Not only was the rent too high ("Fifty dollars!" exclaimed Mrs. Bishop. "How are we going to pay that?") but there was something in the spirit of the place that did not fit. P.Q. had no work. No money was coming in. He was about to start a new business, in linen supply. He had to have room. It was less discombobulating to move immediately than to put it off, try to make do in this cramped neighborhood bungalow, and then have to move later. It was the first time P.Q. had ever so visibly had to take responsibility for the family.

A lucky thing happened. A woman named Mrs. Kanukaris had a house she was about to sell.

Mrs. Kanukaris's maiden name had been Wanda Rupee. She was the white-trash widow of a café Greek whom P.Q. had met when he first came to Ephesus and who had died two months later. Mrs. Kanukaris, inspired by his death, had started an embalming and funeral parlor with him as her first customer. She threw a big funeral and invited everyone to come to it. She had put her husband on display, secretly complimenting herself on the good job she had done making his big nose look little. She wept large tears and put a small, modest sign, KANUKARIS FUNERAL HOME, out by her house on Main Street. She stuck three little stars of mica after HOME so that they would shine at night in automobile lights. Soon colored people began to send their dead to her instead of to other funeral parlors. It was the first black and white parlor in Ephesus. She put out a larger sign in front and tacked a huge electric clock on a cedar tree, with red and blue neon lights to signify to people that their time was limited.

Mrs. Kanukaris was a wheeler-dealer and a braggart. P.Q. secretly admired her for this, and Mrs. Kanukaris looked up to P.Q. She even listened to him respectfully when he gave her advice on how to run her business, although the last thing she would have done would have been to take it. But he was more educated than all the Ephesus professors put together. He spoke to her, whereas they did not, except at funerals.

When P.Q. met her on the post-office steps, talk went around to houses. She thought of the old house in which she had stored coffins. Now that she had built a coffin-display room onto the parlor, she thought of selling the house. But, she said, she might offer him a deal instead. If he would put in the bathtub (it had sink, toilet, kitchen sink, and electricity), she would let him have it for fourteen dollars a month on a year's lease. There was only one trouble with it. But that should not bother unprejudiced Greek Yankees. It was right in the middle of Niggertown.

"It's a relief to know we have hit rock bottom," said Urie, propping her foot on a stone. She used the same stance as in the picture of "The End of Their Oceanic Life."

"Yes. We can't go any lower, Mamma," said Irene.

The Bishop family had come to inspect the house. They stood at the bottom of the weed-infested driveway. The girls surrounded their mother. About six feet away Mrs. Kanukaris, whom Urie had already christened Kan-of-Kerosene, was talking to P.Q. He cocked his head toward her affectedly, pretending to be engrossed in every word she said.

". . . More people are dying now than ever before. Now you take medical science. Instead of being a deterrent, that's a boon to my business. It's kept I don't know how many people alive right up to this very moment, and I'm making a killing on them."

"We'll take it," said Mrs. Bishop loudly.

Although the house was located across the railroad tracks, it was separated by two acres of land from the shanties of the Negro section. It stood on a knoll. Oaks and butternut trees shaded it. A crumbling stone well stood in the yard, protected from the weather by a peaked roof supported on four posts. There were three other outbuildings. A yellow one-room cabin, Mrs. Kanukaris explained to them, had been an outside kitchen in Civil War days. Its roof hove slightly, and some of the tin shingles were dropping off. There was a bleached, bony barn, from which protruded wisps of hay like stuffing. And there was a shed.

The house was a weathered, broken-down farmhouse, which had been added onto several times. A living room opened onto a frail and tottering porch. Another room opened onto a wide shack kitchen. The addition section was a hallway, wide as a room, which led down to the bathroom, an afterthought. On the other side of the bathroom was a bedroom. The house had a second story, but there was no stairway to get to it. Two ancient and crumbling chimneys gave the house its sole support. The floors tipped away in all directions from them. The roof was tin. The underpinnings were rotted. The windows were irregular with cracks in their seams. Panes were broken and rags stuffed in. The front steps of the porch were rotted. Cracks between rotted boards opened to the inside of the house. Walls and ceilings were tongue-and-groove boards. Once they had been glued with newspapers to keep out the cold, but the newspaper had been torn away.

"This is one the oldest houses in Ephesus," announced Mrs. Kanukaris, tramping through the rooms before them. "Of course it wasn't no good to begin with. You know, a man got shot right at this kitchen sink. The man that owned this house shot him right through this window on account of his having moved in here with his no-good wife. He was shaving."

Loco Poco gave a delicate titter. Mrs. Kanukaris looked in her direction and then moved into another room.

"This is a Niggershack," whispered Irene, trying out the sound of it.

It was the extravagance of its lowliness that made it suit the Bishops. Not that it appealed to them, but that it personified their predicament. After Thalassia, a regular house would not do. The rottenness, the many outbuildings, the forlorn red field, the slatternly, abandoned house, the nearness of the Negro section, beckoned fallen angels. They had to be received on earth. Their adventure was beginning.

Mrs. Bishop made a few feeble attempts to avoid confrontation with these facts by talking against Mrs. Kanukaris. "I don't like that woman. Just because she married a Greek and made money, she—I don't know what!"

But she gave up. "Get rid of that woman," she mouthed to P.Q., making motions with her hands.

And when, looking out the window, she saw P.Q. piloting Mrs. Kanukaris down the weed-choked driveway, she set to. "Jump up and down on that floor," she ordered Loco and Urie.

"Why, Mamma?"

"To see if it will hold the grand piano."

They jumped. Satisfied, she roved the rooms, a faraway look in her eye. "Your rooms will be there," she told Loco and Urie, pointing to the hallway. "P.Q. and I will be upstairs. You, Irene, can have that bedroom."

"But there's no stairway to upstairs. How will you get up there?" asked Loco.

"I don't know how yet."

"Rooms!" shouted Urie. "There are no rooms here! I want my own room too, like Irene!"

"After all, I'm the oldest."

"But this is just one great big old stinking hallway! How am I going to sleep with Loco Poco snoring and people coming through my room to go to the bathroom?"

"Curtains," said Mrs. Bishop with soft inspiration, "make rooms."

Mrs. Bishop liked cloth. She had always collected it. Before the textile industry moved out of New England, she had frequented remnant shops. She had kept piles of cloth in the storeroom at Thalassia. They had grown and grown.

She knew material. She knew bolts, yards, leftovers, weaves, warps, shapes, sizes, textures, Paisleys, Chinese prints, copies, plaids, and so on. She always felt goods. She could tell the quality by the feel. She wrapped, knitted, and folded cloth, squeezed it and smoothed it with light-ning-like fingers. After they lost their money she still bought cloth. Some-times, if a thing was cheap (meaning it was never higher than fifty-nine cents a yard), she would buy it, her heart beating and her breath coming fast. Although her doting on cloth entered the realm of sinfulness, she always rationalized it. Cloth was a basic of life.

When Mrs. Bishop experienced her first epiphany about cloth, she was five years old. She was playing sheik with her seven-year-old sister in the Victorian dining room. She looked up and saw the gray-green velvet por-tieres. She ordered her older sister to take them down.

It took three hours. They dragged a love seat in from the parlor. They put a chair on top of the love seat. They put a stool on top of the chair. She stood holding this wobbling scaffold while her sister mounted. Tiptoe-ing like a dancer in her patent-leather shoes, she climbed up and meticu-lously unhooked twenty-five embroidered holes from twenty-five silken hooks. On the last hole the whole thing, portieres, stool, chair, and love seat, fell down on top of them. One hundred pounds of velvet drowned them in darkness. They lay for a moment in silence. Then they began to dig a tunnel through infinite fur. It seemed interminable. When they saw the first ray of daylight, everything was awry. The stool had spun to the bay window. The chair was upside down. The love seat was tipped against the wall.

They spent an hour erecting a framework of dining-room chairs. Tug-ging and pulling, they hoisted the portieres upward and over the chairs. They created an Oriental tent in the Sahara. The afternoon was waning as they sat ensconced inside the tent upon a knitted blanket Clara had found in the linen closet (made by her great-grandmother in New Hampshire in 1822), looking out the one small aperture. The gas lights went on outside.

Flickering light penetrated the tent. It caught the gray-green fur, turning it silver. They pretended it was the moon. The whole tent became magical, and Clara wove a mystery about the sand outside, how the world was becoming colder with the cold moon, and how they were warm and safe in the tent and needed only the light of the moon. The desert sands, mysterious and velvet, grew colder and colder outside.

Suddenly they were discovered by the housekeeper. There were a shriek, loud exclamations about ruin, a flying of hands, and in a flash the Oriental tent was whipped away, revealing two child fakirs and a pile of chairs. Mrs. Bishop smiled for many years, thinking of that moment. After her father had died, she put away the gray-green portieres. She tried to teach her own children the magic of cloth tents. She even up-ended her own dining-room chairs and made one with her two patchwork quilts. She sat with them in it when they were small, and wove stories. But she enjoyed it more than they did. Now the portieres were on the moving van, coming to Ephesus.

In the reprobate Shack Mrs. Bishop began to feel enthusiasm. She clasped her hands together. She began to run from room to room. The girls followed her. Taller than she was, they trailed after the excitement which leaked out of her eyes. She waddled a little. She knew something no one else knew. She had the power to beguile this poverty into a harem of riches. Out of the walls, to whose dusky boards and peeling texture she paid no more heed than to the girls' skeptical and downcast faces, she saw the family's entrance into the real world of riches and tapestry. Having accepted this magic so many years ago, she felt as though she knew the tapestry of the real world. She had been brought up with money, and she did not only not believe in it, she did not even mind not having it. She minded it only for them.

Mrs. Bishop, under this spell, was suddenly transformed into the child of her daughters. She was conveyed by a power as unbelievable to them as child's fancy. Her longer life, corridored by memories, was proof of her being of an order older than they could conceive. It was as if she had given birth to them only incidentally and had been put upon earth for them to steer, to guide to a place where significance would be revealed to them all. For, though they did not believe, they wanted her to show them. They would be the handmaidens to this purpose, she the goddess. Even if she was more naïve than they, they surrounded her as pilots of a baby princess who was promising to deliver them of their hard times. She had inculcated them into an experience simply to pilot her, who was used to a rich and generous, wealthy, tapestried, and now extinct world, which, though gone, might possibly be nursed back to life through her. Her enthusiasm was contagious.

"The first thing to do is to make the frame," said Mrs. Bishop to P.Q. "We've got to have the rooms made before we can do any moving."

"Before we even get the bathtub?" asked Urie.

A look from Mrs. Bishop silenced her.

P.Q. got three two-by-fours out of the shed. Mrs. Bishop measured on the floor with her feet. She pointed to the place. He hammered the two-by-fours to floor and ceiling.

"All right. Now put cross sections here and here," she ordered.

She got thumbtacks out of the tin box under Loco Poco's dolls, which had been brought in the car. She rummaged in a carton box which had been strapped to the top of the Pontiac.

"Yes. I knew it," she breathed, easing out the two tapestries. She held them up at arm's length.

When P.Q. was finished, she began tacking. They were to be double ply. She held the thumbtacks in her mouth. Since these were to be Loco's and Urie's rooms, she made them help her. They held the edge of the material to the wooden frame. Old-fashioned eighteenth-century ladies danced minuets with bewigged and powdered-haired men in silk knickers. The walls formed under their eyes. On the inside of her room Loco had a wall of dragon-and-unicorn cloth. On the inside of hers, Urie had the eighteenth-century dancers. The tapestry facing outward toward the newly created hallway was a thick woven material with purple and yellow thread designs.

"Look! Look!" Mrs. Bishop cried. "What beautiful rooms!"

"Mamma! We can cover the dining-room walls too!"

"It's fabulous!"

"I wish I had a curtain room too," said Irene.

"I'm going to put our Hawaiian bark cloth right over this living-room wall!" Mrs. Bishop said.

"And look, we can put the Paisley shawl on here to cover up this dirty hole!"

"Hahahaha! Mamma! It's too good to believe!"

"I told you so."

"It's beginning to look like an insane Arab palace."

"A Byzantine palace, not Arab," P.Q. corrected.

On August 24 the moving took place.

At seven in the morning P.Q. traded off two small oil heaters for a big four-legged bathtub and some half-inch pipe. The moving van arrived at Ransome Street at seven-twenty. Mrs. Bishop redirected it to the new house. She sent Loco Poco along to show the truck-driver.

At seven-thirty P.Q. hired Bartlett's junkyard dump truck and one Negro man. Driving the Pontiac, he led the beginning of a cavalcade. Bartlett's dump truck followed him, bearing the bathtub.

At eight-fifteen P.Q. drove up to the Shack. Loco Poco was standing in front of the grand piano, which was sitting in the yard next to a honeysuckle bush. She was playing two-fingered "Träumerei." She took one look at the bathtub and jumped in ecstasy.

"Oh, P.Q., it has lion's paws for feet!"

"Go home to Mamma and tell her to pack up the stuff in the house. The dump truck is coming to get it in five minutes."

"How shall I go? On foot?"

"Yes. And when that is finished, tell her to get over here fast."

Loco Poco was so exalted by all the activity that she ran down the driveway backward, imbibing the sight of P.Q. supervising the Negro and the moving-van man unloading the bathtub. They carried it with its feet sticking into the air. She stumbled by a honeysuckle bush and then began to run. Two minutes later Bartlett's dump truck passed her on its way to the same place.

At the Shack, P.Q. studiously ignored the moving van. Their privacy was exposed. Furniture was stacked against the butternut tree. A cooking stove was perched on top of bookcases. Springs and mattresses leaned against them. On top of the pile was Loco's powder-blue bedstead, its legs pointing to the sky. Mrs. Bishop's prized papaya-wood bowl sat in a light fixture. P.Q.'s four-legged radio straddled it. He extricated the radio and turned his back on the whole dormant, racked, helpless heap of their personality's utensils. He carried it, heaved it up the rotten porch steps into the living room. He plugged it in. He turned it on.

A broadcaster announced: "President Roosevelt appealed today to King Victor Emmanuel, to Hitler, and to President Moscicki of Poland, suggesting that direct negotiations be carried on between Germany and Poland. Arbitration or conciliation . . ."

"Where shall I put this?"

"Put it there." He pointed to a shady spot by the trunk of the butternut tree. Then he picked up a broom. He began whistling softly as if nothing unusual were happening. Carefully he swept around the legs of the radio.

". . . Poland agreed to conciliation by a third party. Meanwhile in London today in the British Parliament, the House of Commons met in special session and voted practically dictatorial powers to . . ."

"Where do you want that?"

"Put it over there."

Bartlett's dump truck jounced up the driveway with boxes and books, screeched to a halt on pressed weeds, and disgorged—red, hot, and dusty —Mrs. Bishop and Irene.

"What is that loud noise?" called Mrs. Bishop.

"I'm listening to the news."

"My piano is out in this dirt."

"That's all right. Everything comes out in the wash. Where do you want these things?"

"Have them take them in."

Mrs. Bishop took charge. P.Q. put down his broom and helped with the big furniture. The Negro and the moving-van man grunted.

The stove went in. The refrigerator went in. Chairs went in. The drop-leaf table went in. P.Q.'s steel desk went in. The wicker sofa went in. Three beds went in, leaving two stacked by the butternut tree.

An hour passed.

Loco Poco and Urie returned with the second load in Bartlett's dump truck.

"I don't see how it can all fit in," said Mrs. Bishop.

Two bureaus went in. Bedsprings went in. Mattresses went in. The mahogany glass cabinet went in. Boxes went in.

Loads were carried one after another. The rhythm accelerated. Loco carried bedspreads and the papaya-wood bowl. Urie carried the dragon candlesticks. Irene carried cloth. Loco carried the toaster and art supplies. Urie carried books. Irene carried books. Loco carried silver. Urie carried books. Irene carried books. Like ants they plied to and fro.

Another hour passed. The moving van, disgorged, began to look hollow. The house filled up. Bartlett's dump truck made two more trips. There was one more trip to make.

"At the same time," the radio said, "England and Poland signed a pact of mutual assistance. Albert Forster has been proclaimed 'supreme head' of the Danzig Free—"

P.Q. put down his broom and turned off the radio.

In the silence Urie said, "And now the piano."

Mrs. Bishop turned her back. P.Q. put his shoulder under the round end. The Negro man lifted the keyboard end. The moving-van man edged under the sounding board. Urie and Irene moved with P.Q. on the back end. They swerved. They trembled like pack animals.

Loco supervised with a pussy willow.

They grunted. They edged up the rotting porch steps.

"This way, this way," croaked P.Q.

Into the living room. Gingerly.

"Easy. Easy."

They set it down in the far corner where the main joist of the floor crossed the room. It sank into place.

"It's safe, Mamma!" cried Loco, waving her pussy-willow wand. "You can look now."

Mrs. Bishop turned.

At that moment Bartlett's dump truck bounced up the driveway. The brake shrieked, but it could not stop in time. It grazed the stack of furniture piled by the butternut tree. Loco Poco's powder-blue bedstead catapulted upward, reached the apogee of its slow-motion arc and broke into six pieces on the ground. A small puff of dust arose.

"My bed, P.Q.!" cried Loco Poco. "It's busted!"

"It's nothing," crooned P.Q. "It'll all come out in the wash."

C H A P T E R   3

"Mamma, I don't want to sleep in a coffin!" said Loco.

It was Urie who had discovered the coffins. She and Loco had gone exploring. It was that moment of half-light before dark sets in. Mrs. Bishop was cooking macaroni, their first meal in the house. The light was shining through the screen door. They crossed the broom sedge to the barn. As they creaked open the barn door, the first thing they saw was an old pump organ backed up against bales of hay. Its keyboard shone like false teeth. Urie tried it out, playing "Drink to Me Only with Thine Eyes." Loco began to sing with her high, reedy voice. Her foot touched something. She bent down and pulled a flute out from under the footpedals of the organ.

"Look! A flute!" Loco wiped dust and horse manure off it on her dress. "It's mine!"

At the same moment Urie spotted the coffins, nineteen of them stacked up in back of the hay bales.

It was Mrs. Bishop's idea to try the bedsprings on top of one of them.

"A perfect Procrustean bed!" said P.Q.

Loco Poco could not go to sleep that night. She lay huddled on the bedsprings. All alone in the darkness and closeness of the curtains she lay staring. Outside the wind began to blow. The branches of the trees above the house gnarled their arms and batted their leaves. Cool air sneaked through the rotted underpinning and inflated the curtain partitions of her room. In the next tapestry cubicle Loco could hear Urie breathing in sleep.

Suddenly there was a crack like a gunshot. Velvet footsteps scrambled madly over Loco's head. Loco held her arms rigid to her body and did not breathe.

In the next cubicle there was a stirring. Urie had waked up. Loco listened.

Urie listened. What was it? She heard silence and then strange breathing.

Suddenly there was another crack. Then silence again.

As if a signal had passed between them, Loco stretched her neck, staring into the dark.

"Urie," she whispered.

"What?"

"What was that noise?"

"A nut fell on the tin roof."

"But there were footsteps."

"A squirrel ran after it."

"Oh." Loco laughed strangely.

There was a silence.

"Remember the ocean?" said Urie.

But Loco did not answer.

"Life is very strange," Urie persisted.

Still Loco did not speak. At last a shamed whisper came. "Do you think dead people have been in my bed?"

A flit of smiling malice lighted Urie's face in the dark. "Yes, they have," she whispered conspiratorially. "Kan-of-Kerosene had to fit the right bodies to the right coffins. Often she had to put dead people in it that didn't fit." Urie's improvisation on Mrs. Kanukaris grew. She described an old Negro convict who had been put into Loco's bed. She imagined Loco's delicate Minoan eyes drinking in her words. "Actually he had been in the Medical Building as a cadaver. They had already hung him up by the ears and covered him with formaldehyde. But when they started to use him for dissecting, they found out that he was no good for that purpose because he had had some dread disease, so they got Kan-of-Kerosene to bury him. But when she tried to stuff him in your coffin he was too big to fit. So she began to stuff and stuff until—"

"You're making it up."

"I am not!"

"You are!"

"All right then. If you're such a lily-livered coward that you don't even believe what I say, I won't tell you any more." Urie, smiling, turned over.

Loco Poco was heartened by Urie's derision. She fell into a fitful slumber. She dreamed that she was in her coffin. Above her was the bulbous face of Kan-of-Kerosene. "Got to get him in here. Got to cram him in!" said Kan-of-Kerosene. The body of the dead Negro sank on top of her. She struggled. But raw chemicals smothered her nostrils. She extricated a black arm from around her neck. The head of the Negro man fell on her chest. Everywhere she tried to move, he obstructed her. Suddenly she heard her mother say, "The reason I don't like that funeral woman is because she hung around here to spy on us moving, and she actually told me she'd murder my husband if he picked any apples off the crab-apple tree. As if anyone would pick those wormy apples!" But Loco could not see her mother, and her mother did not know that she was in there beneath the Negro. At that moment Kan-of-Kerosene discovered Loco Poco in the coffin. Grinning, she put her hand over the side, picked the dead Negro off her, and hung him up by the ears.

Loco woke up. She moaned.

Urie shot awake. "What's the matter with you?"

"Oh, Urie!"

"Don't cry!" begged Urie. The floor buckled under her footsteps. The partitions moved. Loco's coffin bed went down. Urie felt for the curtain flap of Loco's room. She took another step and entered. Loco's coffin bed rose slightly. Loco looked like a bent flower. Her crying was so primeval and hopeless that Urie could not bear it. Had it been daylight, Urie would have been embarrassed by her own tenderness, but the night, the darkness, the strangeness, the new house, the new conditions, made her only want to comfort Loco.

"Don't make that noise. Do you want to wake up everybody?"

"Will you come into this coffin with me, Urie?"

Urie snaked herself up against Loco's shoulders and sat on the bed. They did not say anything.

Between Loco and Urie there was a special and unbreakable bond. To Loco Poco, Urie was frightening and individualistic. She could mesmerize and intimidate people. She *was* the goddess Urania. If anything went wrong, Urie had strength.

To Urie, Loco was a kind of baby sorceress. When she was little, people patted her curls, oohed and ahed over her, and paid no attention to Irene and Urie. Friends of P.Q. had always given her extra sticks of candy. A painter had painted her picture. Once the Bishops went on a sea voyage, and Loco Poco won a prize in a potato race on deck, although she had come in last, because she had ravished the judges with her solemn beauty and her dewlaps of laughter, and they created the prize for her. Loco accepted these kudos unaffectedly. She never doubted that she deserved them. Loco Poco had a strange streak. It was as if she were separated from the world's doings. She was abstract. She was preoccupied by something that was going on behind appearances. As if there were gold lurking behind her eyes.

One day Urie made a black book of virtues and vices:

Loco	*Urie*
lazy	bossy
sly	messy
foxy	ambitious
gets away with murder	smart
doesn't do dishes	hard-working
no ambition	plenty of effort
scaredy cat	inspired
gets sick often	healthy
can't stand noise	strong
cries a lot	good wisecracks
neat	intellectual
beautiful	funny
cute	not so good looking
comical	does dishes beyond what ought to be
cries when teased	good actress
can't take it	tough
peculiar (peculiar-queer, as if tuned in to Mars)	plays piano
	practices
funny	rational
sheep (no, lion, but in sheep's clothing)	leader
	brave

Urie showed the black book to Loco Poco. Loco read it solemnly. Then she laughed. Urie looked at her, became infected, and laughed. The black book had to be thrown in the trash.

Once Urie had committed a crime against Loco. After they lost their money, the last big present Mrs. Bishop had given to anybody was a tricycle for Loco. The tricycle was a deep wine-red. Loco loved it. She rode it so much she became part of it. She rode fast. Her feet flicked, spinning around with the pedals like lightning. Urie took this tricycle one day in a spasm of cold anger and wheeled it to the bank of the three-mile pond. Loco ran after her as fast as she could, to save the tricycle.

But at the edge of the pond, she stopped. With great deliberation Urie let the tricycle go. They both watched, fascinated. The crime, the protest, the loss were suddenly merged into awe, as the wine-red tricycle disappeared beneath the surface. Loco turned to her, caught in the collusion.

"Do you think it will live down there forever, Urie?" she asked in the ensuing days. She thought of it, breathing and shiny, deep in the bottom of the pond, its friends the pond weeds.

There was beauty and guilt in the death of her tricycle. It bound her to her sister. She would never tell.

Mrs. Bishop wanted to know where the tricycle was. "I don't know where it is," said Loco. "I must have left it somewhere. It might be at"— she looked with huge frightened eyes—"at the bottom of the pond." She was about to be punished for carelessness when Irene guessed, and told.

When Urie was confined to her room every night for a whole summer, the sentence made a deep impression on Loco. The transitoriness and the ephemeral life of matter were superseded by Urie's Spartan forbearance in the face of punishment. Loco would come up every night and amuse her. They laughed and giggled until they forgot that Urie was in prison. Loco became Urie's familiar, her conspirator, her ally beyond jealousy. One day they found a dead pheasant in the woods. "It's beautiful, Urie. Look at it! Let's make it sleep! Like my bicycle. It wants a home to be dead in!" Urie organized a funeral. They picked flowers, invited Irene, and dug a hole, made speeches when they laid it in and covered it. Urie owned Loco in a realm beyond anyone's knowing or beyond their ability to express. Yet she was bound to the mysteriousness in Loco with a speechless passion.

"See? A coffin's nothing!" said Urie.

The answering snuggling tightness of Loco's arms around her neck comforted Urie. They let their faces float in the cold darkness, gobbling up the strangeness that thrust them together, the fear, the fantasticality of their new house, and their unbefitting downtroddenness. What would ever become of them? wondered Urie. How strange were their two bodies, clinging together in the night. She thought of Loco, wondering what it would be like if she were Loco with Loco's tears on her cheeks and Loco's breath in her throat.

Loco smiled a self-indulgent smile against Urie's chest in the darkness. Then she fell asleep, and Urie was left awake and alone.

Loco dreamed an old dream. She was sitting in a daisy patch. She was fat with a white dress, and instead of having black hair, she had yellow hair. It was Eastern Point. The sun was streaming. A breeze was blowing from the ocean. She was in the world of grass. She was ostensibly a baby, but she knew that she was not; she was a daisy.

She put out her hand to tease the other daisies. They nodded back to her. This gave everything the sense of never-endingness.

Until this night, at the age of ten, Loco could not remember the beginning or the end of this birth of her daisyhood. There was a secret to never-endingness. Now she knew the secret. Everybody knows the secret from the beginning, but the form which the secret takes differs from person to person. Loco knew the pheasant and the tricycle. She knew that they lived. Every person makes the words with which the secret of never-endingness is described, and it differs from person to person. Because of this, each person believes his secret to be different from the other person's secret.

Loco was a daisy because her white dress was petals, her yellow hair refracted from her baby skin like the yellow fur center of the daisy. And her eyes were like the sky. At the time she recognized herself as a daisy, she was not aware of the infiniteness of anything. Irene and Urie were laughing somewhere nearby, unaware. Their laughter and existence accompanied her daisyhood, along with the drumming of the insects and the swish of the ocean on the grass blades. Everything was very simple and she was at home. As the tricycle later was at home with the pond weeds.

When the universe expanded, when she had become ten years old, she recognized her secret. She was a daisy. She would tell this secret to Urie someday, but because she was asleep she had to put off the moment of sharing it until some other day. Perhaps tomorrow.

CHAPTER 4

"Do you know what the worst feature of this house is?" asked Urie.
"What?"
"These linoleum rugs. Only cheap people live in houses with linoleum rugs."

"Yeah. Look at these dirty purple roses."

"Hasten, Jason, bring the basin. Errrrrrrgh! Too late. Bring the mop."

Mrs. Bishop, although reflexively uttering, "I wish you wouldn't talk like that, Urie Bishop," absorbed their point of view. She could avail nothing against their glee of Cassandraic doom. The linoleum rugs could not be taken up because the house was riddled with termites. In the middle of the night they could hear tiny, intermittent chain-saw noises as the termites worked laborious as Communists digging the Moscow subway. Underneath the floorboards were nests of sawdust. They discovered, the first week, that termites not only sawed wood but bit people too. Loco complained first, and then all of them were bitten. P.Q. invented a cure. Rub yourself with Fels Naphtha yellow soap. P.Q. ignored their snobbism. He did not see purple roses. He saw insulation. But he said nothing. He did not want the subject of heating to come up. They would have to buy an oil heater before winter.

The Bishops had not paid the moving company yet. And it would require quick work to get enough money to eat, without thinking of other things. P.Q. surreptitiously worked three nights one week behind the counter at Nick Vlahakis's greasy spoon. This was a dire extremity which cost him his pride. He never told the family. In his own mind he did it not to earn money but to do Nick a favor, with the secret object of borrowing money from him until the first linen for the business arrived.

"Why you come to this place, Ephesus, anyway, P.Q.?" asked Nick, a grizzled ex-wrestler from Phraxos. He had the resentful but sincere curiosity of an underling who, no matter how much money he lends, knows that he will always be despised, and for the very reason that enables him to lend: his work. Nick worked from six in the morning to midnight for his money and could conceive of no other way to get it.

"To raise cypress trees for telephone poles," answered P.Q.

"Why you not do it, then?"

"It takes two hundred years for one cypress tree to get big enough."

"Hahaha," Nick laughed. "You're a case. No wonder I heard them college boys saying you named P.Q. because it stands for peculiar."

P.Q. was in a good mood. He laughed uproariously.

On September 1, Germany invaded Poland. Across the fever pitch of fixing-up that was transforming the house, P.Q. transported the radio down the buckling hallway to the bathroom. He plugged it in to the light socket in Loco Poco's room and listened while he bored holes in the floor for the bathtub pipes. The broadcasting voice of H. V. Kaltenborn gave momentous importance to every nail, screw, curtain rod, and carpet. War was imminent. Each blow of the hammer signaled it.

"You don't think those termites would eat my Oriental rug, do you?" asked Mrs. Bishop, sticking her head through the bathroom door.

"No. Only wood," said P.Q., turning the awl.

"All right. That is the solution to hideousness, then," said Mrs. Bishop. They laid down the Parsons' Oriental rug, covering the entire living-room linoleum. The event corresponded in momentousness with the transformation in Europe.

"It is superb! See, the legs of the piano sink down into it, just like they should!"

"It looks just like our old house, Mama!" whispered Loco.

"It's unbelievable!" said Irene.

P.Q. put the faucets in the bathroom. But when he came to the plumbing, two days later, he felt unsure of himself. He hired a plumber, an old Negro with gray stubble and a big wrench in his hand. It took P.Q. five hours to ferret him out and jew him down to the price he could pay. He stood over the Negro while he worked. The Negro had bad eyes. P.Q. had to place the mouth of the wrench where it was supposed to go. Then the Negro would turn it. The Negro went under the house to push the pipes up through the hole. But he worked much more slowly even than P.Q. Also he was not sure which tool to use for what. P.Q. had to make the decisions. They tried out different tools. Once they cut the pipe wrong. They had to cut it again. P.Q. advised, pointed, explained. He put great enthusiasm into his pedagogy. At last after many hours the pipes were threaded and hooked together. P.Q. turned on the faucet. Water spat, trickled, and then spewed forth.

"Hooray!" cried Loco.

But P.Q. held up his hand for silence. The radio was announcing that Great Britain and France had declared war on Germany.

The bathroom became as silent as a church. Loco perched on the toilet seat. Urie sat on the edge of the bathtub. The Negro stood upright against the wall, holding the wrench reverently in his two hands. Everyone looked at P.Q.

The fact that the Negro was there made everything more important. The Bishops, in the tradition of Garrison, Thoreau, and Harriet Beecher Stowe, were intellectually unprejudiced. But there had never been any Negroes on the North Shore. Since the "colored" water fountain the girls had become curious. That they lived in the Negro section had now become a fact of importance.

"In those countries the peoples are fools out of ancient and narrow-minded habits." P.Q. spoke with loud and specific sententiousness. He did not look at the Negro at all, but directed his remarks. "Instead of looking at the United States and seeing how to do things by joining all their countries together and having a United States of Europe, they just do the same old thing they've done for thousands of years, just like apes. They fight each other, kill each other, grab each other's land, and step on each other's big toe. Even apes know better than that, don't they?"

"Yas sir."

"You know what's the matter with them?" P.Q. asked the Negro.

"What?"

"They're ignorant. Instead of looking at the United States and seeing how they could have schools and teach every man how to read and write and know how to do things so nobody can fool him, they keep the poor people down. Here people like you and me can go to school and then nobody can fool us. We can vote for whom we want. Then we don't need to go in and kill each other like that."

"You absolutely right, sir. I thinks so too."

After the Negro left, P.Q. did not talk about Europe. He moved the radio back into the new elegant living room. He sat among the wall-hangings, the Oriental rug, looking at the familiar pictures, Amalfi, the picture of the Yosemite falls, and the picture of the three-masted schooner. In the soft, swimming lamplight June bugs, moths, millers, and other flying insects whittered, having sneaked their way through the rags stuffed still in the broken panes. They cast giant moving shadows on the board walls. Silence followed the declarations of war. There was a preternatural calm.

"If we're ever going to have a real dining room, we'll have to stop sleeping in it and move into the upstairs room," said Mrs. Bishop.

It was Mrs. Bishop who decided to make the outside kitchen into P.Q.'s office. She ordered Urie and Irene to clean and dust it with brooms, mops, and cloths. Then she laid down an old hooked rug that had been in the family. They made a sofa out of another of Mrs. Kanukaris's coffins. Triumphantly Mrs. Bishop covered it with the very portieres from which she and her sister had made the Sahara tent. She decorated the sofa with pillows made out of old Mr. Parsons' plaid opera cape. Urie made a bookcase out of orange crates, and they moved out some of P.Q.'s Greek and history books. The china umbrella stand full of P.Q.'s canes, the picture of the fisherman on the beach with the two boys pointing, and the golden mantelpiece clock made the concocted office so beautiful that Loco began to use it as her own private playhouse and filled it with dolls. P.Q., though he hated dolls, liked them as artifacts of Loco.

On September 5 he wrote to B. F. Bopp Toweling Company of West Virginia for 123 yards of dice-grain toweling and 50 yards of unbleached denim. He enclosed the sum of $30, which he had saved for the purpose from Nick Vlahakis's loan. This would give Nick a share in the investment, he informed him to make him feel good. Then he sent to Atlanta, Georgia, for grommets and a small punching machine.

The exploration of the territory that they were reclaiming from trashiness and erosion did not extend to the shantytown down the road. One day Irene said prissily, "We should not call it Niggertown. We're supposed to be unprejudiced."

"Well, we can't call it Negrotown," said Urie emphatically.

They made up the euphemism "Sociological Conditions."

Hearing that a white family was living up on the hill, the Negroes blossomed from their shacks almost like flowers. Their black eyes stared up from the bleached white dirt of the road. Their red lips and pink hands waved like petals. Their smell, pungent and sour, mixed with the drenching perfume of the flowers. Their curiosity was creeping and palpable like the summer. It mirrored the sky, which hovered low over the environs, like a skin pressing the atmosphere close upon them.

But the Negroes were separated by the denseness of bushes and the expanse of the broom sedge. The Bishops tried to know them. They walked down to the road to speak. But the Negroes were elusive. When the Bishops got near, man, woman, or child would disappear into the dark, greasy hole of a hovel. Loco followed a child one day. But the child got away. P.Q. told her after that not to follow Negroes.

So the family forgot their existence. They became a backdrop. Sometimes in the evenings the Bishops went out to the barn. Urie played "Fairest Lord Jesus" and "Holy, Holy, Holy" on the pump organ, and they sang. One night when Loco whispered, "Sociological Conditions is listening to us," they became aware of a strange silence over Tin Town. They waited. Then a guitar began. Negro voices started singing. They were like a secret signal of the Negroes to the white family, like the answer to a smoke signal.

But the extent to which the family were aliens was not known until one day when Mrs. Bishop sent Loco Poco to buy some pinto beans at a Negro store in front of the railroad track. A woman named Lucretia Pile ran the store, a voluminous woman, with nonadhering fat which floated and bob-bled as she moved around the barrels, drinking a Coca-Cola.

"I would like a peck of pinto beans, please," said Loco.

"Ya'll'm."

Lucretia Pile waddled to the barrel, picked up the beans, waddled back to the counter, foraged for a bag, and then poured the beans into the bag.

When Loco said thank you and left, a group of children were gathered in the road outside the broken screen door. They were flapping, jumping, laughing, and caterwauling words. Loco tried to understand, but the words were like a foreign language. The children stopped talking and, exploding with laughter, ran away. The only thing she could make out was "blinto screams."

When she got home she gave her mother the package. She sat down at the dining room table and put up her elbows to think.

"What ails you?" asked Mrs. Bishop.

"Mamma!" Loco said softly. Mrs. Bishop waited. "I think those Socio-logical Conditions were aping me."

"What do you mean, aping you?"

"They aped the way I talk!" said Loco, beginning to be surprised her-self. "But I don't talk like that! They mimicked me!" she repeated, amazed.

In the middle of September the Bishops decided to sell the Pontiac. The decision was agreed upon by both P.Q. and Mrs. Bishop. P.Q. wanted to buy a laundry truck. They did not need the Pontiac. They needed a laun-dry truck.

Nevertheless, the day before P.Q. drove the Pontiac to Bartlett's junk-yard, where he was to receive fifty dollars for it, Mrs. Bishop regarded it mournfully. It was the last tie to their former life, the vehicle that had brought them to Ephesus. She felt as if she were burying part of her own life. But since the future of the family hung upon it, she pushed aside her thoughts and looked away.

A certain nebulousness characterized the formation of the linen supply, though P.Q. had local customers lined up. This was because he insisted on thinking of the business as a fully capitalized affair, with a fleet of running trucks, a staff of drivers managed by a supervisor, and a fully worked-out contract with a laundry. P.Q. talked to Greek café-owners and Jewish mer-chants in this vein. He had no contract with a laundry.

The discrepancy between vision and fact did not bother the local mer-chants. They had nothing to lose. If P.Q.'s service was no good, they could return to the monopoly. Meanwhile there were several points in his favor. The war in Europe was going to change things. There was talk of the repeal of the Neutrality Act so the United States could sell to the warring nations. Increased production and services would be needed. There would be fortunes made by nuts and entrepreneurs. People liked the idea of an underdog with gall pitting himself against the established monopoly.

P.Q. evoked a strange reaction in people. He did not play by the rules of the game. He spoke of esoteric subjects when he was supposed to be talking money. He mentioned Plato, Byzantine Church history, or John Dewey to ignorant people. Some felt he was making a fool of them. Others felt that he was the fool.

Yet there was something behind his ice-blue eyes that gave people an excited feeling. He was not a snob. Therefore he must be attacking the system. He struck a reactive chord because, neither professor, Communist, nor bohemian, he was operating in the world behind the system, a world where no one would admit to living. He dressed like a dandy in worn-out banker's clothes unsuitable to hot streets. His shoes were always polished, no matter how many dirt roads he walked. The crowning glory was that he pretended to be unaware that he was strange.

There was a bookstore on Main Street called the Libido Library, run by two bohemians, a fat Appalachian country boy from the mountains named Hoke Tabernacle and his wife, a New York Jew raffishly called Mamma Mia by students. The town rumor was that they were Communists and that Mamma Mia had organized thirteen cells throughout the state. Hoke looked like Buddha. He sat in the store all day, barefoot. He did no work. He read books, with his chair propped backward on two legs, his bare feet on the rungs. Mamma Mia ran the store. When Mamma Mia wasn't looking, students stole books.

One day P.Q. stepped in and banged the door loudly. Hoke looked up.

P.Q. said, "You are both dirty. You ought to rent aprons from me, at least four a week. You can dust your books and sort them without dirtying yourselves up. Then you can arrange them on the shelves. You'll be able to sell twenty per cent more books when you know what you've got in here. Then you'll be making more money, you'll be clean, and you can perform more Communist good."

Hoke set down his chair. He burst into admiring laughter and began to clap. His clapping tipped over a big dusty stack of books teetering on the counter. They crashed. Mamma Mia came to the front of the store to pick them up.

"Anybody that's got the gall to come here and call us pigs, Mamma Mia, we ought to do business with him," said Hoke with a pridefully illiterate drawl.

"What do you say to that?" asked P.Q., bending over to help her gallantly.

"Will it make more money?" she asked, grunting.

"It stands to reason," said P.Q.

"And how would you know?" she said, raising her red face accusingly.

"Because I'm one of the chosen, too."

"Chosen for what?" she asked derisively.

"For anything that anybody thinks people are chosen for."

"What are you, anyway?" asked Mamma Mia furiously.

"Who knows?" P.Q. shrugged. "How can anybody be sure? When I was picking my way through the goat turds in Khartoum, Africa, where I was born, my old grandfather told me I was a Greek, and my old grandmother told me I was a Jew. Of course it was their secret. How could I know? But the only people in the whole place besides the natives and the British were the Greeks and Jews, and since they were always stealing from each other, they hated each other. Such an environment gave me a wide scope of vision."

"Okay. We'll take," said Hoke. To Mamma Mia: "Maybe the man will buy a book."

When the linen came from Bopp Toweling, Mrs. Bishop organized an outdoor sweatshop. She made a cutting table out of one of the barn doors. It was loose. She instructed the girls to rip it off. They did this with glee. Then they transported it to the spot outside the kitchen door which she had designated for the sweatshop. Irene took one end. Urie took the other. Loco got underneath and walked as if holding it on her head. She was invisible.

"P.Q. says the either-or philosophy started by Aristotle is crap," said Urie. "But in this case it's true. Either this business makes money or we sink into starvation."

These words scared Irene. Her eyes enlarged to bubble size as she struggled with the end of the door, but she could not say anything because she was afraid of dropping it.

"We have sunk so low that we live in Sociological Conditions. To sink into starvation couldn't be worse," came Loco's voice, slightly muffled from beneath. Her invisibility lent a perverse exhilaration to the words.

"You eat more than anybody else in this family," retorted Urie, reinforcing the paradoxical myth that went: "Isn't it funny how the smallest member of the family is always the one who eats the most!" It accrued truth by its repetition. "Humph! I'd like to see you if you really had to starve!"

"Do you really think we could starve?" came Loco's voice again. This time it was subdued.

"Well, look who had to go on WPA. Don't you remember them throwing stones at cans in the water when they were supposed to be cleaning up the beach? And this country is supposed to be the land of freedom, equality, and opportunity. Haw haw haw."

"I mean *starve!*" Urie's non sequiturs simply waved Loco on like a red flag. Her feet began to run, twinkling as fast as a dachshund's, as the older sisters walked faster. "I mean shrinking bags of skin and bones like those skeleton people you see in India."

"We can always go on welfare, can't we?" screamed Irene in desperation. "Hurry up!" she shouted. "I'm going to drop this end. And you, Loco, get out of there. You aren't doing a thing!"

They set the barn door on two sawhorses by the kitchen door. Mrs. Bishop had discovered the sawhorses in the shed.

"All right, you, Urie, tack these patterns to the cloth as I lay it out here. You, Irene, can begin cutting." The patterns were made out of newspaper. They were patterns of aprons and chefs' caps. "Loco, bring the cloth out."

Next to the barn-door cutting table, Mrs. Bishop placed her old drop-leaf table. It was her favorite for sewing. She put her electric sewing machine on it. She inserted the electric cord through a hole in the screen door and plugged it in the kitchen. An assembly line began. Urie pinned. Irene cut the first piece. Mrs. Bishop sewed the pieces together.

The conversation on starvation resumed. They had to shout over the clatter of the machine. Finally Mrs. Bishop lifted her foot off the pedal. There was a sudden preternatural silence.

"If you can't talk about anything better than that, keep quiet."

She began the machine again. Their thoughts went underground.

Irene's right, thought Urie. No, they would not starve. There was always welfare. Thus Aristotelian limitation did not seem so dire. P.Q. was really correct.

The momentum of production veered them into a different arena of thought. Talk of starvation was really an exaggerated cover-up for the more impending worry: school. The Bishops dreaded the thought of that day which lay before them, of completely new people, a new environment where they would be strangers, unknown, unrecognized. They were afraid. They flung themselves into production of aprons and caps with a will, as if the great white piles of linen, the endless pins shining in the sunlight, the crackling paper, the drone of scissors, the scream of the sewing machine, the chattering of the needle, the growing piles of recognizable aprons would stave off the day.

"Cut three layers at a time," Mrs. Bishop said.

Work went faster and faster. Irene changed places with Urie. Irene pinned patterns. Urie cut.

"I want to cut, Mamma. Why can't I cut?" asked Loco.

"Your fingers aren't big enough."

"Yes, they are."

"It's too hard for you," teased Irene. "Don't you remember, even Mamma lost the nerves of her thumb for three years and couldn't feel a thing because she cut too many dresses out."

"You can hem later," said Mrs. Bishop as a sop.

The coming of the grommet machine saved Loco. It arrived two days later. There were seventy-five aprons sewed and hemmed, ready to have the grommet holes put at the hips, where the apron-wearer could insert strings to tie the apron around the middle. Mrs. Bishop tried out the grommet machine. She taught Loco how to do grommets by making her practice on the *Wall Street Journal*. A story on the possible effect of the embargo on sale of goods to belligerents was specked with golden hole-eyes.

When Loco began in earnest with aprons she made only two mistakes. Carefully she tucked her lower lip between her teeth and conducted the grommet stamping with surcharged deliberation. But as she became better she did it faster and faster. She did it in rhythm. In the rhythm of the stamping, over the chatter of the sewing machine, she amused the family with imitations. She imitated a woman getting out of a girdle, Eleanor Roosevelt eating an apple through a picket fence, and a blind beggar falling off a cliff.

P.Q. arrived at that moment to survey the sweatshop. He was very proud of the progress, but he said no word of congratulation. He had bad news. It turned out that the laundry truck cost more money than the Pontiac had brought.

"After we have robbed Peter to pay Paul! I don't see how you're going to conduct this business!" Mrs. Bishop stopped the machine. The words echoed across the dirt yard with tragic majesty.

"He can use our uncle's bicycle," said Loco.

Mrs. Bishop threw her a threatening look.

But Loco's joke turned out to be prophecy.

P.Q. made two wire baskets out of the insides of two chewing-gum machines that had been discarded at Bartlett's. The bicycle was an ancient blue vehicle that had belonged to Mrs. Bishop's brother-in-law, now dead under peculiar circumstances. Mrs. Bishop always said he had died from syphilis, calling his mistress's name on his deathbed, because his wife had forced him to be a Christian Scientist. The main thing about the bicycle was that it was made of wood, and it had pedals without a chain, which could not be stopped and could be pedaled backward.

"Well, this is the first time the absent treatment paid off," said P.Q., trying it out. He wobbled around the yard, bumping over the roots of the butternut tree.

"Do you mean to tell me you're really going to start this business on that bicycle?" asked Mrs. Bishop with her hands on her hips.

"It's only a temporary measure. Until I get the laundry truck."

"How can that bicycle hold up under the load of those aprons?"

"It's simply a temporary measure," P.Q. repeated.

On the day that the business began, everyone gathered in the dirt yard outside the kitchen door to watch him go. Loco and Urie stuffed the bicycle baskets with the aprons. Everything was ready. The aprons were in. The caps were in. The cutting table was dismantled and the sewing machine put away.

P.Q. was carefully dressed in his brown business suit. He wore a tie. His brown felt hat was placed carefully on his bald head at an angle. His shoes were highly polished and gleamed as he placed them on the pedals.

Mrs. Bishop's attitude was now transformed. With great admiration and in a historical tone of voice, as if to remind the children of this moment that they should always remember, she said, "I think it is really something to be able to start your own business on a bicycle."

"It's only a temporary measure," P.Q. repeated.

He mounted. The bicycle sagged. A wire pinged as he jounced over a root. Everyone was silent. They all held their breath. He jounced over the roots, down the driveway, and into the road, the bicycle baskets flowing with the sparkling white aprons. As he disappeared across the railroad tracks, he personified that individual existence, that culmination of tradition and labor, that Bishopry that was, like themselves, about to be launched into the unknown.

PART II

CHAPTER 5

The town of Ephesus was called the oasis of the South. This was because of the university. The university vied with the University of Georgia in claiming to be the oldest state university in the nation. It had a liberal tradition. There were only three thousand students. Everybody knew everybody else. Tuition was cheap. Many students were poor. Learning was respected. Philosophy was on everybody's lips. It was a last outpost of Jeffersonian simplicity and Greek humanism, and it was respected throughout the state.

Stories were told about how many miles famous alumni had traveled by mule or walked barefoot to get their education. Spirit and tradition were contagious because of the perfumed leaves and lawns. The campus was centered around an old well, over which had been built a fresh white canopy with columns. Old North and Old South were dormitories that had been designated state landmarks and planted with plaques. Dogwood perforated spring like snow. Oftentimes classes were held outdoors. Teachers came from the North and West and spread the school's fame. It took on a cosmopolitan air.

Ephesus had pride in its democratic ways. It was forced to defend itself each generation from accusations of being a hotbed of Communism. It put out plans for countering erosion, unemployment, and tenant farming. Its mystique was contagious. The Shakespeare authority of Ephesus had been a hog-farmer, who interspersed footnotes with hog lore. He had taken up Shakespeare, he said, so he would never have to leave Ephesus. Another man connected with the university had written a book about Ephesus called *The Magnolia Tree in Heaven* and afterward committed suicide. Ephesian wits said it was because he had no place better to go. Everyone knew that the F-sharp of the bell tower was flat, but people had heard it so much during supper hour at Swine Hall that the false scale had become real to them and they preferred it.

Juxtaposed with the Apollonian dignity of the town was an underside, frenzied, eccentric, and passionate. It existed because, as in all college towns, most of the inhabitants were young, and people were fervent in their ideas and tried to live them. In the twenties a Middle Westerner named Herbert Boll had established the Folk Blood Movement. He got the college to build a true Dionysian outdoor theater out of native stone, and there he put on Euripides and Sophocles with choruses of drawling coeds dressed in cheesecloth costumes and followed by gnats. This was not popular. So he decided that the drama should be indigenous. A school of playwriting grew up under him which featured tobacco-spitting mountaineers, exploited Negroes, mill workers being persecuted by scabs, witches, mountain conjure women, and tenant farmers holding the state's red earth in their hands, like Scarlett O'Hara's father, poeticizing against painted backdrops of pine trees. The theater was acclaimed nationally, and drama conventions were held there. It happened one year that a student murdered his friend in a rooming house and then rushed to the Folk Blood Theater and shot himself. Soon after people noticed that the stones of the theater were turning red. Although the color was from iron in the stone, not blood, the movement got its name from this. Afterward the theater became a focus for two more murders, a suicide, and a strike. But at Ephesus everyone accepted the bizarre as a natural part of life, and although people made the most of these episodes for gossip, wisecracks, and telling the year by, they acted urbane.

A one-track railroad brought coal in once a week for the university power plant. This railroad track separated Ephesus from its adjunct, a settlement called Haw, originally Saxapahaw, Indian for "Dirty Feet in Muddy River." Although Haw was the original settlement, a weaving mill had been put there in 1910. The mill had gone out of business during the Depression, and the low brick building sat like a ghost, in the middle of the town, its great windows broken and squinting. Twisting black machinery still sat inside the mill. Sometimes children sneaked in to explore. Otherwise its silence remained unbroken except for field rats that forayed in from the railroad tracks, skittling around the forgotten piles of lint, or swallows that made nests in stacks of defective BVDs.

Haw was a scattering of mill houses clumped along dirt roads. Each mill house teetered on four stones at the corners. There were no foundations. The dirty white clapboards were stained red on the bottom from clay. Yards were grown up with weeds, choking bushes, or kudzu vines that had multiplied dangerously. Paths had been worn through the yards by bare feet. These paths were more traveled than the roads. The tin roofs gave off a feverish luster on hot afternoons in summer when the sun began to go down. People sat on their broken porches. Through the groan of their swings they stared out of sharp faces, the color of turnips, and they chewed tobacco. Underneath the houses dogs howled in their dreams.

It was in its relation to Ephesus that Haw was peculiar. It was the pole of a dualistic universe, the servile, dirty, ignorant underdog to Ephesus. The Ephesians ignored it. They let it stand ugly in the sun. But the Haw people knew the lacy lawns of Ephesus, the magnolia-tipped excellence, the green aspirations of the university, the promise of its halls, the entice-ment of its books, the lushness of its arboretum, the secret of its learned-ness. And they had no part in it. Despised, out of work, they sat like liv-ing ghosts in the sun and watched when the professors rode by.

In the town of Haw lived a family named Walley. The father, Eames Loomis Walley, was a furnace-repairman who had worked for the mill. Loomis Walley had bowed legs and a face that was dustmop gray. Nothing had ever happened to him in life. He had finished the fourth grade. He had married Henny Pinney McDonald. And he had one child, a boy. When the mill closed down he bought the house he was living in cheap and started raising bees. By selling honey and doing odd repair jobs he supported the family.

Henny Pinney Walley had been a bright student with fitful ambition. She had finished the eighth grade. She married Eames Loomis Walley just to marry. Although she loved her child, her dissatisfaction with married life became the theme of her existence. As Loomis became more dun-col-ored day by day, she became faded and bleached in the years of marriage. She nagged. She tried to pump ambition into her husband, but he was sat-isfied with things as they were. At last she resigned herself. She became happier and began to dip snuff. The only trace of her former aspiration was the name she gave her son: Zebulon, after the entrepreneur and aristo-crat Zebulon Vance Alamance, former governor of the state.

From the beginning Zebulon Walley was favored. His face was as brown as a corn husk. He was curious, with big ears and a blue intelli-gence that covered the horizons of everything. He was also independent and went his own way. The Haw influences fell off him like water off a duck's back. From the first day of school he was bright and willing and he spoke good grammar.

The matter of grammar separated him from the other Haw children. Yet there was some element in Zeb's personality, something easygoing that made the other children accept his good grammar without condemnation. They did not think he was affected. They played with him as they played with anybody else. And they gave way to his peculiarities of brilliance and to his superiority as if it were natural. For he did not claim to be a leader. He lived and let live.

Below the Walley outhouse, buried among the beehives and the honeysuckle near the edge of their yard, was an ancient chickenhouse. It's boards were rotten. It had a tin roof. The first day Zeb used this chickenhouse as his "dwelling" he was six years old. He came home with his corduroy pants caked in chicken droppings. Henny Pinney told Eames Loomis to clean the chickenhouse up. Eames Loomis cleaned it. He made a new floor for it out of some second-hand lumber left in the mill yard. He covered the wall with samples of wallpaper which he tore out of a Montgomery Ward catalogue.

It was because of this little house that Zeb withdrew from his family. He began to bring himself up. He improvised his way of life. As he went beyond her, Henny Pinney sighed and gave up. She began treating him differently, not paying him much attention. She did not fancy herself a maternal type, anyway.

People knew Zeb was smart, from the very first grade. All during his self-bringing-up it was simply accepted as natural that he should take his bed out to the little house, that he should only eat his meals and take his bath in the regular house, that he should become a boarder to his own mother, and that his privacy should be respected. Nothing he did surprised anyone, although the facts of his bringing-up were distinctly unusual.

He always brought his report cards home dutifully, but he actually interpreted his own good marks to his mother and father. Once he asked his mother to buy him some lead cars and trucks from the dime store. She did. He worked out an entire highway system based on a map of the roads of Haw and Ephesus. Then he walked the actual roads and said that the map was fallacious. After that he lost interest in the lead cars and highway system. He turned to painting. Through special favors from the teachers in the Haw school, he gathered up piles of drawing paper. He drew butterflies, portraits, and landscapes. By the age of eleven he had an orange crate full of drawings. All the mothers of Haw wanted him to sketch portraits of their children. He did.

The experience with the drawing paper gave him an appetite for collecting. Unable to get any more paper from the teachers, he began to steal. Once for nine weeks he brought ten pieces of paper home every day. The storerooms in the elementary school became objects of surveillance. So he stopped stealing drawing paper and turned to books. Out of necessity, reading took his interest. For six weeks he drew nothing.

He read everything. The first thing he read was Max Brand. He decided to work his way up from trash. He moved to Jack London. He interspersed this with the Hardy Boys. He discovered H. G. Wells. After flipping from H. G. Wells to the Bobbsey Twins, he gobbled his way through the Nancy Drew mysteries and back to Grimms' Fairy Tales. The teachers prescribed good literature, so he took up the great mutineers and the Greek myths. Reading created his world. The door had opened. He looked up from books and found it incredible that Haw people believed life to be porch-sitting, squeaking, or going to school. He read Suetonius at the age of twelve. At thirteen he discovered the novel *Thunder on the Left* by Christopher Morley. It told of the ocean, which he had never seen. He tried to imagine it. It was something alive. The only water he knew was that which he poured into his washtub when he took his bath in the hallway. During his bath he began a sonnet. He had discovered the sonnet form in the fourth grade.

"Let not the metal sides of tubs deny the ocean." What rhymed with ocean? "Let not the metal sides of tubs deny the ocean. From my metal tub alone I can envision motion far beyond the . . ." Beyond what? It was too far even for him to imagine. He wanted to know.

Now that the world of books was more real to him than the precincts of Haw, or reality, books presented a double possibility. Possession of them in his little house became a realm tangential to the realm that he attained within their covers. There were far more books to steal than there ever was drawing paper, so the very contemplation of the world stuffed with books for him to steal made life ecstatic.

Zeb was perfectly aware that stealing was wrong. But, as with other Haw myths, he paid only as much attention as would prevent his getting caught. When he went to the library to check out books, he checked out three and took four. His little house became a library. He had to move his bed to a different side to fit all the books in. Because of the stolen books, his little house became sacrosanct and all his doings took on an intense mythical import. He knew exactly what books were in the public library, which he wanted to have, who read what, what would be noticed, and what wouldn't. He did not even rationalize his actions to himself because he took it for granted that the world existed for him to discover and appropriation was simply a convenience for a transferral of things that ought to belong to him already. Riches are for those who know how to use them was his opinion.

Between people in the Haw library who knew that books were being stolen and people who knew Zeb's little house was progressively filling with wall-to-wall books there was no collusion. Though people knew Zeb Walley was stealing books, and that books were being stolen, as with field rats in the Haw mill, nobody cared. The discrepancy in ethics, since it dealt with a virtue, "love of books," was sloughed over. Since Zeb was a pride to the community, his stealing was almost a virtue. An old town doctor and three retired schoolteachers, aware that he stole, gave him books. Eames Loomis and Henny Pinney called Zeb's increasing library "all them books that people give you."

Zeb knew that he was free. He could do and be anything. People agreed with his own evaluation and considered him a special case. In the morning he read Sherlock Holmes. In the afternoon he helped his father get the honey and picked some scuppernong grapes. Nothing was inconsistent with anything else. After Paul Dombey's death agonies, he drew a butterfly. The main thing about Zeb's happiness was that, being inconsistent, it was shallow. He never pondered over anything. He gobbled. He evaluated nothing.

But there was a streak of devotion in him. He believed in God ardently. He loved Jesus Christ. He even thought of himself sometimes as that lamblike man and boy, for did not everybody love him and give him things? He was spared sin.

At the same time his curiosity got the better of his devotion. His mother, although a scoffer, sometimes took him to revivals. They were a way to get out of the house, she said. Each time, imbued with the rhythmic screams about lambs and blood, he desired to rush up along the yellowed grass of the ground and be saved. It was the one thing he dared not do, because of his mother. Thus, entranced, he concentrated on the fat neighbor woman, Mrs. Bessie Suggs, a fifth cousin of his father's, who rose like a performing elephant, knocking over camp chairs and speaking glossolalia. He wanted to find out the unknown tongue. It was a gift, he knew, even though his mother called it gobbledygook. He believed that contiguity to Mrs. Suggs might give him the answers, so he took to following her for two weeks after the revival was over, until she became suspicious. She turned around in the road and eyed him.

"You go home," she said. "And quit doing like that, or I'll tell."

The power of her regular speech seemed to him so tremendous that he turned right around and obeyed, not even explaining or asking her the meaning of the unknown tongue. It was the only thing he had ever been foiled in. But he knew that sometime a time would come when he would know the unknown tongue.

He had no particular friends. He did not exhibit preferences. But as time went on there was an older girl named Quira Crabtree, who lived three houses up from him and had often taken care of him when he was little, who formed a preference for him. She had a limp from childhood rheumatic fever. The limp and a pale, freckled face, black hair, a glamorous way of smoking cigarettes and of modeling herself on Tallulah Bankhead, made her exotic. Sometimes at night she came to his little house. They sat with the night millers flapping against the screen, and she told him what she was going to do in life. He was twelve years old at this time, and she was fifteen. She had had boy friends for two years. They were not even high-school boys, but some were Jews and some writers from New York. She said she was going to be a blues singer. She might start out as a typist. First she was going to work in the Vieux Carré in New Orleans, and then she was going to work on Madison Avenue. She dropped these names with attenuated carelessness, knowing that, although he did not know them, he would be impressed, for he was not like other Haw kids.

On the day of her graduation from high school her father abandoned the family. She came over, very pale and nervous. Her fingers trembled holding the cigarette. She had already woven a ballooning romance about the abandonment: her heart had followed that big strapping man into the world; wherever he was, she would find him, perhaps when he was so old he would not recognize her, and she would tell him how she had not only forgiven him, but how she would have done the same thing if she had been he. For Haw could not contain him, or her either.

She began to pet Zeb. She pulled his head onto her shoulder, marveling that he should be her only friend in her own home town. To hear Quira talk gave Zeb an ecstatic anxiety. She was the only one in his life that had ever connected a real life (her own) with the world of books (his own). He held her tight. She cried, and then she laughed, shaking her hair.

When Zeb went to high school, his childhood ended. He did not see Quira much, for she had enrolled in college and began to work as a typist for a professor in the Folk Blood Movement. It was a big step to enter high school, for the high school was in Ephesus. All Haw children graduated to the world when they graduated to Ephesus. For Zeb it was the beginning of a strange life. He became anonymous. He became thin. He lost his baby fat. He became serious and smiled less often. But his curiosity flourished, and for two years he sailed along, as absent, as voracious as he ever was in Haw, but unknown, because no Haw kid was anything in Ephesus. So all his life's energy turned inward.

CHAPTER 6

By the time Mrs. Bishop made inquiries about school, it had been in session for three days.

"I knew it," said Loco Poco. "All the nigger kids disappeared."

"Well, why didn't you say something? Who would have thought it would start on a Wednesday? Well, no matter. You'll be ahead anyway with your background." Mrs. Bishop began making plans to make a new dress apiece over the weekend. "You can start on Monday. That will just give me time."

"Mamma, maybe we ought to go right off and get it over with," said Irene anxiously.

Curtains were all right to create their house. But Mrs. Bishop, with her romantic personality, would make clothes that were ingenious, exotic, beautiful, unconventional, and would run the risk of making her daughters look ludicrous.

They were just beginning to be aware of this. They had no experience with the high-school herd. School life had always been unreal, compared with family life. They had always been protected by the Pontiac and the big house. So they bowed to Mrs. Bishop's way.

Pouncing, cackling, clapping her hands in glee, she unearthed from her carton boxes an Indian print for Irene ("Nobody would ever think of making a dress out of this! It will be stunning!"), for Urie some black velveteen that had been an old evening dress of her own, and pink organdy for Loco Poco. All Saturday and Sunday she sat in front of her chattering machine. It rocketed like an express engine to get the dresses ready on time. Irene helped her.

"I don't think these hems should be this long, Mamma!"

"Yes, they should. They're all right."

Urie hated sewing. She made a face when she had to try her dress on for the gores to be measured. But Loco, uncritical, was excited and donned hers, ran up and down the dining room in pride, her back bobbing with a big pink tie that looked like a tail.

"There now. Wonderful!" Mrs. Bishop beamed. "I think you look beautiful!"

On Monday morning she clasped her hands. Her daughters passed through the broken screen door, one by one. She beamed as they made their way down the path. On her face was the same expression with which she had viewed P.Q. riding across the roots with his bicycle full of linen. She beamed when they reached the road. She was still beaming when they disappeared across the tracks.

In the schoolyard the buses were beginning to arrive.

"By their trucks ye shall know them," said Maddox Stein, a student teacher of English on ground duty. Buses were referred to as trucks. Only Haw kids and country kids came on trucks. Ephesians walked.

The Haw truck was large, hot, orange, and fat. Dust trickled off its back tires and mudguards. Black letters, HAW SCHOOLS, were branded on its rump. It groaned up the driveway, jouncing, swerving into the ruts. It uttered a final grunt and stopped.

Boys in cheap brown trousers emerged. Among them was Zebulon Walley. Some of the boys were chewing gum. Their faces were pimpled. Two spat when they got out. They had graduated to plug tobacco. The girls were limp and wan. Their hair was frizzed. Although they had talked loudly on the road from Haw, they hushed up on the school grounds, knowing that they were among Ephesians.

The crowd of Haw kids dribbled into groups and walked past the separate groups of merchants' and professors' kids from Ephesus.

Maddox Stein opened the doors and posted guard for the mass entrance when the bell rang. Now that the ludicrous aspect of the caste system had dimmed, he was no longer interested.

Zeb had spent the journey from Haw reading Robert Browning. Although school had been in session only three days, already he was immersed in the world of books. A sense of great fortune and possibility possessed him. He felt that he was on the brink of something. It was indescribable. He did not feel that school was school; it was a mere representation of something, a framework for something. What, he did not know. He kept waiting for an event to happen, for the world to make a sign.

Had he known that Maddox Stein had at that moment just said, "By their trucks ye shall know them," he would have been amazed. He believed teachers were unbiased—especially Yankee ones, still students themselves, but graduated from sheeplike high-school prejudices. Zeb had faith that the stranger could see through all caste. The stranger was endowed with the seeds of light which germinated truth.

At that moment the event happened. It was eight-forty-five a.m., September 27. Though it was completely different from the way he had expected the sign to be, it validated everything.

Girls studying under the columns looked up from their books. Ballplayers hollering dropped balls and turned around. Idlers stopped frozen. Speech was cut off. Everything became so silent that a vagrant automobile making its way up the hill became a thrumming sound in the silence, through which the footsteps of the approaching Bishops became a loud, rhythmic clack.

No one would have looked at them if their fear and self-consciousness had not called attention. But they were painfully self-conscious. They walked with the dignity of whooping cranes. Their faces were stony and strange. Their posture was Caryatid-like. Their gait was even and *marcato*.

As soon as they noticed that everything had stopped and focused on them, they began to rigidify in their Beethoven procession. Irene's Indian-print dress began to flap below her knee with audible regularity: one-two-three, one-two-three. She tried to stop it, but could not. Urie heard it. Irene was galvanized with shame. What to do?

"Stop!" whispered Urie.

They stopped.

Zebulon, staring, frightened, held his breath.

Mr. Stein, speechless, withheld his malicious smile for the suspense of what worse was to happen.

"They're looking at us!" Loco whispered. She tried to disguise this childish wail by emitting it through the side of her mouth like W. C. Fields. But it bounced over the cement walks, the cement steps, the cement hall, heard by everyone.

In desperation Urie barked, "Go."

They started up again, robots, formal, didactic, strong-necked. But where were they to go? They were headed straight for the brick wall. Their rectitude was so adamant that they were hopelessly trapped in it. They could not make an about-turn without being delivered up to the thousand-mouthed laughter.

They passed within three feet of Zebulon. Clothed in their autonomy, naked in this stupendous cynosure, their image congealed upon him. Magnificent puppethood. He saw perfectly well soft sprouting girls, like other girls, but he did not believe it. Look at the way they were dressed! An Indian, Joan of Arc, and a black Shirley Temple. They were the Three Fates! Unable to distinguish, he fell in love with them all.

Someone else had the same idea with a different twist. "The Three Stooges!" It was like a voluptuous fart, bringing forth titters and gasps of shock.

Maddox Stein began to feel the climax of the symphony and got ready to let his malice extend into a smile.

Just as they were about to crash into the brick wall of the school building, whereupon they would have had to turn, would have had to face the firing squad, the bell rang and saved them.

"Listen," said Opal Granger, secretary of the Hi-Y, to Olive Akers, daughter of the Associate Professor of Chemistry, at recess. "Those pore things. We've got to do something."

"They obviously come from a good family," Olive said.

"There they are standing there so strange and nobody talking to them at all."

"They're terribly shy."

"They don't know how to act."

"I wonder where they come from."

"They look intelligent, even if they are dressed like—that."

No one mentioned the Three Stooges comment.

"Listen, girls," said Opal in a louder voice. "Let's call a Hi-Y conference over here. We can introduce ourselves to them. Make them feel friendly and wanted. We're the representatives, really, of Ephesus High. We ought to show a good example."

Carmen Watson snickered.

"I don't think it's a laughing matter, Carmen," said Opal.

"How would you like to come to school dressed like that?" asked Olive virtuously.

"How did they get dressed like that in the first place? Ugh. They don't even wear lipstick! Creeps!" Carmen cringed with a grimace.

"All right, Carmen. You've had your joke. Now let's see you act more befitting to the standards of the Hi-Y."

"Oh, honestly, Opal!"

"I mean it, Carmen."

Carmen turned away. She knew when to quit.

Urie, Loco, and Irene, conscious of the movement afoot, clung to each other and stood on the gravel, trying to keep their backs to the enemy so that they could ignore it. The Hi-Y girls moved forward. There were thirty of them, soft, nubile, with smiling, rosy girl-faces, white socks, saddle shoes, and sweater bosoms glistening with the fraternity pins of the Boys' Hi-Y. Lap. Lap. Lap. The sound of sixty Christian footsteps. Loco Poco tried to pretend it was not happening. She would not even have been here, but her assignment to class in the elementary school was delayed till after recess because the secretary had been called out. A derisive smile curled one corner of her lips. She hypnotized herself into the trance of a sea gull, and though her pink ankle sock had fallen down over her patent-leather shoe, she was not attending to frail human foibles: it had become her claw.

"What shall we do?" asked Irene in a desperate voice.

Urie, forced to answer for Loco's disappearance and Irene's terror, flung up her eyes, facing the converging army. She cursed Irene. She licked her lips. She took a large breath. She clenched her fists.

Fragrances of Kampus Perfume leaked through the pitying oncoming eyes. Body pressure, lollipop colors of virtue, the friendliness of town-girl girlhood, the upsweeps, the pompadours, the mascaras, the thrilling verdure of multicolored lipstick smiles closed them in. The army stopped in a semicircle around them.

"Hello," said Opal Granger, her voice, roseate and promising, sliding out of her lipstick.

Veins stood out in Urie's temples and her wrists. Suddenly she turned scarlet, but she could not speak.

"I'm Opal Granger, and we, I mean, all of us—we belong to the Hi-Y. We saw you standing here, you know. So we thought since you all were new to Ephesus High somebody should—I mean, we decided we'd step up and introduce ourselves." There was a pause as Opal caught her breath charmingly and smiled with a public expression. "I'm Opal Granger," she repeated. Still there was no sound. "And this is Olive Akers."

Olive Akers took the ball. "Hello," she said.

For a moment the silence was awful. Then Urie moved her tongue from her palate. She cleared her throat. "Hello," she answered.

There was a visible rustling along the ranks. A new round robin began, as full of suspense as the Three Stooges march.

"I'm Nancy Parker," said the next girl.

"Hello," answered Urie.

"I'm Gert Bynum."

"Hello."

"I'm Sheila Barker."

"Hello."

As the names continued to come, Urie had to lick her lips to get enough saliva to continue saying "Hello." She thought of stopping. But the break in the rhythm forbade it.

"I'm Frances Ward."

"Hello."

"I'm Ora Mae Sissingoss."

"Hello."

Now everybody began to fear the end of the soft, insensate half-whispers of names.

"I'm Bewdella Burns," said the last one, blushing.

"Hello."

The Hi-Y girls waited, having given of themselves, having risen to their own expectation, having accomplished that insistently perfect thing. Now their tongues were half suspended as they waited in silence, hanging awkwardly in midair.

Urie cleared her throat. "We are very glad to meet you," she began formally. "This is my sister Irene. Irene Bishop."

"Hello," said Irene.

"And this is my younger sister, Lo—Sylvia. Sylvia Bishop."

But Loco did not speak. Instead, she spun her eyeballs to the top of her head. The girls did not know what to make of this action.

"And I am Urie Bishop," said Urie hurriedly to cover the *gaffe*.

"Oh, Urine," Opal gushed. "We're so glad to welcome you to Ephesus High. You must—"

"Not Urine!" whispered Olive Akers in a shocked voice.

At the sound of this word, pronounced twice with the accent on the second syllable, there was a silence, then a high-pitched titter.

Urie blushed to the roots of her hair. "That's Irene. I'm Urie," she blurted. "My real name is Urania. Urania. Urania!" she repeated again, lifting her lips in pronouncing it, just like P.Q.

"Oh, I—I'm sorry," stuttered Opal Granger, completely lost to grace.

A dark silence fell. No one knew what to say.

At last, rousting around to snatch anything to rescue them from this impasse, Urie fastened onto the sight of Bewdella Burns's blouse. It had two painted heads of Robert Taylor on back and front. Not only did Urie not think it was pretty—it was ugly, cheap, and putrid—but also, in general, Urie did not care about clothes at all. At this moment, however, clothes were all she could think of. Clothes: the freakery, exotic and unfashionable, that Mrs. Bishop had made them display upon their backs so proudly. Clothes obsessed her. Clothes she used to embrace hypocrisy. Clothes inspired her enthusiastic and inane voice.

[55

"That's a very pretty blouse you're wearing."

"Thank you. You must wear it sometime."

Shame was galvanized and determination was born. To wear Bewdella Burns's Robert Taylor blouse! The insult was all the more unbearable because it was unintended, and Urie knew it. But she was suddenly swaddled in the thought of Bewdella Burns's blouse next to her skin. She cringed to escape Bewdella Burns's sweat and smell. Christian charity, Christian pity would have to be exploded. And then it would have to be peeled away, layer by layer, and discarded like an onion skin.

CHAPTER 7

The class had already assembled when Urie Bishop walked into Zebulon Walley's class. She presented a slip of paper from the principal's office to Miss Hagood. Miss Hagood pointed to an empty seat. The seat was only two away from Zebul. She walked stiffly. She jerked as if her kneecaps hurt. She held her chin up. As she came nearer he fancied that he could feel the steam of her resistance. He had never felt this way about any girl. She *interested* him.

He was aware of being suffused. Everyone was staring at her, but she noticed no one. He thought: Why doesn't she look at one person straight in the face? Just one flash of recognition would stop their staring.

He bent toward her. His eagerness was a palpable presence shining out from him. His eyes were brimming. But she refused to notice him.

She reached her desk.

She pulled her dress down as she sat. She scarcely breathed.

The lesson began. The stares died down. Suspense, fed only by motion and revelation, waned. Urie disappeared behind the transparency of her eyes. Everyone became bored.

Only Zebul remained transfixed. For the first time in his life he felt the rise of necessity. He felt the spirit of pursuit. If the world would not present itself to him, he would have to go after it. But what would he say to her? How could he make her notice him?

Loco was put into the elementary school, a gaunt brick building next to the high school. From the moment Loco departed, the sisters' lives took on a different dimension. An understood agreement grew up among them not to talk to each other or have anything to do with each other on school property. The Hi-Y welcome had taught them that separately they would blend into the school atmosphere, whereas as a family they would be hounded for peculiarity. Irene and Urie only nodded recognition when they met each other in the halls. For the rest of the time it was as if they were strangers. But this cabal of silence only intensified their reality as a family and gave to their separate school lives an air of unreality.

Irene blended into the school scene more quickly than the others. She was aloof yet nonchalant. She did not care about making friends. When she talked to anyone it was about paraphernalia rather than personality. She talked about pencils, books, equations, quadrants, or verbs. On her first day Mr. Pankhurst gave a test in geometry. She made 9. She felt neither ludicrous nor shamed. After all, she said at home, they were ahead of her in the book, weren't they? After that day she spent every activity period getting special help in Mr. Pankhurst's room. The sight of her through the open door poring over geometry made her a fixture in everybody's mind. People became bored with her. She became accepted. Behind her smokescreen of nonchalance, her reticent self was left alone. No one noticed that she was a beauty, and no one thought that she was peculiar any more.

On the first day of elementary school Loco Poco drank everything in eagerly. She flitted around the schoolyard, or she stood completely absorbed. She stared at the big boys. Big boys had hair the color of horse-buns, which they greased and combed into curls and arranged over the red pimples in their necks and cheeks. She smelled them. They smelled like old spoons. They had humps in their cheeks. Why? What did they have in their mouths? What was the secret wadded inside?

There was a huge, clumsy red-haired girl named Faye Gormel standing by the swings. Loco went up to her and asked, "Why do those big boys have humps in their cheeks?"

Faye Gormel started to answer, but she did not talk fast enough.

"Are they eating something?"

"It's plug tobacco," said Faye Gormel in a sheepish voice.

Loco made her tell her everything about plug tobacco. It was bigger and better than gum. It made you spit. Notice how the big boys spat. They wrapped their tongues around the plug and wopsed it up in their mouths, moving it to one side, back of their teeth, and around, making the hump move. Loco asked Faye if she had ever tried it. Faye said yes and tried to tell Loco what it tasted like. Red Man was the best, the type her daddy used. But women used snuff and wopsed it into the gums on little twigs. So she couldn't use plug tobacco. Inspired by the begging, drinking, impressed eyes of Loco, Faye Gormel bloomed. No one had ever looked twice at her before. But now, with her new, refined, miniature friend, she even confessed her secret desire: to become a white-coated hair-care demonstrator in the dime store. Loco and Faye marveled together. Faye became Loco's instant devotee.

On the second day of school a group of children surrounded her. "Bum bum bum. Where you from?" they shouted, going around her in a circle.

"Thalassia!"

"No! Say 'Pretty Girl Station.' "

"Pretty Girl Station," she answered.

"What's your occupation?"

She thought. "Making aprons."

"No. No! Say, 'Knock a nigger down.' "

"Knock a nigger down!" She laughed deliriously.

"Get to work!" they shouted and pushed her to the ground.

Shocked, she stood up, brushing off her dress, facing their hoots and laughter.

"But I'm not a nigger!" she protested, standing on one foot, placing the other on top of it.

"She's a dark-haired Shirley Temple," said one of the teachers in the smoking room.

"She may be a troublemaker," answered another.

"She's gifted," said Mrs. Wadiscloff. "She came out one-fifty-three on the Stanford-Binet."

"Well, she's awfully cute and she knows it," said another.

"She has awfully peculiar mannerisms, that's all. Mixed with that accent."

On the third day of school Miss Bogue said that because so many people did not know how to spell her name, she would now write it on the board.

"B-O-G-U-E," she wrote, pointing to the letters with a painted red fingernail.

"Bogue," she pronounced.

Loco tittered.

"Is something funny?" asked Miss Bogue.

Loco stopped smiling. She started to blush. The red flooded her face and her neck. She said, "I always laugh at U's."

"U's?" repeated Miss Bogue in a strange voice.

"No. UE, really."

"Why is UE funny?"

"It has something to do with tails wagging. Dog's tails!"

The class laughed.

Loco Poco's blush was gone, and now Miss Bogue began to blush. She suspected something vile, and she opened the Arithmetic III book quickly. "Turn to page fifty-four," she said.

Later, in the teacher's room, smoking a cigarette, Miss Bogue began to recover. UE is usually preceded by a Q, she thought. Maybe that is where she got the idea of a tail.

But while Loco disturbed teachers' logic, her lopsided personality infected the children. Girls began vying for her friendship. She dispensed it with grace, making all her favors even, so no one got jealous. She was generous, even merry. The big boys, at whom she continued to stare, became entranced by her. She made them feel like Calibans. But even their own ugliness came to have power to them, so they began doing tricks in front of her, standing on their hands, and roughnecking smaller boys who threw spitballs at her. She rewarded them with ravishing smiles. One redheaded and ungainly youth brought her a pogo stick and taught her to bounce to the gymnasium on it.

Yet some of this mystique was based on pure misunderstanding.

One day Faye Gormel had to stand up to speak an oral theme. It was very poor. Loco listened very carefully, putting one hand up to her ear to absorb every stuttering line. Lines were repeated. Whole sentences were repeated. Every sentence seemed to begin with the words "I think."

"I think I am moderately good," said Faye Gormel. "I think so because my family thinks so. I think that to be good is to be wise. But other people think. . . ."

Every time Faye Gormel said, "I think," her countrified accent made the words sound like "I thank."

At the end of the theme Miss Bogue called on Loco Poco to comment on Faye Gormel's theme.

"Faye Gormel's theme is excellent because it is about gratefulness. It shows the best manners of anybody I have ever met in my life. Manners based on feeling, which is what they ought to be."

The tone of Loco's voice was so enthusiastic that the class, drawn along by it, sensed in Faye Gormel something which they had never suspected before. They looked at Faye Gormel.

Faye Gormel blushed. The cataclysmic pink flood against her ugly red hair was so shocking that the class became silent. They were moved. It was as if Loco Poco's mere presence were a catalytic agent to bring out the depths of feelings, stirrings that were usually unheard, unthought of by

[59

most people. The class began to clap. Even Miss Bogue felt a lump in her throat. There was a victorious feeling in the depths of her being, that feeling that arises when it is manifest that the underdog has won.

One day in the RRR program (Readiness, Respectfulness, and Reading-ness) Miss Bogue assigned a written theme. The topic was "My Personality." She allowed twenty minutes.

"My personality," wrote Loco "is strange. I am said to have quirques by my family. My biggest quirque they call insane. It is to have thoughts. My thoughts are my own, meaning no one else has them. They are called quirquey for that reason. For instance, I see Tootsie Morn. Tootsie Morn was first pointed out to me by father, P. Q. Bishop, in the back yard when I was three years old. Everybody said it was not true, that he was fooling me. But I saw her. She looks somewhat like the blue fairy. My sisters claim she is not true. There is an example of what I mean by saying quirques. Tootsie Morn is true though. I see her and she does not speak. I often poque my sister if she harps too much on quirques. Though you may think I am the mousy type, you will see from this then that I am not. For you have a peeque into my personality. As a P.S. I am not in favor of personality tests. Sylvia Bishop."

Miss Bogue trembled with outrage when she read this theme. Then the one mitigating factor came to her. If it was true that the father's name was really P.Q., then it was possible that the quirques—quirks, Miss Bogue corrected her inner vision—came from the tail on the Q of his second initial. Could someone so innocent be so knowing as it sounded?

Three days passed. Zebul had still not succeeded in getting Urie to look at him. He knew that he had to act.

He analyzed the situation carefully. He went over his assets and liabilities. He decided that Hawdom was his main liability. He would have to eradicate all signs of Hawdom from himself.

But how could he do it? What were the signs of Hawdom?

Hawdom was bad grammar, poverty, and mill psychology. But the only public proof of Hawdom was to come to school in the Haw Truck. Zeb would have to stop using the Haw Truck.

On the next Monday he got up at six o'clock. He stole into the house before anybody was awake and took a bath in the washtub. It was like an initiation. He dressed in the same cotton pants he always wore and his same dirty sneakers. But because he felt so clean, he seemed new to himself.

Long before the Haw Truck would pick up people at the railroad tracks, he started out. He imagined the kids getting into the truck. Would the driver wonder where he was? Yes. They would all ask. They would wonder.

The day was already hot at seven-thirty. Premature sun-rays thrust out along the footpaths where the mill houses sat dry and listless. He decided to take the railroad tracks, shortcut to Ephesus. He walked two ties at a time.

He came to a certain honeysuckle bush that he knew. Dew still pearled it. He spoke "Pippa Passes" into the leaves. His soul vaulted for a moment out of the thick sweetness, picked up over the drone of the morning bees and encircled him with happiness. Impulsively he thrust his head into the bosom of the honeysuckle. He threw his arms around it as if to embrace the blossoms. They filled his senses. But he interrupted the bees, causing them to rise incensed and angry. He did not move. He kept embracing the bush. A gush of dew spilled on his forehead. At last the bees settled down. They began buzzing contentedly again.

He went on.

As he came to that invisible spot that separated Ephesus and Haw, his mind kept mulling on what he should say for the first words. He could not think. He would play it by ear. All he had to do was follow the track. Leave Haw behind. The words would come to him.

In front of him he saw the smokestack of the power plant, and far to the left the bell tower. All of a sudden he stepped on something squashy.

He jumped. At the moment of the jump, still in the air, he saw the body of a Negro. He had walked on his hand!

Zebul felt his skin move unpleasantly, like a snake's, as if he were trying to shed it. When he landed again on his sneakers in the cinders, he wanted to run. But instead of running, he forced himself to look down.

It was a thin, pock-marked, rickety man of about forty, dressed in gray rags of trousers and an old khaki army shirt. His face was ash-colored. Two buttons were missing on his trousers. And in the ditch lay an empty bottle of rotgut. The torn nostril of the Negro, cut in some old razor fight, gave him a ghostly leer. The eyes were upturned.

Zeb forced himself to study the drunk Negro. He hung over him like a murderer. He moved around him, inspecting. He dwelt upon him for two or three minutes. He bombarded himself with the sight.

He looked at the upturned hand. His sneaker had stood in this hand. The hand was white as if the whiteness of his sneaker had rubbed off on the palm, or as if his footstep had worn the black off the palm. Such a connection made Zeb sick. But he forced himself to apprehend it. From this hand he, Zeb, had arisen erect, sneakers, cotton pants, shirt, blooming, full-bodied emblem of youth. Into life. He mythologized. He began to laugh. The laughter made sweat break out on his forehead.

Suddenly he could stand it no longer and he ran away. He ran with the nimbleness of a rabbit. All the while he ran, the experience conveyed itself to him as a trial, a preliminary to what was now going to happen. Yet the moment he stepped onto the school grounds, it was as if it had not happened. He felt buoyant. He was ready.

When the fourth bell rang he went up to Urie very solemnly in the hallways and said, "I stepped on a nigger's hand."

She tensed as if she expected another Three Stooges comment.

"What?" she asked faintly.

"I say, I stepped on a nigger's hand," he repeated.

"Where?"

"On his hand!"

"Where was the nigger? I'm asking." She asked this loudly. People turned around to stare, and when they noticed who it was and that she was saying "nigger," they were amazed.

"The nigger was on the railroad track. Dead drunk," said Zeb in delight.

"Then he didn't know you stepped on his hand."

"No."

"Ugh!" Her voice sounded pleased.

Now Zeb began to spill everything to her fast. "It was a sign," he said.

"A sign of what?"

"Of being born again," he whispered.

Her transparent blue eyes wavered. Her silence was full of doubt.

"I can imagine being born again, but I am not religious," she said cautiously.

"You're not?" He was wide-eyed. He had never heard anyone say such a thing in his life. "What were you brought up as?" he asked.

"Congregational."

"What's that?"

"You mean to tell me you don't know?" she said kindly, but scandalized.

"No. Is it Christian?"

"Course it's Christian. It's Protestant."

They found footholds in this conversation as in a mountain. Yet neither was fooled by the other's strangeness. They were both intrigued by the other's exoticism. Each thought himself sophisticated and the other ignorant.

"All right, then, you were raised a Christian," he said, recapitulating.

"It's funny you should bring up this conversation," she said, "as I have been thinking of nothing but Christianity since I started this school. Everybody practically is brought up as Christian in this country except for Jews. It is a freak of fate that I'm not a Jew. I practically am. But I'm not so narrow-minded as to believe any of that hypocrisy. I am a rationalist," she explained.

"And you don't believe in Jesus Christ?" breathed Zebul.

"Oh, he might be a good man and all that, but Socrates was better. He never went around spouting about all the good Christian deeds he did to others. And at least he didn't let himself be crucified like a fool. He did it himself."

It was like passing the witch's gingerbread house in an express train. It was too fast to catch all these goodies.

"And you don't believe in God?" he asked, his voice rising tremulously.

"God?" she said, her lip curling with derision. Now that she had started on this path, a sense of excitement had betaken her. It was the first time since they had moved into the Shack that anything she had said or done made sense. The very reaction of this boy to her answers was enough to inspire her, to make her see that what she said now not only was true but had meaning for the future of her life. "No," she answered loudly. "God. Adam and Eve. All that stuff. How can anybody believe that pack of lies? Do you really believe man *fell* because he *learned* something? That's what the story of Adam and Eve means. It means man is doomed the minute he *knows* anything. Such a religion is not only stupid, it is criminal. You know what my father calls the Bible?"

"What?" he said, mesmerized with shock.

"The history of Jewish criminality." A smack of self-satisfied euphoria flashed her lips in a smile.

The bell rang.

He bent forward to her.

"Do you realize," he said, "that this is important? When I said I was born again, I did not mean like in a revival tent. Do you realize that ever since I saw you coming into the school I wanted to . . . have you for a friend. Then it happened that you came to my class. For instance, that was fated." His furred, conspiratorial, ecstatic voice drew her into his arena. "But I didn't dare speak to you!" he confessed. Time pressed on them. They felt the closing, yet neither moved. They knew that they would defy time. "So first I decided to de-Haw myself . . ." She did not know what that meant. As he had rushed past her Christianity remarks, she had to rush by this. It was not details that were important. She understood him. "So I did de-Haw myself by walking to school. I always knew I would tell you that I was a Haw-yoo, though. But then I stepped into the nigger's hand. It was horrible!" He almost giggled. "It was the reverse of Venus coming out of the foam of Jupiter's you-know-what—"

"Aphrodite. Zeus," she corrected.

"I mean—that I encompass horror, the most abject and servile putridity imaginable on earth. But that I had to do it. See? I wouldn't have been able to speak to you if I hadn't done it. You don't know that, but I do. What would I have said?"

She opened her mouth to speak. But he would not let her.

"You're gonna be my friend!" he whispered.

They ran, just as the bell started to ring again. Nimbly, triumphantly they made their home room before the bell trailed away. This time he moved to the seat next to her.

Urie did not tell either Irene or Loco about meeting this boy. He might be a drip or crazy for all she knew, although she saw he made 98 on the first physics test.

The very fact of keeping her acquaintance secret from the family, however, forced her into herself, and she put up barriers against him. Had he known where she lived when he told her the story of the nigger hand? Why had he told her? His presence was so eager, so entreating, that she backed away from him. Everywhere she went the figure of Zebulon Walley stood before her. A week passed. She hardly spoke to him.

He was disappointed. Instead of becoming his friend, she became covered over by a mist of pride. Her blue eyes were transparent and so light that it made him feel inferior when he looked into them. He wanted to ask her, "Why are you so proud?" But he did not dare. Even though he had pretended not to come from Haw, he still did, and from that psychology it was perfectly right that she would not want anything to do with him.

One day, girding his loins, Zebul made another frontal attack. "I bet you don't know this town very well," he said to her after school.

"No."

"Have you ever been to the campus?" He put on airs, telling her. "I mean really, all the buildings, et cetera."

"Well, not exactly," she said.

"I've practically grown up on the campus," he boasted, although he had only been there once or twice in his life. "I tell you what. Let's go there. I'll show it to you."

64]

At first she was evasive.

"I'll show you," he egged. "We can go Saturday morning."

At last she agreed.

"I'll come by your house at ten o'clock. Where do you live?"

For the first time he noticed strange oblique lights crossing her eyes, like the shadows of white clouds passing across the sky.

"Down there." She pointed vaguely from the schoolyard.

"Where?"

"At the end of Pergamus Avenue."

"Near the power plant?"

"Yes. But further," she added with quiet deliberation.

"What? You mean on Pack Mill Road?"

"Yes," she said softly.

He looked into her eyes. Deep, deep he tried to fathom her. He could not believe a white family lived in Niggertown. Yet he did not dare to ask her outright. Deep as he looked, he found nothing.

"Shall I come and get you at your house?"—uncertainly.

She said, "I'll meet you right at the railroad track at ten."

That night Urie broke the news. Loco and Irene were studying at the kitchen table. She stood at the threshold. She drew a breath.

"There is this boy, and he is meeting me at the railroad track Saturday morning and showing me the campus of this town."

Loco and Irene raised their heads like gunshot. Through the amazement in their eyes they remained as silent as mastodons.

One fledgling poking a nose out into Purgatory. Making a connection with the world? What would happen? Would they too enter the world? Would Bishopry be drawn into the world? That it was a boy was the threatening thing. Irene should have been the one that went with a boy first. She was the oldest. Or Loco, the only one of them who was interested in boys. Boys had never entered their family life. The only boy they had ever known was Edward Blake, the son of the caretaker of Leggetts' estate. They had learned the physiognomy of boys from him. He had urinated in the coal pile in Thalassia's basement, had boasted of his penis power and waved it like a flag. Later they had learned the facts of life from an enlightened pamphlet called *Your Daughter and Nature,* which Mrs. Bishop had given them, and through individual consultations in the Pontiac front seat with their mother, facing the ocean. Ever after that they had ignored the fact of boys, shunting off Edward Blake as filthy-minded and dirty-fingernailed. Urie, particularly, could not bear boys. She was embarrassed when she had to pass drugstore loiterers and, imagining that they called her a pig, called them pigs. They made her conscious of having two rumps, a posterior manifesting a femininity she did not want to claim. When they looked she could feel her own buttocks take over her entire body, ballooning and flapping.

Therefore the fact that it was she, rather than either of the others, shocked them. If it were not a betrayal, then it must be a prognostication.

A deceptive, multicolored female ambivalence choked the silence. In Irene's eyes fear for her younger sister turned into jealousy.

But in Loco's face there leaked an expression of uncontrollable excitement. "Is it a date?" she whispered.

"Of course not!"

Urie sat down and opened to *Julius Caesar,* pushing her mouth into a derisive yawn.

A long interval passed in silence. Then Loco whispered fervidly, "Does he chew plug tobacco?"

"A-a-a-ch!" snorted Urie.

They all laughed.

CHAPTER 8

Urie was early. She stood in the dirt road, dressed in an unsuitable black velvet skirt. The sun, already high in the molten sky, refracted off the tin roof of Lucretia Pile's store. Inside the door hole, through the baggy broken screen, was darkness, exuding a dank smell compounded of sour sweat and earthen beans. Two passing colored women eyed her furtively.

"What she doing?"

"Look like she praying in the middle of the road."

They disappeared into the maw of the store. Inside, a melody of Negro voices began.

A half-eaten watermelon lay exposed and bled on an upturned barrel in front of the store. The dust in the road was pocked with shining black seeds, and flies buzzed and seated themselves on the rind. All around, the sun was brilliant and searing, pouring a scorching light on the hills in the distance, thrilling the railroad tracks into fire-ribbons, and settling the baked earth of the road so that Urie could feel the heat through her shoe soles.

Zebul came up the railroad tracks. When he saw her he began to run. He arrived out of breath.

The unspoken mystery of where she lived caused an embarrassing silence between them. He pointed to the railroad tracks.

"See those railroad tracks?"

"Yes."

"Railroad tracks are basic to American life. Remember them. They opened up the country. But they made the dividing point between people. They are the crux of everything. By your position in relation to railroad tracks you are crap or noncrap."

She sensed what he was up to, but she did not say anything.

"It was not more than a quarter of a mile from this spot that I stepped in the nigger's hand," he said confidingly. "Have you ever heard that old cliché, living on the wrong side of the tracks?"

"Sure."

"Well, here is the dividing line. Right here." He drew a line with the sole of his sneaker in the dust of the road where they crossed the tracks.

Suddenly Urie saw that he was right. She had never thought of it before. She opened her mouth, but she could not think what to say.

"Which side do you live on?" he asked.

"This side."

It was true, then!

"Well, you literally live on the wrong side of the tracks," he announced. He stared at her significantly.

Her long, straight, aristocratic nose and soft, wide-open mouth awed him. Her blue accusing eyes inspired him.

"I live in the middle of Niggertown," she answered him, lifting up her chin the way she did at school, and pronouncing her words in the careful, strange accent she used. "So that proves your point. But I come from a place different from this, where people are not prejudiced, so I don't care whether I live in Niggertown or not. Nothing can make me low, because I don't believe people are lower or higher unless they *act* it."

He was strangely moved.

"I am not prejudiced either," he whispered, squinting against the sun. Then in the same whisper he continued, gathering up the same breathless concentration in winding her into his conspiracy as when he had told her about the drunk nigger. "I am different like you are different. Because I come from Haw. That must be why, without even knowing you lived in Niggertown, I told you about the nigger hand. Just from osmosis. I'm talking about what people think, not about what is! You understand what I

[67

mean? There is something fated about my meeting you and about my knowing you would be my friend. And here I don't even know you. Yet here we are in the world, and I understand everything about you, and you do me, even if we don't know anything!"

In the silence a dozen eyeballs, disembodied like black and white marbles, peeked out of Lucretia Pile's baggy screen door at them.

"The beginning of the route of triumph and success," he told her, "leads that way"—he pointed up Pergamus Avenue—"to Ephesus. Everything gets better and better. The houses get bigger. They don't have tin roofs. They have real shingles. The road to degradation, ignorance, and stinkingness lies that way—to Haw. The houses get crappier and crappier. The roads turn into dirt. All the roofs are tin. And there are many chinaberry trees."

"Which is worse? Niggertown or Haw?"

"Haw."

There was a long silence.

"Where do you want to go first?" he asked. "Ephesus or Haw?"

"Ephesus," she said.

The first sight on the route was the power plant. As they passed it, they inspected it. He talked about it, describing it with adjectives. It was a giant, cannibalistic power plant with its tall, dithyrambic brick chimney which sucked, ate, chewed, and spewed out smoke from the coke which the weekly freight train brought in.

Next to the power plant was the university laundry. It had a water-refining tank behind it. Little jets of water spurted up into the sunlight, causing rainbows.

"There are the fountains of Versailles," said Urie.

They walked down Pergamus Avenue until they came to the Ephesus Inn. They entered the campus. It lay manicured and fresh as a newly cut sandwich, its tea-party lawns sliced by red brick gutters and paths. On the campus they became hushed and inspired.

They went to the Old Well. It was a colonnaded oval where a shining bubbler spurted a winking jet of water. It had been the first well of the university in 1858. They took a drink out of it.

A bell rang. Students came out of yellow brick buildings and sauntered to their next classes. Zebul and Urie followed the students to the book exchange. Students hurried to and fro, buying Coca-Colas and notebooks. One student bought an ice-cream cone and licked it. Zebul and Urie turned around and went out. Urie remembered the ice cream P.Q. had bought the first night they came to Ephesus. She pushed the ice-cream cone out of her head.

"Do you wish you had money?" asked Zebul.

"Yes," said Urie.

They went through an asphalt courtyard until they came to a yellow brick building. They peeked through its large oval windows.

"This is Lombard Hall." His tone as tour guide had taken on a semblance of great authority.

He tried the door. It opened. They went in. They smelled the cool, fresh meeting house. They sat down on the white pews, saying "Whew" and fanning themselves with lecture programs that were inserted in the hymn racks. Then they left.

They walked down the main campus toward the library. The chime in the bell tower rang eleven o'clock.

"I am going to college here," confided Zebul.

"You are?"

"Yes."

"How will you pay tuition?"

"Maybe I'll get a scholarship."

"Does it cost much?"

"About seventy-five dollars a term. And there are two terms in a year. If I don't get a scholarship, I'll get a self-help job."

"You can get jobs?"

"Sure. They have this thing called NYA, like WPA, which makes jobs so indigent people can go through college. Maybe I will work in the library."

Below lay the library, eight Greek columns with Doric capitals, great graceful glass doors like reflective eyes.

"The library is the focal point of the university," he said.

They walked step by step toward it. It was the shape of the Parthenon. The smell that came out the swinging doors toward them was cool, bookish, and echoey.

"Let's go in!" he whispered.

"Are we supposed to?"

"Of course!" Actually he did not know whether they were allowed or not, but because she questioned, he bade, his authority staked on it.

Step by step they mounted the stairs. They stopped under the columns, looking upward.

"Isn't it beautiful?" he asked, reveling.

She walked away from him to a column and knocked upon it as if to say "Open, Sesame."

"What are you doing?" he asked.

"Knocking the column."

"Why?"

"To see if it is fake."

He was shocked. "What do you mean, fake?"

"Haven't you ever tried the columns of the Baptist church?" she asked.

"No."

"They are all fake. They are made of tin cans."

He thought it was marvelous that she should know facts like this. They walked through the portico, knocking on each column.

"They're real. They're all real!" he said in triumph.

"Yes."

"Let's go in now."

They entered through the glass doors. Once in the elegant foyer, they were awed by the tallness of the high green dome, the marble floor, the chiseled staircase, the cold draft, and the whispers. They clung near each other, inching toward the carved banisters that led to the second floor, the Main Library.

"Are you a bookworm?" she whispered.

"Yes."

"I am too."

There was a naked statue of a Woman of Learning with nothing on and a book in her hand. She stood at the bottom of the stairway near a glass display case showing pictures of textile machinery.

"I am going to this university too," Urie suddenly announced.

Her words felt momentous. These were the first words since the Bishops had arrived in Ephesus that gave a definite direction to her future. Yet the minute she had spoken them, it seemed settled and lost all importance. On the way upstairs they passed a drinking fountain. They bent down and drank out of it.

"This is the fifteenth fountain we have drunk out of on this campus," said Zebul.

"On this campus they don't have any fountains for niggers," said Urie.

"That's because there aren't any."

"Do you know what my sister did in Richmond, Virginia?" Urie asked. "She almost drank out of a Negro fountain because it said 'Colored.' She thought it was pink water!" She poked Zebul, and suddenly he began to laugh. They laughed feverishly all the way up the stairs. Then they clapped their mouths, looked away from each other, then controlled themselves, gulping and blinking until they were worn out.

At the top of the stairs there was another statue. It was of a naked boy faun taking a splinter out of his foot. He had a wicked look on his face, and his big toe pointed to the card catalogue.

"Urie," said Zebul.

"What?"

"Let's take out a book!"

"Can we?"

"Sure."

"But what if it's just for college students?"

"All they can say is No, isn't it? We'll say we are students. They'll never know whether college or high school."

"How old are you?" she asked.

"Thirteen, but my birthday is in sixty-four days."

"I am one month older than you," she said.

"Be very nonchalant," ordered Zebul.

He headed for the card catalogue. She followed him. He opened a drawer. It was like a mouth opening. They stared at the names, thousands of them slipping before them.

"I'd even work typing commas on these cards," whispered Urie, "if it would pay for my tuition."

He closed the catalogue. Ponk, it sounded.

"Sh-sh-sh," she warned.

He opened another drawer, *"Tad* to *Try."* He moved the cards. He came to TOLSTOY, COUNT L. There were hundreds of cards under Tolstoy. He chose one: *My Confession.* He wrote the number on a slip of paper.

The attendant behind the check-out desk, a fat student with pimples and green skin, looked over at them.

"Come on. It's your turn now," whispered Zebul.

She moved to the catalogue and flipped past Tolstoy. Her eyes caught on: *"To the Lighthouse,* V. Woolf, auth." She took the slip that Zebul handed her and wrote down the name and the number. Her heart was beating. She peeked over to see if the fat attendant was still looking at them. He wasn't.

Clutching their slips, they moved to the big oaken desk. Behind was an opening into the stacks, filled with book trolleys and stacks for cards. The fat student was gone. A huge clock above the desk stared down at them, its fingers pointing: eleven-fourteen. A man with warts came to receive their slips. Urie's toes curled inside her shoes. Zebul stared at the clock, pretending boredom. They waited while the man disappeared into the stacks. They did not look at each other. After what seemed an interminable time, the man with warts reappeared. They still did not look at each other.

As the man with warts lifted a stamper to stamp the slips he asked, "Are you students?"

"Yes," said Zebul.

He banged the stamp on the slips and then on the books. Urie's eyes were riveted to the spot, just next to her name and her address, which she had written illegibly in case there was a question. Then the man handed over the two books. Urie's was a dark, small wine-red edition. Zebul's was a green so dark as to be almost black, frayed at the corners, with a plastic binding out of which threads protruded.

"Don't run," warned Zebul. Clutching the books, they passed through the huge reference room. Miles of shelves. Miles of encyclopedias. A thousand long tables with lights perched like Florida birds. Outside huge vaulted windows were the banner-blue sky and the leaves of archaic trees whirling brilliantly like batons. They passed the faun, the Woman of Learning, ran down the stairs, by the glass cases of textile pictures. They pushed their way out the glass doors, ran through the columns, and catapulted down the stairs two at a time. Suddenly they were free on the sporty green campus, their books in their hands. They laughed in triumph.

After the victory of the books their mood changed. Everything seemed anticlimactic. They walked slowly toward Haw. At the power plant they took the railroad track. It was past noon. The sun was high and molten in the sky. They were both hungry, and the heat put them into a stupor. But instead of departing from each other, or going home to eat, they continued almost aimlessly down the baked, flat streets, through the heat-drowsed footpaths, past the ugly, empty mill squatting by the tracks. Mindless air seized them. Heat rose up from the cinders and gravel. Sweat rolled down their faces.

Urie could see right over the flat stores to the sky. She noticed the sag, the props at the corners of mill houses. She smelled dust, gasoline, chickens, and tobacco. She inspected. She bent down to look under a house.

"They have no underneaths to them," she said.

A woman on the porch stopped swinging. She leaned forward and spat a globule of snuff-saliva into a can. It landed with a conspicuous, meaningful plop.

Zebul wanted to laugh, but he did not dare. Although it seemed as if they were wandering aimlessly, he was leading her to his secret place, a sawdust pile back of Polk's Lumber. He did not want to take her home yet. He had to get her used to Haw in small doses.

Yet, though he was lacerating himself, he was greedy for all her reactions. He was in that state now that he was feeding upon her. As they walked he told her about Haw, explained about the mill, the footpaths, the unemployment, and the inferiority complex. He seemed to take a perverse pleasure in her repugnance at Haw. It corroborated some dark and hidden feeling in him.

They passed through a footpath into a yard. A wire clothes line hung motionless with a wash of underwear. There was not a sign of a breeze to make it tremble. Flies buzzed promiscuously. All at once a dirty yellow dog lifted its albino eyes from the underside of a house and stared at them. Growling, it grinned and stalked them. With a thin, servile yelp it attacked.

Urie reared back, frightened. Zebul lifted his arm threateningly and aimed a nonexistent stone.

The dog screeched as if it had been hit, and then, with its tail between its legs, it withdrew into its smelly lair. It barked at them from this safety.

Hypnotized, Urie seemed to wake. The sun was so high that she felt faint. Sweat rolled down her temples and formed beadlets on her upper lip. All at once, ensconced in the ugliness of the silent tin mill roofs, reflected like the tin in the sun, she felt that she had never been anywhere but here. It was all, though strange, familiar. The paths where she had never been before, she seemed to know. She hated the place, loathed it, desired to be free from it. Yet all the while she followed down the paths, in back of the houses, along a scraggly cedar fence, past the sheds of Polk's Lumber Yard.

"Where are we going?"

"I'm going to show you a secret place. It's a sawdust mountain. It's mine. I go there lots of times. I see everything from there."

As he had skirted the subject of her house, she skirted the subject of his. She did not want to go to his house. She did not want to meet his family. They would be white trash, like the woman who spat in the can, like the albino dog.

They passed another shed, inside which half-hewn pine lay, weeping pitch. Everything smelled strong, hot, and metallic. Every now and then a buzzsaw would start to shriek and then taper off into a metallic drone, like some human insect.

"Say something about this town," he demanded.

"What?"

"What's your impression?"

"The stores are ugly."

"I know."

"They are too low. You can see right over them."

"I know it. They are awful."

There was a silence. They arrived at the sawdust mountain. In her mind Urie had thought that it would be new-blown, orange and fresh. But the saw chips had blackened with the sun. They looked dead. It looked like slag. She hesitated to move forward on it.

"Come on. Let's go up."

He tried to help her, but she pulled away. "I can walk," she said with lonely distaste.

The sensation of walking in the sawdust mountain was strange. It was like quicksand, shifting, like sponge rubber. The spume of silvered wood pulp had spouted out of a tin pipe at the top, which led from the tin-roofed shed. The smell of the mountain was like sweet, rainy wood. But the nearer they approached to the top, the hotter under the sun it became. Sawdust filled Urie's nostrils. There was not a breath of air. As they rose they could see the shimmering roofs, the water tower of Ephesus, and some loblolly pines growing in a ditch below Haw. At the top they sat down. Haw seemed only an eroded crossroads, with salt-and-pepper dots of houses.

"You said there were chinaberry trees."

"There. See?"

The silence was profound. She looked at him, trying to grasp the essence of this boy in relation to this place. She felt estranged. Silent. Separate. Where was she? Whom had she come with? Who was he? Why was she in this horrible place? How could it have happened that she had gone so far from the ocean to end up in this limbo town with only this symbolic book in her hand to establish her relationship to the lighthouse of herself?

"This is the town of Haw," he said recklessly. "And I'm a Haw-yoo."

He wanted to break her open like an orange. He wanted those speckless blue and empty eyes to speak. Afraid, hypnotized by her, he waited.

But she said nothing.

"What do you think?" He pumped her.

"I don't know."

"Say!" he said.

"Say what?"

"Something!"

"I thought that dog would bite us."

"They never bite if you act like you'd hit them. Or kick them."

"Why?"

"Because everybody kicks them all the time. They're trash dogs. They're cowards. They're like their masters."

She looked at him. He was ugly too.

"I know what this town is," he said.

Still she was silent.

"Ignorant and dull." He primed her. As the sweat drained down into his shirt collar his voice seemed to become heavier and heavier and his demand greater.

"Why don't you say something about it?" he insisted.

"What?"

"Anything that you think."

Again silence.

"Say. Say."

Silence.

"I know already. But you have to say."

After the whisper of the sawdust, the itch of tires on the dusty roads, the whack of the sawmill, her words seemed like the last whisper.

"It's the ugliest, horriblest, most lowdown town I have ever seen in my whole life. It's the end of the world."

The merciless purity of her words struck him with demonic, lacerating euphoria.

"Do you know true beauty?" he asked in that scarcely articulated tone that people use when they feel that they are about to be initiated into a great mystery.

"You can't have beauty in the burning sun."

"What's true beauty?"

"Where the ocean is. Where it's cold, and so powerful that storms can take you over."

"I wish I could see the ocean," he said after a long, long silence.

"You mean you have never seen the ocean?"

"No."

An actual living being so ignorant! She stared at him with an expression of distaste. No wonder he acted as if she were on a pedestal. Buoyed up by the thickness of her own ego, sweating in the steam of his adulation, almost feeling her solid as melting, she began to speak. Although she was a witness telling him, she said, the only live witness to the known universe was the ocean. To talk of the ocean was to make an ovation to power. The thing about the ocean was that it always wanted something.

The ocean was all desire, rocking between continents and creeping obsequiously on the beach in the calm days, as if to hide its desire with the balm of the sun. What did the ocean want? She herself had always wondered. What did the ocean want, she wondered in the winter, that it moved all the time? What did it seek with its endless bleating waves upon the beach? What did it say when it thundered over Brace's Rock, wrenching its heart out into thundering crashes, into spumes of beady, freezing drops that sought the sky? What did it desire with all its force?

But it betrayed itself in winter. Its awful discipline, its tides, which came up and receded with one hour's difference, summer and winter, retired to the background. And it lay dour, gray, denuded of all the twittering land birds, the thistles, sweet peas, marsh grass, sweet land grass, and wild roses. Only its cold licking seaweed shone like Medusa's evil hair on the gray rocks. Below you could see blue mussel shells. Its waves were short and choppy. It lay in wait for a storm to churn it to ecstasy.

This ecstatic betrayal, P.Q. took them to witness. She remembered a time when Loco Poco was only four years old. They went to Maynards', a French-fairy-like abode perched behind Brace's Rock, a landlubber's conception of safety, a stone castle, prey to the brutality of the sea's ecstasy.

P.Q. held Loco's hand. The gale lashed the sea to a towering rage. It drew itself back and burst with torrential force. They stood on a high rock. They held hands like a charmed fairy circle. All around them the sea gushed with falling waters. It sucked away. They were on a rock which became a small, frail pinnacle when the waves smashed. It threw spray thirty feet above their heads.

None of the children was afraid to be so close. They looked up at P.Q., watching his magnificent evil eyes gather in ecstasy when the wave moved toward them. Then their hands clenched.

"It's coming! It's coming!"

"Keep quiet!" shouted P.Q.

The wild, billowing tongue piled up, ready to break. Urie kept her eyes wide open. It slammed. The sky was rent with shoots of vicious foam. It doused them. They screamed with laughter. The sea salivated, rested a second in satisfaction, and then withdrew its gorge, giving them that second of rest from its unbearable and cruel rapture. Then it sucked on them. It began to gnaw away their souls in its recession. It sucked their eyes out of their heads and their vitals out of their stomachs.

Urie tried not to go with it. She spat, a token, to prevent its taking her. She was careful to spit the way of the wind, hiding the action from P.Q. For P.Q. had an eye on all three to see that their souls *were* the sea's. He wanted them to follow it.

"Sea, I am here. Take my superb spit, but don't take me!"

Her spit dissolved, but she was gone too.

Later, when they went home, the house had a strange, unnatural, unhealthy quiet after the tantrum. How did it happen that the furniture, once so familiar, seemed so strange? It was as if a hundred years had passed in the one hour's connivance with that storm, and they had returned, like Rip Van Winkle, to a strange land. Every object had changed its significance. The grand piano was silent and staring. Surely it had never been capable of Chopin! It had never uttered lullabies. Not Brahms. The old whale harpoon of soft bent iron which they used as a fire-poker stood gravely against the bricks. The polished floor was silent as death. The big rug was silent. Only a small mound of dust, uncaught by the mop, waved as one of the turmoiled breezes, diluted, estranged from the full force of the gale outside, sent it into soft and feeble signals. But it was only fitful. It gave up its waving and lay down dead again against the rug. The sofas sat solid and fat as two middle-aged ladies with their slips showing. Even their pillows, awry, as they had left them before they went out into the storm, were untouched. It was incredible. Outside the storm raged, but it was muffled. Sad, transmuted. The flavor of glory was only a memory. The windows shuddered. The blinds whacked. Everything was lonely. They sat now like still mice in the large and silent house. Ghosts heaved and sighed through them. The flames of the fire, exacerbated by gusts, writhed fitfully.

P.Q. read them Cassius's speech about Caesar, from the very play that Miss Hagood had assigned them now so many years later. P.Q. pretended the fire hearth was a pulpit and quoted, imitating an Orthodox priest. At first they wanted to laugh. But it was an explanation of the ocean. That beauty was contingent on desire, and desire, to be beautiful, had to exert power. Any kind of power.

" 'I was born free as Caesar: so were you,' " she quoted.

> "We both have fed as well, and we can both
> Endure the winter's cold as well as he.
> For once, upon a raw and gusty day,
> The troubled Tiber chafing with her shores,
> Caesar said to me, 'Darest thou, Cassius, now
> Leap in with me into this angry flood
> And swim to yonder point? Upon the word,

Accoutred as I was, I plunged in
And bade him to follow. So indeed he did.
The torrent roared, and we did buffet it
With lusty sinews, throwing it aside
And stemming it with hearts of controversy.
But ere we could arrive the point proposed,
Caesar cried, 'Help me, Cassius, or I sink!'
I, as Aeneas, our great ancestor,
Did from the flames of Troy upon his shoulder
The old Anchises bear, so from the waves of Tiber
Did I the tired Caesar. And this man
Is now become a god."

"The injustice of it!" cried Urie to Zebul, now recalled to the sawdust mountain, the heat, the ugliness. But she cared no longer. She was transported. For she had swallowed Cassius, hook, line, and sinker. She was Cassius. Cassius was the hero; Caesar, the weakling. Yet here was Caesar treated as a god. It was unfair. She would be like Cassius; she would outlast the Tiber, the ocean, to bring in the weakling Caesar, the weakling who had made the challenge and failed. She wanted to challenge and win. She wanted to win.

And so the ocean, because it was so lethal, so powerful, so merciless was the epitome of beauty. It was the only thing fit to worship, an enemy that could, with one slap at the shore, demonstrate humanity's weakness. The ocean never stopped. It was a design of eternity, she told Zebul on the sawdust mountain, in which she had been cradled, inhuman arms which had presented her to the world. That was what pure beauty was. Nothing fake, punky, and sawdust like his mountain in this drab, beaten Southern town, but the ocean, which, if it took a mind to, could demolish this dump with one small wave.

CHAPTER 9

"What happened?" Loco asked Urie breathlessly.

Although Loco asked the question, Irene was fastened onto Urie's face for the answer. Her eyes were avid, yet as cold as a pterodactyl's.

"Nothing," answered Urie.

"What did you do?"

"Nothing."

"What was it like?"

"What is this? The Spanish Inquisition?"

Irene's mouth closed. A shade came down over her consuming eyes. She turned her jealousy inward, imprisoning her hatred for the strange, interloping boy.

But Loco paid no attention to Urie's rejection. Didn't Urie sooner or later always tell? She could not resist impressing or boasting or confiding to Loco, and Loco knew she could wind her around her finger.

So she began to follow Urie around like a dog, attracted by the light daze in Urie's eyes. Instead of asking her openly, she stationed herself in out-of-the-way places such as thresholds, the hallway to the bathroom, the kitchen steps, so that she could slip the questions to Urie as if they were not questions. It was not characteristic for Urie to be secretive. Was that proof of the mystique of malehood? Loco wondered. Had the difference of boys, about whom Urie denied any difference at all, caused her to change her personality from being aboveboard and derisive to—what? Loco wanted to find out everything.

Like a gnome, she would simply be there when Urie went by. "Is he good-looking?" "Did he like you?" "What was the first thing he said?" "Do you like him?" If Urie began to answer even one, she would be hooked.

"Shut up!" Urie cried finally in impatience. "It's nothing like what you think at all. In fact you don't even think, or you wouldn't ask. It has nothing to do with boys as boys."

Yet Urie's protest was muted. She had a pleading, almost reflecting tone. This subordination made Loco aware that Urie's withdrawal signified something more subtle and momentous than she had even imagined.

That night Loco lay in her bed, holding her old Teddy bear. Her eyes were wide open. Urie lay on the other side of the curtain. Loco could tell she was wide awake. She concentrated on Urie's breathing.

All of a sudden a strange emotion overtook Loco. She became aware of something almost as indelible as the impression of the Teddy bear upon her chin, of Omniscience. Urie would not tell her. But Omniscience knew. Omniscience seemed a great and fantastic personage, a relation of Loco's, for he knew what she thought too—he even made her think it. Thinking of Omniscience, the power of Omniscience, Loco had suddenly the most powerfully tender feeling for Urie. She could feel Urie's soul and see her entire entity, just as if it had a form. Urie thought she was holding a secret away from Loco, away from everybody. Yet Omniscience knew. Urie did not know that Omniscience knew. If Omniscience knew, what did it matter if Loco didn't know? Loco desired to tell Urie this discovery more than anything else in the world. For the fact that Omniscience knew the secret that she did not know, and that it was unimportant whether she knew, but that, although she did not know the secret, she knew that Omniscience knew, made her feel closer to Urie than she had ever felt in her life.

She raised herself on one elbow, holding the Teddy bear tight and smiling. "It doesn't matter if you don't tell, Urie," she began in loving excitement.

"Oh, can't you turn that broken record off!"

"Because I'm not supposed to know. But I want to tell you something, Urie. There is somebody who knows."

Silence. Urie raised herself on her elbow and stared into the darkness toward Loco. She waited a long time in silence.

"Who?"

"Omniscience."

Urie was furious that she had been hooked. The very burning eagerness and tenderness of Loco's disembodied voice drove her wild. "Ever since I got back it's been one long blah-blah-blah to get you off my back. All I ask is to be let alone, and you wake me up in the middle of the night to blab your bogeyman all-knowing palavering just to try to get me to tell. Well, I won't—"

"But I don't want you to tell me. That's not it at all. I told you it doesn't matter if you don't tell me. I don't even want to know. But there's something, Urie—"

"Shut up!"

"But I want to tell you. Urie, it's how I know you—"

"You and your crazy all-seeing eye!"

Loco began to tremble.

"You have a straight wire to God's horse-mouth?" Urie belted out, carried away with her cleverness.

"You shouldn't say—"

"Put another nickel in."

"Oh, you stink! Just when I'm trying to tell you something important. You can just go to hell!" shrieked Loco. Her fingers were tangled in her hair in a paroxysm of desperation.

Urie plunged her face into her pillow and laughed.

The next day nothing was changed on the surface. There was always a recognized family framework for fights and a recognized family framework for alliances. Outside these regular routines, breakfast, dressing, dishes, homework, books, walking to school, were carried on as usual. Urie, having been purified by baiting Loco to anger, pushed her out of her thoughts.

But Loco became subdued. She was shocked that she had told her favorite sister to go to hell. She was no longer angry. But she was afraid. She had been cast into a foreign land, using Urie's words against Urie. Direct confrontation, fighting at the wall, was a world where Loco felt afraid not only for herself but for Urie. For she knew that she was right. Urie was wrong. That was why Urie had laughed with triumph when she had got her to swear.

The next afternoon she took the flute from under her bed. She cleaned it with silver polish. She stuck toothpicks in its holes, as if she were picking its nose. She cleaned out the gunk of chicken manure and fastidiously scraped it onto a rock. Then she learned the scale. She began to practice feverishly. She took off her shoes and went barefoot into the field. She sat down under the Bone Tree. She played.

Every day she played. She never played a melody, although she could play anything by ear. Instead she played a series of notes, notes without rhythm or melody. The sound was always tentative, though it was loud and clear. She blew strongly into the flute to get a note without tremolo, very flat. The sound of each note was the direct opposite of her personality. It was as if she were after something in sound. Each time she blew she wanted a note she recognized. Such an achievement was not obtainable as melody. For melody existed in time and employed distentions and suspensions of harmony and rhythm that were dynamic. But Loco wanted this one note, something static and representative of Forever.

"It's horrible," said Irene, blocking her ears.

"Why don't you play something?" asked her mother.

"She plays just this one note over and over," Irene carped.

"But it's like butter."

Whenever the family wanted to laugh they repeated the word "butter" over and over to themselves until it lost its meaning. Mrs. Bishop had taught them to do it. Inanity gave a feeling of euphoric self-justification. The world was wrong. They themselves were the kernel of the universe.

"To me music is a pattern in time which tells a melodic story," said Urie affectedly. "You have to have obstacles to get over, so you have to arrive at crises. You have to have crescendoes. Only that way can you arrive home. When you get back to *do,* you have the victory. Life is these stresses and strains. Life is dynamic. It is not these one-shot static imitations of fake eternity."

Loco blushed at Urie's pretensions. Urie was wrong again, trying to prove she was right. Loco wanted to tell Urie, but Urie was so strong and loud, so full of qualifications and justifications, what good did it do to argue? Paradoxically, Loco was also filled with admiration for Urie's terrific force and passion.

"I don't care. It sounds like a funeral," said Irene.

"But she is Persephone practicing to come out of her hole," said P.Q.

The rescue tore Loco from her defenses. A smile shattered her frail white face. She threw her arms around P.Q.'s neck. "Yes. I'm making the hole wider," she whispered in his ear.

Urie and Irene looked the other way. They were always embarrassed by Loco's effusions.

This special bond between Loco and P.Q. at this particular time had justification beyond the fact that Loco was his favorite. P.Q. was at a stalemate in his business. He was bored by it. If anyone mentioned linen, caps, trucks, money, aprons, or the necessity of getting a furnace for the winter, his reaction was an uncomprehending and sarcastic stare. Then he walked away, as if the matter were too banal to discuss, and turned on the radio.

The United States Neutrality Act had just been amended. America was selling arms to England on a cash-and-carry basis. The last week in October a rumor started in Ephesus that the Navy was going to take over the university. This rumor had originated because there had been a meeting in Washington, D.C., between Dr. Rob, the university president, and the Secretary of the Navy about the possibility of establishing a pre-flight school in the university in case of the expected increase in the military forces.

Every night P.Q. turned on the radio. His life became a concentration on waiting. Correspondents stationed in London talked about the Phony War. The Great Event was always about to happen. When it would be or what it could be, no one knew.

P.Q. did not talk about the war. He just kept his ear glued to the radio. At night he would walk to the university library to consult the day-old *New York Times*. Meanwhile in the house he became more and more a gigantic, preoccupied presence around whom the children had to be careful not to be silly. No one dared to ask him mundane questions. Even Mrs. Bishop kept silent. Secretly Mrs. Bishop knew he was using the war to keep from facing the facts of life in Niggertown with no money. But for the peace of the family, she told herself, she had to keep still. It was a measure of P.Q.'s total mystique that, though there was no demonstrable war and his position appeared spurious, in fact his effect became more and more significant. His waiting began to have the quality of something more profound even than war, something supernatural. That he was an empirical

82]

rationalist made this paradoxical. And the family, almost resentfully, began treating him with the respect due a Cassandra.

Only Loco Poco dared distract him. Almost in return for his rescuing her from Hades as Persephone, she announced next morning at breakfast, "I think I saw Tootsie Morn!"

P.Q., throwing his napkin on the table, rushed outdoors after her.

"She must have followed us here," said Loco conspiratorially as she beckoned him around the barn.

Irene, Urie, and Mrs. Bishop followed them with their eyes.

"They're crazy," grunted Irene.

But Urie and Mrs. Bishop kept quiet. For the Tootsie Morn game had lost all sense in the realm of the real, and the game had become Truth. P.Q. and Loco returned flushed with triumph. Loco had seen Tootsie Morn, and her face was diaphanous as she jittered and hopped at P.Q.'s knee.

Mrs. Bishop said, after the girls had gone to school, "I don't think you should encourage her in that Tootsie Morn business."

But P.Q. gave her the same annihilating stare he would have accorded anyone who had announced that a war did not exist in Europe. Then he mounted his bicycle with grandeur and pedaled down the driveway.

CHAPTER 10

Not only was the experience of friendship too dynamic, too *in medias res* to tell, it was like seeing the back of oneself, as if one were the moon. What had been dark but omnipresent suddenly became clear and illumined. The fears one had dreaded suddenly became open. Exposed in cold moonlight, the emotion's values became negated.

The shame of living in Niggertown was acceptable in the family. That shame revealed to an outsider was another thing. Revealing to an outsider was revealing to oneself. The only qualification in Urie's shame was that it involved the family. It was the Bishop shame she had offered up to Zebul. She had acted independently. She felt slightly guilty, as if she were a betrayer.

At the same time she was excited. For in the last-go-trade was posited a challenge, some immense possibility, secreted in arrogance. Something was in store for her in her friendship with Zebul.

Since Loco had been cured of asking her questions, Urie was free. On

Sunday she tried to read *To the Lighthouse*. It was boring. She read the first three pages five times, then peeked to the back of the book to see if they ever were going to get to the lighthouse. Then she gave up. Nothing happened. Everybody in the book was dull and peculiar, living, removed in some rare, dead world. On Monday she took it to school with her.

"I couldn't wait to see you!" shouted Zebul, running to her in the schoolyard. "I tried to read *My Confession*. It's all about not believing in anything and it goes on and on and it is absolutely boring."

"Guess what! I tried to read *To the Lighthouse* too. I can't stand it!"

"But it's about the ocean!"

"It's awful."

"I tell you what! Let's switch."

"Okay."

During algebra, Urie kept looking around the class. She thought how different school was from what it had been in the beginning—all because of Zebul. She discovered he was looking at her. There was a devilish slash to his mouth. He made a conspiratorial grimace at her. In it there was the challenge that lay at the heart of their cabal, the same exciting cast of face that he had exhibited when he had told her about the nigger hand. She almost laughed out loud.

Later in the day, in English class, Miss Hagood assigned a theme. It had to be written in twenty minutes. Afterward Miss Hagood would call on volunteers to read.

What should she write about?

She looked at the faces around her. She remembered the trepidation, the dread she had felt of high-school kids. Now, buoyed by her image in Zebul's eyes, she saw them as a sea of faces in whom she could float easily, which even she could manipulate, shock, tear, or burst, like balloons in the water. Who are they? Why did I think they were important? What do I care what they think? They're nothing compared to me! Why, I know universes! If they only knew what I knew! She remembered suddenly how it was she who had unleashed that lash that had whipped courage into Bishopry when they had arrived in Ephesus at the end of everything. Like a vow: "We're going to crack this town wide open!"

Among the faces she saw Zebul's again. He was staring at her with a dull, almost totally expressionless face, completely different from the challenge he had given her before. He had not written a thing on his paper. She tried to make out what it was that was in his face, but she did not understand. It was almost as if he were hidden, bidding her to find him, to rouse him, to surprise him, to exist for him, as only she could do. This attitude scared her. And it became incumbent on her to make manifest to everyone that very thing which she had already told him. It was for his sake, to set him back in recognition again.

She knew!

Something took hold of her. It was like opening the sluice gate of her destiny. She went rushing down her own channel toward it, her words brushing at the edges of paper like water at the locks. Words resounded in her head. She breathed softly. At the end of the period she laid her pencil down.

"All right. Who will volunteer?" asked Miss Hagood.

No one raised a hand.

Urie began to twitch her head in such a way, eager, nervous, inspired, that Miss Hagood noticed her at once. It was inevitable. She was chosen, as she intended and had known she would be.

She stood up. The silence was taut. She was conscious of Zebul's eyes. A fantastic haughtiness took her and swept away all traces of stage fright. She thrust up her head, licked her lips, and began.

"Last night I dreamed I went back to Thalassia again," she started, reveling in having copied her first line from *Rebecca*. She was aware of her power, aware of her already transcendent acting. "Thalassia, the house where I used to live, elegant in the morning and huge against the ocean. Our house had fourteen rooms and forty-nine windows. It stood exactly as it used to before I ever left it, before I had to dream it to make it real. Thalassia means House by the Sea.

"Some people believe that certain attitudes dictate the type of houses people live in. But I believe that the type of houses people live in does the dictating. The only name we could name the house where I now live is Athalattia. Athalattia means House away from the Sea. This house is situated in this town, past the railroad tracks, on a hill overlooking Negro town. It is old, rotten, leaning, and peeling, with two chimneys, a tin roof, and a sagging porch. It is the oldest house in town, and as the owner said of it, 'It never was no good nohow.' "

The class laughed. The hair stood up on Urie's arms. The people whom she despised now became a magnificent spectrum for her power to play on.

"Athalattia dictates to me. It says, 'You will not let anybody else do that which you can do.' We try to fix it. But we cannot spend much money on it, for it is too old to fix and not worth it. It says, 'You will not attempt to patch me, fix me, or improve me, because I am manifest and proud in my putridity. I am even worse than those houses which mill-workers live in. I have excellent hubris. I am a historic house. I am the first house ever built in this town. I existed before the Civil War and I never was a mansion. I am the poor house of a poor dirt farmer of the Piedmont who went away to fight against you and lost. My owner was not only trash, he was a cuckold. His wife began running around with some other man. I contain the bullet hole where my master missed the lover as he was shaving over the kitchen sink and hit me. I have an old tin roof upon which no cats run, only squirrels and chipmunks. I dictate the season of the year when the nuts fall down upon my tin roof. They report like pistol shots. My porch is about to fall, nor shall it be mended. For it shall fall when it wants to fall, nor shall it be helped or hindered by you. For you, you occupants, you will realize that you use me when I have been un-used. You shiver in me through my holes. You laugh at my rottenness. You swelter in my lack of insulation. Yet you do not own me. You merely rent me. And renting me, I stand or fall by my age and my pride.' "

Across the silence burst a whiplash of applause. The handclaps were uncontrollable.

Urie sat down.

In the silence Miss Hagood said, "This theme is the most excellent that we have heard in Ephesus High School for many years. It has echoes of both the novel *Rebecca* by Daphne du Maurier and of the play *Richard III* by Shakespeare."

But Urie discounted the silences, the handclaps, and Miss Hagood's breathy, trembling eulogy as the obverse side of the coin of the Three Stooges remark. Luxuriating in her triumph, she wondered how Miss Hagood could have allowed them the license to clap.

She was aware of Zebul's breathing.

Outside in the hallway she could hear the voices, rampant and excited.

"She's a genius!"

"What was all that clapping in your class?"

"What does hubris mean?"

"What does cuckold mean?"

"She's fantastic. She's brilliant!"

Opal Granger came up to her and said, "Oh, Urie, you must invite me some time to your house. It sounds out of this world. That was an abso-lutely brilliant theme!"

Afterward, walking home, Zebul looked at her with an eagerness in his eyes so beseeching that it approached a quality somehow vicious. He said, "You are a great writer, Urie. You did it. Just like when you told me about the ocean. You are absolutely terrific!"

Her smile was slashed, triumphant, burning under his adulation.

"You will turn out to be a famous writer," he said.

"But I don't want to be a writer. I'm going to be an actress!" she answered. "As an actress you can be everything, but a writer can only be one thing. I want to be everything. I *am* everything!" And then, ecstatically: "Zebul, do you know it's because you challenged me—because of the dividing line of the railroad track that I did it. It was inevitable. I told them before they could find out. Now they can't find out because they already know. Do you realize?" she said. "You can make people take anything!"

There was a cabalistic flavor to their bond. They were both incognito, each recognizing the other and being the only one to do so. Although from the moment of reading her theme, Urie was "in," was acceptable to the high-school crowd, this meant only that all harassment and experimentation stopped. Her shy and fearsome façade of Bishopry still cut her off. Thus her energies went increasingly into her friendship with Zebul.

Unknown to Urie, Zebul, since her ocean evocation, had become obsessed with the idea of P.Q. He tried to imagine such a father. He could not. He wished he were lucky enough to have a father like P.Q. P.Q. became mythical. Zebul could imagine him standing on the rock the way she described him, holding the whale harpoon. But to Zebul the whale harpoon was a trident, and P.Q. stood for Poseidon Q. So he lived for the time when she would invite him home. Then he would be able to meet P.Q.

With almost unbearable enthusiasm Zeb did the wooing. He treated Urie like a jewel in a forgotten attic. He turned her this way and that greedily, observing her in different lights. He went over each trait of her, each appearance, almost turning her upside down.

When they walked together from school, they always went up Pergamus Avenue as far as the railroad tracks. That was where he left her. He witnessed her in long, trailing, lumpy, ill-fitting clothes. He was always strangely moved. He thought of her as his classic, his discovery. Her voice, sometimes disdainful, sometimes conspiratorial, sometimes soft, high, whisperingly enthusiastic, entranced him. She had an aristocratic nose, a ludicrous feature. But when she was with him her originality transformed the nose into an emblem of weight and grandeur. He stood in awe of her. Her growing fame, her strange dresses, and her long nose were all part of her brilliance. He could not imagine her dressing like other girls, any more than a gazelle could be a cat.

She used this power of exoticism over him to the hilt. They discussed their backgrounds and ambitions. His were inferior to hers. She agreed that he did not know the world at large. She did. She knew vast strata of society.

But a reversal took place. The more she talked of what she was, the more she desired to know what he was. Where before she had been repulsed by the thought of Haw, there began to rise a quixotic curiosity. As the lowdown house had been the only house possible after Thalassia, now it was revealed that Zebul Walley, a Haw-yoo, was the only possible friend. For they were both alike in being strangers to their social positions. She was a displaced person relegated to Niggertown. He was a displaced person propelling himself out of Haw. Eagerly she asked him to tell her of Haw. Before, she had talked. Now he did. She soaked up his descriptions. He took her more and more often through the baked streets. She wanted to know about trash, lint-headery, redneckery, and poverty. Going with him, she felt initiated. Her repugnance wore off. She began to abandon herself to the lowly.

"I want to know the trashy. I want to understand the trashy. I want to realize the lowest of the low. And you can tell me."

Far from being insulted by these words, he felt honored.

The next day he decided that he would take her to meet his family. He was nervous. So was she. But she walked trustingly beside him down the railroad tracks. They were on such terms of friendship that she was confident his deepest nature was closer to hers than to his own family's. When they left the dirt street and walked up the porch steps, she placed her feet carefully. She pulled up her head. She took on her most polite posture.

"Mamma!" called Zebul.

In the dark parlor with its sagging floor she stared to a board hallway. The mother entered. And then the father.

"Mamma and Daddy, meet my friend, Urie Bishop."

Urie put out her hand.

Eames Loomis was embarrassed to shake hands with a schoolgirl. He moved his big feet backward like flourbags and stared at them. Then he slithered his eyes to look at her again.

"I reckon you're new to the South."

"Yes."

"Must seem strange to you, don't it?"

"Oh yes. But it's very interesting."

Eames Loomis garrumphed into fake laughter.

Henny Pinney resented Eames's being the fool to this girl's highfalutin airs and being embarrassed by handshaking. But she stared at Urie too. "Must be interestin' compared to what you seen—have seen," she added, correcting herself in a loud, affected social voice. "Since you seen all those things up North. But I guess you'll get used to it."

"Oh, I am getting used to it." Urie tried to hide her patronizing tone under even more politeness. But she knew Henny Pinney did not like her.

Henny Pinney did not like the shell-blue of Urie's eyes, in which she saw her own inferiority reflected. She was irritated by this awesome adolescent, who was a misfit with her head in the clouds, just like Zebul. Yet malevolently Henny Pinney enjoyed snobbism by association. In her heart she cackled that her son had picked a fool, a girl so unattractive she couldn't get another boy, but that the fool was high-class.

Later, after Eames bade her to come "set with us for a meal of chicken and bacon and biscuits," Henny Pinney saw her off as if they were foreigners. She and Eames Loomis hashed Urie over. Eames Loomis agreed with his wife. Zebul was growing up. His boy had a girl friend, even if she was peculiar.

"They talk bad grammar," said Urie as Zebul led her down a path through the scuppernong grape arbor.

"Yes."

"Why don't you?"

"I don't know. It just happened that I knew and spoke good grammar from the very beginning. From osmosis. Daddy only went to the fourth grade. Mamma went to the eighth. She's ashamed of him that he only went to the fourth."

"Ashamed?"

"Yes."

Suddenly he turned around. A sheaf of grape leaves framed his head, and behind she saw a group of peeling white-painted boxes buzzing with bees.

"Not that they're dumb."

"Oh, I know that they're not dumb."

"Daddy's not dumb, even if he did only go to the fourth grade."

"I know, I know," she whispered, almost embarrassed for her former forthrightness. "They never had the opportunity."

But he suddenly cut off her excuses. His eyes were fierce and cold and large. He would not allow her kindness and her patronage.

"It's just people," he said. "They're stinking, that's all."

She seared with the recognition of his shame—the hapless pillory of all nondoers, nonmovers, dopes, and willful self-wasters. That it described his own parents was the secret between them. They were equally displaced: this was the augur of their fantastic future.

"Come on," he said. She understood that that subject was over and the new one begun. In the silence she timed her footsteps to his. He pushed his way through the last of the grape leaves. He led her gently through an inferno of bees. They came to his doorway. It was covered with the leaves of a honeysuckle. He turned around, giving her a new, lightning-light smile. Then quietly, but so swiftly she hardly followed his motion, he opened the door.

"This is my little house," he breathed.

It stood before her, the space of it, small but filled with all the paraphernalia of his being, the wallpaper, the books, the lines of shelves, the desks, a high stool, his paintings hanging on the wall. It was close, packed, alive with the stillness of a secret universe.

She was swept into it, as into a conspiracy. She was conquered. Filled with envy, she stepped into it as if into a chapel.

"It's superb!"

He was imbued with her shock of recognition and envy; all his former half-apologetic trepidation at the explanation of his parents, all his Haw-yoo-dom, dropped away from him. "You think so. You really think so, don't you?"

"Yes."

He let her pore. She gazed. She perused. "I never saw anything like it. All those books!"

She turned, and her nose made a profile against the one little window etched with cobwebs.

"They're mine."

"All yours?"

"I collected them. Look. I have drawing paper too. See?" He showed her where he put it. He opened up his cupboards. He took out his secret knickknacks. He showed her everything. They went through a sheaf of his drawings. He explained to her how he had come to live in his little house. He beamed. He flashed. He showed her his compass, his desk chair on casters. He grinned. Carried away with the impression he was making, with her expressions of envy, surprise, admiration, he was eloquent. He made her sit on the high stool. A feeling of domination over her possessed him. At last his life was justified.

"To think! In the midst of this dumb, stinking, dull, lint-head cotton mill town, this!" she exclaimed.

"It's a secret oasis. A secret haven. Heeheehee. It's a universe. Like Faust's," he said, prodding her.

"You can do anything in here!"

"Yes. That's just it," he breathed. "I can do and think anything in here. I can go to the farthest limits of thoughts."

For almost half an hour they sat. She did not say much. Then they turned to the subject of his drawings. But she interrupted him to ask questions, how he happened to make butterflies, and why he had not painted his mother and father. There was no rhyme or reason to her questions. She just asked anything that came into her mind. All of a sudden she asked, "How did you get all these books?"

"I stole them," he said. And then he laughed a high, clear treble of delight.

She was aware of shock. Yet the quality of her shock because of her impressions, because of the little house, the conquering spirit of it, and because of his laughing, delighted eyes, was different from what she had ever thought of herself. For instead of feeling criminality, she fell at once into his view of it.

"You stole them?"

Fear, disapproval, shame, and criminality were fake attributes placed upon such an accomplishment by a hypocritical world.

"Yes."

"But why haven't I stolen too?" she asked.

"I don't know."

"It's so natural. You mean you got all these books . . ."

"Yes!"

"But I never thought—I must not have the guts," she said.

"That's just it. It doesn't take guts because it doesn't entail fear. If it entails fear, then it's a crime. But this isn't a crime. I make use of these that fools that never dreamed of stealing couldn't."

"I can't get over it," she said, feasting on this new vision of him.

As the days passed and he thought of the new development in their relationship, Zebul felt himself half suspended and waiting. Now that he had shown her his parents, would she show hers? Having doled out his parents with this licentious, artless generosity, he had no notion but that she would.

For the first time he mentioned it to her.

"I would like to meet P.Q.," he said.

"Oh, you will."

"When?"

"Sometime."

But more days passed, and there was no sign.

Most high-school people hate to reveal the tacky intimacies of their family life because it degrades their shining images created in the school-yard. But Zebul sensed that it was the reverse with Urie. Again, he began to have his doubts. Was she still ashamed of him? Perhaps she did not want to bring forth P.Q. because he was as yet too great a treasure to bestow upon him.

Once more he mentioned it.

"When will I get to meet P.Q.?"

"Soon," she repeated evasively.

But as weeks passed and nothing happened, the nigger house up the dirt street began to take on shades of grandeur as great in his imagination as those mansions and estates which Urie and her sisters had explored in their youth.

C H A P T E R 11

"Where's Loco?" asked Mrs. Bishop.

Dinner was ready. She had sent Loco to Lucretia Pile's for a loaf of bread half an hour ago.

"Hoohoo! Loco!" she called out the baggy screen door. It was late Indian summer but the day was freakishly hot and the sun searing. The sound penetrated the stifling hot air of Saturday noontime somnolence and died. It brought forth tag-end Negro titters. She waited another five minutes. Then she sent Urie after Loco.

"Come on, Irene. If nobody else is here, at least we can begin." Mother and oldest daughter sat down to eat hot cheese macaroni. But there was silence between them.

That morning Mrs. Bishop had looked in the mirror. Her teeth were beginning to blacken around the edges. A black half-moon was forming in from the gum on her front tooth. As she took each mouthful of macaroni she was aware of teeth and chewing. Paying a dentist was impossible. She shoved the necessity ruthlessly out of her mind. The decay of her teeth, instead of a fact to be faced, became a criminal thought to be avoided. Luckily no one in the family had noticed.

It was not only teeth. It was groceries and electricity and winter and keeping warm and birthdays. Loco would have her eleventh birthday on

November 5. A month after that was Urie's. Presents. Loco needed underwear, even with her hand-me-downs.

Money was like a squirrel cage. You could not stop running.

P.Q. had not bought a laundry truck yet. Without a truck the business could not expand. It was all very well to keep saying it was "temporary," but P.Q. diverted himself from the burden of bicycle-riding and unbefitting duties by becoming the gadfly of Ephesus. He joined students' tables in the cafés where he delivered the new linen and collected the old, engaging them in daily dialectical discussions about far-ranging subjects such as John Dewey, Eleanor Roosevelt, Saint Francis of Assisi, and Thucydides. But this did not increase his customers.

A gamble had to be taken, for winter was coming. They needed a heater, and Mrs. Bishop knew P.Q. would buy a truck before a heater. Twenty-five dollars had to be raised. Mrs. Bishop mulled through the cheese macaroni on how to raise it. The only thing she could think of was selling some of her things. Some of her grandmother's silver might bring something, the dragon candlesticks, perhaps the whale harpoon, or perhaps the porcelain china Chinese vase which they used as an umbrella stand. In her mind's eye she saw Laurelo's Wildwood Gift Shop opening its doors and engulfing these treasures as the whale did Jonah, coughing up and spitting out twenty-five dollars in one-dollar bills. What were things? Mrs. Bishop thought, swallowing three strands of macaroni without chewing them. P.Q. needed the truck if they were ever going to make enough money just to get the heater to keep warm in winter.

Suddenly there was the sound of footsteps. Urie banged the kitchen screen and ran into the room. There was a strange expression on her face.

"Well?" Fear made Mrs. Bishop's eyes bright above the half-suspended, trembling fork where her macaroni waggled.

"She's stuck." Urie grimaced as if to keep from bursting out into laughter or crying.

"Stuck?"

"She can't leave because the road is too hot."

"You mean she went down to Lucretia Pile's with bare feet?" screamed Mrs. Bishop.

"Yes."

"Well, you get her back here this very instant."

"But how, Mamma?" asked Irene, watching the ax fall on Urie this very moment without justification.

Mrs. Bishop got up, walked two steps behind her chair, spotted the dragon candlesticks on the mantelpiece reflecting the glass of the picture of

Amalfi, decided to sell the "things," turned around with such force that the comb fell out of her hair, and screamed, "The wheelbarrow!"

All during this pantomime, Urie had been thinking with resentment how she would have to carry Loco's shoes and socks to her. Irresistible. She turned around and ran to the shed. The moment she put her hands on the wheelbarrow, she burst into hoots of laughter. As she ran, propelling the wheelbarrow over the driveway roots, her heart raced with delighted excitement at Loco's impending disgrace.

Loco's face glittered through the warped frame of Lucretia Pile's screen door with the paleness of a Fra Lippo Lippi painting.

"Mamma's mad," Urie told her at once, trying to control her guffaws. "I haven't seen her so mad since we've been in the town of Ephesus."

But Loco did not seem to take in these words. She was so captured by the idea of riding in the wheelbarrow, like the empress of China, conveyed by Urie the coolie, ricksha man among Sociological Conditions, that she too began to hoot with laughter.

She entered the wheelbarrow with gingerly grace. She scooched at the bottom on her haunches like a cat. When Urie lifted the barrow, she lost her balance. She sat down, clutching her thin legs against her chest, the bread woggling by her feet. Negro passers-by laughed.

"It's a riot, Urie!" Loco giggled. "Go faster."

"You're going to get it," warned Urie.

For the first time thought of the future came into Loco's mind. She became quiet and bounced up and down as they entered the driveway. Urie pitied her. She began to be more careful of how the wheelbarrow jounced over the roots. She arrived at the kitchen door, parked carefully by the step.

Loco stepped out of the wheelbarrow and into the kitchen door. Before the specters of her mother and Irene she appeared in her bare feet and her black, moist, shining curls, holding out the bread.

Taken aback by this vision of innocence, Mrs. Bishop put her fork down menacingly and arose from her chair. Forcing herself against her own impulse, she began loudly, "How many times have I told you not to go barefoot?"

Loco's face began to change under the onslaught, yet it seemed to grow more innocent. Her eyes enlarged, dwarfing the pale complexion of her temples and cheeks. A blue vein above her ear began to throb.

Her frailty began to affect Urie so that she was filled with remorse and was about to beg her mother to stop. But it had the opposite effect on Mrs Bishop.

"I've told you and told you and yet you pay no attention and go out like that. What do you think I'm talking for? Oh, you needn't act so innocent. I know perfectly well your foxy ways. You just say yes, yes and go right on and do what you please, not caring for a soul in the world. It serves you right to get stuck. Maybe it would have been better if you had just been forced to walk down that street and burned your feet to crisps—"

"But Mamma, all the kids do it!" protested Loco, beginning a wail.

"I'm not having a pack of pickaninnies in this family!"

"Not just Negroes. White kids do it too."

"What kind of people do you think we are?" Mrs. Bishop spat. "It's hard enough to keep up standards living in a place like this without you acting like Negroes or white trash from Haw. They don't know any better. You do. From now on, you wear shoes. If we don't have one other thing in this family, at least we have shoes." But she turned away from the sight of Loco's shuddering shoulders, saying, "Put the bread down for goodness' sake!"

All the resentment Urie had harbored against Loco because of her questions about Zebul was suddenly melted at the expression on Loco's face.

In her cubicle that night Urie thought: We are not supposed to be prejudiced. If Negroes are as good as we are, why can't we act like Negroes? If Haw people are as good as we are, why can't we act like Haw people? But we can't and we don't. We're hypocrites. That's all.

Urie thought of Zebul and his stealing. She thought how she had so easily joined in his laughing explanations. And in the secrecy of her tapestried cubicle, wallowing in her own hypocrisy, she delighted even more. Yet it was trashy to steal. She had never done it. It was what people did who had low standards.

She tried to think of Zebul in total essence. But for the first time she felt that there was something frightening about having given him her most precious, secret essence, the ocean. Should she have confided in him? He was self-admitted trash. Maybe she was like the ancient Egyptians, who held that one must never mention the word they called God, for the power of its sacredness could be diluted and leak away. Would the ocean become less real to her now that she had told it to Zebul? Had she been casting her pearls before swine?

A blinding light was falling upon family attitudes. Yet after this episode Mrs. Bishop was more stringent about their duties in the house than before. They had to make their beds unfailingly. They had to sweep under them every day because in this shack dust formed in mountainous heaps. They had to wash the dishes after every meal. They had to do their homework immediately after supper. Loco Poco never again went out without her shoes.

But the nature of living in such a house defeated the standards. The family was like the British dressing for dinner every night in tents in darkest Africa. No matter how much they swept the floor, they could not keep it clean. For it was so corrupted with its topsy-turvy boards and cracks that its consistency was made of the settlings of dirt of ages. The Oriental rug was now molded into the dirt form of the floor. Only the top of it could be cleaned; otherwise the infinite need for infinite cleaning would be revealed.

Every day P.Q. used the yard for airing the dirty linens before taking them to the laundry. He laid caps, aprons, and tablecloths out in the sun from the barn to the end of the driveway. Spread on ground and gravel like fishnets, they gave the aura of a sea of white. Startled Negroes thought that snow had fallen, even though the temperature was 76 degrees. The family walked over the linens on the way to school. P.Q. rode over them on his bicycle, leaving thin tire tracks.

The dirty linens gave off a stench that was peculiar and unforgettable. They smelled like hot, smoking metal. It was a strange smell, for it did not fit the filth of the aprons, which came from the blood of hamburger meat, grease from frying, dust, nosewipings of kitchen help, chicken droppings, machinery oil, and overflows of syrup, catsup, flour, mustard, eggs, tomatoes, and pie wipings.

P.Q. never offered a reason for airing the linen. Once Irene asked him why, but he answered her question with a loud and significant belch and buried himself in the depths of the *Wall Street Journal*. After that, because it was a *verboten* subject and P.Q. was known as the cleanest and neatest person in the family, it was accepted that it was an act of meticulousness caused by the fact that he did not want the smells rising from his bicycle baskets to envelop him while he was traveling. It became as acceptable as eating and sleeping.

The night of Loco's birthday, Urie was preparing for bed. It was after midnight. Loco had long been asleep, holding her new notebook and a pair of shoes, presents, tightly under the covers. Urie carried a flashlight so that she did not have to put on the overhead light and wake Loco. In her left hand she carried a coat-hanger, for she wanted to hang up her skirt in the closet off the dining room. She was walking down the tapestried hallway, when suddenly the beam of the flashlight shone on a rat straddling the top board of the framework partition.

The rat's face was monstrous in the glare of light, its whiskers shining.

Its legs, outlined, looked like the legs of the bathtub. Its tail was long and prehistoric, coiled like cable wire and shining dully. Urie could see its heart palpitating against the cold fur. The rat was wrinkling up its nose. It had just crept to a slow halt. There was no way of knowing whether it would dart like lightning or attack in the next second. Its eyes seemed beadily blind. But its face contained a vile knowledge behind its mask of suspense, of its entity as a harborer of lice, fleas, and disease, its paws as treaders of garbage, and its mouth as scavenger. She stared at it. It stared at her. Trapped in only four feet of space with the rat two inches from her face, above her head, she was afraid to move. She was filled with loathing and fear. If she only had the coat-hanger in her right hand!

She made the attack first, slamming awkwardly upward with her left hand. The coat-hanger struck something. There was a terrible squeaking scream. But the rat was gone from the beam of light. It catapulted off the frame, fell on Loco's bed with a plop. Urie could hear the paw steps scrambling on the coverlet. Then there was another scud. The rat dropped to the floor and scuttled out a hole with rattling claws.

Urie swung the light through Loco's curtain and caught her sister opening her mouth in a moan. Loco shaded her eyes from the light beam. "I thought I was the clock in 'Hickory Dickory Dock.' "

"It's gone."

"What was it?"

"A rat or something."

"Rat!"

But Urie could tell Loco did not believe her.

In that moment she suddenly thought of the coat-hanger, pointed the light at it, imagined blood, and dropped it in a fit of repugnance. It clanged to the floor. In the darkness the two sisters listened to the silence.

But Loco, at the edge of sleep, forgot, turned over, and fell into a doze. Urie, shivering, got into bed.

In the morning she announced the rat at the breakfast table. Loco looked at her in shock, holding her cereal spoon in the air.

"It's those dirty linens!" said Mrs. Bishop.

"Oh, it's only the coming of autumn," answered P.Q. "The field rats wanted to find some good new shoes to wear."

He laughed. Loco rose, slapped his face, and breathed a laughing snort into his ear.

Two days later P.Q. brought home two huge German shepherd dogs. One had a mane like a lion. The other was young, half grown, and tumbled and barked in the yard with uncontrollable enthusiasm.

"Do you think dogs catch rats?" asked Irene.

But no one paid any attention to her.

In the steaming power of their manes, tongues, limbs, snouts, legs, the dogs became like gate wardens, powerful enough to ward off any enemy, let alone scavengers like rats. So nobody asked why P.Q. had brought them.

He named them Scylla and Charybdis and fed them with bones which he brought home each night from the cafés. Urie took over the younger, Scylla, teaching it to sit, heel, and walk. Loco loved them extravangantly and treated them with lavish indulgence, washing their faces and paws in fits and starts to keep them clean, and kissing them on the eyes. They followed Loco, like Mary's little lamb, walking beside her with velvet footsteps, licking her sneakers. She played games with them, inviting them to imaginary tea parties, placing bones in tin plates, and laughing with glee because they tipped the plates over and stole the bones.

But the advent of the dogs caused a change in the relations of the Bishops with the Negroes. The Negroes were afraid. They cowered when they passed. They walked on the far side of the dirt road. They looked at the Bishop house with eyes rolling with fear. And the dogs, seeing their effect on them, slavered viciously at the edges of the honeysuckle bushes, excited into gargantuan barks and threats, baiting the Negroes from afar. They were the final lid sealed on the castle of hypocrisy.

But sometimes, shivering in bed in the growing cold nights of autumn, Urie wondered if the rat would return.

CHAPTER 12

"You have dogs!" Zebul discovered this one day. He had taken to walking Urie a few steps beyond Lucretia Pile's after school.

"Yes." Urie's smile flickered pride.

At that moment a Negro man shambled by. The dogs turned away from Urie to bait him. They wrinkled their mouths, pointed their noses, smelled at him, and yelped ferociously. Cowed, he hid behind an oleander bush.

"Stop that," ordered Urie.

The dogs stopped barking. The Negro passed.

"P.Q. brought them," she said offhand.

"For watchdogs?"

"Of course not. They're not watchdogs."

"But they hate niggers."

She stared at him curiously. Then, to get him off the subject, she told him their names.

For some reason the dogs, the fact that P.Q. had brought them and named them Scylla and Charybdis, excited Zebul. It seemed to him more and more inevitable that he should meet P.Q. Yet Urie had still promised nothing. What was the obstruction? Was she ashamed of him? He could not believe it.

He gave up asking her directly. He began dropping allusions: "When I meet P.Q. I will tell him so-and-so . . ." Or: "P.Q. would like such-and-such . . ."

One day he said, "If Scylla and Charybdis bit me, would P.Q. think me an undesirable?"

Urie was offended. "What do you think P.Q. is? Superstitious?"

One day Urie and Zebul walked home a different way. They took the bed of the railroad track, which had once led from the power plant to the water tower and was now abandoned. Past the water tower, they climbed up a steep bank to get to an old bridge. Urie stopped on the bridge, leaned on the white fence railing, and spat onto the tracks below, where they had walked only moments before.

"Are you pretending it's the ocean?" asked Zebul softly.

She did not reply. Then, as if she had thought about it a long time and it had brought back the memory of the Egyptian gods, she turned to him. Her eyes were dead. She imitated an old tramp woman exhaling the last corrupt dregs of the last cigarette in the world, and she walked down the sidewalk. Then she turned again.

"Do you mean to tell me you really believe in God?" she asked.

"What?" asked Zebul, stunned. His heart began to race.

"Are you so superstitious that you believe in God?"

"Superstitious?"

"Yes. Superstitious."

Suddenly she raised her head. She began, "How do you think people came to believe that folderol? Because they were hardly any better than animals. They didn't know it was lightning, so they thought it was God. That's what they called God. When their crops failed and they starved to death, they couldn't believe it was their own stupidity, so they attributed it to God. Look where Christianity first came in—in Corinth, Greece, which was a big port town filled with old ladies, prostitutes who were so poor they were starving, and sick people. And when that stupid Saint Paul told them not to worry, they might starve now and suffer but they would go to heaven after they were dead, why of course they swallowed it hook, line, and sinker. But to think people are such suckers as to believe that stuff now! I can't fathom it."

He stared at her directly, facing her incredible insults. For a long time there was silence.

"Do you really think it's so stupid?" he asked.

"Yes."

"But I never *not* believed in him!"

"That's what people do. They never think."

"Where does the wind come from?" he asked.

"Do you believe they come from Aeolus's bag?" she said scornfully.

"All right, then. The wind comes from the meeting of different temperatures, creating different currents. But where does temperature come from?"

"You're supposed to be the scientist, not me."

"Yes," he said. "They are the elements of earth and atmosphere." He became pensive. "You mean," he said "the only reason for God is the failure of science?"

"The way I see it," she said, "is all knowledge is like sticks into infinity. Each stick of knowledge stops somewhere, but it is not because it can't be known. It's because it is *not* known. But just where it stops people say, 'God.' Think how stupid!"

He thought. It was as if an infinite and fearsome red carpet stretched out before him. But as yet he was only playing with the idea.

"Don't think of knowledge," she continued, pleased that she had made a dent. "Think of goodness. Is there such a thing as goodness?"

"Yes," he said tentatively.

"Is goodness what people think it is?"

"What else could it be?"

"You dope!" she screamed in triumph. "Look what evil the Church has done. In the name of God they have committed butchery, owned houses that sponsored prostitutes, cut off people's hands, tortured Jews or whatever they wanted to call heathen. And they are good!"

He sensed P.Q.'s thoughts behind all her words. But it was all true. Shaken, Zebul left her at the railroad track and pursued a thoughtful path home.

Three days after this conversation Urie invited him to go home with her for the first time.

She was withdrawn, in possession of a vast universe which he was about to know. He caught her nervousness. Scylla and Charybdis approached Zebul suspiciously at the bottom of the driveway, sniffing his knees and ankles. He felt suffused and could hardly breathe. The dogs were not like Haw dogs or nigger dogs. He bent down to pat Scylla and saw that the dog had a sense of humor under its leonine power. Encouraged, he grabbed the mane and said, "Good dog."

The dog made whining noises of enthusiasm. Since Urie had cracked the surface of his life, everything had led to this moment, and all the mystical fervor of his being had been rerouted from his ideas of God to this driveway, through these dogs to what lay within this house.

He followed her past the outside kitchen house, past the well, to the screen door. The dogs heeled. Urie opened the door.

P.Q. was in the kitchen, washing his hands at the sink. All that could be seen of him was the back of his trousers, his shoelaces spread out on each side of his polished shoes like whiskers, and the important crook of his elbows. It was as if he were doing alchemy.

The kitchen was lopsided. The stove had a thick block of wood under its left legs to make the burners level. Yet it was still awry. As Zeb stepped into the kitchen a board buckled under his weight.

Behind P.Q. he saw an Indian rug that was tacked upon the wall to cover the cracks. He saw a picture of Gertrude the Cow, which Loco Poco had pasted over rust spots on the refrigerator door. There was also a picture of a huge and pitiful rabbit with only one shoe, which Irene had painted in green on the dining-room door.

"P.Q., this is Zebul Walley," announced Urie. She swallowed and plunged in almost haphazardly, as if, now that it was happening, she did not care about the result.

P.Q. turned a quarter-circle. Zebul saw that he had a long, scary nose, like a pope's. The nose was bald and marked with important pores, which were like hieroglyphics to Zebul. P.Q.'s head was an almost entirely bald skull. His face and neck were crinkled leather. The bones of his skull made a perfect cage for his eyes. They looked out of it like omens from some carved altar. The eyes bored into Zebul.

But P.Q. lifted his soapy hand, upon which bubbles still glowed, and pointed his finger to the dining room.

"Go in there," he ordered, "and I will come."

He mouthed these words with an air of articulated suspense, separately, so that at the end of the order there was a total triumph.

This respite was mitigated, however, by the sounds of scurries and whispers in the dining room. Loco, having found out that Zebul was at last in the house, had gone wild. She had run from one side of the table to the other, peeked, hid her face at the thought of what was coming, and then begun to laugh through her fingers. She had been eating a chocolate brownie in a green dish. As Zebul and Urie came into the dining room, she took a soup spoon, balanced the brownie on it, and lifted it to her mouth.

Zebul blushed. "Hi," he said.

"Hi," said Loco.

"Hi," said Irene.

Loco giggled. Urie gave her a warning sign behind Zebul's back.

Irene was looking for a lost geography paper. The moment Zebul entered, she began to dramatize the impossibility of ever finding it, pretending that Zebul did not exist. She hardly looked at him. She poked through papers in her briefcase. She looked on P.Q.'s bookcases, under papers on an upturned orange crate that was P.Q.'s business file, and then she looked in P.Q.'s steel desk.

"I can't find it anywhere," she kept repeating.

No one paid any attention to her.

Loco Poco, after her first foolishness, devolved into rapturous excitement at the sight of Zebul. In a teasing, portentous voice she said to him, "This brownie is old." She wrinkled up her nose charmingly and mysteriously so that Zebul would know that the word "old" was the password. But Zebul was embarrassed by her attention. He turned away from her and looked around. First he stared at the tapestries on the cracked boards. Then he stared excitedly at the picture of the monastery at Amalfi.

Irene was removing a stuffed turtle from behind the mantelpiece clock.

"You don't expect a geography paper to be there, do you?" carped Urie.

"It could be anywhere," Irene answered sententiously.

Zebul found what he had been looking for: the whale harpoon. It looked like a corroded black iron arrow, leaning by its point against the fireplace.

At that moment P.Q. entered. He walked grandly, like an opera star. Zebul turned around, and P.Q. turned the full light of his attention to him. He stuck out his hand.

In the handshake Zebul became caught up in the power of P.Q. The fact that P.Q. was ludicrous made him only more powerful. This handshake was the reverse of Urie's handshakes to his parents. Zebul's face grew hot.

"What did you say your name was?" asked P.Q.

Zebul was about to answer, but Urie said, "His name is Zebulon V. Walley."

P.Q. put up a finger. "Do you need a lawyer?" he asked Zebul.

102]

Zebul began to grin. It was the wrong move. P.Q.'s mouth turned down, rejecting levity.

Overloud, Zebul answered, "No, sir."

Zebul had the feeling that Urie was being cut down like a rose, and his sympathy for her welled up in him.

When P.Q. saw this, he was pleased. The harsh wrinkles of his displeasure sharpened, increased, deepened, until the same wrinkles that had thrown threat now showed formidable pleasure at Zebul's consternation. Concealed behind P.Q. lay the will to push, pull, squeeze, wheedle, demand until his victim was roasted and ready to be served, or had found his hind legs and was up and fighting.

"So you don't need a lawyer, eh?" said P.Q., hanging upon Zeb, beaming like a fantastic and egotistical medallion.

"No."

All in the room became subservient and silent for the performance. Zebul, shocked, saw that Urie was hanging, fascinated, upon P.Q. Instead of bleeding or being bowed, her blue eyes were shining brilliantly.

Loco was also fascinated. Her nose twitched.

"What is your name?" asked P.Q.

"Zebulon V. Walley."

"Where do you live?"

"Haw."

There was no change in P.Q. at the name of Haw. Didn't he know the significance?

"What does your father do?"

"He's a furnace-repairman."

Zeb drew his hand to the side of his corduroy pants. He felt the little rinds of cloth. There was a dew of sweat on his upper lip. He felt that now was the time to explain. "My father's uneducated," he said in a fast voice. "He only went to the fourth grade."

Urie observed his brave words like a statue, admiring and silent.

"Well, that's nothing against the poor cuss," said P.Q. "That doesn't mean he isn't a good man. He's a good furnace-repairman, isn't he?"

"Oh, yes."

"That makes it incumbent on you to show these people something if you learn anything. When you know something, then you can help your own people."

"They're narrow-minded." He faced P.Q. greedily, splaying himself. If P.Q. was different, let him show his difference now. "They're bigoted," he said.

"All people are bigoted until they have studied things and read. What do you think? A donkey's going to eat apple pie when he's spent his lifetime eating grass?"

Zebul laughed dizzily. He knew he should defend his father from being a donkey, but he loved the idea too much.

Urie and Loco pealed with laughter.

"Do you think the donkey is going to sit in the classroom and learn the Preamble to the Constitution?" asked P.Q., basking in his success. "Why, he'd have to learn to read first."

"He'd have to talk," chimed Zebul.

"Yes, sir. So you can't blame the poor cuss for not having his own government for donkeys, can you?"

P.Q. waited until Zebul had the conversation fully on his back. The room took on a different timbre of sound.

"The important question is," said P.Q., "what you do."

In the softness, silence of the room, everything was electric so that Zebul was aware of the broken seams of it and the soughing of the autumn trees outside. He felt that he understood everything. He understood P.Q. at the storm's eye demanding the souls of everyone in this room to be rooted in the sea.

P.Q. had turned and was looking out the window, his nose silhouetted against the sky. It was as if he hardly knew now that Zebul were there. He turned Zebul's presence off from him at the very moment that he had hit the nadir and kernel of him. At the moment that he spoke of Zebul's destiny, he refused to recognize it.

Zebul's awareness of himself, left alone, thus become so tremendous, so enlarged, flung out by P.Q., that it actually seemed to quiver, molten within the walls of the house. He thought: Why, this is the most important thing, this feeling, that has ever happened to me. For I am I. I recognize myself. I am going to do something. I am going to penetrate something! I am going to cause some tremendous change. I understand everything now!

He did not move. But in not moving, he suddenly became aware that Urie recognized his power. He felt her blue eyes burning, growing larger, living like two dangerous blue suns.

CHAPTER 13

The minute Zebul had disappeared out of sight down the driveway, the family faced one another breathlessly. It was an occasion so naked in personal reaction that Urie remained half-hidden in the corner, trying to pretend she did not care. But her cheeks were burning and her eyes had an avid, almost distracted look as she glanced from one to the other.

Mrs. Bishop politely said he was a "nice boy." She was less interested in Zebul for himself than for his effect on the family. Then she asked P.Q. if he didn't think so too?

But P.Q. yawned. After a long time he said, "Yes," in a loud voice. It was as if, having created a performance, he were no longer interested. The proof of the pudding would be for Zebul to take his advice and the child become father to the man. For P.Q. saw the beginning of one of those silly girlish conversations that he hated, and he withdrew at once, leaving them a huge free space quivering with his premature contempt, which they would have to blot away by their silliness.

"He reminds me of a goat in corduroy pants!" breathed Loco.

Then it started, the ritual of hashing over, of lingering on phrases, of creating Zebul anew, of comparison, reaction, and interreaction upon the new element in their family.

He butted and danced on hind legs and threatened arguments with his head, said Loco. Also he smelled like cracked-wheat bread. His personality was the color of blue or orange, she could not decide which. "Which?" she asked Urie.

Urie answered orange. Urie was wary of Loco, however, for, although irresistibly drawn to her metaphors, she did not want to be contaminated by them. Even more, she wanted to shield Zebul.

Loco was carried away by her gossip about Zebul. An hour after he was gone she began mimicking the way he had stood in the dining room and inspected the pictures.

Mrs. Bishop did not like the effect of Zebul on Loco Poco. The flashing vision of an eleven-year-old acting gaga, that quality of febrile prettiness in Loco that had captured adults from her birth, entrained into sex with such a promise of audacity and wanton impulse, scared Mrs. Bishop. Of all the girls, she was most afraid for Loco. Yet Loco was only a child!

"I don't see why he wears those corduroy pants, Urie!" Loco repeated.

"How do I know?" Urie said with defensive loftiness.

"They go ponk ponk when he walks!"

"Why do you have to concentrate on details like that? It's so lowdown he wouldn't even bother with it."

"I didn't think he'd be so talk-talky. He even squeaks his corduroys in rhythm to his arguments." Loco went off into peals of laughter.

"If you don't stop that silly business, you can just go to your room!" warned Mrs. Bishop.

Throttled in public enthusiasm for Zebul, Loco took her enjoyment in private. She began discussing him excitedly at night, when she and Urie were in their separate cubicles. Sometimes she spoke of him as if he were one of their mother's relics. Other times she made him up as she went along.

In the darkness Urie humored Loco. She found a kind of secret pleasure in the darkness, hearing Loco play Zebul like an instrument. The true Zebul was a person with whom she was now somehow more intimate than with her family—even than with Loco, her breathing-confidante-sister. The darkness served to obscure the true Zebul. It abstracted and compartmented him. The Zebul whom Loco talked about was something else, and she stored up the gobbets and impressions to tell him later.

"If Zebul is a goat for an animal, what musical instrument is he, Urie?"

"He's an oboe," said Urie. Clear thoughts and clear confessions. Last-go-trade of shames. Transcendence.

"No."

"What, then?"

"French horn," said Loco.

"It's the same thing."

"Well, almost." Silence. "Do you really think he's orange?"

"Yes."

"No. I've thought it over. He's not even blue. He's brown. There's something completely brown about him." Loco got the giggles.

Urie tried to think of him as brown.

Loco said he had jug ears.

It seemed to Urie that she had almost arrived at the point of seeing Zebul as brown when she fell asleep.

Of all the family, Irene was the most silent on the subject of Zebul. She was surprised. She liked him. But although she saw at once that he was completely and totally Urie's, he no longer threatened boydom. Thus she was no longer jealous. She lost her fear for Urie. For Zebul and Urie, she knew at once, were not what man and woman were to each other. Having passed the test of no rules, having been accepted by P.Q., having entered the ranks of Bishopry, he lost force as a boy. For in Irene's mind malehood meant separation from Bishopry. A male, in Irene's secret thoughts, grew to be a clear image of a prince or a movie-hero-like person who would be alien to Bishopry, unacceptable to P.Q., an enemy, but a rescuer.

Irene's new and secret life now began. The day after Zebul's visit she stopped at the Center Drugstore on the way home from school. The kids were clustered around milkshakes at the counter, but she ignored them. She beelined for the magazine stand. She picked up *Photoplay*. She stood and read about Dick Powell. For a half an hour, absorbed in the details of his married life with Joan Blondell, she stood there. He was stepfather to Joan Blondell's daughter Leslie, from a former marriage. She studied the picture of Dick Powell. She stared at the crow's-foot wrinkles of smiling laughter that spoked out from the corners of his eyes, until at last she recognized that she loved Dick Powell!

After this meeting with the Bishop family, something happened to Zebul. It seemed to be as a direct result of his confrontation with P.Q. Yet there was nothing at all in that meeting that could have been said to point directly to it as a cause.

It had entered the period of autumn when the sky became dour and gray. Hints of a dark, doomed, rainy winter leaked through. Yet through the gray, moist, cold, almost green atmosphere autumn blossoms presented a lacy, blooming aspect. The second-flowering myrtle, late honeysuckle, and pink flowers that suddenly sprouted leaned delicately against feather toadstools. To see these things flowering and trembling like incredible bride frivolities in the gloomy weather was exotic and perverse. Clouds lowered. A green and evil light like snakes' eyes beamed from the sky, threatening lightning in every corner of the world. The blossoms laughed with pastel innocence and climbed toward the black branches just as if they did not know they were about to be raped by the weather. And the day was suffused by the flowers' smells. Instead of walking home with Urie, Zebul suggested that they go to his little house. When they got to Haw, he took two pieces of raisin bread from the kitchen, and they took them to the little house. They sat down on his stools and they ate the raisin bread without butter, in silence.

He was looking at the wallpaper. It was blue with crisscross patterns of brown lines. It was stained in two places where the rain had leaked through.

Suddenly he saw that Urie was right. There was no God.

First he became cold. Then he grew alarmed. The concept of no God took hold of him. It opened up a giant maw. It was scary, dark, and terrible. He was standing on ground that was no longer ground.

He looked into her piercing blue eyes, so strange and fathomless in her face. They had not changed. She was chewing the raisin bread. He saw the tendons in her neck straining a little when she chewed. The small hollow between her collarbones pulsated evenly, but not in time with her breathing. There was a yellow spot—he saw it very distinctly—where she had dropped some honey from breakfast on the front of her dress. To think! She knew there was no God, and yet she lived. She chewed raisin bread—his raisin bread. She lived. It did not change her one bit. While it changed everything for him.

Yet she did not even notice that he could scarcely breathe. The blood roared like a waterfall in his ears. He could not swallow, so he put his raisin bread in the drawer next to his scissors. Burning tears rose up to his throat and were threatening to come out in his eyes.

"What's the matter with you?" she asked tentatively.

He kept his face away from her. "Nothing."

He made sniffing motions like a dog. He was ashamed of himself. He could not bear her delicate, rising puzzlement, her curiosity, her palpitating.

Why am I ashamed of myself? he wondered. If there is no God, then there is nothing on earth to be ashamed of! Crime, stealing, Hawhood, white trashiness, masturbation, ignorance, my father going to the fourth grade, servility, love, or even hatred. Nothing. Yet here he was blushing, almost crying.

For the first time he began to suspect Urie—of what, he hardly knew. I thought she would be my friend, he thought. But now she has taken God away from me. And I picked her out just to do this to me!

Reason argued with him: "But you never knew what God was in the first place!" "But he was there. At least I thought he was!" he protested to himself helplessly. "You were superficial," Reason said.

Then he saw that though he thought that he had believed in God, he had not really thought of God at all. He had only accepted him. Now, at the very moment that he could have believed in him, he was cheated. And it was Urie who had brought this realization to him and at once appeared, by virtue of her preaching No God, to have become far more religious than he had ever been. For she cared. Now that he cared, now that she had forced him to care, he saw that she was right. He could not believe in God.

He pushed himself out of the chair, ignoring her, and loped over the empty floorboards. He went in circles around and around his little house in front of her, experimenting with his muscles, his knee joints. He bent his knees. He flexed his wrists. With the disappearance of God, all these motions had suddenly become all-important, because they were pointless. Yet they were the only thing of him, himself, Zebulon Vance Walley, that he knew.

Just as a masochist lover embraces the beloved one who has deprived, betrayed, and wounded him, finding in his beloved the only source of assuagement, only to have his revilement repeated, and with it the hope that such suffering demands, Zebul sought out the Bishops. In exact proportion to the loss of God, he desired the Bishops. If there was no God, and the Bishops had brought this realization to him, then the Bishops must be the key to what it was that substituted for God.

So instead of leaving Urie at the railroad track, Zebul formed the habit of going home with her in the afternoons. The moment P.Q. arrived, Zebul would enter a new harmonic. He breathed in P.Q.'s being. He plied him with questions. He was burning, eager. He egged, baited, and flattered P.Q. He turned him on. He beguiled him. He argued with him.

Mrs. Bishop was glad P.Q. had a new interest. Often Zebul stayed so long that she just asked him to supper. She said with beans and corn one more didn't count. But she wondered what his people said. Henny Pinney and Eames Loomis asked him where he went so often. His same old answer, "Urie's," they accepted without understanding.

Zebul's singleminded, one-track pursuit fitted P.Q. to a T. It flattered him. But, even more important, it gave him a new ploy in his struggle to ignore the creeping threat of a failure. As Zebul blotted out God to pursue non-God, P.Q. blotted out the thought of the truck he couldn't buy and the heater he had to buy. He placed Zebul up against Mrs. Bishop's harping on the subject. With Zebul in the house, the heater seemed to him no necessity at all. Argument took the place of heat.

P.Q. did not think of Zebul in relation to Urie. He was interested in Zebul as the reflection of every evolving youth, the raising of a generation, the proof of the strength of America, infinite possibilities in magnitude. He liked it that Zebul came from the ignorant. Only the low and the ignorant could attain the scope to be free. Such was his contempt for the well-cared-for, pruned-of-mind, pretentious youth of the stultified middle class sheltered into petrifactions and stunted because they had never had to crawl in the universe. He was interested in youth as rising. To him Zebul was the name of youth.

So he began to depend upon Zebul for his truth. When Zebul had not come home with Urie he would ask, "Where is Zebul?"

Or: "Tell Zebul to come here. At three o'clock tomorrow afternoon. I want to see him."

"But we don't get out of school until three-thirty, P.Q.!"

"All right. Three-thirty, then."

If he forgot the next day what it was that he was going to tell Zebul at three-thirty, he made something new up. He talked to Zebul of laws, literature, and ethics, but as Zebul did not mention God, P.Q. did not mention business or war.

Zebul rode P.Q.'s slow tempo, his pontifical, overwhelming force, like a surfer. He had to withstand the total power of his style, so he argued. It was almost a take-over. P.Q.'s method was accumulative, massive, and stupendous. But Zebul always countered. In the friction and abrasion of P.Q., it seemed to him, he was escaping his terrifying vacuum. He was launched into P.Q.'s dialectic and beguiled in P.Q.'s spell. He had to learn the rules as he went along. As he grew used to the game, he became so entranced and so nimble that it seemed easy in its danger. He had to defer to P.Q. because P.Q. dictated the limits. He could not interrupt P.Q. because P.Q. held up a forefinger. He had to refrain from contradicting because P.Q. would steamroller him down. He had to keep from sarcasm because P.Q. retired from insolence in silence. But these very curbs on his own power challenged his quicksilver mind.

Urie was shoved into the background, her shell-blue eyes alternating between vacancy and delight. Yet instead of being jealous, she was inspired by this relationship between Zebul and P.Q. She breathed on her fingers and bit her fingernails, watching them. She trembled with excitement.

At first she identified with Zebul, who sat before P.Q. with enlarged, dilated eyes, waiting to be pounced on. She breathed in Zebul's inspiration. She had a fierce, protective attitude toward him. She wanted him to give the right answer. She felt she had to be there to prompt him. But he never failed. His rhythm, so attuned, became so quick, so conspiratorial that in the end she veered toward protecting P.Q.

It was at these moments that she could not resist. She had to enter the argument herself. She jumped in like a pouncing bird with her talons outstretched.

But, far from having the effect she desired, she had the opposite. P.Q. stopped talking. Triumph jumped out of his slashed smile. "Aha!" He seemed to gloat as he turned around. "You have broken the rules."

"But P.Q., say something. Don't stop talking! I'm not fooling. I didn't say it to argue. I didn't say it to shut you up. Talk! Say something."

But he only smiled in infinite silence.

"But I really want to know. We really want to know! Don't we, Zebul!"

"Yes," echoed Zebul, a mendacious smile on his lips.

"You know, it's getting chilly at night now," said Mrs. Bishop one evening. "We're just going to have to do something about heat."

"Look at this." P.Q. read loudly from his newspaper to blot her out.

Zebul, who was sitting with Urie on the couch, having just pointed out to her where Mrs. Ramsay died in *To the Lighthouse*—"in a parenthesis, and she's the main character!"—looked up eagerly.

" 'Is there justification for Germany's territorial claims? An Inquiry into Geopolitics.' Dr. Helmut Boehm of the philosophy department, lately of Heidelberg University, for the affirmative. Dr. Sanders of Political Science for the negative. Come on. Let's see what these fools have to say. Get your hat."

"But I'm in the middle of the hem," sputtered Mrs. Bishop.

"Come on. Let's go, Zebul. Up. Everybody!"

Zebul jumped up, raring to go. Urie followed. Loco was excited as a circus. Mrs. Bishop grudgingly pulled the plug out of her sewing machine. She was angry. Half stamping the floor, she was still putting on her coat as P.Q. with gestures and waves pushed her out the door.

Only Irene did not go. "I refuse to fail geometry," she announced.

Memorial Lounge was full. P.Q. led the family and Zebul importantly to the front, seated them on the fattest, most comfortable sofas in the glare of everyone's eyes. People had been too polite and nicey-nice to seat themselves in these prominent chairs. Zebul sat between P.Q. and Urie. He was very self-conscious and put his hands respectfully on his corduroy knees. But Loco, on the other side of Urie, kicked her sister's ankle. Urie clutched her hands tightly, giggles pressing against her closed teeth. She was glad Zebul was with them. Now he would see what it was to belong to a good family. Bishopry was posing a threat and a mock and a promise to the respectability of Ephesus. P.Q., she knew, was going to expose some soul-jolting fact.

P.Q. paid great fake attention to the two initial speeches. Dr. Sanders was a red-necked professor with orange hair and bad teeth. He spoke poorly with an ignorant accent.

Dr. Boehm's speech started with an "Although." His light, kindling blue eyes and handsome nose moved above a fastidious display of English. But his turns and curlicues of wit were heavy through his guttural accent, and he overplayed his charm. He placed sparkling smiles where they did not belong. His front was hiding a ponderous, didactic personality. Although Hitler was certainly unconscionable, he said, and what was going on with the Jews a crime of international import, nevertheless, Germany had a point in her territorial claims. Dr. Boehm brought up the case of Japan, growing populations, overpopulation of areas and overcrowding that could not be solved by democratic processes and that had been ignored by humane governments. The concept of geopolitics might have solved these problems, had it not been for the war.

P.Q. inhaled loudly and threateningly, causing stares.

Zebul blushed. He felt as if he belonged to the Bishops, and through his red face he felt a fierce pride as, for the first time, he gave a flickering glance to the crowd.

In the rebuttal period Dr. Sanders was beaten hands down.

The debate was over. The audience was allowed to ask questions.

People were polite. For half an hour noncontroversial questions were directed to Dr. Boehm. At last, when it was late, P.Q. raised his hand. The student moderator pointed to him.

P.Q. stood up. In a voice which indicated that he was a great authority, looking over his nose, over the sea of faces, he said, "I would like to ask the professor from the University of Heidelberg where the concept of state arises from?"

Dr. Boehm was startled. He saw threat in P.Q., but was not sure where the attack would be. He answered in a winding dissertation about Greek classical states. In Western culture, the idea of state was presumably from the Greeks.

"I beg to differ from the professor from the University of Heidelberg," said P.Q.

Mrs. Bishop looked sidewise at the ground. For the first time Zebul was unafraid. He looked with his huge, clear, fighting eyes at P.Q. Urie held her breath. Loco looked at P.Q. with glittering excitement.

"The concept of state comes straight from the Jews," said P.Q.

Dead silence. People suspected he was a crank or an anti-Semite. Dr. Boehm rested on one leg, half relieved, his face very white.

Zebul wanted to laugh out loud. Only two weeks ago he too would have acted like these people, but he knew P.Q. now. Oh, it was good. He wished he could rub his hands like Uriah Heep.

"Unfortunately," continued P.Q., "the Jews are the ones to suffer from having their idea exploited by the Germans. I am afraid the professor from Heidelberg errs in his statement that Greece was a fatherland. As we all know, Athens was named and settled for Athena. When you have a female goddess in top place, men are too busy worshiping to set themselves up as dictators. Give the ladies their due. Athens existed by the dialogue of its citizens asking each other what was good for their donkeys and what was good or bad for their property. They used the vote to establish their right and wrong. No man took the place of God. They had their goddess. Even when Plato came along and mixed up Socrates' thinking and kicked the poets in the behind, he didn't claim total authority for the state. It was Moses that started it. From the very beginning he received the Thou Shalt Nots straight from God and made them into law by command. Then he started leading the Jews out of Egypt to the Promised Land. The only trouble was, they couldn't find it. But while they were looking, the idea of state became hypostasized. The Germans latched onto the idea. And while the poor Jews have been looking ever since, they put it into action. They put into practice and are crucifying the very Jews whose idea it was. Geopolitics is the same thing. The Germans want to make an absolute out of a theory of how to divide up the world so they'll get most of it. They've already done it with the state, now they're doing it with the land. And all in the name of morality. What is morality?" P.Q. waited, like a teacher, to see who would answer. "Well, unfortunately there is no such thing as morality. The individual is the only morality. In this country we have learned that. In America the state is like a spiderweb. It stretches and stretches and stretches without breaking, while people like us argue what morality is."

P.Q. smiled. His mouth was still open.

Someone in the back row began to clap. There was another motion of applause from the left side of the room. And when the moderator stood up, announcing that the debate was over, the whole room burst into applause.

Zebul and Urie, their hands clutching each other with conniving triumph, backed out the entrance, followed by Mrs. Bishop. But P.Q., accompanied by arching, preening Loco, like a familiar, was receiving handshakes from the people as they filed out. He bowed and beamed like a hero. As a grace note, he shook Dr. Boehm's hand.

"You ought to be teaching at the university." Mrs. Bishop chortled as they crossed the campus.

"Did you see, that German had golden teeth, Zebul!" said P.Q., ignoring the implied criticism.

"He probably got them from a Jewish dentist!" Zebul hooted in complicity.

P.Q. roared.

Loco Poco jumped up and down like a kangaroo, too full of glory to speak.

Who cares what the penalties of living on this earth are? thought Urie euphorically. P.Q. was right. Zebul had seen it! Bishopry was transcendent. Stove, cracks, dirt, rats were simply the stones in the rapids of motion. If your canoe was smart enough you could shoot them!

"I'm part of this family," whispered Zebul in Urie's ear.

Overhearing this secret remark, Mrs. Bishop felt one of those shoots of happiness that justified all of life. Who cared about the Depression, leaving the ocean, P.Q.'s bad luck, P.Q. riding with the linens on the bicycle, the beans and corn, the drafts, the rotten underpinnings, the bricks that were threatening to fall down the chimney, even the heater? The coming of Zebul had brought that ingredient into the family, like orégano in a recipe, that stabilized its overriding femininity. At last it was almost as if P.Q. had a son. It did not matter who Zebul was or what he was—only that he was a boy. Mrs. Bishop felt chauvinistic, almost impersonal about that. For the family was more than any one individual in it. Zebul had inspired P.Q.

Yet the sudden vastness of the evening affected their gloating righteousness. The dome of stars was above them. Everything was cold, clear, and sharp. The blaze of kindly light from Memorial Lounge seemed a memory. And the occasion of the evening was the war.

Urie was amazed. Soon she would graduate from high school. What would the world be? Would there really be war? Was it possible that the United States would get into it? She looked at Zebul to see if he too thought of the war. But he was looking upward, his eyes larger than the stars. He ignored her, knowing her to be his, now that he had made that remark about his belonging to her family.

Urie remembered what Miss Parron had said in the eighth grade. Miss Parron had a melodramatic theater voice with a fake British accent. The United States saved the world for democracy in 1918, she had told the class. There would never be another war.

Suddenly, as if she had read Urie's mind, Loco Poco turned to P.Q. and with a face glittering pale asked, "We won't get into the war, though, will we, P.Q.?"

Urie looked at P.Q. for the answer. She saw Zebul staring at P.Q. They waited for a long time.

Then P.Q. answered. "I don't know."

Urie was conscious that Loco was clinging nearer to her than before, and it seemed that her step had become slightly faster.

P.Q. seemed a tiny matchstick of humanity placed up against the breadth of stars. Above them stretched the gigantic scope of the planets' forces, unbelievably vast. Yet such was the dignity of P.Q.'s answer when the chips were down that it gave to mankind something profound, triumphant, above but not opposite the performance of the preening triumph in the lounge. Urie felt the sensation of heartbreak. She shivered.

C H A P T E R 14

There was something about Zebul's amalgamation into the family that put Loco Poco in an anomalous position. P.Q.'s time was more and more taken up with arguing with Zebul. Zebul provided his distraction from business. Zebul also took up Urie's thoughts. Loco's confidential relationship with her sister thus became inactive, yet deeper. Since Loco was the youngest, she had always been set off from the rest. She had been more isolated in her position, as well as more favored.

The truth of a family is like the truth of an ocean. It is a series of movements in which themes occur and recur. With the advent of Zebul, P.Q. and Urie swung toward a polemical period. They spent days and nights arguing on the coffin beds. The focus of their discussion was always Plato. To Loco, arguments were as slow as snail tracks. She could get to the same place without them. She spurned verbal fencing like Zebul's and Urie's. Whereas Irene sat engrossed and impressed by all arguments, in silence, Loco Poco whistled, laughed, or dropped witty remarks into them. She would take her flute in the middle of a dialectical argument, and as soon as a person had made a point she would mock it with a grace note, a bombastic Beethoven finale, or a musical punctuation. She made Zebul and Urie furious. But P.Q. egged her on, even when it was he she mocked.

Zebul's pervading presence had a subtle affect on Loco. All the whimsical musings she had formerly told Urie, she now told him to his face. She criticized his corduroy pants. She teased. She begged him to let her walk on his feet as he walked, so that she could see how it felt to be a puppet. She tickled his ears with broom grass. She smiled. She made faces at him. She bounced her head and her face before him, insisting to know if he thought she was beautiful.

He tried to ignore her. He was slightly afraid of her. Such gross flirtation from an eleven-year-old secretly embarrassed him. He waved her away, or he kicked the air in front of him, as a threat that he would kick her. Instead of being offended, her eyes became as large and excited as a cat's. She would run behind Mrs. Bishop's drop-leaf table and, pretending to be occupied with schoolwork or painting, she would keep giving him looks. At times she was deceptively quiet. But the more quiet she was, the more she made him aware of her. He hated this because it made him a fool. She loved it. She laughed.

The more attention she focused on him, the more he tried to avoid her. He hove to Urie. He was one of the few people who was repelled by Loco rather than attracted. This made him a novelty to her.

One afternoon when Urie had gone out to feed Scylla, Loco said, "Walk me around on your feet, Zebul."

"No." He was engrossed in *Crime and Punishment*.

"Why?"

"I'm nobody's slave."

"Yes, you are."

He looked up. "Whose?"

"Urie's."

"And you're P.Q.'s stooge."

They both laughed. Perversely, strangely, they both recognized these insults as compliments.

When Urie came back, Zebul was relieved. Loco noticed this and laughed up her sleeve.

One day a strange smile crept to the corner of her lips. She asked them daringly, her eyes jittering, "Are you two in love with each other?"

"Oh, for God's sake!" moaned Zebul.

"Don't pay any attention to her."

Zebul complained to Urie. This made Loco laugh. She danced between them, over furniture, like Fred Astaire and Ginger Rogers, holding out her arms and flitting around about them, aping them like a clever wasp. Urie would banish her with threatening gestures. But Zebul would always get angry. "Come on, let's go. We can't do anything with that fool around here!"

"Oh, my poor fool is dead!" trilled out Loco, misquoting King Lear, clasping her hands together and drooping over like a dead lily.

"She's crazy! Let's go to my little house."

"What do you bother looking at her for? Don't even look at her. That's why she does it."

"How can you help looking at such a creature as that?"

"Hahahaha!" laughed Loco.

"She's just crazy. She always has been. Don't listen to her."

And then to top it off Irene would scream, "Mamma! Loco's prancing around here bothering everybody!"

"If you people can't get along any better than that, I give up!" shrieked Mrs. Bishop.

Paradoxically, as she grew farther and farther away from Urie, there was a level where Loco and Urie operated in almost totally silent yet profound understanding. What the content of this understanding was, neither knew. Yet it grew greater the more Urie got into cahoots with Zebul. It was as if Loco were the mirror of their friendship, in some little-sister, Greek-chorus, mocking sense.

With all her gaiety, Loco grew more and more alone.

School, for her, let out half an hour earlier than the high school. She always walked home alone. She looked at the mailboxes facing the road each day. These mailboxes invited, begged for something. What was it? One day she opened a mailbox marked G. P. MANNERING. It was gaunt and empty. She was sorry for it. Hoping to fill it, she dropped a stone into it. It echoed. She sang the first eight bars of "My country 'tis of thee" into it. Then she closed it up. The next day she picked a pine cone off the road and put it into the box. The following day the pine cone was gone. G. P. Mannering must have received it! She was ecstatic. What an effect! As if in the back of her mind there was an awareness that tampering with mailboxes was a federal offense, she kept her mailbox diddlings secret. With the coming days and the volume of mailboxes, she grew rapt with the number of possibilities. She thought of the mailboxes as sad and empty mouths. Their inanimacy was even more touching, they were unlike weak and hungry birds in the nest, opening their craws for worms from their arriving mother, because the people behind the mailboxes were unknown, like ghosts. She was giving presents. What to put in which box was the exciting problem. She judged the presents by the names. Although parsley was the natural thing to put into Mr. Walter O. Parsley's box, you could not do it. What, then? She ruminated. She knew when a Negro in a mule-cart passed slowly, allowing time for the mule to issue its warm droppings on the road. She waited till they were gone. Then she wrapped a turd carefully in an autumn leaf and put it in Mr. Parsley's box. It was as if she were baking a cake. The next day she could hardly wait till school was over. The baked mule turd was gone!

In late November she caught a cold. Mrs. Bishop kept her home in bed. Loco whiled away her time playing dolls belatedly and singing, even fluting in her tapestry cubicle.

From time to time Mrs. Bishop flipped the curtain doorway and looked in on her. She examined her tongue, gave her large handkerchiefs, and looked at the pale, almost yellow face whose black eyes now had specks of yellow and dark lines under them. "It's not only the cold and no heat in this house. You don't eat properly," complained Mrs. Bishop, reminded by Loco's heart-shaped face of the cat in the Cat's Paw ad. "You always play with your oatmeal in the morning."

Loco, who liked having a cold and nursing herself with silken indulgence in her bed, wailed with a secret smile, "I can't help it."

"I don't like it," said Mrs. Bishop to P.Q. "Something has to be done about heat in this house. I talk and talk and talk and . . ."

But P.Q.'s deliberate withdrawal drowned her words as a futile babble. She felt like a hen going around in circles for at least an hour after its head is severed.

After Loco Poco got well enough to go back to school, she met Miss Picke.

Miss Picke was an old lady who wore ankle socks and sat on stone walls. Loco had noticed her ever since she had been in Ephesus, but because the old lady was a town character she had been afraid to speak to her. On this day the sun was so warm and the tree leaves were so red with late autumn that, filled with enthusiasm, Loco Poco stopped by the stone wall in front of Sigma Delta Epsilon, where Miss Picke was sitting.

"Hello."

"Hello," answered Miss Picke, blinking.

"It's a beautiful day, isn't it?"

"Yes." Miss Picke smiled for thirty seconds and then stopped. But she stared at Loco Poco through her thin gold-rimmed glasses.

"Why do you sit on stone walls?" asked Loco.

"I have often asked myself that question," said Miss Picke. "I am the only white woman that does so. All the rest are nigras. It may be that I am lazy like them. But I like to look at things."

"You reminded me of Humpty Dumpty, but of course you don't look like him."

Miss Picke nodded, and the conversation turned back to Negroes.

"From the bottom of the ladder you have absolute freedom," Miss Picke told Loco. "That is why the nigras are lucky, although they don't know it. Though they are the inferior race, they know the truth of things because they don't have to keep up a lot of appearances. You mentioned Humpty Dumpty. Actually I have always thought of myself as Humpty Dumpty. I can see everything from here. But I take great care not to fall." Miss Picke gave a coarse, leering smile that revealed two crooked gold teeth. "Humpty Dumpty was a great witness. People should never have worried about gluing him together again. The cracked, like the nigras, realize things that other people are completely deluded by."

Loco Poco was impressed. "What's your name?" she asked.

"Miss Picke."

At home Loco trumpeted her discovery of Miss Picke. That night she improvised on her name. "Miss Picke picks her teeth."

"No. Miss Picke pokes a pickaninny," improved Urie.

"Loco Poco is Miss Picke without a pocket," said Irene.

"No. A pig without portfolio," said Urie.

Loco started again. "Miss Picke picks her toe. Miss Picke is a toe-picker. A tag-picker. Pig my tag, you filthy rag! Isn't that good? Miss Picke picks up her ragtag, but I pick up my stick. One, two, rattle your Picke."

"Three four, pattle your poke, you Picke-puking Loco Poco!"

Loco Poco laughed deliriously. "Aren't you glad her name is Miss Picke?"

But it was when Loco Poco came home one day announcing that Miss Picke was rich and a Ph.D. that P.Q. pricked up his ears.

"Rich? How do you know she's rich, the poor cuss?"

"Because she comes from ancient Alabama aristocracy, she told me so, and she's going to start a fish-and-nuts store at that abandoned gas station at the curve at the edge of Haw."

"Right in the middle of Niggertown?" Urie hooted. "A Ph.D. in Nigger-town? Either she's crazy, or you are!"

"You should be careful whom you talk to on the street," warned Mrs. Bishop. "You can't just go up to anybody and speak."

"Of course she can," scoffed P.Q. "How're you going to learn anything unless you ask questions. That's one thing I do. I go anywhere and ask questions. Ask Miss Picke to come over here sometime." He trumpeted his words over Mrs. Bishop. "We should invite her to supper."

The next day Loco asked Miss Picke, "What does it feel like to be old?"

"Don't you know the cells of the body change completely every seven years? Every seven years you have completely different cells than you did seven years before. That means you have to count age as one year for every seven. I am ten and a half years old. Any other system of counting is wrong."

"But you are still old."

"I look old, but I never looked good anyhow, so I don't notice one difference." Miss Picke closed her mouth with a plop to signify that she would not discuss that topic any more.

"Why do you want to have your store in the middle of Niggertown, since you're prejudiced?"

"You should call it the nigra section."

"The Negro section."

"Although nigras are inferior," said Miss Picke, "they like to eat as well as anybody else. I can improve their economy. I will buy catfish from them and sell it to them, which will bring the whole nigra economy up. The nuts I get cheap from my own plantation."

The first report cards came in. Loco made six C's, two B's, and a D in hygiene. She had two A's, one in music and one in art. Miss Bogue had written in the column marked ADDITIONAL REMARKS: "If Sylvia would pay as much attention to her schoolwork as she does to the periphery of things, her motivation problem would be solved. Her I.Q. is very high and she has an attractive personality. But she appears to be in a dream. It is difficult to get to her. Perhaps there are problems at home . . . ?" Miss Bogue had written three significant dots and an even more significant question mark at the end, whose flourish gave Mrs. Bishop dread and electric fear.

"Of course Urie made all A's but one, but look at me," said Irene to Loco in motherly tones. "I made six A's, five B's, and a B-plus in geometry, and I don't have as high an I.Q. as you do. But did you see me fooling around? No. Why, I almost made an A in Mr. Pankhurst's class—from hard work—and you know I made a nine on the first test! But the way you do! I don't frankly see how you even made the A in music, the way you play."

Loco's disgrace was too terrible to be discussed. Urie looked at her in disbelief. Urie formed a perverse hatred for Miss Bogue, who dared to excavate Loco Poco and invade the sanctity of Bishopry. But Loco had let the family down. How could she do it?

Mrs. Bishop, closing her mouth tightly, went about the house in silence. The only word she said about Loco was to P.Q. "I am worried about Loco."

P.Q., finishing shaving, put his razor on its particular place behind the mantelpiece clock. Secretly he was proud of Loco for her bad grades. Teachers were country ignoramuses trained to be robots in the system.

"Oh. It will all come out in the wash," he said, looking at his face in the reflection from the clock.

Loco Poco kept out of the way. She took to chewing gum in school and sticking discards under tables where she thought Miss Bogue would sit. But, as always, she was a polite little girl, and she performed these recalcitrances less in the spirit of retaliation than of preoccupation. She was gay and subdued by turns. The day after the bad grades her behavior was so dizzy and daring that the whole class laughed. She was more beloved by her classmates than ever before.

That afternoon, as she returned home, the sun was just beginning to go down behind a western hill. It was still warm, for the autumn sun was so hot that it heated barn, broom sedge, and earth, and the heat remained far longer than the sun. She got her flute and went to sit on a large stone beyond the barn. Out of sight of the house, she took off her shoes. Ever since she had been forbidden to go barefoot, she had done it in secret. A bee hummed. The air was still. The sound of the flute, playing no particular air, was so flat that Loco felt she was becoming disembodied in the sound. She let herself go into it. By breath she departed from the earth into the sky.

Suddenly the sky took her whole attention. Although the sun was still shining brilliantly, the entire sky was filled with speechless black clouds. The edges of the clouds caught different hues of the waning sun and became pale, with a foreboding contrast of darks and transparencies, like a photograph negative. Everything that should have been white became black. Everything that was black became white. The clouds' reflection in the sun at that moment came creeping over the broom sedge like presences. The earth became darker and darker. But in her transformed eye, it was lighter and lighter. At the same moment the silver of the sun cast ghastly reflections at the edges of the clouds, darknesses whose transition hinted that there was a hole which, if the eye, or the piercing sound of Loco's flute, could penetrate it, would prove to be the aperture leading to paradise. Yet it was the very fact of ghastliness, impending doom—a thunderstorm, perhaps—that made the idea of the paradise possible. In all these feelings Loco Poco did not stop playing for a moment. She was in a galvanized state, and she did not even notice the pats of powder from Scylla's paw steps as the dog bounded toward her. He had to lick her face before she would stop.

CHAPTER 15

Mrs. Bishop made her decision. As soon as P.Q. had gone out of the house, she called the girls together. They were going to collect all the old family things, she announced, and take them over to Laurelo's Wildwood Gift Shop and sell them. They needed a heater for this house. Well, they were going to get a heater for this house.

"What good are *things,* anyway?" she asked with chivalry.

"But Laurelo's Wildwood Gift Shop is run by Gail Potter's mother!" screamed Urie.

"So what?" said Irene.

Gail Potter will see everything and know! thought Urie. But she kept quiet.

Loco Poco was excited.

Irene obeyed Mrs. Bishop blindly, like a sleepwalker, as if she were not aware of the humiliation.

There were two china plates, two matching Victorian figurines of shepherd and shepherdess which had sat on Mrs. Bishop's father's mantelpiece, a small hand-carved sandalwood box from China, a large blue and white striped china umbrella stand, the dragon candlestick, the whale harpoon, and an Oriental dinner gong with a monkey stick to hit it with. When Mrs. Bishop put the monkey stick in the box, the realization came over Loco.

"Let's keep the monkey stick, Mamma!"

Mrs. Bishop ignored this. She dashed around, ordering the girls to dress up nicely. "You, Urie, wear your velvet suit."

At that moment she spotted the Teddy-bear spoon in the silver drawer. She took it out and put it in a paper bag with the small things. The Teddy-bear spoon had been fought over since the children were small. But because Loco was the youngest it had become hers now. After her mother had refused to answer about the monkey stick, Loco knew that no pleadings would alter anything. She stood by the doorway, pleading with Omniscience not to let the Teddy-bear spoon go.

"I suppose I could get rid of my mother's diamond ring too," Mrs.

Bishop was saying aloud to herself, "but I was going to give that one to Irene, my own to Loco, and the one with the rubies to Urie."

Urie bent down to see a spot in a crack in the floor. Irene looked at her feet.

Mrs. Bishop put on her best pair of white gloves. They made her look strangely stylish. As they left the house, ironically, the sun had stretched into the late morning sky and the weather had again turned Indian summer hot. Urie and Irene had to carry the blue and white umbrella stand. They covered it with brown paper so that people on the street would not know what it was. But as the parade of girls and goods started up the dirt street, the paper kept slipping, and shiny white and blue doves, naked and elegant, were revealed beneath. The family made a sight in the street, Mrs. Bishop leading, with a box in her left arm and three paper bags clutched in her right hand. Urie and Irene held their heads high, the umbrella stand clasped tight in their fists. Their throats were rigid, pressing down their humiliation. At the railroad tracks Urie kicked at Irene and said, "Go on. Go on!"

"It's awful!" whispered Irene.

"Mamma!" complained Loco, who was carrying the shepherd and shepherdess packed with papers making the package puffed up under her chin. She could hardly manage the whale harpoon in her other hand.

Mrs. Bishop turned around.

At that moment a great rumbling truck loaded with pine slabs lumbered across the railroad tracks. Its tires picked up loose dust at the side of the road. Loco saw at once that they were Cat's Paw tires, and she felt that they were a sign. Maybe the Teddy-bear spoon would not go. Maybe even the monkey stick—

The driver saw the white suit and white gloves that Mrs. Bishop wore, and the flock of girls lined up in back of her. He let loose a tremendous blast of his horn, drowning them in complete annihilation. At the same time he opened his face into a wide grin. This gave the appearance that the sound of the horn had come from his huge bulky body out through his gaping mouth. "Whoooo!" he shouted out the window as the pine slabs jiggled against the creaking sides of the truck. There was a swish of hot air. Clouds of dust engulfed them. The sun poured down on the white dirt. Dust mixed with the sweat on their brows. Little curls became matted at Loco Poco's temples.

The girls noticed that their mother had no idea of the indignity. Somehow she refused to notice that the truck's commotion was due to their parade.

"Irene, you switch with Loco now," she said.

"It looks awful to carry that!" harped Urie, as they set the umbrella stand down in the dust.

Irene almost snatched the packages out of Loco's arms. Loco picked up the umbrella stand gingerly.

It was ten minutes past eleven when they reached the post office. People on the street stared at the parade. Eyes focused on the shape of the umbrella stand going by. Suddenly the post-office doors swung open and a fat man stood on the post-office steps, staring at them. He wore a pin-striped suit. His jacket was open. His stomach protruded with authority. His watch chain danced gracefully from his waistcoat.

"It's Major Hoople," said Loco.

"Shut up," said Urie.

"Why?"

"Because that's Opal Granger's father."

"So what?"

"He teaches archeology!"

The fat man sensed that he was being talked about; an expression of righteous suspicion dimmed his stance. With feigned unconcern, he turned away from the parade.

But Loco Poco could not bother with Urie's concern for important people who had no meaning to her. She stumbled forward, thinking worriedly of the Teddy-bear spoon. Urie wanted to laugh. The humiliation was beginning to make her turn vicious, and she was glad Opal Granger had a fat father.

Across the street, Mrs. Harriet Ransome entered from the stone walls of the campus. She perched like a bird on the curbstone, eying the parade with beady interest. She was the wife of Dr. Lacey Ransome, professor of William James, and head of the National William James Society. He was a Unitarian, she a Quaker. But she was the most do-gooding person on the entire campus, and, sensing a family in need before her eyes, she darted forward, skittering, chattering before the light, bowing involuntarily to Mrs. Bishop.

Urie and Loco looked at their mother. Faced with Mrs. Ransome's attention, her head rose. She opened her mouth to smile. For the first time her daughters noticed that her teeth were black. Mrs. Bishop's smile was crooked, because she did not open her mouth all the way. Then, under Mrs. Ransome's chirping attention, she turned her eyes away.

"I wonder what in the *world* they're doing," an unknown lady said to Mrs. Ransome when she reached the other side of the street.

Mrs. Bishop hitched her gloves and began to walk faster, forcing Loco and Urie to pick up their speed.

At twenty minutes past eleven, the Bishops arrived at Laurelo's Wildwood Gift Shop. The heat poured into the street. Five austere elms stood in Wildwood's yard, drooped their leaves hankeringly over the roof, and cast a dusky shade over the white columns facing the street. A sign painted in blue letters directed strangers to a flagstone path that led to the shop in back. The Bishops rested for a moment and mopped their foreheads. Mrs. Bishop could not believe that it had been so cold in the night. It was a quiet spot, cool in the shade. Across the street, in front of the Episcopal church, kids were roller skating. At the traffic light where Pungo met Main Street, town automobiles came to a shrieking stop. Suddenly bells from the bell tower rang far away. All these noises seemed outside the orbit of Laurelo's Wildwood Gift Shop and what would happen there—only a prelude in the mysterious quiet, signifying what would happen. The elms were deceivingly protective. The columns were mysteriously commanding. The windows were dark and shutterless, hinting at a dusky cool interior where all noises in the world were obliterated. In there Mrs. Potter and Gail Potter lay in wait.

"All right, you stay here," ordered Mrs. Bishop, settling her dress around her hips and pulling up her white gloves.

Loco and Urie set the umbrella stand on the pebbles.

Mrs. Bishop knocked.

How could they stand it! thought Urie. How undignified they were, standing out on this street with their goods to be sold, their hands outstretched. She prayed that Gail would not be here.

She could not look at Irene.

Loco thought of the Teddy bear. The spoon was right in that paper bag, on Main Street by the Episcopal church. All anybody had to do to see it was open the paper bag. Think how many cereals it had spooned into her mouth. Now it would never spoon anything again!

Urie looked at Irene.

Irene was thinking of paper bags. Paper bags were humiliating because they rattled. They were always full of personal things. Irene knew Urie was staring at her, but she would not look back. Someday, Irene decided, she would be the mistress of a large colonnaded house, with a husband. She would go fox-hunting, play a tuba in a symphony orchestra, and entertain top people and movie stars. She would never touch a paper bag again.

Urie was excoriating Irene in her mind. She never knew what was going on. She was a fool. She was not humiliated, because she didn't know any better. Thank goodness Zebul could not see the Bishops now. They were a pack of tacky drips, and if it were not for Loco Poco's looks and her own brains, they would be banished from the earth. Dark, queer, horrible misfits, they beat any matchstick girls or Orphan Annies.

Mrs. Bishop made a sign to them from the porch.

Urie and Loco picked up the umbrella stand. Irene began to march. They entered.

Mrs. Bishop's dress was wrinkled. Sweat showed through in half-moons under her armpits.

There was a tiny tinkling bell on the door of the shop. It faded once they were inside.

Mrs. Potter stood at the far end of the shop. She was tall and thin like a black ghost. There were two wrinkles over her eyes, and two strings in her neck where it met her collar bones. She kept a cigarette dangling from old-painted lips, to hide the fact that she was a ravaged beauty. Urie stared at her. She could not believe Gail Potter's mother looked like this!

"My daughter is a friend of Gail's," announced Mrs. Bishop in hopeful tones. They echoed through the dusky shop and died in the silence.

Lush honeysuckle bushes covered the windows outside, muffling all sound except the humming of some bumblebees, blotting out the light. Tall dark candlesticks, looking like Mrs. Potter, ancient plates, and silver jugs shone in the dark. There were tarnished fireplace apparati hanging from a wooded wall. Ageless chandeliers hung from the ceiling, one of which caught the drafts made by the parade of Bishops and uttered a muffled tinkling sound. An old Napoleonic desk with coy, polished mosaic work stood in the corner haughtily as if to disparage the goods that the Bishops had brought to sell. Tall chiffoniers sailed dark and deathly as barges. Two bleak mahogany bookcases with glass panes mocked them in reflection. On tables covered with white paper were thousands of breakable valuables, figures that were exact copies of that which Mrs. Bishop held out so hopefully to Mrs. Potter, sparkling golden dishes, glass serving spoons, dancing picture frames, elephant bookends, snoring lily-white doorstops, heap upon heap of vases, and a pair of castanets. Five tables of these objects vibrated before their eyes. The silence held them in its spell. They hardly dared to breathe.

"Yes," said Mrs. Potter in answer to Mrs. Bishop's ploy using Urie's friendship with Gail to sell at a higher price. But Mrs. Potter's voice was harsh, cracked, and full of doom.

Urie blushed.

Loco became afraid.

Mrs. Bishop held out her figurine.

Mrs. Potter lighted a new cigarette. She crushed her old one out in a porcelain ashtray, hung the new one from her lip, and received the figurine.

"Two dollars," she said.

Irene's face remained imperturbable.

"But I thought—" protested Mrs. Bishop.

"It's really not worth that to me. You can see they're really quite common, and I'm already stocked with same."

When Mrs. Bishop took the Teddy-bear spoon out of the bag, Loco Poco sucked in her breath. It brought only a dollar. Loco watched her mother place it in Mrs. Potter's old white-creamed hand. The imprint of the bear's ears remained in Loco's eyes.

Mrs. Potter made prices on the rest of the family relics. She treated each one impersonally, letting her cigarette ashes trail down upon them like dust unto dust. She tried to be gentle in her bids. But feelings had been dismissed long ago in her business. When they came to the china umbrella stand, Mrs. Bishop bade Irene and Urie to strip off the brown paper. At last the one choice item stood reflecting the ghastly green color of the shop. Mrs. Potter eyed it with one unmoving reptile eye.

"I thought perhaps twenty-five dollars . . ." began Mrs. Bishop in bright, faltering hope. Her hand was half outstretched. Her body tried to block out Mrs. Potter's own competition, those candlesticks, chandeliers, the Napoleonic desk, the chiffoniers which already cluttered Mrs. Potter's Laurelo Wildwood Gift Shop.

"Well, I would not have offered over fifteen for it, but I'll give you seventeen," said Mrs. Potter.

When it was over, and they opened the door into the blinding sunshine, feeling weak with lightness, not having to carry the paper bags, the Teddy-bear spoon, the candlesticks, the figurine, the umbrella stand, Mrs. Bishop had $23.50 in her hand.

"Who wanted that old stuff anyway?"

"But you said it would bring at least thirty dollars!" said Irene.

Suddenly Mrs. Bishop laughed. She turned around like a dervish under the butternut tree by the Episcopal church. She put her hand out, stopped whirling, and, touching the tree, laughed and laughed and laughed until tears flowed down her cheeks.

Infected, the girls began to laugh too. They laughed all the way past the Episcopal church, past the post office, past the power plant, and when they finally arrived at their own baggy screen door the $23.50 seemed like a glittering fortune. But it was not enough to pay for the heater.

CHAPTER 16

"What do you think P.Q. thinks about the war? For real?" Zebul asked Urie.

As they walked home in the orange sun, Urie was glad Zebul knew nothing about the Laurelo Wildwood Gift Shop humiliation, and she seized upon the subject he had brought up with avidity, for it made her forget.

"That's just it. He doesn't know."

There was a strange look in Zebul's eyes, something different. Something brimmed in them. Hate. His mouth was a slash. There was a soft covering of down above his lip which she had never noticed before.

"Then it's true," he said softly.

"If P.Q. says he doesn't know, that means there's a real chance of us getting into this war. Think of it, Zebul!" Urie began to become enthusiastic, feeding his strange hateful look with her own rebellion, covering over impotence with passionate wonder. "In the eighth grade at Eastern Point I had this teacher, Miss Parron who talked with this affected British sing-songy accent. She said, 'We will never have another war, for we have saved the world for democracy!' She made us all rejoice that we were spared the horrors of war. War was extinct. I believed her, because she was a teacher. Back then I always believed teachers. They had to be right because they were teachers. Look!" She held her arm out to Zebul so that he could see the hairs of it rising electrically. "It absolutely gives me goose-pimples!"

They were at that moment approaching the power plant.

"Listen, Urie," said Zebul. As he had seen her hairs rising, now she saw again the down on his upper lip profiled against the reflection of the sun on the bricks.

"What?" she whispered.

"I don't believe in God any more."

She bent her head near to him as if they were entering a church. Her heartbeat drummed against her awed silence, but there was the faintest sparkle of satisfaction in her face.

"You don't?"

"No."

"Why?"

"I don't know exactly. It has something to do with you—you and P.Q."

"Me and P.Q.?"

But she stopped abruptly, and he looked at her with accusation.

She continued to wait for him to explain himself. Then she began to breathe quickly. In rapid, quick syllables she said, "Try to think. When was it that you first didn't believe?" She acted as if they were both trapped and she was looking for a path out. "When? Was it just this minute?"

"No. It was sitting in my little house with you, looking at the wallpaper."

"That day? Was that why—"

"Yes."

"But you must figure it out!" she said, alarmed at the look on his face. "And exactly why. Why did you change?"

"I am no longer in a position to speak in innocence," he told her in soft and ultimate doom. Although the words were affected, they simultaneously moved over into a harmonic of articulateness that did away with the phoniness of language itself, in a spirit of faith in a language which they could both handle as young athletes did their muscles. "For," he continued, "I have become rational and knowledgeable, so how can I judge a past where my innocence was pure ignorance?"

He loved the troubled shadows over her blue eyes. Now that he had confided in her and spread his guilt at losing God upon her, his suffering was abated. His loss of God was transforming itself into some kind of triumph by his very talking about it. He actually began to feel good for the first time. He talked longer and faster. He drew her closer to him. He was glad, not sorry, he said. Ultimately it was truth he wanted. He did not want Christian lies.

Well, who could they believe? he asked her. It was necessary that they find out for themselves. Look at the teacher who had said there would never be another war. Look at P.Q. Even P.Q. did not know whether there would be a war or not. Maybe he, Zebul Walley, would have to go to war! He became almost triumphant. See! The world was something different from what they had been brought up to believe! Everything they had been brought up to believe was being revealed as a lie!

"P.Q.," said Urie, coming home from school one afternoon alone.

It had been such dry weather that P.Q., fearing fire, was spraying the yard and the sides of the house with the garden hose. There were no hydrants past the railroad track. If Negroes' houses caught fire, they burned to the ground.

"What?" asked P.Q., absorbed in his task. The pebbles glinted dizzily in the late-November sun.

"Do you believe it is bad to destroy people's religion?"

P.Q. paused in his watering. Although he knew immediately that Urie was referring to Zebul, he pretended to be ignorant of that fact. He brought the spurting nozzle carefully down to the rotten edges of the kitchen door, concentrating carefully on making a neat stream of water to cover every portion of the crumbling wood.

"Your question is muddy the way you have asked it. What is religion? What is religion?" he repeated. "You have to make a distinction between church and religion."

Impatient with this didacticism, Urie almost decided to go into the house that instant. She shifted her books from one hip to the other.

"I mean if a person believes in God and goes to the Baptist church. Then suddenly they hear about Zeus and Apollo and they read Herodotus and then they start reading Plato and they see that people asked themselves questions, and then they begin to ask questions themselves and they begin not to believe in the God of the Baptist church."

"Aha!" he shouted. He lifted the hose up toward the rotting chimney. The water sparkled with victory. "You mean they have begun to read!"

"Yes."

"Reading is what?"

"The beginning of education."

"The beginning of education," he repeated. "And education is what?"

"The end of superstition."

"The end of superstition!"

As the water spurted in the sunny air, glistened, and arched into a rainbow, spattering in drops on the tin roof, she wanted to join in hosannas. Silently, laughing, clapping in imagination to hordes of spectators, she kicked open the baggy screen door. At that moment P.Q.'s stream of water, having loosened the mud around one of the chimney stones, toppled the stone. It careened, rattled down the tin roof, bounced over Urie's head, and crashed to the ground.

As it brought up an ecstatic little pat of dust, she and P.Q. laughed out loud. He was right. Why had she wavered? If people didn't know it, they were fools. Zebul was better off. Hahaha! She laughed. Hahaha, spattered

P.Q.'s water drops on the tin roof, just as if a piece of the chimney had never fallen.

When Urie and Zebul took *To the Lighthouse* and *My Confession* back to the library, they checked out other books. Almost every day they went there. They spent hours reading at the long tables. Soon they became known by the librarians and the students who worked behind the oaken desk. No one dared to ask them if they were students again, for, once they had been issued books, no one dared to discover that a mistake had been made. So Urie and Zebul attended the great marble halls without fear, and soon they began to experience a proprietary attitude toward the library. They met sometimes after supper and went there. Some nights they stayed till eleven o'clock, when the library closed.

How dare the library close! thought Zebul one night when a mournful-faced student traversed the halls, ringing a cowbell like a town crier of old. The cowbell was last call and came after the lights had been dimmed three times to signify that people must go. All around Zebul people stood up, rattled paper, banged their books, stretched, yawned, and scratched.

Zebul found Urie at a long table by Larousse encyclopedias in French on the other side of the library. She was squatting on her haunches on the seat of the chair.

"I don't sit," she explained to Zebul, "because this chair is made to fit your form." The chair had a raised proturberance in the middle of the seat.

"Some night let's stay here all night," said Zebul, making a face at the disappearing cowbell-ringer.

"Oh yes, let's do!"

"We can hide in those cubicles in the reference room!"

"That's a marvelous idea, Zebul! When shall we do it?"

"Sometime. I don't know—"

"When you say something, you have to do it," she said. "You can't just sit around."

Life was, thought Urie, an endless series of movements, as in a symphony. At the end of the first, a second movement came into existence, an entirely different movement from the old one, predicated on something completely new. See how the old life, the Ocean Life, had passed away. She only kept it inside her, waiting with faith for someday when she could play the strands again.

"Listen, Zeb," she said. They were walking toward the grand staircase. "Aristotle says man is a social animal. Do you believe it?"

They passed the Woman of Learning. Zebul thought hard.

"America changed the pattern of everything," he said. "It caused the birth of the individual and the conception of the individual as progenitor of society, rather than the other way around, so maybe it has disproved Aristotle."

"Then you think America has actually changed man?"

"Yes."

"I think you're right," she said excitedly. "Listen. This was the only country on earth that was founded on principles of an excellent society—with a paper, I mean, on which it is written down. To wit, the Constitution."

He liked her saying "To wit." He became excited.

"Man for the first time in the history of his species," he said, "came to a virgin land where, alone, that is, as one of his species, he set out to conquer—nature."

The echo of the cowbell rang out of the depths of the labyrinth below the stacks. They started down the staircases. Below them the statue of the boy picking the splinter out of his foot was shining in the already dimming light. Something about their discovery of man as an individualist, about their wish to practice their individuality, abetted that spirit of inspired recalcitrance that suggested staying in the library overnight. The sound of the cowbell died away. They stopped in front of the naked boy, wanting something ineffable. Wanting to stay there forever. Wanting to disobey, in this freedom of silence, the memory of the bell.

Urie patted the bare foot of the statue.

"I dare you to kiss his toe," whispered Zebul.

She gave him a sweeping look. "I am not afraid," it seemed to say. It affected Zebul strangely.

Then she bent down. Her hair parted behind, revealing the nape of her neck. He saw two tendons standing up, protecting the darkened, tender channel between, a mysterious place. She kissed the statue on the toe. In spite of a sudden squeal of laughter that escaped out of her, this act had great tenderness. Then she raised her head and looked at Zebul.

Her triumph overwhelmed her with embarrassment suddenly. She blushed. Then she ran. She disappeared out through the glass doors into the darkness. He saw her legs flash greenish-white in the strange light. The doorway glinted like a signal, reflecting transparent, then swirling and swinging backward, closed after her soundlessly.

He rushed after her. He felt a special chill that contrasted strangely with that rise of suffused sensation. He knew she was going to hide, and he felt that it was ultimate, that he might lose her. He pushed open the door.

The night enveloped him. He could not see in the darkness. Bushes made stiff silhouettes against the marble columns. Below, the bicycle rack stood like prison bars. The night was green and magic and the cold campus street lights shone. Above, the moon was unearthly and large.

He saw a hand on the column. He crept forward like a tiger. Suddenly his head was five inches from her cheek, next to the column behind which she had been hiding. Her hair seemed golden and liquid under the moon, in contrast to the hard, chuckling laughter of the dry, evergreen wizard magnolia leaves.

"Urie."

"What?"

"I see you under the moon."

It amazed him, what he was going to do. These words had been whispers. He took her hand. He pulled her after him, down the portico and over the steps downward, running. At the bottom of the steps, by the bicycle rack, were two silhouetted wheels. It was as if their inanimate bikes were alive, listening to Urie and Zebul through their spokes. The magnolia leaves glistened, mirroring the moon.

"Let us vow, Urie," he whispered, staring directly at the moon. His voice was thin, devout.

"What shall we vow?"

"Always by the light of the moon, let us vow to pursue truth."

Staring at the moon, he repeated his words, "I vow always by the light of this moon, this moon, right now—to always pursue truth."

"I vow," she repeated after him. Half of her wanted to laugh, half wanted to cry because of the solemn, frail importance of this vow in this age with Zebulon Vance Walley. "I vow, under this moon, standing under with you, Zeb, no matter where I am or whatever happens, always eternally for the rest of my life to pursue truth."

PART III

CHAPTER 17

"Boy, I'm never going to spend another Christmas vacation in this house." Urie shivered.

"What will you do?" asked Loco.

"I'll worm my way into one of the dormitories, where I'll be warm every minute of day and night."

The others, drawn in by the intensity, believed her words prophetic.

The colder they became, the louder, more vicious and volatile their conversation. Where would they put their Christmas tree? Since they had no money, what would they give for presents?

They built a huge fire in the fireplace. Flames roared up the chimney. A sound of sucking and spitting accompanied them.

"Be careful," warned Mrs. Bishop.

"It would be a good thing if this house burned down," declared Irene.

Their fire became larger and more voracious. The supply of wood from the shed diminished.

"We've got to use our initiative," said Urie. "Remember how we foraged the beach for driftwood?"

"Well, what can we do?" asked Loco. "There's no driftwood here."

"We'll make some."

That afternoon they pulled out the first plank in the bottom of the barn. Five nails shrieked and catapulted into the grass. The innards of the rotten hole exposed a crawling mass of termites.

"Driftwood is nothing but rotten wood, fallen off the face of the earth into the sea," explained Urie.

They pulled out some more and threw it into the fire. It made blue flames.

"It's marvelous," said Loco, huddling on her knees before it.

At first Mrs. Bishop pretended not to know they were burning up the barn. She turned away from their chortlings, cooings, sniggerings, and triumphs. But at last she could not resist.

"We're using manufactured driftwood, Mamma."

"Hand-hewn driftwood."

"Straight from Kan-of-Kerosene's barn!" teased Loco Poco.

Mrs. Bishop broke down. "Hahaha!" she laughed. She slapped her knee. "That woman will never miss it."

When P.Q. came home, he ignored their crowing. But Loco confronted him directly. "We're burning up the barn, P.Q."

He went to the living-room mantelpiece. He did not speak. He looked behind the French clock. He took out his razor. He went to the kitchen and filled a glass of water. He brought it back to the mantel. He took his brush out carefully from behind the sixth volume of the *Encyclopedia Britannica,* dipped it in the glass of water, doused it with shaving cream, mushed it into a good mixture, and soaped his chin.

"It's good to police the property," he said.

The problem of Christmas presents irked them. At first they talked about it. Then Irene and Urie went into moody silence. Only Loco Poco continued to talk about it. They told her to shut up.

One day she said, "What's the first line of *Little Women?*"

" ' "Christmas won't be Christmas without any presents," grumbled Jo, lying on the rug,' " replied Urie, falling for the bait.

"You fool!" flung Irene.

"Heeheehee," laughed Loco.

Urie ignored it. "I'm going to paint Squeers Cheese boxes and give them for teatrays," she said.

"Oh God!" groaned Irene.

"How stinking!" said Loco.

But Mrs. Bishop's voice—for she had overheard from the kitchen—singsonged, "Why, that's a wonderful idea! You could make marvelous embroidered Chinese scroll designs."

"Or a snow scene," called Urie.

"I'm gonna put a bunny on mine," said Loco.

"You claimed it stank."

"Consistency is the hobgoblin of little minds."

The next day Loco got out the oil paints and seated herself on the floor before the fire. She painted five boxes black outside and red inside. Then she began the first white bunny.

"I'm going to give one of these to Miss Picke," she said with growing excitement.

Three days before Christmas, P.Q. stamped into the house. Knowing that his footstamps were deliberate, everyone looked up.

"Look outside," he announced.

In the yard stood a brown, round-cornered heater with triangle-shaped holes in the top.

All the girls ran out. Together with P.Q. they hauled the heater into the house. They grunted and groaned under the weight. They set it in the middle of the dining-room floor.

"Where did you get the money?" asked Mrs. Bishop.

"If we put the stovepipe up the chimney, we won't be able to use the fireplace any more," interrupted Urie to blot out the question.

So P.Q. made a round hole in a piece of tin. He stuck the tin into the windowpane that had previously been filled up by a brown rag to keep the wind from blowing in. In order to get maximum heat, P.Q. hung the stovepipe on wires along the entire length of the ceiling. The appearance of this stovepipe traveling along the ceiling, in contrast to the elegant furniture and pictures, the piano, the picture of Amalfi, and the glass-cased china cabinet, accentuated the contrast of log-cabin poverty and high elegance in the room.

"Where did you get the money?" asked Mrs. Bishop.

"First rags in the window. Now stovepipe," said Irene sharply.

But P.Q. ignored everything. Mrs. Bishop, Irene, and all words. He made a great formality of lighting the heater.

First he lit the match. He turned the dial. He squinted. Then he dropped the match into the mica-embroidered door. They waited. Nothing happened.

P.Q. peeped in.

"It didn't take," whispered Irene.

"Keep quiet," said P.Q.

They took breaths. He began again. He took another match from the box. Carefully he opened the mica-embroidered door again. They waited. Deliberately he struck the match. He held it in his hand so long that Loco almost gave way. Then, slowly, like Lady Dedlock in the night, he moved it forward toward the mica door, moved it into the maw of the heater, stopped, and dropped it. Nothing happened.

He lit another match. He held it into the hole. He looked.

They waited.

"I see oil," he said.

Mrs. Bishop moved backward.

"Be careful," she warned.

He dropped the match.

All of a sudden there was a heaving sound. The stove, as if first hiccuping and then belching, said: Pwoooooo!

"It's caught!" raved Loco.

"It's working!"

"We have a stove!"

"Just think!"

They felt the corners, rounded, ugly, the shape pretentiously low-bourgeois, the color of all space heaters, the roundness of all phonies, and as it warmed up, and they felt the warmth with their fingers and stared at the warmth as it emerged through the sharp triangular holes at the top, they laughed, jumped, and breathed it in!

"We'll be warm, Mamma."

"We won't have to burn up the barn any more."

"I know it, darling." Mrs. Bishop's voice was melting.

They patted the stove. They caressed its bourgeois fatness. They stroked its rounded corners. They discussed how ugly it was. They brought up Prometheus. They talked about fire and heat and the meaning of them to humankind.

"Let's have a party!" Irene said.

"I'll invite Miss Picke!" said Loco.

"Why yes. Haha! That's an excellent idea!" P.Q. joined in, to everyone's surprise. "Poor old cuss. I bet nobody has ever invited her to a party in her entire life!"

The party was held on Christmas Eve because it was Sunday. Festivity would divert them from their lack of presents. Besides, P.Q. hated Christmas because of its sentimentality. He assigned Zebul to write a paper on virtue, based on his reading of the *Meno,* to be read publicly for the occasion.

"But won't Zebul's mother want him home on Christmas Eve?"

"Oh no!" assured Zebul. "She can see me at supper. Then I'll come right over here."

Mrs. Bishop decided to hold off supper till seven o'clock, though Miss Picke was due at six-thirty, and Zebul could eat twice.

That afternoon the girls cut a cedar tree from the woods beyond Sociological Conditions.

"This is the measliest tree we have ever had for a Christmas tree."

"What can you expect of a cedar tree? Ugh!"

"Don't worry. We'll just load it down with the lights and stuff, and nobody will ever notice."

They had brought three carton boxes of Christmas decorations from the

North, including three old popcorn chains which they had sewed themselves as children. P.Q. sat reading the paper, ignoring them, the fire flickering on pictures in the rotogravure section of Russians and Finns frozen to waxworks, some locked together, their bayonets within each other's bodies, some frozen half standing, some in crouching positions in the ice-covered forests. Urie noticed these pictures as she stood back to admire the Christmas tree, but the success of the red and green lights cast everything into fairyland. Loco Poco wrapped her Squeers Cheese box present for Miss Picke and rushed out to get her. Mrs. Bishop hung up five old woolen stockings on the mantelpiece, including one for P.Q. and one for Zebul too. The stockings would deflect attention from the fact that each girl got only one good present apiece. She had tangerines, apples, pairs of socks for each girl, toothpaste, bobby pins, shoelaces, and soap bars. That night after the party she would fill them, and the stocking necessities would be the main feature for Christmas morning.

It was dark at six-thirty.

Loco Poco piloted Miss Picke, as if she were a freighter, through the screen door. "Here is Miss Picke!" she announced.

Miss Picke's iridescent ankle socks glowed strangely in the Christmas-tree lights. She lifted her head and squinted at P.Q.'s outstretched hand.

"Ah, Miss Picke, we are so glad to meet you! Come in!"

She blinked again like an albino owl, her granite head wobbling on its foundation from his handshake. Then she uttered five inaudible words, inspecting her surroundings with one sidewise glance.

"Won't you take off your sweater?" asked Mrs. Bishop, rushing from the Parker House rolls.

"Oh, no. I never take it off."

No one could think of anything to say.

"It must be cold out," said Mrs. Bishop.

"It is."

There was another long silence.

"We are having Parker House rolls and honey," said Loco.

"We always have them for Sunday-night supper, even though this is Christmas Eve," said Urie. "They're good."

"They're cheap," said Loco.

Miss Picke paid no attention to the dining room. It could have been a bathysphere, a movie house, or a gas chamber. Her lips were blue, but she did not even glance at the Christmas tree.

"Sit down." P.Q. pointed.

She sat on the coffin bed. Her bifocal glasses made her eyes look pasted on in layers. She had to lift her whole head to see anything above waist level. Buried deep in her eye sockets were her real eyes, so white, so meek, and so mild that they attained an eerie, malevolent significance in the Christmas-tree lights. In addition to her layers of eyes, her shoes seemed to have two tongues apiece, and she wore a filthy white apron. Her gray hair was shingled in back. The ends were frizzled, and each strand stood up separately in the air, with no relation to the next strand. She looked like a ninety-year-old Orphan Annie.

P.Q. stationed himself at a significant spot in front of the roaring fire. He began various subjects. First he introduced the weather.

Miss Picke let this subject drop dead.

He bought up the values of living in a town like Ephesus.

Miss Picke said, "Yes."

He mentioned Mrs. Eleanor Roosevelt.

Miss Picke looked disgusted.

He spoke about donkeys and told a story of roaming around on donkeys in Africa as a boy.

Miss Picke neither smiled nor answered.

The more monosyllabic Miss Picke became, the more ingratiating P.Q. acted. He laid on Old World charm with a trowel.

"Loco Poco tells us that you are a writer."

"Only quasi."

"Quasi is better than none."

Miss Picke opened her mouth wide and laughed abruptly and inappropriately. Then she stopped.

P.Q. preened at his success. "What is your book about?"

"The book was a thesis for the Art Department. I am getting my Ph.D. in art."

"But I understood that you are a philosophical writer."

"I already have a Ph.D. in philosophy." Miss Picke poked a horned forefinger in her hair and scratched. Simultaneously she emitted a large, tube-like breath, as if a pump-organ were hidden back of her nose.

"Are you combining art and philosophy in this thesis?" asked P.Q.

"I am studying under Dr. Helmut Boehm," answered Miss Picke.

This non sequitur produced an air of electrifying suspense. Everybody hung upon her next statement.

"The subject of the book is 'The Algebraic Interpretation of Leonardo da Vinci,' " Miss Picke continued. "My original studies were in mathematics. I have been veering more and more toward art. I got the Ph.D. in philosophy because I wanted to study under Dr. Helmut Boehm. The Art Department advised me that the dissertation was of a quality which, if revised, ought to go to a publishing house."

The family breathed in admiration of her grammar.

"I write stories on the side. They are published in the *Black Heart Quarterly*. But they are just diversions, little things which I think and see. I see a lot, just looking from stone walls. Anyway, back to the subject, I revised 'The Algebraic Interpretation of Leonardo da Vinci' and sent it to Houghton Mifflin. I wrote it in iambic pentameter. I was trying to devise some way for the style to mirror the content. Style must not mirror content, however. It must become content. The reason she heard about it"— Miss Picke shunned saying Loco's name out loud, as she shunned all antecedents—"was that last week Houghton Mifflin returned it."

"What happened?" burst from Urie.

"They said that it read exceptionally smoothly, but that they did not understand it. They said that they could not find a place for it in their company's publishing list."

In these words Miss Picke's voice snarled upward as if she were a machine gone out of whack. She reeled in the grip of her Alabama drawl, and then stopped. Her mouth and cheeks continued to pulsate.

At this moment, like a *deus ex machina,* Zebul appeared. He bounced through the kitchen door. His face was red from the cold. He entered the arena of Parker House rolls, reeling hungrily.

"Aha! Zebul!" called P.Q. in relief. "Miss Picke, I would like to present Zebulon Vance Walley."

Miss Picke gave Zebul a hard look. "I know him."

"Did you bring it?" questioned P.Q. eagerly.

"Yes sir!" Zebul held the papers out triumphantly.

"All right, then. Stand there."

P.Q. pointed to a spot before the hearth. As soon as Zebul stood at the spot, P.Q. announced, "Zebul Walley will now read a paper on the subject of good and evil as demonstrated in the *Meno*."

P.Q. sat down ostentatiously. But he had an afterthought. He stood up again, saying, "Miss Picke is a writer. She will be the judge."

"I am no judge!" snapped Miss Picke.

"I mean only in a manner of speaking, of course," added P.Q. with an oily smile.

Urie blushed.

There was a great silence. The family leaned forward again. Zebul, used to the Bishops' religious reverence for all individual spokesmanship, gulped.

"Is Evil or Wrong-Doing Punished on This Earth?" he began. "Is Evil or Wrong-doing punished on this earth?" he repeated for the first sentence.

As he read, his words became louder. His expression grew more confident. By the third sentence he had even attained a flashy authority.

In an analysis of this query one must first ascertain the meaning of punishment. Punishment is a penalty inflicted on an offender as a retribution, and incidentally for reformation and prevention. Punishment is, then, the deliverance from evil, an advantage attained by the enduring of pain.

Let us consider murder as an evil. Mr. A. murders Mr. B. after having meditated for some length of time. Mr. A. has a conscience, however. He is overwhelmed by what he has done. He repents. He is horribly frightened, not only of being discovered, but by what is to happen to him. He is haunted by the memory of the murder. He satiates himself with debaucheries and liquor to forget his trouble . . .

Loco Poco, pleased with the words "murder," "debauchery," and "liquor," twitched.

He loses his former ability to do his work well; financial difficulties ensue, and finally domestic disturbances. Mr. A., because of his evil act, has brought a hell upon himself—a hell, a consequence of his wrongdoing.

Let us, on the other hand, consider Mr. X, a disreputable gangster, a menacing public enemy, and a crafty killer. He lives in a good house and has stooges to carry on his culpable deeds. Mr. X is a hardened criminal. He is neither afraid of the law nor the afterworld. Having lived this life of riches and comfort, he dies of a sudden heart attack. He has experienced no hell on earth; he has felt no such intolerable anguish of conscience as has Mr. A. He has definitely not been punished in this world.

But in actuality Mr. X does receive the greater punishment and lives in the more unhappy state, for it is he who enjoys the fruits of his crimes. He that is not purged of evil. He who is not delivered from wrong. And in living in evil and basking in injustice he is actually receiving his greatest punishment.

Whereas Mr. A is happier than Mr. X, who, in not being punished is punished. For he who receives punishment is actually punished and also purified. And he who is not punished truly is punished by not being purified.

A total silence greeted this work.

"All right, the floor is opened for discussion," said P.Q.

"You have fallen into a horrible error!" accused Urie passionately. "You hinted that there was a heaven!"

"I did not!"

"Then who enacts the punishment?"

"The punishment—"

"You made tautistic statements."

"Tautological," corrected Zebul.

"You stated that Mr. X received greater punishment than Mr. A simply because he was not purged in this life. What is this? The fall of man?"

"I said nothing about the fall of man. I simply discussed the fact of good and evil as beyond the sense of feeling, of the *feeling* of good and evil."

"But that demands an other world!"

"No. No! Just because you—" But Zebul broke off. Frustrated, he turned to P.Q. His blue eyes were half beseeching, half furious. "What do *you* think of it, P.Q.?"

P.Q. put his forefinger and thumb at the tip of his nose. He pressed. The imagined execrability of the stench perpetrated by Zebul's theme gained from the delicacy of this gesture and the length of P.Q.'s nose. Loco tittered with laughter. Irene began to bray.

"That's all right," soothed P.Q. "You have to get it wrong before you can get it right. Life is trial and error. You will do better next time."

"But what's wrong with it?" sputtered Zebul.

"You didn't read Plato, because you had the habit of Jewish criminology. When you're in the habit of 'Fear thy God,' you can't sing and dance for your God, can you? But it will all come out in the wash. You will see. And what is your opinion, Miss Picke?" asked P.Q., turning grandiloquently toward the coffin seat.

Miss Picke's eyes opened. She stared out, startled, from a sudden twitch of hair.

"Supper is ready!" announced Mrs. Bishop, unaware, at the kitchen door, that Miss Picke had been asleep. Miss Picke's face fascinated her. She must, she thought, check the picture in her 1910 copy of *The Hunchback of Notre Dame*, given her on her tenth birthday by her father. Miss Picke looked like the third gargoyle.

It was only when they went in for supper that the reason for Miss Picke's invitation to the supper party was revealed. P.Q. danced attendance on Miss Picke, escorting her, overwhelming her until she twitched to get away from the grandeur of his attention.

The sparkling linen tablecloth drooped almost to the floor on the side where it tipped downward. But the silver gleamed at the sides of the plates, and the marshmallows, half-melted white eyes, disguised the tipsy angle of the cocoa upon which they floated in the bone-china cups, even though every marshmallow in every cup looked at the ceiling sidewise.

"Miss Picke, will you sit here, please?" said Mrs. Bishop.

Miss Picke sat down. P.Q. sat next to her. And as they began to eat, he introduced the true subject of his concern: investment.

"The subject of how to capitalize businesses is one which is interesting. You, for instance, run a fish-and-nuts store at the edge of Haw. Did you think of this as simply an outlet for the produce of your land in Alabama?"

Miss Picke put a Parker House roll in her mouth and merely grunted.

P.Q. began talking about the linen-supply business. People had erroneous ideas about business, he said. Business was the other half of service. Production profited everybody. It was a fluid process. He waxed eloquent about the possibilities of his linen supply. He mentioned no figures. But he talked about it as if he were Pausanias witnessing the possibilities of the world. He could expand it across the southeastern seaboard with the proper capital. Everything was in organization. He talked about organization, about how you could have twenty trucks and be freed of having to take care of the details, so that you could spend your time building up your list of customers. Or even a hundred trucks. There was no limit to the possibilities, because there was only one company in the entire area. He got carried away with his words and, plunging higher and higher into his rhetoric, he electrified the family with the enormousness of his possibilities and the enormousness of his gall in having seen in Miss Picke the secret answer to his prayers.

At seven-thirty Miss Picke twitched against the sea of their distended eyes, saying, "Kaltenborn is coming on."

P.Q. got up, dismissing his pursuit, like a fly who has got away. He turned the black dial. There was a crackle. Kaltenborn announced in a trembling, evocative voice that there would be a special program devoted to the *Graf Spee's* sinking in Montevideo last Monday.

It was at this moment that Miss Picke and P.Q. merged for the first time in the evening, an image of their connection for all the future visits of

146]

Miss Picke to the Bishops' house. Double and immobile, they sat together, two sphinxes guarding the door to the mansion of war.

"The war has begun in this hemisphere," whispered Miss Picke, laying her Parker House roll down on the plate. She put her chin in her hand. Honey trickled down her fingers.

P.Q. turned the knob. Kaltenborn crescendoed. Disembodied, from the outer world which Zebul had just described, he drowned out family, Ephesus, Christmas, cocoa, and all in his twining tremolo.

What is the *Graf Spee?* wondered Loco, shuddering in the massive, boring, prophetic weight of P.Q.'s and Miss Picke's reverential attention. She felt in a city mesmerized by words. *"Graf Spee . . .* British destroyer . . . fire . . . burned . . . disappeared." What was the *Graf Spee?* Was it destroyed? Had it got away like Miss Picke? Was it true the war had begun? Where was the war?

The honey rolled meticulously to Miss Picke's wrist. As her mouth opened in concentration, Loco concentrated on her jaw hinges. Miss Picke breathed loudly through this jaw.

"You know what I think?" trilled Loco, trying to get P.Q.'s attention.

But P.Q.'s face was turned to stone.

Loco turned to Urie.

Urie was excited, breathing fast, flushed, and looking at Zebul in secret collusion. They were on the brink of adultery, thought Loco. They loved war. War was the future of the world, where they would be adults. War looked like the twin stone faces of P.Q. and Miss Picke, keepers of the pieces of information, stray knowledges, which mankind must pick up forever, as Sisyphus did his stone, to piece together to know the unknown truth that lurked behind the radio, behind Kaltenborn, behind the cocoa, the Parker House rolls, and the marshmallows. The *Graf Spee* was a Nazi whale, not, like Moby Dick, white, but black as Chicken Little's sky, black, black and resounding with the doom sound to which everyone must bow.

At that moment Urie twitched. Surfeited with this crescendo of sound, she sighed. She turned. Zebul fidgeted. Irene fixed the pleats in her dress. They looked each other. Loco felt the triumph of Cinderella's awakening. She signaled. Oh, let them look at Miss Picke's open mouth.

Mrs. Bishop, also weary with endless words, suddenly became conscious that the fire had turned to ashes. She shivered. "My, there's a draft in here!" she said.

Loco let out a dollop of laughter.

Contaminated with Loco's jiggling eyes, and the thick huffs of Miss Picke's breath through her gargantuan mouth, Urie began to hoot.

Irene clapped her hand over her own mouth. She tried to look away from Miss Picke.

There was a side-splitting guffaw from Zebul.

"Joy to the world, the Lord is come!" said Loco significantly.

P.Q.'s pupils moved in his eye sockets until they came to focus on her. "Go to your room!" he said.

Unable to believe her disgrace on Christmas Eve as his favorite, Loco arose and shook out her curls confidently. "But—" she laughed deliciously.

P.Q.'s eyes rolled back to the radio.

She had to go. Past the stove, past the table, past the Christmas tree. Her shakes of laughter stopped only when she opened the hall door. Mrs. Bishop looked past Miss Picke's mouth and said, "She can't stay in there. It's below freezing."

Urie saw Loco frozen, a laughing wax dummy on her bed, like the Russian soldiers in the forest of Finland.

Miss Picke, her mouth permanently opened, stayed glued to the fried light of the radio dial, lost to the world.

C H A P T E R 18

P.Q.'S business did not improve in the New Year. But the less money it made, the more he saw its possibilities. He kept a small looseleaf notebook of hen scrawls in which gas payments, weekly payments to Gag Booch, shoes, and pinto beans were all entered without discrimination. By mixing family expenses with business expenses he provided a cushion against knowing exactly how much he made. He never mentioned figures. Details gave the world a static appearance which was false, which conflicted with his trial and error view of the universe. Some weeks he made as much as thirty dollars, sometimes no more than fifteen. But he never actually knew. The family was always behindhand. The electric bill was not paid on time. The water department sent three last notices that it was going to shut off the water. Yet no one would think of asking P.Q. the facts any more than anyone would have lifted the Oriental rug to sweep under it. The family threw themselves into their schoolgirl doings to avoid all thought of it.

By February the underpinnings of the barn were gone. They had to start tearing down the wall. Since these boards had not rotted yet, they had to pry each one out with a crowbar. A hole opened up. The girls kept the excavation on the far side of the barn so the destruction would not be noticeable.

"What we don't know won't hurt us," said Loco philosophically.

But, although the hole delighted them, it also scared them. They stopped calling the barn driftwood. Guilt arose in them. The fire seemed now an extravagance that presaged some coming day of retribution. Therefore they tried to control themselves.

Most of the time they refrained from having a fire. Since P.Q. turned the heater off at night, they sat in coats and scarfs. They also sat on their feet to keep them warm. They tried to do their homework in a hurry, so they could go to bed. Only in bed could one get warm.

One evening as Urie came into the dining room, having donned her eight-year-old L. L. Bean parka in her darkened bedroom, where the tapestried curtains billowed from the icy wind through the cracks in the house, Irene looked up from her geography and announced, "The rat is back."

"How do you know?" asked Loco Poco.

"I saw it at the outside water faucet."

"Why don't you kill it?" asked Urie sarcastically, picking up *The Merchant of Venice*.

"What with?"

"That old BB gun in the shed."

This remark successfully shut Irene up. The stove, recently lowered, began to tick, making the room, deserted by both parents, seem strange and empty. All motivations that had governed their lives before the stove had been cut off now ceased to function.

"Brrrrr," said Loco, draping herself over the metal of the dying oil stove. "What do I remind you of?"

"The Jukes and the Kallikaks," said Irene.

"Who are the Jukes and the Kallikaks?"

"Two feeble-minded people they found in North Carolina in eighteen eighty-four. They had so many children that they polluted the population of the world and now there are about eight hundred and fifty-three Jukes and Kallikaks. They counted them all up in statistics, and they are all feeble-minded."

"I'm not a Juke and Kallikak. I'm Kayo."

"Yeah, like I'm Moon Mullins," said Urie.

"Who's Irene?"

"Andy Gump," said Urie.

The stove ticked fitfully. It was like a heart-flutter of the house. But finally it died. The wind howled through the toothless gums of rotten boards. There was a brilliant moon staring at them through the pane of glass above a rag with which P.Q. had insulated the window sill.

"Do you realize," said Urie, "that living in such a way in the U.S.A. of this century, in this nigger shack in the cold, right next to these Sociological Conditions, that we could easily become criminals, stupid, or insane?"

Loco and Irene both answered yes.

But the thought inspired them. They all began to talk and estimate whether or not any one of the three of them would be the one out of ten people in the country who would end up in a mental institution.

"If it's anybody, it'll be Loco," said Urie.

In the silence a tiny grinding noise began, as if far-off insects were eating into the edge of the planet.

"The termites have begun again," Irene said in fretful ululations of Chekhov.

"They eat to keep warm," said Loco, trying to cheer herself up.

At that moment a stone fell down from the inside of the chimney into the cold fireplace. It thudded loudly. They jumped out of their skins. A moment later dried mud splattered against a piece of tin they used for the shutter, and sprinkled the floor.

"It's from those fires," accused Irene. "They're rotting the inside of the fireplace."

"So what!" scoffed Urie.

"Not only will there be no barn, but the chimney's liable to cave in too."

"When Kan-of-Kerosene finds out about the barn, what do you think she'll do?" asked Loco.

"She can't do anything."

"She might sue," said Irene. "Oh, I can't stand it!"

"Go to bed, then," said Urie.

"Yes. After all," said Loco, pleased by Urie's recklessness, "we're no worse off than people in pioneer days. Why, we have electric lights even."

The conversation turned to the subject of Lincoln and other famous persons who were born and graduated from log cabins. Who had read by firelight? Who had practically starved but had been a success? Who, like Jane Eyre and Dickens characters, had broken ice in their washbowls in the mornings to wash their faces? Recklessly they clasped their own ludicrousness to their bosoms.

"You know what?" said Loco. "Peter Ashe always knows when I come to class. Even when he can't see me, and he has horrible vision, thirteen-fourteen. He's practically blind."

"How?" asked Irene.

"He smells me."

"Smells!" uttered Irene, shocked.

"Yes. I smell of kerosene."

Urie put her two hands up her opposite sleeves. She put up the hood of her parka. She returned to reading.

Loco put her hands around the light bulb to warm them up. Now that it was so cold in the room, their breaths frosted the air. Loco steamed her breath against the light bulb in her hand, pretending to be a jinni. She squinted her eyes to make the steam grow larger.

"You're making it dark in here!" screamed Irene.

"Go to bed, then," aped Loco sweetly.

"I have to finish this geography."

Urie chimed in on Irene's side. She turned to Loco with an angry face. "Besides, what are you doing? Nothing. Just because you make rotten grades is no reason to force everybody else to do it too. You're nothing but a big nuisance! All you do is get in the way."

"And get on people's nerves!" added Irene.

Loco drew her breath in very tight and then made her mouth a circle as cigarette-smokers do. She squinted her eyes again, and the steam of her mouth was actually an iridescent circle. The only concession she made to their complaints was to take her hands off the light bulb so that the light returned, illuminating the dusky wooden ceiling.

Loco was still thinking of famous people and ancient days. She thought of Louisa May Alcott. Long ago on Eastern Point, when she had wanted to play Jo herself, she had had to play a combination of Amy and Beth, because of Urie, who not only directed the play in the garage, but who had seized the part of Jo for herself. They had charged admission and Urie had thrown sops to Loco, saying that every actress wanted a death scene like Beth's, plus that as Amy she had the opportunity of personifying evil, so she was better off than either Urie or Irene.

The silence was cold. Their hysterical jokes, carpings, criticisms, and aphorisms had taken them to a plane of unreality in the freezing night and still seemed to echo among them, as their own mood went into a Greek tragic fall.

"Money is the key to everything," said Irene with soft bitterness.

"I know how we can make some money!" said Loco.

"How?"

"By singing in churches."

"Us! Sing in churches!" Urie uttered a paralyzing shriek. "We! Transvaluate the values of the universe, after having preached No God on every street corner!"

"I didn't preach it," said Irene. "You did."

"Who will hire us?" brayed Urie.

"Opal Granger's father!" rushed Loco enthusiastically.

"You mean you expect me to use my influence to get that black-robed, fat-faced Major Hoople of the Episcopal church to hire us to *sing?* That purple puking pig of uppity piggety!"

"We'll bill ourselves as the Three Atheist Angels," said Loco slyly.

"And cast our pearls before purple swine!" said Irene.

Their laughter jittered against the walls. Loco Poco's eyes curled like a cat's. No one noticed the increasing puffs of wind that pulsated against the freezing bones of the house.

An hour later, when Loco Poco and Irene went to bed, Urie sat alone in the dining room. She crouched into her parka, thinking. The only things extant were her eyes, fastened on the page of her book, and her nose, which stuck out over the collar of the parka.

She imagined how it would be when she went to bed. She would have to take off her parka, strip off her skirt, her blouse, her socks, and her shoes. The idea of the cold was unbearable. She imagined herself stark naked. She would have to clothe herself with her damp, freezing flannel pajamas. It would take her fifteen minutes to begin to be warm. Her feet would be ice-blocks. Her flesh would be like a picked chicken, all goosebumps.

There was nothing worse, she thought, than to be cold and dirty. Why was one cold? Because oil and wood for fires cost money. Why was one dirty? Because one was too cold to take a bath. Hot water was necessary. Water had to be heated.

Thus she reasoned, as she traced these things back to poverty. Poverty equated with futility. Futility was worse than hopelessness. You worked, you tried, you tried, you worked. Nothing was accomplished. Could you ever clean the Oriental rug? No. Poverty decreed cold and dirt.

If you were cold and dirty, you would never be accepted by other people. Even if you were accepted, you had to keep from them the important fact of being cold and dirty. Thus separated from other people, you could never confide in them, even though they liked you. For if you confided, it must needs be that you would confess you were different from them.

Under your thick clothes, which you wore to keep warm, you were really dirty, for you could not bear to take off your clothes in a freezing bathroom to take a bath every day, as all Americans are advised in Hygiene II.

To be hot and dirty is exciting. Hotness implies that the juice of life has worked to the apex. There is virtue in that. It is a height of accomplishment. If you are hot and dirty everything becomes reward, for the ultimate consequence of being hot and dirty is a bath. Cool waters splash you and you emerge, cool, clean, and refreshed, able to look at that which made you dirty as something as great as the igneous work of secret lava that changes the earth's surface.

Or to be cold and clean. This has the advantage of icy, barren virtue— that state where life is done with, imagized by ancient sages, austere people ready to die, and misers who have desiccated and dried up, their dirt transformed to sparkling coin. To be cold and clean is to be enshrouded, ready to be enshrined.

But to be cold and dirty is paradox. Dirtiness creates rage. But coldness calcifies the rage. Life is dirt, but the joy of life is warmth. The bitterness of life is cold. This sends hatred to the tombs, where the flesh hides it like stone but, being flesh, shivers and raises goosepimples at its own self-repulsion. The memory of warmth is extinct. Calcified rage brings on perversity. Pleasure returns in a strange package. Deceit, lying, putting things over on people, bringing people down without their knowing it, stabbing in the back, hitting and running, obsequiousness, underhandedness, stealing, Uriah Heepishness. The Match Girl and Sara Crewe are vice in virtue's clothing. Dirtiness in shrouds of cold is vice in virtue's clothing. The same thing. Thus, when one is cold and dirty the only pleasure is to dream of great revenge, the world's demise in an apocalyptic holocaust upon which the dirty, cold person can mount triumphantly, rip off his filth, display it with flagrant patriotism, letting loose his own human stench at last to bask in the molten heat of catastrophe, having nothing more to hide. Only this way can one become equal and known.

But such a dream is hard to satisfy. It would cause total destruction, total change.

Meanwhile, Urie thought, staring, galvanized by the power of these thoughts, but shivering, life goes on. The cold and dirty person remains cold and dirty. Anger enlarges like a gallstone. He has to hide more than he can act. He acts in little covert movements every day, always dreaming, always shivering, always stretching out cold hands to the lukewarm stove, always hiding his nose under his collar, hunching his arms into his sides, knowing that these pitiful defenses of his flesh's goosebumps and shivers are giving off the rank smell of unwashed perspiration, weeks-old wool, unwashed misery, stale servility, and the odor of unrecognized hatred.

Such ugliness can never be rectified. For the conditions are always and always the same. If you fix one stone, another falls. You brush, but it is the dirt that supports the rug.

She could not bear it.

But how was she going to get out of it? How could she transcend it? Yes, she had the strength of youth to continue day after day, extolling her vices, seeing through the world with her X-ray eyes, peopling the vices of others with her sharp laughter, and covering her own shame with viciousness and wit.

But she needed the future fast. Suddenly a feeling of such intense longing swept her that she stood up. She desired the day when they were through with this hopeless house. But where would they go? Everything in their lives was lived for tomorrow. She wished for a present, a today where she, Urania Bishop, could come to life, where everything would be legator, and the world, the world of the war that was coming would take her up in its affrighted waves and swim her on top of its foaming sabers, exciting weapons which she knew already how to handle, taught by the winter storms, her first beloved enemy, and toss her free. The only thing that could defeat the Depression was the war. Come, war!

Such a future was beyond money, beyond dirt, beyond impotent adolescence so filled with power and so powerless to act.

I don't want to be famous, she thought. I don't want to be rich! I don't want to work, to prove, to fight. I just want to be what I am!

The only solution was to get through school quickly. If she were already in college, studying for her B.A., things would not be so bad. Fantasies of speeding through the rest of high school assailed her. If she could ask for an exam in Latin, she knew she would pass the year without having to take the course. Also an exam in English to cover English III. She was going to Mr. Huntsucker, the principal, and ask him. As soon as the reports came back—she would have to have received all A's—she would ask him. If she could only finish high school in one more year, not two!

She closed *The Merchant of Venice*. She put out the light. In the darkness she stood for a moment. Then she opened the door into the curtained hall. In the freezing cold she shivered. The floor sank under her weight, even though she tiptoed. She lifted the curtain to her room.

"Let me love what I hate!" she said grimly.

The wind sucked through the winter night outside and breathed on her, inflating the curtain of her room like a sail.

She thought of Loco Poco and Irene and P.Q. and her mother. Slowly she zipped down her parka, ready now for that dreaded act of undressing for which she had rehearsed so long.

CHAPTER 19

Spring came. Germany invaded Norway. In Ephesus green shoots burst up. Forsythia, japonica, dogwood, and Judas opened, separate thralls of bloom, sending a perfume up around the Shack. There was a maniacal reversal of freedom. By the time the Low Countries were occupied, it was hot in Ephesus.

Urie wondered: Why did I put all my effort in trying not to be cold? I wore myself out. What for?

There were no more oil bills to pay. The luxury of being warm created a revolution. The girls put on shorts, hooked up the hose to the outside faucet, and sprayed each other. P.Q. moved the radio to the open window and sat outdoors listening to it.

In May, as the radio announced that 215,000 men were being lifted one by one off the beach of Dunkirk, clouds billowed in the still air and held the country in the thrall of blooms. The sky hovered moist and low. The atmosphere was close, enfolding them in summer like the skin of a tepee.

"It's so beautiful it makes you drunk," said Mrs. Bishop.

Negroes blossomed from their shacks almost like the flowers. They ambled black against the bleached white dirt with their red lips and pink hands waving like petals. Their smell was pungent and sour and contrasted with the flowers. Scylla and Charybdis lifted their lips furiously at them as they passed. The Negroes cringed and circumnavigated the road by the Bishops'.

At night their music suffused the air: guitars, clinking bottles, and hymns. Inspired, Urie, Zebul, Loco, and Irene resurrected the pump organ. They played "Fairest Lord Jesus" and "Drink to Me Only with Thine Eyes." Loco played on her flute. Whenever the Bishops played, the guitars stopped. An eerie communication of music and silences grew up between them. The Bishops knew that across the hill and down in the valley the Negroes were listening to them. One Saturday night there came a cacophony of women's screams, and then the sounds of men shouting.

"Somebody's getting cut," said Zebul. "They're cutting each other up with razors."

Loco stared, frightened.

Later an owl hooted in the woods.

Half an hour later a guitar began again and a solitary voice sang.

The secret signals of the black race, like Indian smoke rings on mountain tops, were all the more profound in this suffused night dark, since they knew that they should never meet and never know the persons who played and screamed. In this thick, palpable atmosphere new magic was infused into the destiny of the family. Lassitude combined with restlessness. They all had a greed to seek, to explore, or to appropriate.

The last week of school, Urie went to Mr. Huntsucker's office. Mr. Huntsucker was a pussycat principal who fought in what he considered a dignified way for progressive education. He was the tool of the university department of education, but official professors who taught the high-school curriculum looked down on him. Professors whose sons and daughters attended the school were impatient with him. He had to put up with student teachers. Some of the old, traditional teachers thought he was weak. But he met all these burdens with a syrup of milklike human kindness which he passed off as authority.

Urie was nervous. She had dressed up specially in her black velvet dress with the hood.

"I thought I should ask you," she said, taking on a proper sense of humility as she sidled up to his desk. Her cheeks burned. "I am capable of doing the work, I know that. The thing is, I really need to finish school as soon as possible, because with so many of us in my family to go to college —well, you know, if I go earlier, it won't cost so much all at once. You know." She stopped. "With my sister Irene and then Sylvia too." She stopped again. "What I mean is, I would like to ask you if you think it's possible to—if it would be possible if I could be given an examination in Latin Two and English Three? And if I passed them, could I graduate next year?"

Mr. Huntsucker always spoke in terms of "helping the pupils to understand themselves," or "helping the individual to recognize his own needs," or "helping by means of guidance and counseling rather than by direct command." Mr. Huntsucker remembered overhearing Urania Bishop telling two other girls in the hallway, "Do you realize that I live not less than one fourth of a mile away from you? You live in Southwood. And I live in Niggertown. Did you realize that Negroes lived so near Southwood? They own the entire western end of town. In fact, the Negroes can see all the way to Mount Airy." Mr. Huntsucker also remembered the time Urania Bishop had read her theme on living in Niggertown.

"Well, let's see, Urania. Let's check your credits."

He leaned over into a file drawer to pull out her record. She was already famous in the school, but he repeated it anyway as her mouth tried to restrain itself from looking smug. "You made A's in English and reported on *War and Peace*. Mmmmmm. Dr. Byrd notes this was not advisable till senior year. Now, what about Latin? A, A, A, . . . hmmmmm, all A's." He turned to her, his mouth mincing and lapping. "There are very few students," he said, "with your sense of drive and talent, Urania. Of course, I would not prescribe skipping classes as a general rule, but because of your excellent background and general education, I can see no point in trying to prevent as homogeneous a learning situation as possible in your case. I'll speak to Dr. Byrd and Dr. Griffith about this. As far as the technicalities of credits go, we ought to arrive at a fair appraisal, since your transfer has put you in a peculiar position."

"Oh, Mr. Huntsucker—" Urie began.

Mr. Huntsucker smiled liberally. "I wouldn't want to make this a general rule, you understand. But every day the world changes, progresses. We are becoming different."

"When do you think I would know something?" Her heart beat.

"I think the best thing would be if you would check in with me in the month of August. I'll be up to my shirtsleeves in work, right here."

"Oh, thank you, Mr. Huntsucker. Thank you!"

She ran all the way home, whipping her velvet hood in the air. That night she went to Zebul's little house.

"Zebul, Huntsucker's gonna let me take special exams in Latin and English, and if I pass, I'll graduate next year! I'll go to college early."

Zebul was shocked. The bang of the door, the dogs' barking, Urie's disheveled appearance, and her act of slamming her books on his table made him jump.

"You've got to do it too!" she announced.

He stared at her. A string of hair fell down over his ear and pulsated. His lips began to sharpen conspiratorially. Everything about her, her translucent eyes, her harnessing herself into this sudden crystallization of her future, her lucidity, her triumph, inspired him.

But seeing his reaction, Urie suddenly became scared at her own success. How fragile power was!

"Zebul, what is the world?"

"What do you mean?"

"Look at the world. There are no rules, no solidity, no substance! See how I can do anything I set my mind to do! Observe how triumphant I am! Yet what is that? All it is is success. Nothing. People are weak!" she said, almost inconsistently. "Therefore it is necessary to discover what the world is and why people live in it."

She made the decision at dishes. She pushed the gray string mop up to its neck in the glass and squirted dishwater on Irene's feet.

"We'll start with the Episcopal church and work down. We'll charge five dollars a time."

Loco, who had been pretending to put the dishes away, seized a dishcloth and began wiping. "What will we sing?"

" 'Panis Angelicus.' "

"That's Catholic."

"Major Hoople loves high-church junk. When we do it in the Baptist church they'll be too dumb to know."

" 'O Love That Will Not Let Me Go.' "

" 'Liebestraum.' "

"We'll make up the words to it. I know. 'Dear God, dear God.' "

From the day of Irene's eleventh birthday they had always contrived money-making schemes. Combined with belief in Horatio Alger (work would make you succeed, all you had to do was have brains and elbow grease, strength of character would win the day), the visualization always caused a frenzy of premature glee, and that was in part a motivation for their successes.

Their first scheme had been the selling of pond lilies. Every morning they had risen before dawn, before the lily heads had opened. They had gone on the pond in a boat. Muskrats had watched them with frightened whiskers. They knew every lily patch. They picked the ones with long stems. Their hands had slid down the slimy tubes. After picking a boatload, they brought them to the cellar, where they wrapped them in bunches of ten and fifteen in waxed paper and tied them with elastics. Then Mrs. Bishop transported them to the business district in their old Pontiac. They stationed themselves at important street corners. There were the suckers, the good, and the crumbs. They categorized them. Loco always brought in the most money because of her cuteness.

Another money-making scheme was playing music at summer hotels. Mrs. Lumkirk, their music teacher, had a set of eight English handbells, manufactured at Whitechapel. They were practice bells for learners of English bell-ringing. The girls learned to ring changes from reading a Dorothy Sayers mystery story called *The Nine Tailors*. Urie learned a spiel about the ancient art of bell-ringing which impressed the manager of the Turk's Head Inn. He hired them for one engagement. Borrowing the bells from Mrs. Lumkirk, they conducted their performance on a long plank summer porch overlooking the ocean. Old men and women sat on wicker rocking chairs and listened. The girls made five dollars. Dressed in identical pongee dresses, they smiled back when the ancients with moles, crooked lips, and printed dresses smiled through their eyeglasses, false teeth, and ear trumpets. They played "D' ye Ken John Peel?" "Oranges and Lemons," and standard changes. Their success resulted in other engagements at different hotels, and this money made up part of the sum they gave P.Q. for his send-off to Ephesus.

This new scheme was absolutely contingent on Major Hoople. If he told the Espiscopal church to pay them five dollars for singing, the Episcopal church would pay them five dollars for singing. They decided to accost Major Hoople directly after church, after he had sung a special solo and was in a good mood.

"I'll do the asking, and the rest of you keep shut. Whatever you do, don't you dare laugh!"

Loco wore pink organdy. Irene's dress was made of blue rayon. The material had lost its gimp and gave her a dilapidated appearance. Urie swathed herself in the black velvet dress she had worn to Mr. Huntsucker's office.

They clicked on the flagstones with their Cuban heels. They had pocketbooks.

"I can't stand gloves," whined Loco.

"You're lucky we didn't make the decision to wear hats," threatened Urie.

They entered the church self-consciously.

Their "girliness" reached its apogee when they picked the pew (near the front) where they would sit. Pink, gauzy, romantic, Little Evas, Little Nells, Beth Marches, Shirley Temples, all the archetypes that Major Hoople would be a sucker for. It was a symbolic and dangerous realm into which they were entering.

They sat down. They folded their hands in their laps. They were very quiet. They bent their heads in a quasi-prayer position, meek and mild. Meanwhile their beady eyes were darting forth like insects, devouring all the church hypocrisies.

"Look, there's Opal Granger!" Loco pointed.

"Shut up."

"But maybe she would help us with her father."

"Yeah. Like a fly in a horse's mouth. I know what I'm doing. So just keep quiet and don't attract her attention. Do we need a lawyer? The whole reason for accosting Major Hoople in this church is to keep him from humping and hawing."

The church organ suddenly trampled the vintage. The music was like a giant vacuum cleaner sucking the congregation into its maw. Major Hoople made his entrance. He beckoned and billowed in his robes. The choir followed his striding figure like medieval scourges. His *basso profundo* competed with the footpedal bumps, though his pie-dough face and button of a nose belied this sonority. He held a long bass whole note until the choir got to their seats. Then he semaphored for them to sit. When he sat, his bench squeaked.

The church service was very boring.

But during the second responsive reading something happened. Amy Grispin White, the 1935 woman golf champion of the nation, arrived, accompanied by her mother, Amy the Older. Six feet one and a quarter, Amy Grispin, favorite native daughter, had elected to return and live in Ephesus after her second divorce. Amy the Older was a prominent Ephesian Episcopalian whose family went back before the Civil War and had donated the Journalism School to the University when Amy Grispin was born. Loping in her brown oxfords, her nose curling aristocratically high above the fake pink hydrangeas of her mother's rhomboid hat, the golf champion exaggerated her lateness by deliberate shrugs. Her mother led. They could not find a place to sit. When they turned into the eighth pew, Mrs. Pony Porter did not move fast enough. Her hydrangeas bristling, Amy the Older paddled farther front and entered the pew in front of the Bishops. She curtsied to the altar. Her hydrangeas jerked. Amy Grispin genuflected low. Her knees cracked.

The Bishops were transported by this proximity. Urie almost forgot her reason for attending church.

Thank God we didn't wear hats either, thought Irene, staring at Amy Grispin's bare head. She wore her hair in a bun with brown hairpins the size of horseshoes. "Golf champions are the nation's natural arbiters of fashion": Irene made up *Ladies' Home Journal* maxims, examining Amy Grispin's tweed jacket shoulders (heavily padded) for signs of dandruff.

Loco Poco was so excited she was afraid she might pee. She clutched her legs together and wove back and forth dangerously.

Prayer was announced.

Who would grovel to the ground, even on royal red velvet kneeling benches? The Bishops moved forward on the pew and bent rigidly.

But Amy Grispin and Amy the Older lowered themselves all the way down. A moment later Amy Grispin's brown oxford shoes with embroidered leather tongues appeared like phantoms beneath the Bishops' eyes, the final culmination of the gigantic spans of lower legs which she had inserted, like two pipes, beneath her pew. The prayer was long. The oxford shoes moved and rumbled beneath the spitting syllables. Then they unhitched themselves slowly from the feet beneath, rolling sidewise. They spun and finally came to a stop, bottoms up, one near Urie, the other near Loco.

Amy Grispin White's feet were naked, brown as golf clubs, and tough as jonquil bulbs. The feet had a peculiar odor. Irene and Urie sniffed.

But Loco had no sense of smell. She was disappointed when, at the end of the prayer, the feet were retrieved. She had fancied planting them and raising a crop of golf champions.

But the shoes remained. They were tempting. Loco kicked hers to an upright position. Urie scowled at her. Loco returned a beatific smile. She had saved the shoe from drowning. Through the rest of the sermon she concentrated. She forgot Major Hoople. She forgot everything. It became incumbent on her to do something with the shoe. At the end of the last hymn she knew what. She picked it up and inserted it secretly (toe pointing to heaven) into the book rack between the hymnal and the prayer book.

The recessional trumpeted. Major Hoople arose, signaling the choir to stand.

Rising for the hymn, Urie whispered, "As soon as this is over we'll beat the crowd to the choir box and accost him there. Get ready."

The voices rose in horrendous triumph. The sound bounced off the vaulted ceiling and crescendoed to the end. The minister's voice whispered. It was the last prayer. "Amen," said the congregation.

Urie, poised on her haunches, motioned to Irene and Loco.

But at that moment a caterwaul rose in front of them, exploding the silence. "I've told you and told you not to do it," whined Amy the Older, "but you go ahead and do it every Sunday!"

At the split moment of these words, Urie spotted the shoe in the book rack. Amy Grispin White was on hands and knees underneath her pew. The congregation was galvanized. Loco Poco, caught guilt-faced by Urie's shocked stare, clapped her hand over her mouth.

Urie ran. Behind her, like dervishes, Loco and Irene followed. The congregation stared after the three vanishing sisters suspiciously. Outside the church, they darted into the arboretum, raced past the greenhouse, and came to a breathless stop under the Ephesus Oak.

"You hog!" screamed Irene, facing Loco in tears. "How could you do it! You've ruined everything!" She stalked up the street, clattering in her high heels, saying, as if it were a curse, "Go home alone. I refuse to walk with a person who has thrown our entire future to the winds!"

"I couldn't help it, Urie," Loco whimpered servilely. "I just looked at that shoe and I couldn't resist." Her eyes had the false ingratiation of a cat's.

Why should she absolve Loco's guilt? thought Urie. Yet secretly she was relieved. Now she wouldn't have to beg from that fat, grunting, and forbidding fool Major Hoople.

The two sisters walked up Main Street. They turned left on Pungo. Urie's silence and the new harmonic born of Irene's abandonment drew the two together. In Urie's moody stillness, through their own footsteps, Loco's occult power began to bloom. From this senseless and whimsical defeat, it seemed everything had been planned from the beginning. Without a word they fell into a mood of inane and hungry drifting. It was as if they understood that now that everything had been reversed, now that the plan had fallen through, it did not matter. That, in fact, they had been released by some superior design. Thus the sights and sounds around them fascinated them even more than usual. They stopped, having come to the Baptist church, and stared at its phony columns.

"It doesn't seem as if we had ever been anywhere but here in Ephesus, does it, Urie?"

"No."

"Let's go to Visigoth Castle sometime."

"All right."

As they walked they began to feel that they were not in the power of their legs, but that it was the power of the breezes, the cinders, the leaves' beckoning that drew them forward. They could just as well have turned left as right. They were in some immense tract of freedom which expands the distance that can be conceived of, to interplanetary space.

"Isn't it good!" breathed Loco.

"Isn't what good?"

"Freedom."

Urie looked at her younger sister and suddenly felt herself half drowning, half thrilled by the fact of drowning in the opacity of those dark eyes. She would never get to the bottom of Loco. Her delicate head was framed by blue sky and green magnolia.

Therefore she began to tease Loco with insistent, profound cruelty.

"But if it is true that we have never lived any place but Ephesus, how is it that we have memory of Thalassia and the ocean?"

"I know. Isn't it funny?"

"I remember the ocean distinctly."

"I do too. And it's even longer for me!"

This untruth Urie understood immediately. Thus she did not contradict it, for it was too important a conversation to disrupt thought processes by being exact.

"But what if it was never true?" she said insistently.

"You mean untrue that we grew up by the ocean?"

"Yes."

Loco thought for a long time. Then she said, almost gaily, "What would it matter if we *know* we did?"

Squinting her eyes against Loco, Urie suddenly saw the outlines of her body trail and dissolve, snaking through the leaves and the cold trees like smoke or a jinni.

At that moment a silver bus embossed with black letters drew up in front of the Ephesus Inn.

"Look!" whispered Loco, catching at Urie's elbow with her white glove.

This gesture Urie was to remember forever afterward, for it seemed the epitome of Loco's charm to her. There was nothing significant in it. It was simply that it was completely ingenuous, completely unthought, that it escaped from Loco, that "Look!" as if that very moment were expressing the entire purpose of Loco's life on earth, and she was embodied in that moment, in that enjoinment for the earth to look, in that one quick, capricious, generous, and unconscious gesture.

A group of officers alighted from the bus. Most of them were United States Navy officers. But there were some with strange uniforms. Four older men wore blue-gray trousers and jackets with black braid. And there were two sailors with flapping white bell-bottoms and red pompoms on their berets.

"It's the Navy!" breathed Urie.

"But what are those ones that look like clowns?"

The officers' hats gleamed in the sun. Their epaulettes were like jewels. But the foreign officers kept to their own group, and the sailors at the fringe in attendance. Conversing informally, they dotted the inn lawn like flocks of birds.

"Free French!" guessed Urie, agape. "Those blue ones, I bet they're British!" The very saying of these words made Urie tremble. "It's because

[163

of the war. The war!" she mouthed to Loco, as if her explanations could make her understand.

The officers moved together, streamed up the brick walkway, past the wicker chairs into the Ephesus Inn. One by one they disappeared through the colonial door.

The girls hung, mesmerized, against the stone gates of the inn.

"Let's explore!" These words, spoken by Loco, who always was the most scared, the most titillated, the first to end up saying, "Let's go home," again returned Urie to the strong memory of those days when they used to explore the winter houses and rendered this moment, the officers, Ephesus, everything, unreal. She moved forward. A sensation of expectation, almost of fear, made her mouth salty.

Loco followed her eagerly. They walked consciously in the footsteps of the officers. They passed the wicker chairs.

"Won't Irene be sorry she left us?"

"Uhuh."

"Boy, she doesn't know what she's missing!"

"Uhuh."

"I wish I could find some of those clown sailors. I like them."

Loco began to giggle excitedly.

Urie stopped before the door, reached out her hand, leaned forward, and pushed hard. A Negro porter in livery stood directly inside the lobby. They entered an atmosphere of Oriental rugs, dark green stuffed furniture, and fireplaces. Urie looked straight at the porter's face and went by haughtily as if she were looking for someone. She stared at a bronze plaque over the fireplace, which said: "The cornerstone of this building was laid in 1902 by John Rathbone Russell, president of this University from 1898 to 1911, Governor of the State, 1914–1918."

They looked for the Navy officers. Only two were visible, silent at the registry desk, holding blue uniform bags.

"Let's take the elevator!" whispered Loco.

They darted forward. They passed the Negro again, ignoring him. They entered the lift.

Giggling, Loco pressed a button. The doors closed. They breathed, gulped, and burst into a loud spasm of laughter. The doors opened. They were on the third floor.

The hall was long, covered with a dark carpet, its walls a colonial cream color. An infinity of closed doors stretched the length of the hall. They had never explored a hotel before. They did not know what to do next.

"Remember when we talked gobbledygook to those two old crabs on the beach?" breathed Loco.

Five years ago, when Loco was six years old, she and Urie, coming home from the beach, had approached two brown-tweed, white-haired old ladies walking the windswept walk above the rocks with silver canes. With innocent faces, possessed by some sudden inspiration, they had asked them, "Bin stooler gloppety Marblehead in my stonk bell?"

One old lady had put her ear trumpet to her ear. The other had looked shocked. The girls had had the audacity to repeat this question, letter perfect, before running away.

"We must open doors," announced Urie, breathing, inspired now. "One of these doors contains the key to our future life."

Loco's eyes opened wide. "Let me try first," she whispered.

"All right."

They tiptoed down the carpet, Loco first. She put out her hand slightly. But she allowed three doors to go by. She almost chose the third; then at the crucial moment she darted to the left and chose a fourth in that direction she had completely ignored till then. She put her hand on the brass doorknob. She turned. Then she opened the door wide, in a fast but stealthy move.

A fat man dressed in shorts and garters, with beer foam upon his upper lip, gaped at them like a shocked rhinoceros.

"Sorry!" trilled Loco. "I must have the wrong room." She banged the door shut.

The sound echoed. They ran down the hall. A mahogany staircase rose at the end. The sound of their footsteps pounded against the wall, echoing like heartbeats.

At that moment they heard the door open. They sidled around the corner out of sight. They held their breath. The fat man bounced into the deserted hallway. "Hey, honey! Come on back here!" he called.

They tiptoed, crossed the staircase and hid under the landing.

"Where are you, honey?"

Loco opened her mouth to laugh. But at Urie's expression she grew scared and, with her fear, grew sober. The footsteps lumbered toward them loudly, and then, halfway, stopped.

"Well, you sure were cute, you little mean old lobster," the man mouthed. "And you didn't even come up to a grasshopper's knee."

Urie made gyrations of her head and rolled her eyes to show that the man was drunk.

Then the footsteps began again, in the opposite direction, heavy, clomping, and uneven. There was a pause, indicating that he must have looked the length of the empty hall again. Then the door closed.

They burst into dry laughter. Loco hung over the banisters, her black curls trailing and bouncing.

"His garters were red. Did you see?"

It took them five minutes to compose themselves. Loco wiped her tears on her gloved knuckles.

"It's my turn now," said Urie.

The hall, when they returned, had changed. They were more frightened and cautious than they had been the first time. Now that they were separated from sunlight, everything they had ever known seemed to disappear from reality—Ephesus, the Baptist church, Sociological Conditions, the campus. The length of the hallway with its closed doors had become the entire universe. The elevator stood open, dark and ominous. The Navy officers, the wind, the leaves that had led them here, seemed far away. Concomitant with this sudden turn in the conditions of their being were those agreed-upon rules which they had contrived at the beginning of the adventure. They had been led here. They must follow the last bidding. An air of seriousness, even ultimacy, encompassed them. Everything depended upon which door Urie chose.

Loco stood back, giving her free rein.

Urie chose a door. She paused. She stood before it.

Then involuntarily, just as Loco had done, she turned to the next door on the opposite side. Her hand grasped the doorknob. She had no qualms about this gesture. She turned. She did not act stealthy. It seemed that she had reached the eye of the hurricane. As she pulled the door open, she expected someone she knew to be inside, something completely known, something ordered, as if the universe were suddenly to fall into place.

In the room sat one of the foreign officers. He was sitting at a table with his coat unbuttoned. He looked more than thirty-five years old, thin and weary, with sandy-gold hair. He looked like a defeated Confederate officer in the Civil War because he had no tie and his uniform did not fit. His cap was upended on the table, sad with pale yellow braid.

The officer looked up slowly, unbelieving, into her paralyzed stare. He was crying. Tears glistened in the cavity of a wrinkle which led from the dark circles beneath his eyes to dewlaps below his cheeks.

The fact that by opening a door she could have shattered privacy and immobilized nakedness was unbelievable. Yet she had done it. It was simple. She stared for a full moment, unable to move. Then she closed the door softly and ran.

"What was it?" Loco flew into the elevator beside her, just escaping being crushed by the doors, for Urie had pressed the button without even waiting.

"What did you see?" cried Loco, pursuing her through the lobby.

Finally on the sidewalk she caught her. "What was in there?"

"I don't know. Some kind of officer. He was crying."

"Crying?" Loco's essence curled, twisted, and twined Urie as if her older sister's vision could be ingested into her.

"Yes," repeated Urie.

"But why?" asked Loco.

They walked, speechless, a long way.

"It was grief incarnate," said Urie in a peculiar voice. And she descended into silence again.

Loco, afraid, did not dare interrupt the silence.

CHAPTER 20

The following Tuesday a shot rang out close to the house. The boards shuddered.

In a split second Urie thought: The lover is a ghost come back to repeat, through the same kitchen window, that act that killed the owner of the house.

Mrs. Bishop muttered senselessly, "Mrs. Kanukaris!"

Everybody rushed to the window.

Irene stood, half planted in a little water-filled trench of stagnant overflow, lowering the BB gun from her eyes. At her feet in the mud a large rat flopped in death agony, its underbelly flashing pale white and its claw feet throwing up brown spitballs in their pulsating.

"I made a perfect shot!" she said, coming white-faced to the screen door. Then she slowly put the gun back in the shed.

"What a peculiar thing to do!" said Mrs. Bishop.

But Urie and Loco were both stung with admiration. Their estimation of Irene went way up.

"How did you know it was loaded?" whispered Loco.

"I didn't. It just was."

In the following days Loco became so voluble in praise that Urie was jealous. Pleased with the admiration, Irene began to boast. She boasted so much that at last Urie, with a perfect replica of her mother's voice, said, "What a peculiar thing to do! There was perfectly good rat poison in the cabinet. What was the use of wasting shot?"

Irene smiled faintly. Her creamy-white complexion became a shade more beatific.

A week passed.

On Wednesday, Irene announced that Mrs. Lacey Ransome had invited all three to tea.

"What for?" croaked Urie.

"To see if the United Christian Church wants to hire us as a trio."

"What!"

The meeting of Loco and Urie's eyes, which usually signaled their embarrassed concurrence in cringing at Irene's un-Bishopian pretensions, upon which they spat, was at this moment a junction of shock. To think that of all three it had been Irene who had taken the lead! Irene by such a dire step to change their fortunes!

"But how—What did you—How did you do it?"

"You mean you mentioned hiring, getting paid—money? You told *that* to Mrs. Ransome?" uttered Urie disbelievingly.

"Of course!" Irene affected a completely phony smile. She tossed her head with fake nonchalance as she had seen grown-up women who aped movie stars do.

The June day was hot and clear. Loudly Urie began to joke about God-dom, fools, and putting it over in the pulpit.

"This is what you call 'Rooking Mrs. Ransome.' "

They had not told P.Q. or Mrs. Bishop. For the first time in Ephesus they were taking up the raveling edge of their condition and trying to knit it back. And, with tacit agreement, they did not want their parents to be witness. Urie had not told Zebul either. This exercise in churches for money was irrelevant to her pursuit of truth with him, and she did not want her cashing in on God to complicate the issue.

They left the house all dressed up, in the same dresses they had worn to the Episcopal fiasco. They covered their hope and trepidation with a loud gaggle of chatter. Their dresses swished as they jumped over a rivulet of mud.

The church was an ugly red brick edifice facing an empty lot on Pergamus Avenue. As they neared, its pointed stained-glass windows looked at them accusingly.

"Oh look!" screamed Irene. "Loco Poco's shoes are covered with mud!"
Loco bent over.

"Don't touch them. You'll get your clean white gloves muddy!"

Only Irene would use old-woman's adjectives, thought Urie.

"Well, what'll I do?" moaned Loco.

"You'll just have to go in that field and wipe them off on the grass."

Irene and Urie waited. Loco smiled wryly like a dog at a fire hydrant.
She went to the middle of the field. Studiously she wiped her feet in the
grass. She felt as if she were kneading dough.

"You did it enough!" screamed Irene, furious at the image in Loco's
mind.

"I'll die of hysteria when we start 'Dear God, dear God,' " warned
Loco.

"Hurry up."

People were walking into the church. The three girls stood at the edge
of the vacant lot to make last touches. They patted their hair in place.
They ran their gloved fingers along their front teeth for tartar. They picked
the seams of their stockings straight. Then they assumed paralytic smiles
of piety. Again Urie and Irene pushed the bait, Loco, ahead. Aware of her
position, she began to strut glitteringly.

"Don't do that!" whispered Irene.

The church door stood open. Inside was dark. Suddenly Mrs. Madie
Oggs, a pontifical church lady, swayed out of the gloom. She wore an imposing purple dress ruined by polka dots.

"We're so glad to see you girls. We were so pleased when Mrs. Ransome suggested it. Now if you will just see Mrs. Owens, down by the chancel there . . ."

Mrs. Ogg's voice was a perfumy, voluminous whisper. People turned
around to look. She herded them down the aisle. She used her painted fingernail to prod Loco forward, by pointing it into the small of her back.
Loco wriggled. She went faster; then, like a twisting snake, she began to
run in tiny steps, looking around at everyone with a fresh, excited face.
Irene and Urie, knowing everyone was staring, blushed.

Mrs. Rubella Owens stood by the altar to meet them. She was a gan-
gling woman with a bony face and a lantern jaw.

"Do you want robes?" she asked.

"Robes?" said Loco excitedly.

"No," answered Urie.

"Do you want accompaniment?"

"What accompaniment?" asked Urie, alarmed.

[169

"The organ."

"We sing a capella."

Mrs. Rubella Owens was impressed but nervous. She opened her lantern jaw and made an ugly smile.

"Sit in the sixth row of the choir box," she ordered. "At the signal of my arm you will know when to sing—at the end of the responsive reading, after the sermon."

The organ sounded a loud moolike chord. It was inferior to the Episcopal organ. It made the windowpanes rattle. Velvet church creaks split the wood-beamed ceiling, and the church gave off a smell of purple dust as it filled up.

Suddenly Loco poked Urie. Mrs. Lacy Ransome had entered. She sat in a right-hand pew. She looked at them.

"Look grateful!" mouthed Irene.

The organ suddenly stampeded like a herd of bison. People's whispers were trampled to silence. The minister entered. Rubella Owens made a semaphore with her arm. The choir exploded through a door in the rear of the chancel. Their silk choir robes snapped.

Urie felt hair rise at the back of her neck. Irene's impassive face was a balm to her. But Loco, hanging upon the choir so eagerly, made her want to laugh.

The organ pumped repeats so that the choir could all get to their box. A fizzy gray-haired woman brought up the rear of the line. She was in the last stages of buxom decay and was pouring forth a soprano shriek when she arrived at her seat.

Amen.

Silence.

The congregation sat down.

It seemed as if many eons passed. The church service was long. The sun peeked through the stained-glass windows, outlining the lazy dust particles, red, blue, and yellow, as they hovered in the air. Everything became suspended. Everything took on the color of the stained-glass windows— women's hats, faces. Everything, disembodied, seemed to float, like the dust particles, above the pews. Loco became one of the grains of dust. She floated slowly above herself, turning pink and then yellow. Helplessly she felt herself drift toward the mouths of the congregation. She saw how the dust was being inhaled. Would she too be sucked up these nostrils? Her expression became intense and white. The veins of her temples began to throb violently, fragile blue channels. She was transfixed, trying to keep from being inhaled.

"Forget not Thine own," said the minister.

Suddenly Loco wiped the sweat off her forehead, breaking into a glittering smile. Rueful, she looked around to see if anyone had noticed.

It was time.

Rubella Owens made the sign. She forked her thumb and forefinger into the shape of a sickle and raised it above her ear.

The three girls stood, trembling. Urie kicked Irene's foot. Loco peeped questioningly into Irene's eyes.

Irene was the pitch-giver. She had perfect pitch. But at this moment, although she had risen with them, she seemed oblivious—creamy, well-fed, half-smiling, remote.

Urie kicked her again. With no change of expression, Irene sang, "Do." The "do" was liquid, small and pure. Urie and Loco breathed relief.

The congregation cleared their throats nervously. Hung upon the sight of the three young, uncertain faces, they stared, half blank, half fascinated, preparing themselves for a disgrace.

Urie closed her eyelids once.

They counted a beat, almost audibly.

Loco cocked her head.

" 'Jesus makes my soul to flourish,' " they began, " 'be I ill or sorrowing.' "

The congregation suddenly found something endearing to assauage their nervousness: the small one, fairy-fey, peeking delight from black frightened eyes.

The voices were thin, reedy, pure as straws in the wind. The faces were white with effort. Irene was still expressionless. She had the soprano. She was the leader. At the end of the fourth measure her head pulsated backward. They picked up.

Urie sang alto, Loco tenor, but in a descant higher than Irene. This gave a frail flavor to the Bach chorale. The sound became irresistible. The congregation was full of suspense, and there was that dead quiet denoting the fear that if anyone breathed too loudly the vision of sound would be blown away.

> "That I may my spirit nourish,
> Let me firmly to Him cling.
>
> "I have Jesus, who doth love me,
> He is mine though far above me,
> So I shall not from him part,
> Though rude sorrow break my heart."

The capture was certain. Loco trembled.

Beyond the sickening words, beyond the notion of surrender to a Jesus demanding doom, demanding death, loathsome Jesus, Urie soared. She had to pretend he was Apollo to make herself do it. Apollo was the only god remote enough, impersonal, beautiful enough to make her want to let her spirit cling or be nourished. Caught, her alto grew too strong. She had an impulse to push Irene.

Irene crescendoed.

It was marvelous. Legato love. Legato power of love. It was a lake upon which they three, ice-swans, suddenly saw themselves reflected, clear as a photograph. They were a reality unto themselves. The mood was even more apparent when they modulated, the chromatic so beautiful that it was unbearable. After the change had been accomplished, they flew fantastically free, in pure power.

Irene smiled.

Urie suddenly looked at the congregation. Straight into their eyes: Is it not beautiful?

The congregation was caught. Mrs. Madie Oggs's harness of Sunday dominance broke. She was suddenly a middle-aged, burlap-skinned, fat woman whose wrinkles hung like broken strings, whose blue, wet eyes were her only real feature. She looked like a crinkled beach ball, thought Loco.

At the end of the Bach, the congregation was still.

Irene went down five notes for a new "do." It was for "Liebestraum."

Loco scratched her anklebone silkily with her sandal toe. She must not laugh. If she laughed she would do peepee and all would be lost. Urie looked at her warningly.

Loco tipped her head sidewise. On "Liebestraum" she had the lead.

"Dear God, dear God," they sang.

Loco's voice trembled on the brink of laughter. Her lips went loose. Then she took a trembling breath. With this breath she blotted out all the people. Her voice went clear, high, transparent.

Everyone was paralyzed. There was not one demur, no trace of tremolo. Loco's eyes followed her voice. They disappeared up into her head. Urie and Irene, intense in the chromatics of the harmony, stared at her, scared. The congregation no longer smiled at Loco. For she had turned from a beautiful child to a simple instrument.

We are on high, thought Urie, and we have done it.

When they finished, the silence was strange and rapturous.

"Look! Ten dollars instead of five!" shrieked Irene, opening the envelope at the railroad tracks.

Pulsating with screeches, gloats, rubbings of hands, kisses, golden looks, hand-claspings, they danced in the dirt road, leaving hieroglyphics of their triumph.

"This sure is better than selling the things."

"It is marvelous!" raved Mrs. Bishop as they stood in a circle, boasting and flashing the ten-dollar bill.

"Mrs. Ransome will get us engagements with every church in town."

"The wife of that jackass that looks like a big frog?" asked P.Q.

"Yes."

"Poor cuss. Married to a frog like that, and all he does is talk about Henry James."

"William James," corrected Loco.

"We might end up with a hundred dollars!" claimed Urie.

"What is money?" said P.Q. "Money is only a stand-for. It doesn't exist. It is a symbol for goods or service. It is the fact that you are giving ignorant people an opportunity to hear beautiful music for the first time in their lives—that is a service."

But to Urie it was no service, it was a glittering example of the stupidity and hypocrisy of the world. She stuffed the money in their brass rooster bank and let no one touch it. Three days later Mrs. Madie Oggs called Irene at the high school and engaged them to sing every third Sunday for the rest of the year at ten dollars per engagement.

"Let's go for a walk, Mamma!" said Loco.

Something about the tone of voice in the sweltering day, the possibility of breaking the airlessness of the day, filled Mrs. Bishop with enthusiasm. She got up from her sewing machine. She giggled. She put on her shoes.

Irene led the way. They walked toward Sociological Conditions. From the porches, black faces stared in wonder.

The parade of Bishop women, their footsteps powdery pats, was like a celebration of some lost female rite. Yet they were unaware of their appearance in the dreamless afternoon. An old farmer went by in a Ford specked with dried red mud from hubcap to hood and left them in a cloud of dust. Mrs. Bishop stuck out her tongue.

"This reminds me of when I was a little girl, when I led my neighborhood pack. They were all boys, and one of them was the Saltonstall boy.

We used to put pistol caps on the trolley tracks on Massachusetts Avenue, and then we'd hide behind lamp posts until the horse-drawn trolley came by and hit them. Oh, it was the grandest noise you ever heard!"

"Mamma, remember when we were young we used to make up poems about people we knew?" said Loco. "Remember that afternoon on the piazza and we made up all those rhymes about Mrs. Von Dunkle and rhymed them with uncle and carbuncle?"

"And junkle!" said Urie.

"We laughed for eight hours," said Irene.

Mrs. Bishop planted her feet in the road, put her hands on her knees, leaned forward, and laughed deliciously.

"Make one up now," egged Loco.

"Make one up about Mrs. Ransome," said Urie.

They waited for her moment of intense, silent thinking.

"Mrs. Ransome ate a pellet. All the neighbors round could smell it!"

The atmosphere of the day had become like that day they had first entered the Shack, when Mrs. Bishop had discovered curtains as the solution to poverty. She, a dumpy, small, wobbling figure, was the center of the group. The girls were clustered like spring roses around her, celebrating her, egging her recklessness. Yet she seemed their baby, an unlikely princess with governesses to pilot her. They were old and cynical. That was why they adored her recklessness and inspiration so much. Gay, uncomplaining, Mrs. Bishop was only playing the game of poverty. They, who knew the reality of poverty, were the ones who had to protect her from their belief in it. Their poverty would never be ended until their way of life was ended, until they left home. Their mother's and father's bequest to them was poverty, an outrageous gift, whose frills, whose tapestries, papaya-wood bowls, and irons, harpoons, grand piano, window chairs, and candlesticks were embroidered with the history of the most classical and high-thinking life of historical America. Mrs. Bishop was incapable of suffering from this poverty as the girls did.

"Look!" she said, pointing. "There's a path that leads into the woods! Let's explore!"

They turned. Large padded leaves shaded the blinding glare of the arching afternoon. Mrs. Bishop began philosophizing in loving, excited tones. How good it was they had come to the South! Even though their house was inferior to Thalassia, they would now have a chance to get a good education, a better education than she had ever had. In her day people believed only in finishing schools. They were stupid. "But you! Why, you people have a real opportunity. You know more now at your age than I did when I was twenty-eight!" She began to embroider on the theme of their luckiness. Losing money was unimportant, she said. "Of course I would like you to have this or that, but what do you need all those things for? Half the things I was brought up with were foolishness. Why, when I think how I wasted money!"

The profusion of these thoughts in the secret woods was like a litany expanding the moment beyond its existence, and the girls, feasting on their mother's glittering joy, breathing these words in, rashly insisted on believing them for this occasion, barring off from the edge of their consciousness the truth that smote their hearts. They jumped into her joy as if it could erase the truth.

Loco Poco darted ahead like a hummingbird. Suddenly, turning around, looking exactly like her mother, she whispered, "Look! A haunted house."

They ran up the hill to see.

The house stood in a clearing. It was a replica of a Swiss chalet. A second-floor balustrade engirdled it, supported by rotting square colums. The paint on the house was peeling, giving it the moldy appearance of a shedding camel. Its windows were gaunt and blind, furnished with ragged yellow curtains and brushed by the hanging branches of mammoth oaks. Its disintegration was consummated in the wild weeds and grasses grown up through the porch floor, and in the trooping honeysuckle stifling its banisters. Yet it was not old—perhaps only sixty years old. It was a pretentious imitation of ante-bellum style gone to seed quickly and now presiding over that fake jungle, so near to Niggertown that it excluded all possibility of pedigree.

"It's ours! All ours!" shouted Loco.

Urie gave the rallying cry: "Let's explore."

But Mrs. Bishop put up her hand. "Wait," she warned.

They turned around.

"But no one lives in it!" protested Irene. "You can see that!"

That their own past life was resurrected in this degraded condition so near to them, waiting to be explored, sent them into a state of febrile exultation. It was as if they had a chance, for the first time since they had been in Ephesus, to connect their old high life with their fallen condition. They froze Mrs. Bishop's warnings.

"It—it might be rotten!" she said feebly.

That was nothing. They ran toward it. Their steps were quiet, excited, fast, subversive, and dangerous as Indians'.

"Be careful!" Mrs. Bishop warned again.

But drawn irresistibly, she followed them, half panting in the sun, pushing bushes and vines out of her way.

Loco knocked on the front door.

The sound was hollow. An unknown quality of the former occupants of the house swallowed up the sound so that only the second-rate, stupendous obtuseness of sad mimicry and frills was left, vibrating in the sun.

Loco knocked again. They waited.

"Come on," said Urie impatiently.

They sneaked around the porch. They swarmed like ants. They peered through rotten windows. Clouds reflected in the warped pane.

Then Mrs. Bishop caught up with them. "The kitchen door is open," she said.

Everything changed. Mrs. Bishop took over the lead. Slowly, as if she belonged there, she pushed the door ajar. She entered.

The game became more exciting. In deference, the girls followed her. Everything had the seal of approval. Trespass became sanctified.

It was dark inside.

Mrs. Bishop stopped in a long, dim hallway. A strairway led to an upper floor. The sound of the wind drowsed through the broken screen.

"My eyes are becoming accustomed to the darkness," she whispered.

She moved forward again. She went into a parlor. There was a zither sitting in the corner, covered with dust. The room was lined with long glass bookcases, which, although full of Scott's novels, Victorian volumes, and religious books, reflected their entrance. The furniture was broken. A chair stood upside down, one leg broken. A sofa had been vandalized.

"A family lived here," said Mrs. Bishop tenderly.

She leaned down. A coat was draped over the sofa arm. A needle and thread hung from a half-sewn button.

"Look. This sewing kit came from the Saint Louis World's Fair in eighteen ninety-eight. Look at the gold-embossed letters. That's the one my father went to!"

But the girls separated from her. They went their own ways to explore. Loco and Urie rushed upstairs, giggling with excitement. They swarmed through the bedrooms greedily. Irene went into the kitchen, poked through silver drawers and cupboards. Urie found a typewriter, an old Underwood standard model of 1933. Loco tried the beds. Then she opened a file. There were folders of a business that made printing machines, owned by a Dorset O. Count in Harrisburg, Pennsylvania.

The sounds of tapping, picking, examining, laughing, and rustling alternated with large silences. A room roared with silence. Loco Poco thrust her face into a doorway and laughed.

"If you were going to steal something, what would you steal?" she whispered.

"The typewriter!" answered Urie. "Then I wouldn't have to use P.Q.'s."

For an hour they explored.

Then Irene called down the hallway that the sun was going down in the west.

Each returned to the others. Amazed, after their own separate, outrageous, vicarious sprees of ownership, they seemed weary as if they were spent with the ghosts. They tried to find their mother. She was in an upstairs room.

"It's so late!" she said, surprised.

Slowly they went out the door onto the porch.

Mrs. Bishop turned to lock the door behind her. But there was no lock. She put a stone against it.

In that act the girls saw that she had become a stranger to them. The candlesticks, the umbrella stand, the Teddy-bear spoon—all the artifacts of her existence seemed to be left behind her eyes, obstructing her from them. They could not dislodge her from that disembodied existence, which she now seemed to have left behind in the Count house.

As they traveled back through the woods again she said, "Why did they leave the doors undone? I wonder where they are. Why did they leave? Who are they?"

They reached the cart path leading to the road.

"It's a crime to leave things in that way just to go to rack and ruin. It would almost be better to have taken some of those things. I should have taken the sewing kit that came from the Saint Louis World's Fair. I could have saved it."

"Come on, Mamma," said Irene impatiently now. "We've got to get back to the road before this place gets pitch-black with night."

C H A P T E R 21

In July, Irene and Urie decided to do typing for money. They put up a printed advertisement on the college bulletin board, announcing that they would type papers, theses, or dissertations for ten cents per page. Irene's first paper was on the balance of chemicals in cesspools. It was by a

Chinese student in the School of Public Health, and Irene had to correct the English. Urie thought the idea of how certain sewage bugs ate other sewage bugs, thus keeping a harmony within cesspools, was profound, and told Zebul.

When Urie's appointment with Mr. Huntsucker came in August, she went to the high school in fear and trepidation only to find out that a program of acceleration was being instituted throughout the state because of the impending call-up for military services. Examinations were held, and Irene, Zebul, and Urie took them and passed. Irene was eligible for college after Christmas. Zebul and Urie were eligible the next school year.

"Thank God for this war," breathed Zebul. "Only one more puking year of high school!"

"Just think, in one more year you'll be drafted maybe, if we get into the war."

But it had no reality for them. The battles had not yet begun. So they turned their attention to finding the "answer to life."

"I wonder if President Roosevelt knows the answer to life," said Urie.

They made up a list of adults to ask. It included P.Q., Mr. Huntsucker, Dr. Boehm, Major Hoople, Miss Picke, Henny Pinney, and Mrs. Ransome. They actually did ask Miss Picke, Henny Pinney, and P.Q., but the answers they got disillusioned them.

Miss Picke told them the answer to life was minding your own business. P.Q. went into an oration that stretched over three days and focused on production, service, and education. Henny Pinney told them they wouldn't be asking if they didn't stick their heads in the clouds.

"It is hopeless," said Zebul.

"We know more at our age than any person that I can think of over fifty-one years old," said Urie.

After that they took up quotations.

" 'The unexamined life is not worth living,' " quoted Zebul.

They chewed, mulled, repeated, discussed, masticated, fondled, even kissed Socrates' line. They did this at all odd hours of night and day, while walking, while studying, while sitting under trees. They felt the line might turn out to be the secret formula. If only they could conjure it, perceive it at the correct moment, it might reveal the universe to them. They were sensual and aesthetic about it, like eating cotton candy nonstop for a week.

They quoted other quotations. " 'How could a child of mine spoil an arrangement of perfection?' "—Mrs. Ramsay's line when Prue took the apple from the bowl of fruit in *To the Lighthouse*.

Yet the world continued to turn, and its discrepancies were dizzying in their number. Zebul organized topics. They analyzed the discrepancies under these topic headings. The gap between lip-service and the truth waited behind every lie to make itself known to them in these topic discussions.

"Let's take up the topic of injustice today," said Zebul. "Maybe we can find out something."

"All right." Urie organized her thoughts methodically. "I am poor. But it is not only the fact of being poor. I am also educated. Now P.Q. knows more than other fathers. He is educated."

"Yet rednecks, hot-dog operators, waiters, mill workers, and furnace-repairmen like Daddy make more money than he does," said Zebul in a singsong voice to set the dialogue, to tee Urie off.

"It says that if you honor work and work hard and aren't afraid of crappy jobs, you will be a success."

"It says, though, that if you are educated you will be a greater success than hot-dog operators and rednecks. For you understand the world when you are educated."

As they conducted these dialogues, they breathed together, and their eyes were wrapped into each other's glittering faces.

"Yes! What does a mill worker understand?" asked Urie.

"Nothing."

"I understand the world, for instance."

"But you just said you didn't. That's why we have been asking adults for the answer. How can you be so stinkingly inconsistent?"

"You know what I mean."

"But the fact that you understand what you understand means nothing," said Zebul. "It does not matter about subjects and predicates to get a job in a ten-cents store."

"But even that is not the reason for feeling injustice!"

"What is the reason?"

"I don't know. But look, Zeb. I know education is the reward. But I don't see anybody giving P.Q. a job! He knows Socrates, Nietzsche, Mrs. Roosevelt, economics, the Byzantine Empire, and botany, but does that get him any money?"

Topics became connected with geography. For they carried on their discussion mostly while walking.

Places became of great significance. Some places were the sites of great discoveries. Other places were important because they drew forth certain associations. The railroad tracks were always the place for a discussion of Negroes, heat, or injustice. The library was the site for discussions of hypocrisy and crime.

Some places were good places. Others were bad. Each had its particular aspects. Another topic they discussed was the value of places. The more they walked and talked, the more they felt that Ephesus was their domain. They analyzed the tracks, the roads, and the paths of the town. The railroad tracks, the chip pile, the secret waterfall, the library, and Coble Hill were good places. Bad places were the milk bar, the Baptist church, Lucretia Pile's store, the Main Street of Haw, and Pack Mill Road.

One day Loco Poco attached herself to them on a walk. Zebul complained loudly. "Has she got to come everywhere we do?"

So Urie in compliance warned Loco, "Okay, you horned in on our walk. Now the least you can do is to keep your trap shut and not horn in on our conversation."

They went to Visigoth Castle, a fake replica of one of Ludwig's castles in Bavaria, built by a college secret society. It was ordinarily a lovers' trysting place. There was a stone bench at the very edge of the Fall Line, brinking a seven-hundred-foot drop to forest and farmland below. This had once been the prehistoric sea, and crustacean shells were always being dug up in the flat, feathery forest of green pine and tobacco that stretched below.

"Oh! the ocean!" trilled Loco, stretching her hands over the edge.

"Yah. I dare you to jump!" said Zebul.

She did not so much jump as drop. That was the last they saw of her until, trembling with fear, having climbed down on thin toeholds in granite rocks, holding on to thorn bushes and honeysuckle creepers, they found her, laughing deliciously, on a moss promontory fifteen feet below.

"You could have been killed, you fool!" whispered Urie, the beads of moisture glistening on her upper lip.

Zebul stared at her strangely. He did not understand how she had done it. Had her fall been broken by a pine tree? Had she seen the moss below? Why hadn't she broken a leg?

Ever after this he viewed Loco as voodoo. She had not been afraid. She had made no distinction between her action and herself.

"She's like an extinct animal," he whispered to Urie. "How did she do it?" Then he turned to Loco. "How did you do it?" he asked.

Loco, sensing his new interest in her, played up to him. "I didn't do it," she said. "I *was* it."

"Insane," muttered Urie.

One evening Urie and Zebul were sitting on the platform of the old well. It was dark. Loco came out of the house and, seeing that they did not want her, she headed toward the carpet of dirty aprons and coats that P.Q. had spread upon the yard, and began dancing. Something in the manner of Loco's actions with these linens attracted Zebul's and Urie's attention. Between dancing motions, she stooped, leaning over, to inspect something.

"What are you doing?" Urie asked.

"I'm examining filth. Ugh, what a stench!" she said. She bent down farther.

Into Zebul's mind came a vision of himself the day he had met Urie, when he had stooped down to examine the drunk nigger.

But Urie fell in at once with Loco's ambience, and that cabal of their sisterhood pre-empted her attention away from Zebul. She arose and went to the spot where Loco was examining filth.

Zebul was aware of the darkness and the sea of white, strange shapes —fishnets? waves? whitecaps?—and the two girls floating about them. He was mesmerized into silence. He refused to join them, as if, as he observed their sisterhood in their strange occupation, something important was about to come into his mind. Something which Urie personified already, which he was about to discover.

The scene was beautiful. The girls flowed and flitted. The femininity charmed him. Their figures and the aprons and coats melded into each other in the gathering dark until the linen became more radiant than the girls.

It reminded him of a snapshot which Mrs. Bishop had showed him once of the three girls as little children. They had worn flower wreaths around their heads and white dresses blowing against the backdrop of the ocean.

Zebul could not understand what Loco and Urie were saying to each other, for they spoke in ravished, giggling tones, in their wheezy, wind-reed voices, which were like whispers.

"Do you realize, if it hadn't been for us, no dirty nigger could have made this apron filthy with crap? Because we sewed every one of these."

"I put the grommets in every one!"

"I can't tell hamburger grease from egg yolk, can you?"

"Look, Urie. Chocolate pudding!"

"How can you tell?"

"Look! Peeee-ee-ugh! I wish it really had the smell of chocolate pudding."

Loco laughed. Urie laughed. Their tinkles, suddenly to Zebul both the same, floated up like bells. At the same moment that they seemed to have merged into the darkness he heard the kitchen door open. Mrs. Bishop's figure was outlined against the baggy screen door from the light inside.

"Could you kiss this apron, Urie?"

"Ugh."

"I could kiss it."

"Why should I kiss dirt?" asked Urie pugnaciously.

"It would be wonderful," Loco said. "It would taste like a chocolate-pudding kiss."

All at once Mrs. Bishop, searching in the darkness for them called, "What are you doing out there?"

They jumped guiltily, and the spell was broken.

"Come in now," called Mrs. Bishop. "It's getting very damp."

As they sat around in the kitchen, too hot from the open oven, which had just dispensed Parker House rolls, Zebul knew what the something was. Loco and Urie, completely divorced from that spell that had so mesmerized them, had forgotten filth and the aprons. But Zebul had discovered them.

After supper he got Urie away from the table. He told her, "You have discovered the Cult of Ugliness!"

What was ugliness? she asked herself. Why had ugliness become important? "This is important!" she whispered, seizing him by the elbow and pulling him, as if he had created Archimedes' deduction from displaced water in the bathtub. Urie reminded Zebul that their first conversation had been this. He had asked her if she had seen True Beauty. "Do you remember?"

How could he forget? It seemed a thousand years ago now. It was engraved upon him, like initials upon a tree.

"What is the difference between beauty and ugliness?" he asked.

"It's in the eye of the beholder."

"But that's a big cliché."

"I know that. Yet Greta Garbo is an example of beauty. *Everybody* knows she is beautiful. Nobody disagrees. Even I think she is beautiful," said Urie. "So there must be some recognizable beauty."

"Who cares about beauty?"

"Beauty is crap."

"Beauty is sentimental."

"Beauty is only talked about by old ladies. It doesn't belong in the modern world."

"Beauty has no place with technology."

"Puke on beauty."

Their comments, however, were a cover-up for that element of their psyches which remembered its once complete domain. Talking about beauty simply made it slip away. When they had fallen, beauty had escaped. Beauty was something in the past. It might exist again in a utopian and unobtainable future, but it did not exist in the present. Its strange quality was that it was recognizable. But the moment they recognized beauty, it hurt them. They were made so sad by its loss that they were almost at the point of tears. For now that they had grown up, its remembrance only conjured its loss. Just as in the photograph Urie, Loco, and Irene had been beautiful against the ocean, so once Zebul had been beautiful. He had been happy, indestructible, impervious, as when he had never known that Haw was a lowdown place. And Urie had been beautiful looking at the uncomprehending reflection of herself in the sun and water of the ocean. But she had ended up in Niggertown. Reality had come to them. Beauty had gone.

Thus all hope lay in ugliness. For beauty was dead and flat to them. The world continued to preach the way of beauty, but it was a hoax. Such beauty was an untrue replica, a shroud of known beauty, like the pictures in Sunday-school pamphlets. Their way lay in ugliness. There was something forbidden in ugliness. People preached against it. People turned away from it. Ugliness lay untouched, available, unwanted by others, free to them, undiscovered.

So Zebul and Urie began to seek out ugliness. Dead ugliness, old ugliness, new ugliness, smelling ugliness, lonely ugliness, desperate ugliness. They talked ugliness, breathed ugliness, and lived ugliness.

Through the shoots and blossoms of waning August they went for walks, ignoring the perfume, and searching assiduously for ugly places. They went to the sewage plant. They stared down through grilled iron rails into the water gutters of the town. They walked through Niggertown, counting outhouses. They peered into the open maws of shacks. They looked at lonely chicken-wire fences that surrounded the power plant. They picked up discarded candy-wrappers and other refuse in the road to inspect it. They placed their fingertips against rusty barbed wire until it pricked them.

"You know why we seek ugliness?" he asked her.

"Why?"

"Because the world is ugly. And now that we are in life and see the world all around us, we know that we must find out everything about the world."

"It is part of our search for truth!"

"Yes! But the real truth is," he whispered, "there is no difference between beauty and ugliness at all."

A strange thing happened. As they sought out ugliness, they actually began to like it. The power plant became a place of strange, even exalted comfort. They began to discover in the smelling, the stinking, the hideous, the deserted, the neglected places, something secret. Since everyone else despised, ignored, deplored, or spat upon these places, the secret element of ugliness took on for them this positive flavor. The more ugly or more deserted a place was, the more virgin, untapped, and potent was its possibility.

"Ugliness is juiciness."

"The very dirt, like Number Two, reeks. That is what makes it juicy. If it weren't describable, it would be nothing."

"Then the Cult of Ugliness is proof against nothingness!"

"No. It is more important than that. We are operating in a universe of cause and effect. Our destinies are involved in the Cult of Ugliness. It proves our power!" said Zebul.

For ugliness was the reverse of beauty. To cultivate ugliness meant to tap the pulsating essence of which both beauty and ugliness were manifestations. As they cultivated ugliness, as they identified it, as they actively began to love it and join themselves in it, they felt themselves enlarge in mastery. They were breaking down the categories that fooled their compeers.

One day just before school began Zebul asked, "Am I ugly?"

It took bravery to do this.

She would have answered "Yes" at once. But, as if to make him aware that her honesty was burning him into the elect, she looked at him coldly. She inspected him closely. Why was he ugly? she asked herself.

"Yes, you are," she finally answered. "In the first place, your hands are ugly because they are dirty. In the second place, you always wear those corduroy pants, which are practically caked onto you. They make that ponky noise when you walk so I always know who is coming in school."

He looked down the road. She could see that her words affected him deeply, because she could hardly hear him breathe. Then his hands began to tremble.

But after three minutes of silence he began to speak in a precise voice which indicated that he was subordinating his emotions to truth. "My ugliness has the squalor of poverty in it."

She agreed, admiring him more and more.

"The dirty hands, for instance. Also the corduroy pants. But I will not think about the squalor. I will deliberately not think of it. I have more important things to think about."

And that slow, lacerating burn which she knew in him so well finally conquered as a strand of hair fell over his plum-shaped eyes.

They grew closer in this laceration of personal shames. It was as if they had faith that bringing the Cult of Ugliness straight into themselves would accomplish something in their knowledge of the world. Thus they were willing to experiment this way with each other.

When school opened that September, all the repulsion of that school world served to reinforce their discovery of each other in their plane of analytical isolation.

It was Urie's turn.

But she did not ask him to call her ugly, as he had asked her. Her awareness of her own ugliness came in an indirect, ignominious way, almost as if the presence of the Hi-Y brought everything to her again, so that she could not justify her shame and resentment.

One day after school, when they had climbed the chip pile she blurted, "Are you my boy friend?"

"Don't use those words."

"But . . . I'd like to have a boy friend. I always wanted a boy friend and never had one."

He turned away from her.

"I'm only telling you because I'm honest."

"That's weak," he said with disgust.

"Don't you have respect for fact?"

"I mean the fact that you want a boy friend. You only want one just because everybody else has one."

"I don't!"

"You just want to fit in!"

"I don't!"

"You do too. And you never will. So why do you even want to try?"

When he turned to see her eyes, vacant and blue as an idiot's and as large as the sky, he was afraid of what he had done.

"How could you want to fit in?" he cried viciously. "You are better than they are!"

No answer.

"They are dumb!" he screamed.

No answer.

The silence petrified him.

"Think of Olive Akers. Does she know who Tolstoy is?"

[185

"No."

"Does she know you?"

"What do you mean?"

"Does she have any idea what you are? Who you are?"

"No."

"But she goes to the Milk Snack. If you want to be like everybody else, you want to go to the Milk Snack. Do you want to sit in the Milk Snack? Do you want to joke with Bill Ticken and Don Mackey? Do you want to date Don Mackey? Do you want to be in the dirt column?"

Yes, she did. Urie began to laugh hysterically. It drove him mad.

"Milquetoasts. Andy Gumps. Chinless dullards. They are stereotyped. You want to be like them! But you can't. You have a long nose. You are ugly, you think. But you are beautiful. Your long nose is definite. It's definable. It's long, straight, and shapely. You are definite. You are so definite, Urie. But they call that ugly. People like a squat coed queen sitting on a float with a rubbery nose and dumb eyes and red rubber lips, smiling, and crown her the queen of Ephesus. They parade it around. But you are original."

Urie stood up. "Don't praise me!" she said.

In his final blaze of glory, born of his refusal to allow her into the ranks of the millions with normal desires, he spun his relentless and cruel words.

"Not only are you original, but every act you do belies that you want to be like them. You cultivate ugliness. You dress horribly. You act like a witch. You act so much like a witch that you look just like a witch. It is very peculiar. You cannot be ordinary, and since you pretend to be ugly, your ugliness is not ordinary either. You are a freak. You capture people and absolutely amaze them with your ugliness! Urie"—and he lowered his voice to a whisper—"that's why ugliness is necessary!"

She stood staring at him with hatred.

The nadir of heat that these igneous thrusts, these dynamic pulls and pushes brought them to tempered them. The contemplation of their shame, an illicit act together, brought their relationship to the strength of steel. They became welded in a way neither had ever imagined the first day they had made their peregrination to Haw and discussed True Beauty. To have reached such a depth of exploration of ugliness that they could have plumbed the depths of each other in this way was mysterious to them.

They knew that, having said these things to each other, they would repeat them over and over, like incantations in a mystery. Together they had arrived at the rehearsal of a mystery. Sometimes they actually talked of themselves living in the mystery, so real did their exotic plane of life become to them. Here they were, in the world, floating around among the artifacts of nature, teen-agers, milk bars, parents, home-economics classes—all the appearances of real life. They snortingly confided to each other how psychologists would say that they had an energy to master the world based on the sexual power of puberty.

Zebul said these words distinctly: "The sexual power of puberty."

And between the everlasting crescendo of terrible longings, terrible anguishes, and their obsession with the pursuit of ugliness, there seemed to be implied some gesture, some deed, some unspeakable act that would culminate and define the nature of the universe. An act that would put a stop to the tension of their interminable pursuit and spill them like gods to that remembered place, like the extinct Sargasso Sea at the end of the Fall Line, where gods lived and breathed.

C H A P T E R 22

*K*ings Row came to the Pick Theater the last day of September. It was this movie that catapulted Urie and Zebul into that deed that had seemed so inevitable that summer.

It was Saturday, and they looked longingly at the pictures under the marquee. Robert Cummings stood on the stile with Cassie Tower, played by Betty Field. Ronald Reagan was making love to Ann Sheridan on mailbags in a train depot. Her black-stockinged legs were waving in the air. Claude Rains was looking evilly out the window of a creepy Victorian house.

Usually Urie and Zebul never thought about movies. They knew they could not go. But in that way in which high-school students learn the underdrift of the new world before it arrives, they had heard rumors of *Kings Row*.

They passed the marquee. They did not speak.

In back of Dowson's, Zebul squinted against blinding sun. "We've got to go to *Kings Row*."

"We can't spend our *savings* on movies when we have to save for college!" Urie was alarmed, thinking of the brass rooster.

"Coca-Cola bottles, fool!" was Zebul's answer.

Making money for such a specific purpose as movies was a new view of life for Urie. Movies were pleasure. Movies were dispensable. Movies were immoral. They required money. They were a waste of time. Empty

Coca-Cola, Nehi, Pepsi, and RC Cola bottles from people too lazy to take them back to collect the two cents made the reverse pole of waste and extravagance. To retrieve one waste to commit another seemed marvelous. Not only was it cheap, it was trashy. It demanded complete dedication to spendthriftism of time. It involved wallowing in every ugly place that they had sought in the universe—empty lots, high dusty grasses, gutters, parking lots, trash barrels, basements, and store backs.

Zebul and Urie threw themselves into the occupation with the same zeal that they had in studying. They separated to cover more territory and find more bottles.

At twelve noon they met in back of Dowson's to compare.

"You only got five!" accused Zebul.

He had found nine. They had achieved only fourteen between them.

She was so mortified that he suggested the old trick of the trade: steal empties from the cases back of the store, go cash them in in front. Dowson's was onto this trick, though. They had to go to the back of the A & P. In an empty case there they found nine more. They took them to Dowson's. A beefy man looked at them suspiciously from Dowson's counter. But he handed out the forty-six cents.

What should they do? they pondered. Movies cost thirty-five cents each. They had to get twenty-four cents more.

"Let's steal it," said Zebul.

There was a long silence.

"Where from?" Urie whispered at last. Her face was white in the hot sun. Her knees felt deliciously weak.

"From the Episcopal church," he said.

Her eyes glittered and met his in one supreme moment of understanding. Where else did you think I meant? his eyes seemed to say. Where else but the church could you mark the meaning of theft and waste?

They walked through Main Street and down, the same way she and her mother and sisters had walked to the Laurelo Wildwood Gift Shop. They approached the church. Its green lawn grass blades shone in the afternoon sun.

Zebul led the way. They entered by the cloister. He clanked his hobnailed boots on the stones. The echo of his noise beat strangely in the ears. He did it again. He was trying to test the universe, exploring the qualities of time and space.

"Shshsh. They might hear you."

But he paid no attention. In his eyes was something she had never seen, a strange, antagonistic power that was refined to an ecstatic pinpoint of light in his pupils. She was spellbound. She felt that she was with a stranger whom she was following blindly, utterly dependent on his power and untouchable because of it.

They entered into the old church, where, now darkened from the outside, this triumphant antagonism seemed to expand in front of her eyes.

"O replica of truth, created by the blind, open up to us your false money, your sterile, fake gold. Conception of fools, we despise you. We pity you, for your existence is the existence of chimeras!"

At the end of this speech he uttered a snort of secret pleasure.

"Shut up! I'm going to die on this spot if you keep that up!"

At that moment he spotted the poorbox. It was hand-carved, made of mahogany in the shape of a birdhouse. It was nailed to a wooden beam that held up the balcony, which had been used during Civil War days for the slave congregation.

"There it is!" He pounced on it. He jiggled it. "There *is* money!"

"But how are we going to get it out?"

Zebul discovered that the box would move all the way around on the pivot of its nail, like clock hands. He turned it upside down to jiggle the coins out. The clank-jangle sound expanded in the depth of the little church, where Loco had hidden Amy Grispin White's shoes, where they had first tried to waylay Major Hoople for a job. The clank echoed across the beams and down the perfumed pews.

"I'm afraid," whispered Urie.

"Shut up. Get my jackknife out of my pocket."

She pushed her hand into the pocket and found the jackknife. "It's lucky you didn't lose it. There's a hole in your pocket."

"Open it."

She handed it to him open.

At that moment a dime fell out of the upside-down slot.

"Look! A dime! And I didn't even have to poke with the knife."

"This is a cinch!"

"Now we only need fourteen more cents!" He inserted the blade of the knife into the slot. The motion was professional, light, deft, and swift. He moved the blade back and forth, trying to feel the coins.

"Mmmmp!" he breathed.

A quarter fell to the stone floor. Urie grabbed it while it was still rolling.

Their triumph was so assured that they now became tight and professional in absorbing, as if a wasted motion would jeopardize everything. They were concentrated. He took the quarter from her hand. He turned the coin box right side up. He took a large dirty handkerchief out of his left-hand pocket and wiped the coin box affectedly for fingerprints.

"Give me the dime." He put the dime back into the poorbox.

For the first time since they had begun stealing, he grinned. "I give this act meaning," he proclaimed. "We only need twenty-four cents. We take the quarter. We return the dime. The act becomes pure. You understand?"

She nodded.

When they left the church the sun blinded them. They could hardly see.

"Brrrr! Do you realize how cold it was in there?" whispered Urie.

Walking up Main Street, they began to giggle. They grew very warm. The change of temperature created a sense of unreality in them. They did not even think of their deed. The soles of Urie's feet began to absorb the white heat of the sidewalk through her sneakers. The appearance of everything was normal. Yet it was as if they had embarked on a course of action that included all poles. Freezing church, molten sidewalk. Theft, the mask of virtue. Poverty, the chimera of poverty, extravagance, flinging to the winds seventy cents. Dark. Blinding light.

"If we had tried to earn that money for something important, we could never have done it in three hours!" she said.

"But movies *are* important," he argued. "Movies feed our brains. We have brains superior to the multitude. We will make something, create something, out of this movie. We ought to be able to go to it. It is unfair not to be able to go to it. We need it. It's a necessity. Don't we deserve it more than other people, since we will *make* something out of it? It is more important, even to the world, for us to go to this movie today, than for fifty people to donate fifty dollars to fifty churches in fifty days."

He was silenced by the fact that they had arrived at the Pick. A fat girl sat in the glass booth, chewing gum. He handed the money in. Two pink tickets flapped out of a metal clip like tongues. A penny rolled down from the change machine.

"We have this penny left over. You take it."

The moment they entered, the air-conditioning enveloped them in ice-cold darkness. The penny was still sweaty from Zebul's hand. They went way to the front and sat down. In a few seconds the picture began. The credits came on. There was still sweat trickling down Zebul's collar. There was sweat all through Urie's hair. But the sweat was cold now. All trace of the world of searing sunlight had vanished. They became sucked up into the ice-cold screen world with almost religious exaltation.

Zebul became Parris Mitchell immediately. Mrs. Bishop was a fat Maria Ouspenskaya; the Chopin Preludes were simply transfers. Zebul decided to be a doctor. P.Q. was even Claude Rains, and Cassie-Urie was revealed to be his incestuous victim.

Next to Zebul, Urie fought not to be Cassie Tower. Maybe Loco was, or a combination of them both, but not she alone. For half an hour she foiled Zebul by becoming Ronald Reagan, but then sat up, choking back her scream, when he felt the blankets and found his legs were gone. It was the worst moment of the film—even worse than when P.Q.–Claude Rains committed Sophoclean suicide after Cassie Tower went crazy and drowned.

At the end of the movie they were weak. The sun was still pouring down. The heat was atrocious. The world welcoming them from the cold wind-machines of darkness was glittering and unrealizable. It had been revealed to them that afternoon of their greatest license as the reverse side of their dreams. Dirty psychology. Counterfeit. There was weakness behind genius. There was madness behind logic. But the glamour of these miseries, like the dazzling heat and freezing darkness, outlasted all other impressions that year. When the ordinary life of their limitations, their family routine, their school life, their mundanities salved that glimpse of the danger lurking behind the pursuit of the highest, only the glamour was left. It beat in their veins with the same rhythm as the experience: light—dark; heat—cold; theft—extravagance.

One day in the Negro graveyard on the railroad tracks, which marked the halfway point between Urie's and Zebul's houses, Zebul said, "Now that we've committed crimes, we've got to do better in school this year than last year. Not only must we continue to make A's, but we have to really learn. Books reveal the secrets of the universe."

"What you're saying is: not only must we steal, we must also learn."

"I'm saying: not only must we learn, we must steal. We must learn in the day and steal in the night. We must accomplish the poles of both!"

So they became magicians. They cast three balls in the air and caught them simultaneously. The ease of the feat confounded them. They brushed past every apparent logical inconsistency. They said it was in the name of a higher truth.

Urie was elected editor of the literary magazine, *The Scroll*.

"Extracurricular activity is crap."

"I know that, Zebul Walley. You don't have to tell me."

"Those kids on *The Scroll* and the *Proconian*. What do they do? All they do is repeat their fathers' opinions like parrots."

But Urie could not resist the honor.

When *The Scroll* was ready to be mimeographed and there was not enough material for its pages, Zebul helped her. They both wrote stories, poems, and jokes. Zebul stayed up late those nights during the year, working in the brilliantly lit little school office, clacking the mimeograph machine to get the magazine out.

One day Urie said, "Let's send *The Scroll* to the President."

She knew Zebul would say, "What is the President? History is false. Let's not confuse ourselves with sociology."

But instead, a look of secret inspiration crossed his face. There was something outrageous and grandiose in this idea that appealed to him— like stealing.

That night they stayed up late. Zebul stole a sheet of expensive Bond paper from Huntsucker's office and began composing a letter.

Oct. 19, 1940
Ephesus High School

The White House
Washington, D.C.
Dear Mr. President:

As members of the graduating class of Ephesus High School we are pleased to present you with this current issue of our literary magazine, *The Scroll* . . .

"I can't believe we'll be in college next fall, Zebul, can you?" Urie suddenly interrupted with utter irrelevance.

"Shut up. Let me finish typing this letter!" "We sincerely hope that you like it," he wrote. "Like it"? or "enjoy it"? he wondered.

"Like it," said Urie.

He put down "like it." In the next paragraph he finished.

With all good wishes we are

Sincerely:
Urania Bishop, Editor
Zebulon Vance Walley, Associate Editor

Later that night, when they dropped the package down the chute at the post office, they felt melancholy. They were empty after the rich excitement of writing it.

"Do you think he'll read it at breakfast, or at supper?"

"At breakfast, over orange juice."

"At the White House, or at Warm Springs?"

"Crap. He probably won't read it anywhere at all!" said Zebul with perverse self-contempt. If he could not be initiating, then at least he could cruelly stamp his own productions. "What do Presidents care about us? Do you really think a President cares?"

"You mean you led us on for nothing?" Urie kicked him.

"Well, it was your idea, wasn't it?" He laughed.

In the next five weeks, they forgot it.

Almost at Christmastime, a letter arrived, addressed to *The Scroll,* Ephesus High School. The envelope said *The White House,* and it had no stamp.

Urie saved it secretly in her blouse, and that afternoon she and Zebul opened it in the Negro graveyard.

The letter read:

December 20, 1940

Dear Miss Bishop and Mr. Walley:

The President was delighted to receive his copy of *The Scroll* and wishes to thank you for sending it to him. Although he is very busy, he wanted me to give you his thanks personally.

He is always very interested in what the students of the nation are thinking and doing.

With warmest regards,
Marguerite LeHand
Secretary to the President

For an hour Zebul and Urie sat in the graveyard, poring over this letter. They commented and remarked upon every sentence in it. Urie said that it was a strange miracle to think of the President reading *The Scroll.* Zebul said it was funny for the President even to say the words: *The Scroll.*

The President became almost sacrosanct in their minds. He was like balm to the misanthropic rebellious questioning they had dedicated themselves to. When they looked at the President's pictures in the post office they felt warm and inspired almost to the point of tears. There seemed to be no rhyme or reason to this sentimentality. It was against their stated creed of logic. But they did not care. All they knew was their feelings. They gave way to them. They believed that the President really was noble. He would take care of their country. They loved his aristocratic voice and his easy smile. All those ideas that Urie had been brought up with against

[193

the NRA, WPA, and PWA now changed in her head. A benevelent father image began to replace the dry, chopping dogmatism of P.Q.

She kept her love for the President secret. She would not have dared to reveal it to P.Q., for he would have thought of her: the poor cuss. In fact, neither Urie nor Zebul ever showed the letter to anyone. They put it in Zebul's little house, in his correspondence file, in a special place. And there, together, was the only place that they indulged their growing love for the President.

One day Urie impulsively told her sisters about the *Kings Row* church theft. She described everything in detail: how cold it was, how Zebul had tipped over the box, what Zebul said, how hot it was on the street. Mrs. Bishop was in the kitchen. P.Q. was not home. Urie spoke in a low, quick voice, accentuating every word.

Two things happened because of her telling this. First, a new image of Zebul as an outlaw began to form, tinged with danger, grittiness, foreignness, and meanness, intensely effective. If he had been important before because he was a boy, he now became even larger because he was a thief. They felt all the orgy of licentious freedom in the idea of theft, while the onus of wickedness fell on Zebul.

The second thing was that the world opened up for Loco and Irene just as it had for Urie. Urie, by telling them, was solidifying the idea of that act. By their acceptance it became not only legal but possible in the future. Not only was the act of stealing to get things they wanted; it was the living proof that the system could be beaten. Money was ostensibly the insuperable obstacle to their lives. But stealing meant money was nullified. The world of barriers was nullified. The possibility was wide open before them. It was easy. You took what you wanted. The prospect was dazzling.

The style of Urie's telling was at first like a black mass—Urie the preacher, Zebul the image, stealing the chalice; the substance was justice, and the deification of the act a resurrection to that life of freedom they had lived before they ever came to Ephesus. Stealing showed that the world was not the way people said it was. It furthermore justified their poverty by showing that it was not hopeless. Its justification lay in the fact that they were unjustly deprived.

But beyond the theology, the simple fact that Zebul and Urie had actually gone to the movies on stolen money and that they could do the same delighted Loco and Irene. The hypocrisy of trying to be good was demolished. It became the same thing as burning up the back side of the barn— an extravagance, a freedom, a delight, a beautiful wickedness.

Loco cackled and jumped up on one foot and then the other with glee. "Where shall we steal?"

"The ten-cents store."

"No! Count's house."

"Oooooh! It's scary! I'd really be scared to do it."

"Loco, you stole Amy Grispin White's shoes."

They brayed.

"The whole thing is, you can't get caught."

This commotion of joy brought Mrs. Bishop smiling to the edge of their group. As one who senses by the changes in intonation, in the laughter, that something very important has happened and is being enjoyed, she wanted to share it with them. She was like a child again, that rapt princess asking to be surrounded by them. She asked breathlessly, "Who got caught? What did you do?"

They hesitated in a pause of silence.

Then Loco said, "Mamma, Zebul and Urie stole money from the Episcopal church and guess what! They went to the movies on it!"

There was great awe in Mrs. Bishop's face. The news scared her. She was silent.

Urie and Irene studied her expression for definitive disapproval. But seeing that she was scared instead, they became inspired. They became reckless. It was the exact opening they needed to begin the work of conversion. Urie went to work. She repeated the black mass. But this time it came out pure comedy. She could not help it. Something about her mother's being scared enticed her to embroider it. Everything was included, the theology, the reasons for stealing; she enacted all the details until the whole episode reeled before Mrs. Bishop's face like a Charlie Chaplin pantomime.

Mrs. Bishop, in spite of herself, began to laugh. It really was like burning the barn. Outrageous. Funny, although it continued to scare her. Her fear made it even funnier. Everybody knew it was wrong to steal. What mother would ever say it was right for her family to steal? Yet she was too honest not to admit these feelings. Her loyalty to her family came first. The amoral aspect of her nature was brought out.

"I don't know what people would think about me, but I just don't care," she said. "We are different, that's all. I'm not saying it's good to steal, but what do these old hypocritical fogies know anyway?"

Irene and Urie hooted in triumph.

It was the same as with the Sawyer medal that Urie had won in fifth grade. Or the booby prize that Loco had won in the potato race on the maiden voyage of the *Cristobal* in the Panama Canal because she was so cute with her long black curls. Stealing was not stealing to Mrs. Bishop. It was another discovery that the family had made, a perverse variation of Horatio Alger. If the church had to be stolen from to succeed, then go ahead and do it. Sometimes young people had to go to the movies. It was good to outwit the world.

But stealing did not become a reality until one Saturday when Zebul suggested that they go steal candy and cookies from the dime store to eat while listening to records in Hill Hall.

He planned the major blocking as if it were a ballet. Irene was decoy. She had to go to the cosmetics counter and ask for Stench Oil, a nonexistent deodorant, diverting the clerk while he and Urie picked and stole. Loco was to walk up and down and be a watchdog. If she saw anybody beginning to look Urie and Zebul's way, she was also to request something they did not have.

"But I want to actually steal!" she protested.

"You can't this time," ordered Urie strictly.

"If I ask for Stench Oil, they'll know it's a gag and they'll be suspicious," complained Irene.

"Make up any name you want. But be sure they don't have it!" snapped Zebul, impatient. People ought to have ingenuity and make up their own improvisations.

"I know! Call it Armide!" suggested Urie.

The last instructions Zebul gave were to Urie. "There's one thing to remember. You have to be absolutely blatant. Don't try to hide the goods. Wave them in the air if necessary. Talk while doing. And then walk out holding them right out in broad daylight."

On signal, they swarmed into the dime store. Zebul and Urie waited for Irene to engage. As soon as they saw Irene's mouth asking for the Armide, they moved forward. Loco jiggled up and down the aisles, half giggling, half talking to herself. Her eyes darted blackly in and out, catching the lights of the popcorn machine. She stubbed her toe against a lady's foot.

"Oh, excuse me—" she began.

At that moment she saw Zebul signal to Urie. She looked away and jittered past the lady, who stared, believing the child to be feeble-minded.

Zebul and Urie made their selection. Zebul concentrated on hard crackers with raisins in them. Urie took fifteen chocolate candies resembling overblown cow turds, which she knew were filled with lumpy, heavy peppermint cream. Zebul filled his pockets. Urie filled her skirt pockets till they bulged, and then filled one more hand with candies, and the other with the raisin crackers.

"Let's go!" Zebul ordered. Picking up another pile of crackers for good luck, he shouted, "Loco, come on! What are you doing over there?"

Irene, seeing them go, behind the shaking head of the Armide clerk, turned and followed.

"Did you get the peppermint candy? Did you get it?" demanded Loco, pecking at them.

"Shut up! Not here!" warned Zebul. Loco was so elated that she wandered into the street in front of an automobile. Adeptly she stepped out of the way as it slammed on its brakes.

"I feel pregnant, I'm so loaded down." Urie giggled.

"You look fat."

"You waddle." Loco snickered.

"I do not."

"If that car had squashed Urie, peppermint creams would be mashed all over Main Street!" Loco laughed. "You did get 'em, didn't you, Urie?"

"Yes."

"The orange Snickers too?"

"I wouldn't think of stealing trashy orange Snickers."

"But I wanted some. I told you I did!"

"These chocolates are melting. Ugh! Hurry up!" Urie pushed.

They swarmed into Hill Hall. Zebul made Irene sign for Beethoven's "Eroica" and the "Appassionata" Sonata, plus the Brahms Fourth. He and Urie ran up the stairs and chose the record cubicle farthest from the main door. They slammed the door, knelt on the floor, spread out the goods, sat down around them in a circle, and then put on the light.

"Oh, the chocolates. Oh, mmmmmm! Oh, it's marvelous!" cried Loco. "I never had so much fun in all my born days."

They began to laugh. They laughed until tears streamed down their cheeks.

Then they put on the "Eroica" Symphony and began to eat. They gorged themselves. Zebul turned the sound up loud so that no one could hear them eating or chortling.

When the "Appassionata" Sonata began they fell into a subdued mood. Zebul took a Number 2 pencil and wrote on the wall: "We died inside while listening to the Appassionata." They all laughed at this.

When it came time to go, they tried to pick up all traces of the chocolates and raisin-cracker crumbs. But Loco's last half-eaten chocolate was left. Nobody noticed it. It was round and fat and still had her teethmarks in it.

Many weeks later they told Mrs. Bishop about this escapade.

For this one rehearsal made them initiates. It opened the sluicegates. It was not that they would keep on stealing. It was that they had stolen. They could steal. They had proved it.

The open espousal of stealing made a palpable difference in their family life. But there was a strange feature of it. They never openly told P.Q. or forced him to answer. He heard them telling Mrs. Bishop. He was reading the *Wall Street Journal*. But he did not move or crackle the paper once. He refused to acknowledge. He acted as if he did not know. He heard every word perfectly, but he pretended he didn't. He ostentatiously ignored everything about the subject.

People learn on their own, was his presumption. He did not believe in morals, punishment, or commands. They would learn better by doing. Furthermore, he did not admire docility in children. That was why he always took perverse pleasure in Loco's bad grades. Stealing, however, he looked down upon as beneath his contempt. So he refused to confront it. His own questionable activities, his relentless search for some woman to invest in his business, was, in his view, part of the constructive process of service and profit.

Thus the family took careful pains to protect P.Q. by not confronting him with their new-found pattern of freedom. They finally did not talk about it around him. Or they stopped laughing and talking about it if he came into a room.

C H A P T E R 23

"Urie, we're having Hi-Y initiations on Friday. We would like you and Irene to join." Opal Granger issued this invitation, sticking her head into the *Scroll* office, just after Christmas vacation.

Urie and Irene discussed it. Mrs. Bishop stopped her sewing machine and listened. She tried to control the glimmer of exultation that lit her eyes.

"It's crap," said Urie.

"Yeah."

"It's crap, *but*."

"Yeah," said Irene.

"It's crap, but we better join it."

"Yeah."

"Oh, the price of success."

"Yeah. And we've got to make black robes," said Irene.

"Black robes!" cried Urie. "I forgot the black robes!"

Mrs. Bishop made the Hi-Y robes out of leftover black cloth which she had saved since they had dressed up as witches for Halloween and walked with lighted pumpkins along the beach.

"We should have had these black robes when we sang in the church!" said Loco, watching Irene try hers on.

"They're perfect!" raved Mrs. Bishop.

The sight of Mrs. Bishop's blackened teeth in her triumphant smile smote Urie. The awfulness of her mother's pleasure was a cage. Yet she laughed an unholy laugh of complicity.

The ceremony was held in the home-ecomonics room annex on Friday, January 23. There was a green carpet on the floor, and the room was fixed to look like a living room so the students of home economics could sweep it, fix it, and decorate it. Pictures hung on the walls, and sofas sat on the floors waiting.

The girls wore soft cashmere sweaters and skirts and saddle shoes. Urie and Irene stood near the doorway, their robes in paper bags. They felt dry and scared.

"Okay, girls, let's start the meeting," called Muffy Playhorn, the Hi-Y adviser, a Phys. Ed. teacher.

Girls sat down on the sofas and floors in groups. One girl began talking about dues, funds, and expenses.

Ora Mae Sissingoss asked, "Has anyone a suggestion to add to the motion of spending two hundred dollars to help with the Senior Prom?"

Judith Hedgebeth made a resolution that they should spend the same money to aid "some poor person or something for Easter instead. You know," she said.

There was a discussion to and fro. Finally a vote was taken. The poor-basket vote was defeated in favor of the Senior Spring Prom, with an amendment to raise ten dollars at the next meeting for a poor basket.

Olive Akers tiptoed across the room to Urie and Irene. "Your recommendation will be coming up next," she whispered importantly.

Before the words were out of her mouth, Opal Granger whipped her platinum-blond hair in a sporty gesture and announced, "All right, girls, now we come to the initiations."

Everyone turned to stare at Urie and Irene.

"Will the candidates please leave the room?" said Opal Granger. "It's the rule that all discussion of candidacy remain secret."

"You all go to the girls' room and put on the robes," suggested Olive Akers. "This is only a formality. They don't really say anything—but you're not supposed to listen. I will call you when it's time."

Irene and Urie blushed. Then they fled.

The door closed upon a trial *in absentia*. They were excluded. But they were relieved. This brought upon them a sense of unreality. They stood upon the garish white tiles of the bathroom. They put on their robes. They waited.

Urie stared into the rose-colored mirror. Her complexion was bad from cold weather. Her skin was beginning to scale. Her lips were pale. She looked at Irene. Irene's cowlike, stubborn silence annoyed her. Irene looked like a nun.

"What do you think they're saying about us?" asked Irene nervously. "What if they reject us, now that we made these robes?"

"How can you be so stupid?" said Urie scorchingly. "Would they have asked us to join their dirty Christianity club if they were going to do that?" Suddenly she approached Irene closely and significantly. "What if they knew what we were really like? Thieves and liars." She laughed loudly. Irene's eyes flashed.

At that moment the swinging door opened. "All right. You can come in now," called a voice.

Urie gave one last look into the mirror, trying to put her hair into place. Then she switched her robes into a run. Irene followed.

When they re-entered, the room was dark. Five candles flickered upon a table. All the girls had put on their robes and were transformed, changed from supercilious, giggling high-school girls into white-faced owls. Everything was deathly still. A thousand eyes with blades of flame reflected in them stared at Urie and Irene. They were like a disguise. The room was a hushed, obscure cavern of masks.

"Will the two initiates approach the altar?" said the voice of Opal Granger.

Urie looked but could not see her. She assumed a Machiavellian meekness. She stared back at the starers with velvet ferocity. Suddenly someone put a lit candle in her hand. Someone else put another in Irene's.

"Go forward," ordered the voice.

She and Irene traveled forward. On the carpet, their footsteps made no sound.

Something hideous was beginning to happen. Under the guise of the robes, the darkness, the flickering candles, there was a noise like a stifled hoot. The quality of it was disguised. Was it a laugh? A sob of agony?

After this the silence became more profound, as if there were a promise of some exposure.

"Kneel," ordered the voice.

Urie paused, thinking of refusing. Was it true that the ceremony was a prurient, indecent enjoyment of victims in the fruity candlelight? What was she being initiated into? What was this organization, this Opal Granger, this Hi-Y to be initiated into?

She knelt down. Irene knelt beside her.

The act of doubling her body to this position made her emotions suddenly weak. She felt like crying because of the indignity. Her mind doubled likewise, and all the effort and heat involved in preventing the rape of her worshiping instincts turned perverse.

I will be sincere to myself, whatever! she vowed to herself. She hated the Hi-Y. She wanted to crucify their professions of pity, intimidate their curiosity, foist off their rape. She crossed her eyes, looking straight at the candles. Then she looked at the horde of eyes staring at her, but she could not see anything.

A voice whispered, "Repeat after me."

It was Opal Granger. Urie saw her clearly, holding a typewritten paper at an odd angle before the candle. Opal read in a voice of doom: "I, Urania Bishop, do take the oath to respect the Christian qualities of reverence for God, devotion to Jesus Christ, respect for adults, and love for all human beings on earth."

I, Urania Bishop, Urie retranslated silently as she repeated Opal's words, do take the oath to abominate the quality of reverence for God (for reverence of Untouched Pure Supergod), hatred to Jesus Christ (the fake perpetrated to keep everybody mushy sheep), critical appraisal toward adults, and hatred toward all human hypocrites on earth.

"I do swear," Opal read, "to the best of my ability to act out these qualities in the framework of my home life, my school life, and the life of my social encounters in the fellowship."

(I do swear with all my brilliance to mock these qualities in the framework of my stinking, horrible, putrid life and the life of my social encounters in all crapping fellowship.)

"With all the humility of my heart, I will try to love and to do good unto all."

(With arrogance in my heart, I will be sure to hate and to do rotten unto all. Oh, let me enter my own heaven, where vileness, do-goodiness, and hypocrisy cannot enter!)

She wanted to laugh, unaware that her voice had grown so strong and authoritative in double-edged hypocrisy that she had achieved a strange dominion over the act of abjection.

One night Urie woke up to hear Loco Poco sobbing. Her heart beat with fear at this sound, and she clutched her hands together under the blanket.

"What's the matter with you?" she whispered through the curtain.

"I don't want to be killed!" sobbed Loco.

"Killed!"

"I'm afraid we will get into the war."

"You mean to tell me you're crying because of that?"

"Yes."

"You're a fool."

"Well, what if we do?" persisted Loco.

"Go to sleep."

"I don't want to go to a concentration camp."

"How can you go to a concentration camp? Are you a Jew?"

"P.Q.—"

"What P.Q. says and what P.Q. is, is something absolutely different. Don't you know—"

"But *if* P.Q. is —"

"Let P.Q. be a Jew. *I'm* no Jew. I can tell you that!"

Urie rolled over and closed her eyes tight. Loco stared at the shepherds on the curtain, trying to pierce to the state of the absolute. As always, since they were disguised from each other's sight, the souls of the sisters were magnified to each other. Loco tried to see through the shepherds to where she knew Urie, in her adamant silence, was projecting invulnerability as a talisman. She raised herself on one elbow, her eyes now dry, and asked, "But we *could* get into the war, couldn't we?" The sentence was declarative. Urie opened her eyes. She held very still. "So what?"

"What if we lose the war?"

"Pah! We can't lose the war!"

But why couldn't they? wondered Urie. The glib reasons: we are the richest country on earth. We are the creditor nation. We are the most powerful. We are great because we are a democracy. Democracy will inevitably save the world. We wouldn't think of going into the war if the President and all the leaders of the country didn't believe we could win the war. They know. They must be right.

But why should she believe this, when the process of her life with Zebul was the discovery that all these edifices were lies?

The next day she asked Zebul. He too traced the glib answers.

"You're being an inconsistent fool," she told him.

But Zebul and Urie could not care. They were not afraid of war. They wanted it. The coming of it brought them, on its outer rim, nearer and nearer to the metaphysical heart of history, pulling them in with its exciting, centripetal force. It dissolved their fifteen-year-old self-conscious separatism and flung them into membership with history. So they refused to think of its outcome.

After that evening Loco Poco never mentioned the war again. In the darkness of that spring she tried to entice P.Q. away from it. When he was listening to the radio she curled between his arms and legs. She kissed his chin. She banged her fist in the palm of his hand, trying to dislodge him from Kaltenborn's clutches. Ever since her twelfth birthday, when Coventry was being bombed and she had played a kazoo in P.Q.'s ear trying to blot out the thudding of bombs on the special radio report, she had tried to fight his withdrawal from the family into the war. But he was like a stone. He did not tell her to go away. But she got up poutingly. She went to the kitchen. She knelt by the legs of the kitchen stove, staring at his rock face angrily. She played loudly on the tissue-paper-covered comb, beating her foot, while Tobruk fell and the British entered Bengasi, until Mrs. Bishop almost dropped a hot pan of Parker House rolls on her head.

Another strange habit she began that spring was the eating of flowers. She never told anyone in the family, knowing that they would laugh. But it came to her that if you ate flowers war could be averted. It was easy then, because the daffodils came out while Rommel was pushing the British back in North Africa, and there were Japanese quince, forsythia, and Judas blossoms. The dogwoods came out. There were many daisies, and they would last all summer to eat—the petals. The insides were too bitter. She looked forward to roses, whose petals she could suck, and after roses she would eat zinnias. They would be horrible, but they were flowers. She was afraid of fall. By her birthday in November there would be no more blooming flowers. She knew berries and grasses were no good for her purpose. She prayed for Tootsie Morn to raise winter flowers next year, and late in the winter some snowball bushes might put out thick, sweet blossoms, which she was counting on till next spring came and perhaps the war would stop.

But Loco Poco's life was dislocated that year. She had looked forward to the day when she would be in the same school with Irene and Urie. Now that they had been accelerated into college, she would be going to high school alone.

At the end of April she tried to ask P.Q. about the fall of Greece. There was a black headline in his outstretched *New York Times*. But he would not speak. The moment of recognizing that Greece was important to her was the moment it became impossible to communicate with it. Did that prove P.Q. was not a Jew? Two weeks later in the second week of May Loco Poco saw a picture of Rudolf Hess standing in a field with his parachute behind him. Its strings were the spokes of his halo. She cut the picture out and pasted it in a scrapbook. Rudolf Hess was a secret black angel of peace. She decided to pray. She knelt in front of her scrapbook that night. She stamped Tootsie Morn by imagination onto the blank page opposite Rudolf Hess and begged them to resurrect P.Q. from silence, banish war, and make up flowers for next winter. In her mind's eye she dreamed of them raising an army of fleas so powerful that it would force the people of all countries to scratch instead of shoot.

Mrs. Bishop claimed Loco was spoiled and P.Q. had spoiled her. The fact that she was so popular with her classmates and acted like a queen among them did not satisfy Loco. Friends were easy. Like opinions, they were cheap. Popularity, love, laughter were lavished upon her, and she gave them back easily. But she felt this all to be dispensable. She was searching for something. And instead of regarding her peculiarities as hampering, she indulged herself in them.

That spring she changed. She was twelve and a half years old. Her physical shape changed. Little beginnings of breasts sprouted on her chest. She stroked them with glee, jumping around on her colt legs, giggling. She purred like a cat that she was growing into adulthood like Irene and Urie. Just as her fervent caresses of P.Q. embarrassed the two older sisters, so did Loco's ardent delight in her own puberty. They looked away to ignore it.

Sometimes she ran down the curtained hallway to the bathroom, naked to the waist like an Indian, walloping her palm against her hooting mouth in a rain-dance call and reveling in the tender shaking of her new breasts. Other times she rubbed herself lasciviously against the curtained walls of her room, completely naked, pretending she was a moth trying to get out. Caught in these sensations, arching herself, she tried to aim her small pink nipples in the semicircles of the shepherd's crooks. But cold weather stopped her wanton action. It was still too cold to run around naked.

Her exhibitionism took a secretive turn. She used to borrow the flashlight. At night, after she had warmed up in bed, she turned it on, not to read secretly as Urie had done in past days, but to examine her own body. First she pointed the light at her breasts, aiming at a nipple, touching it and examining the delicate hole in the center. Then she pretended she already had the large breasts of a woman. She also pointed it to her groin, where baby hairs were sprouting. She could feel the spear of light against the hair, and when the inside of the aperture began to tingle, she opened it up with her fingers and rubbed it. When she became so excited that she thought she would burst, she put the cold flashlight between her legs and pressed it, reveling in its cold hardness.

She tried to tell Urie about this masturbation. "Guess what. Did you ever feel the sensation of when you rub yourself on cloth? It feels just like—"

"Keep quiet."

"Why?"

"Because."

"But it's good."

Once long ago Urie had told her she was evil. The sky was gathering with poopoo. It was black. There was a thunderstorm coming, but Loco Poco, five years old, had believed it was poopoo. The world stopped, became green and absolutely silent. Then a tree whipped. The poopoo would fill the sky so completely, said Urie, that at last God would drop it. It would fall upon Loco and she would be buried, first up to the ankles, then up to the knees. She would try to move but she would be stuck. It would grow higher and higher until she was covered up to the chin, and the stench would be so bad she would not be able to stand it. And at last it would even cover her head and she would die of suffocation. At the time that she was five years old Loco Poco believed this story, ran crying to her mother, and, as in the episode of the tricycle, Urie was punished.

But now Loco laughed. "Urie, did you ever see Zebul's thing?"

That perverse streak in Loco that exacerbated its source made her whimsies as tenacious as Urie's ambition. She laughed out loud at Urie's shock.

"Quit blabbing that stuff!" warned Urie puritanically.

"I'd like to see it," continued Loco in a serious voice.

In this game at Urie's expense, Loco pretended that instead of being horrified, Urie had asked her why.

"I want to see what it would do," continued Loco. And then suddenly, almost laughing, she asked with fake innocence, "What do they do when they make sexual intercourse?" She knew perfectly well, having carefully analyzed all the pictures in *Your Daughter and Nature* by Dr. E. O. Rowan, which her mother had given her three years ago. Reaching the crescendo in her monologue: "I'm going to feel it sometime."

The outrageous in Loco so shocked Urie that she was almost afraid of her. She wanted to hide her head under the pillow. She blushed. Loco, like Irene, was becoming a cross to bear. How did Loco come from such an inhibited family as the Bishops and act in such an unrestrained way? Was she crazy? Would she become a sex fiend or prostitute? What would ever happen to her?

Just before spring vacation the report cards were issued. Loco made three C's, two D's, and an F in civics.

"I don't understand you," exploded Mrs. Bishop in a frenzy of anger and fear. She darted and wheeled about the kitchen as if she would attack Loco. Loco stood on one foot by the kitchen table, hanging her head. But she was waiting for her mother to expend the energy of her anger and forget again. "Miss Nickle says you chew gum in class and throw wadded paper. Where do you get this gum?"

Such erratic non sequiturs guaranteed Loco's ultimate escape. But she had to suffer the whole family's analysis of her poor marks, as they asked the old refrain, why Loco, with 159 I.Q., according to the Stanford-Binet Test, should be such a disgrace.

Only P.Q. remained unperturbed. "Everything will come out in the wash."

"Yes. We know you," muttered Mrs. Bishop. "You *like* her to make bad grades so you can laugh at the teachers."

P.Q. and Loco masked a look of collusion.

That night in bed, as though to get back at her for forcing Zebul into a sexual framework, Urie asked her, "Don't you care?"

"Huh?" asked Loco sleepily.

"How can you bear to make such low grades?"

"I don't know."

"You don't care?"

"No."

Loco stared brilliantly into the darkness. She was sorry for Urie that she cared so much. At the same time she wanted to laugh hilariously. But as Urie was waiting in imperious silence for her to diagram herself, she suddenly thought up an idea.

"I don't care"—she took a large breath—"whether a sentence"—another large breath—"has a"—another large breath—"verb in it or not"—another large breath—"or whether an adverb modifies a noun"—another large breath—"or what—"

"What are you doing?"

"I'm trying to breathe in the same rhythm as you are."

That answer was so beautiful it broke Urie's heart. It was the same as harmonizing in church. Loco was the greatest person in the world to sing with. But Urie refused her sudden and stupendous admiration for Loco's wicked cleverness.

"You're just trying to change the subject!"

"I am not!"

"Really, Loco, do you mean to tell me you're *not* interested in verbs?"

"No. They bore me."

"But they're basic to the power of thought. You can't even think if you don't know verbs."

"I don't care."

"Look at you. You think Rudolf Hess is good"—Urie blasted the secret in her face— "when he's the fourth Nazi after Hitler."

"He's in Scotland right now bearing offers of peace!" cried Loco ardently. "He flew. The verb: 'flew.' The secret black angel flew!"

"Yeah. And he's evil with horns. They've got him in a prison right this minute."

"No, they don't!"

There was a long silence. And then Urie recapitulated the real subject.

"I'm talking about thinking. Don't you want to think?"

"No. I think thinking is crap. Feeling is all."

The moment Urie heard the words "Feeling is all," she knew that something as important as "the Cult of Ugliness" had been said. But she persisted.

"Aren't you interested in anything?"

"Oh, yes!"

"I mean in school," said Urie hurriedly.

"I hate school."

"Aren't you interested in Shylock?"

"No. I hate him."

"Well, you can hate him. I mean, it's fun to like to hate him. I mean, to know him and—"

"I know all of it!" Loco suddenly sang passionately. "I know it before I read it. I recognize it. I don't need to read it. Why do they call such things great? Who says they're great? I think it's silly, when you know everything and then they try to teach it. So what's the use of studying?"

"But it's exciting!" defended Urie with passion. "It's exciting to read something and then to see that it's true."

"But that's not what's true," said Loco.

"What do you mean?"

"How do I know what I mean?"

"*What* is true?" insisted Urie, clipped now, harsh.

But Loco did not know anything now. She wanted to laugh about Urie's eagerness for truth, when it wasn't truth she wanted. She and Zebul were both the same. All they wanted was to put things into a scheme. That was not truth.

She nuzzled her nose in the blankets. She was sleepy.

A long time later she heard Urie say in disgust, "You're crazy."

She smiled in the dark. In back of her eyes a vision came to her. All was dark, exactly as it really was. It was like a great cave. Yet farther out, just at the periphery of existence, it seemed that she could see fantastic shapes of light. It was as if the cave had opened onto a panorama. The shapes, gargantuan and moving like mists, drew her to them. She thought that they were Greenland's icy mountains. Yet they moved like mists rather than mountains. And the quality of their light, wraithlike, bright, almost icy light, in such contrast to the darkness where she lay, contained a most delicate quality, as if it were a call echoed from some far place in a time she could not place, either past or future. Had she come from this fantastic place? Or was she going to it? What was it made of? Was it mountains? Or was it mists? She tried to get nearer to the aperture so that she could get rid of the darkness around her, so that she could enter and explore the shapes of light.

The strange thing about this light was that it had precisely the same mysterious ardor as threatening thunderclouds, only in reverse. For it was the clouds that exuded the light and moved round about, whereas in an impending thunderstorm the clouds were the darkness threatening.

"Oh, please don't disappear from my sight," she whispered to the vision. But her very plea, as if denying the impending happiness that threatened her, an ecstasy frighteningly imminent, suddenly made the vision go away.

She could not get it back. She fluttered her eyes. Then she went to sleep.

PART IV

C H A P T E R 24

Everything changed for Zebul and Urie when they went into the university that fall. They made a lightning-like shift from the juvenile world to the adult world. Yet they were both still not quite sixteen, so they had to study fiercely the first quarter and had no time to contemplate their new station in life.

They had lived the summer in the fever of their new life. Urie saved sixty-five dollars from typing. Zebul had made money too, working on his father's cousin's farm in the western part of the state, for eight weeks, on tobacco. He wrote momentous letters daily, composed more for posterity than for Urie. "The Nazis have just attacked Russia and here am I describing cows grazing at the edge of the lake and the azure haze of distant mountains. What does P.Q. think? It seems strange the war is getting bigger and bigger."

When he came back two days before freshman orientation in September, he was brown from the sun. They met in an elevated state in which the mystique of their friendship suffused the details of their first days at the university. They remarked on the faces of every student in the registration line, the exact words of Travis, the NYA man who assigned them to their self-help jobs, the expression in each of their professors.

"Remember when we first declared we would come to this university?" Zebul whispered.

"And now we are in it!"

Urie was assigned to a job in the catalogue department of the library. Zebul got a job typing in the Philosophy Department. There was one difference in their status in the university. Zebul had a scholarship, and Urie did not. The university did not give scholarships for girls in the first two years. But instead of causing jealousy or guilt, this welded them together in a cocoon of protection against the absurd. The technicalities of the university were ludicrous against their larger loyalty and admiration. They were aware of the drama of their lives beyond the university, yet for that very reason doted on every detail, inhabiting their studenthood as if these roles were the touchstone of their grown-up lives.

Two days after her sixteenth birthday, Urie went to Winston Dormitory to pick up a term paper in social work to type. Every extra job was extra money.

It was Sunday. The three girls had given a bad performance of "Adoremus Te" in the church. Loco and Urie ganged up on Irene and dinner had taken especially long because they tried to learn a new song over the dishes. Their repertory was down to zero. They had used up every song, including "Smoke Gets in Your Eyes," substituting "Christ" for "Smoke," so Loco had, on instructions, stolen a complicated anthem from the high-school glee-club room.

"It's sol *si* la, there, not sol *sol* la. Can't you learn that?" spat Urie to Irene. "Hurry up, for God's sake. I've got to pick up that paper, and she said it was twenty pages. And I've got to get it back by eight o'clock. Plus that I've got to write this theme on *Paradise Lost*—"

"I don't see why you said you'd do typing if you don't have the time," interjected Mrs. Bishop from the dining room.

Urie threw her a dirty look.

It was almost four o'clock before she got to the dormitory. The day was slipping into late shadows, and the lights were already on inside. Urie remembered how more than a year ago she had boasted she would never spend another Christmas vacation at home, and now another one was coming. She looked around furtively.

The paper in her hand said the name she had copied down from the bulletin board: Sophie Binney, 103. She knocked on the door. Inside the room were women's voices. The radio was on. It played the organ music of *A Lamp at Your Feet,* a special Sunday religious program. Social-work students *would* listen to that, she thought. They were older women, usually county welfare workers, often religious, who came from the sticks for special courses and wrote hicky papers with bad spelling. Urie had typed two during the summer.

The door opened, and a gray-haired woman looked out.

"I am Urie Bishop," said Urie.

The woman had the paper in her hand, ready. But instead of giving it to her, she stared through her glasses, holding the door wide open with her right hand, and said, "They dropped bombs on Pearl Harbor."

"What?" asked Urie.

"The Japanese."

Urie immediately thought of Jack Pearl. Her embrace of the trashy through Zebul had given her this appreciation of jewels as objects. Besides Opal Granger, she wished she had known a Ruby or that the Pick Theater could have been called the Bijou. Yet she knew perfectly well that something momentous had happened.

There were three other women in the room, two young and one elderly like Sophie Binney. One was sitting on the bed, putting on stockings. Another was studying at a desk, with the light on. And the third was fixing her curlers in front of the mirror.

The young one at the desk swished her sharp nose and orange hair around, saying, "It means war. They've been interrupting the programs all afternoon."

"She doesn't know what Pearl Harbor is."

"Pearl Harbor is in Hawaii. Hawaii," the orange-haired one explained.

"No," said Sophie Binney. "It's a place in Hawaii where we have a naval base. There are a whole lot of battleships in the harbor, and they don't know yet how many—"

"The President is in conference and he is going to address the nation."

Urie noticed that the radio was colored brown and that the little dial mouth was lit. All the women were focused on her excitedly, as if some ghost were animating them, their arms halfway in the air and a special, strange, friendly look on their faces. The vision of the woman's open mouth forming the vowels "ah-ee," "ah-ee," for Hawaii, stayed in her mind after she had taken the paper and left the room with her promise to return the finished typing by eight p.m.

She started to run home but she got tired by the Ephesus Inn. It was not that she wanted to announce the news, or to find out if the family knew, but she had contracted a sense of unreality from the women, into which the ordinary details of trees, gravel, and power plant flowed frighteningly.

The family knew. Irene had visited Mrs. Lacey Ransome and rushed home. P.Q. was listening to the radio, and for the first time she heard the news flashes interrupting the regular programs. Everybody turned to P.Q., waiting for him to make a pronouncement on the meaning. But he turned off the radio and yawned, presenting them with a vacancy.

"We are in the war at last. That's what the meaning is, isn't it, P.Q.?" prompted Urie.

"Yes, I guess so."

The hungry to be fed with a radish, like Scarlett O'Hara! She began typing with ferocity and finished Sophie Binney's paper in one hour and thirteen minutes—unheard-of speed, she boasted, an average of 3.6 minutes for each page. "And I had to do two carbons, too!"

Zebul came for supper. They put the radio on again, and Zebul and Urie did not dare look at each other. Zebul went with Urie to take the finished paper back to Sophie Binney. They faced each other in the glare of the street lights, naked as at their first meeting. In the revelation of impending war, they harked back to the fall of man. It was not the fall of man, but the fall of Satan they had been living, the fall of the Bishops to the Shack. All that they had learned from injustice, tenacity, work, the Cult of Ugliness, stealing, courage, and indomitability was revealed to have a reason. Everything came into perspective. Events now coincided with their personal history. All they had hoped for was true. They forgot P.Q. still thinking in his sphinx chair, Mrs. Bishop listening and looking around at everyone, Irene doing her calculus, Loco Poco looking lost like a blown-away leaf. By the time they arrived at the dormitory they discovered they had written Urie's *Paradise Lost* paper.

The next day they listened to the President's declaration of war. When they heard the words "unprovoked and dastardly attack," every injustice of their lives, all that they had been dedicated to by their vow of truth, welled up in those lyrical aristocratic syllables. Their past was justified in this vision of the future. Everything was as they had imagined. They were young, immortal, and right. They were truly going into a war that they now knew they had been born to fight. So be it that the family was made small by this stunning blow of history. Zebul and Urie as individuals were meshed into it and made large. P.Q.'s silence, his final withdrawal, was the sum of his knowledge. Did Cassandra preach mortality? But whoever heard of such a thing as the Japanese attacking the mightiest nation on earth? Too huge and powerful to inhabit their sixteen-year-old bodies, Urie and Zebul jumped into this new, accelerated universe and became speechless.

But in the second quarter of school, excitement gave way to lassitude, and in the intermittent changes of the campus around them—the graduate schools diminishing, all the students classified for service, people in Ephesus saying that soon the town would be nothing but a bunch of freshmen and old professors limping around—they realized their position. They were only sixteen. As freshmen they were years away from the important events.

The long-time rumor about a preflight school came true in January. The Navy commandeered two lower quadrangles of the university for dormitories, took over half the classrooms in Malden and Peabody, and began construction on special buildings. The gymnasium was used by the Navy in the mornings, and Faulkner's Field was turned into a drilling ground. Ten units of the Free French Forces came into town as part of a liaison program between the Allied forces for preflight training. But all the strange sights of cadets, sailors, and senior officers only served to accentuate the unimportance of Zebul's and Urie's existence. They were dwarfed in the heady blossoms of uniforms, strange accents, the hints of the dimmed-out world of war suddenly burgeoning all about them.

The week after spring vacation, a feeling of restlessness assailed Zebul. He had finished his assignment for Advanced English I, a theme in the style of Dean Swift. In the theme he had made a stupid, evil Gulliver go to a dentist. He had written it from the point of view of Gulliver, and all the knives, picks, tooth-cutters, and drills were like Lilliputians, clipping, poking, and pounding his rotten teeth. It was a marvelous theme. He wanted to read it to Urie.

But she was working in the library and would not be free until six. He went and peeked through the glass panel into the catalogue department and saw her straining over a catalogue card in her typewriter. She was erasing something. Her tongue was curled in the corner of her mouth, and Miss Marsh was hanging over her shoulder, pointing to the card. He tried to be Urie and suffer the sound of Miss Marsh's talking noise in his ear. Miss Marsh had a dry palate and whenever she talked, her tongue stuck to the roof of her mouth, the sound coming out in a series of gluey clicks.

Zebul, unable to catch Urie's eye, turned away. He left the library and wandered toward the bell tower. Unable to share his euphoria at his theme, he turned melancholy. He switched his blue notebook to his left hand. It was getting warm for March. Sweat formed triangles at his elbows. His hair, like wet ringlets of ripe grapes, quivered over his forehead. The warmth of the end of day grazed his earlobes in slight breezes. It was five o'clock, and the bell tower began to play hymns.

Ever since he had lost his belief in God, he too cringed at the flatness of the F-sharp.

> Fairest Lord Jesus,
> Ruler of all nature,
> Oh thou of God and man the Son,
> Thee will I cherish,
> Thee will I honor,
> Thou, my soul's glory, joy, and crown.

He wished he could cherish and honor something, but Jesus was ruined for him. He was post-Christianity.

From the tennis court came the sock of balls. Oh, he wanted to do something. He wanted to hit the perfect ball, floating around silent, almost slow motion. He smiled dreamily in this fantasy. But he was a stinking tennis player. The sweet smile that fell out of his parted mouth shone against the beaded moisture on his upper lip and clung to his soft male fur wistfully. He hung motionless against the cage wire of the court. He wanted to do something. What he wanted to do was secret. For it was a secret that he was great.

Thoughts of the meaning of his life, which for all these months he had suppressed, now blossomed again. But he did not know what to do. He left the tennis courts. He looked at the bell tower once more. Its clock face hung lonely against the sky, bonging out its flat and melancholy tune. With all his purity and love he wanted to abjure its faults and bong it to greatness.

He thought of the bell tower. It was an ugly Arabian shape. A millionaire named Morris had given it to the university. The millionaire had made his millions manufacturing shoes and galoshes. Zebul imagined the millionaire dying as emptily as Ivan Ilyich. Now all that was left of him was the bell tower, which provided self-help students with a job from five to six, playing hymns on the fake keyboard of the carillon at the bottom of the tower.

Zebul could bear it no longer. He left the bell tower. He ran down a gravel path toward the Tin Can. Maybe he would run five laps around the indoor track till Urie got out of work. He did not do that. Instead, he turned down into the woods toward the Geology Building, until he came to the Armory.

The Armory had been taken over by the Navy. It was used for gymnastics, and math and weapons classes were taught there. Some French cadets, from the Free French Forces, were also quartered there. The building was an old nineteenth-century one, made with ash-gray stone.

He saw an open door in the basement. He decided to go in and look around. It was dark. At first he could not see well. But the coolness and darkness soothed the tenuous, heat-laden melancholy that the bell tower had produced in him. It smelled green. He liked the Armory.

He stepped in on the gymnasium floor. He was conscious of his heavy breathing. A door was open at the far end, which let a spoke of light in. The light caught the tile edges of a vast expanse. The Armory's shiny mosaic walls seemed to tilt. He was entranced. It began to be a holy place to him. He nodded. He smiled radiantly, making his exaggerated breaths echo back to him against the tile walls. It was a place fit for his greatness. He felt himself expand. He stretched out his arms to devastate the distance and the silence. He felt himself become gargantuan. He imagined his form from a distance, small and outlined in the sliver of holy light. Then he noticed some lockers at the other end of the vast stage. He walked toward them. He was conscious of how he walked. At first he frolicked, jumping up and down like a goat. Then he walked with great dignity. He amazed himself with his largeness and dignity. His footsteps echoed in shorter and shorter sounds until he arrived at the lockers.

He opened one. Inside hung one of the French cadets' uniforms. The French uniforms were strange. The pants were white with very wide bell-bottoms at the ankle. The jackets were blue wool with very large collars. The hats were white with huge red pompoms on top. Zebul had watched the French cadets on the campus.

He was eager to try the uniform on.

He stripped off his shirt. He pulled on the woolen blue. The pale collar crossed his back like a flag. Then he looked around. He had a feeling someone was looking at him.

Silence hypnotized him like the pupil of an eye. But it was not a person watching him. It was God, that old God, that ultimate, defied God whom he had abjured, who inhabited this Armory, attempting to catch him like a flea. "There is no God," he whispered to himself, taking off his pants.

The bell-bottoms were made of wool. They were rough and scratchy. They had buttons instead of a zipper. They were so tight that he began to jerk and jump to make his loins smaller. For a moment he felt that he was Charlie Chaplin, with the bell-bottoms flapping around his ankles. He giggled. Then he put on the hat.

The moment he assumed the hat, he assumed another identity, although he knew that he, Zebulon Walley, who had been loved by God in another age, still could never escape his destiny as *himself*. But since there was no God, he got solace from the hat. The hat gave him great possibility in that place of immensity and strangeness. It filled him with power.

A voice suddenly interrupted him. "What are you doing here?"

He bolted around.

There was an officer standing in the sliver of light at the far end of the Armory. Only his outline was visible. The Navy cap with its visor sliced into the ray of light, colorless but with authority. The officer was slight, but his shadow elongated eerily upon the polished floor as if painted by an omniscient pencil.

Zebul knew impersonating a member of the armed forces in wartime was a federal offense. In his fear his first thought was losing his scholarship.

"I—I was changing clothes."

His defensiveness was despicable to him. Yet floating in the super-real world of the Armory, he noticed that his fear had made the words garbled and they sounded like broken English.

"What platoon are you in?"

How much had the officer seen? Would he turn on the light? He had to prevent him from approaching.

"Third!" he answered.

"I don't seem to remember you."

"I was moved from the seventh yesterday," he improvised, transforming the broken English to Charles Boyer sounds.

"From which?"

"The seventh?"—accent on last syllable.

The officer's first footstep made a muffled, tentative sound. The light in the Armory was changed by the elongated shadow and splintered into patterns like liquid birds flitting against the walls.

Zebul could feel the sweat dank and cold in the roots of his hair. The hall was so vast he estimated it would take hours before the officer would be upon him. But this fact paralyzed him. With discovery imminent, he felt dead. His body's moisture was something that had occurred in a distant past. He breathed. He felt the small hairs of his nose jiggle. He bid good-by to the sound, as if even his own hairs were ghosts. The nearer the footsteps came, the softer they sounded. He turned, blocking the open locker so that the officer could not see his clothes. But he did not dare shut the locker for fear that would prove his guilt.

The Armory was now very dark, and the footsteps stopped. How far away was he?

Zebul turned around to look.

The officer's face was white, and the eyes looking into his were dead. But behind their deadness lurked another quality which Zebul could not understand. The man was slight, no taller than Zebul. His bearing was refined and weary.

In Zebul's mind flashed the thought that this officer not only suspected, but actually was enjoying the suspicion. Why had he not put on the light? Why had he walked so slowly across the Armory floor? Why had he stopped so far away?

Is it possible? thought Zebul. He knows I'm not a cadet!

Suddenly he blushed, a deep blush that rose from the base of his neck. But in the duskiness no one could see the blush. Everything was so far-fetched that he wanted to shout: I'm not a French cadet. I'm not French at all. I'm a Haw-yoo from Haw. My name is Zebulon Vance Walley.

But at that moment the officer said, "Well, go ahead, then. Change!"

And, his gaze increasing in intensity for a second, so that there was an air of roving mercilessness in it, he waved and with a small shrug turned. His footsteps were louder as he walked toward the sliver of light from the open door where he had come. Without another word, he disappeared.

Zebul did not move for a long time, and then, somnambulistically but quickly, he changed back into his own clothes and ran out the doorway into the courtyard of pines.

He wanted to tell Urie. But for some reason he could not do it. Instead of meeting her at six, he wandered abstractedly home.

Why had the officer refused to expose him? Zebul knew that when people were in a position of authority, they had to castigate trespassers, for trespass denied their authority. This was a Navy man. Why would he use the military to flaunt authority? Or was Zebul dreaming? Had he really fooled the officer?

Emanating from some deep-seated and unknown part of himself came an intense desire to have a new suit of clothes. He had never cared about clothes before in his life. Now suddenly he remembered what Urie said about his corduroy trousers making that ponky sound. "Corduroys will wear forever," his mother said. But he could not buy clothes. He would never be able to buy new clothes until he graduated from college. But before then he would probably be in the Army. Then he would not have to buy clothes. He would wear a uniform. And suddenly, when he had never cared before, he saw himself as a poor boy, deprived because he could not buy new clothes like the fraternity boys. This vision was totally strange, even despicable to him, and although before he would have met it with impatience, with fierce scorn, now he gave it wide berth and he pitied himself.

The next day at noon he met Urie at the Book Ex. He bought a chocolate milkshake for fifteen cents to eat with the battered peanut-butter sandwich he had brought from home. As they talked he noticed that his hand, holding his green book-bag, was right next to an open box of Mounds on the counter. He could easily have stolen two packs. No one was watching. But he deliberately rejected this golden opportunity.

He led the way to the sunlit asphalt courtyard and sat down on a green bench.

"What do you think you are?" he asked her in a mean voice. "What other people think you are, what you think you are, or what you really are?"

"I am *me*." She was chewing her sandwich. He could see pink bits of tuna fish between her teeth.

"Yes, but what are *you?* I gave you three possibilities. In the name of reason you will have to admit that the answer you gave me is simply *faith*."

Her blue eyes glittered. He saw that she could not answer the question. He had beaten her at her own game, by rubbing her nose in *reason*. He felt derisive. But she smiled ruefully. And then she packed the argument away, as if she were stuffing a handkerchief deep in her pocket. It was a peculiar, sweet, feminine gesture, and he knew that in some future time it would come to rest, like a chicken to roost, in his heart. But he could not think of it at that moment.

That night he planned to tell her. She came to his little house to study. She bent softly over Shakespeare sonnets, mouthing them in whisper breaths. Her presence irritated him. She seemed peculiarly soft and fragrant. But it was her very warmth he could not bear. She was oblivious to his feelings, and this made him feel even worse.

Outside, the bees were buzzing with upstart noises lulling among the honeysuckles in the rich silence. It was still March, but it was hot. The street lights wove opulent shadows on the white dirt street. Everything was surcharged, rich, perfumed. This exacerbated him. As the people of Haw went to bed, the windows of the mill houses became dark. It was the perfect time to tell her. Now he and she were absolutely alone.

He could not do it.

The breeze was indescribably sweet. The frogs now took over the abandoned evening, filling it, full-throated, with their symphonic croaks. He got up and banged the door shut.

"Why did you do that?"

"I hate that huge, globbing shadow."

"What shadow?"

"That one."

Her surprise, her eyes docilely following his pointing finger, made him even more irascible. His loneliness was boomeranging back.

He had to tell her.

"Urie—" he began.

But suddenly he saw that if he told her, he would be catching her in some dark and unwholesome web where she would be *contaminated*.

"Which shadow?" Her innocence increased that wave of protectiveness that he had felt, and he answered with a flood of relief, "That one."

The shadow of a thick magnolia bush writhed upon the white moon-struck ground. It looked like a huge lopsided rabbit trying to escape from the clawlike fingers of a mammoth maw tree whose top branches were moaning among the telephone wires. The shadows were moving as if in perpetual motion because the perfumed breeze was moving the bush and the tree in the eerie street light, illustrating, he saw, his own everlasting predicament.

"It's magnificent, Zebul! Why haven't I ever seen it before? All the times I have been here!"

The golden hair down of her upper lip shone against the darkness of the windowpane from his lamp. She liked it. How could she like anything so sweet and full of terror? He wanted to protect her. He had not told her. Yet the picture was on the ground before her.

"Close the window!" he ordered.

"No!"

"Close it!"

"I will not. What's the matter with you?"

He gave up. He pretended he did not care. He went to his cabinet, took out his bamboo pen, and dipped it in India ink. He made a perfect sketch of a skeleton head. He put crossbones and printed the word DEATH under it. He cut it out with scissors and pasted it on an empty bottle he had saved from the dump.

"What are you doing?"

"I'm filling up this bottle with cyanide," he said, getting the bottle from its place on the shelf. "With cyanide which I stole from the chemistry building. And sometime, when I feel like it, I may commit suicide."

"Would you really do it?" she wondered in a whisper.

"I might."

His stare at her was detached and cold. It was a stare which came from the core of him, and by which he meant to bore to the core of her. He felt great power in this manifested strength. Suddenly he was dying to smile, to initiate her into the marvel of himself in his barren courage.

He began to pour the colorless liquid. He held his breath, trying not to smell it, though he caught a whiff as of bitter almonds. But its very innocuousness gave him power. It thrilled him that only a whiff, and he could die.

"You're doing it for effect," she said.

"Nevertheless, it's real," he answered, smiling, grandiloquent and cold.

In retrospect the incident in the Armory came to Zebul to have the quality of a dream. The officer became chimerical, enlarging out of all proportion. By April he began to fancy that something very close and intimate had happened between himself and the officer. He knew that the incident was important to his destiny just as he had known P.Q. was. He knew in the way one knows something is imminent, the way the world changes indefinably in the moments before a thunderstorm. The air of the universe became subtly changed, so that all the familiar objects became strange and new.

He had escaped something awful and entered into something indescribable. His escape made him feel both fear and delight. But the incident demanded its finish.

A feeling of suspension transferred itself to Zebul's outer life. His Gulliver theme made an A-plus. It was read to the class as an example of what an advanced freshman could do. As the weeks passed toward the end of the quarter, Zebul made two more A's in English and an A in French. He developed a passion for French. He tossed off these successes as if they were nothing. Yet he was transported. And the very fact that the kernel of him was so clear and still in expectation, in contrast to these noisy, new academic triumphs, made him giddy. His excitement spilled into Urie and infected her.

One day they were walking home after classes. It was late afternoon in the full blossom of spring.

"Just think. We are beginning to emerge from the chrysalis of anonymity. We are becoming recognized. Do you feel as incognito as you once did?"

"It's because college is absolutely different from high school," said Urie. "In those days we were ugly misfits. Now we are beginning to be something."

"No, everything!" he corrected. "There is no beauty. There is no ugliness. There is no injustice."

It was very hot. Mrs. Lucretia Pile was sitting out on Pack Mill Road on a nail barrel in front of her store. Beside her a group of Negroes lolled lazily in the dirt; an old man sat on a broken cinderblock in a patch of kudsu.

"We are white and Protestant. Just think. There is no better thing to be. Why, we are successes! We can look down on niggers and Jews and be approved of by society. *Pauvre Nègre. Pauvre noir!*" he sang celebratingly. French as of French cadet. French as of A-plus. French so they could not understand it.

"Hahahahahahaha!" supplied Urie in rhyme.

> "*Pauvre Nègre, pauvre noir,*
> Hahahaha, hahaha."

They perfected it and began to dance in time to the beat.

"How'm!" said Lucretia Pile, entranced. "Yoohoo. It sure done got hot, ain't it?"

"Hi, Mrs. Pile."

"*Vous l'appelez Madame,*" Zebul accused Urie. "How do you square that with your prejudicial tendencies?"

Lucretia Pile, riveted with fascination, scooped up her belly in her two hands and then deposited it in a more comfortable position on her lap. Two other Negro women came up to listen in on the gobbledygook.

"I don't have such tendencies. Their potential is as great as ours, but it is unexploited," answered Urie.

"What that crazy talk?" asked Lucretia, wagging her fat head with admiration.

"It's French," said Urie.

"My'm. My'm."

"It's French like a football cheer," said Zebul. "*Pauvre Nègre. Pauvre noir.* Hahahaha, hahaha."

> "*Pauvre Nègre, pauvre noir.*
> Hahahaha, hahaha."

A group of Negro children came running to repeat it. Everybody began to laugh and slap his backside. Even the old man sitting on the broken cinderblock got up and sang it and laughed.

CHAPTER 25

The next Sunday, Zebul brought *The Gioconda Smile and Other Stories* to the circulation desk. He had been in the library all afternoon. It was one of those too rich and ravishing days when the smell of honeysuckles had penetrated the hall through open windows. Suffusing perfume denied the rows of books, mustiness, and parchment-gray faces.

Suddenly Zebul saw the officer. He was standing right next to him. The officer was dressed not in Navy whites but in off-duty civilian clothes.

Zebul did not see him all at once. He saw his hands first. They were neat, strong hands, faintly tanned from the sun. The fingers were long, with excellent lines, and the line of muscle from thumb to wrist stood out boldly. The backs were covered with a fur of gold-colored hair. The officer was holding an old, tattered book called *The Variables of History* and was preparing to put his name and address on the call card.

Zebul controlled a reflex motion to jump. A wave of fear flooded him. It was three weeks since the incident in the Armory. He thought of running.

But the officer, sensing a disturbance in the person by his side, suddenly looked at him. Up to this moment the officer's face had been serene, liquid, dreaming. But at once an expression half puzzled, half guarded came upon it.

As he faced the officer's gaze, Zebul's fear changed to hope. He doesn't know me. Because of the uniform! The officer might not recognize *him* without the French cadet uniform, but *he* recognized the officer. He adjusted immediately to the gray sports coat and trousers. But the revelation of the officer as a man fascinated him. It broadened his whole concept of him.

Now, irrationally, with the same progression of emotions as he had followed in the Armory, he wanted the officer to recognize him. His gaze became eager.

The effect of this eagerness again changed the officer. His hazel eyes grew aloof. From behind the iris screen, the pupils reflected a strange and sharp curiosity.

At that moment the undergraduate library clerk came to the desk and asked, "Yes, sir? Can I help you?"

The officer broke off staring to write his name.

Zebul slid his eyeballs westward and down, like a convict. "E. Bostwick, Town," he saw.

The attendant stamped the card.

The officer looked at Zebul once more with an enigmatic, almost mocking turn of his lips, and then walked off. His footsteps were smart. They had the knowingness of a cynosure—even more, the provocative beat of having made a conquest.

Had he recognized Zebul? Zebul noticed he was trembling, and then he flushed under the clerk's eyes as he almost wrote E. Bostwick on his call card.

Early in the evening, just after it got dark, he whispered to Urie through the baggy screen door into the familiar smell of corn and beans, kerosene oil and girlish perfume.

"It's you!" she whispered.

"Come on out."

She slipped out the screen through a thousand millers batting their wings. She brushed them off her face.

"Yes. Phoo! It's too bright in there. It's too hot."

He led the way down the driveway toward the railroad tracks. She followed. He was wearing his hobnailed boots. He felt in a dream, floating, for the air was too thick with honeysuckles. Though he clacked the boots heavily to weight him down from the feeling of half ecstasy, half fear, he felt disconnected even from his own footsteps. Disconnected from the earth.

"The next time you see me, I may be in prison."

"What?" she breathed. "Did you do it?"

He knew she meant had he finally stolen the microscope which he had decided it was necessary for him to steal ever since he had made the decision that he was going into medicine.

"No, I didn't do that."

"What did you do?"

She was filled with a dread so acute that it actually thrilled her. She looked into his face, knowing that what he was saying was terribly important.

"This officer. I met this officer named E. Bostwick. . . ."

All fear dropped away from him. But the way he told it seemed crucial to him. The sequence of events. He wanted to make her understand that beyond the details of the cadet uniform, the getting caught, the being saved, the fear, it was the officer, E. Bostwick, that was important. So he rushed through, fumbling, eager, and intensely articulate. She lapped up each detail with an expression of enthralled admiration, made more intense by the hint of moonlight shining on her lips.

"It's not that I was really afraid—about the police. After all I'm still a minor. Besides that, I didn't go out of the Armory and parade around the streets or anything. But it's this man. He's something!"

"What do you mean?"

"You'd know what I mean if you saw him. He—"

She waited, but he didn't go on. She was now woven into the complexity of the mystery Zebul had presented. She abandoned herself utterly to Zebul. She began to ask questions, to ply him, which was exactly what he wanted.

"Is he handsome?"

He ignored this question. "It's as if he *knows* something."

"Knows what?"

"Something that nobody else knows."

"You mean—about you, in the Armory?"

"For instance, I think he knew I was not the cadet."

She waited with stunning silence.

"And not only that—"

"What else?"

"That he liked it."

"Liked what?"

"Liked that I was not the cadet. And that I was impersonating one. And that I was putting something over on him."

Urie was fully roped in now, caught. He had mesmerized her and in the process knew an unbounded freedom to explore at last the thoughts he had been harboring for three weeks. "Because now this time when I met him at the library—"

"You mean you've known him this whole three weeks and you never said one thing!" It dawned on her.

Her incredulous face broke in on the free expansion of his thoughts. He grinned defensively.

"If you hadn't seen him again today, you mean you would never have told me?" she whispered.

"I would have told you, but—" The grin made him a wicked old chimpanzee. It covered his shame.

"But we vowed always to pursue truth. You have broken your vow of truth—"

"This *is* the data of truth!" he conceded, trying to clarify her ridiculous charges without telling her that they never vowed to *tell each other* the truth. "But how did I know it had to do with ultimate truth. How do I know even now? Besides, there was something awful about it. I did try to tell you. That night when you saw the maw-tree shadow eating the rabbit. I *wanted* to tell you. But I didn't want to contaminate you. I wanted to *protect* you!"

Her resentment went underground, hiding in the darkness. They walked on in silence.

"Where are we going?" she asked sullenly.

"To the Episcopal church." He plucked it out of his head, as if it were a bingo ball.

"Just think. It's been a year and a half since we stole the money for *Kings Row*," said Zebul, trying to mollify her.

But it was centuries. They were full-fledged now upon the road for which that had been their initiation. Urie was glad he said it. It brought them back to the breathless magic of themselves. The imaginary figure of E. Bostwick, which stalked over them like a handsome, cold, powerful dream, receded. The church itself became primal and it beat Bostwick back into oblivion.

The cloister was well lit. But the naked light bulbs had been changed. They were placed under the eaves now. Zebul assailed the magic with squinting eyes.

"Come on. Let's go into the old church."

They passed through the creaky door and walked under the slaves' balcony.

"Let's play the organ."

"Do you think anybody'll hear?"

"At this time of night?"

They approached the organ in reverent silence. It was dark and massive in front of them. Only its pale pipes glowed silently from the cloister lights. They had to grope their way to the bench. Zebul's hand roved until he found the switch.

A red light turned on like an eye. The organ came alive, wheezing. Zebul pumped the footpedals. The bellows began to roar with wind. He played the major in C.

Together they sang "O Love That Will Not Let Me Go."

It was strange. At first they were aware only of the dangerous, massive night around them. They were two tiny specks singing against the dark night. But as they sang they began to become passengers in harmony and the organ a camel upon whose back they swayed. They lost the sense of their bodies' traveling across a desert of black ink. They became tremendously pure. Allied with the red eye, everything spread out infinitely from their center. They began to see strange shores and strange suns. The yielding of their flickering souls was actively a momentum of love. Their wills became superannuated.

When the hymn stopped, they came back to their bodies, intensely aware of the sensation of the hard bench where they sat, and the nearness of their two bodies. The organ purred in the silence.

"Let me play," whispered Urie. She pushed him.

How strange, thought Zebul. He moved over. She has breath like the organ. She is sweet. Again he did not want Urie sweet. She is alive. She is sitting near me and I am sitting next to her. I am alive.

She played "Drink to Me Only with Thine Eyes." Neither of them sang, for they had already made their testimony. They had let their animal carry them, pulling in the beauty of the night. But Zebul thought the words as Urie played them. He tried to see her in the dark. The moon made a hollow in her upper lip. He thought she had a furry, dreamy expression. But he could not see her eyes.

Urie thought of nothing. She could play the organ better than Zebul. She did not press it so hard. She let it play her. On certain chords she let it hurt her with ecstatic modulation. She ended up unaware of what happened, sitting with limp hands.

He did not know what to do next. He did not want to murder the spell. But they had to do something else. Nevertheless, they sat there waiting for a long time. Then he took the step. Feeling very cruel, he found the switch, flipped it off, and watched the red light die. The organ gave one last expiring groan. Urie closed the walnut lid tenderly over the dead keys.

They tiptoed down the velvet rug. By now their eyes were accustomed to every listening pew, every pane of medieval glass, even to the tubes of the extinct organ, which seemed to be watching from the hollow holes at the top. Since by the death of the organ they had caused the night to come to life, what should they do with it?

"Go on," he said in a strange voice.

The door to the cloisters shone pale and scary with light.

"What are you waiting for?" He pushed her out into the light.

"But I wanted to kiss the organ good-by!" She had to catch her balance from the push. She laughed. "Pig!"

His face was horned, Machiavellian, glittering, and brilliant. She was suddenly conscious of him as a being exactly like herself. She looked like him! She had never noticed it before! She moved toward him, giggling. She was being sucked toward him. She did not know what she was going to do when she got to him. Kiss him?

But he would not let her come. He put out his hand and stopped her by the shoulders in a shadow made by the arch blocking the naked light bulb. They froze for a moment, her magnetic motion in limbo.

Then he let her come. *She* moved. At the last minute she stopped. So he touched his mouth to hers experimentally. He tasted it. Her lips seemed different from what he thought they would be. They were soft. They were also clinging. He grew breathless. When she wanted to go away from him as if she were scared, he actively pushed her away. At the same time he slid his arms over her neck to hold her.

He did not know what to say.

"You're beautiful." After the Cult of Ugliness, this was phony. But neither bothered to think of that.

They tried again, kissing, feeling each others' lips, breaking apart, looking at each other, kissing. They were filled with a lightness amounting to inanity. Then they were filled with wonder at the inanity. At last their legs ached from standing and their heads became dizzy.

The next day they met at the library, and the sun was so bright they had to squint. They stared into each others' faces to see if there was any trace. Each looked utterly familiar to the other, yet each was strange.

"Let's go a new way home," said Zebul. "One we've never been before."

They chose the woods below the bell tower. They figured they would come onto Pack Mill Road below the Count house. On the way they did not talk. They crashed through the underbrush, each thinking his own thought.

On a ridge in the woods Zebul suddenly stopped and said, "About last night. We have to make it immortal."

She opened her eyes in surprise.

"Well, it *was* immortal, wasn't it?" he asked.

"Yes."

"And now it's gone, isn't it?"

"No! It—"

"So now we have to make it immortal."

"But how?" Her whisper was fearful, as if he were going to make a suicide pact.

"Write it down." He repeated to her, "We've got to write it down on paper!"

"But it is what it is what it is what it is, like Gertrude Stein said—"

"See! You can't even find a word for it. We can't go around making definitions! How can you call it any word? That's why we have to write it, to evoke it, with words around it, not it, to try to approximate it, otherwise—"

"But aren't we going to—"

"Is last night now?" he asked brutally.

"No. But *it* is. It *is!*" she protested.

"If *it* is, God is!" he snapped with evil triumph.

He was immediately sorry for this victory. His voice changed as he leaned over her bent head. "That's why we have to make it and give it form. We'll make it indelible!" He stopped as an idea made him knit his eyebrow into a T-square. "Urie! I know what. You be Sybil in it. I'll be Attis. She's a different goddess from any we have ever identified ourselves with!"

The moment he mentioned Sybil she wanted to be Athena. But she waited too long to disagree.

"Have you got your notebook here? Gimme!" He ripped two sheets from the brown canvas looseleaf she clutched, and sat down on the ground.

Her disappointment switched into another gear. She felt the beginnings of excitement. She sat down six feet away from him.

Zebul wrote free association. He ended up: "Kiss, kiss, lips, kiss, I Attis, lips, breast, lips nigger road honeysuckle road, kiss, the vaulted ceiling, light of naked bulb, perfume, oh kiss, kiss, Urie-Sybil, kiss me. Kiss, kiss me, kiss." He held it out to her.

She blushed to have her breasts mentioned on paper. Her face was hot, but she had to admit, "It's good!" She began to write: "Sybil in a sandbox sat." She wrote, weaving a poetic story about Sybil from the day she became aware of existence as a child in a sandbox to this night in a church when she became aware of conjoinment by a kiss.

Zebul was ecstatic at its epic tone. He started talking in affected, passionate sentences about how he and Urie were so different, but how they were complementary, and how each conception of that evening was more because of the addition of the other's conception. He caressed her paper. Then he caressed his own.

Later in his little house he typed them both on separate sheets of green paper which he had had in stock since the days when he stole from the elementary school. From that time on, he carried the green sheets everywhere he went.

CHAPTER 26

Now that Urie and Irene were in college, Mrs. Bishop felt sorry for Loco Poco. She was at loose ends. She frittered around the house like a butterfly. Once Mrs. Bishop had seen her eating a morning glory.

Mrs. Bishop was sensitive about Loco because she felt guilty. Not only had she been incapable of doing anything about Loco's bad grades, but she had seen Loco become progressively wilder and more flagrant as she began to enter womanhood. She feared for her now that there was no school and she had the whole summer on her hands. P.Q. would never think of doing anything, so she had to.

A profound change had come into the family, Mrs. Bishop felt, this year that Urie and Irene had been in college. It was as if they had left home, even though they still lived there. They had become hard, impatient, compared to themselves in their high-school days. Urie had scraped up money from typing, which, added to what she had hoarded from last summer, would pay for two courses in the first summer session, and she swore she was going to finish college in three years. "There's a war on. You can't just sit around. I'm not going to end up working in some dumb defense plant!" Irene, influenced by these words, also registered for summer school.

Mrs. Bishop felt a sense of loss, as if she were expendable. Not that she had time on her hands, for there were always new aprons and caps to make. But the business felt like a losing proposition. P.Q. was making no more money now than when he had started. Here, all around them, things were changing. Ephesus had gone on the war economy, had grown larger because of the influx of the Navy. A new war plant was reported to be moving into the old mill at Haw. Even Zebul's father was making money; he had been hired as a machinery-repairman on an Army base fifty miles away and came home only on weekends. There was constant talk about a second front in Europe; Molotov was coming to Washington for conferences with the President; and all P.Q. did was listen to events, as if listening meant something *per se*. But what Mrs. Bishop saw was delusion. Why did P.Q., who *knew*, fail to make any more money in a world where the Depression was over and everybody was cashing in? What good did knowing do you? She remembered when he had not batted an eye last summer at the news that the British had finally evacuated Crete. P.Q. reminded her of North Africa. For two years now the British and Rommel had roved back and forth over the desert, capturing and recapturing the same places. Getting nowhere.

More money was needed now, even with Irene and Urie paying for their own tuitions. There was their lunch on the campus. Fifteen cents apiece was not enough for lunches, but that was all they were going to get. And they were each going to be thirty-five dollars short when it came time to pay the bursar's office. They got their books second-hand, yet even these cost twenty-eight dollars. Mrs. Bishop felt irascible, incompetent. She never got a chance to talk with the older girls now. So she projected some of this dissatisfaction upon Loco.

Mrs. Bishop's concern was even deeper. There was a secret side of herself born of these feelings that she refused to recognize—like her teeth. Sometimes she sat and thought about the Count house, and those things still lying neglected in that abandoned place. It was more than a year now, and nothing had been done. The Count house was still abandoned. And those things still there, rotting.

In May she spotted a squib in the *Ephesus Weekly* about a special program sponsored by the university symphony for talented high-school students.

"Oh, look here!" she said to Loco. "Why don't you try out for the symphony orchestra?"

"Yeah. Maybe they'll pay you," said Irene.

"Sarcasm isn't necessary, Irene."

"It says 'talented.' Do you think she's talented?" persisted Irene over her mother's shoulder.

Loco looked at the article in the paper and did not bat an eye. She was like P.Q., thought Mrs. Bishop—no acknowledgment. Yet the next day after school Loco went to the Music Building with her flute in her hand.

Dr. Napod Nagy was the director of the University Symphony Orchestra. He was a Hungarian who had escaped from Europe via Lisbon, a distant relative of the Heidleziggers, a family that had recently come to Ephesus and established a strudel shop next to Hoke Tabernacle's bookstore. Dr. Nagy was a tiny, ageless man with beautiful brown skin and delicate pink fingernails. His movements were quick, and he spoke atrocious English.

When Loco Poco peeked through his half-open door, he was writing on some music paper, singing, "Booboooboo," through purple lips. She did not dare go in.

He spotted her. "What do you want? What do you want? Come in and say," he squeaked.

She opened the door, went in, and stood like a cow. "I want to join the symphony orchestra. Like it said in the paper."

"You play flute?" he said. He made his eyebrows prance up suddenly like two ballet dancers. He put his pen down and squnched himself up in his chair so that his feet did not touch the ground.

"Yes."

"You are beautiful. Ah."

Loco accepted this matter-of-factly, as she did all kudos, and waited.

"Well, play, so I can see if you're good enough."

She played "Three Little Fishies." As with Amy Grispin White's shoes, she could not help herself.

"Why play that?" He picked up his pen sulkily and waved it in hieroglyphics in the air. "Are you ignorant, that you should play that to me? You are ignorant," he decided.

"But you'll let me play in the symphony, won't you?"

"You don't play good. Your tone is flat, flat, flat."

"But I want to!" she pleaded.

"You need lessons. You blow too hard. Give me," he said.

He took her flute and blew it low so that it had a mellow, throaty *vibrato,* just the opposite of his personality.

"But I don't like *vibrato.*"

"You got to have *vibrato.* I haven't no time for lessons. Though, try it." He gave her back the flute. She put it to her mouth, blew very low, affectedly, aping him, and came out with a perfect *vibrato.*

"Why you not take lessons?"

"No money," she said.

"I got no time," he said, "and you got to have lessons. I won't have you in symphony orchestra blowing like that. You have to play solos. The only hope is for you to follow me around. I show you how when I get time, between letters, fixing scores, conferences, chewing out rotten people and players, at steps when other people waste my time, and so forth. You may be beautiful, but you can't get away from everything. You got to know right and take the rotten with the excellent. You come down here and spend all day, eight hours a day, five days a week. I'll fit you in. No other way."

Loco was radiant. At home she announced the news, hopping around the kitchen.

"I've been accepted! The only thing is, he's forcing me to play with *vibrato.*"

"I told you those flat notes made a horrible sound!" said Irene.

For the first time, Mrs. Bishop thought, Loco Poco was fascinated, dedicated to something.

The next day she started training. She became Napod Nagy's familiar. She followed at his side, three paces distant, with her flute in her hand, and in strange places, in halls, thresholds, basements, even outside that same music room where she and Urie and Zebul and Irene had eaten the stolen dime-store cookies and candy, he made her lift her flute and practice passages. He had her copy the flute part in Ravel's "Bolero," and they walked in time to the rhythm. Neither Loco Poco nor Dr. Nagy thought there was anything funny about the method of these lessons. They became so entrenched in music and rhythm as they sang, blew, and marched their way around the building that they were unaware of people's attitudes. Secretaries in the department make jokes. Opal Granger's father, who was teaching a course in liaison with the Music Department on Greek choruses in ancient drama, named her Nagy's Poco Piper. Some graduate students made up a rhyme:

> Napod Nagy picks his pipers pixie.
> If Napod's pixie's really Loco Poco,
> Does Nagy prick or poke
> Her in the nicht?
> Or is this really all the piping in his bag o' tricksie?

Mrs. Olliphant, Chairman Rankin's secretary, said, "Bad taste." Music librarian Verna Watson said, "Gross favoritism." "It's absolutely disgraceful!" said the first violinist, Losey Blainton. But Payton Almirer, a tenor, said the two looked like dwarfs, Nagy the smaller one.

The method of these lessons gave Loco Poco freedom, and because she continued to despise and scorn that throaty *vibrato* that he made her play, she nagged, sulked, and quarreled in the corridors.

"Why do I have to blow it like that?"

"That's the way it's done."

"But I hate that tone."

"Don't be ugly. You beautiful. Keep quiet except for flute."

"But I don't want—"

It was only when he waved at her imperiously with the clutch of papers he held in his hand that she was quiet.

"Go in that room and practice the sixteen bars of 'Eroica' till ten past four when I finish that conference. Then I come to pick you up, and you better sound good."

Once, outside Dr. Rankin's office, when he made her finish the solo to the very end, he praised her.

"You're getting good."

"But that dirty *vibrato* is—"

"You keep quiet about dirty *vibrato*. Listen to your nose hairs!" he squeaked in his itchy voice, pointing with a pink fingernail up his nostril. "You listen to the wind when she sing in pine tree. No wind blows straight!"

Loco did listen to the wind in a pine tree. It was true. Vibration made things waver.

She became very good at note-reading after that. And the first session in a complete rehearsal of the orchestra deflected her dissatisfaction. Dr. Nagy made her sit in the very front section of the wind instruments.

"Your beauty catch all them audiences in the eye. If they ain't got no ear, they got an eye. That's half the battle, believe you me."

"Do you let me play because you think I'm beautiful or because you think I can play good?" she asked petulantly.

"What's the difference?" he asked, ripping open a letter that he had just received.

The orchestra was so big around her that it was thrilling. She could hardly bear it. She got so excited in the first rehearsal she tipped over her music stand. Nagy shouted at her, and she almost stuck her tongue out. She forgot about the flat, the absolute tone that she had sought for so long. With the orchestra she was as delighted as she was with her own playing, and she stared around her, her hair bobbing and waving, as she almost clapped for the violins or the trumpets when they took the lead, or even the triangle when it came in on an unexpected beat.

She raved at home. Everybody gathered around her.

"I knew it would be marvelous!" beamed Mrs. Bishop. "I told you it would be!"

After this no one heard her trying to get that flat note any more. She became intensely proficient and technically brilliant, and sometimes she would pick up the flute at night and wheedle Haydn or Mozart out of its holes, like a virtuoso mouse.

P.Q. loved it. Sometimes he picked up his paper at night and looked under it to observe her playing, as if it were the curtain of a theater.

"That Dr. Nagy is a card," he praised. "He may be a Hungarian midget, but he is as great as Mitropoulos!"

CHAPTER 27

On the first day of summer school Zebul came face to face with Bostwick. He had just finished registering and was walking on a footpath which people had trod through the grass as a shortcut under the confederate soldier. Bostwick was headed toward town, dressed in Navy whites.

Zebul stopped dead on the balls of his feet.

Bostwick hesitated and then, perplexed, stopped and faced him.

"Where do I know you from? Are you the cadet that I saw in the Armory back in April?"

"Yes," Zebul breathed. He was aware of the bathing light, of a squirrel that ran up the trunk of the tree above the Confederate soldier's head, and of the sudden glint of the water fountain under the canopy of the Old Well. "But I wasn't—I mean I'm not a real cadet. I'm not French. I'm not in the Navy at all."

All the rules of life demanded that this information be ingested and register a reaction. Was Bostwick angry? Would he now report Zebul? Would he give him a warning? Or would he let him go?

Bostwick's expression did not change, except for a slight withdrawal. Zebul stared at him, frightened. Out of the pale face, Bostwick's eyes seemed to lift themselves and float above their sockets.

"Aren't you— Are you going to do anything?" he asked him.

Bostwick's eyes inhabited their sockets again. They were softer.

"Are you a student here?"

"Yes."

"What year?"

"Freshman."

"Where do you live?"

"In Haw—over there." Zebul pointed.

"You live at home?"

"Yes."

"How old are you?"

"Sixteen."

Again Zebul waited. Bostwick would be a fool to be satisfied with literal answers. But Bostwick looked bored. Zebul's heart, like a lover's, began to feel a wound at incipient separation. If Bostwick left that moment, there would never be a confrontation. He could not bear to go unrecognized.

"You—you knew I wasn't a French cadet!" It succeeded. The look of boredom was replaced by a hint of interest. But Zebul did not dare go as far as collusion. "Even then. Right in the Armory you knew!"

But Bostwick's manner was correct. He gazed at Zebul, forcing him to carry the ball still further.

"Why didn't you report me? You're a captain in the military. You're supposed to report any infraction." Zebul was pleased at his own ingenuousness. Just as he had sensed Bostwick entering into his impersonation, now he sensed him entering into the challenge.

"You take the position that I am a representative of the law?" Bostwick's manner gave no hint of bending.

"Yes. And I acted against the law."

"You think I'm the law?" Bostwick's nostrils flared slightly, and his mouth went up at this question. Zebul gave way to enthrallment. He could feel the roots of his hair tingle. "No man is the law. It's far too simple to make me the slave of a law which you are now indulging yourself in pretending to defy. Your cosmic egotism is absurd. Naïve. What importance do you think your trivial crime has in a world—a world as evil as Hitler? You've blown it all out of proportion."

Zebul blushed. He could not think of anything to say.

"Also," said Bostwick, "I'm not a captain. Still a lieutenant." His rueful smile seemed to go back to some other life, some thin life which he had succeeded in forgetting during this interlude.

Seeing only that he was leaving, Zebul blurted, "Are you—"

"I'm not going to report anything. Consider the incident closed."

But he left before Zebul could tell him that that was not what he cared about at all.

He was in a half-abstracted mood all that evening at Urie's.

"Millions could be made," said P.Q., "if someone translated the diaries of what went on in some of these depraved courts."

"What courts?" asked Zebul.

"Catherine the Great's."

"Dirt!" said Urie.

"Yes, but dirt sells!" Glad of the opportunity to break his preoccupation with Bostwick, he faced Urie.

"For instance," continued P.Q. "There is this memoir written by Charles François Philibert Masson. It describes intimate court doings, the murder of Peter by the knout, the torturing of some court ladies on marble slabs in the basement, all kinds of indescribable doings. You wouldn't believe it! All the details of the twelve lovers of Catherine the Great."

Zebul began to slaver with interest.

"Of course, you do not know seventeenth-century French."

"He could learn that in a minute," retorted Urie.

"They use *ois*'es for the *ais*'es of the past tense," said P.Q.

"Phooey. A cinch." Zebul was derisive. "But how do you know it's so juicy?"

"Look yourself." P.Q. handed him an ancient brown book with a pattern of red and blue scrollwork. Its yellowed pages were as rotten as old cheese. "This is what you use for the basis. When you finish, we'll have the typed version bound by the library. Then we can send it off to Houghton Mifflin in my name and yours."

"What kind of stuff are you getting them to do?" Mrs. Bishop asked P.Q. just before he went to bed. "I don't think that's very good." She had seen Loco Poco's expression when she was supposed to have been doing her homework.

But P.Q. paid no attention. Life was trial and error. Everything was dynamic. People should be exposed to all things, and they would find their own values, like creatures in the ocean.

Urie too was disapproving, but for different reasons from her mother's.

"What are you doing this for? Money?"

"Why?" countered Zebul, refusing to fall into any more traps that day.

"Because if it's for money I would approach it with skepticism. Skepticism," she said, lifting her lips in P.Q.'s gesture. "After all, P.Q.'s record for money-making leaves a lot to be desired, and if you go to all that work and nothing comes of it, well—I'm just warning you."

"Your cosmic egotism is absurd," said Zebul, experimenting with the line. "Naïve. It's far too simple to think that anyone does any one action for one simple intention."

"What are you doing this for, then?" repeated Urie.

"Art for art's sake," he mocked.

"Dirt for dirt's sake, you mean."

He refrained from laughing, saying, "Well, you don't have to do it just because I am."

But she did. She took his dictation on the typewriter. Every evening he sat at the table with the tattered old French version of the book. When he came to a part he could not get, he showed her. Together they figured it out. It was a strange game, full of suspense. Sometimes there were asterisks, and they could only guess the horrible details. The elegant style of the writing contrasted with the candor of physical details and mitigated them.

His friendship with Bostwick was consolidated at the same time. He had to play it cool, for he did not want Bostwick to think he was pursuing him. For three days he frequented the path where he had met him, but there was no sign of him. Nor did he know what he would say when he did see him.

On the fourth day they met by the Confederate soldier.

"This must be your route on Thursdays," Zebul said joyously.

Bostwick seemed neither pleased nor displeased to see him.

"You may think it's odd for someone sixteen years old to be so interested in you, Bostwick. But do you know that you are the only adult I have ever met that I could talk to?"

"How do you know my name?"

"I saw it on your call slip. At the library that time."

Bostwick nodded.

"And do you know why? Because you are the only one who can see beyond appearances."

Bostwick did not halt the friendship which Zebul thrust upon him, although at any moment he could have done so.

One day Zebul followed him, talking, all the way to the house where he lived. Zebul was amazed at its tackiness. It was a run-down house with two sagging board steps, on McCauley Street. Bostwick lived in two rooms on the second floor.

"Do you want to come up?" Bostwick asked.

Zebul followed him. To think that a Navy officer lived in a place like this! Zebul inspected carefully. There were a bedroom and a living room with an old brown sofa. There was a card table, which was untidy, with Ritz cracker crumbs and a half-empty peanut-butter jar upon it. This untidiness did not fit with Bostwick's immaculate appearance. It thrilled Zebul.

Zebul sat down, feeling strangely shy. Bostwick made some cocoa on a hotplate. They drank it out of blue mugs. The sun floated into the room. They began to talk about Schopenhauer. Zebel lost his shyness. Once in the conversation Bostwick laughed. Zebul stared at him strangely. It was the first time he had ever heard him laugh. The laughter was openhearted. It made Bostwick vulnerable.

It was at that moment that Zebul decided to show Bostwick the two Attis and Sybil themes. He took the green sheets out of his schoolbag and laid them before him, like a gift, in an act of supreme confidence. He held his large boyish hands together, forming a gobbling prayer in his heart.

Bostwick read them. The clock ticked. Through nervous sidelong glances Zebul noticed how Bostwick's hair was overgrown at the back of his neck and formed a nape over his Navy collar.

When Bostwick finished, he looked up. "So you're in love," he said, and then, softening his voice, added, "Or think you're in love."

Was he being callous? Or tender? Zebul blushed. He could not believe Bostwick had used the expression "in love," which he connected with high school and dime store. He grew redder and redder under Bostwick's rude gaze.

"I don't know what you mean by that. I didn't expect—"

"Is she pretty?"

"No!" Zebul grew alarmed. He picked up the themes in his trembling fingers and began stuffing them back into his bag, trying to melt away from Bostwick.

"Of course you don't know what love is yet, do you?" Bostwick's voice was soothing.

"No."

"That's why you wrote that, isn't it?"

"Yes." He despised his docility.

"But you didn't want these kinds of comments from me, did you? You wanted me to comment on the style, didn't you? Not the content."

"Yes."

"No, you don't really," contradicted Bostwick softly.

The sun slipped below the window sill. Zebul stared, trapped between daylight and night.

"Does she know you gave them to me to read?"

"No."

"Are you going to tell her?"

"Of course."

Bostwick had the stance of a master after he has decided the fate of a recalcitrant slave. His eyes were weary. Instead of looking into Zebul's eyes, he looked at the same point over his head.

"Well, you have pleaded your age to justify all your unconventional acts, even this one of making a friend out of me. As ingenuous as that is, from now on your age is irrelevant. I shall not treat you according to it. It bores me with its purity. So don't expect special favors. I'm treating you like a soul. Even Steven. That makes you handicapped, since you have no experience. Well, maybe not." Bostwick gave a harsh laugh. "Experience could be pollution. Then I would be the weaker one."

Just as Zebul was enthralled again, Bostwick said, "You know, you regurgitate your soul more painstakingly than anyone I have ever known. You have great pride in your vomit."

Zebul's face froze. He was unable to believe that anyone could say such things to him.

Bostwick wore an open, calm smile.

"Well, look who's here! Alcibiades himself! What's the news in Syracuse?" P.Q. greeted, stressing the rhyme heavily as Zebul entered the door that evening.

The familiarity was reassuring to his bruised ego. The loudness was clean. The intrigue was wholesome. He had interrupted a family discussion on the subject of Mrs. Polenta, a new friend of Loco Poco's. Mrs. Polenta was a trustee of the university symphony who lived in the Ephesus Inn. She had taken a shine to Loco, was fat, wore lipstick up to her nose, and wore corsets whose grommet holes could be seen through her dresses and made her look like a giant chestnut burr. P.Q. had listened to Loco's imitations with a view to inviting Mrs. Polenta for supper at some future date to sound her out and see if she would put money into his business.

"You saw him!" pounced Urie.

"Yes, I did," he said in a strange voice. "I went to his house. He lives on the second floor of that gray house on McCauley Street, that old beat-up place."

The group broke up. P.Q. settled down to read the paper. Headlines on the Battle of Midway flashed on the upright page forming a wall to cut him off from them. Urie hated the war in the Pacific. She hung on Zebul with the same hypnotic fervor that he had hung on Bostwick. Ever since he had taken to hunting for Bostwick, Urie had been jealous on one hand and mesmerized with the myth of Bostwick on the other. She wanted to meet Bostwick too. She wanted Zebul to hurry up and make friends so she could meet him.

"We sat and talked. He is strange. I didn't know what to think of him. He said he despised my age. He said I traded on it." Zebul began to present an intense, exaggerated picture of everything. He told the incident in an abstract, disconnected way. He felt unreal. A strange thing was happening. The traitor Alcibiades. He began to see from Bostwick's point of view. In showing the Attis and Sybil themes had he betrayed Urie? "I showed him our Attis and Sybil," he said.

She continued staring at him. "Why? Why? Why did you do it?"

"I don't know."

"But—"

"I don't know why. I just did."

She did not register surprise. Nor disappointment. No emotion at all, except the same strangeness he felt himself.

"He wondered why I did it too. He asked if you knew I was showing them."

"He did?"

"Yes. I told him I'd tell you."

They sat staring at each other hypnotically.

"He crucified me," said Zebul suddenly.

"What do you mean?"

"I don't know. He just crucified me, that's all. I'll tell you later"— making a motion with his eyes to indicate the presence of the family. Then he went on in a conversational tone, "We talked all about Schopenhauer when I first walked in. We—"

"Schopenhauer," said P.Q., letting down his paper slowly, with emphasis. The words "crucified" and "Schopenhauer" had formed the stunning impression. "That Jew. He never got his behind off the wailing wall. Crazy. Who is this Bostwick, anyway? Is he a Jew?"

"No," said Zebul, and he and Urie laughed insanely.

C H A P T E R   28

The Attis and Sybil had become a pubescent marriage pact. For the first time in their relationship, Urie catered to Zebul. Now that he had gone outside the family and become interested in Bostwick, he had seized the initiative. And she was the one who had to follow. She was congealed in his actions and committed unquestioningly to his maneuvers with Bostwick. She hated Bostwick. Yet it was a fact that Bostwick belonged to her as much as he did to Zebul. It wanted only a meeting, a consummation.

She understood also that in some way she was Zebul's ace in the hole. Because Bostwick could not belong fully to Zebul until he met Urie.

It would have been easy to arrange a simple meeting. Zebul could have taken Urie to the Confederate soldier, and it would have happened. But Zebul was fiercely idealistic. It was very complicated. He talked about it night and day. The time and the place had to be perfect. They discussed the Fall Line, Poker Hill, or the Negro graveyard.

Urie grew very nervous. The figment of Bostwick enlarged in her mind until she grew afraid of him. The plan was also humiliating. She felt like some statue in a museum, about to be undraped.

But despite all his talk with Urie, Zebul had not even broached the subject of such a meeting to Bostwick.

That night as the June bugs pounded against the screen door, Irene said in a strange voice, "Look at that."

Urie looked up from her assignment in Victorian Literature. Loco, who had been painting a sheep curiously resembling Dr. Nagy, lifted herself on all fours from the Oriental rug, careful not to tip over her pot of water.

"Why, it's that sewing kit we saw at the Count house!" said Loco.

Mrs. Bishop, behind her sewing machine, was stitching the final gores of a navy-blue skirt for Loco's first public performance in the symphony's summer series. The machine stopped. The pinked edges of the blue material quivered. Only the strange jitter of the June bug against the screen broke the silence.

The sewing case was secreted in a hollow place in the bookcase just above Scott's novels.

"Where did it come from?" asked Irene.

How could Irene be so stupid? thought Urie. Slipping between her different universes, campus, Bostwick, Zebul, family, with the ease of gears, she turned her eyes on her mother.

A second later Loco and Irene followed suit.

Mrs. Bishop blushed, fighting the thralldom of their eyes. She lifted the presser foot, turned up the needle, lifted the cloth out, and held it at arms' length, pretending to fit the two gores together.

"I got it," she said.

"You mean you stole it?" Loco tinkled.

"Well, I was darned if I was going to let everything go to rot in there. The Count place is in litigation, and the relatives are fighting, so nobody can do anything about it, and that's why everything is left there like that."

But that second of the blush had revealed a weakness as intimate as Mrs. Bishop's teeth. It was a thousand times worse than all P.Q.'s faults combined. What troubled Urie was a new, hidden side of their mother. It was all right for them to steal. But their mother? And they had taught her! Already disconcerted at the changes in herself and Zebul, the interloping of Bostwick, the instability of her conceptions of herself, she felt the one steady center of Bishopry was Mrs. Bishop. Now she was chimerical!

"That's not all I stole!" Mrs. Bishop accentuated the word "stole" defiantly, as if she were rehearsing a passage as difficult as Loco's passage in the "Eroica."

This smote Urie. But Loco moved to her mother like a bee to a flower. "You stole other stuff?"

"Yes. I stole *The Last Days of Pompeii,* T. E. Lawrence's *The Seven Pillars of Wisdom,* and *East Lynne.*"

Mrs. Bishop ran to the bookcase, took out *East Lynne,* showed it to them, and then cradled it to herself.

"Mamma, it's marvelous. When did you do it?"

"Last week."

"In the nighttime?"

"No. In the afternoon."

Loco was beside herself with delight. She stood up, clenched her fists to-

[243

gether, and broadcast into them as if they were a microphone, the voice of Irene Wicker, the Singing Lady.

"As Mrs. P. Q. Bishop crept up the stairs of the haunted mansion, the ghost of the Count appeared in the waning afternoon, saying, 'Lo! The blue fairy has come! Though she be in the guise of a thief she has come to save us from—' "

"Hush, Loco!" But Mrs. Bishop was beaming. "Just because I stole doesn't mean you can do it too. Or broadcast it all over kingdom come. For goodness sake, don't tell P.Q. I did a thing like that. He would think it was terrible!"

In spite of her trepidation, Urie laughed. The sound jittered in the June night and contaged Irene too.

"In other words, don't do what you do, do what you preach."

"Exactly."

"But that's horrible hypocrisy, Mamma."

"No, it isn't! It's the best thing she ever did!" cried Loco, flinging her arms around Mrs. Bishop's neck.

"Maybe it's a bad thing to tell you I did it, but I had to." Mrs. Bishop's face smiled against Loco's dark hair like a flower. "I couldn't stand the thought of those things going to rack and ruin."

The next day Zebul went to Bostwick's. But Bostwick was not in his room. He was in the garden back of the house. He was dressed in tennis shorts and a beige sweater. There was a can of paint on the ground and a new brush, and he was digging at the roots of a small runty pear tree.

"I came to see you," announced Zebul. He was slightly nervous, yet charmed by the garden, which was very private.

Bostwick turned around. "Oh, hello." He smiled but continued his digging. He explained that he was trying to fix the pear tree. "I'm going to put lime in here. I want to see if I can save it."

Zebul was disappointed at Bostwick's preoccupation with the tree. "What's the paint for?"

"To make a ring here to keep off the insects."

"Shall I do it?"

"All right." But Bostwick did not look enthusiastic. He pointed to a screwdriver, with which Zebul opened the can.

"How far up do you want it painted?"

"Oh, I don't know. Wherever you think."

Zebul indicated four feet from the ground. Then he dipped the brush. He noticed that Bostwick's shovel action was very neat, biting the earth with tiny nips and lifting it slightly so that more earth was turned over in small particles than it would have been had Bostwick put muscle into it.

Bostwick finished digging and dipped lime from a burlap bag around the roots of the tree. He took great care not to let the dust flick Zebul's paint job. He passed so near that Zebul could see the pores in the skin of his legs. They were a dark brown color, with sandy hair so thick and opulent that it seemed like fur. Zebul's legs were longer. The hair was young and soft. His muscles were harder, but not apparent like Bostwick's. He had a curious desire to touch Bostwick's leg. It horrified him. At the same time he had a hilarious desire to laugh. Bostwick's legs were manly and beautiful. They impressed him.

"Why do you want to save this tree so much?" he asked perversely. "Do you have a desire to do good to it?"

The moment he made this remark he was aware that up to this point there had been a tender and dignified reserve in the day and that Bostwick knew he was referring to himself. The garden secured a silence which almost proclaimed itself in sound. Their activity was imbedded in restrained reverence more powerful than either of them. Yet Zebul had cut into it.

He felt a sense of pervading loss. Now it was almost dark, and Bostwick's legs had dimmed. The fire of his hairs had turned subtly and was disappearing, becoming merely silhouette—what had been full-bodied and mysterious in the bright sunlight.

"Not good. There's no such thing as morality. Only taste, emotion, and constant change. I like to be an effecter of change."

His words sounded tall and lonely to Zebul. Hadn't he and Urie both hitched themselves like racehorses to the world of change? To beat the system by shooting the rapids of change?

"There are so many acts," said Bostwick in his strange, musing voice, "and so many changes, that you can't see where cause begins and effect ends. I had the choice of chopping it down, propping it up, or forgetting it. This was hardest. So I did this."

"But this tree doesn't even belong to you!"

"Well, you could say I was bored, in other words," said Bostwick wryly.

He is noble, thought Zebul.

"Bostwick, I told Urie. I told her about showing you the Attis and Sybil! She—I don't know what she thought! No, I mean, that brought you closer. She is terrific. She lives in this house and her father is P.Q. He was a great influence on my life when I was younger. They live in Niggertown. I never met anyone until I met her and P.Q. and that whole family. Until I met you now. And now you have to meet her. Do you want to?"

"Of course. Very much."

"I will introduce you to her!"

In the dusk Bostwick's smile had a triumphant cast. But in another light it seemed not a smile at all, only a breaking of the lips as if something had stirred him, an effect which he despised.

The meeting was scheduled for Thursday, a week to the day. It was to take place at Bostwick's room, or in the garden. Zebul was to bring Urie.

"Why his place?" she asked pleadingly.

"Because of the cocoa."

The idea of cocoa mollified her. It was the only human thing she had ever heard about Bostwick. Drinking cocoa was a definite act by which one could avoid the baldness of confrontation.

C H A P T E R 29

Urie finished work, put the cover over the typewriter, and, without saying goodnight to Miss Marsh, sneaked out of the catalogue department. It was already Tuesday. There were only two more days. Already she had spent the weekend worrying about what dress she would wear. She was being sucked into arbitrary sex categories again. Until Bostwick became a person, he was a Navy officer. A Navy officer was a man. A man looked at girls. She was a girl. A girl was dress. Dress was a girl. She, who hated dress and girl, was forced into that plane of existence. On the other side of the mirror stared a pathetic witch in tatters, passing itself off as a teeheeing fake.

She sat down in the reference room to sweep herself clean by reading "Sarah Bernhardt," page 2138, volume 5 in the *Encyclopaedia of Biographical Personages,* 1650–1900. She lit the light. She read for ten minutes. Then she became aware of something. She looked up.

Zebul was walking toward her from the rotunda, accompanied by the Navy officer. His face was blushing and eager, and he was talking animatedly, striding in an unnatural, superior, masculine way. He was so preoccupied that he did not notice her.

But I'm not supposed to meet Bostwick now! she thought. She rose electrically, turning her head half away so that she could escape before Zebul spotted her.

But Bostwick was looking at her. Calm, derisive, he was staring right through her as if she were a stick of furniture. She could not look away.

She was mesmerized. Bostwick was the Grief Face she had opened the door on in the Ephesus Inn that summer!

"Urie, I—we—didn't expect to see you here."

Zebul tried to adjust to the fact that the whole scheme of meeting was changed.

There was a three-second round of glances and communication. Urie, her mouth a round O shape, was staring transfixed at Bostwick. Bostwick looked to Zebul questioningly for a confirmation of the meeting. And then he turned toward Urie, leaned his head slightly, and smiled, waiting for the introduction.

"Bostwick, this is . . . Urie Bishop. Urie, this is Bostwick."

Catalyzed by Bostwick, Urie did not alter her expression. This time he was a regular Navy officer. But it was the same man. How could he be smiling? Doesn't he recognize me?

Zebul was flashing his cabalistic, intimate, "Urie, this is it!" look.

"How do you do?" murmured Bostwick. He was faintly mocking, as if they were children and he condescended to play their game. But Urie's stare piqued his interest, and a glimmer answered out of his usually pale gray eyes.

Why doesn't she stop staring and say something? thought Zebul. But the very fact that she stood in that dream-stance justified him and surpassed his greatest expectations. He felt like a creator, for it was he who had envisioned the reality of this. He wanted to shout to both of them at the same time: "See! I told you! It's just as I said." To Urie: "See how great Bostwick is! I told you!" To Bostwick: "Now you can see why we wrote the themes. See how different she is!"

Urie knitted her brows, still staring. "How do you do? I'm glad to meet you." This polite whisper masked her mendacity. Maybe the tears blocked his eyesight. She was aware of Zebul's triumph beside her, but though she looked at him, her expression was stonelike. Zebul had no idea. Zebul did not know the truth. Everything was unreal. She went into a suspended state, a place of divine irresponsibility above them both. Zebul was impressed with her poise. She could feel it. In other circumstances she would have been triumphant or laughed at his attitude. But she was still staring at Bostwick.

[247

It was only when they were walking down Pergamus Avenue that she came to any sense of the present. They walked three abreast, Bostwick in the middle. Bostwick and Zebul were talking about Leibnitz, another Jew. She was quiet. From the corner of her eye she saw Opal Granger going into the physics building. Opal saw them, stared, and then disappeared into the building.

She began to realize: I'm walking down the street with a Navy officer! Blood flowed from her heart into every part of her body. It tingled in her fingers. She felt all the parts of her body separately. Bostwick was shining in a great light, and this light was covering her and covering Zebul. The light was of miraculous power. Yet it was not only the uniform. It was the essence of Bostwick. She was transformed from misfit and misanthrope to a high echelon. All that which had been unacceptable in her before, yet which she had always known as the source of her greatness, was justified. In this state she became smooth. The power activating her muscles began to come from outside her. Even her walk was silky. Zebul too was walking along with insidious ease, as if he knew what she was feeling. She was happy.

It was all the more poignant because she had a sudden intense longing to know Bostwick. To talk to him like Zebul. To lose herself communicating rather than contemplating.

They were walking as if they had a destination. But they did not. They were still on Pergamus Avenue, but they had just turned left. They crossed the parking lot in back of the Ephesus Inn. Two garbage cans stood outside the kitchen door.

Suddenly Zebul gave her the opportunity of throwing herself to the winds. He spotted a cabbage in the garbage can.

"Look! A face!" he cried, interrupting the conversation on Leibnitz. "It's looking at us!"

"It's got a cap on!" said Urie deliriously. Substitute the cabbage for the enigma.

Bostwick seemed faintly bored by their affectation.

But Zebul, with an unerring instinct for the mode of involvement, persisted. He grabbed the cabbage out of the can. He turned it in his hands, examining it. It was large and hard, with tight green curls. There was a deep semicircular slit in it, like a mouth. It took on identity. It smiled at him solemnly.

"Why do you spose those nigger cooks threw it out?"

"Maybe the mouth was a rotten spot," suggested Urie.

"Why do you say 'nigger'?" asked Bostwick softly.

"Because I'm not supposed to."

"I live in Niggertown," informed Urie, loud and glib.

"Yeah, she lives in Niggertown."

"When we first came down here, we went to Sears Roebuck and my sister saw the fountain with the sign 'Colored.' She started to drink out of it because she thought it was pink water!"

Again Urie thought this hysterically funny. She laughed.

Vaudeville was the ultimate revenge against mystery. Bostwick could have been the President, he was so high. Melt down Bostwick. Arrest him with charm. He was smiling slightly. Zebul played the straight man. The sun was beginning to go down, and the afternoon became red.

"It's Potemkin," Zebul told her, inspired.

"We've been translating these memoirs about the court of Catherine the Great," she explained. "We see everything as characters in it."

"Pretend you're Catherine. Kiss it," ordered Zebul.

If he had to be treated rudely to keep them from seeming wooers of his splendor, let him be treated rudely. The redness tinging the curls of the cabbage made it possible. Familiar things became transformed and fantastic.

Urie took the cabbage carefully. She looked at it, pretending to fall in love with it. She concentrated. Then she placed her mouth on the slit.

She giggled. She lifted her eyes to see Bostwick's reaction. His decorum was frightening, but his nostrils flared slightly against the gray pallor.

Zebul was spellbound, she saw out of the corner of her eye. Later he would praise her.

She caressed the cabbage's hair. She thrust herself into final schizophrenia. She closed her eyes. She imitated Bette Davis kissing Paul Henreid. She abandoned herself. She moved the cabbage first right, then left against her lips. She wheeled her head against the sky in different positions to perfect the frame. She wanted to scream with laughter. But she was trapped in her role. She lavished long and sultry kisses, hot and torrid kisses.

Out of her ruthless eye above the performance, she saw Bostwick's expression. There was a dark interest in his opacity, like the reflection of black seaweed on the ocean's face. Yet his disguise was perfect. He did not move a muscle. Perfect, cream-marble gravity. She tried to connect this sheathed visage with her congealed memory of him staring at her, weeping.

Urie intended to tell Zebul, but she did not. Was she revenging herself on him for the three weeks he had kept Bostwick secret? She did not tell

Loco either, and Loco had been with her when it happened. It was evidence of her separation from Loco during this period that she did not tell her.

As for Bostwick, either he was pretending that he was not the Grief Face, or he did not remember or connect her with that moment. It was incredible to her that he did not remember, even though it was two summers ago. Yet she was inclined to believe it. The discrepancy in uniforms bothered her also. What was the uniform he had worn then?

Ever since Zebul had met Bostwick, Urie had been drowned in significances. She could not make head nor tail of anything. Bostwick had appeared. Zebul had kissed her. They had written the kiss down for immortality. Their immortal written kiss was the agent for Bostwick's friendship. And now the meeting with Bostwick, only to discover that she had known him before Zebul had!

Zebul ran to her on the campus the next day to discuss the meeting. "It was obscene!" he raved in triumph. "You were marvelous! I thought I would die, you were so funny. You went into that other harmonic. Urie, you will be a great actress!"

"What do you think he thought of me?"

"He thought you were marvelous. He liked it that you didn't talk. He was fascinated."

"I feel funny. Do you?" she whispered.

"Yes."

"Why?"

"I don't know."

"Zebul," she said solemnly, taking his hand, pressing his wrist in her palms so that she could brand him with her fingertips, "we are the most marvelous things in the world." She wanted to blot out the importance of Bostwick, whose influence was the mechanism of this newness in which they viewed each other. Zebul understood this perfectly, sitting in a chair in an empty seminar room, and he remained immobile, allowing that moment in the late afternoon to punctuate itself into their consciousness.

She buried the mystery deeper inside herself. In the next days they became giddy and speculative by turns. They hashed Bostwick over endlessly.

"Do you think he's handsome?" Zebul asked.

"Yes. He is smooth and silvery."

"Like a moth at night."

"He denies the supernatural, doesn't he?"

"Yes. He's a skeptic."

"He's the color of supernatural."

"What color is supernatural?"

"Battleship-gray. With ivory tinges showing through."

The discussion of Bostwick as a color led Zebul into another fantasy.

"Bostwick has been touched by something," he said. "Most people have been touched by the world, but the only thing the world has done to them is to make them robots. But Bostwick is not a robot. He must have been touched by some forbidden thing."

"What forbidden thing?"

"I don't know."

"The war? Do you think something horrible has happened to him in the war, maybe?"

"That's why he's battleship-gray."

Zebul saw in his mind the battleship, the antiaircraft gun, the rope mesh of panoplies, the grillwork of the caterpillars, the cranking wheels of tanks clanking on a deck in the North Sea. Upon this montage stood Bostwick, naked except for rough, muddy boots. Bostwick's flesh was tender. Zebul saw his naked body facing antiaircraft guns. The pupils of Zebul's eyes dilated.

"What are you thinking of?"

"Nothing."

"Tell."

"He has elements of sainthood and sinhood."

"All we do is talk about Bostwick, Zebul. We're making a mountain out of a molehill."

"No, we're not. We're Mohammed about to make a mountain come to us."

C H A P T E R 30

From the moment Bostwick's first penetrating, even cold glance upon her, Urie became aware of a most intimate connection between her soul and her body. It made her wriggle to escape, as if Bostwick's cold, gentle, adamant, yet haunted consciousness might possess her forever in some alien atmosphere, as a moon. Yet his ivory coldness, his very altitude, drew her. She and Zebul described him as a moth. But she was the moth.

When she was alone at night in her tapestried cubicle, he was with her.

Behind his screened face, the arrowlike sculpture of his chin, the marble concave between his collarbones out of which soared his neck, he was always standing over her with effortless ease. She desired the secret of him. But she did not have the courage to go for it.

Beside him Zebul seemed an unformed puppet with his attempts to raise himself out of his awkward childhood into the secret adulthood that Bostwick represented. Yet when she was with Zebul she was consumed by euphoria. They were more intimate than they had ever been before. The influenced of Bostwick filtered through Zebul's consciousness. Something was let loose in her. She felt breathless. She blushed. She laughed. Her toes danced. She was all girlish delight, revolving around Zebul until he was dizzy.

"You are more beautiful when Bostwick is with us or when we talk about Bostwick," he told her. "You love everything. You love me more. I even get afraid of you. I even worship some hidden fabulousness of you!"

She burst out laughing rapturously, protested, "Don't talk to me like that!" and ran away, instigating a game of hide-and-seek. He pursued her. When he caught her she upended her blue eyes at him. Her pupils were very small, and the whites of her eyes enormous.

"He affects you. That's all I'm trying to say," he persisted.

Her wooing of Zebul with this recklessness unleashed in him a new and amazing feeling of power over her. He knew perfectly well it was Bostwick's influence that had uncaged Urie. But he was not jealous. Instead he appropriated Bostwick. He used Bostwick to dominate her. And his feeling of power contained an excruciating, tender regard for what Bostwick had released in her. It was as if Bostwick were working as both the subject and the object within him.

One night, late, he chased her through a grape arbor on the old Poker property, under a persimmon tree, by a barn, to Poker Hill. A dray horse was out by the moonlit barn, chewing hay just like an old man. It pawed the ground with its front hoofs and looked at them furiously as they ran past. It was far past midnight. Zebul was sucked completely into the ludicrous reality of the chase. The shocked eyes of the dray horse made him laugh. But he put on extra power, a last painful surge of power. There was nothing ahead of them but the sky.

She let him catch her on the brow of the hill. The sky was so huge it would divert him from inspection of her. Zebul had a weakness for the sky.

They lay on the white grass, panting. Stickles of grass pricked their backs through their clothing. But they did not even scratch where it itched.

Even Bostwick could be exorcized by the sky, thought Urie, trying to dominate the specter of him by thinking of the words of "Renascence."

Finally Zebul stopped panting and laughing.

"Bostwick's not everything, you know, Zebul," said Urie in a soft voice. A slight begging tone crept into it. "Don't make him too big!"

He flung away from her, to separate himself from her. He became hard. He could feel his Satan self coming on. He attracted her with his Satan self, his wild, cold, glittering, horned smile. She quoted Edna St. Vincent Millay: " 'All I could see from where I stood/was three tall mountains and a wood.' " He gave his slippery, Satanic eel's smile to the face of the earth.

Zebul's Satanhood was the reverse side of his euphoria. He was delighted by the effect he had created on Urie through Bostwick. Where was it leading him, though? He refused to pursue that thought. He felt that she was jealous of him and Bostwick. That she should be so afraid of Bostwick that she had to warn him—this excited him.

He controlled the threefold universe, exactly as if he were a successful Phaëthon. He saw himself as Phaëthon, driving with the reins in the solemn ritual taught him by Apollo. Having met Bostwick, having wooed him, having almost lost Bostwick through ignorance, and having now aroused in Urie a girlish, rhapsodic Aphrodite who blushed under Bostwick's look but gave herself exclusively to him, who begged him to diminish the importance of Bostwick even, he began to be completely enmeshed in the sense of his own power. He felt for the first time that he had proprietary rights over Urie. And was she not taking refuge in his power? Zebul knew Urie as both Athena and Aphrodite. He was witness of her rising Aphrodite-dom. Yet she was really Athena. He could never lose her in Aphrodite guise, for she would never give up Athena.

Far off the bell tower rang.

"It's one o'clock. Do you realize it?" Urie was scandalized.

They began to walk home. The moon lit the whole world, glittered softly on the leaves of the gigantic heads of trees. Houses peeped out of the earth's verdure of bushes, trees, and grasses. All humanity seemed extinct. The windows were dark. They came to the power plant hovering in silhouette mutely above Niggertown. Not even the kerosene lamps in Negroes' houses burned. They were confronted with total silence. The moon, though, glowed on the white road, making it the sands of Araby. Soft powder rose from their heels. The road was still warm from the day's heat. They cut through broom grass behind the railroad tracks.

There, instead of going home, they sat down in a field. Having sat down, they discarded all idea of going home. They threw out the frame-work of night and day. They were launched into paradoxical freedom. They felt graceful in this freedom.

"Here. Taste this." Zebul picked a blossom from a wild rosebush.

She sipped it. She moved her tongue over the petals. It tasted slightly sweet, with a strong, bitter overtaste. Zebul tasted it too.

Nothing was decided upon. There was no agreement. Zebul traced Urie's collarbone with his finger. He was like a teacher. He used the same worshipful manner toward subject matter that he used in explaining the difference between the English and Italian sonnet.

"I want to see your breasts, Urie."

"I'm embarrassed," she whispered.

"You can't be."

He undid her blouse and pulled it till her shoulders were naked.

Their rising breaths touched each other's cheeks, but they did not kiss. The moon streaming down gave their experiment an uncanny quality. It was a face watching, yet receiving nothing, merely furnishing the pale, in-tense light that enabled them to see. A leaf made a brushing movement. Its shadow moved down Urie's white shoulder, following the swell of her breast to the edge of her bra. He leaned forward and put his arms around her. She pulled like a statue away from him. Back of her shoulder wing-nubs, he found hooks and eyes, and undid her brassière.

Urie was unable to maintain the inviolateness of her flesh. The garment fell away and trapped her arms. Her nipples were revealed above the cloth. She shivered. Unable to bear the light of the moon and Zebul's eyes, she hid her naked trunk against his chest. He held her tight for two or three minutes. Their hearts pounded. Then he pushed her away and propped her up, like an *objet d'art*. Strands of broom straw glistened behind her, like the spokes of a halo.

For a long time he sat in wonder, staring at her lithe, supple stem, her nubile power, her breasts blossoming her nipples silkily, her wide and childish shoulders curving around her beauty. His stare, as wide and time-less as the moon's, did not seem to be capable of conceiving its end. To-morrow he had a French poetry exam. He could not enclose this inevitabil-ity into his consciousness. Tomorrow would he be ashamed? He could not encompass his shame, nor her shame, nor their doubts. He entered into a state of being which shut out the recognition of her personality. There was deep in him a worship that he knew to be unfitting in a young boy. It was age-old. He was a living vehicle of appreciation.

Left alone, Urie felt the hair of her arms and tiny bumps of her flesh rise. Her nipples hardened slightly.

To think this can be happening in Niggertown. I am Urie, not beauty. No. I am beauty. Am I breathing through my nose? Is my breath seething and scything? Ants are sitting under us. What do they think? They don't blush at me naked. Do I have an exam tomorrow? Why am I sitting? I don't even feel the air on my shoulders any more.

She became a pose crystallized by the moon. All embarrassment left her. As her nipples expanded again, two velvet mouth-sockets that desired touch, vibratory instruments, she herself became ardently hard. Her eyes became vague, in tune with the moon's face, as if her pupils had somehow become disengaged from their fields of white and congealed. She rose to the moon's light. She indulged in the moon alone. She arched her shoulders back, presenting herself full. Terrible clarity, a force of full identification.

But something broke in Zebul. He lifted himself above her on his knees, in a state so vulnerable, so aspirative that he felt like sobbing. She looked straight into his eyes, but gave no sign of recognition. He could not believe it. He had made her a statue. The statue cut him off.

Suddenly he envied her. She exemplified desire, yet she was hard as a star. She was luxuriating, he begging. The steady, strong rise and fall of her breath brooked no touch.

Very slowly he began to caress her shoulder. He barely touched her. His fingers followed the contour round and down her breast. She sat up.

"Don't do that!"

But he was now so engrossed in the velvet realms of his hands' caresses that he began to perceive the containment of her entire body in his hands. Her nipples hardened.

"Look, they got hard!" he whispered.

She looked down.

"That's what happens in sex."

"Don't do that. I feel so strange. What's going to happen? I don't understand it!"

And suddenly she threw herself on him, pushing him backward on the ground, covering his face with her torso. He was immersed in her. He felt as if he were drowning. Her breastbone crushed his forehead. Her whole weight was too heavy. He began to struggle. They grappled. A moment later they were lying on the grass together, apart, looking at each other strangely.

The next morning when Urie came to breakfast, Mrs. Bishop asked, "What time did you come in last night?"

The seven-thirty news was on. P.Q. had pulled his chair away from the table to listen as the broadcaster said, "The FBI is planning an investigation of the two thousand and ninety-five federal government employees named by the Dies Committee on charges of subversive and un-American activities. . . ." Mrs. Bishop stirred the oatmeal in the hot pan and spooned it into Urie's bowl. Then she returned the pan to the stove.

"Late," answered Urie.

"Two-thirty in the morning." Mrs. Bishop thudded the wooden spoon onto the bottom of the pan and forgot to turn off the burner.

Urie calmly spooned dollops of oatmeal into her mouth, noting Loco Poco's arrival just in time for her disgrace. She was beaming on her with shining piety as the radio talked about suspicions of fifth-column activity. Mrs. Bishop stood in the doorway, her hands on her hips, facing Urie accusingly.

Loco Poco stirred the oatmeal again, spooned some into her bowl, and told her mother, "It's going to burn on the bottom."

Mrs. Bishop paid no attention. "Where were you?"

"With Zebul."

"Until two-thirty in the morning?"

"Yes."

Urie chewed with more deliberation, aware that her rhythmic insolence was succeeding.

"What could you possibly have been doing with Zebul until two-thirty in the morning?"

"The usual."

"What kind of answer is that?"

How dare her mother be so naïve? The only reason she could ask such a question was that she would never suspect! It would require shouting straight into her face, "Sex!" The irony was that she could confront her mother: "And what about your stealing from the Count house that you don't want P.Q. to know?"

How complicated life had become with these secrets! She could not tell the truth to her mother because her mother would not want to know. She would be embarrassed. It seemed to Urie that her relevant life had passed into another realm now, in which she was hopelessly separate from the rest of the family. Even though the same daily things went on as they always had, everything had a different meaning. Her fury secreted helpless nostalgia.

"Mamma, do you want me to flunk? Good God! I have an exam this morning, and here you keep harping and I'm going to be late!"

It was a necessity to leave, to beat her mother's begging handgrips from the gunwales of the departing ship, like Saint Augustine.

"All right! Go!" shouted Mrs. Bishop. "Eat and go!" As Urie snatched her jacket from the hook: "The only time you're ever here is when you eat or sleep. This place might just as well be a garage!"

As Urie passed the windows, she saw Mrs. Bishop turn her anger onto Loco Poco. "Do you mean to tell me, Sylvia Bishop, you just stood there and let that oatmeal burn to nothing!"

PART V

CHAPTER 31

At the beginning of the second summer session in July, there was an influx of freshmen. By now Urie and Zebul, veterans, looked down upon
them with pitying scorn.

Zebul had got hold of an "office" on campus. It was a seminar room in
the bottom of Malden Hall. He had answered a request of Dr. Boehm's,
the German whom P.Q. had made a fool of so long ago, for a student to
type a paper. Dr. Boehm wanted the typing done where he could supervise
it closely, so he set Zebul up in a seminar room in the philosophy building
with a special small table and a typewriter. Long after the paper was completed, Zebul continued to work in the seminar room. Dr. Boehm forgot to
take the typewriter away. He forgot everything, once his own work was
done, and even became so used to Zebul's being there that he assumed that
there was a reason for it separate from himself. Other professors in the
building got used to seeing him there too, and assumed that he was still
working for Dr. Boehm.

Entrenched, Zebul set up a little bookcase. Urie brought her books,
Zebul his. Neither one of them went home any more except to eat and
sleep. Although classes were held in the seminar room during the day, students were specially deferential to the anonymous "owners," thinking them
graduate students with privileges. They carefully put back into the bookcase the books Urie and Zebul left out on the table. They always returned
the room to the exact shape in which they found it.

Zebul and Urie worked out a plan for anyone who asked too many
questions. They always said, "I am typing a manuscript for Helmut
Boehm." The use of the first name, Helmut, always worked. Dr. Boehm
was so formidable that anyone who used the first name *must* be of the
inner sanctum. Questions always stopped right there.

At night the "office" was like a lighted box. It was half underground,
with two windows that opened out into two cement troughs, above which
were the ground and magnolia bushes. Often Zebul and Urie entered by

the windows. They would be seen heading for the magnolia bush. Then suddenly they would vanish into thin air, like characters in a fairy tale. Each knew if the other was there at night, for the light would be shining significantly, as if the campus were a storm-tossed sea.

But Bostwick never visited them at their office. That would have meant a committal of friendship on his part. Such an admission was still a mystery. There was a tacit agreement that Zebul and Urie were suitors and Bostwick, by dint of not refusing them audience, was still the object.

They often met Bostwick in late afternoon by the Confederate soldier. It became a habit to walk home with him and to sit in the garden talking before they went home.

One day Urie asked, "What does the E. of your first name stand for, Bostwick?"

"Edmund."

The name immediately took on a magic, noble effluence. They connected it with the good hero of King Lear.

"Do you have a middle name?" asked Zebul.

"Holland. That was my mother's maiden name."

"Is your mother alive now?"

"Yes. she lives in Pittsburgh."

These facts, rather than illuminating Bostwick, seemed irrelevant. Nothing grew from them; nothing connected.

Bostwick's attraction for them was based on his paradoxical combination of glamour and passivity. He was a representative of the war, which for the first time they had direct congress with in him. His passivity made him a mystery.

"Were you ever in action?" Zebul asked one day in a low voice, trying to seem casual.

"Yes."

"When?"

"I was navigator of a bomber before I came here."

"A Flying Fortress?"

"No. Before that. Six months after the war began I went into the Canadian Air Force. I was in England. That's when I was on missions."

Urie and Zebul were astounded and silent. They were contemplating England, thinking how they had been in high school. "Did you drop bombs?"

"Yes."

It was incredible. They hardly heard when he told them with a self-deprecating smile that he had been called "the civilized man" by Englishmen, who were surprised at his austerity and coolness because they believed all Canadians and Americans to be excitable and violent, as in the myths of young countries.

"Did your airplane ever get hit?" Zebul whispered.

"Yes, once. But it got back to the base all right. One engine."

"In England?"

"Yes."

The war, England, became magic. But they did not dare to ask too many nosy questions after this, for he often seemed reluctant to talk. He offered generalizations instead.

"War allows you not to have to justify your existence. Loudspeakers, assembly lines, ten thousand echelons of machinery springing from factories from Baltimore to Los Angeles speak louder than one man. War merges people in a definable, cataclysmic process which, because it is dedicated to victory by the road of death, acts the same as the power of God in history. It even eats up time. Consciousness is simplified. Look at you two, for instance. You don't have to think twice about what you are going to do. You're going to be a soldier, and you"—pointing to Urie—"will be doing something for the war effort."

I'm going to be a WAC captain, Urie thought. The war has to last till I'm twenty-five.

But he did not mention being in action again. Once he told them that the essence of war was being on a bombing mission.

"The suspense is like a hollow ball, in the center of which you sit, just as you sit in the airplane. It's a vacuum. But it seems inconceivable that there is any life outside it. If you asked me, I would say I never had a life before a bombing mission. When I was in it, I could never conceive of a life after it. Yet here I am now, in another life, such as it is—here in Ephesus."

How could he stand such a small, dumpy place? they wondered.

"How did you happen to come here, Bostwick?" asked Urie.

"Well, once we got into the war they needed anybody who knew anything. I'm American. They needed trained men."

"Were you ever in Ephesus before?" Her heart beat painfully.

"I was once here in nineteen-forty when I was liaison officer between the Canadians and Americans. They were in the planning stages of a flight school here."

Caught in momentum, she was shocked when Zebul interjected innocently, "Why did you join the Canadian Air Force in the first place?"

"Why did I join?"

"Were you patriotic or something?"

At that moment Bostwick's eyes seemed far away at the corners. It was indescribably sad, the echo of beauty behind the deadness.

"Well, just say I wanted another life from the one I was living."

The present was nothing for him either. Urie and Zebul felt small under his gaze. A tremendous, painful desire filled them. They wanted to create something important for him so that his eyes would not steal away to that other place. They wanted to stop his eyes from saying: No, this is not life here. There is nothing living, nothing important, nothing to hold me here. Life is there, where I want to be—that other place his eyes beheld when they went to the corners of their sockets, leaving only his beauty behind.

Zebul and Urie were perfectly aware that they were foolishly romantic about Bostwick. The miracle was that a Bostwick really existed who fitted the description of their fantasy's romantic idol, and that he actually bothered with them in real life. It was frightening, such a materialization of one's aspirations. For that reason the relationship that grew among them was less a friendship than the unraveling of the mysterious elements of Bostwick. Their doubts were in ratio to their idealization. They continually looked at him, examined him to see what he really was. To see, in fact, if he were really true.

"Do you think Bostwick has any friends besides us?" Zebul asked Urie one night in their office.

"No. I don't think so."

They watched him. He never talked of anyone. He hardly ever talked with other officers or joked with them. Just as his past was unreal, so was his present, except for his friendship with them. Yet girls on the street looked at him meltingly. Middle-aged women acted thrilled at the opaque bleakness of his eyes. And businessmen trusted him. Zebul and Urie believed he was aware of this effect of himself upon others, and even acted the way he did to promulgate it. Sometimes he would turn his eyes squarely onto a passing person, as if he might consume some meaning from him before he passed by.

"Why do you think Bostwick bothers with us?" asked Urie at last. "No other grown-up is interested in sixteen-year-olds."

"Aren't we interesting?" Zebul looked at her as if she were a traitor. Then he began to boast. He reminisced about their pursuit of Bostwick. They had allowed him to make fools of them by the Attis and Sybil themes, even. Perhaps they were Bostwick's only reality in Ephesus. Urie was very quiet. She was thinking about how she had never told Zebul what she knew.

But in most of the conversations among the three, it was Bostwick and Zebul who talked. Urie remained silent, a presence rather than a partner.

One day Zebul read Bostwick a poem he had written. It was about the ocean.

"Well, what do you think of it, Bostwick?"

"I think it is extravagant, silly, affected, and irresistible."

Urie looked at Zebul to see how he would take this reaction. He was excited, smiling.

"Bostwick, you could say anything about me or my poetry and I wouldn't mind it, because you disbelieve in words, don't you?"

Bostwick nodded.

Suddenly it began to rain. Zebul had to rush out to get a geology book he had left in the garden. Urie and Bostwick were alone in an embarrassed silence.

"Do you like his poem?" asked Bostwick gently.

"Yes."

"Why didn't you write one too?"

"He's the writer. Not me."

"You know that's not true."

"Well, I grew up by the ocean. I don't have the same attitude as he does at all."

"Neither did you have the same attitude at the Episcopal church."

She blushed deeply and looked at the floor.

"Don't be embarrassed."

"I'm not!" she blurted in a shaky voice. When she looked into his eyes, she saw that he was teasing her.

"Has Zebul seen the ocean?" he asked.

"No."

They began to laugh delightedly, and at that moment Zebul returned.

Urie felt strange. For it grew on her that Bostwick's interest in them was in their alliance. He could not do with one or the other only. He needed them both. It was their alliance that gave them strength in his eyes. Their pooling of their youth, sex, and energy gave them a dimension that neither had alone.

Once Urie and Zebul had an argument in front of Bostwick. It was about poetry. Urie argued for purity in poetry. Zebul scoffed. Under Bostwick's eyes they quarreled with far more violence than they would have alone.

[265

"What do you think, Bostwick?" asked Zebul.

Urie could have whacked him. Why should Bostwick be the deciding factor? Why should they play into Bostwick's hands? But in spite of herself she too turned to Bostwick.

Bostwick's passivity forbade him to make alliance with either. In fact, he allowed them to play against each other, reveling in the quarrel, watching them at last drift inexorably together again, like magnets. His presence gave them an anchor point to play their differences against. It was safe. It was proof of their unbreakable union.

In that poetry quarrel Bostwick told them a paradox. "Young people can't be pure. Only middle-aged people are pure. They know what life is. They have accepted it, so they are the pure result of the laws of nature on earth. They're simply their reactions. They've learned the limits of life. But everything is possible to young kids, even the conception of immortality, for they haven't discovered the limits of life. If you don't know life's limits, then everything is before you. Everything is complex. Your reactions are not you. See how impure the young are? They haven't even become used to the earth. They retain foreign elements, being untrained, untempered by the laws of earth. Maybe they act in response to other laws, laws unrecognized by the middle-aged, or forgotten. So, until the young become tempered, beaten, melded like metal by earth's laws of suffering, change, growing, and loss, they are going to continue in their capricious, inconsistent, unformed, and uncharted path. And middle-aged people, caught in simplicity, their consciousness captured by the physical laws of the earth, will always witness these dartings, pushes, flings, passions, false fears, and falser confidences with condescension. Or with hatred. Or envy."

Zebul pondered Bostwick, marveling at the strange way he used words.

But suddenly Urie startled them by asking, "Do you think we come from another place, then, Bostwick? Before we're born, I mean?"

It was the first time she had ever talked to him like this. She felt some intense sympathy streaming from him, and she could not bear it, for it was as if she had fallen into a trap. And she had. For Bostwick only smiled, and he never did give an answer.

That night she said to Zebul, "I wonder if Bostwick is married."

Zebul was arrested by the thought. It had never occurred to him before. He became restless and jumped up from his chair. "He couldn't be."

"Why not?"

"He doesn't act like it."

Urie returned to her book. But Zebul refused to look at the dilemma. He was tormented by the idea of Bostwick's being married.

"Maybe he's divorced," he said hopefully.

He wanted Bostwick to be divorced. He arranged his mind to this possibility. Then he began thinking about Bostwick's really being married. There was a sharp pain in his chest, but he continued to think about it, forcing himself not to care. But what if Bostwick brought his wife to live with him in Ephesus? Finally Zebul arrived at a point where he could bear the reality of Bostwick's being married if only he never brought his wife there.

As they left the office that night he said, "I'm going to find out if Bostwick's married or not."

"How?"

"I'll ask him."

But he did not do it. He could not bring himself to.

But there was another element in their relationship with Bostwick that both were barely aware of. He was developing the forbidden in them.

From the very beginning his connection had been made to an oblique sexuality that they gave off: Zebul's impersonation, the Episcopal-church kiss, the cabbage. Then it was mirrored back to him first- and second-hand by means of their acting performances and poetry. It achieved an echoing force by its relationship, which reinforced the sexuality without ever bringing it to an act. Their innocence allowed the games and the works of art, and a feeling of great accomplishment was engendered in them.

But after they left Bostwick they were extended in this impulsion, whose force they did not understand. The rhythm of their necessity increased. The force seemed to promise total transmutation or total annihilation. The momentum of their universe changed and grew in possibilty. But it also opened up an abyss. They became aware of the sexual in themselves. They were wrapped in it, as if it were the crucial end of their breathing. It forced them more and more to the brink of art. And in doing so, it led them to a vision of depersonalized divinity (horrible) or of catastrophic smallness (horrible).

They tried to coddle, to comfort each other with their personalities as they used to do. But they could not blot out their evening together under the moon. It had confirmed the realm of depersonality between them. They talked more and more about sex.

One night Zebul gave Urie an illustrated lecture on the orgasm in man and woman. He made pictures on the blackboard in the office. He used the words "orgasms," "vaginas," "penises," "sticking it in," "pulling it out," and "coming at the same time." Urie sat at the seminar table, glassy-eyed.

"I think you are afraid of sex," he accused her.

"No, I'm not. The only thing is, you talk about it all the time."

"Me?"

"Yes."

"Who asked me to outline the five stages of genital excitation in complete coitus? You! All I did was answer your question!"

The figures on the board taunted him like Andy Gump. He carefully erased them before they went home.

"Read Freud," he told her as they approached the power plant. "Freud is the one and only influence of the twentieth century. Who are we to dispute the reality of the twentieth century? If there is no God, then let us find out what reality is. Even if we find out that it is only that state that is agreed upon by the majority of the people on earth, why, we have to find out, don't we?"

"What if it *is* only that, and nothing else?" asked Urie.

"Why have the funeral before the person dies?"

The next evening after this conversation Zebul appeared at their office window from the outside with news. "Guess what!"

"What?"

"I just overheard this 'feelthy' conversation in Hoke Tabernacle's about a book that tells people everything. They keep it locked up in the Vault and it's called Krafft-Ebing."

The Vault was a room on the basement floor of the stacks in the library. The letter V printed on the upper right-hand corner of catalogues cards was a sacred frightening hieroglyph denoting that a book was kept in the Vault.

"We've got to get down there."

"How?"

"You can do it. Just get the key from Fats Pollard when Jackass Jackson's gone home. If anybody asks, just say Miss Marsh wants you to check some catalogue cards."

The next day at five o'clock they went to the library. It was time for Jackass Jackson to leave. He got his umbrella, checked his wristwatch, looked at the round clock above the circulation desk, and took his coat from the back of the chair. Then he disappeared down the stairway.

Urie waited a beat. Fats was leaning over Due Books.

"Fats," she said. "Give me the key to the Vault, will you?"

He looked at her.

She yawned.

He opened his soft mouth as if to ask something. But he changed his mind. He went to Jackass's desk, opened the drawer, fumbled for the keys, and brought her one with a little clip on which was written VAULT.

"Thanks," she said. She walked to the stack door, paused, and gave the signal to Zebul.

He left the Woman of Learning and met her.

"I didn't have to give any explanation," she whispered.

Never apologize. Never explain. His terseness disguised exultation.

They went down five dark, narrow iron stairways. Their footsteps clanked as if they were in a lighthouse. On the second floor they emerged. The *New York Times* lay on black shelves, the years 1915 to 1935 bound in large black leather sheaves, upon which were printed golden letters. Newsprint leaked out of these bindings and died in crumbs on the floor. But the mass of these twenty years, signifying more than all the years Urie and Zebul had lived, acted as insulation in the dark. They became afraid. Zebul switched on a stack light. All the world receded. Everything was soft. There was not the faintest whisper of danger. They were ushered to a strange freedom, the like of which they had never known. All the world of classes, Jackass Jackson, hurrying students, the bell tower, Loco Poco, town, Franklin D. Roosevelt, automobiles, lights turning on in the streets, stores, people hurrying home for supper—all these familiar sights and sounds were gone. No one knew where they were. They could have screamed. No one would ever have heard. They were buried alive, like mummies in an ancient catacomb.

Their hearts beat strangely. Perhaps their abandoned state was the sin. Zebul had the impulse to turn back. Urie's mouth was dry.

But it was a serious pilgrimage. They came to their goal at the end of bookcases 820–930.4 by the Dewey Decimal System. The Vault door. They looked at it. It was oak with thin strip slats. Zebul inserted the key. He turned it. The door opened easily. Urie found the light and switched it on.

The room had the air of a captain's cabin in the frigate *Constitution*. Oval-shaped, paneled in oak, with high bookcases full of leatherbound volumes. A comforting, elegant room. A board table stood upon a red carpet, with benches, like a refectory table. Everything about the room bespoke an absent owner.

They closed the door and locked it behind them. They were brittle with fear. But curiosity led them on. They looked for Krafft-Ebing. It was easy to find. Everything was alphabetical.

[269

It was as large as a photograph album and very old. The pages were yellowing. There were ancient marks in it where people had penciled things and others had erased. The print was large.

They took it to the refectory table. They sat down and opened it carefully, almost as if it were sacred. They were like two birds at a dish. They pecked. Each read at a different place, holding the middle pages up in the air respectfully, waiting for the other to turn.

They became engrossed.

"Look at this," whispered Zebul.

She read:

L, aged thirty-seven, clerk from tainted family, had his first erection at five years when he saw his bedfellow—an aged relative—put on his night-cap. The same thing occurred later when he saw an old servant put on her night-cap. Later, simply the idea of an old ugly woman's head covered with a night-cap was sufficient to cause an erection.

Their faces when they turned them to each other to laugh presented a ferocious fake vivacity.

"That's nothing. Look at this," she said.

In a provincial town a man was caught in intercourse with a hen. He was thirty years old and of high social position. The chickens had been dying one after another, and the man causing it had been "wanted" for a long time. To the question of the judge as to the reason for such an act, the accused said that his genitals were so small that coitus with women was impossible. Medical examination showed that actually the genitals were extremely small. The man was *mentally quite sound*. There were no statements concerning any abnormalities at the time of puberty, etc. (Gyurkovechky, "Mannl. Impotenz," 1889, p. 82.)

They sat very still.

"How could he do it?" asked Urie.

"I don't know."

"Could you do it?"

"I don't know."

Time passed. They had acquiesced in the world of distortion by bending themselves. They belonged no more to the upper world of Ephesus, Haw, their families, Bostwick, and the university. Krafft-Ebing, a doctor with golden teeth from Grimms' Fairy Tales and the weird, scientific, plundering mind of Dracula, spoke in a broken translation. The presence of the authorities and jailers was all around them. There was no choice between Krafft-Ebing and the authorities. They breathed harder and harder, their deformities exposed. They had to get out of this elegant room and pretend that they belonged to the upper world. But they could not move.

"Look. Latin," said Zebul, pointing to page 1878. "Case 20. Tirsch, hospital beneficiary. It must be real bad. Most of it's not even in English."

They read:

Case 20. Tirsch, hospital beneficary of Prague, aged fifty-five, always silent, peculiar, coarse, very irritable, grumbling, revengeful, was sentenced to twenty years imprisonment for violating a girl ten years old. He had attracted attention on account of outbursts of anger from insignificant causes, and also on account of taedium vitae. In 1864, on account of the refusal of an offer of marriage which he made to a widow he developed a hatred toward women, and on the 8th of July he went about with the intention of killing one of this hated sex. Vetulam occurentem in silvam allexit, coitum, poposcit, renitentem prostravit, jugulum feminae compressit "furore captus." Cadaver virga betuloe desecta verberare voluit in quetamen id perfecti, quia conscientia sua haec fieri vetuit, cultello mammas et genitalia desecta domi docta proximis diebus cum globis comedit. On the 12th of September when he was arrested, the remains of this meal were found. . . .

"What meal?" asked Urie.

"He must have cut off her breasts and her vagina and put it in a plate and ate it up like spaghetti."

Urie got up. She almost fell against the door, shaking.

"Are you going to get sick? Don't you get sick in this Vault, Urie!"

"I'm not."

"You look—"

"Let's go—"

He put the book back. He switched off the light. His knees were weak. He locked the door, and as he stared, frightened, at Urie's face, ashen and drained of color, he saw that the second-floor stack clock said five-fifteen. How could it have been only fifteen minutes when it was a lifetime?

Two days later, alone in his little house, Zebul saw that he was a homosexual. It came over him in the same way and with the same clarity that he had recognized two years before that there was no God. The only difference was that Urie was not present. He had never accomplished coitus with Urie. That was what was at the kernel of his obsession with Bostwick. That was why he imagined him naked on a battleship. That was why he had wanted to stroke his legs. That was why he was jealous of a possible wife!

Most boys had screwed women by the age of fourteen. Especially boys from Haw. He was almost seventeen. Gag Booch said he had screwed fifteen women in one year at twelve, one for each month plus two for Christmas and one for Thanksgiving. Therefore there was something wrong with him, Zebul.

As a homosexual he tried to imagine himself kissing and fondling Bostwick. He tried to imagine Bostwick kissing and fondling him. This made him blush, and he became excited. But his imagination burst at this point and became blank. He could not imagine any acts of sex. His chest was constricted. He was in agony. He looked at the bottle of cyanide, knowing that now was the time to take it. But he could not do it.

He turned to Urie. But ever since Krafft-Ebing, she had become very dreamy and distant. When he searched her eyes they were vacant blue shells. The experience seemed to have left no impression.

One day, experimentally, he thought of telling her in a rueful voice, "That Krafft-Ebing makes you feel you have every perversion in the book. I even think I'm a homo." But he did not.

They were walking home on Pergamus Avenue. She continued walking doggedly, pulling her thin brown jacket around her as if she were being brave.

For a week they were more or less speechless. They did not meet Bostwick. It was always Zebul who decided the days they should go to Bostwick. But now everything was suspended.

One evening after a sociology examination Zebul went to the office. It was already dark, but there was no light shining. Instead of entering by the window, he went in the main doorway. The building was silent. Everyone must have gone home. His footsteps echoed as he went down the stairs. For one moment he thought he heard a sound in an upper hallway. He stopped and listened, but he heard nothing.

In the office he decided to wait for Urie. To while away the time, he decided to read *The Last Puritan*. He read for half an hour, and then he closed the book. He was disturbed. He jiggled his feet under the table. His shoelaces were untied. He watched the shoelaces flap. Then he began dreamily to write a poem.

LOOSE-ENDED SHOELACES

My heart is like a shoelace
Untied.
My foot has grown bigger,
My mind descried
An end to Being,

My seeing an end
Which demands to be broken.
I demand infinity.
What shall I do?

He stopped writing. He wanted Urie. Where was she?

Suddenly he thought that he and Urie must do something. An act was required. Something huge, outrageous. Something to break out of the chains of reality. What? The sexual act itself? Or . . . Suddenly he thought of stealing. He had not stolen anything for two months. He had never stolen the miscroscope he had promised himself. They must steal something, dare something. Break something! He thought of the bank in Ephesus. If they broke into the bank they could get thousands of dollars. And how easy it would be! At night the town was dead. Dan Tatum went home at six o'clock. There were only two policemen on duty every night, stupid Haw-yoos. They played cards in the police hut next to the Pick Theater. All one had to do was lure them out of the hut, conk them over the head with a crowbar, tie them up, and stuff them back in the hut. Then the bank would lie free for plunder. No obstructions. Why had no one done it? It was so simple, that's why. No one had ever thought of it.

Far off the bell tower struck nine o'clock. Had he been reading for three hours?

It was time to go home. If Urie had not come by now, she was not coming. Although he knew quite reasonably that she had gone home without coming to the office, he became alarmed. He folded his poem carefully and stuck it at page 180 of *The Last Puritan*. He then changed his mind. He did not want his poem in *The Last Puritan*. He did not like that book. Something about it reminded him of Bostwick. He took it out, held it for a moment, and then opened his book of Shakespeare to the sonnet, "Let me not to the marriage of true minds admit impediment" and stuck it there. This symbolized the permanence of his relationship with Urie.

He switched off the light. He closed the office door behind him and climbed the stairs in total darkness. On the first floor light from the street lamp streamed through giant windows and formed patterns on the corridor floor. Suddenly he heard the sound he had imagined before. He stopped. It was a strange, wheezing sound, like a gasp. He heard it distinctly.

But he was sure there was no one in the building. He looked up the dark maw of the staircase. No lights. Carefully he tiptoed toward the sound, past the front door into a darker corridor, which led to the east staircase. He passed Dr. Helmut Boehm's office—Department of Philosophy. His sneakers muffled the sound of his footsteps.

The noise suddenly came again, this time very near. There was a broken noise. It was a human voice. Suddenly he saw Urie clearly. She was sitting on the fifth step of the east staircase. She was perfectly etched in the eerie light coming through the round window on the landing. She was sobbing. Her hair was like wilted taffy in the light.

"Urie!"

She stared at him. Her face, unrecognizable, was puffy and swollen. Her eyes were as large as oyster shells.

"What's the matter with you?" he breathed.

She was silent for a long time. Then she said, "I overheard something awful in Dr. Boehm's office."

"What?" His heartbeats were beginning to pound in his ears.

"Dr. Boehm was talking to Dr. Scolimowski. Dr. Scolimowski attacked Plato and the New Testament, and then he said—"

"Well? What?" Zebul was desperate.

"Jesus Christ was a homo!"

"What?"

"And the disciples. They were all his—things!"

How could she have come to discover the same thing as he had? He, about himself; she, about Christ. It was all true. All along he had known it. Urie, who never cried, was crying. The walls of his certainties fell around him. He stared at her naked grief.

"But what do you care?" he cried, blasting through his amazement to comfort her. "You hate Jesus Christ!"

"I know it!" she cried, her voice breaking. "But I didn't *want* to hate him!"

CHAPTER 32

After a while the effect of Krafft-Ebing wore off. Their identification with sexual perversion, recognized and sealed in silence, began to slough off with the mere passage of time. It was as if they were awakening from a submerged state of anesthesia. The sounds of the classroom, of footsteps on gravel walks, P.Q.'s cough in the morning, Mrs. Bishop's scolding, Irene's calm pronouncements, and Loco Poco's squealing laughter returned. And with the return of sound came a promise that qualities like love and aspiration could not be reduced to irreducible sexual detail.

Urie found herself thinking about Bostwick all the time. At night she strained her eyes against the darkness, imagining him framed by the hotel doorway, weeping. Bostwick as the Grief Face took on peculiar relevance. Why had he cried when he was here before? Was it a particular sadness, or the sadness of the world? Why was she so afraid of him that she could not even ask? Everyone seemed pitiable to her. From Prague to Sioux Falls people were helpless against centuries, separate, desperate, or poor. She and Zebul had believed that their strength, youth, ugliness, and alliance could beat time and nature.

As the days passed the image of weeping Bostwick began to fade. She began to see him as she wanted him to be. He was leaning near her, his hair parting, his forehead and his chin just above her eyes, like an actor on the screen. She was immersed in his sympathy and interest in her. She imagined that he was really in love with her, or falling in love with her. She melted at this vision of him and blushed alone in bed. He, knowing she was afraid, pursued his path toward her with gentle insistence until that moment that he would exact from her total surrender—a surrender which, in fact, she could not imagine giving to anyone.

That was why she was Zebul's partner for eternity. Surrender was foreign to her, she believed. Zebul demanded her obeisance to a sterile moon, to an abstraction, not to himself. They were novitiates, each ecstatic in proportion to his lashing of the other toward avowal. All their sexual experiments were rehearsals for another thing.

She tried to analyze Bostwick's fascination for her, and he became the subject of symbols which she tried on him like hats. Weeping Bostwick, Hamlet, Christ with thorns. Satan from *Paradise Lost*. She said to herself: Bostwick doesn't love me. That's not what is real. This is what is real. The Shack. The coverlet. Loco Poco snoring. She poked her head out, listening to the night and to the breeze against the tapestry walls. Soon it would be autumn, and she had never noticed! Soon it would be cold. I am here alone. Bostwick is not here. I am making it all up because I am in love with him. She saw that she had even made herself up. She was like butter melting, clinging to its shape even while changing, flattening out to a spot, and she had no implements, no fork or spoon to scoop herself back up with. She did not even have a dish to define her. Life, she thought, was the process of growing sides.

She rubbed her nose and, as if it were Aladdin's lamp, another vision came to her. This time Bostwick's head was at a different angle. It was not above her; it was underneath, his forehead at the level of her chin. His eyes were lowered. Every now and again he looked up at her. His eyes were very light and brilliant, full of laughter. His hair was soft and golden as a baby's. She had only to reach out to caress it. Each separate strand was visible to her imagination, its texture intensely soft, in exact ratio opposite to his power. This image frightened her because it was the reverse of the former image.

In this image she was again a vessel from which all attention was draining and flowing toward him. But, as if he were a warrior-king with his head in his mistress's lap, his power was all the more fearsome for being vulnerable. He lay at her side, open and unguarded. Did he intend it to be so? Or was he careless? Was he inviting her to touch him? If she put her finger upon him, would he envelop her and cage her with his power? Or would he instead lay its infinity upon her as a gift, a mutuality of exchange? Did Bostwick's giant power conceal his own need? Was this why he lay by her side, his hair parted so carelessly, giving her the gift of himself as if by accident?

In her imagination she was just about to touch his hair. Inside her breast there was an actual ache because the impulse was so strong and sweet. She was filled with surprise at the nature of herself, that she had such maternal feelings. She viewed her shy desire to exercise protection over this master with disbelief. She thought her talent for such love slender, but it was a talent she had never believed she possessed until this moment.

She smiled happily to herself, sticking her face again out of the covers. The curtains rustled, and Loco Poco drew a tendril of breath in allegiance with the wind. Urie thought of Thalassia and her other self, the pre-Ephesian self that had ended with Zebul. Feel the wind. It would grow cold again. But who cared? It was all a chimera, her old self, the house, crazy poverty, studying, the memoirs of Catherine the Great, the curtains, the creation, Loco's breath gone into the breath of the wind. The same breath of the wind which had sneaked up the sleeves of her parka, the same into which she had cast her spit as a child by the ocean. What would Bishop Berkeley say? She concentrated carefully, half smiling, as if to penetrate the phantasmagoric quality of what people called real, knowing her only reality to be her fiction of Bostwick.

"Look what I found, Urie!"

She read where Zebul pointed in the *Cambridge Encyclopaedia of Gods and Goddesses.*

The Unspeakable Mysteries. Chapter Nine. Just on the frontiers of classical belief and cult was the great Asiatic goddess Kybele or Sybil, with her cult partner, Attis. Kybele sprang originally from the ground and was bi-sexual until the gods reduced her by surgical methods to a female. She fell in love with the mortal Attis. He fell in love with her. But she drove Attis mad, and he castrated himself, whereof he died. The goddess repented of her harshness, and Zeus granted her prayer that the body of Attis should never decay. The little finger should continue to move and the hair to grow. From the severed part of Attis sprung up an almond tree of marvellous beauty. These beliefs were prevalent all over Asia Minor from Trebizond to Ephesus.

"Not only is it beautiful," averred Zebul on the way home from the library, throwing his *Bourgeois Gentilhomme* up in the air gaily like a juggler, "but history proves that the conventional limits assigned to man, sexual, as well as political, moral, and every way, are sheer delusion." He was in an exuberant mood, and as they approached the power plant he was trying to consolidate the genius of his relationship with Urie by pointing out how they had stumbled on this framework of the Attis-Sybil cult without realizing how profound an expression of themselves it was in archetypal form. "I wonder what the ancients really did in the ritual," he said. "They always tell about mysteries in history books, but where can you really find out? I mean, the real details!" In his enthusiasm he vowed that he would find out, and when he did they could re-enact it so that they could understand it. You could not understand anything about modern civilization, he said, if you did not understand these pre-classical rituals, for they were the basis, through drama and through churches, of Western experience. He was aping P.Q., but he knew it and liked the fact.

At the railroad track he changed the subject. "Hey, Urie, let's invite Bostwick to your house."

She was silent. Fear assailed her and she closed up like a clam.

"We could have him at night for Parker House rolls." He grew in enthusiasm.

"I knew you would start in on that," she said at last.

"Start on on what?"

"Inviting Bostwick to the house."

"Well, why not?" He pretended to be surprised. "Don't you want him to come?"

"I don't care."

"Well?"

"Well, nothing." But her derision was defensive.

The next day, as they were eating their sandwiches by the Old Well, he said, "Remember how long it took you to invite me to your house because it was a niggershack? You're always scared to invite people." He smiled sweetly, remembering.

"I am not."

"Well, why won't you invite Bostwick, then?"

She did not answer. She kept on chewing like a cow and would not budge.

It took two more days, when his asking had turned subtly to nagging, for her to reply. She turned her blue eyes squarely upon him.

"P.Q. won't like Bostwick."

"Ah, so that's the real reason!"

"Nothing's the real reason."

"How do you know he won't like Bostwick?"

"I just know. Bostwick is the type that P.Q. hates."

"P.Q. hates everybody."

"He doesn't hate you."

"No, he doesn't hate me," said Zebul thoughtfully, beginning to pride himself on the thought.

"That's because you're a Haw-yoo."

"So then what do you care if he hates Bostwick?" snapped Zebul, vengeful.

There seemed to be more and more that Urie had to hide from Zebul, and more and more she had to hide from P.Q. To be morally bound to hate whom P.Q. hated, yet not to hate, to love, to give with P.Q.'s gibes, yet cringe when the silver ligament of herself was torn. To bring one's conflicting loves to joust with one's conflicting loyalties. It meant nothing that Zebul gave as the ultimate argument that Bostwick could never become a friend in depth until he saw the depths of their beginnings.

CHAPTER 33

Toward the end of August, Urie and Zebul finished the translation of *Memoirs of the Court of Catherine the Great.*

P.Q. was ecstatic. He showed the two typed copies to Mrs. Bishop and then went to the stationery store and spent $1.50 for blue binders. "Now let's send it off!" he announced.

The force of P.Q.'s enthusiasm became stronger to Zebul and Urie than the memory of their nightly efforts. Zebul typed on the title page: "Translated by P. Q. Bishop." In fact it seemed to them as if P.Q. had really done the work, not they. P.Q. paid for the postage, and on Monday morning they mailed it to Houghton Mifflin. They unanimously picked Houghton Mifflin because that was where Miss Picke had sent her manuscript.

After they mailed it, Urie and Zebul felt let down. Their minds were empty and they could not think of anything to do. As they came up the driveway they saw P.Q. spreading the dirty linens in the yard. Idly Zebul began to sing, making motions with his hands and feet. He bent to the ground, wriggled, and spread out his arms.

"What on earth are you doing?" asked Urie.

"I'm creating the ceremony of the Sybil cult as practiced by the Lydians."

Urie pulled a branch off the hickory tree and stabbed him. "Die, then."

"No. I'm going to do a prance of death first."

He tried to do *entrechats,* grunted, failed, and then clutched his stomach and reeled. Urie made up an accompaniment in the unknown gobbledygook that she and Loco had used on the two old crabs on the beach.

P.Q. ran up to them, his forefinger outstretched. "No! You can't use white-trash glossolalia. It has to be in Greek!"

"Oh, P.Q., you're ruining everything!"

"No. He's right!" said Zebul.

On the spot P.Q. made up a speech in Greek for Urie to say when Zebul fell to the ground dead. He circled around Urie, waving his arms like a theater director, teaching her the Greek and making her say it the way he said it.

O Cloud Gatherer, behold what I have done. In killing Attis I have killed myself. Zeus, Zeus! Though I represented the whole earth, I have killed mine own self. Never can I look again into the face of Attis and see that which was mine. I shall never again know love. O Zeus, save me! Bestow your power upon me, for although Attis is dead, my love is alive. Zeus, make some sign that my life exists!

Loco Poco ran out of the house in her old cheesecloth Halloween costume, blowing on her flute. Seconds later Irene came, unable to concentrate on Modern Civilization. They watched Zebul writhe, dying.

Out of these improvised beginnings developed a pageant. P.Q. checked the details of the real ceremony in the library and made up all the speeches in Greek. He omitted sex references. Loco and Irene were appointed priestess-narrators to explain the events in English. Both danced. Loco danced while piping music she made up on her flute. Urie had four monologues. Zebul had the solo death dance. And P.Q. was the director.

"We need a Zeus," said Zebul.

It was P.Q. as Zeus that provided the *coup de grâce*. Since Zeus was invisible, he had to hide in the barn. He delivered Zeus's speeches in Greek through a megaphone that Loco made out of old shoebox cardboard. The effect of the megaphone was to expand his voice into something unfamiliar, disembodied and eerie. Everyone was drawn into the Zeus prevailing beyond P.Q.

"I'll tell you what let's do!" raved Loco. "Let's have a performance at night and invite people. We can use those old hubcaps in the shed for reflectors and put electric lights in front of them for stage lights!"

"Yeah! Let's have the Ransomes. Lacey as well as Mrs. Ransome!" said Irene.

"And Mrs. Polenta," added P.Q. "Why don't you invite Mrs. Polenta. Think what her reaction would be to a real musical play based on the Attis-Sybil cult!"

"I'm going to invite Dr. Nagy, then, and Miss Picke!"

"Yes!" seized Zebul. "And I'll invite Bostwick!"

Urie felt the sting of Zebul's triumph. A cold feeling assailed her under his wide, beaming eyes as she envisoned Bostwick witnessing their tacky house, their cheesecloth costumes, and most of all this Sybilline fantasy played out before his eyes.

"I don't want to act Sybil in front of all those people—"

"Aha! She wants to save her art for posterity!" mocked P.Q.

It was too late.

The pageant snowballed the following day, because of P.Q. He stopped by a table in Nick's greasy spoon when he heard some students complaining about a Greek assignment Opard Bigelow Granger had given them. "Dr. Opard Bigelow Granger knows as much Greek as my big toe," he announced, shifting an armload of caps to his shoulder.

The students gawked.

"If you want to know how the ancients talked, come to the Sybilline ceremony taking place across the railroad track at the end of Pergamus Avenue next Saturday night."

"What's a Sybilline ceremony?" asked one student.

"Why, man, come and see. It's better than that old-time religion you go to in revival tents." He shifted the caps, picked up some aprons, and left.

"Dirty fertility rites," whispered another student.

"That's Pee-Q-liar Bishop, the gadfly of Ephesus."

"Jesus. He insulted Major Hoople!"

By evening the word was spread. The next day Opard Bigelow Granger stopped P.Q. by a NO PARKING sign in front of the Pick Theater.

"Harrumph. I've heard that a performance of the Sybilline ceremonies is to take place at your home." It was the first time that Opard Bigelow Granger had ever spoken to P.Q.

P.Q. minced forward, a greasy smile spreading over his skull from his eyes toward his cheeks. "Why, yes. Would you like to come? I want to issue you a special invitation if you are interested. Mrs. Polenta will be there, and Dr. Nagy is coming. Would your daughter Opal like to come too?"

"Harrumph. Why, yes."

That night at the supper table P.Q. imitated this meeting. He waddled like Opard Bigelow Granger, and Urie knew that all was lost and that Bostwick's coming was inevitable. But perhaps, she thought, her scalp prickling with trepidation, it would be better with a lot of people around. P.Q. would be too busy to stick his fangs directly into Bostwick. Then maybe he would not get to know him and not get to spread his withering scorn of Bostwick into her heart.

Some people were invited earlier than others. Zebul saw to it that Bostwick was one. Mrs. Polenta was the other. Zebul invited Bostwick for four-thirty to guarantee the tête-à-tête with P.Q. Urie was afraid to object.

On the day of the performance P.Q. assiduously refrained from picking up the sea of aprons, caps, and tablecloths.

"For goodness' sake, hurry up and get those linens off the driveway," warned Mrs. Bishop. "People will be coming pretty soon."

"There's plenty of time." P.Q. was nonchalant.

No one could understand what perverse streak lay in P.Q. that it seemed he *wanted* people to see these articles of his business. All the preparations were made. Mrs. Bishop had mixed five quarts of Kool Aid with two quarts of grapefruit and pineapple juice which had been on the A & P's "reduced" shelf because the cans were bunged in. She had also baked Toll House cookies to be served as refreshments after the performance. The costumes, the hubcaps, the lights, P.Q.'s megaphone were all ready. Irene and Urie knew exactly what chairs were to be rushed out and what blankets—for there were not enough chairs—so that people could be seated on the ground. The day was spectacular, with a hot sun refracting on the sea of dirty white linens, dazzling the eye.

At four-thirty Bostwick arrived, piloted by Zebul. The dogs' barking roused everyone. P.Q. was not ready. He was shaving by the mantelpiece clock.

Urie rushed out of the house, smiling and blushing, followed by Loco and Irene.

"Hello," she said shyly.

Bostwick's eyes were so light, almost yellow, floating between his half-closed lids, that they lent him silent power. She saw reflected in them the toppling house, the oak trees, the linens, all the paraphernalia of their queer poverty. The mocking victory in Zebul's gaze confirmed the unreality.

Irene, after one look at Bostwick's handsome face, swept forward, put out her hand phonily, turned into Greer Garson, and said in the quavering tones of a heavenly hostess, "You're Bostwick, aren't you? Welcome to our manse."

Urie stared.

"I'm Irene."

"How do you do?"

"And Bostwick, this is Loco Poco," introduced Zebul.

Urie turned to watch Loco greet Bostwick. But Loco was staring at her with an estounded expression in her eyes. She did not even say hello to Bostwick. She stared at him, then stared back at Urie with such an expression of comical accusation that Urie, beet-red, turned away.

At this moment Mrs. Bishop came out of the house. Urie saw immediately not only that Mrs. Bishop was impressed with Bostwick, but that he thrilled her and induced in her that confidence that Bostwick always induced in middle-aged women. She darted forward and then stopped. The dirty linens were stretched from the kitchen door to the well. Mrs. Bishop had to walk upon them to reach the spot where Bostwick stood. Everyone noticed how she walked. She was too fat for her beautiful legs and ankles. Each step, outlined against white, posed the threat of tipping her over. She proceeded at a controlled bounce, like a lead-weighted clown, keeping her lips firmly shut over her blackened teeth.

At the moment she arrived to shake Bostwick's hand, Loco Poco sidled up to Urie, inserting a loud whisper into her ear. "You're in love with him, Urania Bishop."

A problem now confronted the group. Mrs. Bishop went into a tizzy of confusion. To get into the house it was necessary for Bostwick to walk upon the dirty linens. It was one thing for the girls, for Zebul, even for Mrs. Bishop, but for Bostwick! No. Something in his aristocratic stance, in his coolly reflecting, half-sympathetic eyes brought Mrs. Bishop face to face with her comedown in life, symbolized by the linens. There remained the option of picking up the linens in front of Bostwick. But who could dare do it?

P.Q. appeared behind the screen. He opened the baggy door slowly, like an emperor. There was a moment of silence, a waiting, as if everyone expected him to to move forward out of the house, into the yard, to the spot where Bostwick still stood for the greeting. But P.Q. did not move. He pretended to be unaware.

"This is my father, P. Q. Bishop," announced Urie in a whisper.

Bostwick smiled. He moved forward.

Like vassals, the others also took a step forward.

Bostwick paused.

"Come eean," prompted P.Q.

But Bostwick was uncertain at the edge of the sea of aprons.

"That's all right. Walk on the linens."

It took another second for Bostwick to make the decision. Then he planted his polished shoe on its first gingerly step. It was silent, soundless in its eminence. One foot followed the other in ten soft and silent footsteps across the nosewipings of the universe, and the significance of Bostwick's royal black shoe upon priestly velvet was transfigured.

P.Q. shook his hand in absolute triumph. "How do you do! I'm so glad to meet you after hearing so many wonderful things about you." "Wonderful" or "awful"—despised Anglo-Saxon words pulled out of P.Q.'s hope chest of hypocrisy for conformist situations.

"I can't think what." Bostwick gave a small self-deprecating laugh as P.Q. pulled him into the kitchen and propelled him up the hill in the floor to the dining room.

"Sit down. There." P.Q. pointed to the coffin couch.

Bostwick sat obligingly. P.Q. remained standing. As the others poured into the room, he indicated where they were to sit too. They sat with the docility of roosting birds.

"Well for instance," answered P.Q., "I hear that you are an authority on Schopenhauer and Leibnitz." And for the first time in his greeting P.Q. poured forth the full power of his eyes, sucking Bostwick into his gaze like an octopus.

It was worse than Urie had ever imagined. Every joint in her body ached, and to exacerbate the situation Loco Poco inched up behind her left shoulder, feasting on every discomfiture of Bostwick, every word of P.Q., every expression in Urie's face, like a bewitched midget.

Zebul's eyes became febrile. But Bostwick remained liquid and graven. "Hardly an authority," he said gently, refusing to recognize P.Q.'s baiting.

"Have you read Plato, Mr. Bostwick?" Self-denigration, the mark of the aristocrat, was the greatest of P.Q.'s *bêtes noires*.

"I'm afraid Plato is the granddaddy of us all."

It was unfair. How could Bostwick know that he had to praise Plato immediately, praise him not by words but by some passage of a Dialogue that would immediately relate to the present situation? But still, Bostwick should have known not to use the word "afraid," as if Plato not only had not been surpassed but had possibly led the world astray. Did Bostwick *want* crucifixion, neglect, the wastebasket, defeat, the Grief Face, doom? Urie tried to intervene.

"Bostwick means—"

"Aha, you have a lawyer, Mr. Bostwick!"

"But P.Q., you're not letting Bostwick develop the argument his remark implies—" began Zebul.

"Two lawyers!"

"History teaches—" began Bostwick in patient tones as if finally, his defenders batted down, he would consent to play the game.

"May I interrupt you one moment, Mr. Bostwick?"

"Yes."

"How can history teach? You are using a hypostasis. *Ypostasis,"* said P.Q. in Greek. "High up stop. An absolute. A contradiction in terms. Mr. Bostwick, where were you born?"

"Harrisburg, Pennsylvania."

"What did you do before you became an officer in the Navy?" P.Q. pronounced "officer in the Navy" in a mock-exalted manner.

"I did some organizing work in unions. And then—I became a broker."

"Which comes first? Thought or speech?"

"Ooooh! Mrs. Polenta's car!" screeched Loco.

A fat maroon Packard swerved up the driveway, approached the dirty linens, careened, and slammed on its brakes. Scylla and Charybdis jumped up from the shed, lunging into the interruption with barks. They attacked the tires. The family left Bostwick in mid-sentence and rushed to the windows. Loco ran out of the room and out the kitchen door.

Having slammed on the brakes to prevent the car from running over the linens, Mrs. Polenta made a mistake. Her foot slipped off the brake onto the gas pedal. This reverse of her expectations, the motion of going faster rather than stopping, enticed Mrs. Polenta to press harder. The car went insane. She was forced to steer. She steered with total occupation. She missed the kitchen door, bounced off the side of the shed, twisted the wheel, and headed back for the well. The fat tires lapped up the aprons in their wake. The aprons came alive and did a Maypole dance around the well. Inspired by their spinning and writhing, Mrs. Polenta chose the one course available for a perpetual-motion Packard. She circled the well. For her first three revolutions she kept the Packard on course. But, unnerved by her success and her increasing speed, she cut closer to the well-posts. On the fifth revolution she hit. The post groaned. The roof heaved. The Packard shuddered to a stop, The structure swayed, one pole following the other in a domino-fall formation, slowly, until the well-house froze at a tipsy forty-five-degree angle over the car.

"She's trapped in the machine," whispered Mrs. Bishop hoarsely to P.Q.

Everyone rushed out amid howling dogs. P.Q. sauntered. After strolling under the edge of the displaced roof, he leaned into the car, turned off the ignition key, and opened the free door for Mrs. Polenta to emerge.

"That darling old well! Oh-oh-oh! I've ruined that darling old well!"

"We never could use it anyway," offered Loco. "Six puppies fell in it before we came, and poisoned it."

"So charming!" wailed Mrs. Polenta. "I thought it was snow on the ground."

"It was just about to fall anyway," said Irene.

"I don't know what's the matter with me!"

"We'll push it back up," comforted Zebul.

P.Q. paid no attention to these noises. He took Mrs. Polenta's arm and pulled her out the Packard door. Then he set her upon her Cuban heels and feasted on the sight of her.

She was a fat bohemian with a pleated Hawaiian skirt, a peasant blouse, and white shoes. She exuded expensive Tabu.

"How do you do, Mrs. Polenta! So here you are! The famous Mrs. Polenta! I have heard so much about you. That you are a student of the Pupul Veh and the power behind that wonderful organization of harmony, the University Symphony Orchestra! We are so glad to meet you! We have been waiting to meet you for weeks."

"Oh, Mr. Bishop. I am so impressed at meeting you too!"

She gave herself up to his flattery with elephantine gratefulness, and those same Anglo-Saxon words that had slithered out like snakes to Bostwick were now delivered with creamy success into her ear. He turned her toward Mrs. Bishop with an affected concentration which did not betray one ounce of his pleasure in her having delivered herself so securely into his ambitions for her millions.

Bostwick was standing alone by the kitchen door, a tiny smile lurking at the edge of his grave lips.

Suddenly Zebul was aware of Urie staring at him with eyes so icy blue that he paled before the accusation in them. Maybe she was right and P.Q. could *never* like Bostwick. Why? Because he was a man? But he could not bother to argue with her now.

"Come on. Let's push this well back up," he said.

Urie put her shoulder to the well-post. Zebul and Irene each took a well-post. They pushed. The well creaked and resumed its upright position. Urie breathed hard.

She could not bring herself to look at Bostwick. Even when she heard her mother order Loco in a whisper to pick up the linens, even when P.Q. moved Mrs. Polenta's car away from the well and parked it neatly by the barn on the grass, even when the yard was miraculously clear of the dirty aprons and she could hear P.Q. inside the house talking small talk, "bringing Mrs. Polenta out," Bostwick seemed far away, untouchable, unfathomable.

By eight o'clock it was dark and the moon was streaming eerily upon the dirt road. Niggertown, the improvisational quality of lights strung through the trees, the hubcaps set up before the grass stage, the audience chairs, Victorian furniture carted all over the country to arrive on this field, the swishing of the trees, the lightning bugs, the smell of hickory nuts, and the breathlessness of all the Bishops gave the evening a strange, titillating atmosphere.

Dr. Napod Nagy was the first to arrive. When Mrs. Polenta saw him she clacked across the yard and embraced him with a squeal. He almost disappeared into the depths of her peasant blouse but shook himself out like a scared spider and backed away. Loco Poco saved him.

"You look very beautiful tonight," he said nasally.

"I made up all the music for this performance!"

"Yeah? Well, I hope it's as good as you look."

Loco Poco trotted him to meet her mother and father. He had to make his feet go double-time to keep up with her. Then she told him he could choose the place he wanted to sit. He chose an old child's painted rocking chair which Loco considered her own. It had come down through the family from Mrs. Bishop's syphilitic brother-in-law. Dr. Nagy moved it to a crooked, rocky place where he believed Mrs. Polenta could not climb, and he sat down in it and began rocking.

Dr. and Mrs. Lacey Ransome were next to arrive.

"Oh, what a wonderful scene!"

"Do sit down," said Mrs. Bishop.

Lacey Ransome stared through golden spectacles at Dr. Nagy rocking and then chose the one other rocking chair, a Boston rocker with a barrel-cover and pillow covering the broken-out seat.

Five students arrived. No one knew them or had ever heard of them. But P.Q. greeted them ostentatiously. They sat on a blanket.

"Do you think that boy is cute?" whispered Irene.

Miss Picke arrived in her winter sweater. Everyone gawked at her and no one spoke except Mrs. Lacey Ransome, who cheeped, "Oh, it's so nice to see you, Miss Picke. Isn't it a lovely evening?"

Miss Picke gave Mrs. Ransome a stonelike stare. Loco Poco piloted her to a seat next to Dr. Nagy, where each ignored the other, Miss Picke clearing her throat three times, and Dr. Nagy tapping his purple fingernails on his rocking-chair arms.

Wanda Rupee Kanukaris arrived. "Why did you have to invite that woman?" Mrs. Bishop whispered.

But P.Q. treated her as if she were the Queen of Tonga, introducing her particularly to Mrs. Polenta.

"Thank God it's night and she can't see the barn!"

Other students came. Nick of the greasy spoon arrived. Gag Booch. Faye Gormel, Loco's white-trash friend. There were some bohemians from the university. One boy who was a Communist sat next to the wild-rose bush. He was always exhorting people to sign petitions for the Trenton Ten, the Oxford Five, or the Wadesboro Three.

Out of sight of the gathering, beyond the hedge, Negroes heard the increasing hum of tea-party voices. They came out of their houses. They crept up in the darkness toward the Bishops' knoll. They were lured by the appearance of university people in Niggertown as if by lotus-eaters. They hid behind their rotting columns. They secreted themselves in bushes.

"The niggers are out!" Loco whispered excitedly.

"How do you know?"

"I can hear them!"

"God, I hope they don't start up guitars or begin cutting each other up with razors!"

"Just think! They'll see our performance!"

At that moment Opard Bigelow Granger and his daughter Opal approached. Unaware that they had passed like bison within three feet of Lucretia Pile and five of her children squatting in the ditch, they stepped onto the Bishop's driveway.

"Welcome to the Sybilline ceremonies!" hailed P.Q., raising his arms like Stokowski.

"How madly unique this all is!" said Opal to Urie.

Dr. Opard Bigelow Granger swayed his bulk to and fro. He nodded to Nagy, bowed to Lacey Ransome, smiled at Mrs. Polenta, gaped at Miss Picke, and claimed a chair. But he did not sit. For at that moment he noticed his students arrayed like leaves on the ground. He grunted. P.Q. cocked his head with fake *noblesse oblige* and spoke patronizingly of the coming performance. "A little thing. . . . Gives one a small idea of what the real thing was. . . . Something we worked up ourselves to give it reality. Why, I wouldn't be surprised if right this minute there aren't a few dozen old Negro women parked out on that grass who are going to be scared out of their wits by this devil-worship!"

Dr. Opard Bigelow Granger sat down.

"Are you scared to walk home alone at night?" Opal Granger interrupted Urie.

"Oh no." Thank God she had never begged for the Episcopal-church singing job.

But Urie could not think of that. For she had gone into a strange harmonic, and nothing seemed to have any reality. For all through the rising momentum of anticipation, the increasing hum of the audience, the separate voices, the cooing, the clearing of throats (Mrs. Ransome, Mrs. Polenta) she was aware of one person only.

Bostwick stood leaning against a tree with folded arms. Sometimes he leaned down and spoke to Mrs. Ransome and Mrs. Polenta. But most of the time he stared into the sky. The tree lights shone on his hair, and his eyes were hollows. It seemed to her that the audience, so strangely enthusiastic (did they, the Bishops, know so many people in Ephesus?) existed merely as the sounding board for her solo to Bostwick. She became aware that she was going to play solely for Bostwick's benefit. Just as with the cabbage! All these people lured to this place for different reasons, none of them friendship really! All for Bostwick.

She did not care about Zebul's triumph in Bostwick's presence. She did not care about Bostwick's defeat by P.Q. She did not care that Loco had discovered her secret. She did not care what P.Q. thought. She did not even care what Bostwick thought. She had watched Zebul sprint to him at odd times during the evening to keep him company, and she despised Zebul. She laughed in an apogee of derision.

Suddenly Loco signaled her. It was time to begin.

The lights went up on the stage area. There was a pause. The audience waited. P.Q. walked casually to the center of the spotlight. The hubcap reflections focused on him. He spoke slowly, definitely, his Byzantine tones accenting every word with precision. He introduced the performance. In the darkness tiny titters of laughter escaped from Loco Poco.

Urie threaded her way behind the crowd. She had to make her entrance from the small ash tree. She waited nervously, knowing that Zebul too was standing in the dark by the barn, preparing for his entrance. Behind P.Q. strange sounds of the flute began. Loco appeared in the stage lights in her trailing cheesecloth garments like a wraith, her flute at her lips. Her legs twinkled to the weird Oriental sounds; her torso swayed in the hubcap flares. She took center stage, and P.Q. unobtrusively disappeared.

It was at this moment that Urie became aware of what her role in this performance meant. She, Urie, was going to betray Zebul in front of Bostwick's eyes. If Zebul had been necessary to Bostwick for his appreciation of Urie, now he would be demolished. Only she would remain. As Sybil she could not enact a twosome. All the criminality she and Zebul had built together, all the love, she would pulverize before Bostwick's eyes. Out of the ruin of their twosome she would emerge, a girl obsessed with Bostwick, waiting for Bostwick, willing to do anything for Bostwick. Would she be desirable to him as Sybil was irresistible to the ancient millions?

Zeus announced Greek through the megaphone.

Zebul crept through broom grass and made his entrance. In the light flares he looked like a scrawny stranger. He stood in front of Mrs. Bishop's Venetian tapestry with gondolas. He began his joyous leapfrog dance. Suddenly the evening breeze moved the tapestry and the gondolas moved.

The audience was very quiet. Urie heard a separate sound like a high whine from Miss Picke's direction. She felt broom-grass stackles pricking her ankles. How glad she was she was speaking Greek. No one would know if she made an error, even Major Hoople, who did not know modern pronunciation. She began the ululating sound for her entrance. Loco and Irene made three dying falls. The music stopped.

The moment Urie walked into the hubcap footlights, feeling the burn of the lights mixed with the strange velvet breeze, a power betook her. It was scorn. Transcendent scorn. Burn the Grief Face. Annihilate grief. Her stance was splendid. She strode like a goddess. Also her enunciation of the Greek was perfect, just the way P.Q. had taught her. She became P.Q. Burn out of P.Q. his scorn for Bostwick. Everything but admiration for her. Steady. Clear. She approached Zebul. They did their *pas de deux*.

Somebody laughed with delight. Was it Mrs. Ransome or Opal Granger? What was Bostwick doing? Was he spellbound?

The death weapon was neither sword nor wand. It was a slip of tobacco. They had all agreed on the tobacco slip because it was green and graceful, the opposite of death. She had rehearsed the death motion so carefully that she knew it perfectly. She did not touch Zebul. She brought the leaves delicately, teasingly in front of his face. He fell, writhing. Loco and Irene came out of the background, ululating and dancing as Zebul died, explaining the death in English to the audience. Zebul gave one last twitch. Dead.

Loco and Irene withdrew. Urie waited a good long time, and then she gave her Sybilline soliloquy about love and everlasting life, taking the role of both male and female in a mutant state which everyone must worship. She stared out into the audience with a hideous grimace of tragedy which she knew to be sheer triumph. She aimed it directly at Bostwick.

After the loud, enthusiastic clapping, the curtain calls that they improvised on the spot—Zebul got up from the dead, the tree lights came on, the hubcap lights went off—Urie, Irene, and Loco went to help Mrs. Bishop. They carried trays of Kool Aid and cookies out. Glasses tinkled. Everybody started talking at once. P.Q. strode through the groups.

"You did not use the Erasmian pronunciation," Opard Bigelow Granger said.

Snatches of P.Q.'s arguments came to Urie as she picked the glass and five cookies to take to Bostwick at the tree. "It has never been proved . . . fake pronunciation . . . I made the translations. . . ." The scorn and triumph born of hot lights and hatred of Zebul's triumph and P.Q.'s excoriation were rolling off her. She was like a water-color painting still wet and wrinkled from the water.

"Oh, Urie, it was fantastic! Such a Worth-while Evening!" She almost tripped over a root trying to keep Opal from following her. Some of the purple juice brimmed over. She looked up into Bostwick's eyes, and they blinded her. Did he recognize? Did he understand?

"You were wonderful. All of you!" he said, taking the glass.

She could hardly breathe.

He continued talking. He laughed about how Zebul must have enjoyed dying. It was small talk. She wanted the important thing.

"Bostwick," she said.

"What?"

"You don't care that everything's funny, do you?"

"I like it."

But it was the importance of Sybil that she demanded he recognize.

"Don't mind P.Q.," she blurted. "P.Q. can convince anybody that black is white and—I mean, even when they know it's a lie. I mean, P.Q. is right, even when he is wrong—"

In the distance she saw Zebul coming, so she had no time. He arrived breathless, laughing, throwing himself gloriously into the praise he knew Bostwick would give him, when Urie said, "I have to go get the cookies."

It was Sybil that was important. Why hadn't she let Bostwick say the first word about P.Q.?

In the morning, awakened by the buzz of flies, Loco got out of bed and went to the scene of last night's entertainment in pajamas and bare feet. She discovered thirty-nine watermelon rinds on the edge of the road.

"I knew the niggers were eating watermelons!" she announced at breakfast. "I smelled them!"

CHAPTER 34

The next day Zebul could not find Urie. It was the first time after a Bostwick episode that they had not immediately rushed to hash everything over together. He looked for her everywhere, in their office, at home, in the library three times, searching every room, every chair. So he gave up and turned his attention to Bostwick. But he could not find him either. He went to Bostwick's house, knocked a few times, and then went home.

The next day when he saw Urie in the Book Ex yard, something was different yet strangely familiar about her. She blanched as if she wanted to escape him, but when it was too late she put on a mask.

"Are you mad?" he asked.

"Yes, I am."

"Just because I brought Bostwick to meet P.Q.?"

"I told you he wouldn't like him."

"Well, you don't have to be that mad!"

Her reticence, the enlargement and silence of her blue eyes, suddenly struck home. But instead of retaliating with anger to her anger, Zebul had a strange reaction. He was inspired. Everything he had envisioned when he first saw Bostwick and imagined them in the relationship of three had in fact come true. Even if Urie did not tell him, her esteem for Bostwick, her love, was something that he, Zebulon Vance Walley, had created. He was seeing his own creation come to fruition. It was like the Attis and Sybil. He had arbitrarily chosen this goddess and god from his head. Now they had become an event! Also he recognized what Bostwick had not recognized, that Urie really was Sybil. And as Sybil she was taking on Bostwick's attributes!

A strange thing happened in Urie when she saw Zebul contemplating her like a cat that has swallowed a canary. She was glad she was betraying him. The fact that she had turned into a deceiver pleased her. Not only was she deceiving Zebul, but she was deceiving him as a direct result of his having introduced Bostwick to P.Q. The more disloyal she became, the more delighted she became. She felt no guilt. Instead she opened up. She changed from her silent, evasive manner and became dashing. She told Zebul about the watermelons, and they laughed.

The balance of power in the threesome changed to her advantage. Forced to disregard both P.Q. and Zebul, it was as if she were taking up her own destiny in regard to Bostwick. A process of truth, it seemed, was going to be revealed to her alone.

Anyway, what *was* there to tell? Her dreams were her dreams alone. As for Zebul, as they had sworn their vow to truth, he, with his adamant and glittering devotion to her, would in the end have to embrace her love for Bostwick too. Had he not led her to it? Had he not demanded it? Was he not taking pride in it? If she had made up a superhuman Zebul, the Zebul she had had an intimation of in the moonlight, he would have to become this Zebul. He would learn to own the new truth of her when it had been accomplished. Had not that, all along, been promised in their vows of truth to each other?

A strange euphoria took her. The new fall semester was beginning. She seemed to see things around her for the first time. She walked to classes rapidly. She understood the professors at once. She did not have to ponder on what they said, to judge whether it was truth or untruth. She gobbled pertinent information and dismissed the rest. Two weeks passed, bringing her into the meat of her courses. She wrote her papers quickly and well. She even talked more rapidly than before.

Yet intense anxiety underlay this excited state. Zebul was only background to the decision forming in her mind.

That Wednesday night she started out for Bostwick's house. Her chest was tight and her throat knotted. She could hardly swallow. Her footsteps on the sidewalk of Pergamus Avenue hardly touched the ground. They crackled and skidded on the gravel. Her face was burning. She tried to listen to her footsteps, but instead her ears began to ring.

What would she do when she got to Bostwick's? Would she tell him how she had seen him in the Ephesus Inn long before she had met him? Would she ask him why he had been crying? As she walked she made up fantasies. She arrived at the corner of McCauley Street, and the fantasies exploded out of her head. She turned around and ran toward home. At the power plant she stopped. She was panting. She leaned her hands on her knees and broke into laughter. To think she had been within five houses from Bostwick! She stopped laughing and walked soberly home. In bed later, she lay and thought.

She was scared to go to Bostwick's. She was not ready. When she really did go she would be scared, but not that totally. It must be beautiful when she saw him. A modicum of fear was acceptable in beauty. But fear and beauty were too limitless for her to apprehend in this state of necessity.

The next day at noon meal when Irene told the news that Maddox Stein had been killed in the Battle of Midway, deflecting a tonguelashing Mrs. Bishop was doling out to Loco Poco for using half a bottle of catsup on her beans, Urie was skeptical.

Irene's tone was idle. "Guess what! Maddox Stein was killed in the Battle of Midway!"

"But that was in June."

"Well, he's been dead for three months."

"How do you know it's true?"

"Mr. Huntsucker told me."

"How does he know?"

"Some professor told him, I guess."

"How did you happen to see Huntsucker?"

"I went back there for my Phys. Ed. record to get out of taking tennis. What is this? The third degree?"

But Zebul had heard it too in some roundabout way through Henny Pinney, who got it from a secretary in the Department of Education, which kept track of all former students in the teacher-training program.

"To think that Maddox Stein would be the first person we would know to be killed in the war!" breathed Urie.

"It's unbelievable," agreed Zebul, marking the passage of his ideal: from Maddox Stein, that student-teacher, stranger, Yankee whom he believed to be impartial, to Bostwick.

"I wouldn't believe Maddox Stein would even be a soldier, let alone get killed!"

"Yeah. To think he's been dead three months and we didn't even know it."

"To think he's the first person we know to be killed, and him being so obnoxious!"

"A sniveling Jew!"

"I wonder if he was a hero."

"I wonder if he knew before it."

"That just shows. You better join the ASTP. Or be an officer."

"I can imagine officers like Bostwick being killed, but not Maddox Stein."

Now that Maddox Stein had no more life to live to make his destiny change, his leer was frozen forever in Urie's mind as the bell rang, saving her at the head of the parade of three Bishop girls from banging into the brick wall.

It was late Friday afternoon when Urie made her decision. She was typing at the catalogue department, and Miss Marsh had wheezed into her ear from her dry palate, "You'd better do these four over. Subject headings, remember, are typed in red."

"I have to leave an hour early today, Miss Marsh."

The fleeting thought of Zebul came to her mind. How amazed he would be, if he came to meet her, that she was not at her regular place.

She grew scared as she approached Bostwick's house, but she pursued her course doggedly. At the open screen door she listened. She did not knock. There was no sound, yet she could have sworn that Bostwick was there. The house breathed him. She sneaked into the hallway, listened again, and climbed the stairs furtively. At the top she saw that Bostwick's apartment door was indeed open. Her heart began to beat uncontrollably. But a revelation in the daytime is not so formidable as at night. At night you commit yourself more inalienably. You have to burst through light bulbs, go from pitch-black to blasting light. There is more reality in unreality. And there is no limit to nighttime familiarity. But the day would show to Bostwick that she was really Urie. He would know Urie as Urie in the day, and it would be she alone without the magic of darkness that would acquaint Bostwick with that unknown of herself that she desired in this revelation to him.

She knew she should have called out to him, but she could not. Through the open door she could see a blue cup on the table. The door to his bedroom was open. She went into the living room and peered in. Was he there? She thought she heard a movement.

"Bostwick," she called in a faint voice.

One more step and she saw him lying on his bed. He was dressed in his khakis, with boots. His coat was open. When he saw her he craned his neck as if to concentrate on her glittering face.

"Urie!"

"I called you."

"I haven't seen you for ages. Where's Zebul?"

"Uh, I didn't bring him."

"Well, come in!" In her mind she almost believed he asked her: What do you want? "What time is it?" he asked.

"About five-thirty I think."

The mentioning of the time was unreal to her. Didn't he have any idea? Her revelation was going to have to be radical. She began to suffer. Her throat was tightened. The necessity, now that she was really facing him, became more intense than she had thought.

The bed was not made up. He was lying on sheets. There had been a weary look on his face when she interrupted him. The combination of this elegant weariness with the messiness of the room and the wapsed-up sheets was incomprehensible to her. Yet she looked down on the wrinkles of the sheets, coveting them simply because he was lying on them. She did not look into his face at all, only at the wrinkles in the sheets. Her eyes had a pleading quality.

"It's late, isn't it?" he said, beginning to get up.

Some strangeness flashed over his face, a shadow of knowledge in his ice-gray eyes. He stared at her questioningly.

Her throat was filled up and she could not speak a word.

She turned red. All at once she noticed his boots, which had been propped on the iron bedstead, swinging to the floor. Everything was extravagant and unrelated in her. Suddenly, just like the wrinkles in the sheet, she wanted to avow her love for his boots. But she could not put the idea into words. She had a desire to embrace the boots, to put her cheek against them because they were foreign, hard, thick, coarse, just the opposite of his soul, she thought.

"What is it?"

"I love you!"

"What?" His voice was loud, quizzical, but strange, as if he had understood perfectly but in fact was forcing her to repeat herself.

"I love you. Oh, Bostwick!" She suddenly knelt on the floor beside the bed. "I love you so much." She could hear herself flop. She could hear her own voice, half in a groan, half in a whisper. All the performances she had ever given, from the first day of school through the Sybilline ceremonies—and now this began to seem like a performance. Her very sincerity made it fake. She wallowed in awkwardness. Still she did not yet embrace him, embrace his legs, his boots, as she craved to do. She took the sheet in her fingers and twisted it.

"But Zebul. What about Zebul?" An angler, who sees the fish flop out of the stream to his feet, he refused to pick it up.

"I love *you!*" For the first time she looked straight at him.

"You can't love me."

"Why?"

"Because I don't love you."

Up to this point her single-minded and aggressive enforcement of the gift of her love, whether or not he wanted it, had assumed total possession of the ventricles of her action. Her strength was so great that she was sure that her *need* alone would break him down. But now she was surprised.

"Not at all?" Her voice was rasping and dry.

"Of course I love you, but— Get up from there."

"Are you married?"

"No." He moved as if stung. The bedsprings jounced.

"But you were, weren't you?"

"Yes."

"Did you get a divorce?"

"My wife died." Bostwick grimaced and his eyes looked helpless above his mouth.

At that, suddenly seeing the light of day, that his wife had died, and that was why he had been crying in the Ephesus Inn, Urie melted, grasped his hand, buried her face in his knuckles, and then began kissing them passionately.

"Did you have any children?"

"Urie, get up from there." He pulled his hand away.

But she, feeling one thing snatched from her, hurled herself forward in an orgy of desperation and grabbed hold of his boots. She groveled, she grasped them tight, shut her eyes so hard she saw stars, and pressed her cheek against the shoelaces.

"All right, get up!" he said in a stony, even cruel voice. "Don't do that. Stop that!" And he lifted her up by the shoulders.

At this change from words to physical grappling she burst into a paroxysm of sobs. It was an explosion of exhilaration. A fight. His hands were very strong and very firm, but not cruel like his words. A fantastic declaration of war. She did not care what he thought. It was her will against his. He lifted her to the bed. She threw herself against him, crying, sobbing, and kissing anything she could get hold of, his buttons, his loosened tie, and at last his neck. It was a strange sensation. His neck was soft after his boots. She had worked her way through all the accouterments of his officerdom, to that. Was it the secret of him? But his body was strange. Hard, unbending, and quiet. His quietness infected her. When her sobs were done, she rested. Then she sneaked a look at him.

"Zebul should see this performance," he said, letting her go. His expression was grim. He got up, went to the living-room door, closed and locked it. This action seemed to belie his words.

"It's not a performance!" But what was he going to do? Talk to her? Straighten her out? Or make love to her? She felt naked after this orgy of touching to be sitting alone on his bed untouched.

"This entire relationship has gone farther than it should have. You and Zebul—"

"Zebul doesn't own me. You—*you* make up that he and I are together. *He* made it up and then you took it up!"

Strangely, he laughed a laugh of bitterness. "Don't you feel any feeling of guilt?" he asked.

His face had a salacious expression. It was unbecoming to her conception of him. In the back of her mind she knew perfectly well she was forcing Bostwick to turn away from her. Perhaps now he was going to become kind, fatherly, and full of nobility. Perhaps he was going to transform her from a lover to a devotee. She saw herself at the age of thirty remembering her first and strongest love, for she would worship him even then for not having let her make love to him.

But he stood with his back to her, thinking up things to say. "What do you want of me? I'm too old for you."

"How old are you?" she asked.

"Thirty-eight."

He was twenty-two years older than she was and—she totted rapidly—only thirteen years younger than P.Q.! "That's not old," she lied. She thought rapidly of his having been on the earth for that long a time. The clock ticked loudly. Suddenly she felt guilty for fear he could read her thoughts as she was reading the clock face: five-forty-five. Only five-forty-five!

She rushed up from the bed toward him. "But age is nothing, Bostwick. You know it isn't. You don't know me. All you know is that stuff, those performances that Zebul and I played for you. You made him do it. And he made me do it. But I am something. By myself. I am something, even if you don't know it. You will see. I will do anything for you, and then you will know. If I give you everything, you will love me! I know you will!"

"I do love you already." She could actually see the click of the decision in his mind. "And off you go. Out." He pivoted her by the shoulders toward the doorway.

But she lifted herself on tiptoes and caught his mouth in a kiss. She did not move or touch him. She did not put her arms around him.

He pulled his head away and stared at her. There was a fold in the skin of his cheeks, below his mouth, which gave to his face a harried expression.

"All right," he said. He held her arm hard above the elbow and walked her to the bed. "Then take off your clothes." He took off his coat. He unloosened his tie, removed it, and hung it over a chair. Then he undid his shirt.

She was shocked. Was he trying to make her go? She became afraid. The bright glint of blond hair on his chest and the perfect hard ivory skin of his belly transfixed her.

"Take off your blouse. Sit down and take it off."

She was so afraid, she began to obey. She undid two buttons. But he was so different from the way she had imagined Bostwick, that she hung upon him, unable to speak. The wrinkles of his sheets, which she had loved so much before, now seemed foreign. She tried to smooth them out.

"You've never done this before, have you?" He turned away from her, went to the bureau drawer, took something out, twisted a cardboard box, and put something into his trousers pocket. She deliberately pretended in her mind that it wasn't a condom.

"Yes."

Yet why had he asked? Didn't he know everything they had done? From the moment he had read the Attis and Sybil theme he knew. But no, he did not know about the evening under the moon!

As she hung on his every movement, almost as if to obliterate herself, he seemed to come into such powerful prominence in respect of her that it really seemed as if she had never known him before. He was completely foreign. He was clinical. He was hard. His being a man seemed so stupendous that she could not believe it was Bostwick. He had turned into an absolute stranger.

"You mean you and Zebul have never played?"

He came toward her now, smiling. She shrank.

"No. Yes."

He sat down.

"Don't be afraid." But his mind was so full of everything he was going to do, hard with confidence, that she shrank when he finished undoing the buttons and drew off the blouse. She began to pant with fear. He took off her brassière, loosened her skirt, laid her down on the bed, her head on the pillow. But he did not look at her body at all. He looked above her head and into her eyes. As she stared back into his yellow pupils she tried to recognize in them Bostwick. But they seemed disembodied, like living animals jerking in their bonnet of lashes, in a head fastened by a neck to a hard, long body that was moving next to her, threatening and heavy. He was still wearing his boots.

"Bostwick!" she pleaded.

"Don't be afraid," he murmured. He kissed her. Then he looked at her body for the first time. "You have a beautiful, fine girl's body," he said. It was such an outside, analytical thing to say that she looked down at it, naked to the waist, and then fastened on to his eyes again, pleading. But he began running his hands up and down over her breasts to her hips, down under her skirt to her buttocks and up again. "Did he do this?" he whispered in a thick voice.

"Yes, but—"

"But what?"

"But not like this."

"How?"

"Not on a bed."

"Where?"

"On broom grass."

"On broom grass?" He took off her skirt now, put his hands through the waist of her panties to her hips and drew her panties off.

"Yes, but don't talk about him!"

"Did he do this?"—stroking the fur of her groin.

"No! Bostwick, I don't want to talk about him."

"Why?" He was sitting up, unloosening his belt buckle and unzipping his pants. He was smiling!

"Bostwick, I love you!" she squealed.

He lay over her and kissed her as if to quell the energy of her mind and divert it to her lips, her breasts, and her groin, to prevent her forcing from him the words of love. She could feel him naked against her. But she could not look. He was preparing his sex to enter her.

"Bostwick, don't hurt me," she begged.

"I'm not. Only a little, maybe, it will. I won't."

"Bostwick, I love you."

"I know."

"Do you love me?"

"Yes, I love you."

He kissed her. She kissed his neck. He ran his palms gently against her breasts. She moved her lips against his neck, his collarbone, his throat. His hands opened the lips of her vagina gently, and pushed in. It hurt. She twitched.

"Shshsh."

"It hurts."

"Relax."

"Don't, Bostwick, don't!"

"Kiss me."

In that kiss he poured himself into her with a slight gasp, holding her viselike for the moment of his orgasm. A convulsive jerk of his neck completed the nervous act. Yet everything was too controlled. She shrieked with pain. And when she jerked bleeding away from him, he raised his body nimbly above her tiger-cat thrust. He held her sobbing. He kissed her face. He was very quiet. She calmed down and finally she raised her face to his neck. He released her gently, got up, and went, naked but for his boots, into the bathroom, leaving her staring strangely at the spot behind the door of the bathroom where he had disappeared.

When he returned they stared at each other. He lay back down on the bed again. They continued to stare. All the force of their being was released into their eyes from the unfulfilled act. She cared nothing now about her nakedness. How strange it was lying inert with pain, her brain fiercely alive behind her eyes. Pride and unreality contested in her.

"It's time for you to go home," he said.

She looked at the clock: five-fifty-five. But she did not take it in.

"I did it, Bostwick."

"Yes."

"I'm glad."

"Yes," he said.

"Bostwick," she whispered, looking up over his perfect furred chest, over the ivory muscles of his forearms into his bleak eyes, "I'm glad it was you."

He kissed her. She dressed. She suddenly clutched his neck in an embrace full of all the passionate love foiled on the bed of sex.

Speechless, she wobbled down the stairway, feeling inexpressibly light, sore, and proud.

CHAPTER 35

U rie pushed her way in through the baggy screen door at her usual gait, trying not to grimace at the pain when she walked.

She whistled "From the Halls of Montezuma" loudly.

Mrs. Bishop was ladling out beans and corn for supper. P.Q. was in the midst of telling how he had met Mrs. Polenta downtown and how she had invited him for supper. He was standing by his place, imitating and describing.

". . . and her lipstick was painted two inches past where her lips stopped, like two arrows pointing in to her nostrils."

"Who?" asked Urie to put them off the scent.

"We're talking about Mrs. Polenta," answered Loco. "And then what did she say to you?"

Urie went to the bathroom and washed her face and hands. She stared at her eyes in the corroded mirror. Her face was red and thin, and her eyes were staring. Why are my eyes red too? She forgot she had been crying. "Sexual relations," she whispered to the mirror. The moment she said it, she dismissed it, as they had dismissed "Sociological Conditions" long ago.

She came out and sat down at the table, her groin sore, her tongue dry.

P.Q. had gotten fully into his part. He had one hand on his hip. He waddled and minced past his plate, where the beans and corn were steaming hot, to the iron standing lamp. He batted his eyelashes betwitchingly at the lamp. "Oh, Mr. Bishop!" he purred. "I'm so glad to meet you. Won't you join me for supper at the Ephesian Grill?"

"And you mean she would have paid?" cried Loco.

It was lucky that Loco was so excited at P.Q.'s story, Urie thought, or she would have noticed. She had to watch out for Loco. Urie was very hungry. She ate three plates of beans and corn, hiding in the hum of supper conversation. I screwed Bostwick. Bostwick fucked me. No. Bostwick screwed me. I fucked Bostwick. No one asked her where she had been or what she had done.

That night P.Q. went to bed early. The girls sat with their mother in the dining room. Urie pretended to study. Irene finished the dishes and began translating Latin. Mrs. Bishop was hemming some new aprons.

Loco Poco was sprawled full-length upon the floor, surrounded by geography papers.

"I wish you wouldn't lie on that rug," said Mrs. Bishop.

"Why?"

"It's drafty. You'll catch cold."

But Loco did not move.

How can they not know? Urie's incredulity gave way to a sense of nostalgia. Up to this day she had always slipped easily between the different universes of campus, Bostwick, family, and Zebul. But this was different. She was Margo after love had forced her out of Shangri-La. In the snow, that frozen, desiccated three-hundred-year-old mummy revealed! When everlasting youth had been stripped away. Reality.

"Well, it's time to go to bed," announced Mrs. Bishop, pulling the last apron out of the machine. She released the needle and pulled the cord out of the wall.

Last week, exactly six days before Bostwick had screwed Urie and Urie had fucked Bostwick, Mrs. Bishop had decided that she was going to use the upper room for a bedroom. There was no way to get to it except from the outside.

"She'll have to go up the way Socrates went to heaven, in a basket," said P.Q. But he constructed a ladder instead from some two-by-fours he found in the shed. He leaned the ladder against the living-room chimney and nailed it to the side of the house. It led to the gable window. It was very rickety.

Urie did not want to move for the litany of Mrs. Bishop's ascent. Her legs ached and her groin throbbed. But she followed the parade.

"It's getting chilly," said Mrs. Bishop, looking at the stars. "You know, I will never get used to going outdoors to go to bed."

"What will you do when it gets freezing this winter, Mamma?"

"I'll cross that bridge when I come to it. Well, good night."

She put her foot on the first rung. The ladder creaked. The girls stood at the bottom of the chimney. Loco held her breath. Urie's fist curled like monkey paws, but she refrained from holding the ladder.

Halfway up, Mrs. Bishop repeated, "Good night."

"Good night," they echoed.

At the top the ladder jiggled. Mrs. Bishop pulled her leg up as if about to make a pirouette. Two stones crumbled and dropped out of the chimney.

"Good night," she said, aiming at and hurdling the window sill.

"Good night."

They waited. Mrs. Bishop balanced on the inserted leg and heaved. The second leg went over. Knocking sounds emerged from the dark hole of a window, and a light illuminated the fathoms within. At last her head appeared over the sill.

"Good night," she said with pride.

"Good night."

In the living room Irene returned to her Latin translation. Loco plunked herself down on the carpet again amid her geography papers. The quiet was profound. There was not a breath of air. Even the insects fell silent. In fact the silence was so uncharacteristically profound as to be suspicious, for usually when the three were together they could not resist interrupting each other with complaints, comments, or tales.

Bostwick appeared to Urie in the silence in a strange new way, physically as a presence, heavy, almost brutal, as unwanted and encompassing as he had been at the moment of penetration, and completely mysterious, not as he used to be mysterious, of the spirit, but now mysterious of the flesh.

"Listen!" said Irene in a whisper, hunched like a witch. "I think Mamma's been stealing again!"

Urie jerked her eyes and Bostwick exploded into atoms.

Loco's expression was strange, a half-smile of guilt, and her dark eyes feasted on Irene.

Urie did not want to hear what Irene had to say. She did not want to reckon with new information in her state of unreality. Irene had the horrid satisfaction that is seen on faces of purveyors of ill tidings.

"Stealing?"

"Stealing from Counts'?"

"No."

"Stealing from where, then?"

"From the grocery store."

The words "grocery store" were insulting and heartbreaking. But Loco squealed with delight.

"Shut up! Do you want her to hear?" And to Irene: "How do you know?"

"Because we've been eating a lot more meat lately. Haven't you noticed it?"

"We had beans and corn tonight."

"Yeah, and we had lamb the night before. Do you know how much that costs?"

The irony of her mother's being discovered, and the exposure of secret lives in the heart of a family, when it was Bostwick she had fucked, and her own new life that lay unsuspected, while they whispered here to keep Mrs. Bishop from suspecting they knew! Everything was changing. Could it be true that in the heart of Bishopry they were losing Bishopry? Was life the losing of Bishopry?

"And we had a round of beef the night before that. And steak on Sunday. She said it was bottom of the round."

"Don't call her *she!*" But Urie herself continued to say "she."

"You know P.Q. doesn't make any more money than he did before. We never had meat before."

"Maybe meat's gone down."

"I don't care. I'm glad she steals," declared Loco. They looked upward, thinking of their mother lying in the room over their heads. "How do you think she does it?"

"With the carpetbag."

"Carpetbag!"

"Yes. I saw her take the carpetbag to the grocery twice. I think she puts the meat in the bottom and covers it up with other stuff, which she pays for. And nobody can notice."

"I love it!" swore Loco. "Don't you love it, Urie?"

"I'm worried," announced Irene. "What should we do?" Her look at Urie sloughed off Loco's bobbing, smiling, puerile irresponsibility.

"Are you a hypocrite or something?" answered Urie. "You know you steal and I steal and so does Loco."

"But what if she gets caught?"

At that moment the silence merged the prospect of Bostwick with the private soul of her mother. She could not worry about being caught. She could not worry about invasion of privacy. Deception was so easy. Nothing was as it seemed. Oh, would Bostwick ever love her, or was it a chimera?

"Maybe we should warn her," pleaded Irene. "Should we warn her, Urie, do you think?"

Oh, Mamma, should they shatter her shame?

"Not yet," she answered with that absolute authority born of complete indecision. Like her pledge to crack the town wide open, something was necessary.

But there was something intensely stupid about the fact that everything had changed for Urie and no one recognized it. The next day the pain was almost gone and there was only a strange feeling about her body, a vestige of Bostwick's body.

The one person she could not bear to see was Zebul. She was afraid. For, now she had committed the betrayal, her most treasured dealings with him were damaged, and all their intimate philosophy was warped and double-faced.

But he nabbed her in the library. "Didn't you work yesterday?"

"Yes, but I left early."

"Well, I learned the names of a hundred rocks yesterday in geology lab, and I wanted to repeat them over to you. I really do have a photographic memory, Urie. It's lucky, since I never studied them at all, and we were given six weeks, and I've got that test tomorrow. Listen." He began the list he had learned.

He suspected nothing! But there was a restlessness in him that was dangerous. He jounced on his legs as they headed toward town. She sensed melancholy.

"I wonder where Bostwick is," he said.

"I don't know."

"I haven't seen hide nor hair of him for almost a week, and he never showed yesterday at the Confederate soldier." Idly he followed Urie into the post office. "I even went to his house, but he wasn't there."

"You went to his house?" She stared hard at the WPA mural of men in overalls. "When?"

"Two nights ago. No, three nights ago. Hey, let's go by there now."

"No."

"Why?"

"I don't feel like it. I tell you what. Why don't we go to the top of the Fall Line."

"Why don't you want to go to Bostwick's?"

"Oh, I don't know."

She diverted him by peeking through the glass of P.Q.'s box. There was a letter inside. She fumbled through her pocketbook for the key and opened it. The letter was addressed to Mr. P. Q. Bishop.

"It's from Houghton Mifflin!" She pointed to the letterhead.

"Open it. It's ours really too."

Dear Mr. Bishop:

Thank you very much for allowing us the opportunity of seeing your translation of the *Memoirs of the Court of Catherine the Great* by Charles François Philibert Masson. Although we found it interesting, we regret that we are unable to find a place for it on our current list. We are returning the manuscript to you under separate cover. Again, with thanks and our sincere regrets. Very truly yours. Charles Hinckel, Editor.

Zebul held the letter, still reading, while they walked down the post-office steps and crossed the street. She read it again too.

"They were interested," he said. " 'We found it very interesting,' it says."

"Charles Hinckel has funny handwriting, doesn't he? I wonder if he's the same one who wrote to Miss Picke."

"Do you believe they were really interested?"

"Why would they say so if they weren't?"

"If they were really interested, why wouldn't they publish it?" He stuck the letter in Urie's brown notebook and walked on down the Kingston Road. "Do you feel futile?"

But she knew he did not expect her to answer. He was going to go into the futility recitative.

"Futility is the worst thing," he said. "Sometimes I feel futile."

"So do I."

"I feel futile right now."

"Me too."

"What is futility?"

"A mood."

"The question is: 'Is futility justified?' "

Zebul thought: If there is no God, there is only reason and poverty. Reason is essentially futile because it is godless. Yet some people in reason's name sacrifice their lives to bettering the materialistic position of man. It was reason itself which made Raskolnikov murder the old money-lendress. It was essentially the futility of life which led to the mirage of bettering it.

Urie thought: If Bostwick loved me, would I have an orgasm? What is Bostwick besides a man? I own part of Bostwick. Can I sneak to his house at night? And how am I to act with Bostwick, now that he is no longer a shared ideal with Zebul?

They walked out on the Kingston Highway. The sun of Indian summer burned them. The highway was an engineering feat executed in the raw, red earth of the Fall Line. It gouged through hills, huge plates of cement tipped toward the Triassic sea. Not more than five hundred yards from where they walked, Loco Poco had jumped off Visigoth Castle so long ago. Since the President had asked people to cut out all nonessential driving, there were fewer cars on the road. They walked in the middle of the

306]

highway, owning the huge mass of cement. In the woods on both sides insects rang. Squat and silent, the highway hung over the void.

"Ever since you convinced me there is no God, everything seems worthless," he complained fitfully.

"It's not my fault God doesn't exist."

A car was coming. Lazily they headed for the shoulder. Everything was so sad that Zebul might just as well know about her and Bostwick, she thought. They walked slowly and spitefully, as if they were being interrupted.

The black Buick tooted. It swerved, giving them wide berth, pressing its brake at the same time self-righteously. When it had passed, it gunned its motor and spurted forward, leaving them in exhaust fumes. They stuck out their tongues.

"Bums," said Urie.

"Yeah. But we're like niggers. Go as slow as we can in front of cars so they have to stop."

"I'm not like a nigger." Urie pretended she was telling him right this minute that she and Bostwick had screwed. What if she really told him? ,

"Yes, you are." Zebul's mind was making a metaphor between feet and rubber wheels, between a heart and a motor.

"Do you really think you would still believe in God if you hadn't met me?"

This was the eighteenth time he had brought God up. But it was always the same. He acted as if it were the first time. This allowed them to keep the same dialogue going, like the Three Bears. Each time it necessitated a different wording and it had different effects.

"Well, maybe I would," he said. "I didn't think much until I met you. And then with P.Q. and all, and my introduction to Platonic thought . . ."

The bleached sorrow he saw burning in her eyes matched his own and, as always, excited him.

"I don't say I would," he continued, "because, maybe without you even coming here, I would have awakened from those hardshell Baptist lies. Goethe talks about the Zeitgeist. Bostwick and I were saying how it always happens that two or three people discover the airplane and the steam engine at the same time, unbeknownst to each other. Zeitgeist means 'wind of the age.' Isn't that good?"

"Are you sorry you met me?"

He smiled cagily. For they had arrived at that moment in the dialogue which he always enjoyed, when he had to make a new paean of praise to her. She looked doubtful, as if she didn't trust him, even as if she were antagonistic to him. He tried to frame it in new words, in some way that would surprise her.

But just as he was about to answer he saw a car coming. It was full of middle-aged ladies from the Ephesus Inn. Instead of saying anything, he dropped his books down on the side of the highway, picked a spot, and stood on his head. As the car passed, he began to pedal his feet furiously in the air. The ladies turned around in bewilderment at this sight. The car wobbled drunkenly. It disappeared around a long curve.

"Zeb."

"What?"

"When you believed in God before you met me, did you know what the meaning of life was?"

He stood up. "Yes," he said.

"What?"

"To be good. And if you were good, you'd be happy."

She was silent.

"But I knew it was crap even then," he said. "Happiness is no fit end for man. People who think they are good are vegetables." His laughter bounced on the highway in the heat and then disappeared.

In the great space of sky and highway, Urie imagined embedded below their feet the shells, petrified sea urchins, snails and corals of all colors, relics of the Triassic sea, dead treasure of the past. Everything became unreal. The memory of Bostwick's body and the thought of Bostwick tomorrow faded away, and she and Zebul became the only beings upon the earth. She looked at Zebul. She was as analytical as Zebul had been with the drunk Negro when he had been born again. She was as analytical as Bostwick when he said, "You have a beautiful, fine girl's body." She became aware of every movement of Zebul's walking, the way his hands and feet jerked awkwardly as he walked. Someday he would die, like Maddox Stein. He would have no movements any more. His khaki pants, bleached from too many washings, would not turn their pockets out on his hips, showing the linings. His pants would never become dirty again. He would walk no longer. He would breathe no longer. He would stand on his head no longer. He would die, like Attis. He would be buried in a Southern grave, and the mound of dirt over his skeleton would be the only trace.

"Urie, I have an idea!"

She was startled. His face was white and foxy.

"What?"

"Go back of that tree there and watch me. Hide. Don't let anybody see you from this highway!"

She hesitated, but she was sucked into it. She ran to the side of the highway and jumped across the ditch. Grass and thorns scratched her knees. She clawed her way up by the edge of a blackberry patch into the broom grass. Her sneaker caught on a thorn and ripped.

Up on the bank, she hid behind the hickory tree. When she scooched down out of sight, a wild smell suffused her. The blood of the blackberry had stained her sneakers. The smell was suffocating. The highway shone in the sun.

Zebul looked forward. Then he looked backward toward Ephesus. He walked forward, looking at the cement. What was he doing? Picking a spot. He picked the right spot and lay down on it on his back. It was the direct center of the right-hand lane of traffic. Why was he doing it? She stood up out of hiding to shout "Do you want to get killed?" But instead of asking, she scooched down out of sight again. A strange thing had happened. His gesture was attaining prominence over all future and all past, and his power loomed. She was bound to ask nothing. He had chosen this act, whatever it was. He had embarked upon it. Its mystique controlled her, as if Zebul, by serving himself to danger on the platter of the highway, were entering her upon some offering to a nonexistent God too.

He looked like a rag doll.

In the distance she heard an automobile. She heard it before he did, because of her position high up on the bank. She almost laughed. She thought if the automobile really did squash him, then she would never have to tell him that she had betrayed him with Bostwick. Stifling her laughter, she began to tremble. She craned upward to look, pushing her hair against some white flowers. He had two or three minutes from the second to change his mind. She turned cold. His frame was inert, tempting the tires. Bloody possums and rags of dogs went through her mind. She remembered the tire that Loco Poco had picked in Sears Roebuck, with the cat's paw to be etched forever along America's highways.

If it really killed him, she would run. Later, after she hid for a while the police would catch her. They would tell her Zebulon V. Walley had been run over by a car. What was the reason for it? they would ask. It was not her fault, she would tell Bostwick. But the police would not believe her.

Above Zebul the sky lay steep and blue. He heard the car coming. He felt the scorched cement warm his shoulder blades. He was Icarus after falling. The car panted. The tires sucking cement made vibrations, still very faint, which were increasing in waves and crescendos. Seething, exhaling. Closer and closer. The tire would go over his head. Succulent tire creasing his brain. He could taste dusty rubber on his tongue.

Suddenly he felt small and helpless. The car turned the bend. Its motor pulse changed. It was too late now. He felt like a fly in the dead and careless silence, untouchable, buoyed as if in air. And he had nothing to do with his will, which had placed him there. He had to do with the endlessness of the sky, which he concentrated on, hard.

It was a small Chevrolet with carefully groomed gilt. It shone and flashed. Urie saw it, but Zebul could not see it. The mirror-like windows and headlights moved forward like blind rays. Something dropped from the car. Metallic, it clanked on cement. Zebul heard it. But the car did not know it. It kept coming. There was no change in its motor pulse.

"What if they don't see me?" he asked himself now that it was too late.

There was a scream of brakes. He felt the lurch of metal in air. He kept his eyes closed insistently. A great crisscrossing and signaling of air current. The car swerved to the left lane and shivered to a grinding halt only inches from his left hand.

The sound of the doors opening was like the popping of corks. Voices and footsteps surrounced him.

"My God!" said a man's voice.

"I almost didn't see him—"

A thick hand waved to and fro in front of his face. He could see a wedding band sparkling and pronging through his tight-shut eyes. The hairs of a nose hissed. He smelled camellias. A bunch of carnations wagged. He sensed varicose veins through a pair of stockings.

"We better call the police."

"But we didn't hit him!"

"Don't touch him."

"No, Alfred. He's a young boy!"

"Maybe he's drunk."

Decisively Zebul opened his eyes. He stood up.

There were two men and a woman.

"Why are you traveling out on the highway?" he asked them accusingly.

"Alfred!"

"What right have you—" began the man, panting with fear and shock.

"What right have *you* to be wasting gas during rationing?" Zebul interrupted.

At the expression of Zebul's face, the middle-aged man heaved his breath back. His neck jerked and he turned stentorian.

Zebul moved back and pointed his finger at them like a district attorney. "Was this trip necessary?" he shouted.

Then he ran. He flew down the ditch and up the banking of the highway. He grabbed Urie by the hand, pulled her running into the cornfield. They hid among the cornstalks, watching. The three people, overpowered by disbelief, wobbled in shock. Then, dispersing like hens, they entered the car from three separate doors. The doors closed. The motor ground, uncertain. The car started up, wove, and slowly, half disabled from shock, gained momentum down the highway.

Zebul and Urie watched till it disappeared down the Fall Line, and then they looked at each other and laughed maniacally.

CHAPTER 36

A week after this incident the manuscript of the "Memoirs of the Court of Catherine the Great" arrived, still neatly bound in its blue covers.

P.Q. told Urie and Zebul, "That's nothing. We can send it somewhere else."

But he did not move to do so. Instead he put it in the bookcase in a prominent place, right next to the first volume of his Grote's *Greece*.

The weather turned suddenly cold, and Urie was beset with her thoughts of Bostwick. How would Bostwick get in touch with her? He knew perfectly well that P.Q. did not like him; he would never come to her house. There was no telephone. He could not call her. These were her rationalizations.

But Bostwick never sought anybody out.

One day in the ten-cent store she bought a ten-cent spiral notebook. That night she put down three pages of questions she had to ask Bostwick, "Topics of Necessity." She had written:

1. How will relationship be pursued? Marriage.
2. How can we be threesome like before?
3. Hypocrisy. Zebul.
4. Will he screw [she crossed that out] make love to me?
5. Talk about sex. It is necessary to talk about sex because I want to be good to him. Will it hurt? If he loves me will I get orgasm? [She

had crossed out the word orgasm but failed to put anything in its place.] It is necessary to talk about this.

6. Does B. love me? Will he ever? Can he? Is this what makes me [The rest of this question was blank.]
7. How can I see him? Will he want to continue with me? What if he doesn't?
8. Will it be at nights?
9. Sex and marriage. I ought not to talk about marriage. Very premature. It is [This ended blank.]
10. [This was left blank.]

At the bottom of page 4 she had written: "Sounds exactly like the Hi-Y. I can't stand it! I am the apogee of a scheming woman in these pages!$ #%!&*$**!"

The next day she secreted this notebook in her skirt pocket and set out to find Bostwick. She went to the statue of the Confederate soldier and loitered as Zebul used to do. She hid herself behind a holly tree so she could decide what to do in case she saw him coming. She scorched the whole terrain with her gazes. She kept being afraid Zebul would appear.

Suddenly she saw Bostwick. She sauntered out from the holly bush, cutting casually across the lawn in the same direction. But the moment he saw her she stopped.

"I wanted to find you." She blushed.

"Come along, then."

"I was waiting behind that holly bush. I mean—I mean I was lying in wait."

"That's all right."

"It is?" She skipped into time with his footsteps, hanging on his smile. "Are you going home?" In a moment she was ashamed because it sounded illicit, demanding, asking for the unaskable.

"I have to stop to pick up my mail first."

"I have to talk to you, Bostwick."

"All right." She took reassurance from his eyes.

They walked in silence through the stone gate and across Main Street. It was the exact spot where Mrs. Ransome and Opard Bigelow Granger had watched the Bishop sales procession to the Laurelo Wildwood Gift Shop. She looked around furtively. Behind trees. In groups of people. In store doorways. She was afraid of the post office. Zebul liked the post office because of its echoes. But that was usually at night when it was empty. He could declaim in the post office like Demosthenes, or sing fake operatic arias, which sounded wonderful.

"What's the matter?"

"I'm afraid of seeing Zebul."

Bostwick's face, which had up to now been purposeful, betrayed a glimmer of fascination. He too began to look around as if Zebul might be standing by a post, by a building, or might suddenly walk around the corner. His manner was open, even eager, as if he would welcome the sight of Zebul, calculated to put any suspicion out of Zebul's mind. There was not one hint of any relationship between him and Urie. But there was no sign of Zebul. They stopped at a dry-cleaners to pick up Bostwick's Navy whites, which he was putting away for the winter. Then they walked past the Ephesus Inn, up Pergamus Avenue to McCauley Street. At his house they pushed through the porch door and climbed the stairs to his living room.

"All right, what is this about Zebul?" he asked.

Urie's questions fell dead to the ground. She did not want to talk about Zebul. She wanted to talk about themselves alone, herself and Bostwick. But she could not. How could she ask him if he loved her?

"I'm just afraid, that's all," she said, twisting her hands.

"But he has to find out sometime, doesn't he?"

"Oh, Bostwick!"

"And, after all, didn't you conceive of that when you came here?"

"All I want is not to have to act hypocritical." And after a moment, to his surprise: "I *want* him to find out!" She said this passionately. "But then I can't go around with him and you like before."

Bostwick took the Navy suit and went to the closet to hang it up. "Well, maybe you can."

"How can I and be in love with you? When it's not me and him making up mythologies of you, making you into something we own, some god, like—"

"Maybe you misjudge all your feelings toward Zebul, and his toward you, and it is not as you imagine at all, but, since he is a creator—"

"Bostwick, don't talk about him." she said with a soft plea. When he turned around she was standing directly in front of him.

"But it was you who said you had to talk to me about him," he whispered, stroking her breasts through her sweater.

"Not him! Not about him!"

"What, then?"

He is seducing me. He is seducing me. She could not speak at all. The important questions of his loving her, and the future, and what would happen to them, would he marry her, fled out of her mind. They seemed beyond the possibility of answering. She was embarked upon the sensations of her own body this time, instead of his. He locked the door. This time his lovemaking was softer and sweeter, slower. So that, with the welling up of her sexuality, she forgot time. It grew dark.

"What's the matter?"

"It's time for supper."

"You have to go home?"

"No. Don't get up, Bostwick."

"But perhaps you'd better—"

"No. I don't want to go home. I don't want to ever. I want to stay here with you forever and ever."

But she did not. She went home without finishing that lovemaking.

The next day what she feared happened, but in reverse. She stopped in their office to pick up her Latin notebook. Zebul was there. He decided to walk home with her, and they ran smack into Bostwick by the Sociology Building.

The air had turned very cold and was a distilled blue. The sun was shining brightly, but there were purple clouds low over the arboretum which presaged a sudden turn to winter. There was a high wind, and this snapped the red trappings of the trees. Crackly leaves swept through the air and swept in pools between their legs.

When she saw Bostwick, Urie hung back. There was an imploring gaze in her eyes as if he would blame her for being with Zebul.

"Bostwick! Where have you been! We looked everywhere for you!" Zebul leaped joyfully.

"Well, I've been right here all the time." Bostwick smiled. His air of modesty was in strange contrast to his enigmatic strength. Urie felt that she was entering some tremendous, straining, important episode in her life. The outside world, the act of seeing the sun and feeling the cold breeze whip her hair was unreal. The only reality was Bostwick. She was trapped in the enigma of him. His actions even took away her fear.

This glad smile was legato. Far from invalidating that "we" of Zebul's, which seemed to Urie now to be a "we" from 1500 B.C., painfully, embarrassingly extinct, it spurred Zebul beyond his own conceptions. Zebul had only to look into Bostwick's eyes and he was on fire from Bostwick's mysterious strength, like a struck tuning fork. He galloped with love for every stick, every pebble, every dark green grassblade shivering in the wind.

"Let's go up this path," said Bostwick. "Where are you going? Home?"

They went back of the Episcopal church and came to a stone wall.

There was a persimmon tree there whose fruit, already ripened, had dropped.

Zebul picked up a persimmon and threw it at Bostwick. "Hey, Bostwick, you're dead."

"You'll get his uniform dirty," warned Urie.

"No. Let's see who can get to the stone wall first," said Bostwick, accepting the challenge.

Bostwick made up the rules of the game. Each stood thirty yards from the wall, one on one side, the other on the opposite. They were to walk toward each other, the meeting-point being the wall, like the net of a tennis court. The weapons were three persimmons. Two of the persimmons would wound. The third, the ripest, would be the death weapon. They could throw them in any order and at any time they wanted.

"You be on my side." Bostwick waved to Urie.

"But that will give him double the chance of being killed."

"Don't worry!" yawped Zebul, glorious with challenge. "Go on. I want you to!"

"It's not fair." Urie hung back, aware of her hypocrisy.

They began without her.

Zebul watched Bostwick's trim figure, scarcely poised. Bostwick was looking at him. Zebul drew from this look divine momentum. Everything was bathed in pure glory, he thought, aware of everything, the sun hanging low just below the purple cloud, a sudden gust of yellow leaves, and Urie watching by the tree.

They walked toward each other, exactly in the manner of a duel.

Zebul feigned a shot at Bostwick. Bostwick neither ducked nor batted an eye. There was a smile on his mouth, and he had not yet raised an arm.

Halfway to the wall, Bostwick raised his arm to shoot.

Zebul fired, but his persimmon missed Bostwick by a yard.

Bostwick threw his with a faint flick. It hit Zebul in the left arm.

"You're wounded."

"Lucky it's the left arm, Bostwick. Haha."

Zebul raised his arm again to draw the second persimmon from Bostwick. It failed. They walked nearer. I could kill him now, this minute, thought Zebul. But, staring into Bostwick's eyes, he had a new feeling, as if those eyes in which he swam so intimately were strangers to him. The force of his desire to win became tremendous. Yet he refrained from using the death persimmon.

Without even aiming, he threw his second persimmon. It just grazed Bostwick's ear.

"You missed," Bostwick said in a low voice.

The persimmon smell had become wild and overweening. Like blood, thought Zebul. He feigned a third throw. Bostwick shot and missed. Zebul smiled maliciously.

They walked closer. Now they were within fifteen paces of each other. Hunting. Barely breathing. Like animals.

"You've only got your death blow left," whispered Bostwick, teasing.

"So have you."

At that there was a strange look on Bostwick's face. Then his expression changed. His eyes said: Let's not play this any more. He smiled and walked so disarmingly to the stone wall that Zebul understood that if he shot, he would betray him.

Bostwick extended his arm over the wall, like a tennis champion. Zebul put his hand out. Instead of shaking hands Zebul felt the death persimmon inserted into his open palm.

"You're dead," said Bostwick.

"Bostwick, you cheated!" he breathed in astonishment.

As they walked in silence back up by the Sociology Building and across the campus to the Ephesus Inn, Bostwick said nothing. Zebul's eyes popped and his face had the bloated look of a blowfish. They reached the corner of Pergamus Avenue where Bostwick would leave. Zebul still could not bring himself to speak. Smiling, Bostwick said good-by.

A cold, unnerving fear clamped Urie's heart. What was the meaning of Bostwick's gesture? Was it a lesson to Zebul? Was it a sign to her? Of what? Suspicions scuttled in her brain. She sensed contempt. She ran from the thought. Bostwick's cruelty was creepy. But just the same, she had only one desire: to go with him. She did not want to be abandoned. She did not want to be alone with Zebul. All the life she desired was disappearing with Bostwick.

"Why did he cheat?" whispered Zebul, staring at Bostwick's retreating figure. "You saw him!"

"If you wanted to know, why didn't you ask him?"

The sight of his turmoil mocked her own.

Before they got to Urie's house it started to snow. The purple clouds had turned black. The sky had become gray. The snowflakes were large and wet, but they swirled madly in the wind.

Instead of going home, Zebul came in. P.Q. greeted him with open arms. "Aha! Alcibiades himself. What have you been doing?"

"We just walked home with Bostwick." Something made Zebul say this, although ever since P.Q. had trimmed him at the Sybilline ceremony everyone had carefully avoided mentioning the word "Bostwick" to him. P.Q. turned away from Zebul. He pretended to look for something in his favorite storage place behind the clock. He whistled. Then he went to wash his hands at the kitchen sink.

The pointedness of this reaction pleased Zebul. He was like a person with a bad toothache who has just cut his finger on a rusty nail. He laughed until his face got red.

Urie shot him a look of hatred.

Loco, who had been drawing Cleopatra's Needle on P.Q.'s steel desk in the waning winter light, noticed and loomed up out of the darkness like a glowing Eyptian cat.

"Who were you with?" she asked.

"Look, it's beginning to snow!" exclaimed Mrs. Bishop artlessly.

P.Q. opened the door and stood framed in the doorway, looking at the black sky.

"Close that door. The wind is sweeping through this kitchen!"

P.Q. waited for two minutes to elapse. Then he closed it. "It won't last long," he announced like a prophet.

Zebul stayed for supper. It was deliberate. The very time Urie could not bear his presence, he thrust his dependence and hostility upon her. In him Bostwick's smile vibrated, Bostwick's triumph redounded, Bostwick's cruelty, Bostwick's essence, exacerbating the question of her own guilt.

"I'm going out to go get wood and build a fire that will *heat* this place!"

"I'll help you," said Zebul.

"You don't need to."

"I want to!"

"Put on your parka!" warned Mrs. Bishop. "And you, Zebul, don't you have anything warmer than that jacket?"

Neither one spoke. Urie grabbed the ax out from under the water-heater. She did not put on her parka.

The ground was already covered with a thick carpet of white. It went over the tops of her shoes.

"It's a regular blizzard!" huffed Zebul.

She ignored him. She struggled through snow-clung broom grass. At the barn she picked her place to strike. With her first blow she used such ter-rorizing force that Zebul said, "I don't see why you need to be so mad! He

[317

didn't cheat you!" Then, as the ax whipped before his eyes: "Watch out!" The board screeched and shattered. "Let me do it!"

She refused to give him the ax. He waited, shivering, snowflakes beating down his shirt collar, until there was a gaping hole. Then he bent down and wrenched the board free. It took all his force. She started on another board.

"Why do you suppose he did it, Urie? There must be some reason!"

"I told you not to trust him. I told you not to make such a big Mohammedan thing out of him!" Her unintentional guile struck her as funny. She laughed, imitating the screeching sound of the tearing lumber.

"Jesus Christ, Urie. If you take one more board out, this barn will fall."

"Is this the church's one foundation?" she asked with rhythmic scorn.

When they were done they piled themselves high with wood. Hot and flushed from the exertion, they pushed their way back through the iced grass and entered the kitchen, dripping and wild. Loco started the fire, and they nursed it until it roared. After they ate supper, Irene went outdoors to test the snow.

"It's up to my ankles!"

"It looks just like Christmas," said Mrs. Bishop, looking out of the window. "Like those 'O Little Town of Bethlehem' Christmas cards. How beautiful!"

All the disparate elements, Zebul against Urie, P.Q.'s dichotomy with Bostwick, Urie's hiding against P.Q. and against Zebul, Loco's creeping suspicion of Urie and Zebul, became localized in an energy beyond any of the separate manifestations. The elements were negative, but the force of the snowstorm was positive. The core of the universe changed. The room grew warm. Everything became intensely still except for the popping and breathing of the fire. The flames were gaudy, and the heat radiated so intensely that they had to move back. Later the wind died down. The flakes fell faster and more silently than before. There was an air, relentless and steady now, as if the snow had set in for good.

"P.Q., you were wrong," cooed Loco, dusting his chin with a kiss and then sticking her face next to the rag-filled windowpane. "It's going to snow and snow and snow and snow."

"I hope it never stops," echoed Irene.

Urie did too. It was as if another presence had come among them, which lurked like a ghost outside and transmuted the depths of her anxiety about Bostwick to a level out of reach of her ability to grasp it.

"Feel how warm it is in here!" breathed Mrs. Bishop holding out her arms to feel.

"It's the same principle as the igloo," said P.Q. "If you cover all the cracks with snow there is no draft, and right in the very center of ice you can create a completely warm place."

"Remember, Urie, that year you said you were never going to spend one more Christmas vacation in this house?"

Urie signaled Loco with her eyes to shut up. To be free of the cold of poverty, free, free, free, without having to break down barns! Maybe she *should* sneak into a dormitory. But some sensitive streak in her forebade her to make this connection. Freedom of nights in a dormitory meant freedom of nights with Bostwick. She could explore him to the kernel and know him and never have to come home and explain. Deep in her consciousness this spark ignited her vision of Bostwick as he used to be.

I will talk to P.Q. about Aristotle, thought Zebul in the silence. P.Q. could excise Bostwick's insult from his consciousness. P.Q. puked on sentiment. He ignored greasy personal problems. P.Q. was as impersonal and brutal as a bleached bone. He did not give a damn for anything. So Zebul leaned forward to speak.

At that moment there was a crash that shook the whole house. The floor buckled, then cracked. The steel desk quivered. In the next room the piano pinged la-do, mi-ti. The picture of Amalfi jerked on the wall. Mrs. Bishop's thimble fell off the sewing machine and rattled across the floor into a crack.

No one moved. All sat quiet, like animals, their motion frozen. An entire minute of heartbeats passed.

"What was that?" Mrs. Bishop asked in a feeble voice. It was as if she were daring a second explosion.

They waited. Then they began to move. But their knees were weak from fear and they felt light and unsteady. They tried footsteps. They looked in the living room. They peered through doors. No one could find anything.

Loco looked out the window. "Oh, there's no porch any more," she said in a strange voice.

"What do you mean?"

They rushed to the window. The porch had ripped away from the house and lay like a drunk in a horizontal farce of itself, imprinted on the snow.

Immediately they put on all the lights in the house and ran outside to look. There was a pale patch where the old roof had been hitched onto the house. Scrabbled husks of foul wood had spat on the snow in jags. Nails were wrenched awry. Broken timber beams and two supporting posts lay in tipsy symmetry. The floorboards were completely caved in. The roof had fallen in a complete mass and not a shingle was out of place—only three rotten scraps, shot up during the impact, peeping like insolent Toms out of the snow.

"The snow on the roof," cried Zebul, "it was so heavy it just caved the whole thing in."

"Oh, Mama, now we won't have to burn the barn!" said Loco.

CHAPTER 37

The house was literally falling down around their heads, piece by piece, and Urie could not concentrate on it. The next morning she knew only that she would have to wait until five that afternoon for Bostwick to get home. The day dragged endlessly.

Though her excision of Zebul was as neat as the division between porch and house, she could feel the pale yellow imprint of his existence on her mind.

In his little house Zebul woke up knowing Urie was right. If he wanted to know what the insult meant, he must ask Bostwick. The sun was high and the snow on the beehives made them look like a colony of gnomes. He put on his hobnailed boots. He didn't have rubbers or overshoes. The snow would probably melt by evening, when Bostwick got home. Already the world was dripping. By noon he could not even see his breath on the air. There were great gaps in the snow and dripping, iron-red mouths of earth were revealed. He waited until the precise moment of five. Then he started walking toward Bostwick's house.

"Bostwick," he practiced, "you deliberately cheated me. I don't know what you mean by it."

In his mind he could not make any reply for Bostwick.

"What do you mean by it?" he asked, to prompt himself.

Walking along, he went even further with the conversation. Bostwick said this. Zebul answered that. Before he even realized it, he was turning the corner from Pungo into McCauley Street.

Urie reached Bostwick's house a few moments after five, the same moment that Zebul was walking the railroad tracks. She knocked lightly and Bostwick said, "Come in."

He was lying on his bed again, fully clothed, as he had been the night she had declared her love. At this vision of him, all her curiosity was suddenly quelled. She felt tender toward him. She walked to him, stood by the side of the bed, and, feeling that she was taking a great liberty, put her hand on his hair, caressing it. She felt very strange doing this. She remembered the dream she had had of him. She was making that dream of him come true.

"You're good," she said. "I love you."

"I'm not good."

"Yes, you are."

"Why? Because I cheated Zebul?" He pushed himself up on the pillow and looked straight into her eyes, ignoring her caresses.

It was as if he knew everything within her. Her love was suddenly fake because she did not know him. She was a hypocrite to Zebul. She was acting maternal to make him, Bostwick, weak. She was guilty, so she had to have him be good. His gaze was both merciless and sarcastic. She stopped caressing his hair. Her lumpen, heavy hand she hid behind her back.

"Why did you do that to Zebul?" she whispered.

"Oh, I don't know. It just came to me to do it."

"Did you want to teach him a lesson?"

"What lesson?"

"Maybe to be foxy and know how to protect himself because you want him to be strong."

"You'd interpret anything I did, whether good or bad, to be good, wouldn't you?"

"I *know* you're good!"

"How do you know that? You don't interpret everybody like you're interpreting me, do you?"

"You *are* good, Bostwick. I don't care!"

Bostwick's eyes glittered impatiently. "Was Zebul angry?" He wanted to get her off the subject of his goodness.

"Yes. No. He didn't understand it."

A slight smile came into Bostwick's eyes, though his lips remained unsmiling.

"Did you do it because of me?" she asked.

"Because of you? Why?"

"Like an insult because—because of what I—I—"

"No. No. It had nothing to do with you." He smiled coldly, even wearily. "I should not have done it."

"But why did you?" It was a great effort to go against Bostwick's despair.

"I am too old to explain myself."

She wanted to pour herself upon him, as before, for his despair was keeping her apart from him. She felt like weeping. She knelt down so her eyes would be on the same level as his.

"Are you bored with me because I am too young?"

Again he looked through her. The same merciless gaze, but this time without sarcasm. "Not because of youth. I am bored because you are alone," he said.

Disbelief made her face pale. She understood that it was not even personal and that Bostwick was the only adult who acted against human sensitivity, as she and Zebul did. Yet at the very moment that he allowed those words "I am bored with you" to enter into her consciousness on the altar of some impersonal truth, he put out his arms to her and held her shoulders. He held her as if she were a statue, but as if to understand himself more. He spoke in musing tones as if he were making discoveries. Though he looked at her face, he acted as if he were seeing the far country, inhabited.

"You are beginning to learn the limits," he said. "But you don't even admit them yet."

I am not alone if I have you! she wanted to shout at him.

"You don't admit what you see and what you know. You refuse to cross the borderline out of youth."

You are alone, she wanted to shout. Not me.

The touch of his hands affected her. He was preventing her from coming close to him with this very touch, and she could feel herself beginning to believe every word.

"You are becoming pure," he said. "You are learning the earth. Because of me. You're learning what you can do and what you can't do."

"Is that bad?"

"Don't use those words, 'good' and 'bad.' "

"I won't, Bostwick. Let me— Don't keep me away from you!"

"Remember what I told you and Zebul about the impurity of the young?"

"Don't you see I love you? What shall I do? What do you want, Bostwick? I'll be anything you want me to be."

"Oh!" he sighed. And then he gave up. His act of giving up was to pull her to him wearily against his chest. He leaned back against the pillow as if the gesture were the seal of his despair.

She clung to him. She allowed herself to be held, hiding her face so she would not have to look at his. But she had lost all her own thoughts and was putting into actual words what he would not say: why aren't you *More?* Why aren't you *All?*

Why was it this way, when he was all to her?

Bostwick's place looked unfamiliar in the snow. Realizing he was there, Zebul suddenly rushed in the front door and ran up the stairway two steps at a time. At Bostwick's door he knocked wildly.

No one came.

He was forced to stop and consider. Everything was very quiet, except for his panting. He tried the door. It was locked.

"Bostwick!" he called.

This was the second time in his life he had come and Bostwick had been gone. He listened. He imagined, because of the sound of his own heavy breathing, that he heard something inside. In his mind's eye he could see Bostwick's apartment. All the furniture, the messy table, the crumbs, the blue mug were lonely.

He decided to leave. He clomped down the stairs. He made this loud noise to comfort himself. He saw that he was leaving his wet tracks on the stairway, and these gave him a kind of vengeful satisfaction. He felt himself turning angry. Not only had Bostwick insulted him. Bostwick had also been absent.

Outside, he stood on the curb idly. Perhaps Bostwick might come home while he stood there. It was while he was standing there that the feeling came over him again, that someone was really in Bostwick's apartment. He turned and went around to the back of the house. He stood by the tree that he had painted. The white paint was as good as ever. Not a fleck had peeled. He looked up at Bostwick's windows.

At the moment when the sound of Zebul's footsteps penetrated the upstairs, Bostwick's arms stiffened around Urie. The knock was loud. As she became afraid, he kissed her. His kissing, his stroking were passionate throughout the knocking. But when Zebul was simply waiting on the steps they increased, almost in time to the sound of Zebul's panting at the doorway. Even through her fright she was amazed. Her eyes rolled, trying to find Bostwick's eyes, but he was too close. When Zebul's call, "Bostwick!" demanded that they do something, a moan rose up from her chest and was stifled by Bostwick's kiss. She gave herself up to Bostwick then, everything in her rising to his touches. She thought of Zebul still standing there in the doorstep of the hall, and she did not care. So that when he left it was anticlimactic. Even though she was aware that he was stamping loudly, and that the sound was growing more distant and hollow as he neared the bottom of the steps. What was important was that the dimension of touch had been created from the surfeit and fear of sound.

Bostwick's ardency subsided after Zebul was gone. He caressed her gently, lovingly. It was as if, in the residue of Zebul's presence, with the stiffening and guilt it had produced in her, he was made freer to pursue sex. He began to rouse her. She felt warm, ecstatic, and lazy. The light changed in the room as the sun went down.

"Bostwick, it's better when it gets dark, isn't it?"

"Yes, it's getting dark."

"Do you think he'll come back?" she whispered. But she was not afraid.

"If he is persistent, he will."

"I love this, Bostwick."

"You do, do you?"

"Oh, I love you so much, I could die."

"Mmmmm."

A few minutes later: "Bostwick, I know you'll never come to my house any more, because you don't like P.Q., but—"

"I like P.Q. exceedingly."

"Then why don't you come to visit me at my house?"

"Because it is another universe. You come to me."

"Will you let me come at night? It's better."

"All right. Come at night."

She seized this scrap of invitation. Maybe he loves me a bit, she thought. His hands were idly caressing the length of her, and she arched, lazily anticipating, indulging herself, yet at the same time storing into herself the silence, the cast of the shadows, the oncoming darkness, the atmosphere of this frame of sensuality, as if to make it eternal. Suddenly she became aware that there was something outside this moment and this frame.

The sun had gone down beyond the bare trees past the horizon of Niggertown, which, the world being stripped in winter, was visible to Zebul from Bostwick's garden. Suddenly he thought of going up and looking through the window.

There was an outside stairway to the apartment adjoining Bostwick's on the north side of the house. Although this was some distance from Bostwick's windows, Zebul decided to try it. The snow had drifted upon these outside steps and had not melted. His boots made clear footprints in it. There might be people in that apartment. He had to be careful. This time he trod softly. He was careful to duck underneath the sills of the adjoining apartment. The last coals of the sun struck Bostwick's windowpanes, reflecting an opaque and lonely orange hue.

He reached the top, which was a balcony of six feet in length. Bostwick's nearest window looked into the living room. But it was four feet out from the railing of the balcony. Zebul straddled this railing. He set one foot upon an outside molding and leaned over to grab the lintel of Bostwick's window. Leaning in this way, he was able to look in.

It was so familiar, yet unfamiliar from this angle. The living room was deserted. The blue mug was not on the table. Why was it not? He was disappointed. It was so lonely, the view, that he grew scared, looking in. He became afraid that the molding would not hold. His entire weight was balanced on it. Also, it was very slippery. The heel of his boot was rubber. He was just about to shift his weight and push himself back upon the upstairs balcony when he heard a sound.

His fingers tightened on the window hasps. The sound was like a sigh. It was not Bostwick. It was softer. Then there came the sound of a voice. A woman's voice! But it was a vague whisper, for the door to the bedroom was closed. Bostwick had a woman in there! Zebul listened carefully for the actual sound of Bostwick's voice, but instead there came sounds of rustling, of movement, and an inaudible murmur. Was it lovemaking?

Zebul became aware of an outcome of some anguish like paralysis. His fingers were freezing. If he slipped, he would fall thirty feet to the ground. Also he suddenly became aware that he was perfectly visible for miles around. The last flares of the sunset were spotlighting his figure, blinding his eyes. He had a sudden vision of himself as the Compleat Prowler, burning in the air, as brilliant as the Angel Gabriel.

He hauled himself back to the porch and shivered. He tried to make his way down as fast as he could. But on the third step down he skidded. He fell down four steps before he caught himself, and the echo of his fall upon the wood resounded in his ears. He banged down the rest of the stairs to the bottom. He tried to collect himself. His face was burning. In contrast to this, his bare hands were freezing. He blew on his fingers and then held them against his neck, trying to get them warm. He stared back up at Bostwick's window, his eyes enlarging in the flares of light. He ran around to the front of the house again, afraid that Bostwick might have heard and come to the window to look. At the front, standing on the curb to the street, he stared at the doorway.

I'm going to wait and see who it is, he thought. I'm going to wait till kingdom come. I don't care. I'll find out.

He took a position across the street, behind a magnolia tree, and began waiting.

"Bostwick! It's Zebul!"

"Shshsh!"

"But if he climbs—"

"He can't see anything. Be quiet. Do you want him to hear?"

Bostwick grew more passionate again. And in the knowledge of the listening eyes and seeing ears, that transposition of all senses which can see nothing, hear nothing, yet know everything, he brought her sensuality to the tip of her body, dispersing the filaments of feeling from the center, and took her. He glittered, smiling and rushing to the climax. They were locked in each other's arms when they heard Zebul fall down the four steps of the fire escape. They listened. They heard the footsteps disappear into scuttling silence. And they heard no more.

C H A P T E R 38

Zebul waited for twenty minutes. But nothing happened. No one came out.

He grew cold. The loneliness and silence enticed him. The world grew dark. He turned into a creature of oncoming night. He was on the outside of everything, he felt. He grew in tune with time. He took on the characteristics of night and all nature. He grew to fear that if he were to see anybody come out of Bostwick's, he too would be discovered and lose some power in his loneliness.

So, chattering from the cold, realizing that his feet were wet inside the boots, he left.

But he did not want to go home. He did not want to go to Urie's, either. For he was discovering something in the breadth of his loneness, and he wanted to know what it was. So he went to the office.

How warm it was in the office! How dark! He was in the darkness, in the clutch of time, reveling in it. Should he put on the light? No. He did not want to put on the light. He was a Prowler. He was an infidel. He was an Outsider, reveling in outsiderdom.

He sat down in a chair. He leaned down and took off his boots in the darkness. His socks were soaking wet. He put them on the radiator. He put the boots on the radiator. And then he devoted himself to the truth of outsiderdom. He sat in the darkness and thought.

What, after all, did he or Urie know about Bostwick? They had made him up. Out of each of his characteristics they had fashioned something to suit themselves. They adulated him because adulation was in them. They had never dared ask him the truth. Was he married or not? Was he divorced? Why had he been so interested in sixteen-year-olds? No other adults had ever been so interested in sixteen-year-olds before. Why was he so mysterious? Did he have something to hide? Why had he insulted Zebul? Was all this withholding of himself for a reason? Was he a success? Or was he a failure in civilian life? Why did he never give these details of himself? Why did he always allow Zebul and Urie to *act* before him? What did he *get* from them? Zebul grew almost inspired by getting down to brass tacks. It took him into the apogee of his outsiderdom.

It was ten o'clock when he put his socks and boots back on. His socks were still damp, and his boots were wet and warm. He left the office by the window. He closed it behind him. Then he headed up Pergamus Avenue.

He was going home. But he went by Urie's instead. It was not that he had the *intention* of telling her what he had discovered, but that he could not refrain from communicating with her. The nature of his communication was larger than the news about Bostwick. It had to do with prowlerdom. Prowlerdom was greater than stealing, for the quarry was unknown, and the truth, therefore, possibly greater.

But the lights were all out at the Bishop house. It was so late they had all gone to bed. He prowled under the trees. He circled through the soggy grass. He went out by the barn. He stood there, looking at the dark house. Then he tiptoed back. He went to the window of Urie's room.

"Urie," he whispered.

He was the only one alive in the dripping night. The trees smacked. The windowpane gleamed palely in the remaining snow. The blood beat in his arms, his neck, all the way down to his wet feet. He was churning. Confronted with this giant body of the night with all its dark ignorance, the drops smacking on the tin roof, the soggy grass, the tongues of wet licking the treetrunks, he felt one with it.

Pressing his face against the pane, he saw Urie fast asleep. One arm was curved outside her quilt.

"Urie," he whispered again.

She turned over onto her stomach. Her face was hidden from him in the pillow. All he could see was the back of her head. The hair parted behind her head. The two neck tendons formed a tuning fork at the base of her skull, lit up by the reflection of snow, casting the concave between them in shadow. It was very mysterious. He was looking at a place that she could never see herself. Anyone else could see it. Another person could see it. The tree could see it. But Urie would never be able to see it. How vulnerable! Strike a person at that secret concave, and he would die in an instant.

No. I must not awaken her, he thought, blossoming into the huge responsibility this gave him.

He actually expanded. Now I am part of the night. And, feeling that he might never communicate with another soul as long as he lived, he took one last look at the secret concave at the base of Urie's skull, and went home.

The next night, instead of telling Urie of his discovery, he went to Bostwick's again. It was already dark, yet the lights were not on. He stationed himself under the magnolia tree on the opposite side of the street and waited. After fifteen minutes the lights came on. He became excited. A few minutes later Urie appeared on the porch.

Staring at her from the magnolia tree, he knew. But he did not believe it.

"Urie, what are you doing?" he said, running to the middle of the street, his hands stuck out like matchsticks.

"What do you think?"

"You and Bostwick—"

"Yes," she whispered. "We were fucking."

He stared stupidly at the house behind her. His mouth was open.

She ran away from him toward Pergamus Avenue.

He noticed Bostwick standing in the hallway. He must have come down the stairway with Urie to see her off. But it was so dark in the hallway that Zebul could not see his eyes. He blanched under Bostwick's imagined gaze, as if it were he who was guilty. Then he ran away as fast as he could, in the opposite direction from Urie.

After moments of running, he stopped in the middle of the street by some fraternity houses. Tears were rolling down his cheeks. A fraternity boy came out from the Doric columns of the Deke House. His soft maroon sweater, out of which his white shirt collar, softly starched, stood up to frame his neck, glowed in the lamplight. He stared at Zebul strangely.

Zebul's brown curls had unrolled and hung in strings down his forehead. He tried to control his sobs. He held his mouth rigid. His fists were curled up tight, apelike. When he saw the fraternity boy looking at him, he hid them under his armpits. His knees were slightly flexed, and his eyes were wild and staring. He imagined himself as he must look and flashed a look of hatred at the fraternity boy. Then he rushed off, his fists still in his armpits, down an alley, under the water tower, by a dirt road to the railroad tracks.

He turned off the railroad tracks by the honeysuckle bush, into the woods below the mill. He sat down on a stone. He began to cry openly. He sobbed for a half an hour and then he stopped. He sat quietly. His body, through with racking, was tired. But his mind was as hard as the stone.

He could not think of Urie or her betrayal. So he separated her entirely from him and tried to think in philosophical language because, he told himself, he was in the grip of an emotion. An untoward emotion.

Nigger spit *is*. That's the truth. But the laugh of a nut on a tin roof is truth too, and that's beautiful. Beauty is truth too, like the old cliché says. But I am not in beauty. I am in nigger spit. Even the fraternity boy looked at me and knew I was in ugliness and nigger spit. Would I be in beauty if I were the fraternity boy? No. For who would I be then? As for him, he sees nothing. He's not in beauty, even though he has a beautiful soft collar. What is all this, then?

He got up. He began walking around the stone as if he were learning the earth.

It's simply the emotion of truth.

He looked and saw a tree.

All life is a tree, he thought. And somewhere at the bottom there is a branch, out of which has grown a twig. And that twig is the emotion of truth. It is nothing. Only a twig.

He tried to turn this discovery around to find something to palliate the smallness of his place in the universe. But he couldn't find anything.

I am only I, he thought. Berkeley questioned whether this stone existed if nobody knew it existed. Now here I am with one foot on it. Nobody knows I am here. Nobody cares whether I cry or not on this stone, because there's nothing but me here. Who cares about my piddling emotion of truth?

He remembered when he and Urie had written about the kiss, trying to make the form of themselves. It was not then that he should have tried to make the form. It was now, when he was alone. But, overburdened by the form that he had already made, he did not have the gumption.

C H A P T E R   39

For four days they avoided each other.

The state of Urie's mind was wide and startled, as if she could not believe what she had done. She replayed the scene in which she had delivered the blow between his eyes until the word, like Loco's tone on the flute, lost all meaning. Because of that, it had to be repeated again. The calling of a spade a spade would seem, like a holocaust, to rip appearances and prepare for the new. But that was operating in a realm too simple.

If Zebul reeled, it was only to dislodge as an image in her mind and spread himself more pervasively than ever into categories where she neither could place him nor had ever imagined him. Even if he were to abjure her forever, even if she were never to see him again, even if he took the cyanide in his bottle and committed suicide to conform to Attis, she would never be able to get rid of him. He had crystallized in her the pattern they shared of trying to understand the truth by naming it.

But she was scared. She wanted to go to Bostwick but did not dare. She could not involve him in scenes of her relationship with Zebul. She had to keep the integrity of her ruthlessness. She could not compound the betrayal. So she remained in a paralyzed state, thrashing about, trying to keep from drowning in her cruelty.

If Zebul had not insisted on writing down their first kiss, she would not have had to insist on naming what she did with Bostwick. It was not his fault that he was not what Bostwick was, but was it her fault that she had wanted him to be? So went her rationalizations. Why had he acceded to all his inferior roles? The trashy. The criminal. The worshiper. He had made her his ally, his friend-criminal, to capture the high by plumbing the depths. But they had not captured the high. That was what had caused their split.

Now she wanted him to come to her to discuss the split. To have an intellectual discussion on betrayal. She wanted him to talk about it just as they had talked about poverty, ugliness, and shame. But the day of the sawdust pile was gone. It was ludicrous.

Could he ask for this rejection by her and laugh?

Could she share that thing more personal than the ocean that she had sought in Bostwick instead of him?

"Get up, dog. Be larger than I am, because I am only human. You've got to be larger for my right to be less! Don't dare be only human. Inhabit the place where, when humanity did not tempt us, we used to live. Now you must live large alone because sometimes I must be human."

At last she had an intimation of Bostwick's definition of purity. With Zebul she had inhabited the cruel world of limitless possibility. Ice, fire, ruthlessness, and laughter. Nothing could be lost because everything was possible. But the elements had force too strong for human flesh and feeling.

What could she say to the human in Zebul she had hurt? She had nothing to say, nothing to offer. So she hid like the yellow Haw dog she had met on her first walk with Zebul. But this guilt was only a disguise. The enormity of her betrayal was only surpassed by the calm, sad steepness of knowing what she had done. She felt no sympathy. She felt only pity, and that emotion belonged to God, if one had existed, not to humans. For the pity was for herself as much as for Zebul.

After three more days she could no longer bear these ludicrous extremes. She went to Bostwick for palliation.

He sat upright in his chair and did not comfort her. His face was pale and calm. He nodded when she told him what she had said and how she had not seen Zebul since.

"What do you think?"

The expression on his face told her that it had all come about just as he had imagined it and that it was their responsibility, that was how the world was. But he would not share with her. It confirmed all his passivity.

She clutched at him. He only patted her gently and held her. He was distant. He had no message for this dilemma. He did not make love to her.

They drank coffee out of the blue mugs and talked about random things until she had to go home.

CHAPTER 40

Zebul decided to steal a microscope. "Actions speak louder than words," P.Q. always said.

That night he went to the Chemistry Building. It was eight o'clock. He entered by the basement doors, went straight to the room where they were locked up, and put on the lights. Large black-topped tables arrayed with Bunsen burners glowed emptily. He found an icepick on a window sill, and, in full view of anyone on campus looking through the windows, began picking the lock in the cabinet. He held the icepick lightly and made tiny scratching noises. Urie as dirt-doer, he thought, would have to offer him an apology so tremendous that she would be incapable of it. What apology could he accept in the realm they inhabited? Apology would confirm him as victim. No. It required a deed so grandiose that apologies, victims, vulnerabilities, even betrayal would curl and disappear like burnt paper.

For the first time in four days he allowed himself to think of Bostwick. Urie had been as weak with Bostwick as she had been with him at the lumber pile, begging him to be her boy friend. If sex was more to her than transcendent form, then she was inferior crap. He had the strength of Saint Paul in his thoughts.

He now understood Bostwick's death persimmon. What coolness to enact a betrayal before the fact, to titillate both his guilt and his sadism! A belated admiration for Bostwick lighted the filaments of his hatred. For his hatred was cold. It had the same ancient quality that had endowed his worship of Urie. If he were impotent—the thought occurred to him that he was impotent with women and was compensating for it by becoming criminal—then his impotence was a mere footnote to his ancientness.

On an upstairs floor he heard footsteps. But he was not afraid. He felt nerveless. Locating the small talons inside the lock, he twisted. He admired himself for feeling nothing, remembering his first meeting with Bostwick in the armory. What idealism he had felt then!

The lock gave. The microscope was there. But it was a very old and large one, and he felt disappointed. But he could not afford to be choosy now, so he pulled it out. It was very heavy. He let it bang on the floor. At that moment he heard the footsteps running down the stairs and the corridor light switch flicked on.

Like a cat he lunged to the light and doused it. He stationed himself behind the swinging door, raising the icepick in his hand. He knew that if anyone entered he would stab.

But the footsteps passed the door and went down the hall. Then there was a silence. A key ground in a lock and a door opened. Zebul waited with perfect control in the darkness. He began to wish that the person would return. Five minutes passed. Then there was a strange scraping noise and the door slammed. The footsteps returned and passed again. Click. The corridor lights went out and the echoing footsteps died.

Zebul did not turn on the lights of the laboratory again. There was enough light from the campus to see. He fastened the locker door and wiped it in case of fingerprints. Holding the icepick through his sleeve, he also wiped it on his corduroy pants before he returned it to the window sill.

The microscope was so heavy he could hardly carry it. He thought of leaving by the window, but that was too melodramatic. He went along the dark corridor and out the door. A feeling of elation filled him. He carried it first with one arm, and then shifted it to the other side.

I can't carry it all the way alone, he thought. It's too heavy. So this was the time to get Urie. She too would be incriminated, as she had been from the first moment he had told her about the nigger hand. He looked for a hiding place for the microscope. He chose a large thick bush with evergreen leaves and prickle thorns. He checked to see that no one was watching. He planted it in the thickest part of the foliage. He tore his knuckles.

Cold and pale, he headed toward the Bishops'. He licked the blood from the backs of his hands. He ran part of the way, his elation sparking his will. As soon as he got to the driveway, the dogs smelled him. He heard knocking sounds as of bones upon crockery.

Loco Poco, feeding them, raised pale lunar curls, cajoling them, and when she noticed him, she waved her hands like wands at him.

"Where's Urie?" he asked.

"I don't know. She's not here, that's all."

"Is P.Q. home?"

"The dogs eat. The Greeks have provided. Amen."

This language meant that P.Q. was home, for he had brought his usual bone ration for the dogs from the Greek cafés. Loco's secret tinkling laughter pleased Zebul. Her unreality was almost impersonal, so that he was drawn in and dematerialized. But he did not have to confide in her. He did not have to talk. Inside the window he saw the damask tapestries hanging in the dining room.

"What's the matter with you?" Loco asked in her spectral voice.

"Nothing."

He went in to wait, to argue with P.Q. But Loco was wrong. P.Q. was not there. Mrs. Bishop said that he had left after supper was over and gone to the library. Zebul picked up the whisk broom distractedly and twirled it three times. He went to the kitchen, took a little wad of bread out of the Bond wrapper, rolled it into a ball, and ate it. Then he went outside again.

The dogs had finished eating. In the distance by the barn Loco Poco was giving them orders: "Arise. Sit. Sit. Arise." The dogs obeyed these commands slavishly. When she told them to sit, they sat, foaming and heaving.

The white heat of Zebul's will was abating. He crept up on her and watched, remembering the time she and Urie had danced on the linens and he had discovered the Cult of Ugliness.

Scylla, bored, went to the hollow tree and defecated, looking at Loco with a sublime expression. As soon as he had finished she picked up a stick and went to poke his excrement, delighted. Then, inspired, she suddenly lifted up her skirt to her middle and squatted down in the same place. Her underpants formed a silvery triangle at her ankles, and her head looked like a mushroom in the moonlight. She began singing while she added her excrement to Scylla's pile. When she arose she shivered. Then she pulled up her pants and started to hop. With the stick in hand she did an Indian dance around the pile of excrement.

>"Ohoho,
>   Tell it. Smell it.
>   Speak upon it.
>   Think of secret thoughts upon it.
>   Go around the Knuckle Tree,
>   Round and round,
>   Three by three.
>   Tell it. Smell it.
>   Cockleshell it.
>   Ohoho
>   Poo poo po."

Zebul could not believe his eyes. He began to choke with laughter and ran up to her with his eyes bulging out.

She stopped her dance, half scared. "Don't tell!" she whispered.

"I will so."

"Promise you won't tell."

"No."

"All right, then, tell."

She threw away her stick. She walked over to the spot where he was hawking and jerking in hysterical laughter and pushed her face toward him in a magical, conspiratorial fashion.

"I don't care if you tell the whole world. If you do, I'll say it was the dogs."

He was disappointed at her change of tactics, and her attempt to win him into her conspiracy. It did not seem funny. He stared at the moon.

"What's the matter with you?"

"Nothing, I told you."

"There is too. I know." A sudden light dawned in her face. "Urie's in love with Bostwick. That's it. I knew it!" But this brilliance changed in a minute. "Ooooh, Zebul! You're crying!" And immediately she threw her arms around him, kissing his hair.

334]

He tried to get away from her. He snatched both her arms to push her away. But he was so far gone that instead of casting them off him, he held onto them instead, not realizing what he was holding. A tremendous sob formed at the pit of his chest, and the act of holding was accompanied by a fantastic emotion that was far away from him, at the top of his head or beyond. The sob traveled up the cage of his ribs. His muscles contracted. It burned all the way up his torso from the inside, and he lost all control of himself. Stars from his eyes punctuated blackness.

Girded for all his strength, she trembled into the intensity of his sob like a sail into the wind, as if it were natural for her to deliver it to the air. The cry erupted from his mouth. His saliva dribbled onto her breast and they both fell onto the ground. She cooed baby words in his ear. The sound he made was hideous.

The anonymity of being soothed in the cold darkness gave him a strange sensation. Far away in his consciousness he could imagine himself despising tenderness. But now his own sobs were delicious. He loved his dribbling mouth. He reveled in his limpness. He was a mere fragile, sobbing boy. He liked the image. The only thing that counted to him was to be close to someone. He never recognized that it was Loco Poco who was holding him.

Even Urie was unreal to him in this state. He abandoned himself lasciviously to total defeat. For the first time in his life he did not seek clear outlines. In the warmth everything seemed round. He desired only to remain forever comforted and unthinking.

But after a while, when he became quiet, he became aware of things, and that the animal he was holding was Loco Poco. The ground, opposed to the warmth of their huddling, was frost-cold, hard. The stars were out. The sky was infinite. She had stopped cooing baby words. His head was in her lap.

He looked at her.

Her hands tightened on his shoulders and shook him as if to get him back to the state they were in before.

"Don't talk about Urie," he warned.

"But I didn't say anything."

"Well, don't."

But he did not move away from her. Contrary to his words, he went back to his old position again, trying to reinstitute the wallowing warmth. He discovered his body was too long for hers and extended in sharp, unprotected prongs. But he lay upon her all the same, staring at the stars, his feet beginning to grow cold. He closed his eyes.

"Zebul." He opened them lazily at the high whisper. "Let me see your dong."

He did not move. Then, incredulous, he made her repeat it. "What?"

"Let me see your . . . thing. You know . . . your . . ."

In this state of anonymous familiarity her switch from baby cuddling to ghostly sexual familiarity had the same unreality as everything else. She was laughing. Her fingers, the same wasps that had shook him, now trailed like vines over his chest and down to the belt of his pants. And he actually unbuckled it and unzipped his pants for her. His own hands lingered by her hands—shocked at her doing such a thing—and funneled her arms all the way to her elbows as she felt him. The moment she touched him he welcomed his lust as he had his sobbing. In some far-off room of his consciousness he knew it was Loco Poco. Yet it hardly seemed possible. He tried to stare at her even to summon his disbelief. But he gave up trying. The same unreality that caused his lust made him abandon himself to it. He gritted his teeth in ecstasy and rose up. Everything was profoundly new, strange, and laughable. Therefore he laughed.

She stared into his face and said shiveringly, "Ooooh! It's big! I didn't think they were that big!"

"It's not that big."

"Eeeeeesh!"

"What are you doing that for?"

"Zebul, you could kill me with that!"

"Well, how can I help it? You're killing *me* right now!"

He was perfectly aware of the inappropriateness not only of the laughter, but of his physical happiness. He was suddenly a full dragoon with vicious saber, and this physical power took him at the inappropriate time of his full defeat, in his heartbreak. It disproved the Bible: "To him that hath shall be given." He was stupendously proud of his erection, and grabbed what gave it to him, not Loco Poco but a thrilling realm of abandonment. Had he thought truly for one moment it was Loco Poco, he would have stopped.

His mind was as vicious, glinting, and hard as his sex. He thought of Urie coming home, or P.Q., so he grabbed the other Loco Poco, whispering, "Come on in the barn."

They ran to the far end of the barn, away from the hole that had been chopped. "Away from the hole. There's a breeze there," he said, delighting in the piny laughter he got from Loco Poco. And they threw themselves down on some old curtain material which had once covered the pump organ and where she had played dolls. There they began to feast upon each other's bodies. Since he was the rider, he got on top of her, hot but light in his power, unbuttoning some of her clothes, moving, looking, kissing and feeling her, all four actions at once. She had plump breasts and small hips, and her skin was so delicate and white that it glowed like a lightning bug in the darkness. Her smell was alkaline, barely perceptible, and the only other color was the pale pink of her nipples. He was surprised by this roundness of her, which bubbled into his hands. But what amazed him even more, for he had never contemplated her physical body as he had Urie's, was her imperiousness. "Eeeeh! That's good. Do that. Do this. Oh, I can see your hairs! Under your arms. Ooooh! You're an albino he-angel!" All this bewitching wit in a thirteen-year-old.

"How old are you?" he suddenly asked, scared.

"Fourteen years old."

"You're lying! You're thirteen."

"No sir. My birthday was November fifth."

And she handled him as adamantly as he handled her; she might have been thirty-eight years old, so wanton and demanding was she. "Ooooh, darling," she crooned when he fondled her nipples. He could see the blue vein stand out in her temple like a worm. "Oh, Zebul, do something. Do something!"

So he brought his hard and fast dong, as she called it, and put it between her legs, huge, fast, slippery, and tricky as a cowboy, almost waving his imaginary hat as he did so because his mount was treacherously ecstatic. He did not go inside her yet because she was a virgin and so was he. But nothing could quell his dauntless virility or take the stiffening out of his stick—not even stopping cold to experiment with her just where it was they were to put it. Nor going slow when they put it there. Since neither of them could believe it, they stared into each other's eyes until in the blaze of unrecognizable pupils their eyes turned up and out.

After that they both ran down and got the microscope from behind the bush, holding it between them, laughing and weaving like drunks all the way down the railroad tracks to his little house.

CHAPTER 41

The next day when Zebul came to the house he met Urie face to face in the dining room, where she was typing the final copy of a social-science term paper at P.Q.'s steel desk.

[337

P.Q. was deriding the rumor that Hoke Tabernacle was secreting a short-wave set inside the beat-up Chickering piano in the back room of his bookstore.

"That piano has as much chance of emitting messages from Berlin as my big toe," he said.

Zebul and Urie both said, "Hi," to each other in cracked voices. Zebul backed away from her blushes and guilty, glittering eyes like a hard-shell crab. For his guilt now matched her betrayal, and, drawn in equal proportion by negative and positive magnetism, without specific intention toward either Loco or Urie, he merely stood there on the substance of his new virility, feeling the incorporation of both poles of Bishopry in him. It was like having unfamiliar feet.

"In fact I pity the Nazis if they have him working in the fifth column for them."

"But I heard the police have searched the place. Twice!" said Zebul loudly and artificially, jumping onto the conversation.

"Yeah," echoed Urie. "But Berlin doesn't talk over it, P.Q. *He* contacts Berlin with it."

"He has a pythia in his piano," offered Zebul.

Urie laughed zanily.

"Pythia in his piano! That's great!" cried P.Q., ecstatic.

"He transmits. But it won't emit. First he has a mimeograph machine in there and puts out Communist literature, and now—"

"It reminds me of when Croesus went to the Pythia," interrupted P.Q., enraptured, "and asked her what he should do to save himself. His enemy was coming to get him. The Pythia let out smoke from her hole in the ground to the top of Delphi and said, 'Yes. Tomorrow at the river I see two mighty armies. One of them will win.' Of course he was so happy to have heard that he was going to win that he immediately marched his army straight to the river and was defeated."

Everybody laughed loudly, seeing Hoke Tabernacle as the general. Thank God for P.Q. Habit was stronger than broken hearts, catastrophe, and guilt.

"People are fools!" cried Urie enthusiastically, ushering in a new discussion. "Would you believe they would believe a story like that? Why, people will believe anything!"

"Police too," said Zebul. "To think people could be so suspicious in this day and age!"

The double edge of their remarks caused their faces to burn. And yet it was exciting, reassuring them that a realm beyond their wildest dreams existed, proving through unbreakable habit the strength of their bond. Zebul stayed for supper.

It was the same as it had always been. Zebul believed it totally. Even when Loco kicked him secretly under the table and made signals with her eyes, he did not believe anything was going to happen. So he was surprised when, after he left, he heard a pattering of footsteps beyond the railroad at the pinewoods.

Sex with Loco, rather than being a palliative, took the place of grief. He had neither time nor place to participate and articulate it. His feelings became drowned in sensation. This second time he not only allowed it but embraced it. The doom at the end of the rainbow he scooped into himself. It was like swallowing an endless ribbon. And he had the delusion that the piper would never have to be paid. The Bible had already been disproved. And no one dreamed of any new connection between him and Loco because habit gave framework to it. His presence at the Bishops' could never be suspect because he belonged to the Bishop family.

In the next week he made love with Loco seven times. In the week after that, twelve. He never planned it. It always "happened." Loco was random, greedy, and insatiable.

They did not use his and Urie's places for trysts, because he could not be sure that Urie would not walk in on them. He did not even have time to think of his sense of sacredness, reverence, and sensitivity. His little house was out. That left the pinewoods. But it was cold outdoors. In the second week of December it warmed up, and they picked open spaces where the pine needles held the warmth of the sun. Loco would always show up at their meetings as if materializing from thin air. She chose a different part of the wood each time. She reveled in teasing as if it were magic.

But she caught a cold from the dampness. He inhaled her snuffling nose, her husky croaking voice, her coughing, scooped her into his inner being at the same moment that she captured him in her genitals. The liquid strings of her runny nose in coitus were perverse delight to him, and he actually imagined the germs as invisible wedding guests. She did not get over her cold. She was completely reckless. She perspired, dried off, perspired, got cold again, and refused to leave off wallowing in his embraces.

"All right. You've had that cold one solid week now, and Christmas is coming," said Mrs. Bishop one day. "You're going to bed."

"No, Mamma, I can't—"

"I told you to rest after dinner, didn't I? What do you do? You go out all hours. I don't know what you're thinking of! You don't even put on a coat half the time."

"I'll rest. I promise. Just one more day. Please, Mamma!"

She bewitched Mrs. Bishop. And the next day she skidded out of sight.

"If you were in my bed with me, it would be all right," she breathed in Zebul's ear. "We would make a big tent. It would be real warm. We would do everything." Neither one of them mentioned that Urie's bed was in the next cubicle.

He was afraid for her daring. He was actually afraid that she would get pneumonia or die of her own greed. Blankets were too heavy to carry around, so he stole a big bathtowel from the Ephesus Inn and they used it for a blanket. After one session of lovemaking he wrapped her up in it and held her against him like a baby until in her wantonness she teased him, taking nips of his shoulders and ears, to do it again. But the bath-towel worked, and she got over the cold.

Lust in such a young and small girl was incomprehensible to him. He ceased thinking of her as Loco Poco, and she became a miraculous sexual presence. The degree of her desire contrasted with her delicacy of body. She was so white, had such transparent skin, such petiteness of ankle, of ear, and of wrist that he could not believe she could bear the force of him. She was also elegant. Her cleanliness, so many baths, so much attention to her face and hair, like a cat's prodigious licking of shiny fur, contrasted with her greedy embrace of dirt, sticks, filthy aprons, and dog-shit. And even the beads of her sweat seemed jewels. She had the fragility of a china doll. How could she stand the gravel, the stickles of broom grass, the coarseness of tree bark? She seemed a child to him. She was so young, he so old. She was so little, he so big. She was so lyrical, he so strong. Yet it was she who was ravenous. With the transparency of a silverfish wriggling with such lightning speed its movements cannot be traced by eye, she tried for the bait he gave her. He was the desired, the darling, the food to be gobbled. She could not get enough of him.

She treated him like private property. She was so direct that he became aware of his own sensitivity. All appearances belied. She desired his rod and staff, but his cup of feelings was extraneous. This greed, since his feelings had been mauled, was reassuring to him. All her sexual movements, sly, delicate, mixed with hysterical laughter, shocked and excited him, but they did not demand emotion of him. He did not have to love her. She grasped him, and he was drenched in her flesh. She was affectionate. She gave him kisses and caresses as if they cost nothing. "Oooooh, darling,

340]

do this, do that."

He could afford to be patronizing in what was left of his mind, smiling secretly, in a different way from his celebrative laughter, for he was transformed. He created separate rodeos day after day.

Never in all his life had he concentrated on separate organs of his body. He had masturbated, knowing, just as he had known good grammar, that it did not make you go insane. But he had always done it idly, as a matter of course. And when he had done it he had thought of far-off things, scenes which he had painted or wanted to paint: butterflies, roses, the sun shining on grasses, his sawdust pile, even the abandoned mill. He never thought of girls or people. Or he thought of stealing things like drawing paper or books.

But now, because of Loco's awe of his sex, he confronted it. He looked at it as if it were separate from him. He upended it, thrust it out, rode it like a hobbyhorse in the pinewoods. It was her praise that made it work. He began to think of it as better, faster, more Olympian than the Titans themselves, who had succeeded in killing Chronos.

She loved it. She doted on it. She kissed it. She fondled it. She made up names for it: bull, ramrod, blockbuster, steamroller, pusher, knobkerry; names completely unsuited to her tongue. He was proud of those names. "You have to make up names too," she said. His names were inferior: stick, staff, sword, spear, ruler, whip, and killer. She said no, it was none of these, it was an Indian rope-trick. She wished she had a dong, she said one day, but now she didn't need one because she had his.

In an afterglow of such appreciation he strutted one day to the sidewalk in front of the Milk Snack, and there he spat into the gutter, imitating the pimple-Romeos of high-school days whom he and Urie had so despised and feared. But it was experimental mockery and he did not enjoy it, for now he had become so thoroughly Bishopian that he could not conceive of himself as anything but special. He thought of Gag Booch. Probably Gag Booch had lied about all those monthly and holiday screwings. Gag Booch went down in his estimation. And even so, what if it were true? Wasn't screwing easy?

So this aspect of his lovemaking, his discovery of himself as a rider whose never-failing pogo stick jumped him, like Paul Bunyan, across mountains heedless of the pass, Loco's valley, became less important to him than the realm he had entered.

The realm was a blind, involving, andante state, dark like nature. All the forces of his grief over Urie went into his inundation with Loco. His life became subterranean. There was only one small part of him operating in the real world. He studied his lessons, passed his tests, conjugated his Latin, argued with P.Q., ate his Parker House rolls, even talked with Urie as if nothing had happened between them. These actions were at the top of him, some sharp, mechanical area at the surface of his existence, atrociously unreal, in which he played the part of a talking doll. He could see himself above, bobbing in the sunlight at the surface, a strange Charlie McCarthy form like the others.

But he felt unreal except in the drowning roundness of Loco caressing him in the sea of sensation. Penises, pine trees, bathtowels, grasses, beads of sweat, gravel, veins, roses, lobes of ears, vaginas, valleys, nipples—all the delicious words were superficial ornaments, shining crackers floating on the surface. Did he love her? Did he not? What matter? Feelings were dead vegetables in the broth. He was surrounded by roundness, tasting nipples with his tongue till they were not nipples, plunging into the sweet meal with both hands, gobbling, gathering, and plowing, sucking honey and stinging ecstasy. But he became a petal as well as a horn. As he drew from her, she drew from him. He was a lake in which she played like a child and then, suddenly demanded of to produce Excalibur, he produced Excalibur erect and shining. It was easy. It was no miracle at all. But its plunge was always downward. And the moment of thrust was the moment of taking in. He was below the surface of the sea, and the animals of the deep traveled around him without form, heavy, massive, blotting out all sound in giant, liquid dark.

They talked only of superficial things. Did the grass prickle? She had mud on her dress. His fur was lighter than his hair. There was a stone in her back.

You just fit.

It's perfect.

We are fitted together to each other, just like perfect shoelaces.

He blotted out the memory of his poem. But the quirk of this pain lying behind him daunted nothing of his enjoyment. He hardly listened. When he did not want to listen, he giggled. She riposted. If he attempted an analytical word, she stuffed grass in his mouth. Transcendence by knowledge was gone. The aims of his life went by the board.

He lied. Loco lied. They cheated. They lied and cheated quite automatically, without turning a hair. The days of right-and-wrong mystiques were purged. They lied to Mrs. Bishop. They lied to P.Q. It was cheap. They were as superficial as sequins.

At the same time his friendship with Urie presented a new, articulate face. They carried out the same kind of conversations they had always had. But now, with duplicity, their relationship actually deepened. Since they were bereft of the ability to say what they meant, everything became profound, achieving layers of meaning or sarcastic, covering layers of unspoken knowledge.

After only one week of immersion with Loco something had happened in Zebul's consciousness. Bostwick had gone dead on him as if dropped down a chute in the back of his head. It was not just a refusal to think of him, it was a fact. If the thought occurred that if this were love which he and Loco were doing, what was it that Urie did and felt with Bostwick, it was so brutal he saw a twinge of stars. He did not desire to revenge himself on Bostwick, but he never wanted to see him again. The curious thing was that he never met him on the streets. And since Urie could not bring the subject of Bostwick up, with all that it entailed—sex, love, the Confederate soldier, the discovery, and Bostwick's reaction to Zebul's discovery— they found themselves in the state that they had been before they had met Bostwick. They talked about the unknown tongue again. The unknown tongue was exciting now because their inner lives had become the thing they could not tell. One day Zebul wrote a nonsense poem.

> Ish danstoboob ye clarafalter
> Bins ball blabben pilterfilter
> Na ye nowns do browns and pee
> > boch grunden not
> > boch brunden
> Not ish pans too froob me milker shalter!

"It's superb!"

"But what's behind it?"

Urie studied it. But she had to go all around Robin Hood's barn to give an interpretation that did not say too much.

"It's German for the fact that humanity talks and does and eats and craps, but in the end everything is futile!"

"That's good," breathed Zebul.

But in her heart she felt his testament: I don't give a damn what you do because all is blabbering gobbledygook. You can crap or pee, but as far as I'm concerned you're no more significant to me than a chocolate milkshake.

"I'm going to answer in Russian. Now figure out what this is!" she challenged.

Shostvok ya!
Poshtock blah!
Ia ne budget pah yoh cornstvock
You me hoodget mah nah schlah.
Bwillstrib flinkstrom
        cvom yoah
            stinkbomb
Swill-blah shrinkbloom
Shostvok ya!
Shostvok ya!
Stinkboom blinkstroom
Poshtock blah!

"Hurrah! Hurrah!" he answered. "Let the world blow itself up with stinkbombs. I know it's all stinking. I can even imitate it. Hurrah! Hurrah! Glorious stinkbomb!"

And she knew he knew it was her personal "go to hell" aria. I can't suffer on your cornstalk. You can't make me suffer from your stinkbombs. So smell your own. Hurrah.

This guessing of each other's inner meanings, as if each could approach what was known to the other but could not be discussed, was dangerous. But they always achieved a perfect degree of balance, never letting the beast escape from the box. It was the rhythm that inspired them. They admired each other. Their private vocabulary and the art they were now forced to use bound them together more indissolubly than sex could force them apart.

The term was coming to an end. Examinations were impending. It was the first term of her college career that Urie had not done her work conscientiously. She had a book report due on the last Monday before Christmas vacation—*Ulysses,* and she had not even read the book!

"Don't worry," said Zebul, who had not read it either. The paradoxical hostility of returning a tooth for an eye instead of an eye corroborated the hot, articulate unreality in which he lived with Urie. It reminded him of a horrible movie he had seen in which someone went up to a complete stranger in a public hallway and said, "How dare you look like someone I hate!" and administered a stunning slap. The affect was hilarious.

That night he went to the library, read the plot of *Ulysses* in the *Reader's Digest of Famous Literature,* wrote a page of outline, gave the major thematic points, and delivered it to Urie, who then converted his material into a book report whose authority was total because it was fake. "Complete bull," she said proudly. She got it back with an A-minus and a note from the professor: "Surely you are being ironical."

"Oh, my God, you put everything upside down!" Zebul accused.

"Well, I got it from you!"

They stared at each other darkly and barked in strange, short laughs.

There was a special commencement being held just before vacation began for students who had accelerated and were being given their degrees before induction. A rumor started that the President was coming to make the commencement address.

"Do you think he will, Zebul?" asked Urie.

"My foot."

But the rumor sparked some restlessness in Urie. She swore that she was going to summer school again this year. That would mean she could graduate in the spring of 1944 and get out into real life.

At the house she paraded this desire loudly in front of everyone at the supper table. The force of its obsession lay in some direct relation to her duplicity with Zebul and her relationship with Bostwick.

"I refuse to be a creeping old lady by the time I get out of school!"

"You are only seventeen years old," said her mother.

"It will be just a few years and I'll be ninety, crawling around on a stick. Don't you realize how fast people can kick the bucket?"

"I wish you would not use such vulgar expressions. They don't become you or your surroundings."

"Don't worry. This stinking house has heard a heck of a lot worse than that! Don't you realize, Mamma, that all of our high school was a sheer waste of time? The whole first year of college is a simple repeat of what we had in high school. Anybody is a fool who can't go from grammar school to freshman year in college."

"This is the ninety-eighth time I have heard the word 'fool' used today."

The family laughed. But Mrs. Bishop sank. The tapestries had failed to hide the walls.

"Well, I suppose you're right," she said sadly.

Urie could not bear this acceptance of her brandished aspirations. The descent into mournful death was punctuated by six gongs of the one clock they had not sold to the Laurelo Wildwood Gift Shop so long ago.

Loco kicked Zebul under the table, but, since he knew he was going to meet her later, he paid no attention. Urie's adamancy on going to summer school affected him with feverish intensity. If she went, he had to go too.

"Where are you going to get the money?" asked Mrs. Bishop.

"I don't know. But I'll think of something."

The rumor came true. Early on the morning of Commencement, December 19, the news became definite that the President was coming. The day was unseasonable, warm, but eerie, and overcast with a yellow light that threatened rain. It was like spring rather than Christmastime. The commencement exercises were scheduled for four o'clock in the stadium, to be moved to the gymnasium in case the rain began to fall.

The town was hushed as preparations began. Zebul and Urie met in their office without exchanging a word. But under their eyes everything became unfamiliar. The streets became jammed with strange vehicles: gray and silver horn-trucks with national broadcasting paraphernalia; limousines carrying notables from the state capital and Washington, D.C. The governor, Navy admirals, mayor, two senators from Washington, the Secretary of the Navy were due to arrive. Black automobiles with Secret Service men and Navy officers fanned out from the Ephesus Inn. Newspapermen came from all the major newspapers in the country. The radio trucks spread wire cables and outdoor lights through the woods from the stadium to the gymnasium on the Kingston Highway. By noon the campus was a walking mass of officials, parents of the graduating class, officers and cadets, students with caps and gowns. The sky grew darker. And because of the expectancy of the occasion no automobiles blew horns, Cadillacs purred like velvet, and people were pulled up out of themselves into a hush all the more amazing because there were so many thousands of them all engaged now in an unfamiliar occasion which they believed to be historical, on such familiar ground.

Minutes after the President's airplane landed at the airport, twenty thousand people were walking toward the stadium. It began to rain. The word was passed, by radio broadcast, by loudspeaker, by word-of-mouth. The ceremony was to be moved to the gymnasium.

Umbrellas blossomed. Ladies with high heels fanned through the woods. Seniors put on their tasseled caps for protection and ran. Businessmen flipped through wet pine trees to beat the quickest path.

The gymnasium was hot with klieg lights. The unfamiliar pink glare smelled of drying clothes, cigarettes, and wet umbrellas. American flags were draped in bunting, dwarfing the thousands of pink heads and hands gathering in the bleachers. A Navy band played. People milled around the floor at the bottom of the stands, competing for folding chairs. A minister stood in robes on the platform, talking with the aldermen as some senators arrived.

Zebul and Urie found places halfway up the bleachers just in time, for the gymnasium filled rapidly, and the roar of the waiting people was muffled within the echoing structure to the same pitch as the former hush had been.

"I'm almost dried off, it's so hot in here."

"Me too."

"We're yards and yards away from where he will come. Do you think we'll be able to see him well enough? Everything is so small down there. I wish we had opera glasses."

"If we could get near to him, you know what I'd do?"

"What?"

"Say, 'We're the ones that sent you *The Scroll*.'"

"Do you think he'd remember?"

"He might."

But even this desultory conversation broke off, and they merely waited, silent, filled up with the heat of the arc lights, fastened on every detail of the gathering senators and Navy officers on the platform.

Suddenly the band played "Hail to the Chief." The figures on the platform moved like leaves. A straggling line of men entered from the doorway on the far left, and a silent hush descended over the crowd.

He advanced like a drunk, one metal crutch at a time, the gleam of the metal signaling in the arc lights to the crowd. He was easy to distinguish, even though bodyguards accompanied him to the sides, to the front, to the back. For his head floated forward, benign and smooth as a lion's out of his cape. The cape's undulations disguised the crudeness at the apex of each jerk as he dragged and then catapulted one ironbound leg after the other. At the microphones he paused. Then he bent down with the dignity of the Hunchback of Notre Dame to unlock his leg braces. He sat down, smiling, and gave a wave.

The gymnasium burst into a tremendous roar of applause.

There were three invocations, by the Episcopal minister, the Jewish rabbi, and the Catholic priest. After the speeches, prayers, and a hymn, the president of the university, bowing to the graduates, the senators, the admirals, introduced "the President of the United States."

Everything was so still that the world seemed stopped. Urie and Zebul looked at him with tears frozen in their throats. He addressed the seniors of the graduating class, ladies and gentlemen, president of the University, senators of the United States, "my new-found alumni." His nasal twang uttered in the fine, lyrical tone, with the patrician jog of head enlarged in the broadcasting system and sounded out beyond the gymnasium to every radio in the country. He made a joke. His voice was strong. He made a speech. But he was a speck. In the distance he was noble and small. A mere man. Very frail. If this frailty was the reality of the ship of state, what was it? What was this myth come true in such a fashion? What was the war, the nation, the world, the future?

Urie and Zebul loved the President more than they had ever loved him before, but it was a hopeless love. He was human.

CHAPTER 42

Christmas came and went. There was something confusing to Zebul in the fact that it was Loco in whom he was drowned instead of Urie. He feared that he might make a mistake and say to Loco what he should have said to Urie, or worse, to Urie what he was already saying to Loco. But in fact it was easy. He never made a mistake. Loco Poco and Urie were such totally different poles of the same thing that they brought out different aspects of him. And he was continually amazed in one aspect that the other could exist in his same body. Just as he was continually amazed that Loco Poco and Urie could be the same thing yet different.

Did he hate Urie? Here he was, acting the same way toward her as he always had, yet had she not betrayed him completely? He remembered long ago when he had lost God, how he had almost hated her. Now he did not hate her as much as he had then. Yet he wondered if he had taken up this subterranean life with Loco simply to revenge himself on her. He was so habituated to thinking himself the captain of his soul, he could hardly believe he had "fallen into" it. What if Urie found out? Did he secretly want her to find out? All these complicated emotions stupefied him. He could not untangle them. He could not extract hate from the larger emotion that had swelled around him since Urie had betrayed him and in which he and she were caught more securely than ever for the reason that they could not say it.

What about Loco? Why wasn't she jealous? Did she have a supernatural sixth sense? Was it delicacy that made her refrain from questions about him and Urie? What did she say to Urie when he was gone, at nights when they slept side by side, separated from the sight of each other by the tapestries of their separate rooms? Thinking of this should have scared him. Instead it inspired him.

One day he moved his head up out of Loco's naked breast and asked, "How happen you weren't killed that day you jumped off Visigoth Castle?"

"I don't know."

He turned her over, put his hand on her throat as if he were going to choke her, and looked into her eyes. "Did you aim for that bank with the moss on it?"

Her black pupils had a coquettish gaze. Lurking behind them was some troglodyte of mockery. "No."

"Weren't you scared?" She went into gales of laughter. "Did you know you weren't going to be killed?"

He humored her, and finally, after a long time had passed, she confessed with a fervor that demanded of him not to disbelieve her. "Tootsie Morn was there." She whispered this.

"You saw her?"

"Yes. She was there."

It was bushwa, but he did not tell Loco so. It was at such points that he felt he was becoming Urie in his relation to her. And his very inability to cope with her on this level fascinated him. Like Urie, he began to develop awe for her. If Urie had seemed to have been impersonated by Loco in allaying his grief, if in losing Urie he had not lost her because he had Loco, now he became, because of or in spite of his dark, sexual entente, Urie. He felt like Urie. He acted like Urie. He had the same attitude of adoration and impatience toward Loco as Urie. Sometimes he even felt that Loco thought he was Urie too.

But she was more imperious and scornful of him than she was of Urie. Bones she threw to his masculinity, a special present. The same as the caresses she gave to Charybdis and Scylla because they were dogs. She was not in thrall of him. She did not love him. She used him. It was amazing to him.

For instance, she never asked him if he loved her. For all her gushings, her demands, her adoration, her obsession with his masculinity, her caresses, her cooings, her kisses, for all her complete abandonment of her body to him, letting him believe he owned it, she did not care a fig for him. He knew every cranny of her body, but he could not possess her. After love she turned away from him. She once made a noise like the flute into the branches of the pine tree.

"What are you doing that for?"

"To see if my voice really does make *vibrato*. Dr. Nagy swears it does. Oh Zebul! Guess what! What we do makes *vibrato*."

He blushed.

"You're a dolt, oooh, my darling!" She smacked in his ear. She ate a flower. "Do you want to know why I do this?"

"Well?"

"Promise not to tell anybody. I mean nobody."

She meant Urie.

"All right. I promise."

"To make the war stop soon."

These words were made more important by the fact that she stared at him solemnly so that he could not laugh. It was scary because in fact the war had just begun in earnest.

"I know you do not believe it. You are pretending," she said in a peculiar grown-up manner. She was disappointed. "I feel sorry for you."

"Does P.Q. believe everything you say?"

"P.Q. is different from you and Urie."

He blushed. It was the first time she had ever spoken to him about Urie and it proved to him that she thought of him as she did of Urie.

"How?"

"When he plays, he believes it, he really does believe it, even if he thinks it's a lie."

Zebul saw why P.Q. loved Loco Poco better than Urie. Loco never made gods of people as Urie and he did. She was impersonal, untouchable, and ruthless, like P.Q., and her fears, delicacy, colds, and fragility were a disguise.

"It's eight o'clock! You're going to be late!" P.Q. always lied about time in the morning. It was only seven, but Urie jumped out of bed guiltily, only to find that Loco was in the bathroom.

"Get out of there fast. I have an eight-o'clock class!" she called, shivering in the hallway.

The irrelevant trivia of living fed into her frustration. She felt wasted by the materialization of her betrayal. Zebul, full of *double-entendre,* seemed to wait for her defeat by Bostwick to capture her in revenge. She feared to lose Zebul, but she feared even more his getting hold of her, making her tell what was between her and Bostwick. Worst of all, she was losing contact with Bostwick. He was more distant than ever. She could not tell him about Zebul. He did not love her. She pined, even in his arms. She did not dare ask the one question, the catalytic question that might give her understanding of the look in his eyes: "Why were you crying, Bostwick?" Through Loco's flap-door she saw the scrapbook open on her sister's bed to that ancient clipping: HESS PARACHUTES INTO ENGLAND. POSSIBLE SECRET TERMS—that shibboleth of long ago.

Because of Loco's dawdling Urie arrived at the breakfast table before her and was calmly eating her oatmeal when Loco appeared. Urie knew at once something was different about her. But it took a moment to know what it was. Loco was wearing lipstick.

No one had ever worn lipstick in the family. Not because it was sinful, but because it was, according to P.Q., silly. Lipstick was like the words "stomach," "God," "throw up," and "love"—taboo, a delusive way of thinking that had nothing to do with growth, education, or improving yourself.

Urie had two impulses as Loco spun her eyeballs away from her with a simper. First, she wanted to announce it. Second, she wanted to protect Loco, to tell her to run away and wash it off before P.Q. saw it.

P.Q. did not notice at first. He had a forkful of eggs and at the moment his eyes turned from blankness to brilliant recognition, yellow strings of yolk slid through the prongs of the fork.

"Come look and see!" he trumpeted. "Loco Poco has painted the barn doors red!"

Urie winced. How could Loco bear such a sarcastic insult?

Irene ran to the doorway to look.

Mrs. Bishop came from the kitchen.

Loco sat down as if nothing had been said, picked up her spoon, and placed a mouthful of oatmeal into her immaculate mouth, making small movements of her lips around the oatmeal. Bits of red paste came off on the spoon and a silent laughter built up to the edge of her eyes, but she only raised them in thrall at P.Q. and chewed.

When breakfast was over and everybody was on her way to school, Urie realized that P.Q.'s culture had been smoothly undermined, and the first new thing since the Freedom to Steal had been instituted. In the next week P.Q. referred to Loco three times, once as an Egyptian mummy and twice as a painted barbarian, but his remarks were as useless as the old pictures of Rudolf Hess.

When a person wants something, she has to dress up and act beautiful. By March Urie had descended to lipstick too. She went to the admissions office with her completed application forms and stood before a fat secretary whose desk plaque said Ada Dee Dowd.

"I'm sorry. There are no scholarships for the summer term." Ada Dee Dowd tacked a kindly smile on her sentence, like a period.

"Oh."

But Urie circumvented this news by holding out the application blank over the name plaque. As a fat, hypocritical Southerner, Ada Dee Dowd examined the application. Her two chins creased to three when she reached the bottom.

"You're only seventeen." She laughed indulgently. "Why don't you wait until fall? Then I am sure we could give you a loan."

"Thank you," said Urie.

The moment she was outside she shucked her dignity as well as her lip-stick, which she wiped off on a Kleenex. She threw the Kleenex away, taking vicious satisfaction in littering the campus with her lip-prints. Two whole years she had been in college, and they would *never* give her a scholarship. It did not matter that she had worked for every cent of her tuition and had as good marks as Zebul. Now, because there was no program of summer jobs, she was in this pickle. Yet it was only seventy-five dollars she needed. Her life hung in the balance over seventy-five measly dollars, and the difference between owning and not owning it was nothing but everything.

These thoughts beclouded a gathering terror at her increasing lack of contact with Bostwick. For instance, she never told him of her growing obsession with school and money. On March 12, when Congress passed Lend Lease for another year, she thought of Bostwick and money. Did Bostwick have seventy-five dollars? What if she told him she needed seventy-five dollars?

But he lived in a different universe. He was not charmed by her queer poverty. He neither laughed at it nor entertained it at all. That part of her life was nothing to him. It only proved that she was an appendage in his universe, a tail to his kite. He was becoming unaware of her. And she loved him so hopelessly that it pained her, a physical pain in the heart, even to think of his money, let alone think of taking it.

She had grown a strange habit concerning adults. She could not bear to see them open their pocketbooks. A week ago her mother had bought a toothbrush for Loco Poco in the ten-cents store. Urie had to turn away because she thought she might cry. Buying was doom. Adults were near death. The more they spent, she felt, the faster they would die. Eating too was like buying. One day she saw an old lady eating potatoes in Swine Hall, forking them up to her mouth, alone at the table, unconscious that she was feeding herself merely to die.

The dichotomy between her unconfessed love for Bostwick, grown so outward now that it had turned into unfocused love for doomed humanity, and her greed for education, school so that she could graduate into life, split her into poles of parsimony and pity. She was so possessed of love on one hand that it threatened to dissolve her, and on the other she was so possessed of hatred that she wanted to tear the world to bits by force of will.

Mashing down all thoughts of Bostwick, his understanding, his money (why should he give either? she knew she did not deserve them), she felt herself grow uglier and uglier upon the streets. She loved this ugliness. She took it unto herself until she became a huge bloodshot carrion with a vile, prodigious, and unscrupulous gizzard and an even more stupendous and filthy beak with which she could swoop down upon dead universities and pick up live secretaries, deans, fraternity boys, sorority girls, and college presidents, hearing them scream in agony as she ate and chewed them up in midair, their blood dribbling over her feathers until she spat out their bones.

She saw a girls' bicycle leaning against Dwight Hall. It had a wire basket on the handlebar. She threw her pocketbook into the basket, mounted the bicycle, and rode quickly down the gravel walk to Venable Hall.

I stole a bicycle, she thought with glee, dismounting, leaning it against Venable. She thought of keeping it. But she walked away, knowing that her hatred could not be quelled even with the thought that the owner would now have to report its disappearance to the police.

An old lady came around the corner of Venable. Pale, dewy eyes shone out of her withered skin. She did not see Urie because she was occupied climbing around the stones of the footpath with a cane. A gold wristwatch dangled on her wrist, and she struggled to hold her large black leather bag. The bag kept hitting her shins. The sun shone down upon a universe devoid of everyone save Urie and the old lady.

The large black pocketbook signaled, and her mind's eye became an X-ray that improvised seven bills within, five in denominations of twenty, two in denominations of fifty—two hundred dollars, wrapped neatly, folded, and pinioned with a paper clip, whose power enabled the old lady to live in retirement at the Ephesus Inn, rocking the afternoons away on the colonnaded porch overlooking Pergamus Avenue. This old lady was innocent of the difference between Urie's being a sophomore or a junior. A year of life. Urania Bishop's destiny.

Urie stopped and stepped behind a magnolia, the tree she had hated since the first day, entering Ephesus, hearing the flat sound of the bell ringing "O Love That Will Not Let Me Go." She picked up a large stone warm from the sun and imagined the sound as it cracked the old lady's egg-skull. The gray hair, silver from old lady's bluing, was sparse so that the outline showed through. She analyzed every faltering step with her young, cruel, microscopic eye.

The old lady noticed her and smiled. "It's very warm for a spring day, isn't it?"

Old ladies sweated, but the sweat was extremely refined, the beads indistinguishable from each other, a mirror reflecting and carrying the reflection of their trembling upper lips.

"Yes." Urie put the stone down in her mind and picked a magnolia blossom instead. The old lady, having achieved the obstacle of the stones with some success, took up her cane again, like a cross, and tottered on her way. She passed the bicycle. The magnolia blossom was brown at the edges. Only lilac was suitable for such an old lady.

C H A P T E R   43

"Bostwick, do you love me?" she wanted to say.

They were lying together on his bed, she in her brown dress, he dressed in his khakis with his collar open, staring at the ceiling. But she did not dare ask it. She knew he did not. Being able to reach him no longer, she had only one desire, to stave off the dreaded day when, in some kindly way, he would tell her it would be better if she did not come again. Ever since Zebul's discovery, he had become very pure and had not taken her again. In all their days of love he had penetrated her only three times. She remembered these times as if they were in another age, and he a stranger. It was only academic, the remembering, for he had never seemed Bostwick to her then. And now he had become the old Bostwick, the Bostwick she had known in the first days with Zebul, the unknowable Bostwick, the god Bostwick.

How could she have allowed herself this passive role with him? She who was so ambitious, so burning, so vicious? And he was even more passive than she. It was incomprehensible! She longed to shake him, to grip him by the shoulders and ask, "Why? Why were you crying in the Ephesus Inn that day? What do you think of all the time? Why don't you see me?"— reminding herself of Isabella in *Wuthering Heights,* when she knew she was Heathcliff. But she did not dare. He possessed the power of his passivity.

She understood how a woman could be a slave to a man. She felt she was Bostwick's concubine because he spoke to her so little, because he was not interested in her, and because he forbade her without a word to interfere in her true life. But she wanted him, even though she had never loved

354]

a moment of coitus, to make love to her, or to get angry, or even to hit her. It was his kindliness that was so terrible to her, for it was the mask of his godliness, which made her fear and be inferior to him.

Now, lying by his side, hovering over his chest, burying her face in his neck, she understood P.Q.'s condemnation of Jews, the One God, the "fear thy God," all of which led to the Wailing Wall. It was a melancholy religion from which Christianity was born. She understood through Bostwick why P.Q., who never stole, never lied, never smoked, and never got drunk, hated the Anglo-Saxons who, through the Puritans, had perpetrated the arrogance of work, duty, and stiff-upper-lippery. Good taste even crucified life. But the alternative? No. For his freedom P.Q. had exacted that they live in poverty. She loved Bostwick because he was the opposite of P.Q.

But even at the age of seventeen, Urie knew that she was in a tragedy with her first love. She was on the fence. One way lay parsimony, stifling discipline, the death of love in passion for love, miserliness and saintliness; the other way lay extravagance, foolishness, lowdownery, common sense, humanity, and children. If only Bostwick loved her, she might grow up to be a woman.

Why hadn't he asked about Zebul? Why did he not mention the fact that he never saw him any more? Why didn't he ask her questions? Such as, did she see Zebul? What did he say? Did he mention Bostwick? Wasn't Bostwick interested? That decadence in Bostwick that had made him love her more when Zebul was near, as if he had desired not one belief but an orgy, not one person but two, that perverseness which had made Bostwick choose out of all the people in Ephesus two sixteen-year-old freshmen whose relationship he had controlled and then broken, had now made him drop his interest in her. If he had been kind to her and cruel to Zebul, there had also been a modicum of cruelty in his relationship to her, both in the way he had made love the first time and in the way he made her take full responsibility for her relationship with him. He never once pursued her. He never once admitted lust for her. He made her aware of her lust for him by trying to give her what she wanted in a sexual manner. When what she wanted was—

She did not know what she wanted. And it was this respite from being held up lone in his eyes and in the universe, made to contemplate herself as separate from him, that caused her to accept with feverish gratefulness his kindliness. That kindliness made her fear him. It was her enemy. She hated it even as she depended on it.

She looked into his eyes. "I'm going to stay with you all night," she said in a low, threatening voice.

"No, it's late," he said, brushing her hair from her eyes as if she were a child. "What will your mother say? It is bad, your spending so much time with me when I—"

"Bostwick, don't hate me!" she whispered, throwing herself on him to blot out his words.

"I don't hate you."

She wanted him to hate her.

He kissed her convulsive arms, made love to her breasts, caressed her until she wanted to die for him. Then he went to sleep.

It happened that in this sleep his head fell upon her arm. She did not move for fear of waking him. Her devotion was reciprocated, she felt, by Bostwick's most unconscious wish. Her arm grew numb. His clock showed two, and then three. Her fingers were now cold as ice, the circulation shut off. But his act of breathing upon her skin was miraculous, and she would have done anything rather than move. She studied his face. Could she get gangrene? At four o'clock he awakened and stared at her in surprise.

She moved her arm behind her so he would not know. But he noticed.

"You should have wakened me," he said gently.

But the pins and needles born of returning circulation made her cherish that arm, as if it had been married to him.

At breakfast Mrs. Bishop was furious. "You didn't get home till I don't know when!" she said.

Her mother never attacked Irene, for whom she was sorry, nor Loco, whose lipstick had passed into the culture and whose disappearance from the house at odd hours elicited mere naggings pacified by kisses. But in her fatigue Urie felt adrenalin rise in her veins, and she was viciously happy her mother had attacked. She held her full spoon as if it were a weapon. She wanted her mother to ask, "Where were you?" She would tell her the truth. She pitied her mother in expectation.

But her mother avoided this confrontation. "You are the most selfish person I have ever known!" she said. "You go where you want. You do what you want. You don't care about anybody in this house, do you? Not even your own father! You treat everybody as if we were too low for such an exclusive being as you to recognize. And as far as you're concerned we're just a bunch of bog-Irish maids to get your meals and provide the bed you sleep in. Well, I'm going to tell you something, Urania Bishop. If you think you can act like that in this house, you've got another think coming."

"I'm going to be late for my class."

"Do you dare sit there and answer me like that?"

"Yes, I do. For God's sake, I have a class and you start nagging! Every time I come in this house you start nagging. What is this house anyway but a freezing, horrible niggershack that we just pretend is something good. The trouble with you is you can't stand it because we're beginning to live our own lives. Do you think other people in college live in niggershacks when they go to college? No. They don't. They leave home and go away and live in dormitories. Well, why don't you get some other interest away from us? You ought to get a job or something and get your mind away from nagging us all the time. We're not going to stay in this house forever, you know."

Urie avoided the look on her mother's face. If it was not an attack, it was the weapon of guilt. "Well, you asked for it!" she screamed, banging out the door.

The whole morning she avoided thinking about this scene. In the afternoon when she returned home she expected a silent truce. This seemed to be the case, for Mrs. Bishop did not speak to her directly. P.Q. was buried in the *Wall Street Journal.*

That night Urie went to bed early, not only to get away from everybody, but also because she was dead tired and her arm ached from last night's adventure as Bostwick's pillow. Mrs. Bishop never entered the girls' bedrooms—a custom ever since the tapestried cubicles had been made. So when she entered at the flap-door just as Urie was about to put out her light, Urie stared at her as if she were a ghost.

"I thought we ought to have a talk," she said in a soft voice, standing uncertainly.

She sat down on Urie's bed and folded her hands self-consciously in her lap. Her dress wrinkled at the hips. Her presence hinted of strange, unallowable intimacy, a naked return of Mother to Baby, whose culmination could only be an embrace. Urie hunched herself into a rigid posture like a stone.

"I thought of what you said this morning. It's so futile. I've tried and tried to talk to you, but I just can't seem to get anywhere."

Mrs. Bishop waited for Urie to say something, but Urie fixed her eyes on the naked light bulb.

"Haven't we always given you people complete freedom? Why, I don't think one of the girls in your entire class in high school had the freedom that you have. Now, I know that things have been hard and P.Q. doesn't make much money, but that's not his fault. The Depression wiped us out and he never had the powers to bounce back like I have. But this isn't what I'm talking about. It just seems to me lately that you've changed. I don't understand you any more. Maybe I've nagged, but I don't mean to. It's just that you're never here any more. And when you're here—I don't know. You used to have Zebul around all the time, but now— Why, it seems to me you're in Timbuctoo, even when you're here. What have I done wrong? Don't you care about us any more?"

The pressure of her mother's body on the bed was the measure of her psychic want. Urie remembered her own gallant words: "We're going to crack this town wide open."

"I have probably put too much responsibility on you—"

Urie's eyes slid like lizards to escape her mother, but she could not avoid her completely. She caught a glimpse. Mrs. Bishop was winding one finger around and around the third finger of her left hand. The tapestry wriggled pitifully.

"How am I going to talk with you?" begged her mother with relentless tenderness.

"You're talking, aren't you?"

Was this the way Bostwick felt when she threw herself upon him, pleading for his love? She understood that humankind demands total surrender for love in modern times, and this understanding was an affliction. Why could she not put out her arms and say, like either a baby or a grown-up woman, "I love you, Mamma"?

"Maybe you're right I ought to get a job." When Mrs. Bishop stood up, the floor went down and the bed went up. "All right. Do things your own way. You will anyway, so there's nothing anybody can do about it."

Urie's happiness was insane at being left alone, and she was careful not to put her foot on that still-warm spot where her mother had sat.

C H A P T E R   44

At the end of April P.Q. bought a truck. It was a seven-year-old blue-paneled truck he got from a Negro who worked for Mrs. Kanukaris. No one knew where he found the money to pay for it, and no one dared ask. Zebul painted in gold lettering on both sides: LYCEAN LINEN SUPPLY. "Lycean" was a word Apollo used for "light." P.Q. pronounced it, Loco Poco said, like LICK-'EM-CLEAN LINEN SUPPLY. Everybody had a go at naming the business. Urie suggested KHARTOUM KLEANERS but was vetoed by Irene because it sounded like a nigger company. Irene suggested ACHILLES LINEN SUPPLY. Zebul said everybody associated Achilles with heel, which meant that the wash would not only come out dirty but would also have been cleaned by "heels." But P.Q. insisted on LYCEAN and did not care how people pronounced it. From then on he conducted the linens by truck and put the bicycle in the shed. It gave an unfamiliar air of success and growth to the business. The weather turned hot. But Urie still had not figured out how to get seventy-five dollars for summer school.

One night the family was gathered in the living room. Zebul was there, lying on the floor with his feet propped up against the coffin sofa. Mrs. Bishop was poking through some carton boxes of clothes. P.Q. was in the dining room, reading a newspaper that sported a picture of John L. Lewis with his eyebrows sprouting out like devil's horns. Ever since the truck, P.Q. read his newspapers standing up rather than sitting down. Therefore John L. Lewis leered from the dining-room doorway on P.Q.'s feet. Irene was telling everybody that she had a plan to go and work in the Turk's Head Inn in Rockport as a waitress for the summer.

"How are you going to get there with no money?" asked Urie sarcastically.

"I'll do it."

"I said how?"

Irene had become more beautiful with the passage of time. Her hair was a magnificent chestnut-brown, which the hot suns of April had burnished to red. Her face had filled out and become more creamy than before. The stubbornness with which she had buttressed her life had given her a mysterious look that was increased when she assumed she was being attacked. She had a full Venus-like figure which testified to secret realms of femininity behind her laconic actions and tactlessness.

"I'll hitchhike," she said, lifting the idea out of Urie's unconscious.

Urie snorted.

"She can do it!" Loco said.

But Urie did not need the contagion of Loco's excitement, for she understood that if Irene had been able to get them singing engagements in church, she was capable of anything. Who knew what she would do? She was so unpredictable she *would* hitchhike. Urie was filled with envy. Why should she go to school this summer, she thought, when she could go hitchhiking instead and beat Irene to the punch? Even with gas rationing you could get rides with trucks and break the barriers of geography. You could escape to the ocean, even if you had to be a waitress.

At that moment footsteps sounded outside. Scylla and Charybdis lunged up and broke into loud barks.

No one who knew the Bishops came the front way. They had burned only a small part of the porch, and the rest was broken boards and shingles, forming a lumber pile on the ground, obstructing the way. In addition, you had to climb almost the height of a person to get in the front door. Yet there was a rap on it. Loud.

Irene opened the door. The face was at the level of her kneecaps. It was Dan Tatum, and from the shoulders down he was invisible, but he waved a printed paper at floor level.

"Won't you come in?" said Irene, as if to a dwarf. The dogs were howling and gnashing their teeth.

"Don't P. Q. Bishop live here?"

"Yes."

Dan Tatum grabbed hold of both sides of the doorway and hauled himself in. He sweated and announced, "I am the sheriff."

The bicycle! thought Urie, even though she had not really stolen it, only borrowed it.

Zebul hardened into a ball like a beetle, rolled over, and tried to hide in the corner. They could put him on the roads for the microscope. He shouldn't admit anything right off. Keep quiet. It would be their word against his.

Loco's eyeballs were spinning in their sockets.

A blush of shame spread all over Irene's face. They hadn't paid the electric bill for four months. Her mother had complained one night to P.Q. Or it was the ninety dollars P.Q. had owed for oil for two years when he had gone and bought a truck?

A large black pistol clung obscenely like a fish to the belt below Dan Tatum's slovenly potbelly.

"Is P. Q. Bishop in?"

"Yes," whispered Irene.

Everyone acted in concert, refusing that impulse to turn his head toward the dining room. John L. Lewis continued to leer as if nothing had happened to change the rhythm and tenor of the evening.

"I'm looking for a Miz Clara Q. Bishop."

"It's not Clara Q.!" Loco informed him.

They would, like Macduff's army, have transformed themselves into Birnam Wood to disguise her, now that the A & P game was up, but they were paralyzed.

"It says right here: Clara Q. Bishop."

"It's Clara P."

"No. It's P. Q. Bishop," argued Dan Tatum.

"P. Q. Bishop. And Clara P. Bishop. P. is for Parsons."

Flailing to extricate himself from the smart-ass pit of pickled peppers, Dan Tatum suddenly spotted Mrs. Bishop on her knees by the carton box.

"I got a complaint against you, ma'am. You was seen goin' into the Count house and takin' things."

"Me? Why I— How could that be?" Mrs. Bishop struggled to her feet. Don't say anything incriminating, Mamma! They wanted to warn her.

"Did you ever go to the Count house and take anything?" Dan Tatum asked.

"Why, no. Of course not."

"You know where the Count house is?"

"Why . . . yes."

"You ever been down in that Count house?"

"No." Mrs. Bishop's face was beet-red. She was panting. "I've gone for walks down there, of course. Maybe somebody, confused, thought that I—"

"You never walked inside that ole Count house?"

"I noticed that it was old and run-down and I thought it was kind of dangerous. It looked as if it would cave in at any minute. And once— well, I thought of going in, but it—"

"Ma'am, I asked you if you gone in?" Dan Tatum issued this insult in a whisper, his head lowered like a bull.

Mrs. Bishop opened her mouth.

The figure of John L. Lewis suddenly folded up as if the presence behind the façade of the United Mine Workers' refusal to go to work had deliberated and decided on the seizure of the mines. P.Q. made his entrance into the room.

"Oh, hello, Sheriff Tatum," he said as if to a long-lost friend. "Won't you sit down?"

"No, sir. I just come on here to—"

"I'm P. Q. Bishop."

"Yes, sir."

"What is that paper that you've got in your hand?"

"I got this warrant—"

"That you wanted me to see. Just hand it here, please."

"This here warrant was issued by the County Recorder's Court of Ephesus, requesting that Mrs. Clara Q. Bishop appear on Tuesday, May fourth, in Recorder's Court of Poltray County on charges of breaking and entering said Count house on lower Pack Mill Road and committing larceny and—"

"Thank you."

The red drained from Mrs. Bishop's face, leaving it an ashen mummy.

Loco Poco twined like a mosquito and began eating her fingers. Irene shook. Urie's brains crackled and shrank like scrambled eggs.

Only P.Q. pretended that a disgrace had not happened. He took the warrant to the same iron standing lamp that had played P. Q. Bishop to his Mrs. Polenta, and there he turned it back and forth under the light, pretending to study it. His nose roared out of his wrinkles like a train from a tunnel, and his mouth spread with great hypocrisy.

"Yes. Well, we will be glad to appear on May fourth. I guess you had a long walk down here, Sheriff Tatum, didn't you?"

"I come in the car."

"You came to the wrong door. That is the door we use," said P.Q., pointing through the dining room.

"That's all right, sir. I'll go out by this door right here."

"Gag Booch is your cousin, isn't he?"

"Yes, sir."

"Is that on your mother's side or your daddy's side?"

"My daddy's mother's. She's aunt to Gag's step-grandmother."

"Well, well, well."

"How many wells make a river?" parroted Loco.

P.Q. turned his face, beaming, upon Loco Poco, clapped Dan Tatum on the shoulder, and invited him to partake of his loud laughter as if at a conclusive joke of Will Rogers. The whole family echoed this laughter, but Dan Tatum looked at his feet.

"I do business with Gag. Yes, sir. What, you insist on going out the front door? Well, be careful, watch your step. Some of that old lumber has nails in it."

Etched in the doorway like a big upside-down heart, Dan Tatum's backside disappeared into the darkness. The dogs barked and began deviling him again.

"I'll come out with you," called P.Q.

"Naw. Ain't no need." Dan Tatum opened up his flashlight and trained it on the animals as if they were war criminals.

Long after the light had become a small bobbling dot upon the darkness, the car door slammed, the dogs quieted, the motor started, and the car zoom faded, there was silence.

Mrs. Bishop faced P.Q. and in a low, intimate voice, as if no one were in the room but the two of them, she said, "P.Q., what am I going to do?"

P.Q. raised John L. Lewis with the same loud rustling noise with which he had folded him, replacing his gaze with John L. Lewis's gaze, and his silence with the message in half-inch type: LEWIS PROPOSES 15-DAY TRUCE.

The next day the Bishop girls talked gaily and vociferously about clothes, food, classes, everything except what was on their minds. But shame had a palpable consistency. They could not look straight into each other's eyes or into the eyes of their mother.

It was Loco who broke the pretense down. That night as Irene passed down the tapestried hallway she asked in a trembling voice through the shepherds' crooks, "Will Mamma go to prison?"

"They can't put her in prison."

"But it's grand larceny."

"It's not grand. It's only larceny," said Urie, who was sitting in her cubicle upon her bed.

"What's the difference?"

"I don't know."

Intense and automatic, the three gathered in Loco's room with the artificiality of a Communist meeting.

"I told you we should have warned her," accused Irene.

"It was my fault. I never knew this would happen. I loved it that she stole!" Loco began to cry.

"Keep still," ordered Urie. "Do you think crying's going to help?"

"But—"

"Shut up. If it had been the A & P it would have been worse."

"But will they put her in jail?"

"No, I don't think they'll put her in jail. They'll let her off with a warning, maybe."

"You mean a suspended sentence."

"They could fine her," said Irene.

"A fine!" This introduction of money brought their eyes to a frantic impasse.

"A fine!" repeated Irene viciously. "They give you a fine. If you can't pay the fine, then you have to go to jail."

"Quit talking about that!"

"Yeah," plumped Loco. "Do you see P.Q. worrying?"

"He's thinking of settling out of court." Irene dealt out the law terms as a shill does cards.

"How do you settle out of court?" asked Loco.

But none of them knew.

[363

"Do you realize," said Urie, wishing to crack their shame open with lucid logic, "that the incredible thing about this disgrace is that it is being perpetrated by lowdown white trash that we have always despised? Didn't we look down on Dan Tatum? Now he has absolute control of our lives. It's enough to make you turn Christian and repent."

"You don't have to talk that junk," said Irene.

Loco smiled like a mournful ghoul.

In the following days Mrs. Bishop turned into an object in their minds. Like a patient admitted to a hospital, whose self fades into unimportance compared to his illness, she became in person subordinate to her crime. She would go on trial like a dummy before Judge Ledbetter. On the surface everything appeared the same. Mrs. Bishop went about her household duties passively. The only sign of anything different in her existence was the fact that, for the first time in four years, instead of sewing for the children, she was making herself a dress. It was white with dark blue polka dots. She had found the cloth that night in a carton box.

What was strange was that Mrs. Bishop, the one person to whom the Bishops would have turned in trouble, was herself the one that had gotten the family in trouble. Urie thought of this. Having opened the door to disloyalty by betraying Zebul, she now had the talent to practice thoughts of disloyalty in their extremes. The more dignified Mrs. Bishop acted in the nadir of family disgrace, the more relentless became Urie's rehearsal of the future. What would it mean? Urie saw headlines in the *Ephesus Weekly:* MRS. P. Q. BISHOP APPREHENDED ON LARCENY AND TRESPASSING COUNTS. "Local housewife, wife of P. Q. Bishop of Pack Mill Road, caught stealing sewing kit and books from Count property. Mother of three apprehended in theft. Mother of three arraigned." Urie tried to think up some quotation Mrs. Bishop would utter in defiance to the charges, but she could not. Henny Pinney Walley now no longer needed to be jealous of the family. Everyone would read these headlines and know. Bostwick first. Then Mrs. Ransome, Opal Granger, and Opard Bigelow Granger, in that order. Urie even thought: I will never get a scholarship now. Everything they had ever built up in Ephesus destroyed. Down, down, down. She built doom in these fantasies like voodoo, but nothing availed the passage of days, and the outrage that finally swallowed up disloyalty was huge, but it was also futile.

A week before the trial P.Q. decided to play his one card. He went to the ABC store and bought a quart bottle of Old Crow. On Thursday he fiddled around the house nervously. In the afternoon he dressed up in his best suit. It was gray and shiny and too big, with very small lapels, an extinct style ten years gone.

"You had better put on a dress," he said to Mrs. Bishop as he took the shoe-polish out of the kitchen cabinet.

"Put on a dress" meant put on a good dress.

"But I haven't finished this hem!" Her eyes popped out behind the sewing machine, but it was from hope rather than fear, for action was being initiated. She finished the hem while P.Q. polished his shoes on the kitchen steps. She did not know where they were going, though she suspected it was to Judge Ledbetter's office, and she decided not to ask until the right moment.

The departure was on foot, for P.Q. had not fixed the bucket seat next to the driver's in the blue truck; it was not fastened to the floor. The ceremony, with the furtive audience of Loco, Irene, and Urie gathered at the baggy screen door to witness the two children going alone into the wilderness, began with the hushed and long-deferred question, "Where are we going?"

"Oh. To the office of that alcoholic illiterate."

The consistency of P.Q.'s silence was as hard as metal, and even Mrs. Bishop's moving blue polka dots could not dislodge any more words. It portended nothing itself, neither that he felt condemnation nor that he felt sympathy. It was Mrs. Bishop's business, and, being hers, was especially not his. This ruthless lack of interest had given Mrs. Bishop a sense of relief at first, and then a desire to tell him the actual truth. But she never did tell him the truth because he positively did not want to hear it. Stealing, like sickness, sex, and affection, was better ignored. Compared to institutional crimes like the Spanish Inquisition, baptism in rivers, or the NRA, it was peanuts. But people could never look into their own faces; they always wanted absolutes.

The actual mechanics of the operation attracted P.Q. He bridged into his character of "big guy" by working himself into a pose halfway between Al Capone and King Zog, with the disadvantage of looking like Pope Pius *after* the Jews were stuck in concentration camps. A disgrace was a bad medium. P.Q. did not mind Dan Tatum because he was a redneck. But Judge Ledbetter, although a cracker, was at the top, and people at the top were to P.Q. crooks. P.Q.'s last weapon was the arrogance of his freedom. He felt no guilt whatsoever about Mrs. Bishop, but it was the same trait that made him ruthless about the unimportance of money.

Mrs. Bishop followed him up a dingy stairway over Nick's grill, eying the brown-wrapped bottle of Old Crow with hope. He switched the bottle to his left hand at the top and swept past a fat secretary filing her finger-nails, straight into the dirty mahogany office.

"It's a long time since I've been in to see you," he announced, never having been there in his life. "This is my wife, Mrs. Bishop."

Judge Ledbetter was surprised. He was a small square man with a red face and purple veins in his nose, a cracker-barrel lawyer who drank from noon to midnight and made underhand money in league with the police from Negro moonshiners. He owned a lot of real estate, half of Nigger-town, and had just wangled a pile of pre-fab housing from the government, which he was renting out at high prices to students. He served in Record-er's Court one day a week. He had had infantile paralysis when he was a child, so, although his legs were not paralyzed, he walked in a strange, waddling way, leaning his body far to the right on one leg and far to the left on the other. He also kept a perpetual catlike smile under his gold-rimmed spectacles, which made his face not so much sinister as unbeliev-able. The icing to all his enterprises was his four second-rate daughters, one of whom aspired to be an opera singer.

"Glad to meet you," he said, half rising. "Won't you sit down?"

"Thank you. Oh, I meant to bring you this before." P.Q. gave him the bottle, and the judge set it on his desk.

"What can I do for you?"

"Well, there is this little trouble. Some Negroes saw my wife taking a walk down to the old Count property, you know. We often take walks down there." P.Q. in the role of American family man sounded phony. "It's very beautiful looking across the Haw—you know—the bridge. You know the place?"

"Certainly do."

"Wonderful site. The view."

"Yes."

"Well, you know these niggers." P.Q. leaned forward conspiratorially.

Judge Ledbetter obliged. "Hehhehheh."

"So the sheriff came up to the house with complaints about trespass-ing."

"Trespass, eh?" Kindly syrup flowed from the judge's mouth.

They discussed trespass. Mrs. Bishop had saved some things from rotting in that derelict dump, said P.Q. After all, the stuff was molding. She didn't realize and never thought about the consequences, the more foolish she.

For half an hour they talked.

P.Q. and Mrs. Bishop sat waiting. Their hands were folded.

"Well," began Judge Ledbetter, "I just don't think I can call it off at this stage. You see, it ain't no nigras that's the plaintiff; they're only the witnesses. It's the state." The refusal had the same consistency and flavor of syrup as the build-up. Judge Ledbetter leaned over and patted Mrs. Bishop's hand. "I wouldn't worry about it, ma'am, if I was you. It won't amount to nothing."

Mrs. Bishop melted like a pancake.

But P.Q. rose, disgusted. His Old Crow, his polished shoes, his cacklings at niggerdom, all in vain.

"Thank you," he told Judge Ledbetter at the threshhold.

"Thank you," he repeated at the top of the stairs.

"Thank you," he mocked at the bottom.

On the street he stepped on Mrs. Bishop's Achilles heel, looking straight ahead with disgust at her playing pancake to Judge Ledbetter's syrup.

"You're walking on my heel!" cried Mrs. Bishop.

But P.Q. did not speak; he looked straight ahead and waited for her to walk faster.

At four-thirty they arrived back home. Mrs. Bishop's polka-dot dress was wrinkled. P.Q.'s shoes were dusty. Mrs. Bishop heated up the macaroni from yesterday, and, without even waiting to change clothes, she and P.Q. sat down at the table. They ate wordlessly.

In the living room Urie pretended to translate the "Song of Roland." Irene threaded her U-Weave It set four times with red yarn before she got it right.

Only Loco Poco refused these hypocrisies. First she peeked and saw P.Q. suck in a long string of macaroni. Then she moved up and occupied the entire doorway with her body.

"What did Judge Ledbetter say?"

Mrs. Bishop waited for P.Q. to answer.

P.Q. waited for Mrs. Bishop to answer. He turned and looked straight through Loco as at an unwanted mule. He returned to sucking in the macaroni string. After a long thought, during which the macaroni string disappeared, he announced, "That dir-r-ty crook. He owns two hundred and fifty niggershacks in this town and lets the rats run around the outhouses. That man is no judge. He is a dead letter!"

P.Q. lifted his lips significantly from his gums and guffawed belligerently.

Everybody laughed obligingly, except Loco.

"If he drinks all that whisky you took him, he will become known as Judge Bedwetter," she said.

At eight-fifteen on the day of the trial Mrs. Bishop hoisted herself into the bucket seat of the laundry truck and waited for P.Q. to slam his door. He pushed his foot eight times to pump the gas pedal, while Mrs. Bishop sat silent. Then he slammed his door. He turned the key. It did not work. He turned the key two more times. Still the truck did not start. On the fourth try the motor caught and he gunned it. Mrs. Bishop concentrated on his ceremonial coaxing of the machine for five more minutes. It was an exhibition of patience. But after they had proceeded down the driveway and hurtled down Pergamus Avenue, after he had driven the right front wheel over the Ephesus Inn curb, almost bumped into Amy Grispin White's mother's Buick on Main, and driven through a red light at the post office, she said, "Why don't you watch what you're doing?"

He gave her a long dirty look, to which she remained unrepentant.

A red motorcycle tried to pass. P.Q. pushed down the gas pedal. In the acceleration the bucket seat upon which Mrs. Bishop sat turned over backward. The motion of its upending was slow and easy, like a rocking chair's. Her feet achieved the height of the windshield and stayed there for twenty-five seconds. The motorcycle passed defiantly and cut in. P.Q. was forced to hit the brakes. She slammed down with a staccato speed in inverse ratio to the legato of her upending. It was as if she had appeared suddenly after a long vacation abroad.

"I thought you were going to fix this bucket seat."

All that anger at Judge Ledbetter, all that ignominious stalling about hiring a lawyer, now she was forced to go to trial with no lawyer at all, she thought, full of self-pity. She knew all lawyers were crooks, but you had to have a lawyer, didn't you? According to P.Q. this was a faulty syllogism.

"Your driving is worse than Mrs. Polenta's." She sniffed.

But her sense of shame was on the brink of transformation. Negligence, frustration, and rejection transmogrified it into a quality of positive value. So that when P.Q. parked the laundry truck in front of the town hall, she was radiant with energy. The milling crowd of Negroes flocked like sheep around the town-hall entrance parted. She alighted from the paneled door of the truck and slammed it behind her. She mounted up the steps through the parted black sea of eyeballs like a ludicrous queen.

"Here! Here it is!" whispered Urie, trembling.

Irene, not daring to steal, had bought the *Ephesus Weekly* from Sutton's and actually paid five cents, but did not dare open it. They were forced to this extemporaneous secret congress of three. And it was Urie who actually conducted the opening.

It was on page 5, toward the bottom of the page, under a headline saying MAN ACQUITTED. There followed a list of the court cases of the week. Mrs. Bishop's was the twelfth and the only one that did not have the word "Negro" after the name.

The paper said: "Mrs. Clara Q. Bishop, for trespassing, entering, and petty larceny. Nolo contendere. 3 months suspended sentence. $50 and costs, fine."

"Nobody'll ever see it," breathed Urie, feeling suddenly weak, sitting on her bed.

"What's *nolo contendere?*" asked Loco.

"The fifty dollars. How will they ever get fifty dollars?" said Irene.

CHAPTER 45

Two days later something happened that drove everything else out of people's minds. It happened in broad daylight. It was a hot day with sheet lightening. Miss Picke was walking from her fish-and-nuts store toward Haw. She was lured or forced into a pick-up truck, carried up Old Route 98 to New Hope Chapel, and raped in the churchyard. She was dead, and her old brown dress was found up over her head. She had been wearing her oxford shoes with the carved tongues, but she did not have on her ankle socks. One shoe was found nine feet away from her body. The second shoe was still on her. Police found flesh and hair under her fingernails. But no one had any idea of who the murderer was.

Everything stopped short when the first news percolated into town. People on their way to the post office, students in transit from one class to another, and professors on their way to Swine Hall for lunch stopped in the moment of discovery. The event became legendary while it was happening.

Loco Poco was in the Music Building. A boy she knew, named Dick Edwards, came in licking a chocolate ice-cream cone, saying, "Guess what! Miss Picke was raped and murdered." Up to that minute she had been intensely hungry. She put down her flute, sat in a desk chair, and listened to details. Then suddenly she thought the words, I want my Mamma, and got up to go home. She did not think of Miss Picke on Pergamus Avenue, but she almost fainted by the power plant. When she got home there was no one there, so she sat on her coffin bed and stared at the shepherds and their crooks.

Mrs. Bishop had been in the ten-cents store looking for pinking shears. When she heard the clerk telling Mrs. Opard Bigelow Granger this news, there was only one thing clear in her mind. This was that it was folly even to think of buying pinking shears when she and P.Q. had raked up everything they had had to pay the fifty-dollar fine.

Urie had gone to Haw to try to borrow Zebul's social-science notes for an exam. It was the first time she had been to his house since she had betrayed him. But Zebul was gone, and Henny Pinney did not know anything about social-science notes. Henny Pinney had just heard the news, and there were three women with her in the yard.

"I thought I heard screams," Henny Pinney was saying.

"Yeah. I heard screams all the way down the highway, but I didn't think nothin' of them," said the other Haw woman. "You know how kids fool around shouting and carrying on in their daddies' pick-up trucks. Even with gas-rationing."

"I swear I actually saw 'em!" said the third woman. "It was a blue pick-up truck. They was fightin' or something. If I'd only known now that that was Miss Picke screaming all the way down to New Hope Chapel!"

Urie stared at Henny Pinney with her wide shell-eyes distended. What had been a distant suspension of dislike now crystallized into superstitious hate. How could this woman be Zebul's mother?

She started walking home fast, congratulating herself on having betrayed Zebul. Her mind was too disarranged to think of Miss Picke at all.

It was only when she got home that she thought of Miss Picke. This was because Irene had just got home, knowing nothing, and asked, "What's wrong with Loco Poco?"

There was a hushed atmosphere in the house. Loco was lying in her darkened room, crying. Mrs. Bishop had just told Irene, and Irene stared at Urie like a ghost. Mrs. Bishop spoke in whispers.

Mrs. Bishop, Irene, and Urie sat in a threesome around the table. They did not speak. A lizard-like silence scuttled between them, and they did not even look into each other's eyes.

Finally Mrs. Bishop said, looking down at her hands, which smoothed out the wrinkles in the tablecloth, "I know. It is so horrible that it makes me sick myself."

They sat in this stunned silence for five minutes, each one turned private and inward. For the respectable people like the Bishops, thought Mrs.

Bishop, and the other families like the Grangers, the Boehms, the Akers, the Lowestofts, who tried to bring their children up reading books and aware of the ideals of love and freedom, steering their children's minds into decent, wholesome channels, even with such errors as her stealing or their living in this shack, unlike the Boehms, the Grangers, the Akers, or the Lowestofts, all the same Miss Picke's murder was less a fact than an intrusion, a chasm in the linings of their lives. Perhaps it was a rehearsal of the brutal organic nature of themselves as men. This was why it was too revolting to bear.

Urie got up and went to her own room and rustled around in her bureau drawer for the secret place she had hidden the notebook in which she had written her plans and alternatives on Bostwick.

She left eight pages after her last entry on Bostwick and wrote: "The Sick Futility Feeling of the World if Miss Picke Can Be Murdered." Underneath she began a paragraph: "It makes all seem worthless. If the world is so bad that Miss Picke has to be murdered, I am glad Mamma steals. Why was Miss Picke murdered? This proves there is no God. If there were a God so mean that people are better than God, then what would be the use of anything?"

She thought. She became inspired. "Aha!" she wrote. "Perhaps Miss Picke deserved to die." She underlined *"deserved."*

It was at that point that Urie began to hate not Henny Pinney, and not Zebul, but Miss Picke herself.

She became aware of Loco Poco's stifled sobs.

"Shut up!" she barked. And her hate of Miss Picke swelled up to preternatural proportions, so that she felt saved, even heady with the discovery that people *must* court their own destinies. There was Loco Poco sniveling, she who had brought Miss Picke into the heart of Bishopry. "Keep quiet!" she wanted to cry again, but she controlled herself, saving and savoring her hatred for Miss Picke.

When P.Q. came home, he did not talk about it. But Urie knew that he had heard.

Later, while Irene was washing the dishes and Loco drying them, her face all puffed up from crying, Urie heard P.Q. answer something that Mrs. Bishop had said in an uncharacteristically soft tone. He said, "The poor cuss."

The next day was hot. Before he had even got to the Bishops', Loco Poco waylaid Zebul. She had been keeping watch with the dogs in the tall grass, and the moment she saw him she rushed out. He knew it had to do with Miss Picke, even though she was laughing, cajoling, teasing him not to go up to the house but to go to the pine grove right now.

"Right this minute!"

"We can't do it in broad daylight!" he said, shocked.

"Why not?"

He paid no attention to her but started walking up the driveway with the dogs at his feet.

"There's no one there!" she said.

And when he saw that it was true and paused, she came and brushed up to him and opened up his shirt, sliding her hands across his chest, across his nipples.

"Come on, Zebul, let's do it right now. I want to do it now, when it's hot, and the pine needles will be warm. Just think of it!" Her breath was thick in his ear and her voice suffused, lilting. He smelled her musky odor permeated with a sweet smell of cold cream and honeysuckle. He melted, had an erection, and at once grabbed her around the waist, his heart beating. In complete inundation of his senses, he was no longer aware of who or what she was. But all the way up the railroad track with the ties exuding giant breaths of creosote and the ribbon rails flailing his eyes like knives of sun, with the salt coming out bathing his temples in sweat, dragging her only a few yards off the path, he asked himself what it had to do with Miss Picke.

She took his shirt collar in her teeth. She was in such a hurry to get at him that two buttons ripped off.

"Hurry up! Hurry up!" she moaned, because he took too much time to unbuckle his belt and draw his pants down from his hips.

He thrust into her the moment his hands felt her breasts. She twisted, sighed, flexed like an animal, caressed him with her body, and they did it five times in a row, she moaning in a low voice and sighing, even grunting, a sound that made him recognize for the first time that it was Loco Poco. They had both gone out of their heads. They were completely exposed, naked in a bare field in the sun. They had been there so long their bodies were red with sunburn.

But she would not leave him. She followed him home.

At the entrance to the honeysuckle bushes, where the beehives sat, she said, "Go on in and study. I'm just going to sit here for a little while."

"Why?"

"Because I like to."

"You can't. Pretty soon it will be dark and they'll be looking for you."

"Oh, go in. I'll tell you when I'm going."

He went in and started doing his calculus graphs. Everything was strange, for the heat was still thick upon the air. He understood nothing. He looked out of the window of his little house. He thought he heard some sounds. Then he turned back to his graphs again. What was she doing?

"It's time for you to go," he said, going to the door. She was sitting, staring transfixed at one of the hives. Her mouth was moving.

"What are you doing?"

"Nothing."

"Tell me."

"I was telling the bees."

"Telling them what?"

"About Miss Picke. If you tell bees about the death of someone, that will prevent dying. Now you won't die, nor Urie, nor Irene, nor Mamma, nor P.Q., nor me."

"Superstitious," he said. He almost took her arm, but she looked at him in such a way that he knew that if he touched her he would be making love to her some more.

"Come on. I'll walk you halfway home," he said. "By the road this time."

But the halfway point was Miss Picke's fish-and-nuts store. Dark, abandoned, it looked like the vacant gas station it had once been before she moved in. He could not leave Loco Poco there.

He walked her to the bottom of the Bishops' driveway, and then he ran home. Later he looked up under "Bees" in his Funk and Wagnall's *Dictionary of Folklore*. It said:

Almost everywhere in Europe and quite generally in rural sections of the United States, people still tell the bees. If this is not done they will either leave or die or stop making honey. This is possibly a remnant of an old European belief that bees were messengers to the gods and notified them of mortal deaths. In Ireland not only are the bees told of a death in the family, but crepe is hung on the hive. The Irish tell their secrets to the bees; any new project is also told them in the hope that the bees will prosper it.

On May 11 the Kingston paper carried the headline: 72-YEAR-OLD COED RAPED AND MURDERED.

"If you think them police are ever going to catch a murderer, you're crazy," said Hoke Tabernacle, hugging his bare feet into his trousers crotch. "Why, an hour after they discovered the body New Hope Chapel grounds were filled with so many police footprints it looked like a herd of elephants had gone on a rampage."

A carnival atmosphere took over Ephesus and gave the news a festive quality. The newest in the chronicle of Ephesian murders deserved wit. The Haw people wallowed in the horrible details, but the Ephesians improvised.

Lacey Ransome inadvertently made the remark in eighteenth-century literature class, while they were studying sonnets, that some fair ladies could be plucked but not picked. Opard Bigelow Granger said that remark might pass muster in the Education Department, but not in the English Department. The Education Department countered with a remark by a graduate student that he hoped Miss Picke had been meet material for the treatment she got. Other puns dealt with being picked up in a pick-up truck, and people who said that they could use such a pick-me-up. The effluvium of the crime brought forth such a hysterical quality that even children joined in it. One child from a good family lay on the ground and imitated the position of Miss Picke when they found her. And Helmut Boehm's six-year-old boy almost beat up the Rockford girl whom he made pretend to be Miss Picke, bringing forth accusations from the other children that that proved he was a Nazi. Gag Booch said Miss Picke had probably tried all her life and finally succeeded.

But there was nowhere in the Bishop frame of reference to fit Miss Picke's murder. After three days they all gathered around the dining-room table while Zebul was there. It was a curious fact that Miss Picke superseded all divisions and thoughts of betrayals among them, bringing them together upon an eerie, unselfconscious plane where they experimented in a ritual devoted to accepting the unacceptable.

"Just think. We knew Miss Picke."

"Miss Picke sat right at this table."

"And Zebul, remember? That's the time you read your theme about murder and punishment. Remember?"

"Plato."

"She sat right here with her mouth open."

"We have known a person who was raped and murdered," said Urie. "It's incredible."

"We have known a person who was raped and murdered."

"Must you repeat that?"

"You have to repeat the reality to even begin to attain the idea of reality."

"No. That's not true," began Zebul.

"I wonder what it feels like to be raped," interrupted Loco.

"Let's talk about something pleasant," said Irene.

"Do you really think she screamed all the way down the highway?"

"If I were raped, I wouldn't fight," said Irene. "You shouldn't fight."

"Last fight in the blue pick-up truck," said Urie, still searching for the proper caption.

"Green," said Irene.

"If it had been a blue panel truck, they could have accused P.Q.," said Loco.

"I thought of going to New Hope Chapel," said Urie. "But I couldn't do it."

"To understand ugliness?" asked Zebul, his heart beating. "To imbibe ugliness?" The same as staring at the drunk nigger, he thought, but he could not say it. Yes. The day had passed for the Cult of Ugliness. In all their adventures with stealing, betrayal, love, ambition, and desire, there had never been a true insult of divinity until now.

"Well, there's one good thing about Miss Picke's murder," said Urie, trying with a hard, inflexible voice to maintain her hatred of Miss Picke, now fast fading, like smoke. "It took everybody's minds off Mamma."

Loco appeared not to have heard a word. "I still wish Houghton Mifflin had published Miss Picke's book, even if it didn't make sense. Don't you, Urie?"

The next Monday six police cars began buzzing around Galbraith's Lumber Yard, two miles out of Haw on Old 98. Word leaked out that Mr. Galbraith was the murderer. Mr. Galbraith had a blue pick-up truck. A broken string of pearls had been found in his garbage can. Also there were fingernail scratches on his cheek and chin. Various Haw-yoos had seen the Band-Aids. Somebody had also seen scratches on his left arm. The police checked the hairs and blood under Miss Picke's fingernails.

Hoke Tabernacle said that these rumors were so cheap that they could not be believed. Therefore people would believe them. Professors did not take stock in such flagrant mythological vulgarities. They even claimed to take no interest in the illiterate germination point of rumors. But it was the rumors' cheapness and vulgarity that made them irresistible to the scientists of Jeffersonianism. As old Ephesians, they understood Ephesus. When the time came that the gods wanted to make fun of Academia they created a pageant in its underside. This was happening now. So old Ephe-

[375

sians, accustomed to the bizarre, rode these details with gusto, for they represented a Pandoric storm of all the diseases of bad taste that were denied the high-minded in such an oasis.

Mr. Galbraith said he did not murder Miss Picke. He claimed that the broken string of pearls came from his girl friend, who worked as a part-time waitress in the bus-station café. Her name was Pearl Ida Bynum. That Mr. Galbraith, an upstart Southern cracker Jew, would throw a pearl necklace —he probably had had the bad taste to give it to her because her name was Pearl—into his garbage can was an excellent detail. The discrepancy that this necklace could have belonged to Miss Picke—who had ever seen Miss Picke wear a necklace?—was overlooked. In everybody's minds Mr. Galbraith had done it. He probably paid Pearl Ida Bynum to back up his story, for he could pay for anything.

By the next Saturday Mr. Galbraith's business was affected. Yet he was not even indicted. At the cost of twenty-five dollars, he took out a full-page ad in the *Ephesus Weekly*. At the top was a headline saying: ATTENTION. He offered a five-hundred-dollar reward for any information leading to the killer of Miss Picke, or to the apprehension of anyone known to be spreading vicious and vile rumors. It was the crowning laugh for the Ephesians. Aristophanes had taken over.

It was not that Mr. Galbraith was less the murderer in any sense, but the advertisement had given the rape and murder a certain dignity. Even wholesomeness. The pure energy of an oldtime immigrant was in this gesture, and it commanded the Ephesians' respect. They even hoped that Mr. Galbraith had been the rapist, for Miss Picke would have been well served to have met her end at the hands of Mr. Galbraith.

No one came forth.

Mr. Galbraith was not indicted.

The police footprints at New Hope Chapel were left to erode in coming summer rains.

C H A P T E R   46

There was a knock at the door of the philosophy office. Urie jumped up from the typewriter, practicing the words, "I am typing a book for Helmut Boehm." It was Bostwick.

"So this is where you are!"

What if Zebul had been here?

Bostwick was in no hurry. He looked around the room in a comprehensive, openly curious way. "Let's get a Coca-Cola."

To connect Bostwick with Coca-Cola was incongruous. She pulled the paper out of the typewriter and put it in her notebook.

The effect was strange, walking with Bostwick into the Y. It was the first time he had ever taken her to a public place. She breathed into the wax cup of ice and watched her breath steam up. Why had he sought her out? He had never done it before. She did not dare ask.

This time, more than at any other time she had been with him, there was leisure, as if time had stopped, to enjoy a primary emotion, pride. To be seen with a Navy officer meant she was a girl, a regular girl, she had a date, she was prettier than other girls, more desirable. She remembered the first time she had had this emotion, when she had walked down the street with him and Zebul. Since then, whenever she had walked down the street with Bostwick, the occasion had been blighted by a fear they might meet Zebul.

Now, miraculously, she and Bostwick walked down the street, familiars with those debutantes the trees, who, fashionable with the shocking, brilliant greens of May, were leaning over them, trying to pick up any scrap of talk they might hear, and clapping their leaves as if flushed, proud of the sight that Bostwick and Urie made.

Olive Akers passed and said hello. Urie nodded casually, as if she did not feel it spectacular to be with Bostwick. Yet it was all true. Was she not having a love affair with him? Was he not testimony that she had captured him whom any other girl would have given eyeteeth to be with? Even though she knew this emotion to be false and the facts different, it was true. It was false, petty, social, and it made her laugh as if she were putting something over on someone—slightly bitter laughter. Illusions always lived in one's own head. Who could believe that a man like Bostwick would drink Coca-Cola? There was lightness in the air. Bostwick was quick. She skipped twice on the gravel gaily, and he held her by the elbow, catapulting her as if he enjoyed her caprices. Miss Picke raped and murdered less than two weeks ago, and here was she, skipping and jumping on the gravel sidewalk with Bostwick, the same place Miss Picke's footsteps had trod. Did she care? No. She could not feel anything. The very ability to have withstood horror, to be in this place doing these things, just as if she had never known Miss Picke, was a miracle that denigrated the individual. Walt Whitman had made the mouse miracle enough to stagger sextillions, but Skinner had trained it with electricity.

They returned to Bostwick's house. But instead of going in, Bostwick led her to the garden, and they sat down in the grass, crosslegged, facing each other.

"Urie," he said in a soft voice, "I'm leaving Ephesus. I got my orders."

Just as she had always known. That was why he had been happy and everything so light and gay. The way she had imagined feeling was the way she now felt. Her heart plunged downward, her mouth drained of saliva, and she felt faint. At the same time there was a burning sensation in her head.

"When do you go?"

"Tonight. At eight."

"How? I mean, what method of transportation."

"There is a bus for officers; it leaves from Faulkner Field."

"Let me go there with you."

She jumped onto forms now, eager, rapt, even supercilious, as if there had never been any relationship between her and Bostwick, as if her only identification with him would be that wartime parting and a kiss at Faulkner Field which, thirty years later, if she could imagine when the war would be over, she would remember.

"No," he said.

The grassblades formed separately, sharp as knives out of the ground. There were three hours left to find out. But she could not think of what to say, what question to ask to find out who Bostwick was.

"Where are you going?" she asked.

"I've been assigned to destroyer duty. I'll have an APO number. I'll give it to you and you can write me there."

But she knew he would never write.

"You're glad, aren't you, to leave Ephesus? Because you didn't like it here."

He took her hand and smiled. She did not want to cry, so she gritted her teeth.

"I want you to know that I never loved anyone as I loved you, Urie. You are the sweetest thing that happened to me in Ephesus."

"Am I?" she breathed. She opened her popping eyes even wider so that no tears would drop down her cheeks, and they were enlarged into a huge, wavering mirror in which Bostwick shook while she pretended she was not crying. He smiled at the sight.

She knew that she could throw herself upon him as on the day she had declared her love. She did not understand why she did not do it. But she had to ask him before he would be gone forever.

"You know I love you more than anything, Bostwick, don't you?" she said, rude and rough.

"Yes, I do."

"I never loved anybody in the whole world like that. But I don't understand you!"

It was a mistake. He looked at the ground. He pressed her hand as if she had never said that.

"The only thing I am sorry about is Zebul," he said. "You tell him I say good-by."

Phony! But she was completely conquered by it, as if in situations of meeting and departure (and she now saw that she would make her life stretch out with them) only words of this degree of phoniness could be said for the reason that reality was uncapturable, shocking, and unrecognized when it came.

"Yes, I will." All she wanted was one signal. "Bostwick—" she pleaded.

"Come on. I've got to pack."

They went into his apartment. She sat on the edge of the couch. Already the place was a strange place. She knew what it looked like without him there. He had occupied it for only a little while, and now he was gone. He had packed most of his things, so there was not much to do. He put shaving cream, razor, toothbrush, and his shoes into the bottom of a bag. He took his uniforms out of the closet and unzipped a big blue clothesbag. An hour passed. Neither of them talked. At last there were only a few minutes left.

"Where did you grow up, Bostwick?" she asked.

"Around Harrisburg."

"Were you like me and Zebul?"

"No. I was alone." He looked at her. "I was very happy, though. I saw everything as yellow."

"Yellow?"

"Yes."

"Was it beautiful?"

"No. Not really."

"I mean did you like it?"

"Oh, yes, I loved it. I was possessed of the color. I think I identified with it. It was me in another valence."

She looked at his face. It was free, happy. It was one of those moments at the end of a relationship when one takes the last chance for that intimacy which has never been achieved.

"Bostwick, why were you crying that day?"

"Crying?"

Was he going to lie now? But he was looking at her, interested.

"At the Ephesus Inn. Crying in a room."

"What are you talking about?"

"You were crying in the Ephesus Inn. The day when you came here the first time. Long ago, when you were a liaison officer. I saw you. I opened the door on you and saw you there crying."

She searched his face wildly, but he shook his head. He looked at the floor. His gray eyes registered nothing.

"Didn't you come in a Navy bus that August? Didn't you? Didn't you go to the Ephesus Inn in the Navy bus?"

"Yes."

"Didn't you have a room on the second floor?"

"Yes, I think so. I don't remember."

"Then it was you!"

He did not attempt to deal with her conflict. In the silence he was quiet.

"Why are you lying?"

"Urie—"

"Bostwick, don't you remember?" she asked in agony.

"No," he said.

"You swear—"

"Listen, Urie. The time has come when I've got to go."

She stood up from the couch primly. The clock said exactly eight. They walked down the stairs and out to the street, down Pergamus Avenue. Her heart was bursting.

"Bostwick, don't go and leave me and never tell me like this. I can't—"

"But you can't think I wouldn't tell you if I knew!"

She looked into his eyes and saw sincerity. "No, I know you would."

Halfway to the Ephesus Inn he stopped and put his hands on her shoulders. "Say good-by now."

"Good-by."

"I will write you."

"All right." Once more she burst out, "Bostwick, you know I loved you, don't you?"

"Good-by."

But she wouldn't kiss him, so he had to kiss her. It was a gentle kiss, like a stranger's. She stayed in that spot until he walked out of sight. When he was gone her sense of relief made her shoulders rise, and she turned around and started for home, her palms and neck wet with sweat. But she felt light.

CHAPTER 47

Loco Poco flipped her way into Urie's cubicle. She was going to ask her something. What?

"Urie—" she began.

But the question fled out of her head. It was not Urie she was looking at, but a sight that she had heard described. Urie's face was white and suffering, her hair the color of taffy. Her blue eyes, staring at nothing, were pouring down a milk of grief. In one second the picture was framed in Loco's mind and she remembered: incarnate grief. She backed away.

"Urie!" she begged, terrified.

The picture dissolved. Urie, caught, turned back to Urie and pulled a pencil out of her wrinkled sheet angrily.

"What do you want?"

"Nothing. But—Urie! What— What's the matter with you?"

"Nothing, for God's sake!"

"But you're crying!"

"*Who's* crying?"

"You are. I saw you!"

At this remark Urie began to laugh hysterically.

"Bostwick's gone!" guessed Loco, and impulsively she threw her arms around Urie's neck, catching her unaware. The laugh dissolved weakly.

But Urie was not like Zebul. It shamed her to cry in Loco's arms. "Get away from me," she groaned, pushing Loco away from her toward the flap-door with all her might.

Loco was not the least offended by this rebuff. She looked at Urie with the same awe and sympathy with which she had regarded her so long ago when Urie was punished for drowning the tricycle.

For three days Loco Poco remained in a strange state. She made no overtures to Zebul. She acted solemn and walked as slowly as a mendicant beggar. It was this act of walking slowly that suddenly made Loco seem her age. It was uncharacteristic. It created a distance between her and other people. Mrs. Bishop looked at her one day and thought: Loco Poco is fourteen years old. She was amazed. It affected everything. It meant that the Bishops had been in Ephesus three whole years. It meant that she, Mrs. Bishop, was three years older. But the strangest thing of all was that, although she had always imagined Irene and Urie grown-up women, she had never imagined Loco Poco growing up. Those quicksilver movements had guaranteed the jinni before child, woman, or old lady, and it was with a feeling of terror that Mrs. Bishop contemplated Loco Poco becoming a responsible woman.

That night Zebul kicked her under the table at supper and made a leering face at her. She looked straight at him as if she were looking at Braque in art class. She hated Braque.

"Meet me later," he whispered when Mrs. Bishop had taken the plates to the kitchen.

Loco Poco slipped out at nine-thirty and headed for the pinewoods. But instead of meeting him in one of her usual ways, weaving into him like a magic fog or bounding like a go-cart out of control, she rushed up to him with news.

"We've got to quit messing around with each other, Zebul."

"What?"

"Didn't you even notice? Bostwick's gone."

Bostwick was gone! When had he gone? Where? How had Zebul gone along, seeing Urie, and not even known it? But it was so long ago that he had made Bostwick die to him, filling himself up with Loco Poco, that the very word "Bostwick" from Loco's mouth had no reality. He could not take it in.

"What's Bostwick got to do with it?"

"What do you mean, what's he got to do with it? Now Urie hasn't got Bostwick. It was all right when Urie had Bostwick, but now she hasn't, so it's different."

"Are you crazy?"

"No."

"You mean to tell me you're being moral?"

Loco made a face.

"You? Ethical?" He howled with laughter, sat down on the ground, and pounded the pine needles with his hands in paroxysms, like a dog. She watched him, waiting for him to get through with these demonstrations.

At last he did. He looked up at her with concentration, half fake, as if to say, Well, you are sure one card. What are you pulling now? She looked back at him solemnly, knowing he still didn't believe her. Then he changed his tactics. He got up.

"Come on," he whispered. He brushed his head, nose, face, into her hair, breathing into her ear.

"Leave me alone, Zebul. Quit doing that."

He stood back, amazed.

"I feel different, that's all. It feels funny now."

"You *are* crazy!" he said.

"I am not."

"You can't just turn everything off. You know you want to do it!"

"I don't."

"That's a lie."

"Well, I don't care if you believe me or not," she said, turning her head sveltely. Feeling success with this new haughty manner, she walked out of the pinewoods to the railroad track.

"Do you realize I could beat you up and rape you and bash your face in and leave you here just like that nigger did to Miss Picke?"

"What nigger? Maybe it really was Galbraith!"

"On this very spot," he continued breathlessly, inspired, "where I stepped in the nigger's hand and was born—"

He choked the words back into his throat. It was the first time he had ever made a mistake.

She bent toward him. She was interested again. "What nigger's hand?" She looked as she had the first day she had met him, when she spooned the brownie into her mouth and used the word "old" as a password without significance.

"No nigger's hand."

"That's proof of the pudding," she said, and she smiled a knowing smile, aware she had caught him in a Urie-Zebul secret.

"What are you talking about?" he said loftily.

He walked her as far as the Bishop driveway and left her there with Scylla and Charybdis.

But he stayed up late that night and thought. Instead of being frustrated by this encounter, he gained a satisfaction from it. For he saw Loco, not in the different way which she had presented to him, but in a caprice more extreme than he had ever imagined.

He knew that in a few days she would be walking like lightning again. She would give up this resolution. For she was a complete weathervane. He knew her as no one else knew her in the world. He knew her blood fire, every wily mechanism of her, every catapult of her sexual nature. He thought of her as a nymphomaniac of the soul, because she gave every bit of her Loco Pocodom in sex. She held nothing back. And she held nothing back of her personality either. This was why she was so simple to deal with. Furthermore, she was fitted to him. Even though she was so impulsive in her twists and turns, she was undevious in her nature. She was not like Urie. He knew that she had loved him from the minute he had walked into the Bishops' door.

The next morning Zebul awoke with a strange feeling. He realized that Bostwick was gone. Therefore he could think of Bostwick.

Actually he did not feel anything toward Bostwick. With amazement he thought of Bostwick getting on a bus, leaving Ephesus, stopping at bus stations, drinking coffee, perhaps brushing his teeth this very moment in some billet on a Navy base. The very fact of Bostwick's existence amazed Zebul. The moment he realized that Bostwick was actually somewhere in the world this morning, he became a ghost.

People of a person's past were called ghosts. Zebul thought of people in his past. There was Quira Crabtree. Quira had left six months ago to go and work in a defense plant in California. Was she a ghost? The fact that he was old enough now to have ghosts in his past was novel and frightening.

He got up out of bed and picked up the bottle of cyanide from his desk and looked at it. The skull and crossbones made a double cross. There was a grace note of pleasure in his pun. Urie had double-crossed him with Bostwick. Now had Bostwick double-crossed Urie with his departure?

Everything seemed changed by the fact that Bostwick was gone. With Bostwick gone and sex between Urie and Bostwick obliterated, new material unwound from his consciousness, and he breathed in his old direction toward Urie.

He went to the campus that morning and looked for her. His doing this was curious to him. He had a desire to mention Bostwick to her. But it was not to rub it in. Not for revenge. No. It was more a matter of curiosity, as if only by her mentioning the word "Bostwick" could he understand the reality of Bostwick as a ghost. Yet he knew that he would not mention Bostwick and never would.

It was curious that ever since Bostwick's coming, whenever he looked for Urie he could never find her. This time he found her immediately. She was walking down a path by Malden Hall, and she did not see him. He watched her walk. He noticed her shoes, how they were worn at the heels. There was a hole in her sweater, and he could see her pink blouse through it.

He called her.

384]

She turned, smiled, said, "Hi," and came toward him. Together they walked to Peabody Hall, talking about Dr. Wakefield's definition of "negative capability." In their office Urie frowned and put a pencil between her teeth, just as if she felt nothing about Bostwick's being gone.

Ever since her betrayal, when he had looked at her, thickness had suffused him and blotted part of his mind out. The awareness of her having gone to bed with Bostwick, slept with Bostwick, caused a constriction actually physical, as if his senses were stifled by a wool blanket. It was not that he had hated her, or that he grieved. It was nothing definite. Only that consistency, thick, soft, and utterly suffocating, which had made him turn away from her. To think of her had entailed Bostwick, and he could not bear it. For it had involved her in the same way that he had been involved with Loco. It was that which was an offense to his perception of Urie.

But now he felt free, as if a weight were lifted from his shoulders, and in its place was an awareness of the infinity of the universe. It felt as it had always been. But it was not as it had always been. For he looked at her with a new consciousness. The Urie that had always been was now entwined by a mystery of what the memories of Bostwick were to her. So that his freedom was permeated with an additional thrill, even a fear, of some sadness which, sooner or later, he would have to deal with. But it had to do with that chance for truth that he felt well up within him, a truth that would surpass sadness and the fall of man.

The next afternoon Zebul went by the Bishops'. He rejected Mrs. Bishop's invitation to supper and stood by the open kitchen door, idly conversing about favorite ice-cream flavors.

"Pistachio has always been my favorite," said Mrs. Bishop. "Oh, my!"

"It's because it's green," interrupted Loco.

"But it's actually made of a nut," said Zebul pointedly, looking at her.

"Peach is my favorite," said Irene.

"I like peach too," said Mrs. Bishop.

"I bet you like strawberry," said Zebul to Loco Poco.

"My two favorite are chocolate and maple-walnut," said Urie. "I hate strawberry."

"Yes, I do like strawberry. But I like pistachio too because it's green and doesn't taste like what it ought to. I like surprising things," said Loco. "For instance, what would you taste like as an ice-cream cone? You'd probably taste like corduroy. Please may I have a Zebul Corduroy ice-cream cone?"

It was exactly as Zebul had thought. She had gone back to the way she was before. She teased him, flattered, cajoled him, and yet all this, passing under the family's eyes like a banner to reassure, betrayed not one hint that she had ever gamboled with him in the woods. She was so open that it was just as if she had never had this other existence with him.

The sky was pale and red.

"Go pick up your things, Loco. We've got to eat. And Zebul, stay if you want."

"No, thank you, but I will another day," said Zebul.

He followed Loco out beyond the barn, where she picked up her music books. He found himself acting in a strange, double-edged way. It was experimental. It was even deceitful.

For though now she did not walk slowly, and did not carry that cloud of preoccupation around with her, though she was nimble, hopping quixotically like a toad, yet now, alone, she made no overture to him.

"Meet me in the pinewoods after supper. At eight," he ordered.

"No."

"Why?"

"I told you."

"Don't you love me any more?"

"Of course I love you. But not that way."

"What way, then?"

"I don't want to do it any more with you."

"With who, then?"

A smile wreathed on her mouth, and she banged the music books in the rhythm of the "Bolero" against her knee, pretending she had not heard.

"If you won't do it with me, you don't love me," he accused.

She merely looked at him from her long lashes with a deprecatory gaze.

He left her at the well, she to return to the kitchen, he to go down the driveway and along the tracks home, his face bathed in the red relief of the sunset, his deceit intact.

By this deceit he unstabilized her. He made it appear that it was she who was being deceitful. And he covered up his own withdrawal from her.

In his mind a strange transversal was taking place. The very withdrawal that she had suggested was now invested in him. He grew thin and thoughtful. It was a transition that reminded him of his transition from baby fat in high school to the day he had met Urie. If he had learned sex with Loco, he was now changing from boy to man by giving up sex with her. He felt thinner. He felt sad. He felt pierce-eyed. He felt thrilled to bursting. He began to conceive of himself as a monk. He could not now submit himself to drowning in Loco's flesh. He had done it before because he had had no recourse. But everything had shifted subtly, and it was Loco herself who had opened up the new dimension. He was aware of the cost to himself, but he could not do anything else. For Loco by that whimsical intent of giving him up had opened to him the vision of himself as a unity.

He would be dependent now on no one. He was free again. He could keep Loco or he could graduate into the promise that he had once had with Urie. A promise that had been changed, threatened, made more stupendous, and finally made extinct by Bostwick's coming into their lives. The freedom was, in fact, terrifying.

And so he repeated his deceit every day for a week, spending all his time at the Bishops', not leading Loco on so much as, by his continual presence, his bantering, his philosophizing with P.Q. and Urie, leading up to the revelation of his decision.

It happened in the afternoon, with the sun still out on the other side of the shed, where Loco had followed to help him bring the ladder with which they were going to replace Mrs. Bishop's bad stairway up the chimney side. He had tipped the ladder to one side. Loco was standing next to him, with her arms out to receive the other end of the ladder. Instead she leaned up against him, her arms creeping about his shoulders. She rubbed herself against his chest and reached up her face to kiss him. She was smiling as she did this, as if she had not a thought that it undid everything she had said before.

Zebul pushed the ladder back against the shed and, feeling himself grow hot all over, reached back of him, got hold of her hands, and unwrapped them from him.

"You are incorrigible," he said gently but strangely, letting her hands go.

For a moment she acted abashed. She looked at the ground and drew a line with her shoe.

"I didn't mean to."

"Whew," he said.

"Pooh," she said.

They looked at each other—a naked look, very strange, because it spoke an agreement that was beyond either of them and stronger in some ultimate meaning than their lovemaking had ever been.

Then Loco burst into a titter of laughter and ran away, saying, "You can carry the ladder yourself, then."

He could be a monk. He could be cold as Bostwick. He could be a master of control. He cast his attention away from Loco, understanding nothing but what he had said about her. She was a genius and an incorrigible.

The next week he plunged himself into his studies. Final exams were coming up.

C H A P T E R   48

That summer Loco played three solos in the concert series. There was a college boy, a senior, named Cory Atwater, who took a shine to her and invited her to the summer's most fashionable fraternity dance. Her head was turned by the attention of the boy, and at home she begged to go. It was unheard of for any of the Bishops to have attracted a scion of society. And for it to be Loco! All the rules of acceptance were broken without cheating, stealing, or lying. Simply by the attraction of the boy. Yet it was entirely unsuitable that a mere sophomore in high school should be allowed to date a college senior. So Mrs. Bishop insisted that he be invited to the house before she would allow Loco to go anywhere with him.

P.Q.'s water and fire tests, undergone first by Zebul and then by Bostwick, were now applied to Cory Atwater. But Loco Poco, long graduated past Urie's state of mind, had no shame about the Shack life. In fact she diddled it as bait in front of Cory Atwater with the insouciance of a cat playing with its mouse. P.Q. made three sarcastic remarks and grunted. Cory was too enamored of Loco to be shocked, and treated Mrs. Bishop with such good manners and enthusiasm that she gave permission for Loco to go. He looked around the house as if there were nothing unusual in it at all.

His good looks, his athletic bearing, his gaiety, his money, and a certain innocence in him about the difference between his station and hers made him irresistible to Loco all summer. He was a football player and was handsome and popular and well known. And in addition to this, Loco had him in the palm of her hand, and the wielding of her power in such circles foreign to her made her heady. At the same time it delighted her that he was so ignorant of music, and she spent hours teaching him all the things that Dr. Nagy had taught her. He paid no attention, could not absorb the meaning of any of it. Instead he saw that he had a child-capricious genius on his hands, and he fell seriously and worshipfully in love with her.

It was she who enticed him at last into inescapable and impetuous love-making.

"Have you noticed, I look like you? You look like me. Our black hair and our black eyes. Why, we could be the same thing. Do you think we are the same thing, Cory?"

Although he did not take such remarks seriously, he could not escape some aspect beyond him which he had never considered before. He was not stupid, although he had failed one course in his junior year, which he had to make up that summer before he could get his degree. And the summer courses were his most successful academically in all his college career. This success, and the strangeness of having his life changed his last quarter in school by a lovemaking wilder than he had ever dreamed of, settled his future in his mind. Although he had joined mildly in locker-room boastings, he had not had many experiences with girls. He was typical of many handsome and popular BMOCs in having a reserve, a shyness that had kept him from profound experience. He was even wistful about it. Was love like this? With all his protective instincts aroused, he was delivered totally into Loco Poco's hands. Unable to imagine a future life without her, he wanted to marry her.

"But how can I marry anybody when I'm only a sophomore in high school?"

He would wait for her, he said, and she would be faithful to him. He spent many hours explaining the future to her. He was going into OCS, and it did not matter where he was. As soon as she graduated from high school, the exact moment, he would come back, or he would send for her and she would come to where he was, provided it wasn't in the Pacific or they hadn't started the second front in Europe, and they would be married. She agreed to do this with all the fervor of Cinderella agreeing to her future with the prince. Everything about Cory was an atmosphere of unreality that boded riches, success, an undreamed-of life in a gauzy future. When he told her about his family, she dreamed of her movie-production meeting with them as a young bride.

The reality of it was that she was enjoying his young body in the same unfettered and enthusiastic way that she had once enjoyed Zebul's. In some way they were even connected in her mind, although they were nothing alike. Only their "boyness" mattered, and the terms by which she maneuvered them. But Cory was outside the realm of her daily life. He was mythological, college, glamorous for the future, whereas Zebul was old, ancient, intimate, like a brother. Zebul was the only one who suspected what was going on. Afraid that he was going to say something about her carryings-on, she turned away from him. She spun her eyeballs in the air.

But he did not say anything. He only looked at her curiously, so that she knew he knew. She was spared having to accuse him of jealousy.

When Cory was leaving at the end of the first summer term, it was he who broke down, rather than Loco. He cried. He held her so tightly and kissed her so long with his football player's lungs completely inflated with breath, that she almost fainted. After that she received a barrage of awkward and impassioned love letters couched in Victorian language, which she answered at the rate of one to five, with piquant expressions. She was matter-of-fact compared with his fervency.

PART VI

PART VI

CHAPTER 49

The summer was more different for Urie and Zebul than any summer had ever been. As soon as the May examinations were over, Urie put all pride away from her and went to beg from Huntsucker again. This time he managed a loan for her from the University Women's Association. "I'm mortgaging my entire future," she told Zebul. They registered for two classes together. One was psychology, and the other was *Beowulf*.

The change between them was never mentioned. The President had spoken, Bostwick had gone, Loco had taken up with Cory Atwater, and they were different. But it was unmentionable. They spent more time together than ever before.

By July, Urie had received five letters from Bostwick. His orders had been changed from destroyer duty to a place on a Navy aircraft carrier. He was in the waters of the Caribbean. The letters were strange. They were warmer than he had been in person. He described the boredom of shipboard doings, Ping-Pong and alerts. He talked about the derivation of words. "Piacular" was one. It meant sinful. "Plethoric" and "sentient" were others. It was as if in retrospect he knew she would have liked such conversation. At the end of each letter he wrote that he loved her. The love words were sincere but general, as if he spoke about himself and humanity, rather than her. Each letter made him seem more remote. And when she wrote back to him, it was a joyless duty, as if she owed it to the memory of her ideal. As the summer retreated, the reality of Bostwick faded, so that after the fall term had started it was with surprise that she received his continuing letters. The past was frozen like a chunk of Arctic land that had split and dropped away. It seemed unbelievable, miraculous that there had ever been a life outside Ephesus, and now all that had departed from Ephesus, i.e., Bostwick, also seemed unreal, a testament of an idealistic past.

"I had a letter from Bostwick today," she told Zebul after medieval-romance class. It was a test for both of them. Her voice was deliberate and dead, and behind the deadness lay an experiment. To raise the ghost to make it die. To drive a spike into the weathered beam that was now the friendship of Urie and Zebul, a friendship so mute, so unexplained, so tested, so stoic that it seemed eternal.

"What did he say?"

"He is in Guantanamo Bay. In Cuba." Zebul waited. "It was a bloodless letter," she continued in grown-up tones. "You know Bostwick. Most of it he recounted how you catapult an airplane off the landing of the carrier."

"What a funny thing Bostwick was," mused Zebul.

"Yes."

"He doesn't seem real to me at all. He stopped being real so long ago that I don't know when he was real and when he wasn't. For you it is different than for me."

"He doesn't seem real to me now either."

But Zebul refused to heed the softness of her voice or the pleaful hint to leave their safe isle of stoic unity. He rejected the closeness of confidence.

"I have been alive ninety years," he announced, looking past her out over the treetops. They were walking the railroad tracks to Haw.

"And I a hundred. Zebul—" She stopped and looked at him. He turned his plum-shaped eyes upon her as if daring her, and she fell stone-silent again, never dreaming that in the new, hard lines of his mouth there was anything more than reminiscences of himself, her, and Bostwick. "I don't believe the past changes one, do you?" she asked softly.

"No. It only makes you more what you are."

"You know what, Zebul?"

"What?"

"I don't even believe in cause and effect. I mean, I understand now why no fifty-one-year-old person could tell us what the answer to life was."

"Why? You mean because it's different for everybody?"

"No. That's a banal idea."

"Then what?"

"I mean, you think something in events is the point of this or that, but it isn't at all. Everything leads up to something that is supposed to be the point, and the whole world thinks: Aha! That's it! That's what it was all for! But it isn't at all!"

He fastened onto her, quickening his steps. "What do you mean?"

"I don't know. But don't you feel that way sometimes?"

"Yes, I do. But I don't even know what you're talking about."

They laughed. They kicked their feet through the dying but raucous leaves. They felt enthusiastic, as if all the world were changed.

At the beginning of September, Mrs. Kanukaris sold the Shack to a Negro named Ellsworth Keck.

"Well at least now Kan-of-Kerosene can't complain about how we burned up half the barn!" cried Loco.

"Yeah. We're finally rid of that woman," said Irene. "Aren't you glad, Mamma?"

"But what's going to happen to us?" asked Mrs. Bishop. "What if this Mr. Keck wants to live here himself? What if we have to move?"

They looked at each other with worried eyes.

"To think we would end up fighting to stay in this stinking hole," mouthed Urie under her breath.

"Where else can we get such a cheap deal?" said Irene.

"That's enough of such talk!" commanded Mrs. Bishop. And turning to P.Q. she said, "We've got to make some arrangement with Mr. Keck."

On Thursday, Ellsworth Keck came to look at his property. P.Q. met him out by the roots of the third hickory tree. He pulled two sawhorses from the shed and invited Mr. Keck to sit on one of them. He sat on the other.

"It's a mighty fine day," he began.

"Yas suh."

P.Q. moved the conversation through the weather to the tobacco crop. Then he talked about the injustice of the poll tax for poor people. At last he brought up the subject of what Mr. Keck intended to do with the house. Mr. Keck shuffled his feet along the gravel. He wiped spittle from a corner of his mouth onto his forefinger.

"I couldn't afford to live in it nohow, as I got me a house of my own, so I reckon it be fine if you was to continue to live in it for a while."

"That's good." P.Q. soft-pedaled. "Now, I tell you what. Why don't you come over again sometime next week, and I can sign a paper on the rent."

The moment that Mr. Keck was gone P.Q. ordered Loco Poco to the typewriter. She was learning to type. He dictated an official-sounding lease, agreeing to pay rent at the rate of eighteen dollars per month for a period of five years. Loco made three errors. She corrected them with a red pen.

A week later Mr. Keck appeared again. This time P.Q. invited him into the house and motioned for him to sit at the steel desk. Then he gave Mr.

Keck the paper to sign. Mr. Keck studied the paper with his rheumy yellow eyes. Mrs. Bishop brought two plates of strawberry shortcake with ice cream, which she served on her best bone china. As soon as Mr. Keck had signed his name on the line, an act which took four minutes of wavering effort, she set the china down on the steel desk. Mr. Keck did not look at her. He bowed his head like a wily dog.

After he had gone they all jumped up and down in self-congratulation. "He signed it. He signed it. We don't have to move!"

"And I typed it. Isn't it beautiful?"

"It's legal, isn't it?" asked Mrs. Bishop anxiously.

"Sure it's legal. All you have to do is have it notarized to make it absolute."

"How much does notarization cost?"

"Oh, fifty cents or a dollar."

"Well, be sure you have that thing notarized as soon as possible. What a relief! I have to get supper!"

P.Q. put the new lease in a manila folder. Every day he intended to take the paper to the notary public, but he put it off to the next day. For he had become parsimonious over the years. He had become chary of every nickel and dime. Allied forces crossed the Straits of Messina and landed in southern Italy and Salerno, and by October, when the American troops had beaten their way to the stalemate of mountains and winter weather at Cassino, P.Q. had forgotten the lease completely.

C H A P T E R 50

Christmas vacation was coming again.

"Remember when you said you were never going to spend one more vacation in this house?" Loco asked Urie.

"I'm not."

Urie's decision was cast on December 14, an evening when she overheard her mother's voice cry in despair, "Oh, no, it didn't all leak out, did it?" P.Q. had opened the oil-barrel faucet to measure the oil. He had not fastened it tight again.

"What are we going to do?" asked Mrs. Bishop in the darkness, not realizing anyone but P.Q. was listening.

There was no answer. The silence gave tragedy substance. As with

Urie's betrayal, how could you defend what you did not mean to do and could not help?

The next day she and Loco staked out the room they would occupy. It was on the third floor of Winston Dormitory. Mrs. Gibbon was the housemother and lived in an apartment behind glass French doors on the first floor. They could avoid her easily, they figured. She would never know they were there. If she did see them, they had their excuse prepared: "I was just returning a book to Kenan Rivers." The room was Number 304. Name cards on the door announced that it belonged to Constance Dodge and Kenan Rivers. They chose it because of the names, because it had a bookcase containing Thomas Carlyle, *Crime and Punishment,* Tolstoy, and Ernest Hemingway, and a bed upon which sat a giant stuffed koala.

"You'll be expelled," warned Irene, "if they find out you're illegally occupying dormitory rooms in Christmas vacation. It would have been all right in high school, but now it's too late."

"Crap!" was Urie's attitude.

It was a measure of their consideration, ever since Mrs. Bishop's trial and the death of Miss Picke, not to involve their mother or P.Q. in any of their illegal doings. But since they were to be gone, they had to tell. Urie stayed in the background, letting Loco's enthusiasm enunciate the decision.

"Mamma, we're going to spend the vacation in Winston Dorm. Urie and me!"

"Do they know?"

"Who?"

"The authorities. The housemother."

"No. We decided to go without asking." Loco giggled. "Our room is on the third floor."

"What do you think of it, P.Q.?" asked Mrs. Bishop.

"Everbody is a free agent." He turned on Kaltenborn.

"They'll be expelled," warned Irene.

"I can't be expelled," said Loco.

"All they can do is throw us out," claimed Urie contemptuously. "That risk is nothing compared to spending one and a half weeks in a warm place."

The night of their departure for the dormitory, Mrs. Bishop made them a lunch of peanut-butter sandwiches, eight fig newtons, and some meatballs from supper, wrapped in waxed paper. They packed their things in their great-uncle's carpetbag, Mrs. Bishop's unsaid blessing to their venture, and she stuffed the paper bag of lunch on top.

"You'd think we were going to California," complained Urie. "We're gonna be right here to eat lunch tomorrow, you know."

But Loco reveled in these preparations. "We can eat in the middle of the night, Urie!"

"Maybe I'm crazy, but I don't blame them for wanting to get away from home this vacation," Mrs. Bishop stated to no one while she was packing the lunch. "Sometimes it is good for people to get away from their families."

On departing, Loco kissed everybody effusively, but Urie walked out of the house, only turning around by the well to shout, "Well, good-by."

The dormitory was silent, permeated with odors of its absent inhabitants. It smelled of girls' hair and carpets. A few light bulbs were on in the corridors. The girls kept carefully to the eastern staircase, far from Mrs. Gibbon's quarters. They breathed as softly as they could, and whispered.

"Feel how warm it is!"

"These carpets are so thick we could sleep on them."

"This is real luxury, you know it?"

"How would you like to really live here, Urie, while you're in college?"

"I do!" To Loco's laughter: "Shut up!"

Some of the rooms were open, lit by the dim light of the corridor. Boxes were piled on chairs. Beds were unmade. Stockings, long dried, hung on makeshift lines across beds. Family pictures stood on bureaus with hair curlers, bottles of pills, deodorants, perfumes, and powders. Girdles hung on chairs.

"It feels as if they had all fled in a second, just like Pompeii," whispered Loco shivering. "It's creepy. What if we wake up next morning and they're all here and we found out we made a mistake and it isn't vacation at all, and they discover us in their beds?"

"Quiet. Do you want Gibbon up here?"

"Urie, I feel like going. I'm scared!"

They found Room 304. They snaked inside. They closed the door, locked and bolted it. Loco Poco dropped the carpetbag to the floor by her feet. They stood in the middle of the room, staring and listening in the darkness. A street lamp from the quadrangle lighted up their eyes.

"Quiet. Listen."

They listened some more.

"Can we turn on a light?"

"Wait." Urie pulled the two shades down, as in an air-raid shelter. "Go ahead. The little lamp on the bureau."

Loco lit the lamp. Bathed in the sudden safety of the wash of light, they let go their breath. They took their pajamas out of the carpetbag.

"Hide the bag under the bed. In case we have to ditch in a hurry."

Loco bent down and pushed the incriminating carpetbag out of sight.

"This bed is Kenan Rivers'. I am Kenan Rivers," she announced, pulling up the bottoms of her pajamas.

"Kenan Rivers would never have a bear on her bed. *I* am Kenan Rivers. You can be Constance Dodge."

A recalcitrant expression came over Loco's face, but she kept quiet. She blotted Urie out of her mind, became Kenan Rivers, got into bed, and pulled the koala in next to her. Urie almost jumped when, turning around, she saw two heads on Loco's pillow.

"Eeek! I thought there was somebody else there!"

They laughed. Urie turned out the light. But they could not sleep. There was no clock, and the darkness obscured time. From time to time they looked at each other, surprised to find the other's eyes wide awake, alert as tigers. They made idle remarks.

"I don't think I'll ever go to sleep."

"I bet I'm sleeping on Kenan Rivers' bedclothes. How filthy, and I don't care."

"You know it's sort of warm in here. It's funny to sleep where it's so hot. In fact, I'm sweating."

Another hour passed.

"What if I have to go to the bathroom, Urie?"

"Go."

"But it will make a noise!"

"Don't flush it, then."

"I don't mean that!" Giggles.

More minutes passed.

"When we leave we ought to put the bear on Constance Dodge's bed."

"And move the bookcase to the other side of the room. They'll think they've gone insane."

They lost all track of time. At some unknown hour in the morning Loco said, "Isn't it funny, Urie? Here we are together, just like always, and nothing's changed."

Urie looked over at her. Each stared so searchingly into the other's eyes that they pulled each other's consciousnesses over each other like blankets and went, reassured, to sleep. Urie dreamed that she was saying "I know it, I know it, I know it," over and over to herself all night. Yet it was paradoxical because all those inadvertent moments that Loco had taken hold of her, on the deck of the liner when Loco had unfairly won the potato race, on the coffin bed, at the Ephesus Inn when they went exploring, and on the mossy promontory below Visigoth Castle, she was at once the same Loco, yet now somehow different. "I know it, I know it" was testimony to the difference.

The next day they awoke very late. The day was gray, and they had no idea of the time. It was two o'clock when they sneaked out and went home.

They whooped with laughter and burst through the screen door.

"Breakfast!" they called.

"Breakfast!" Mrs. Bishop was shocked. "Why, it's almost three o'clock. Do you mean to tell me you slept all this time?"

The second night, although the dislocation in place and time was all the more extreme because they were doing it *again,* they were more accustomed to their room. They were less afraid. They expanded. They dared to listen to the deserted life and creaks of the dormitory for the first time. They closed down the curtains again. They had come earlier. Loco had brought her tin of paints. She got a cup of water from the sink and lay down on the floor to make a squirrel.

"Think of having a sink in your own room," she purred. "Drench yourself in lux-u-ry!"

It was the proximity in dangerous circumstances, always with an ear for strange footsteps, always aware that below, in the humming silence, broken only by fitful creaks now and then, was that figment of Mrs. Gibbon, their official capturer, that brought them closer, brought them to the brink of recognizing that they were sisters, grown-up now, each with some other life the other knew nothing of.

"What do you learn in the crassroom?" asked Loco, beginning a word game.

"How to eat crow."

They both laughed. They played on the crassroom puns: glassroom, passroom, pass-water room, sassroom, grassroom, mass-room-Communists, just as in the old days they had improvised on Miss Picke puns.

"What do you learn in the assroom?" Loco hit upon.

"How to make the ultimate pass."

They both shrieked. But Urie thought it over.

"You used a dirty word."

"What dirty word?"

"You know what."

"That's not dirty," said Loco contemptuously, tossing her curls and adding a red berry to the squirrel's paws.

"Of course it's dirty," said Urie. "And you especially shouldn't say dirty words."

"Why?"

"Because you're the youngest" appeared on the tip of Urie's tongue. Back in the child-world things were so casual they entailed no thought. But she looked at her sister again and said with sudden passion, "Because you are the most refined, mysterious person in the family, and that word does not befit you."

"But ass is not dirty, Urie," said Loco with sincerity. "I have an ass. So do you." Urie blushed. Loco gave up and went back to childish sniggers. "It's a poo-poo putter-outer."

Faulted as a hypocrite, Urie let it go. Loco had not learned the word "ass" in family circles, but it achieved new heights by her saying it. Urie mulled it over intellectually.

"Am I really mysterious, do you think?"

"Yes."

"I'm not either." And then: "Why do you think that?"

"Why did you pick up with Miss Picke?" asked Urie suddenly. "Why do you almost flunk out of school every year? Why did you jump off Visigoth Castle?"

Loco shook her curls. And, having made this incursion, Urie thought of pressing it. She took a breath, but at the same moment—and a long time had actually passed, each unaware of the other and the air thick with thought—Loco looked directly up from the squirrel into Urie's eyes.

"Urie, did you ever do it? Did you ever make love with Bostwick?"

"Yes," answered Urie without a moment's hesitation.

The gate was open. The incursion had been made. She felt an excitement, a spell, a hope that she had never imagined. It was as if all the questions, even the passion, that she had never spent with Bostwick would finally be investigated and some meaning would finally blossom from the unreality of that affair. It was unquestionable proof of Loco's superiority or intuition that Loco should have said "Bostwick," never even considering Zebul. Urie did not think of this twice. Perhaps she might even tell her that Bostwick was the Grief Face.

Loco twirled herself on her haunches over the squirrel and sat excitedly with her legs folded.

"I have too, Urie, hundreds of times."

"You've made love?"—incredulous.

"Yes. Hundreds of times!"

"Who with?"

"Cory."

Loco's bending of her face downward in a dispersal of the spasm of rapture with which she had told Urie seemed incredibly beautiful. It was all that Urie could take in of what was being given her. For she could not imagine her younger sister. And then a thousand trembling images of Loco naked, her curls jiggling, her bare shoulders writhing, her body gobbled by Cory Atwater suffused her. She turned red. She trembled. She tried to get the images out of her mind. And all the time she was staring, her blue eyes fathomless, ostensibly drinking in all the rapid sentences, the laughter, the curls, the sincerity, even the charm which Loco was pouring upward, like the nozzle of a merry teapot boiling over.

"I like it when it's quick. Cory is good and quick. When he touches me I—eeeeh, Urie, it's so good. Did you love Bostwick? Eeeeh, I just love Cory. He's big, but he's good and smooth. He looks like me. Cory looks just like me, and he mades me die. I go up to him to kill him, but what happens, he just sticks in his thing and makes me die. Don't you think it's funny how you go up in smoke, and we did it five times in a row one time, Urie. How many times did you do it?" Laughter. Loco lowered her head again and dissolved in laughter, but then, carried away: "It feels like dying, doesn't it? I could just die and die and die!"

"Where did you do it?"

Loco told her the places, the arboretum, a record cubicle, the woods. "Everywhere!" raved Loco. "Are you shocked?"—seeing Urie's face.

"Did you use anything?"

"Use anything?"

"You fool. You'll be pregnant, and then what will happen? You'll be a disgrace and you'll disgrace the whole family."

"Well, he used something. Don't worry, Urie. And anyway, I'm going to marry him."

"But you're only fifteen years old!"

"I know it. So he'll have to wait. I told him."

Urie threw back her head and laughed hysterically. Loco crept up to her with a mischievous smile, took hold of her elbow, and shook it as if to mitigate the effect of everything she had blurted out like this, or as if to reassure Urie that she would not turn into a nymphomaniac.

"I thought I might be a nymphomaniac," she whispered into Urie's ear. "Do you know?"

"Shut up! I'm going to die if I hear another word!" And Urie leaned back on the bed, shaking in paroxysms of laughter or sobs.

"I've got to go to the bathroom." Loco stood up.

"Go, for God's sake."

"Shall I flush it?"

Urie couldn't answer.

But the moment that Loco was gone from the room, she became calm. She sat up. She was weak. She wiped the tears off her cheeks. Her face was dry and hot. Her heart was beating strangely. She heard a sudden cascade of waters. The pipes shrieked. Her heart stopped beating. She felt in some foreign world, separated not only from P.Q. and her mother and Irene, the family, the Shack, but from Loco too, to whom she could not connect the sounds of the cascade and the shrieking of pipes in this far-off dormitory. And the same incredulity with which she had greeted the fact of Loco's sex life with Cory, she now accorded to the fact that she had not suspected. Of course Loco had done that. Why had she never known that before? Just like the lipstick. Everything. Of course she was a nymphomaniac, whatever that was. The balance of power between the two had changed, because whatever Loco had done and however she had done it, it might now be possible that Loco was at last old enough to say, not it, but the meaning of it, aloud. It was Loco's extreme superficiality that made her so mysterious. Loco's mystery was so tall that it would take an entire lifetime to fathom it. And it was this lifetime that offered such promise to Urie that she felt as if she could not wait for Loco to come back through the door so that they could begin it.

"I flushed it," whispered Loco, stealing in.

"It was so loud Gibbon must have heard it too."

"Do you think so, Urie?"

Loco was afraid again. Everything was so familiar. They sat facing each other shyly. Loco tried to paint the squirrel again. But she couldn't. She dumped the cup of water in the sink.

"Everything's kind of funny, isn't it?"

"Yes."

All through that night they discussed sex. They did not even try to go to bed. They were mesmerized by the experience. They discussed in fits and starts. They did not talk about love, but stuck to the physiognomy of sex. Who put what hand where, what organ where, and when, and how fast. They talked with long pauses, with excited jitters, with disconnected facts, with bubbling laughter. They broke in on each other, winding around the other such feasts of confidence that it amazed them they had known each other so long and never known these things. Yet the very closeness engendered a concentration of solipsism. Each became self-concerned. Each listened with half an ear, for the translation through each of their separate minds became their occupation and lifted them into a blinding common realm where they felt their fates upon the universe to be dependent upon their femalehood. They lost all shyness. Their work, understood and agreed upon by both, entailed no sentimentality. They had no idea of any goal, were simply transported by the revelations of the present. Again Urie had a vision of Loco as an entity separate from the little girl in this room, her younger sister. Loco was as hard and brilliant as mica. Between them both they dwarfed the idea of man and malehood. The hysterical, silly, even unintentional primacy of their sisterhood was the first recognition that femalehood could blot out the very office of malehood which gave it definition. Sublimity alternated with ridicule. They were aware that everything was warped and that they were degenerating into another of their pun games. But they could not let go of it. Even exhausted, they could not make a move toward bed.

"Course, sex isn't everything," Loco mumbled sleepily. "In fact, I don't think it's much at all. Even though it's so good and you die, what is it? I mean, it almost doesn't matter who you do it with."

"How can you say that?"

"Well, I mean everybody turns into the same thing."

Urie was too tired to catch her on the point that, if she had not tried more than one man, how would she know?

"I don't know Cory," she told Loco, thinking of Bostwick. "He's a stranger. That's what's funny."

"I agree that's what's funny. People do it with strangers. You can do it with any stranger, but you can't do it with your own family. Just think of doing it with P.Q. That would be incest. Worse than nymphomaniacs!" Loco tittered.

At that moment they heard footsteps coming up the stairs. They clutched themselves together, holding their breath. The footsteps reached the top of the stairs and stopped.

"Quick! The lights!"

Loco lifted up as if a wind had blown her, scooping up the squirrel paper and hiding it under the bed. Urie ran to the light switch and flipped it. The footsteps began again. They both jumped on their beds at the same time, burrowing themselves up to the eyes in the covers. Urie hit hers so hard that the bed rolled on its casters and hit the wall. It was not loud, but loud enough to be heard in the hall. The footsteps stopped again.

There was a long moment in which they neither breathed nor lived. Then the person opened the bathroom door and it banged. Another silence. After an interminable time without sound, the person opened the bathroom door to come out. It banged, echoing in the hallway. The footsteps began again, this time coming toward Room 304. Urie was aware of her arms framing her head. Loco was as if dead. But the footsteps passed their doorway without a moment's hesitation and continued to the other stairway. There was a change in the sound as the person stepped from the carpet onto the linoleum, and then down the stairway. But Urie and Loco waited fifteen minutes after the sound had disappeared.

"Do you think it was Gibbon?"

"I don't know."

"It's getting dangerous."

"You can't flush the john, that's all."

"But that was hours ago!"

"Only fifteen minutes."

"Hours!"

"If she'd caught us, how could we have said we were returning books?"

Laughter.

"We've got to be more careful, that's all."

Neither of them said more. They fell into deep sleep. On the next day they awoke feeling drugged, with the conversation still going on under the swollen eyes. They were frightened, as if they had been conducting an orgy. Paradoxically the only thing that relieved their anxiety at the realm they had opened up together was the presence of each other. They were like drunks who need a drink. They felt as if they had lived in this dormitory forever; they had begun to hate it, and yet, since it provided the framework for the new ardor each had for the other, and since the realm was incomplete, they needed it more than they ever had before.

They had no idea of the time. They could not seem to wake up. They lay abed dreamily, until suddenly they heard the sound of a vacuum cleaner.

Loco Poco bounded out of the bed in her pajamas, opened the door a crack, and listened, kneading her feet back and forth.

"It's on the second floor, I think."

"Hurry up and dress."

"What time is it?"

"Why are you asking me?"

They hurried, but it was not fast enough. The vacuum-cleaner noise was growing louder and louder, and it was punctuated by banging noises.

"Whoever it is, is doing the stairs. They're coming up here. My God! What if they clean up *this* room?"

"Quick! Get dressed."

They dressed like lightning, stuck their clothes in the carpetbag, stuck the carpetbag back under the bed.

"They won't know whether it belongs here or not."

Then they put on their coats and ran down one staircase while the vacuum cleaner was arriving at the top of the other. Breathless, laughing, they loped down two steps at a time. Just as they were running out the doorway they turned to see, staring at them across a topography of green carpets and stuffed furniture, a fat and lumpy woman whose corsets made bumps stick through the back of her knitted beige dress. Pasted eyelashes flapped over malevolent black eyes. Scarlet lipstick painted a kewpie-doll mouth in a telephone network of wrinkles.

"Gibbon!" they sang, fleeing across the arboretum.

"Who would have thought she looked like that?"

At home they found out it was almost noon, and they dozed before the fire.

"Doesn't look to me as if you got much sleep over in that dormitory room," said Mrs. Bishop.

"We do too!" avowed Urie.

But Loco admitted that the room was a little warm and it was taking her a while to get used to it. Mrs. Bishop knew Loco's foxy ways, and she looked at them again as if she might figure out a conundrum. But their faces looked the same as always.

A restive spirit settled on them, yet they would not give up the idea of the dormitory. Instead of being more careful, however, they were more daring. Loco Poco explored the second floor in the late afternoon. She burst into Room 304. Urie was reading *Crime and Punishment* and jumped a foot.

"There's a Jap in this building! I had to use the excuse!"

"A Jap! Are you crazy? How could it be a Jap if they're the enemy?"

"How do I know? It's a Jap coed and she talks funny with mixed-up l's and r's. Maybe she's a spy."

"Maybe it's a Chinese. They don't have Christmas in China and it's too far to go. I told you not to scrounge around these halls. Haven't you any sense? After the vacuum cleaner? After Gibbon?"

They laughed without any reason. Loco sat down, filled the cup with water.

"I'm going to finish this squirrel."

Something gnawed in Urie's mind. She looked at Loco intermittently, as if there were not much time left for the truth that she wanted from Loco. Loco was not aware of these glances. Instead, as if the dozing day, the drugged sleep, the hysterical sex conversation they had had, had drained her of all that capricious side of her, she appeared completely serene, the exact opposite of Urie, who now that Loco was in the room could not concentrate on *Crime and Punishment* any more. Who would have thought that the unhealthy suspense could fare so badly beside the serenity that Loco's face presented as she breathed shallowly, painting the leaves of the tree in which the squirrel sat?

Loco suddenly put the squirrel painting away and took out another piece of paper. It was something she had meant to tell Urie as long as she had lived. What was it? She began a picture of a daisy, for she had dreamed her daisy dream again, and in the background she heard the laughter of Urie and Irene as some forgotten phantom of silver poplar leaves turned. What was it? Omniscience was behind her ears, behind her head; in fact, Loco was all mixed up with where she was—under the poplar tree, in a dormitory, in their shack home?—but Omniscience had not formed the word that made the secret recognizable. The minute she told Urie, Urie would recognize it. But she had to wait, even though there was something inevitable that they would talk about, as they had talked about sex, dongs, hands, and bodies. But the inevitable thing was what they would come down to after sex. But Urie would be as wrong as ever, and she would make too much of it, and though she was unaware of Urie's glances, Loco felt full of that thing Omniscience was about to put into her ear the word for, and she had this feeling of fantastic love for Urie. She even pitied her for reading *Crime and Punishment*. Rot. Then she thought of her flute and how she had not made one note this entire Christmas vacation. She had not missed it at all.

"Urie, you don't really think P.Q. is a failure, do you?"

"Yes, I do."

"Why is he a failure?"

"Because he can't make money. By his own argument intelligence means the ability to make money."

"Why is not making money a failure?"

"Would you be warm if we had money? If you were warm, would you be hiding out in this dormitory?"

Loco painted the petals carefully. But how could white show against white? She would have to outline them. Or else the background would have to be a color. What color? Dark black? Ink-blue? Like the negative in the storm? But the truth was white against white. If a person could see everything, she could even distinguish white from white. For all outlines were lies.

"Urie," she said, "you've changed."

"I know it," whispered Urie, and her voice sounded as if it would break.

"But you didn't need to."

"Why? How can you be in life if you don't?"

"Don't you think it's funny of us to talk about P.Q. like that?"

"I hate it," said Urie.

"Do you think it makes him little?"

"Yes."

"Do you feel as if the family was littler than it used to be?"

"Yes. Do you?"

"Yes. But it's only because we're talking about it. So it's a lie. Anything you talk about is a lie."

"Like sex?"

"Yes."

They laughed.

"You think they're not little, because you're a wisher," said Urie. "You're a wisher and you don't face facts."

"No. You're the wisher, not me"—steadily, serene.

"Doesn't everybody get old and die? Won't we get old and leave? I know what it is, Loco. You're hardhearted. You don't have any pity."

Again they both looked in each other's eyes and laughed.

"You're scared of the silliest things," said Urie fondly.

"You're scared of even sillier. Tell me one thing, Urie. Does P.Q. think he's little?"

"Of course not."

"Well?"

"I'm glad! Ah, fools, fools!" declaimed Urie, striking herself on the forehead. And then: "Isn't it funny, us talking about ourselves and our family like this? It's the first time in the world we ever did it. Think of us fifty years old. We will know each other and talk like this."

"I want to tell you something, Uria."

"What?"

"I don't know yet. But it's important."

"Well, when you think it up, tell me. Do you ever think of the time when you will be grown up and not be a Bishop any more?"

"It's about Omniscience, Omniscience knows everything," said Loco, feeling the necessity grow upon her more intensely.

"Banal, banal, banal," said Urie.

The next morning on the way out they met Mrs. Gibbon face to face in the hall.

"Haven't I seen you girls in here before?"

"I don't think so," said Urie. "We were returning a book to Kenan Rivers."

"It's not allowed, you know, to go into girls' rooms when they are away. You look familiar. Are you town girls?"

"Well—yes."

"What is your name?"

"Opal Granger."

"And what is hers?"

"Olive Akers. Well, thank you, Mrs. Gibbon. We are sorry we returned the book. But we've got to get home for lunch now or I don't know what will happen. Good-by."

"Good-by," chirped Loco.

Running across the arboretum, they stopped at the back of the Episcopal church.

"How are we going to get the carpetbag and our stuff out of there? We can never go back!"

"Yes," said Urie, "I'll go back. Don't worry. I'll get it. You know we can't ditch it there. It's an heirloom."

That night, after creaking her way up the stairs, sneaking into Kenan Rivers' room alone, standing there with the carpetbag safe in her hand, Urie looked at the lamplit room of Kenan Rivers. Her heart beat strangely. She knew she was the savior of the carpetbag. She knew that there had been no other course to take than to have tried the dormitory out. But she was loath to go, as if she and Loco had left something in there that was not in the carpetbag, or as if the thing they had sought in there had never been told. She turned her back on it, though, stalwart, and ran back down the stairs and home safe.

CHAPTER 51

The buzz of defense spending which had hit Ephesus the year before with the naval pre-flight program now hit Haw. The dead cotton mill was refurbished, shattered glass swept up and carted away, the windows were bricked in, grass was planted, new bushes were set in, and a defense plant opened up to make parachutes for the Army. Farm people moved by droves into Haw, filling up empty mill houses and sprouting a prefabricated cluster of dwellings on the edge of the river. The road to Kingston was paved. Fleets of trailer trucks ground through Main Street of Haw and Ephesus on their way to Baltimore or to Atlanta.

Eames Loomis Walley quit his job at the Army base so far away and got a job as an inspector in the new defense plant so that he could stay at home. With new money he put a bathroom into his house. For the first time Zebul had an actual bathtub in his house. But such an improvement seemed a mere superficiality, dressing to his destiny. He paid no attention to it, did not even take baths in it. His life had long ago been given over to the Bishops and his studies. And now the buzz of activity, the bathtub, and his father's new job were proofs of what he and Urie had envisioned in the beginning, the materialization of what they had studied, stolen, and scrimped for.

The third day of March was classic, gray and windy, with blackbirds wheeling in the sky on their way north. No leaves had budded yet, nor was there a hint of sap. But there was a green, wild atmosphere, and frozen old branches and twigs thrashed in it, black as winter, chattering and clicking above the swaying telephone wires.

When school let out, Loco put her sneakers in a paper bag and started for Hill Hall. It was Thursday, her day for practice. She had left her flute in its case on the lowest shelf of the cupboard in Dr. Nagy's office. She was cold in the wind. That day at school she had lost a button on her old green pea-coat. It flapped open, and even her yellow sweater underneath, yarn grown thin at the elbows, could not keep her teeth from chattering. The wind in its invisible course against the wires, her teeth, and the twigs of trees, signaled her to choose her Fred Astaire personality. She held out her arms and curtsied to each tree, after which she tap-danced a roundabout-face to each and continued on her way. Passing the stone wall where she had conversed with Miss Picke, she kicked each ninth stone, mouthing under her breath as if it were an accomplishment, "Rape Miss Picke. Don't rape Miss Picke. Rape Miss Picke. Don't rape Miss Picke." She was aware of the affect her gyrations were having on passers-by: they smiled and she preened, all the while nevertheless concentrating. She experimented with the steps, trying to keep strictly to the beat of 9/8 time which Dr. Nagy had just taught her. Whenever she made a mistake she stopped and stood, both feet together on the eroded sidewalk, picking up the beat again from the whacks of the twigs on the telephone wires. A double-trailered Van Fleet van, hoisted by its rusty green cab, made a sound of thunder rounding the curve between Haw and Ephesus. It was a symphonic sound and it began the undercurrent of importance to Loco's crescendo as she approached the Baptist church.

The Baptist church with its fake columns was the separation point between the ugly and the beautiful. Across the street lay the campus. She would cut through the secret hole in the armory hedge and take the short-cut back of Swine Hall, which led right to Dr. Nagy's office.

At this same moment Urie was walking toward the Ephesus Inn. She had waited for Zebul in the office, but he had not arrived, so she decided somewhat aimlessly to go home. She pushed her way out through the window by the snapping magnolia leaves at the moment that Zebul entered the main door of the building. He decided to wait for her in the vacant office. She arrived at the Ephesus Inn. She heard the roar of the Van Fleet truck and watched it approach the corner at the Baptist church. If it went straight down Main Street it was headed for Baltimore. If it turned, it was going to Atlanta. It turned. It was taking parachutes to Atlanta. Urie suddenly saw Loco Poco dancing by the church steps.

Loco knew the van was going to turn. It thundered in her ears. In the tip of the field of her left eye she saw its bumper, high as a battering-ram, and she reveled in the patch of rust harvested by rain and time in the dent of the chrome. The street light had turned from green to yellow. It was with her, about to turn red. Caught in the 9/8 time, she teetered at the curb. She knew the truck would brake. She would use the squawk of the brakes as counterpoint to her rhythm, even though she had to threaten it to do this. She concentrated again, hard.

The danger was glorious, like the descant of "Jesu, Joy of Man's Desiring." She wanted to giggle, but for giggles you needed Bach. The light turned red. She stepped into the street, into the walking lane. She looked straight up over the giant, filthy, battered mudguard into the truck-driver's eyes. He was forty years old and he had not shaved. He had brown curly hair, he was smoking a Camel cigarette, and his eyes were blue. His glance back was intimate but surprised.

It was the way of tigers and lions of the jungles to be pure in their powers of devastation. Trailer trucks had the same purity, gassed, oiled, and thunderous in their barbaric machinery. She could not help tempting it, since she had been born in this century, white, soft, and smashable. Properly, the Caliban who would give her the ultimate curtsy, even though his truck would scream to backtrack because of its odd, ferocious powers, was dreamy and soft of soul too. And his shoulders were powerful and muscular, and the backs of his hands were hairy.

If there was any fault, it was the fault of her reflexes, not her conception of the dance. She was too fast. Therefore, instead of braking, the truck tried to move out around her. There was a delicious collision between her 9/8 rhythm and the gunning of the motor. By the time the dreamy blue eyes of the Caliban had registered and he had hit the brake, the change of tactics was fruitless.

Something struck her. Something was smashed, and then she was catapulted and dragged. The brake squeaks did not jibe properly, and what was amazing to her was the simple demolition of the rhythm. All became silence. She was in a cave, protected from the wind and beating twigs, and the atmosphere was very dark. The chassis of the truck shuddered and trembled above her, a relic of the music.

Urie saw this happen from the Ephesus Inn, saw the truck stop, the man jump out of the cab, the traffic tied up, the crowd gather. She sprinted slowly, lightly to the edge of the crowd, floating through it rather than pushing, as passive, as reluctant, as remote, as inhibited as Bostwick.

Even before Loco saw Urie, before anyone dared touch her, she thought of Bishopry. When she noticed that her knee was bent the wrong way, making her ankle contiguous with her hip, she had a vision of P.Q. and her mother bowed and crying because of her death. She was not scared; she was smitten by pity. How could she explain the chimera of it? For the chimera came immediately after the pity. It was clear to her that though she died and was gone, she was not dying. At that moment she saw Urie kneeling down on her hands and knees in the street next to her.

Urie simply could not believe a body could be got up this way, the elbow broken backward, the legs folded the wrong way like a frog's. The only convincing detail of the contortionist's act were two sad strands of yellow wool hanging out a hole in the green pea-coat, from Loco's sweater. Loco's face, by contrast, was very bright and pale and clean and without a scratch, and the blue vein flickered in her temple like a secret signal. Her eyes were dark, bright, liquid. She tried to push herself up on her good elbow and whisper to Urie.

"Don't be afraid," she said. But the surprise was so acute in Urie's eyes that she became defensive. "I couldn't help it"—almost as servile as after Amy Grispin White's shoes.

Loco tried to think up the thing she had to tell. Thank God it was Urie who had come. Urie was the only one of the whole family who might be able to learn it. P.Q. knew it, of course, so she did not need to apologize to him. The 9/8 rhythm floated in her memory along with the clicking winter branches and whispering grasses. She saw that her position under the chassis of the trailer truck was the negative place of her dream of the sky and the world. The place where Urie was squatting, the light coming out in back of her head, was the promise. The symphony could have been marvelous if she had not been so quick and direct, assuming that the Caliban could make his move as quickly as she made hers. She thought she was really a genius, and this was not ego. If it were ego, everything would have fallen in and been indefensible, vain, and untrue. But it was true. Tinkles of laughter came through, and though Urie was actually fading from her eyes, it made it proper. She listened for Irene's laughter too. She did not hear it. She made a small titter to consolidate Urie's suspension of disbelief. She couldn't actually tell her it was true, since Urie and Zebul and their vows to truth through argument and outline always made them say the right thing and form the wrong opinion. She could only hint it, as it had been hinted to her throughout her long, as she now thought, life. She tried to recapture the ghost of the 9/8 time. Urie would not touch her. She was achieving the rhythm. Although she wished Urie would touch her. The grass blades clicked it better that summer, better than these Ephesian tree twigs in that green, promising sky, this almost spring. She could have been a baby, but the 9/8 time, the words "rape," "Picke," "pluck" were beating time, and it had really happened; it had been resurrected to her through signs. But what it was, was:

"I am a daisy," she said as fast as she could, not seeing Urie but knowing she was there. She would have reached out to touch her if her arm hadn't been twisted up.

An ambulance took Loco Poco to the Kingston hospital. Doctors fixed her arm and leg back into the correct positions. Mrs. Bishop went to the hospital in the laundry truck, her hands still floury from making biscuits.

The next day at eight o'clock in the morning Zebul appeared at the house. He did not state that he wanted to go with Urie and Irene to visit

Loco; it was simply accepted. He and Urie sat on the floor of the blue truck, facing each other, behind P.Q. in the jouncing darkness. They balanced carefully to keep their haunches from bruises every time the truck went over a bump, and they concentrated on the classes they were cutting. Irene clung to the dashboard to keep the bucket seat from turning over.

In the hospital room Mrs. Bishop got up from a tan fake-leather chair by Loco's head to greet them in silence. She had spent the night thinking of how they were going to pay the hospital bill so she would not have to think about what had happened to Loco.

Zebul stood by the foot of the bed, his hands clutching the iron bedstead as if it were prison bars. He desired to say something to Loco's grave expression as she looked at them all.

"I know what my favorite ice-cream-cone flavor is," he made up, as if this long-forgotten non sequitur would solve everything. "Lemon and lime." But Loco did not answer, did not even register.

Urie made up the response for Loco as fast as a prompter. "That's sherbet. That's not ice cream."

The next day Loco went into a coma.

Urie was once in the room alone with her. She hung over the bed and called to her. "Loco. Loco. Loco."

Loco moved her eyes upward in her head, for she recognized Urie. But she could not come back to earth to see Urie or make any more pronouncements. Her eyes jiggled as if they were birds hidden in eggs. Then she opened them and Urie breathed right down into them to make the dark pupils focus on her. No good.

Two days after that Loco began to breathe shallowly and fast like a bird, the symptom of brain injury. With those breaths she died.

CHAPTER 52

Zebul was scared to go to the Bishops'. He had been there on every occasion, when he was wanted and when he wasn't, for stealing, drama, fighting, sex, love, and philosophy. He remembered the first time he had been there after the betrayal of Urie with Bostwick, himself with Loco, how Urie had sat at the typewriter and typed. But he had never been there for death.

He came up the driveway and cleared his throat before the kitchen doorway. Urie stared at him through the screen door.

"Hi," he said.

"Hi," she answered.

He came in. He wrapped his hands together and wopsed his tongue in his mouth uncomfortably. He stared at her but could not make up his mind to keep on staring. She had a piece of bread in her hand. He heard a noise in the other room. It was Irene, looking up a word in the giant rotting-leather dictionary. She had it open on the floor. Everything seemed so ordinary that it was unnatural that Loco did not come out from her tapestry room to join them. He was careful not to sit on the coffin couch. He sat on the Boston rocker, the one Lacey Ransome had sat on during the Sybilline ceremonies.

He thought of Loco Poco's name. Everyone had called her Loco Poco when her name was Sylvia. What was the meaning of that? Ever since he had written down the kiss, not with Loco but with Urie, he had sought meaning by the key of words. Now he sought Loco Poco's meaning, since he could never drown in her again and never forget drowning in her and never be Zebul without her Pacific merged with his Atlantic. He sought the word. It was not Sylvia. After all, Loco Poco had only been a way of calling her, a description. But it no longer fitted her now, since she was not on earth. Loco Poco was on earth.

P.Q. came in from outside, banging his feet on the doorstep. He burped once as if to acknowledge Zebul. But there was no mention of Alcibiades with the news.

It was not true, thought Zebul, that P.Q. was now merely this thin, immigrant failure in a business suit, grown warped in the crotchets of his megalomania, delivering linen to Greek cafés and repeating worn-out antisermons to whatever students would listen. Zebul looked at P.Q. carefully to see that he had not lost his power.

P.Q. went to the kitchen sink. Why had Zebul given up God to go over to him? P.Q. lathered his face in the reflection of the clock glass. Why had he found the promise in Bishopry when the Bishops did not have power over life and death? Their metaphysic was broken, yet they would not even say, "Loco Poco is dead."

Urie had tried it in the bathroom, looking into the mirror, practicing as on the day she had practiced "sexual intercourse." "Dead" was easier than "die." "Die" was legato, sad, and evil. "Kick the bucket" was a possible euphemism, less affected than "croak" from George Raft movies.

"Where's Mrs. Bishop?" Zebul asked.

"In the living room."

"She's looking for the plot in the cemetery," said Irene.

P.Q. made a growling noise in his throat, and the three of them lowered their eyes.

Mrs. Bishop entered the room with a paper in her hand and closed the door behind her. A draft of icy air accompanied her. She did not look Zebul in the eye. Her ruined cheeks and loose mouth hung downward off her black teeth like sagging taffy.

He had joined Bishopry, teamed up with them, given his allegiance, his loyalty, been wounded, and become them. It was not true that their power was gone. Surely Mrs. Bishop would say, "Loco Poco is dead."

Loco Poco is dead, he almost announced to make them say it. But he picked up *Main Currents of American Thought* instead and pretended to read it.

There *was* panacea on earth. They had willed him to discover it, this secret thing they could not express. P.Q. was the Socrates of it, preaching it to the innocent and spellbound. They had come to the town like fallen lords, odd, poor, knowing they were fallen, had found this house to pull around them, to work out of, to explore panacea from the position of knowledge. What was this knowledge based on? A dream they had had before they had fallen. Nothing daunted them because they were sure, without God, that they could find their kingdom on this earth. They were humanists. God was for old ladies and prostitutes, the hopeless who, not being able to find life bearable on earth, had to have life everlasting in heaven.

P.Q. said if you discovered all the outlines of phenomena on earth, played them with the knowledge of your senses and the excitement of your intelligence, you would be buoyed into knowledge. You could change the world and be changed in the process. You could move into that place which was your definition, whose outlines could not be expressed because they were of an importance and beauty indescribable in words. Yet words were possible to be known in the future, for you would create words as they described you.

Loco Poco is dead, he almost announced.

P.Q. finished shaving and put on his coat. He went out the kitchen door and drove the blue truck out of the yard.

Mrs. Bishop went to the bathroom.

"Mamma found our plot in the Eastern Point cemetery. It's a famous cemetery. Sophia Peabody is even buried there," said Irene.

"They're going to cremate her," said Urie.

"Who?" he asked dumbly.

She struggled. She said, "The carcass."

"If you buy a new cemetery plot here it costs too much," said Irene.

"The name Loco Poco," said Zebul. "Where does it come from?"

"It's a nickname."

"I know it's a nickname, but where did you get it?"

"From the Lone Ranger. He always called people *loco poco*."

"P.Q. believes in cremation," continued Irene.

"I know that," said Zebul, impatient.

"Mamma is going to take her up there and bury her."

"It costs more to cremate people than to just bury them," said Urie.

"Is P.Q. going too?"

"No."

"He doesn't believe in funerals."

"I know that," repeated Zebul again.

"Funerals are barbaric."

"I know it."

Mrs. Bishop came in from the bathroom and told him, "I am going to take . . . Loco Poco to the cemetery plot that my father bought when he was first married. That was eighteen eighty-three."

"How are you going?" asked Zebul.

"By bus."

Mrs. Bishop went into the kitchen.

He imagined Mrs. Bishop getting on the bus, sucking her teeth in, carrying an urn of ashes. Suddenly an awareness assailed him that whatever was in that urn, ashes, was the body of Loco Poco. Drowning flesh that had drowned him in embraces and kisses, touched every extremity of his flesh, smelled moist, and laughed in his ear. His shoulders began to shake with a spasm, and a tear rolled out of his eye.

When Urie saw Zebul crying, she was amazed. They had come to crack the town wide open. Instead the outside world had swept Loco Poco away, like the ocean. But it was not the worthy enemy, the ocean, which had done it; it was a freak of fate; coincidence. For a thing so large as life to need a thing so small to dent the armor of invincible Bishopry!

"Stop crying," she whispered, leaning down. Irene was looking. Irene's face was crumpling. She was going to cry. Urie did not want to cry. Her throat clamped down on her own tears, and she convulsed her body to its fingertips. She tried to grab *Main Currents in American Thought* before it fell, to clutch it against her from his lap, to hold it for its strength, but as it clattered to the floor she felt mercury in her throat. How amazing it was that Zebul, the stranger to whom long ago she had thrown her pearls, thinking he was swine, should be the one to cry! She put her arms around him and clung to him.

P.Q. made arrangements with Wentworth's Funeral Home of Kingston, although Mrs. Kanukaris had offered to cremate the body for half price. The next day the whole family and Zebul gathered around Mrs. Bishop at the bus station. She carried an urn of shining brass decorated in scrollwork of white porcelain. It was in these seconds before the bus came that the sense of sacredness awaiting its recognition welled beneath them.

Urie thought of how she and Loco had buried the pheasant.

Zebul thought of how Loco had made her excrement holy, adding it to the dog's by the Bone Tree.

Irene thought: It's really true we don't have enough money to go to the place where this urn is going to be buried, but it's not true funerals are barbaric.

It was a waiting-room. It was an unbefitting place whose grimy walls had no remembrance except of anonymous persons coming and going. There was a calendar hanging over the ticket counter with a picture of the President on it.

"The bus is coming," said P.Q.

He took Mrs. Bishop's pocketbook and the urn in his hand while she boarded, and then handed them up to her on the steps, his hand, the same one that had marked the place in Plutarch, holding on a second longer to the urn as if, in spite of his individual intention and by some order he yet refused to recognize, it would be a caress or a benediction.

During the week that Mrs. Bishop was gone, a letter came with a check for fifteen hundred dollars' damages from the trucking company. This paid for the funeral charges, and there was some money left over. But P.Q. refused to say how much, passing over the irony, as he had the death itself.

When Mrs. Bishop returned, Urie and Irene went back to their classes again and P.Q. was already delivering linen in the usual places. Mrs. Bishop hemmed up a new batch of aprons which she had been cutting out at the time of Loco's death. These activities were carried out in a vast atmosphere of disbelief, as if Loco Poco had not died at all but were only gone, in some new scheme like trying out the dormitory room.

Nobody talked about her. No one mentioned her name. Mrs. Bishop did not go into her room, so her clothes hung as they always did, on a rod balanced kitty-cornered over the frames of the tapestry curtains. Her brown shoes peeped below the curtain of her door. They were worn at the toes, the way she always wore out her shoes. Every time someone went to the bathroom, they peered out.

The bleakness that accompanied this regroupment of the family was mirrored in the weather. It was now the middle of March, and the sky was gray and cold. There was no sign of spring. Bishopry became like an army battered by fate. They clung nearer together but ate in silence. They awaited something—a word, perhaps, like that gallantry first uttered at the realization of their fall: "We're going to crack this town wide open." But no one spoke. P.Q. turned on the radio and used Kaltenborn's voice for noise to fill up their metaphysical abyss.

There was a suspense involved in this state, not the banality of who would recognize that Loco was dead. For she was not dead. Yet there was no sustenance to be got from the heart of Bishopry, for if progress, growth, and ultimate panacea were the understood premise of Bishopry, how account for coincidence? Who had ever faced that problem when Miss Picke was raped and murdered? She had been ingested into the culture immediately, as if a bobbin had picked her up in the giant weaving machine of existence and threaded her as a giant joke into the carpet of life.

But now that their mortality was exposed and no one of the remaining Bishops could utter the word to hallow Bishopry above the desecration of Loco's death, they were dancing tightrope on a nightmare. The question that Urie and Zebul had played with all these years rolled to a stop at their feet.

What is the meaning of life?

Urie, sleeping every night next to Loco's silent cubicle, was assailed by terror. She was obsessed by the idea of flesh. Dead bodies. She remembered the first night, when Loco was afraid of the coffin bed and Urie had made up her death by the Negro for her. Zebul said he had arisen out of the dead Negro's hand. Drunk Negro. Not dead Negro. It rained. Would rain leak into Loco's urn? Fire burned. Loco went into ashes. Where was the essence? In the morning Urie could not eat. She would be feeding a body. By noon she was starving. She spent twenty-five cents on a pimiento-cheese sandwich and a chocolate milkshake at the Y.

"Loco is a carcass," she said to herself in words. A carcass is garbage. A person becomes garbage. Trucks do not carry away such garbage. People have to handle it. They burn it and put it in the ground. She thought of Loco, the living, vibrant form of her sister, from whose living eyes she had received signals of the divine. She remembered her in different poses: singing "Jesu, Joy of Man's Desiring," talking to her with those gestures just before she saw Bostwick's Grief Face, jumping off Visigoth Castle, walking on Zebul's feet, kissing P.Q., laughing. She was floating. She was possessed of a secret. She too was obsessed with garbage. They had planted the pheasant. They had danced on the linens. Now Loco Poco was garbage, and that image she had foreseen upon the tire in Sears Roebuck was being stamped endlessly as the seal of her death on highways all over America.

Coincidences were the cause of her terror, she thought. For if God did not exist, then man made his own fate. Had Loco made her fate? Or had she, Urie, made Loco's fate? Or what merciless and random thing outside made their fate?

Their fate: garbage.

Loco, her feet and legs broken like matchsticks. Clark Gable wanted to keep Bonnie's carcass with him. It was a fake. No live person wants a carcass. Urie did not want Loco's carcass. Urie would not look at Loco dead. The last she had seen of Loco, Loco was pushing her eyeballs up into her head, trying to protect the eggshells. Had the birds hatched? Who was this only person, this Loco, the only one except Bostwick whom she had ever courted? Who was her sister, whom she had lived with all the years of her life, witness to the secret of the ardor behind her eyes? She wanted Loco. She wanted to embrace her. She could not embrace Loco. The last time she had embraced Loco was on Loco's coffin bed less than six feet away from her through the shepherd cloth.

The carcass, the body after death, bore no marks of the flesh's ecstatic dances before, so Loco's confessions at the dormitory were rendered execrable to Urie. Ultimate ecstasy ending in ultimate garbage. She remembered Zebul after the first kiss, forcing her to write it down, as if words could transcend the flesh. It was not that Urie was desecrating Loco for betraying them by dying. By this time she had reached the conclusion that there was the Great Merciless Outside, and that *it* had killed Loco and desecrated Bishopry, rendering them feeble as ants stepped upon, or birds swept away by the wind. Loco was stamped out with her secret and her talk of Omniscience. Omniscience. Was that the Great Merciless Outside?

At the table Urie chewed in agony, desiring stones to speak. P.Q. was unfathomable. He looked as if nothing at all had happened.

What is life really like? thought Urie. We all hurt each other. Not because we want to, but because we live. I step on an ant I don't even see. A truck smashes Loco, whom its driver didn't even see. I love Bostwick.

That hurts Zebul. How can I help what I feel? So I didn't love Zebul like that. Could I help it? If you live, you get hurt, you render hurt. And the worst of it is that you can't do anything about it. And then Loco Poco dies. I can't bear her suffering. But she has to. She turns into nothing. Worse than nothing, she turns into a carcass. What is the answer to that?

The last day of March, Urie went to stand out in the field beyond the barn. It was that moment just preceding spring, when the broom grass was dead and limp from frost, when everything was an ugly brown, even the sky, when the melted frost had made everything soggy and no sun had appeared yet in the sky. Scylla and Charybdis ran around her feet. Scylla licked her left leg. Urie thought of Scylla's tongue. It used to lick Loco Poco's face. It is still warm and licking, but where is Loco's face?

She stared at the dead brown grass. She wondered: Did the ocean really exist? Or did I dream it?

Panic overcame her.

She tried to remember every detail. She conjured up the smell at the edge of the ocean. It smelled of tarred corks, bottles dumped off freighters, broken beams from Norway, eggshells from Algeria, and misshapen driftwood broken from branches of the Amazon.

Suddenly she remembered that they had had a lamb. She had forgotten that they had a lamb. Now she remembered. The lamb had followed the three children across the beach. Just as Scylla and Charybdis were following her now. It had jumped over boulders and left broken blue mussel shells in the wake of its hoofs. Once she had seen the lamb looking at itself in the salt-water pool left by the tide in the rocks. This was the pool she had told Irene and Loco was the world, and she had divided its sections into Europe, Norway, California, Greece, Massachusetts, and South America, not recognizing differences between states, countries, and continents. Minnows flashed under the water but did not disturb the image of the white woolly face looking at itself. Beyond the pool the broad, calm ocean bleated on the beach, as uncaring of the silent lamb as it had been of the Bishops on the day of the loss of their oceanic life.

But in her mind its uncaringness in this memory of the lamb was worse than its uncaringness on the day of their departure for Ephesus. The ocean was a mirror of her mind that it had forgotten the lamb. The lamb was a memory of happiness. The lamb had gamboled that day and presented itself to her in this memory all these years later as more bright, shimmering, more quick than anybody could imagine. They had been happy in those days. What had happened to the lamb? Had the Bishops given it away? Had it been killed and eaten with a knife and fork by some other family? And where was the day gone now?

All that was left was she, Urie, who stood on broom grass with two dogs, suddenly aghast at the importance and ephemerality of her own flesh and bones. She was eighteen years old. She had forgotten the lamb. What else had she forgotten? She had forgotten something. She tried to remember it, but she could not. Was it true—now she was afraid—she was going to forget Loco too?

"Who took Loco Poco's shoes away?" asked Irene.

"I did," said P.Q. He took his razor out from behind the block and moved it back and forth on the strop that hung under the mantelpiece to sharpen it.

Did he throw them away? wondered Urie, her heart beating.

P.Q. made a mush of shaving cream in the cup and applied it to his chin. He made two precise movements and stopped. He opened his mouth to say something, but he did not speak. He brushed with three more deliberate movements.

"I gave them to that old nigger plumber for his kids." He scrunched his face into an ugly grimace and brought the blade down in a perfect swipe.

"Yeah. Loco Poco doesn't need them," said Irene with a frightened face.

"They might as well be worn by his kids, the poor cuss," said P.Q.

There was not a trace of any payment in P.Q. for this strength. Urie felt dizzy. She was sweating though it was cold in the spring air. P. Q. was not her father any more. He was not even the father of Loco. He was a pioneer observing the bleached bones of pioneers who had died on the desert before him.

The next day Mrs. Bishop took down all Loco's clothes and gave them away too. She walked down to Tin Town and gave five to each house she saw with somebody Loco's size.

C H A P T E R 53

There months passed, and Zebul and Urie became welded together in the way of habit, a subtle change from the days of old when they questioned every move. It was July. Both Zebul and Urie were to graduate the following spring term. Irene would finish by Christmas.

It came to seem to Zebul as if he had never made love to Loco. He did not think of the idea consciously and it neither activated nor negated his relationship with Urie. He knew he would never tell her, but he did not feel that it stood in the way of his truth with her either. It was like a physical change that has happened in the past, uncapturable in words, incapable of arousing known feeling, simply a fact to be observed, stirring wonder when it is remembered, like looking at a baby picture of oneself, thinking: Was that little thing really me? and deciding: No, not really— even when you knew it was. What Loco had left him with was ingested in him so profoundly that he could not gauge it. He was a man where he had been a boy. His aspirations and sensibilities were hidden in a coarser exterior. This made him more of a totality, more self-sufficient than before, more unneeding of Urie, of P.Q., of Bishopry, of sex, of answers, even, he thought, of gods. Something had withdrawn to the inside of him, leaving a thicker-skinned outer shell. His face was thinner, and consequently his eyes became larger, and his wristbones, anklebones, and shoulderbones, primary armaments of manhood, more prominent, like turrets of a castle. It was both this self-sufficiency and the withdrawal of his self to a mysterious depth that made him prize all the more his daily life with the Bishops, who were so used to him, that, like himself, they could not have said what he was. They did not even think of it. Neither did he. His future was mapped out for him. By Christmas he would join the Army special training program. It was lucky he was smart, he used to say to Urie. Now, not only would he finish college, he would get his pre-medical training and serve as a medic, or even a doctor, rather than have to be a dogface. And he wouldn't even have to pay for it!

The mechanics of Bishopry in the Shack had not changed one iota. Everything had become confirmed in the way it was. Where outside the world had picked up tempo, Bishopry remained poor. Money was floating in the universe. While the number of civilian students at the university decreased, uniformed students took their place, studying political science, geology, meteorology, and pre-flight. Hoke Tabernacle joined up with the Heidle-ziggers and opened a coffee shop specializing in thick, creamy Viennese coffee. In the second month of this enterprise he was so successful he began to wear shoes. But P.Q. did not share in the general prosperity. Something in the sight of these entrepreneurs even disgusted him. He became more voluble in his philosophical talks at Nick's grill, and brought linens only when he felt like it. He grew thinner. He was more ebullient, messianic, sharp-nosed, and haughty than he had been before.

The half-moon of blackness at Mrs. Bishop's gums expanded until her four front bottom teeth were completely rotten. Now she did not try not to smile. She smiled anyway. "I know I look like some witch out of a cave in the Pyrenees, but I don't mind about that."

At the same time a crisis point was reached in her hold over the family. She nagged unceasingly.

"Did you get that lease notarized?" she would ask P.Q.

"It's enough to drive a person crazy, the way you people act," she cried in a rage if everyone were not at the supper table on time. "How can I know how to get supper when you just come in any old time?"

She even nagged Zebul. "You don't keep your shirt tucked in. What are they going to do to you when you get in the Army? They're not going to let you go everywhere flapping and flopping like that!"

By this time Urie had removed herself from her mother and could remain stony-faced and mercilessly unconcerned. For she and Zebul had made a host of new friends.

Only Irene was spared her mother's barbs. She was Mrs. Bishop's mainstay, not because she offered her sympathy or even defended her, but simply because she was there more than the others. Mrs. Bishop looked down on her, felt sorry for her, and depended upon her presence. There was a wave of sympathy at the bottom of Irene's imperturbability.

It was the house itself that symbolized everything.

One day at the bottom of the driveway Urie put her hand out and clutched Zebul's elbow hard.

"Look at this house!" she said, her voice hard and electric.

They stared at its two tipping chimneys, its rotten sagging frame, and the black outline of the porch, which looked like Mrs. Bishop's rotten teeth. The house, having been used to support the fallen, symbolize their plight, been used in its desecration to support their mockery even, had now turned pale, washed-out, thin, empty-looking, even frail, as if it had turned upon itself and consumed itself.

"You know the only thing wrong?"

"What?" asked Zebul.

"Loco Poco should have been killed by this house. If it was going to be coincidence, the porch should have fallen on her instead of her being run over by a truck."

Zebul was shocked. He trembled and could not speak. He pulled away from her. But she stared at him dry-eyed with her lips pulled off her teeth in P.Q.'s gesture, like something predatory, a wolf, and he was overcome by the same old admiration he had felt the day she read her theme about the house in class. And he was strong enough now to feed her vicious freedom with a wall of insouciance so pervading that she uttered a stony laugh and broke her own stance with that punctuation, like an actress untouchable at the apex of a tragedy. There was released in him a great joy in their double wickedness. They were incorruptible after all.

This strength of their now old youth spirited Urie and Irene and Zebul to a sudden spurt of improvement. One day they decided to make a bookcase. Ever since they had moved into the house their books had flowed over. Orange crates, boards with bricks—nothing could hold them all.

"I tell you what let's do. Let's cover this whole wall with the bookcase."

"Yeah. Ever since we moved in here we said we were going to build one. To think it's taken till now to do it!"

They got some old unused lumber out of the shed. They laid the boards down on the living-room floor in the proper shape.

"Good. That board just fits."

"Put that one here. That one can go there. It's warped a little bit. Do you think that will ruin it, Zebul?"

"We've got to do with what we have."

Zebul picked up the saw.

"Are you going to saw right over my rug?" called Mrs. Bishop from the dining room. She was hemming a skirt of Irene's.

"We'll sweep it out," said Irene.

Mrs. Bishop put four pins in her mouth, watching the sawdust cover the worn flower pattern like snow.

They nailed the frame together and raised it to the wall. At that moment P.Q. entered. He looked and said, "That board is warped."

Urie, standing on the king chair propping up the structure, turned around. "Who are you to come in here and say that board is warped?" she shouted.

Zebul had to catch the falling structure.

"You know what you should do?" advised P.Q. "Put that warped board down here where it doesn't show. That will strengthen the whole frame and—"

"For Christ's sake!" shouted Urie, who saw at once that he was right. "We sweat over these boards and we get them all nailed in, and then you come in here and stick your goddamn nickel's worth of—"

P.Q. turned as if no words had been spoken and walked back into the dining room.

"Urania Bishop!" shouted Mrs. Bishop, blowing the pins onto the dining-room table. "I will not have that sort of talk in this house!"

"Well, what right has he to come in here and—"

"Shut up," warned Irene.

"Yeah," corroborated Zebul.

"—and make stinking remarks when we are trying to improve conditions in this dump? Has he ever improved anything? No! Would he ever lift a finger to make a bookcase? No, sir. All he would do is leave the oil spigot open so all the oil can drain out on the ground, just because he can't remember a stinking goddamn thing!"

"Jesus Christ, shut up!" cried Zebul. "I can't hold this any longer."

Urie turned back to prop the bookcase again.

"I will not have anybody talking about their own father that way."

"I will talk any way I want to."

"You goddamn Jesus Christ will not!" shouted Mrs. Bishop, rising like a hen, turning over her chair.

All three looked at each other and broke into raucous laughter.

That evening P.Q. talked about the stock market, meeting Opard Bigelow Granger on the campus, and the defacing of the street statues by Athenian youth in the third century B.C., as if nothing had happened. But the rest of the family was silent. Supper stretched the room to the seams. Mrs. Bishop looked like a ghost. Irene moved about with the dishes like Judith Anderson in *Rebecca*. Urie sat with glazed eyes in silence, unrepentant and weak. Zebul received her stolen glances of collusion with no sign. After supper they studied. No one said a word about the fight.

Fights within Bishopry, Zebul thought, had the aspect of those pirate fights on shipboard in Errol Flynn movies. They demanded prowess and knowledge of the limitations of personality-slaying. They had bravura, and each person involved needed form, style, and the correct slash. Urie and Mrs. Bishop were the most accomplished. But he missed Loco's grace notes. Irene and P.Q. always retreated like blank walls, never pierced, leaving the field to the fighters.

Now that P.Q., the catalyst, had retired, the rancor remained with Mrs. Bishop. At eleven o'clock, when P.Q. had long gone to bed, she came out. She sat down significantly at the dining-room table, dressed in her bathrobe, her hair down, ready for bed.

"I feel as if everything is impossible."

"If you hadn't interfered, everything would have been all right," said Urie.

"I cannot bear to have you swearing at your father."

"But if you hadn't gotten into it I would have stopped. You nag all the time."

"I know I nag."

"Yes, you nag."

"I know it's me who is impossible, but what can I do?"

"Well, I didn't mean to swear," backtracked Urie. "But I just got too mad. Sometimes you have to get mad, especially when you're trying to do something good."

"Mrs. Bishop, you know what? You could get a job!" breathed Zebul.

"I don't have any degrees."

"But you know you have a better education from Miss McCabe's academy than we are getting from this university. Four years of Latin and four of Greek."

"*Arma virumque cano,*" quoted Mrs. Bishop ironically.

"Even a part-time job would be good," egged Irene. "She actually supported us by baking apple turnovers on Eastern Point."

"Seriously," said Zebul.

"It would stop me from nagging so much."

"But you don't want a business, Mamma. You want a job. There's enough businesses in this family. Businesses don't work."

"Of course a job. Even a part-time job. But what can I do?"

"You can read, drive, sew, cook, and translate Greek or Latin, French or German—"

"I've forgotten German."

"You'd get it back in no time."

"Maybe you could translate some of those new texts for the Medical Department. I will look and see."

"Well, you people look and see. It's come to a point where you're absolutely right. I've got to do something."

The following days Zebul, Urie, and Irene looked at the bulletin boards in the Y, at the medical building, and in the Philosophy Department. There was a notice asking for a person to translate some medical work from French, and Mrs. Bishop applied, but they did not hire her.

At the end of July, Zebul saw a notice on the bulletin board for drivers for eight blind students who had come to study social work. Without waiting, he hurried, in the middle of the day, out to the Shack to tell Mrs. Bishop.

That afternoon they all waited for her to return. She came running up the driveway, wobbling on her beautiful legs, unfamiliarly decked with halfway heels, stocking with one run worn carefully so that it was on the inside.

"I got it!" she shouted breathlessly before she had even opened the door. "It was not only driving, but they also wanted a driver who would read. They tested people, and I was the best reader! They said so. I am fast, very fast, and they have a lot of medical vocabulary. 'That's where your Latin and Greek come in handy,' she said. Also my hours are free. I can do it any time during the day! And just think! It pays seventy-five an hour!"

"It's marvelous!"

"Superb!"

"Terrific!" cried Zebul. "And I'm the one that saw the ad!"

"If it hadn't been for you, I never would have got the job, Zebul!" cried Mrs. Bishop, giving him a sudden and unusual kiss. Zebul felt strange, as if Loco had suddenly kissed him.

That spring Mr. Keck came to the house. He planted his running yellow eyes, like two egg yolks, on the rotten boards of the back steps and announced that he reckoned he was gonna have to ask them to leave because he and his family would sure like to plan to move into the house sometime.

"Yes, sir. Yes, sir," said P.Q., holding his newspaper in one hand.

"Thank you, sir," said Mr. Keck.

P.Q. went back into the living room and sat down, burying his nose in the paper.

"What will we do?" asked Mrs. Bishop.

"What do you mean, what will we do?"

"I mean if we have to move out of here."

"Oh, he's only talking," said P.Q.

"Why do you yes them all the time?"

"Might as well not get into a fight over nothing."

"Can he put us out?"

"Of course not."

"Yes. After all we have a lease. You should have told him. What can he do when we have a lease?"

"Mmmmm."

"You ought to get that lease notarized, P.Q."

Yet after that on Sundays, P.Q. would announce, "Come on. Let's go for a ride!"

They would get in the panel truck. They called it a "ride," but P.Q. always drove, and they stopped and looked at land. There was a certain tract of woods, a hill that rose above a stream. It belonged to Gag Booch, and P.Q. always ruminated about how you could get it for maybe three hundred down and pay twenty or thirty dollars monthly.

"Who could pay that when we can hardly pay eighteen dollars' rent?" scoffed Urie.

"You could build a cinder-block house here," said P.Q., pointing on the ground. "Aristotle showed how you should build a house. You make the front look south. Build it on a high place, so it will not be damp. And have the southern exposure, or western, but never north. You could begin with one room first. Build it right here, looking down on the stream, with a window to the east for the morning sun. If you make it out of cinder block you could add on a room whenever you needed it."

Zebul walked around, imagining what trees you would have to cut to clear enough room for the house.

But Urie and Irene stomped soddenly on their feet around last year's leaves, making loud rustling sounds as if to drown out the possibility of all such daydreams.

C H A P T E R 54

In the beginning of August, Urie and Zebul made some new friends. They came to visit the Shack.

"What a fantastically exotic place!" growled Greta Grobersheim.

"This is the real South, isn't it!" breathed Archie Makin, a doctor's son from San Diego, California. "Listen, someday I'd like to take pictures here. I plan to be a free-lance photographer after the war."

"I tell you what! Let's make a movie here! It would make a perfect locale!" Greta Grobersheim was the daughter of a Chattanooga railroad magnate. She was a long, bony girl who trailed around the campus in expensive but unsuitable clothes, trying to disguise her wealth by friendships with self-help students and Negroes. She had written book, lyrics, and five songs for Sounds and Fury, the musical-comedy club, but she was so obnoxious nobody wanted her in his production.

"Yeah!" cried Archie. "I've got the camera, and my friend Jack Lawrence has a projector for rushes."

"We'll have to get permission first," said Urie doubtfully.

"Who from?"

"My father."

"Show me to him," said Greta Grobersheim.

"He's not here now."

But the next day, before anybody had even broached the subject of P.Q. or Mrs. Bishop, Greta Grobersheim showed up with a completed screenplay about a Southern-trash woman with a cretin daughter who falls in love with the hired hand.

"Mrs. Faith Shafter Lowestoft says she'll do the mother, and you can play the daughter," announced Greta.

Urie had trepidations. But that night she asked Mrs. Bishop and P.Q.

"Well, I don't know," Mrs. Bishop hesitated. "If you're going to string wires over everything, how will we eat? Not that that will bother me, but—"

"Mrs. Faith Shafter Lowestoft?" interrupted P.Q. "Ha. I'd love to see that fat old cuss play the part of white trash."

Mrs. Faith Shafter Lowestoft was a rich widow who had brought up five children on an old Mississippi River showboat, had come to Ephesus because of the Folk Blood Movement, had written a three-act play called *The Insurgent Medea,* and was known to hoard canned goods in her basement.

The meeting between Greta Grobersheim and P.Q. took place outdoors in the field by the barn.

"What did you say your name was?" he asked, leaning toward her.

"Greta Grobersheim."

"Greta? Like Greta Garbo?"

"Yes," said Greta with an unpleasant look.

"And you, Miss Grobersheim, are the Aristophanes of this production?"

"Well, I'm more like the Sophocles."

"Ah! Serious drama! And is this the first time you have directed a motion picture, Miss Garbo?"

"Grobersheim."

"Grobersheim, excuse me."

"Well, it's the first time for a movie. I've directed three plays and a musical before this."

"I'm really the director," inserted Archie Makin, rushing past with some lights, stringing wire behind him. "She was the writer."

"I once witnessed the filming of Pola Negri in twenty-degree weather," said P.Q. "She was supposed to fall out of a rowboat into the harbor. They had to dump her in the harbor five times, fully clothed, before they got the right shot. She almost sank twice and in the end looked like a dill pickle. What is this work about?"

"It's about this white-trash woman with a cretin daughter—"

"Cretin, Miss Garbo?"

"Yes."

"What is a cretin?"

"A cretin is a feeble-minded person."

"You mean this daughter is organically decrepit?"

"She is a moron."

"You mean her organism is defective?"

"What?"

"She has nothing upstairs?"

"Yes."

"And what does 'cretin' come from?" asked P.Q.

"The derivation of words is beside the point."

"Then she must not be a cretin. Cretin means the degradation of 'Christian.' Low-class English people couldn't pronounce the French for Christian during the Norman Conquest, and now people think that cretin means—"

"But she *is* a cretin! That proves the tragic universe!"

"Tragic universe? What tragic universe?"

"What she means is—" interrupted Archie, coming back the other way.

"Ah, Miss Garbo, you have a lawyer."

"I don't need any lawyer, I can tell you that. Keep out of this, Archie. Now, Mr. Bishop, the tragic universe—"

"Excuse me, Miss Garbo. But who sees the tragic universe?"

"*Everybody* sees the tragic universe."

"How do *you* know they do? Think again. Who sees the tragic universe?"

"I do!"

"That's better, Miss Garbo."

"Grobersheim."

"Excuse me. Miss Grobersheim. That proves my point: there is no tragic universe. There is only what you see," said P.Q., walking to the kitchen door.

On the day that Jack Lawrence, Archie Makin's friend, came to the filming, a strange thing happened. Irene had just come out of her room into the living room and was crossing the wires of the arc lights, which Archie had spent three hours arranging at the kitchen door, when Jack Lawrence saw her.

[43 I

"She has to be the daughter!" he whispered to Archie. "She's beautiful!"

The production stopped. A fight ensued, with Greta Grobersheim on one side, Jack Lawrence on the other, and Archie Makin in the middle.

"What right has Jack Lawrence to say who is who? Urie's got to be the cretin. She does drooling better than anybody I've ever seen!" Greta had a threatening way of walking, inserting the top half of her body forward at the same time as she catapulted her bottom with grinding tenacity, as if her legs were the treads of a caterpillar tractor. It made her seem to be in two places at the same time.

Jack Lawrence was thin as a giraffe, but handsome. He ignored Greta with mild insouciance.

"Why are you standing there like an unreconstructed heap of tin cans letting somebody else take over the production?" she screamed at Archie. "You're supposed to be the director, aren't you?"

"Greta—"

"I'm warning you."

The house, steaming hot and blinding with all the light reflectors, exacerbated everything. The kitchen was so full of equipment that Mrs. Bishop could not get the noon meal, and it was now two-thirty in the afternoon. The walls were so close that no one could move.

"Greta," said Zebul, trying to reason.

But she trod on this intercession. So Zebul took a slice of bread, spread peanut butter on it, tore it in half, and gave a half to Urie. With glazed eyes they found a place under the piano to eat. Perversely they were excited, for from the beginning they had felt guilty that a creation making use of their artifacts should be abused by a stranger.

"Something awful is going to happen. This movie is going to blow up."

"Zebul, what does it remind you of?"

"The Sybilline ceremony?"

"No."

"Your theme on Athalattia?"

"No."

"What then?"

"The kiss. When we wrote down the kiss. It's using something real to make a fake. Who can make it? Jack Lawrence is right. It *shouldn't* be a cretin! We can't let it be a cretin. Cretins never happened here. If it's a cretin, she doesn't know, and she has to *know* to have a destiny."

"You mean you don't want to play a cretin," said Zebul, testing her.

"I would play a cretin in a minute," answered Urie deliriously. "But we ought not to allow a cretin to inhabit this place where—because it *is* inhabited by something else. Irene will play her."

"Play who?"

"The character!"

"What was Bostwick like to screw?" Zebul whispered. The shouting was increasing in the kitchen, but he fastened onto Urie's blue-shell eyes, inhabiting the new lining of his being. He even by-passed her surprise because he knew that they were going to take over the wreck of the movie now, and all that had passed, all that which he never would tell her, came down to the vow of truth that they had made, no matter how it worked out.

"Even if I could explain it, how can I explain it?"

"What was it like?" he insisted.

"Sex is nothing, even though it's everything."

"That's because it goes away. You have to keep doing it more and more and more, because it goes away."

"No. I think it's the opposite: it's there and there and there and you have to do it because—" But she could not think how to say it.

"Urie, that's brilliant!"

"Have you done it?" she asked.

"Hundreds of times." And she did not remember, fastened on his eyes, that Loco had used the same words.

But why didn't you ever ask me about it before? she was going to ask when all of a sudden there was a crash in the kitchen and Archie Makin's voice said, "All right, Greta. That cuts it. Nobody can say a thing like that to me."

"If the shoe fits, wear it!" There was a sound of footsteps as Greta stomped off. A murmur, then silence.

When Urie and Zebul came out from under the piano, Archie was gone, Jack was gone, and only the camera was left, lying on the floor beneath the oven, Irene draped over it in despair.

"They've all gone and the movie's ruined!"

"That's nothing. It will all come out in the wash!" crooned P.Q. from the Boston rocker, where he was sitting outside under the shade of the hickory tree.

"He's right," whispered Zebul, twisting the dials of the camera to see how it worked. It began whirring. "Whew! There! I wonder how much film there is."

"What about lights?"

"They had them all set ready to go," informed Irene.

"Now, Irene, stand there," ordered Urie. "You're not a cretin. But just pretend that you're calling your mother out the doorway. Look out there. That's right."

"Shall I call out loud?"

"I don't care. It's a silent movie."

Irene stood at the baggy screen while Zebul took aim. Everybody held his breath. Irene, barely perceptibly, said the word "Mother."

"That's good," breathed Urie. "She wants to tell her about the boy but she doesn't know exactly where she is, because she's not in the house, she's outside, maybe. Look toward the barn. Love is what everybody wants. It's as if it comes by the grace of God. That's why she wants to tell her mother." Urie crooned these words in the senseless way of the swans on the legato lake when they were singing in the church, not for the meaning, but for the note beyond the meaning. She was not even aware of the meaning, for the plot was not even worked out in her mind.

After he had finished that shot, Zebul could not let go the new toy. He went out by the barn and photographed the tree where Loco had added her excrement. Then he aimed for the sky, as if seeking something from it.

The next day no one appeared. So Urie, Zebul, and Irene improvised a plot as they went along. They expanded into the spirit of their initial thrust. Since Faith Shafter Lowestoft was not coming because of the fight, they had to shoot as if the mother were just outside the frame of the picture. In addition to this, the film was running out.

That night Jack Lawrence came. He apologized for Archie and Greta. "I thought surely they would have come back by now," he said, looking around.

"Oh, Jack!" Irene Mrs. Minivered.

There were some people, discovered Urie, who mimicked their way into reality, and Irene was one. But for the first time Urie neither cringed nor underrated mimesis. Miraculous, this hoarding of her destiny, which Irene had always known and never mistrusted, that she would be fallen in love with and married and become mistress of a manor, her family fooldom a mirage, even a mirror of a beauty, unrecognized by Bishopry, but not by Irene, that contained herself as a prima manager, merging herself into the event when it happened. It had now happened. Under their eyes Irene was achieving her Minervaness, which her Mrs. Miniver had all these years led her to.

"You played the girl!" he guessed. He did not say "cretin."

"Yes. And now we've used up all Archie's film. Thank goodness you came!"

434]

"But that's fantastic!" breathed Jack, blushing before her. "Let's get it right over to Leacocks' to develop it."

Two evenings later Zebul and Urie sat close together in the Victorian chairs. Irene hung a sheet from the top of the bookcase. But they waited a long time for Jack to thread the machine. Zebul got up for a while to learn how to do it, but the moment the film started running he rushed to sit down again next to Urie. The machine chattered. The twitches of light and shadow were ghastly.

It was marvelous to see the Shack on film. Irene uttered a delighted laugh. But she stopped the moment she appeared on the screen. It was the shot Zebul had taken of her calling out the doorway. It was intensely beautiful. The light was focused under Irene's chin, running like liquid up valleys behind her cheeks, and coming to some point just above the pupils of her eyes, where there was a glistening. It seemed that the glistening was not from the eyes but from disembodied spools of water, more important than the pupils, which were merely looking out the doorway. The shot was held a very long time—far too long for a proper movie. Irene's lips moved. All three, Irene, Zebul, and Urie, mouthed the word "Mother" in the darkness, striving unconsciously to make the movie sound aloud, for they could not unloose themselves from themselves in what had been rehearsals for this moment. In the next moment the scene switched. For a split second they were disappointed, for though the shot of Irene had been endless, yet the moment it ended, it was as if they could not get enough of it, as if some strange thing that had to do with their yearning were ripped away from them before they were ready. Their mouths were still in formulation, trying to make Irene's sound.

The Bone Tree was on the screen. Then an unfamiliar scene of the field looking into the sky. It was evidently very ugly because the light was in all the wrong places. The sun was there. Zebul must have forgotten and aimed directly at it. This made everything look like a thunderstorm, as if the print were taken from a dark place, or trying to escape from the darkness into a thousand haloes too bright to be dealt with. Clouds moved before their eyes and what was the camera, or what was Irene's mind in the movie, was straining, straining to solve the infinity of dealing with the sun, which threatened such radiance.

It was at that moment Urie remembered it. "I am a daisy." Everything should have been astonishing to her, yet the moment she remembered, everything became natural. Instead of straining any more to get out through the tunnel to the edges of the cloud, the light seemed to blind her and turn something inside out in her brain, and she simply hung on with her hands to the figment of a cushion under her in the Victorian chair while something whirled on the linings of the light. She heard a sound like muses laughing in grass blades. She was conscious of this in a *silent* movie. She almost laughed herself, but she refrained, being aware suddenly of the sun as the heart of Loco's daisyhood, forgetting, as she meant to do, to look in the broom sedge of the field to see perhaps if there were real daisies still in bloom there in the photograph which had brought her to remember. But place was irrelevant. Evidence was quite irrational in this state. Everything, everything was turned inside out, the dark being the light, the light being the daisy, the clouds being cloudless, the face being faceless. A fig dropped. It meant there must have been no Grief Face, but a mere figment of grief invested, reaped, repeated, and harvested thereof. All the time the sun blinds the cloud-tree, through whose cavern people look up for their heart. The clouds being the cloudless, the light being the daisy, the dark being the light, there were no events at all. It was a movie.

The picture changed to the inside of the Shack again, and Irene was playing something at the piano. Again it seemed to want sound, but the following shots were insignificant and Urie was disappointed.

She was still holding tight. At the end, when Irene snapped on the light, she did not dare to look at Zebul. What if he had not seen anything? She looked. There was a strange frown between his eyes, and his lips were in his teeth. She signaled him.

They ran out to the field, where at this moment the sun was not shining but the moon, full, as full as the night they had experimented with worshiping together.

"Well?" she demanded.

"You have to be careful, Urie," he answered, taking her hands as if he wanted to turn away from her.

"But what did you see?"

"Something strange."

"Strange?"

"Yes."

"When?"

"In the scene of Irene at the doorway."

"What was it?"

She saw at once that he did not want to tell her because he dropped her hands and turned away. But the next minute he turned full-face and looked not at her but past her to the moon.

"But I saw it too," she prompted, as with the ice-cream cone. Yet she had difficulty. It was as if he were re-creating her as the *objet d'art* again under the moon, another rehearsal of the event which was not going to happen, because it had in fact already happened. In addition, a sense of sacredness to the vision forbade actual words. Was this what Zebul meant? A stream flowed from that sense, a sense that had been there, neglected and fraught from the beginning, past and up to this moment of the moon that they were sharing again.

"I didn't see Irene in that scene," Zebul said. "It was Loco Poco. I swear it looked like Loco Poco!"

But she had not seen that! The moment he said it, she understood it. It was true. The lights on the eyes! And she suddenly felt things she could not find words to tell him. She felt as if she knew a secret. She had always known it. It was something about never-endingness. It seemed natural to her that Zebul knew Loco Poco lived. Every person makes the scenes by which the secret of never-endingness is described, and it differs from person to person. Because of this each person believes his secret to be different from the other person's secret, but everybody knows the secret from the beginning, and it is only the forms that differ from person to person.

"Do you think we can get him to run the movie again, Zebul?"

Every action has to be sacred, Zebul thought, the worst of actions, the ugliest of sights. They had almost touched it, and he suddenly wanted her to know that. How strange!

"Before I go into the Army, let's go somewhere, Urie."

"Where?"

"Eastern Point. I want to see the ocean. Remember, I've never seen the ocean."

"Oh, yes, let's go," she said.

"Promise."

"I promise."

CHAPTER 55

The Bishops did not answer the first two notices to vacate the house. P.Q. did not even bother to pooh-pooh the first one. He merely ignored it.

"We've got a lease, after all," said Mrs. Bishop.

But when the second one came she turned to P.Q., demanding, "What about our lease?"

"It's not notarized," he told her. He told her this with a straight face, as if it were news, so that, just as with his recognition of Tootsie Morn, the mystery of him reared up terrifying before them. What had it cost him to refuse to recognize the death of Loco? Had it been an act of gallantry, like Urie's "We're going to crack this town wide open"? Or was it simple truth? Now did his stone face hide remorse for not having notarized the lease? Or did it deny in arrogance his responsibility?

"You mean to say that we can really be put out of this house?" cried Mrs. Bishop in shock.

P.Q. did not answer, so everybody knew the answer was yes.

During the period after the second notice no one said anything about what was going to happen, except Mrs. Bishop. She referred to it constantly, speaking at first with incredulity, and then trying to make plans. But the reception her words received was complete silence, so that at last, when the air was thick enough to cut with a knife, she burst in despair.

"What are we going to do? We're going to be put out in the street with nowhere to go, and I don't know what will become of us. We'll have to move our things. What's going to happen to my piano?"

"Oh, for God's sake!" Urie exploded because those words were archetypical in her memory. Had those not been the words of Loco on the coffin bed the first night they had slept in the Shack? "You'd think we were the same as we always were! We don't have to have a house! Irene and I are old now. We don't have to live at home if we have no home! And Zebul can keep the piano, while we go and work in defense plants!"

"Don't be silly," barked P.Q. from the radio, which was talking about invading Europe.

Mrs. Bishop was shocked. It was the defense-plant remark.

"You're going to have to see Gag Booch about that land," she said, turning on P.Q.

He had already seen Gag Booch. But he was silent. He refused to deal with anything backed to the wall. Two days later, as if it were an entirely new subject, he told her that he had given Gag Booch twenty-five dollars and that the land was being surveyed. After that everybody put the whole subject out of mind.

On a brilliant Saturday afternoon in August, Dan Tatum waddled up the driveway. The dogs barked ferociously. P.Q. told the dogs to go behind him, but made Dan Tatum step on the airing linens to make his announcement.

"I got a court order here says you people got to be out of this house by Monday morning or we will have to make bodily disposition of household goods and furniture."

"Who will?" demanded Urie, approaching from the well.

Mrs. Bishop also had come out on the kitchen steps, her apron flapping in the wind.

"The town deputies," answered Dan Tatum.

"You mean you're going to put my furniture out on the road?" screamed Mrs. Bishop.

Dan Tatum looked at her, trying to recognize the thief.

"Cain't help it, ma'am."

"Give us until Tuesday, at least," said Mrs. Bishop. "We've got to get a moving van! and they won't do it Monday, if we can only tell them Monday. Say Tuesday."

"All right," said Dan Tatum, waddling away.

P.Q. kept the dogs back until he was in the road.

Urie made the announcement to Zebul with appropriate dramatic underplay in Sociology 53.

"We're being evicted on Tuesday. All our stuff is going to be put out on the road."

"What?" blurted Zebul, so loudly that everyone turned around to look at him. "I mean where are you going?"

"To that land of Gag Booch's," she answered later, on the way to their office.

"Have you paid for it?"

"P.Q. gave him some money and he'll give him some more."

"Have you got the deed in your names?"

"Ask P.Q.," whispered Urie. "He's already built a gypsy tent. We're moving some of the things this weekend. But the big moving is on Tuesday. And you've got to take the piano until we get the first cinder-block room built."

Zebul's eyes bugged out, but he had already in his mind learned to play three of Chopin's études and the Brahms piano concerto. He would force his mother to take it, but she wouldn't object. It would be the first baby grand in all Haw. She always did what he said.

That weekend Irene, Mrs. Bishop, and Urie packed fifty-one carton boxes, hauled from the A & P, full of household articles. Clothes, material, silver, P.Q.'s desk things, Loco Poco's scrapbooks, paintings, and music, the picture of Amalfi, the Hawaiian bark, the Yosemite, the mantelpiece clock, Irene's stuff, and Urie's stuff, and twenty-four boxes of books. Load after load they struggled with, hauling to and from the house, to the laundry truck, to the gypsy tent under the unfamiliar pine trees.

P.Q. got a huge extension wire and plugged it secretly into a public electric box on a telephone down on the road, stringing it through the pine trees.

"It's lucky it's summer," said Irene, "or it would be too cold to sleep out."

But as the Shack became more and more barren, denuded of the Hawaiian bark on the walls, the curtain at the windows, the pictures covering the holes on the wall, there came a different posture in the Bishops' personality. No one asked any questions any more about where they would sleep or what the future was. All motion slid to the present. No plans were made. No doubts were aired beyond the "I don't know how we can ever build a house before winter comes" that Mrs. Bishop breathed upon the impervious air.

Monday was called the Moving. They hired Bartlett's dump truck. Jack Lawrence helped them. He insisted on going down to the university and getting Archie Makin. Ever since the movie had gone up in smoke, Archie Makin had felt guilty. Here was an opportunity, he felt, to make up his fight. But no sooner had Greta Grobersheim heard of the Moving, than she wanted to help too. She rounded up two actors in Sounds and Fury, plus a boy named Bobo who was a psychology major.

Mrs. Bishop cooked two vats of cheese macaroni. She directed the proceedings, reserving just enough silver and the long table for the feast. She had bought paper plates for this occasion.

P.Q. helped only during the removal of the piano onto Bartlett's dump truck. Greta Grobersheim angled herself under one leg, next to the one Negro who was helping. P.Q., Zebul, and the psychology major got under another leg. Mrs. Bishop's tongue hung out of her mouth as the piano began to sway like a bug. They used no levers, no dollies. They made noises like prisoners at Devil's Island. Zebul laughed, and his side fell down two inches before they caught it. The living-room doorsill broke, and the other side of the piano tipped down. They got out the door and into the yard. The piano inched forward to the truck. With one gigantic heave they lifted it onto the bed of the pick-up.

Just before they were ready to leave the house forever, they sat down to the table of macaroni like guests. For chairs they used barrels, the floor, and the piano bench, which was withdrawn from under them as soon as they had finished.

The household goods awaited outside, loaded upon the truck and on top of the laundry truck, having come from somewhere, going now to somewhere else. Loud guffaws arose from the nearly empty house.

P.Q. ordered a fire to be set in the yard to burn up the final trash so that they would leave the place in A-number-one condition. Bobo, the psychology major, built it and stoked it with the last leavings. Old newspapers, unused wrappers, leftover carton boxes, some old remains of cloth Mrs. Bishop had discarded, paper wrappings, all the flotsam and jetsam of five years' living were cast upon this pile.

"Oh my God, that was the best meal I ever ate in all my born days," said the psychology major, lifting himself off the barrel from the long table and putting two hands on his stomach.

"Quick, the silver, the silver!" Mrs. Bishop ordered.

It flashed as five hands flapped it off the table. Someone took the paper plates and heaved them into the fire. Someone else took off the burlap sack they had used as a tablecloth, and the table was lifted as if alive, disappearing out the living room door as if it had become a phantom.

"Let's go!" screamed Greta Grobersheim.

Urie ran to get her pocketbook, which she had left on the window sill of her room. The breeze lifted the tapestry, like sails, gently as the sounds rang in the other part of the echoing structure. She stopped. She stared at the shepherds and shepherdesses dancing. She trembled.

"Leave the tapestries," Mrs. Bishop had said. "They're rotten now."

Loco's coffin bed, denuded of springs, still stood in her room.

"Come on!" Zebul was calling her from the living room.

And when he met her, he saw that it had happened, that same thing, that indescribable thing that he could not make a word for.

In that mysterious place, thought Zebul, where their separate experiments in sex and love and philosophy had coursed into their private beings, those experiments where they had sought separately for the truth they had vowed together, a new round of adventures was beginning. They were repeating, to the accompaniment of Archie's and Greta's and all these strangers' moving, they were repeating in an andante movement like the waves of the ocean, the same rehearsals of their relationship, their aspirations, their roles in the family and in different fields.

"We're the same, aren't we? We're absolutely the same," he breathed.

"No, we're not. We're absolutely different."

"All right. But come on."

They were split apart. Yet the fact of their split had merely widened the horizon of Bishopry to something that they had never contemplated when they had first come to Ephesus. The same remarks with different actions. The same gaze with a different performance.

It was very windy when they got outside.

"What are we waiting for?" asked Urie, stamping impatiently.

Looking back, she saw Mrs. Bishop escorting the big psychology student out the kitchen door, with Loco's coffin bed in his arms. Mrs. Bishop pointed to the fire.

P.Q., the radio under his arm, was walking to the trucks.

But Mrs. Bishop suddenly turned and started running to join him. She had to hold on to her sweater to keep it from blowing off.